THE ETERNITY OF THED

ALSO BY LOGAN YOUNG

The Power of Princirum, Book 3

THE ETERNITY OF THED

LOGAN YOUNG

To Margaret—

~

For your constant encouragement,

and being my first ever reader

~

CONTENTS

THE 8 ELEMENTS

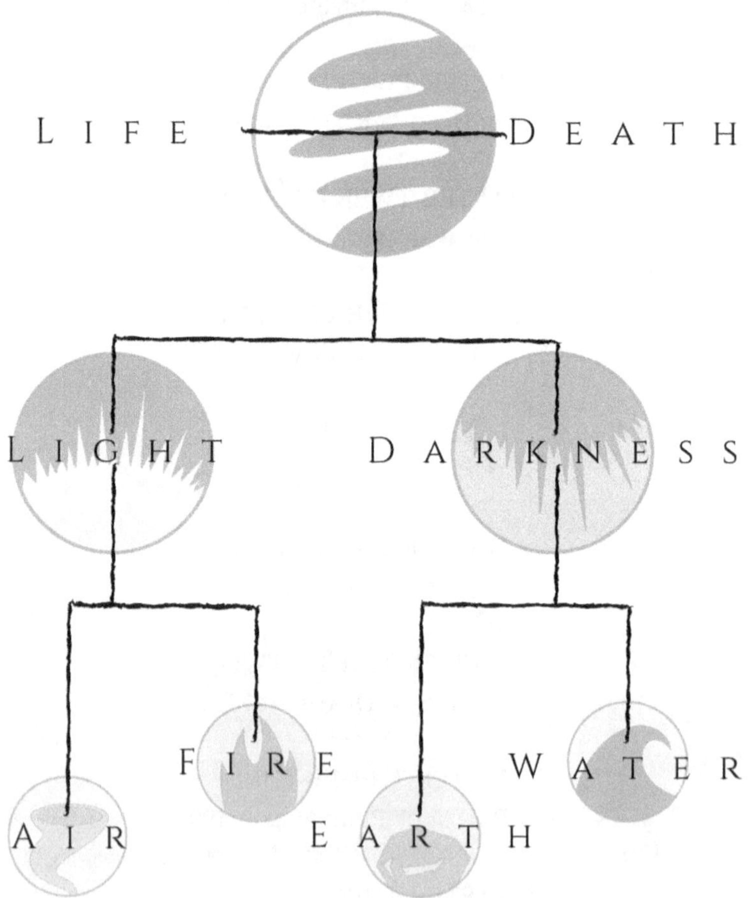

INFERON
IGMONTIS
SOLARIS
LUXMONT
THE CITY OF LUXMONT
THE CITY OF SILVAURA
ALFONBURG
SILVAURA
CRYSTAL PALACE
TERMUBRA
TERADON
CONTELLUS
THE CITY OF CONTELLUS
THE CITY OF TERMUBRA
THE GREAT FORTRESS
UNDARUNCI
WADITA

THE ETERNITY OF THED

CHAPTER ONE

CHAINED IN AGONY

KYM LAY CURLED IN A BALL, HER BACK PRESSED AGAINST THE COLD stone wall. She forced her stiff eyes open, trying to ignore the throbbing in her skull. She tried to take in her surroundings, but like every day, she saw nothing but darkness around her. It had been so long since she'd seen daylight.

Kym sat up—a daily struggle given her paralyzed, dead arms. She forced her elbows, which still had a glimmer of life in them, beneath her, and pressed as hard as she could into her sleeping pad. It wasn't pretty, but she managed to lean herself into a sitting position. Chains rattled in the darkness, but Kym barely noticed. The chains binding her hands and feet were the few constants of her continued existence.

"Another day." Kym's voice scratched in her throat, her tongue dry as sandpaper. She hardly ever spoke these days. Unless she was screaming.

Kym staggered across the room in four uneven steps. She bent down, attempting to grab a fistful of the chains extending from her wrists. Her fingers, of course, were useless. She hadn't felt them in so long—she honestly forgot they were there somedays. But she could pin a chain-link between her palms easily enough.

Kym dragged the thick chain across the stone wall with trembling arms. Carving the scratch to mark the days since the Rulers of Princirum ripped the magic from her took time. Some days, she wondered why she kept counting. If Kym were honest, she liked having something to look forward to each day. It didn't make any difference. Kym should have died that night. She wished she had.

"Four hundred thirty-one," Kym croaked.

Kym's numb hand drifted along the stone wall. She couldn't feel, or see, the grooves she'd carved, but Kym didn't need to. She knew the place well. Chains. Scratches in stone. Pain. Soon, she'd be eighteen—not that it mattered. This little stone box was her whole world now.

Why did it have to be this way? Kym knew the Rulers could have ended it. So why didn't they?

A loud thunk echoed around Kym's tiny world. Kym barely flinched as the sound bounced around her cell, working its way into the deepest, darkest spaces. Hardly a day had passed since she'd woken in her cell at Tenbatter that she hadn't had a visitor. Kym turned to the bare stretch of stone behind her—except the wall wasn't there.

The dark stone had turned to smoke, while flickering green light trickled into Kym's cell. Kym winced, shielding her eyes in the crook of her elbow as tears streamed down her cheeks. A tall figure stepped through the wall, glowing green spirals coiling around her arms.

"You know the drill," the Warden said.

Kym knelt silently on the cold stone floor. She knew the drill. No matter who came into her cell, the visits were always the same. Kym preferred it when it was one of the Protectorate guards. At least they minded their business and didn't speak to her.

And why would they? The Protectorate were warrior priests sworn to protect Princirum's gods. And after Kym betrayed the Rulers, the Pros wanted nothing to do with her. She'd attacked the children of the gods. To the Pros, there was nothing worse.

Kym kept her eyes trained on the ground as the Warden walked around her. Kym braced herself. She couldn't stop the Warden from doing this next part, no matter how much it hurt. Kym's arms jerked forcibly behind her as her chains tightened. Pain radiated through Kym's shoulders and upper body while the Warden continued to pull the chains.

"Ah!" Kym couldn't stop the cry from escaping her lips. The Warden was many things, but gentle wasn't one of them.

Kym was grateful she couldn't feel anything below her elbows. The Warden yanked the chains again, pulling until Kym's arms couldn't move. The Warden pulled up on Kym's restraints, and she rose awkwardly to her feet. The tip of something sharp pressed into the small of Kym's back, and she clenched her jaw, determined not to cry out again.

"Step forward," the Warden hissed in Kym's ear. "And no funny business."

Kym obeyed without hesitation. She stepped through the wall of smoke and out onto the dark landing. A tall man in form-fitting robes stood before her, flanked on either side by two others. The Protectorate knelt and held his hand in Kym's face while the others pointed their spears at her chest. Her eyes fell to the Pro's palm, where a little dish sat full to the brim with crystal clear water.

Kym's tongue grew dry as she stared at the tiny bowl. Her daily water ration. Kym leaned forward, saliva flooding her mouth. The last thing she wanted was to spook the Pros. She knew they were scared of having water near Kym, and she couldn't blame them.

Kym tried to remember her life before Tenbatter, but most days, it felt like a dream. She'd been a Favored—a select group of people in Princirum who magically controlled one of the seven elements: death, light, darkness, fire, water, air, and earth. But Kym hadn't been a regular Water Favored. As the Vanquisher of Water, she'd spent her time fighting death demons all over Princirum. She'd competed in the Calling as one of the Prized, and became known as one of the most powerful Favored in a generation.

That's when everything went wrong. Kym didn't want to spend her life serving and being manipulated by Nila, the Ruler of Water, so she and a few of her friends had tried to leave. Nila and the rest of the Rulers hadn't liked that. They attacked Kym and her friends, Tomark, Kat, and Ashlyn, and ripped the magic from them while they forced Kym to watch.

"Drink," the Pro ordered, bringing Kym back to her surroundings.

Kym placed her lips to the bowl and took a long sip. The warm water had an odd metallic taste, but she didn't care. Kym savored every drop as it slid over her dry mouth. But like every time, the bowl ran dry before she'd had her fill.

Kym knew why the Warden didn't want water anywhere near her. Having her magic ripped from her should have killed Kym. But she survived. And if she lived, did that mean some of her magic remained too? Kym hadn't bothered to try. Magic had brought her nothing but suffering. She was happy to be rid of it. She'd never wanted magic in the first place.

The middle Pro stepped back while the others kept their spears pointed at Kym. Kym's shoulders throbbed as the Warden yanked on the chains, and Kym stumbled back through the smokey door. The tension on her arms vanished, and she fell to the stone floor in a tinkle of metal. Pain throbbed through Kym's torso as the Warden stepped out from behind her. Kym didn't take her eyes off the tall woman, who smiled maliciously down at her.

"Good girl," she said.

The Warden backed out of Kym's cell. She raised her hand, and green Marks glowed on her arm, illuminating the path the Warden's magical energy followed. She placed her arm in the smokey mass and turned it like she was turning a key. The smoke solidified, and Kym was once again alone in her cell as darkness surrounded her.

Kym sighed, her muscles relaxing slightly, and pushed herself into a sitting position. She turned from the stone door, happy to be alone once again. With any luck, she wouldn't have a visitor for a while. At least now she could go about the rest of her day in peace.

Kym kept her food in the far corner of her cell. There wasn't much, just a hunk of bread covered in an odd, grainy powder that coated her tongue. Kym gagged the first time she ate the stuff and refused to take another bite. However, it didn't take long for her hunger to win out.

Kym picked up the bread with her numb hands, holding it close to her face. There wasn't a lot left. She hadn't gotten any new food for three days. Kym knew it was probably for the best. The moldy loaf became hard to swallow after a few days. Whether she got new food or not, this would be the last day for this piece of bread.

Kym yawned and gnawed on her last chunk of bread. When she'd eaten all she could bear, she crawled on her elbows and knees to her sleeping mat. The musty thing wasn't comfortable—it smelled like mold and only took up space in her already-minuscule world.

Kym sat cross-legged on her mat, staring up at the dark ceiling. She'd never actually seen it, but she imagined it was smooth, like the walls and floor. Kym hadn't bothered to try and find it. With her paralyzed hands, she'd never feel the ceiling, even if she managed to touch it.

Kym shook her head. Why did the Rulers bothered keeping her locked up after all this time? She knew they'd wanted to kill her when they ripped out her magic. They'd done it once before to a Fire Favored, and the strain was too much for his heart. So why'd the Rulers lock her up when she survived losing her magic? The thought stirred something in Kym's aching mind. Did the Rulers even know she was alive?

The Rulers hadn't been acting of their own free will when they tried to kill her. Thed, the god of death and enemy of the gods, had forced his way into the Rulers' bodies. He may have influenced their actions that night, but it was still the Rulers who ripped the magic from Kym, and for Kym, that made them just as guilty as Thed. She knew why Thed wanted her dead. She'd spent her whole time as a Favored fighting death's power and influence.

Kym shook her head. Thinking about all of this was pointless since she'd never find the answer. She'd never make it out of Tenbatter, or her cell, for the rest of her life. So why did she keep thinking of the world outside?

Kym lay back on her sleeping pad, yawned, and closed her eyes against the blackness. She needed sleep. She barely got any these days, even though she spent her whole life in her dark, tiny room. Kym knew she needed to try again. What was the worst that could happen? Another nightmare, no doubt. Wandering Nothingness, the land of the dead, would be easier.

~

KYM WAS ALONE. Vast black walls rose on either side of her, stretching up for an eternity, while gaps led to newer, unexplored paths. Tendrils of smoke and fog swirled around Kym's feet, turning her insides to ice and filling her soul with a dull emptiness.

Kym stepped forward, an unnatural silence pressing on her ears as questions filled her mind. How'd she get there in the first place? She couldn't hear herself breathe. Was she even breathing? There had to be something, anything, around her. Kym needed to find her way out. But how could she when she didn't know where she was?

A high-pitched, horrified scream pierced the silent air. Kym's legs froze, rooting her to the spot as dread coursed through her like fire. The cry, although oddly distorted, sounded familiar. Kym's heart thudded in her chest. Whoever made the sound was in pain. She needed to find them.

Kym ran forward, peering down every new path she passed. But all of the paths were just as deserted as Kym's. Kym's heart raced even faster. Where were they? Kym's heart skipped a beat as a louder, more horrified scream filled the air. She was getting closer.

Kym stopped at another opening in the path, and a horrific sight met her eyes. A girl with flaming red hair lay pinned underneath a pile of rubble. Tears covered her shimmering yellow dress in several places, and a bright red stain coated one side of it. Kym stared at the girl, her arms trembling uncontrollably as blood oozed from the glowing yellow Marks on her forearms.

"Ashlyn!"

Kym scrambled forward, tripping over her feet in her haste. She tumbled to the ground, but quickly pushed herself up as more chunks of stone fell from the darkness. They landed on Ashlyn, whose screams pierced Kym's heart like a knife.

"No!"

Kym pushed herself forward. She couldn't let Ashlyn get crushed. But as Kym drew nearer, more pieces of stone fell on Ashlyn, making the ground beneath Kym shake. Kym stopped, staring horrified at Ashlyn. She couldn't save her. Her presence was causing Ashlyn more pain. Ashlyn was suffering, and it was all Kym's fault.

"I'm sorry," Kym panted, tears sliding down her face.

"H-he-help," Ashlyn stammered.

"I want to."

Kym reached forward, and another piece of stone fell on Ashlyn's chest. Her shriek of pain made Kym's insides ache. Kym collapsed, the pain in her chest too much to bear.

"Pl-please," Ashlyn breathed.

"I…"

Grief washed over Kym like a wave. She fell to her knees, and it was like someone had hit her in the chest with a mallet. Another piece of stone fell from above and landed on the pile with an almighty crash. Ashlyn's screams echoed around Kym, working into the deepest parts of her skull. Then everything went quiet.

Slowly, Kym raised her head. Ashlyn and the pile of earth crushing her were nowhere to be seen. Kym shook her head, white-hot tears burning her eyes. Where had she gone? Kym needed to know. She needed to make sure Ashlyn was safe.

A pillar of bright yellow light bloomed in the distance. Kym's heart jumped into her throat as the tightness in her chest lessened slightly. That had to be Ashlyn. Who else could make light appear in such a dark place?

Kym rushed forward, blood pounding in her ears as sweat ran down her back. She needed to stay calm. Ashlyn had to be okay if she was making that much light. She must have found a way to heal herself from all the falling stones. Kym wasn't sure how she'd done it—Light Favored didn't have the power to heal. But Kym didn't care. Ashlyn was safe.

As Kym drew nearer, she noticed a figure laying in the center of the golden spotlight. A mixture of fear and confusion coursed through her like ice as she took in her features. This girl was at least a foot shorter than Ashlyn, with short brown hair and round eyes that Kym knew well. Kat. Kym watched, horrified, as Kat's skin grew redder under the intense spotlight.

"No!"

Kym rushed forward. She couldn't let Kat get hurt too. Kym reached the pillar of light, and something hit her in the chest with the force of a cannon. She flew back, landing hard on the dark ground. Lights flashed in Kym's eyes as she searched for what hit her, but she saw nothing in the strange blackness.

Kym pushed herself up, her fear overriding the pain coursing through her. All that mattered was getting Kat out of danger. But the pillar of light was gone, and so was Kat. Kym looked wildly around, her breath catching in her throat as her heart pounded. First Ashlyn disappeared, then Kat. Where could they have gone?

"You chose this," a soft, gentle voice said behind her.

Warmth spread through Kym's chest as the words washed over her. She knew that voice. Kym spun around, some of her fear melting away. Tomark, his dark, wavy hair falling to his shoulders, stood a few feet from her. Kym couldn't believe how normal he looked, his green eyes twinkling in the blackness. Kym relaxed. If Tomark was there, the others had to be too. They could find them together.

"Tomark," Kym whispered, taking a step toward him. "We need to find Kat and Ashlyn."

"You chose this," Tomark said again. His face was downcast, like he'd just heard the worst news of his life.

"What?" Kym had no idea what Tomark was talking about. She didn't choose to be in this maze. She still didn't know how they got there.

"You chose this," Tomark repeated.

Kym took another step, and bright red flames exploded around Tomark. Kym flew back through the darkness, knocked off her feet by the force of the explosion as Tomark's screams ripped through her soul. She landed on her back, and ringing filled her ears as she scrambled to her knees. All Kym could see was flames. Dread coursed through her like ice. Where was Tomark?

"No," Kym panted, tears falling thick and fast down her cheeks.

Smoke and mist swirled around her. It was so thick she couldn't see the towering black walls beside her. This couldn't be happening. She couldn't lose them again.

"*Your choice,*" said a dark, cold voice.

Kym spun on the spot, the hairs on the back of her neck standing on end. She wanted to find who'd spoken, but the path was deserted. She thought she'd heard the dark voice before. Something about the way it bored into her skull was familiar. It was like the smoke, surrounding her on all sides. She tried to place it, but she couldn't.

"*Your choice,*" the voice said again.

"No," Kym whispered, shaking her head. She hadn't chosen this. She never wanted any of this to happen.

"*Your choice. Your fault.*"

"I didn't."

Kym curled up in a ball, squeezing her eyes shut while she covered her ears with her hands. Why was the voice saying this? It wasn't her fault.

"*Your choice.*"

KYM SAT BOLT UPRIGHT, sweat pouring down her face and back. She gasped, but no matter how many breaths she took, no air reached her lungs. Kym squeezed her legs with trembling arms, trying to hold onto something, anything. Every time she closed her eyes, it was the same.

She'd first dreamt of the maze after the Rulers ripped her magic from her. She wandered around for hours, unable to find her way out. The next thing she knew, she was in her cell for the first time. The parts about Ashlyn, Kat, and Tomark came later.

She pushed the dream from her mind. It was easier if she didn't think about them. Remembering her friends like that—burned, broken, and dying—was too much for her heart to take. At least this way, they were still alive. She remembered seeing them before her ripping, their bodies barely twitching on the glittering white floor of Crystal Palace. They'd been alive then, but were they now? Kym had no idea. If their fate was anything like hers, she didn't want to know.

Kym wiped what sweat she could from her forehead onto her shoulder. How much sleep had she gotten? It couldn't have been more than an hour. She'd try again in a little while.

Kym stood, her chains rattling in the darkness. Desperate to drive the dream from her mind, she shut her eyes and followed the path her feet had tread more times than she could count. Five steps up the long wall, turn, two more steps, turn, five more steps, turn. She'd done this so often she didn't need to feel her way around.

A high-pitched ringing filled Kym's cell, boring into her skull. She turned around, her heart racing as her legs trembled beneath her. Nothing in her cell made that noise. What was going on?

Wham! Kym's head slammed into something solid. She reeled back and fell to the floor.

"Ouch! What the Thed?"

Pain bloomed in Kym's head and tailbone as lights popped in her eyes and the ringing grew louder. She lifted her arms, trying to cover her ears with her paralyzed hands while she searched for the source of the sound. But all she saw in the darkness were the stars in her eyes.

Kym froze, her eyes trained on the specks as her breath caught in her throat. More tiny glowing flecks shone in the blackness, and Kym fought the urge to cry out. She clamped her eyes shut, trying to rid herself of the specks. They couldn't be real.

She opened her eyes and saw more glimmering white dots as the ringing intensified. The specks drifted to the center of the room, collecting like a cloud of stars. Kym scurried to the opposite wall as the particles condensed, forming a glittering white sphere. Kym raised her trembling arms, shielding herself as best she could as the sphere morphed before her.

Thin branches of shimmering white light stretched from the sphere. They twisted around each other, growing longer and longer as the construct took shape. The woman stood in the center of the cell, at least two feet taller than Kym. Her dress billowed around her as she stared straight ahead, her eyes narrow and focused.

Kym glared at the construct of the Ruler of Life, anger burning away the fear inside her while her arms shook with suppressed rage. What was the construct doing there? Kym hadn't seen Zara, or any of the Rulers, since they'd ripped her magic out of her. Why would Zara come to Kym's cell now?

Kym expected the construct to face her, but it stared resolutely forward, its white light flickering in the darkness. Kym narrowed her eyes. Constructs didn't flicker like that since they could only form if the creator's intent was strong enough. So why was this one wavering?

"I do not have much time," the Zara construct said, but there was something wrong with the sound, like it was coming through a worn-out speaker. "Thed's attention is elsewhere, but it will not be for long. His grip on me, and the other Rulers, is strong. I can feel him now, that creeping cold of death twisting around me once again.

"Thed's conquest of Princirum is nearly complete. Much has transpired since your imprisonment. The Favored who opposed us have been forced into compliance. Many of the people openly praise the new world we are building, although they do not know it is Thed who speaks through their beloved Rulers."

Kym shook her head. What was going on? Why would Zara send a construct to tell her that Thed was on the verge of destroying everything? It wasn't like Kym could do anything about it, or even cared. After everything she'd been through, Kym wanted nothing to do with the magical world. And if Thed was on the verge of dominating Princirum, she was happy to be trapped in her cell.

"There is very little resistance to his will. Princirum is on the verge of descending into chaos, and we are powerless to stop Thed. You, however, are not."

Kym shook her head at the construct. Zara telling Kym she could stop Thed was so ridiculous Kym found it almost laughable. She had no magic and was chained up in a cell in a magical prison. But there was one other problem. Kym had no desire to help the Rulers. They caused this whole mess, letting their lust for power blind them to what was happening around them. Their desire for power was why Thed got his foothold into Princirum in the first place. The fall of Princirum was the Rulers' fault.

And why would Kym help the Rulers when they'd never lift a finger for her in return? Ever since Kym discovered her magic, the Rulers made her life miserable. They were the reason she'd spent her childhood shunned after the Protectorate killed her aunt and uncle for speaking against them. They forced Kym to compete in a magical contest by threatening her mother's life. They confined her to the Palace of Water for months when they questioned her loyalty. They had other Favored spy on her, and when she said she wanted to leave, they tried to kill her. Kym didn't owe the Rulers anything.

"You are Princirum's last hope to restore the balance of the gods," Zara's construct continued. "If you fail, we will all be lost to the eternity of Thed. Be ready. Help is coming."

Kym opened her mouth, her refusal ready on her lips, but she was too late. The pure white construct faded away, plunging Kym's cell into darkness. Kym stared at the spot where it had stood, blinking rapidly to try and rid the impression from her retinas. *Help is coming*? Why would Zara's construct say that?

Kym shook her head. There was no way help was coming. And even if it did, she'd tell whoever it was to turn around and leave. She was done cleaning up the Rulers' messes for them. She'd stay in her cell, where there was no magic, no conquering gods, and the only pain was in her dreams. Besides, how could she fight when her body was broken and shattered?

Kym lay back on her sleeping pad, her resolve as solid as the stone walls. The past minute never happened. She must have imagined the construct. She was starving, on the verge of dehydration, and sleep deprived. Her mind was probably playing tricks on her. She needed to try and sleep again. Maybe this time, she'd get a little more rest before her nightmares became too unbearable.

C H A P T E R   T W O

D A M O N

Kym's eyelids were boulders. She hadn't slept a wink for what felt like two days. She lay on her sleeping mat, staring into the darkness above her. She guessed her lack of sleep was a good thing. At least she didn't have any nightmares. However, she preferred the nightmares to the thoughts swirling through her mind.

No matter how hard she tried, she couldn't get the shimmering image of Zara's construct out of her head. Why would Zara, the daughter of the goddess of life, ask for Kym's help? How could Kym fight the power of death if Zara couldn't? Besides, Kym was still determined not to help the Rulers after everything they'd done.

However, that wasn't what concerned Kym most. Zara's final words played on a loop in her mind. *Be ready. Help is coming.* Who could Zara send to help Kym in a magical prison? Kym knew it wouldn't be Zara herself. She, like all of the Rulers, never got her hands dirty if she could help it. And Kym doubted Zara would send a Favored. She'd said the Rulers forced the Favored into compliance. Then why did she say help was coming?

"Stop it," Kym ordered herself.

If someone came to Tenbatter, what could they do? The Warden was the only person who could open the cells. Kym knew the Warden wouldn't let her out, no matter who came. Kym needed to stop thinking about something that would never happen. The Zara construct was a product of her dehydrated, starving mind. No one was coming to get her, and she needed to get on with her life.

Kym pushed herself to her feet, walked to her counting wall, and carved another day in the stone with her chains. She felt her way through the dark to the corner farthest from her sleeping mat. She usually discovered food there a day or two after finishing what she had. The Pros hardly delivered food when she was awake.

Kym found a small hunk of bread in the corner. She rolled the little loaf across her upper arm, and a shudder ran down her spine as the bread's fuzzy surface brushed her skin. Tentatively, she raised her crippled hands to her face, and sniffed. Kym gagged as the musty, bitter smell filled her nose.

Kym shook her head. She swallowed, and her rough tongue dragged across the roof of her mouth. The bread was easier to stomach with water, so Kym returned the little loaf in her food corner. She'd have better luck after her daily drink. Kym wasn't going to die of hunger under the Warden's watchful eye. That would be far too peaceful.

She didn't have to wait long. The stone on the other side of the room rumbled, and she heard the telltale turning of the Warden's arm in the wall. Light seeped into the cell through the smokey entrance, and a Protectorate walked inside. Kym licked her lips as her stomach growled.

Of all the Pros, this one was Kym's favorite. He was always very gentle when he tightened her chains in the hook on the wall. Kym never felt like her arms were popping out of the socket like they did with the Warden. She knelt before he told her to do so. She was starving and wanted to get the whole thing over with.

"Alright," the Pro said after making sure Kym's chains were tight. "Let's do this."

Kym stood as two more Pros stepped into her cell, their spears pointed at her. She fought the urge to roll her eyes at the sight of the weapons, while her mouth grew dryer by the second. The one drawback to the Pros giving her water was they did everything by the book. After all, they didn't have the Warden's magic to keep her in line if anything happened. But oddly, she didn't mind. This was normal, and in that moment, normal was all she wanted. She just wished they'd hurry up.

Boom!

The stone walls quivered as dust drifted down on Kym and the Pros. Yells of pain reached Kym's ears through the smoke door, as did several cries of alarm. The Pros turned their spears to the door in one fluid motion as they shifted their stances, ready to lunge into battle.

Kym stared out of the smokey door, her heart thudding in her chest as her arms and legs shook uncontrollably. What was going on? When she'd visited Tenbatter a lifetime ago, the Warden told her the Rulers reinforced the building with their magic. Nothing could, or should, be able to harm the prison. So what made the building shake?

"Protectorate! *D'naity drah!*" Kym heard the Warden's stern voice waver as she barked outside the cell.

A shudder ran over Kym's skin. There was something in the Warden's usually stern voice Kym hadn't heard before. Fear. But why was the Warden afraid? She was a powerful Earth Master. She and her Pros could handle anything. So why couldn't Kym stop shaking?

"You heard the Warden," the Pro holding Kym's chains barked. "Pro Inali and I can secure the prisoner. You three, go help her."

Kym watched two of the Pros leap through the smokey door and out of sight. Pro Inali appeared a moment later, his spear pointed at the still-open entrance to Kym's cell.

Kym stayed where she was, not daring to move. Pain shot through her back as something sharp grazed the gap between her shoulder blades. The slack in her chains tightened, and pain exploded through her shoulders. Kym gasped, unable to keep her mouth shut.

"No moving," the Pro behind her ordered, his voice shaking.

Anger flashed inside Kym like lightning. She bit her tongue, fighting to keep her anger from exploding out of her. Why'd he cut her? She hadn't even moved, and if she had, she was in no condition to attack him.

More screams drifted in from outside Kym's cell. She stared

through the smokey door, her mind whirring as her spine tingled. What was going on out there?

"Squads two and three, *Agni drah!* Squad one, secure the—Ah!"

Terror coursed through Kym as the Warden's scream filled her ears. Kym didn't know what the Protectorate commands meant exactly, but she knew they attacked when they said "*agni.*" Whatever was happening out there required multiple Pro squads, and by the sound of it, they were losing. Kym tried to imagine what the Warden could want secured, but her fear overrode her reason.

"I'm going out," Pro Inali said.

"*D'lorh,*" the Pro holding Kym's chains barked. "Stay here."

"But Bronix, the Warden—"

"*D'lorh,*" Pro Bronix ordered again.

Pro Inali turned his spear back to the door, his forehead covered with lines. Personally, Kym didn't know why Bronix wanted Inali to stay. Sure, her cell door was open, but she was chained to the wall by her hands and feet. She couldn't get out, even if she wanted to. Given the crashing outside, Kym would send Inali to help.

Two more Protectorate burst into Kym's cell, sweat shining on their faces. Their form-fitting robes were ripped and torn, and one of the Pros had a deep cut down his left cheek. She didn't recognize either of them, but that didn't mean much. Tenbatter had more Protectorate than she could count. But why were they in Kym's cell? Was the chaos outside so bad that they needed to seek refuge?

"What's the status?" Bronix demanded, his voice stern.

"What's going on?" Inali asked, although Kym heard the fear in his voice. "Does the Warden need assistance?"

The new Pros took a few steps inside Kym's cell. With four Pros and Kym kneeling on the floor, the already-small space seemed even smaller. Kym watched the two new Pros' eyes dart around before landing on Kym. A shiver ran down her spine, and she wished she could run away. Did they need to stare?

"She's here!"

Terror surged through Kym as the two new Pros lunged. Inali and Bronix raised their spears, but they were too late. Spears expanded in the hands of the new Pros, which they spun expertly around themselves, filling the small space with whirring metal. They whipped their spears around, striking Inali in the face while flicking Kym's chains out of Bronix's hands.

Kym fell face-first onto the stone ground. Pain coursed through her jaw as cries of pain and the unmistakable sound of metal striking flesh filled her ears. Kym squeezed her eyes shut, her thin frame trembling like a leaf. These new Pros wanted her, and they were fighting the other Pros to get her. But why? Slowly, Kym forced herself up.

Bronix stood in front of Kym, but she couldn't see Inali anywhere. Bronix lunged forward, his spear pointed at the two newcomers. One of the Pros stepped to the side, twirling her spear around her and gracefully deflecting Bronix's spear tip. Bronix reeled back, and from her place on the floor, Kym saw Bronix's eyes widen in shock.

The other new Pro stepped forward, and the back half of his spear collapsed in his hand. He spun his sword around, its tip glowing light blue. The sword slipped between Bronix's arm and grazed his chest. Bronix flew back with a crackle and collided with the wall before collapsing to the floor.

Kym's pounding heart filled her ears. Who were these Pros? Kym could tell they knew each other; they fought without uttering a single word. But that didn't tell Kym why they were there, or what they wanted with her.

The sword-wielding Pro knelt beside Kym, and all reason left her. She scurried back until she hit the stone wall. She stared at him, stars bursting in her eyes. What was he going to do to her? He'd handled Inali and Bronix with such ease.

"Blessed One," the Pro said, his voice worn and gentle. "Don't worry. You're safe."

Safe? The word buzzed through Kym's mind like an angry bee. She didn't know this Pro, who'd attacked his fellows and defeated them with ease. How could she trust someone who attacked his comrades? Whatever Kym felt, it wasn't safe.

Someone burst through the smoke door before Kym could say a word. He looked young, maybe fourteen, with dark brown eyes and matching skin. His dark hair hung in waves over his forehead, which shone with sweat. Something stirred in Kym's memory as the boy drew nearer. Kym tried to focus, but there was so much fear in her mind that it drove away all other thought.

He crossed the room in three quick strides, his glittering white clothes practically glowing in Kym's dark cell. He knelt in front of her, and the sword-wielding Pro bowed his head to the boy.

"Secure the room," the boy said in a quiet, gentle voice.

Kym couldn't take her eyes off the boy as the two Pros stood on either side of the smoke door. She just didn't know his face; his voice was familiar to her too. But where had she seen him? Something stirred in the deepest part of her mind—something about a dog in a cave?

"Hold still."

The boy held his hands over the coil of thick chains beside Kym. She watched him close his eyes and take a deep breath. Pure white spirals appeared on the backs of his slender hands, coiling around five times before reaching his wrists. They wrapped around his forearms several times, then stopped at his elbows.

The boy's shining white Marks ignited Kym's fearful mind. She knew where she'd seen this boy before. She'd found him crouched in a tunnel beneath Crystal Palace as darkness constructs attacked him. He was a servant at the Palace of Life, the home of Lady Zara.

"You're…" Kym croaked.

"Damon. It's good to see you again, Kym."

Damon didn't take his eyes off Kym's chains. She looked down, and her mouth fell open. Glittering white mist seeped out of the chains—life energy.

But Kym shook her head. Damon couldn't be using life magic. That was impossible. Zara was the only person in Princirum who could manipulate life. Besides, Damon was a servant, not a Favored. What was going on?

"You may want to look away," Damon said, his gentle voice strained.

Kym didn't need him to tell her twice. She turned from her glowing chains as a high-pitched whirring filled her ears. There was a flash of white light, the sound of cracking metal, and a shudder ran up her upper arms. Her heart pounding like a drum, Kym glanced down.

The chains that had bound her for over a year were gone, reduced to a pile of metal sand. In the light of Damon's fading Marks, Kym saw her arms properly for the first time. Like Damon, Kym also had spiral Marks on her arms, but hers weren't glowing. Hers were black and sunken, like someone had wrapped white-hot wire around her arms. Even a year later, the scars from the Rulers ripping her magic from her hadn't healed.

Her heart raced even faster as Damon grabbed Kym's numb hands and hoisted her to her feet. She barely dared to breathe as she tentatively took a step. Was she really free?

"You're a Life Favored," Kym croaked as he helped her to the door. "How?"

"It's complicated."

Damon led her through the smoke door. The inside of Tenbatter was just as dark as Kym's cell. Torches sat sporadically on the walls, giving off very little light. Below them, she heard more screams of pain as the fighting continued.

"Syreta, take her to the others," Damon said. "Zayven, push on."

Syreta grabbed Kym's arm and draped it over her broad shoulders. They moved down the winding tower steps, Kym's frail legs trembling beneath her. Kym peered over her shoulder, expecting to see Damon behind her. Instead, she watched him and Zayven climb higher into the tower.

"Where are they going?" Kym croaked.

"They'll meet us at the bottom," Syreta said, her voice heavy. "Fear not, Blessed One. You're—Ah!"

Syreta's grip on Kym's arm slackened. Kym's legs gave way, and she tumbled down several steps before stopping. Kym raised her head, pain coursing through her back and legs. Syreta lay a few steps above her, a massive cut in her shoulder. A Pro Kym didn't recognize stood above Syreta, his spear raised. The spear tip fell, and Kym's heart froze in her chest.

"No!"

Syreta spun like a top, kicking the Pro's legs out from under him in one sweeping motion. He staggered back, teetering on the edge of the stairs. Kym watched, her pulse thudding in her ears as Syreta kicked out. Her foot hit the Pro's chest, and he fell off the stairs and down the tower.

Kym stared at the place where the man had stood. Blood pounded in her ears, and her skin felt like it was vibrating. Syreta had pushed that Pro to his death. Kym's insides squirmed as she continued to stare at the place where his feet had been. Syreta was willing to kill for her. But why? What was Kym to her?

"Come, Blessed One," Syreta winced, hoisting Kym up by the crook of her armpit. "We need to join the others."

"Others?"

Kym's mind raced, the sounds of fighting growing louder the more they descended. Damon and Syreta had mentioned others. But who were they talking about? Kym tried to think of any possibilities. Her first thought was Zara, but that couldn't be. She was still possessed by Thed. But she'd said help was coming. Were Damon and these new Pros it? If they were, that still didn't explain who these others were.

Kym and Syreta reached the bottom of the stairs, and Kym's mouth fell open. Pros lay motionless on the ground, their spears lying beside them, their tips glistening and red. Kym shuddered as Syreta steered her toward the door. She closed her eyes, trying to keep her breathing under control. This was insane. Completely insane.

Kym opened her eyes and stopped dead in her tracks. Two girls, both around seventeen, sat hunched on the ground between two new Pros. Their clothes were ragged and worn, and Kym saw their bones showing through their skin. Their brown and red hair was longer than Kym remembered, and their faces seemed older, but their eyes looked just like they did in her nightmares.

A mixture of joy and dread surged through Kym. She couldn't breathe. Kat and Ashlyn. How were they there? Kym thought they'd died when the Rulers ripped their magic from them. But they weren't dead. They'd been in Tenbatter—just like her. The spark of joy inside her faded. If their time in Tenbatter had been anything like hers, wandering Nothingness would have been better.

"Rest here, Blessed One," Syreta said. She set Kym beside Kat and Ashlyn, then turned to the two other Pros. "Protectorate, *D'naity d'lorh.*"

Syreta and the other Pros stepped in front of Kym, Kat, and Ashlyn, their spears pointed at the stairs. Kym crawled closer to Kat and Ashlyn. Up close, they looked worse than when Kym first saw them. Several cuts covered Ashlyn's arms and legs, there was a large bruise around one of Kat's light brown eyes, and like Kym, their Marks were burned black on their arms.

"You look like crap," Kat croaked, the usual biting edge to her voice even sharper than Kym remembered.

"I thought…" was all Kym could bring herself to say.

"I know," Ashlyn wheezed darkly, a far cry from the light, gentle tones of Kym's memory. "I thought I was the only one here."

"Clearly, you were wrong." Kat shook her head.

"What's going on?" Kym asked.

"Didn't you get Zara's message?" Ashlyn croaked.

"Oh gods. That thing?" Kat groaned. "It was clear as mud."

"She'd said help was coming, and we needed to do something," Ashlyn said.

"We're off to a great start," Kat said, jerking her head to the bodies lying around them.

Kym shook her head. What was wrong with them? Why were they talking about Zara's message? They had far more important things to worry about—like getting out of Tenbatter alive. Kym's brain didn't have enough room for anything else. Until they got out of there, nothing else mattered.

"Here they come," Syreta shouted.

Kym looked up. Damon was running down the stairs, Zayven right beside him. Two more Pros hurried behind them, an eighteen-year-old boy supported between them. The spark inside of Kym burst into a billowing flame. Tomark. His long, wavy hair reached the middle of his back, and his skin looked oddly warped, like melted wax turned solid.

Kym pushed herself to her feet as Damon, Tomark, and the Pros approached. She flung her numb arms around Tomark's neck, his arms hanging limply on her shoulders. Kym pressed her forehead into his chest, and some of the worry inside her melted as the shouts around her faded. Tomark was there, and so were Kat and Ashlyn. They were all alive. Listening to Kym hadn't gotten them killed after all.

"We need to move," Damon said to the Pros. "Before they—"

"Protectorate! *Agni drah!*"

The Warden's voice cracked through the tower like a whip. Kym's arms trembled, and a shiver ran down her spine as the sound echoed around the tower walls. Above her, she heard the unmistakable sound of running feet. The Warden and her Protectorate would arrive any second.

"*D'naity!*" Zayven ordered as Tenbatter Pros bloomed out of the darkness, running down the stairs with their spears at the ready. "Defend the Blessed Ones."

The Pros rushed forward. Kym backed away, pressing herself into the wall as the fight broke out. Kym turned her back on the fighting as Tomark, Kat, and Ashlyn joined her. Why were these Pros fighting to free Kym, Kat, Ashlyn, and Tomark? They'd betrayed the Rulers and the gods by wanting to not be Favored anymore. These Pros, these warrior priests, should hate them for what they did.

Kym opened her eyes a fraction. Zara's Pros moved as one, running around the Tenbatter Pros, their spears constantly twirling around them. The Tenbatter Pros tried to attack, but Zara's Pros knocked their spears gracefully out of the way, forcing them to take a step back. Kym couldn't believe it. Zara's Pros were forcing the Tenbatter Pros back up the stairs.

A glowing green sphere streaked through the air, filling the dark tower with eerie light. Syreta screamed as it hit her in the chest, and she flew through the air. Kym's breath caught in her throat as she watched Syreta slide down the wall. Kym spun on the spot, and the bottom fell out of her stomach. The Warden stood on the stairs, her green Marks glowing, two more earth bolts above her hands.

"*D'naity drah!*" Zayven yelled.

Zara's Pros scattered as the Warden's earth bolts flew through the air. Kym threw her arms over her head, shielding her face from the exploding world around her. She needed to get out of there, but how? She, Tomark, Kat, and Ashlyn could barely move. They were utterly useless. But Damon wasn't.

Kym stared at Damon, his eyes wide as he stood behind Zayven. Anger burned through some of Kym's fear. Why wasn't Damon doing anything? Kym knew how powerful life magic was. Why wasn't Damon using it to help the Pros?

More Tenbatter Pros leaped off the tower stairs. They rushed toward Kym and the others, their spears expanding in their hands. Zayven and two of his fellows stepped forward. The back half of their spears retracted as they directed their swords at the oncoming crowd.

"Get the Blessed Ones out of here!" he yelled, deflecting a spear from hitting Kat. "We'll stay back!"

"As you command."

The two remaining Pros pulled Kym and the others to their feet. They pushed the others toward the door, but Kym couldn't bring herself to move. A Tenbatter Pro lunged toward her, his spear pointed at her chest. Kym braced herself, ready for the impact. One of Zara's Pros jumped between Kym and the spear tip, which disappeared in the Pro's chest.

"No!"

Kym ran forward, her limp hand outstretched as the Pro fell to her knees. Shock and confusion drove the fear from Kym's mind.

Why had she done that? Why was this Pro sacrificing herself so Kym and the others could escape? She didn't even know Kym.

"Stay back!"

Zayven lunged between Kym and the oncoming army. His chest made contact with Kym's, and the whole thing went ridged as he gasped. Kym looked down, and her legs went numb. A metal spear tip protruded from his abdomen as a deep red stain spread through his robes.

"Run," Zayven grimaced. He spun around, disarming the Pro who stabbed him in one fluid motion.

"No," Kym said, her voice shaking. "We're not leaving you—"

"Kym," Kat hissed. "C'mon. We gotta go!"

"I've completed the gods' plan, Blessed One," Zayven said, disarming another Pro and sending them flying back into the hoard with an electric shock from his sword. "But you…their plan for you isn't over."

Kym stared at Zayven as another spear pierced his left shoulder. He fell to his knees, his face full of pain, but he didn't stop fighting. The gods' plan? Kym had given up hope on the gods having a plan for her long ago. The Rulers took away her magic, she almost died, and death was on the verge of destroying Princirum. If the gods had a plan, why hadn't they done anything to stop that from happening?

"Go," Zayven said through clenched teeth. "Fulfill their plan. Restore balance."

"But…"

"Get them out! *D'naity drah*!"

Hands found Kym's shoulders. They pulled her back, and she didn't resist. Kym ran after Kat, Tomark, Damon, Ashlyn, and the other Pro to Tenbatter's massive front door. More screams filled Kym's ears, cutting through her like a knife. Her every instinct told her to look back, but she stopped herself. She already knew what horrors were happening behind her.

The Pro in front of Damon pushed open the door, and light spilled into the dark tower. Tears streamed down Kym's cheeks from her stinging eyes as she ran. She couldn't remember the last time she'd seen daylight. Damon led Kat, Ashlyn, and Tomark out the door, and Kym hurried after them.

"Get them out," the Pro holding the door shouted to someone behind Kym. "I'll hold them off as long as I can."

The pressure on Kym's shoulder vanished as she heard the heavy door thud shut behind her. The Pro steering Kym sprinted past her, quickly catching Damon at the front of the group. The vast green fields and trees were just as Kym remembered from her last visit. A stitch bloomed in Kym's side as sweat drenched her back and her face burned under the bright sun.

"Head for the trees." the Pro shouted over his shoulder. "We need to find cover."

A loud rumbling filled the air, and the ground shook beneath Kym's bare feet. A massive wall of earth, at least fifty feet high, exploded out of the ground. Kym skidded to a stop, her insides burning. She spun wildly around, looking for another way out, but the wall of earth completely encircled Tenbatter. Kym glanced back at the tower, and all the air left her lungs as terror coursed through her.

The Warden stood in Tenbatter's massive doorway. She held one of her arms up while the other clutched a red spot on her side. The Warden staggered forward, and Kym saw the pain on her face. Kym couldn't believe it. How was she still fighting?

"Go!" their remaining Pro shouted, running back toward Tenbatter. "You're our only chance. Restore life and balance to Princirum!"

"Verraph!" Damon shouted, his hand outstretched.

Verraph charged the Warden. Two spears expanded in his hands as he closed the distance between them with incredible speed. Streams of earth swirled around the Warden, glowing bright green as they reached her hands.

"Do something," Tomark demanded.

Kym turned around. Tomark was glaring at Damon, and Kym saw fear flash across Damon's face. Tomark's eyes were narrow, and Kym knew what he was thinking. Damon was a Favored, but they hadn't seen him use his magic to fight. Why wasn't he helping his Pros fight?

"You're a Life Favored, for Pheil's sake!" Ashlyn snapped. "Help him!"

"I—I don't…" Damon faltered, taking several steps back.

"Spit it out!" Kat snapped.

The ground trembled beneath their feet. Flashes of green light filled the air as Kym heard Verraph's scream of pain. She fought the urge to look over her shoulder. Whatever was happening at the tower didn't matter. Kym's only concern was getting as far away from there as possible.

"I don't know combat magic."

Damon's confident exterior melted as the words washed over Kym. Anger reared inside her like a wild animal, clawing at her insides. How could he not know any combat magic? The Favored, regardless of the element, were trained exclusively in combat. Why would Zara send Damon to break them out if he didn't know how to fight? Was he really there to help them?

"For Pheil's sake! What the Thed is wrong—"

"We need to go," Kat cut across Tomark, her voice cold.

Kat sprinted forward, Kym and the others right on her heels. More green light flashed in Kym's eyes as more screams assaulted her ears. Kym didn't have to look to know Verraph had fallen. Kat was leading them to a massive wall Kym and the others were in no condition to climb. The Warden had them trapped.

But Kym kept running, her blood pounding in her ears like a drum. She reached the earth wall right after Ashlyn, who was doubled over, her face green. Kym stared at the enormous wall of stone before her, and her heart fell. What were they supposed to do now?

"Suck the life out of it!" Kat barked at Damon.

"I…I can't. It's too big—"

"Not the whole thing, stupid! Just make a hole we can fit through."

Kym's heart raced as Damon held out his trembling hands and

invoked his Marks. White mist seeped from the wall while bright green bolts exploded around them. Kym staggered into Tomark, her ears ringing. The Warden was going to catch them if Damon didn't hurry up.

The wall blackened and cracked as the life energy drifted into Damon's hands. The black pieces crumbled to dust, and Kym sighed as she gazed through the small hole in the wall. Kat dove through first as a bright green blast exploded against the wall twenty feet away. As Tomark crawled through the hole, Kym chanced a glance over her shoulder.

The Warden was hunched on the ground, one hand holding her stomach, a bolt in the other. Protectorate spilled out of Tenbatter, their spears held high. They sprinted past the Warden, and Kym knew exactly where they were going.

"Hurry," Tomark shouted.

Kym tore her eyes away from the oncoming army. She crawled through the hole on her elbows and fell in a heap on the other side. Kym pushed herself up as fast as she could, ignoring the pain coursing through her. Damon landed light-footed beside her, glittering life energy above his hands.

"What now?" He stared expectantly at Kym.

Kym fought the impulse to kick Damon in the gut. Why was he asking her for orders? Whatever his plan was, Kym doubted it involved losing the Pros he'd brought with him. How were they supposed to defend themselves? They had no magic, no Pros, and clearly no plan.

"If you put the life energy back in the wall, will it fix the hole?" Ashlyn asked.

"Yes, but it won't be as strong."

"Do it," Kat said.

Kym's legs trembled as the glittering white mist floated from Damon's fingers into the pile of black dust. It rose into the air, turned back into solid stone, and sealed the hole as the first of the Protectorate reached it. Kym heard their spears scrape against the wall, along with several louder thuds that must have been bodies.

Relief washed over Kym as her quivering body relaxed slightly. She took several deep breaths, trying to slow her racing heart. She couldn't believe it. They'd made it out, and they were all alone.

"What now?" Damon asked, again looking at Kym.

Kym's insides boiled at the question. Why did he keep asking her for directions? Wasn't this Zara's plan? He should know what to do more than her.

"Now we run," Tomark said.

CHAPTER THREE

A REASON TO
FIGHT

KYM RAN AS FAST AS SHE COULD, HER INSIDES SCREAMING IN
protest. Every breath she took felt like fire in her lungs, but she
didn't stop. She stared determinedly ahead, not daring to look
behind her. She couldn't hear the Protectorate anymore, but that
didn't mean much. They could show up before Kym knew what was
happening and take her back to Tenbatter.

Damon ran a few paces ahead of Kym, Kat, Tomark, and
Ashlyn, his head turning a new direction every step. The worried
look on Damon's face made Kym want to lash out. What kind of
plan was this? It was clear to Kym now that Damon had no idea
what he was doing. Why would Zara send a servant who couldn't
lead or fight to break Kym and the others out of Tenbatter? It really
was the worst plan ever.

"We can't keep running," Kat snapped.

"Where are we going?" Ashlyn panted.

"We're nearly there," Damon called over his shoulder, his voice
quavering slightly. "Just a little farther."

Kym and the others pressed on, never letting Damon out of their
sight. But it was difficult. Kym's year-long confinement and isolation had taken its toll. Her legs and chest seared with pain, and so
much sweat poured down her back that her ragged dress was
soaked.

Damon darted through a gap in the trees, and Kym and the
others followed. A massive, light purple villa stood before them,
surrounded by perfectly manicured trees at least fifty feet tall. A
large fountain sat in the middle of the long drive, splashing faintly

in the afternoon light. Damon sprinted to the front door, and a shudder ran down Kym's back.

"What the Thed?" Kat panted. She stopped so abruptly that Kym nearly ran into her.

"Why are we at a Darkness Master's estate?" Tomark demanded.

"The Masters have been at the palaces for over a year," Damon said, his voice dark. "The estates are deserted."

Kym's eyes narrowed as Damon continued to glance this way and that. Kym couldn't quite place it, but something was definitely off. She knew many Masters, and none of them would leave the comfort of their estates and return to the palaces. Getting an estate was how the Rulers rewarded the Masters when they finished their training. Damon wasn't telling them the whole story, and Kym didn't like it.

"What?" Ashlyn looked just as confused as Kym felt.

"I'll explain inside," Damon said quickly. "I promise."

Kym looked at the others and saw her disbelief reflected on their faces. Could she trust Damon? She'd known him for less than an hour, and Kym didn't know what to make of him. But she knew Damon was right about one thing—they needed to get out of the open if they didn't want to get caught.

Tomark led the others inside. Kym followed Damon through the dark halls and into a large sitting room. Her eyes narrowed as she took in the dim space. Sheets covered the furniture, and dust drifted through the air, twinkling in the sparse shafts of light. The tightness in Kym's chest lessened slightly. This place did look like no one had been there for months.

"Alright," Tomark said once Ashlyn was inside. His voice was hoarse, and there was an edge to it that made the hairs on Kym's neck stand on end. "We're inside. Tell us what's going on."

Damon took a deep breath. Kym watched his eyes dart between herself and the others as he twisted his fingers around the edge of his white shirt. Kym couldn't believe it. Why was he nervous?

"Lady Zara wants us to save Princirum," Damon said in a tremulous voice.

"We figured. She sent us a message and broke us out of prison," Ashlyn said coolly. "But why?"

Kym rolled her eyes. That was Ashlyn's big question? Why did she, and Tomark from the sound of it, care why Zara broke them out? They didn't want to help the Rulers, did they? No matter what Damon said, Kym had no interest in helping the Rulers. Her chief concern was how they were going to make it through the night.

"Zara said it's the gods' plan," Damon said. "You're destined to restore balance to Princirum."

"The gods' plan?" Tomark asked, his voice softer than before.

"Ha!" Kat barked. "Sorry to burst your bubble, kid, but the gods' plan is a joke."

"It's not!" Damon said defensively. "You will save Princirum, and Zara told me how to do it."

Kym suppressed a snort. Of course, Zara told Damon this was all the gods' plan. If the gods had a plan all along, then the Rulers were blameless for the part they played in Thed's rise to power. But Kym knew better. Saving Princirum wasn't their destiny. The Rulers made a mess by letting Thed take over, and they wanted Kym and the others to clean it up.

"Thed cannot exist outside of Nothingness on his own," Damon pressed on before Kat could retort. "He needs to anchor himself to living things to stay in Princirum. We need to break his anchors and force him back to the world of the dead."

Damon's words stirred something in Kym's memory. She'd heard those things before—only it hadn't been Damon who'd said them. She remembered Zara, her perfect features oddly pale as dark black veins covered her face like cracks. Thed spoke through Zara, boasting how he'd forced his way into the Rulers while they were too busy with the Calling.

"How are we supposed to do that?" Tomark asked.

"You don't even know how to fight," Ashlyn said.

"And in case you hadn't noticed, we're not exactly in fighting condition." Kat raised her arm, and Kym saw her hand hanging limp and lifeless from her wrist.

Kym stared at Kat, Ashlyn, and Tomark. Did they actually want to go along with this? It sounded like it. But why? The reason they tried to quit being Favored was because they didn't want to be manipulated by the Rulers anymore. That was why the Rulers tried to kill them.

"Zara may not have taught me to fight," Damon said, "but she taught me to heal."

He stepped forward and grabbed Kym's limp hand. She stepped back, jerking her numb fingers out of his grip. What did he mean he could heal them? She didn't want anything to do with magic, even if it meant healing her. Besides, her hands were beyond repair.

"Sorry," Damon said gently, taking a step back. "I'm not Zara, but I should be able to get your hands working."

But Kym didn't move. Instead, Ashlyn stepped between Kym and Damon. She held up her hands, her Marks looking like black cracks in her skin. Ashlyn's face was set, and Kym could tell she was bracing herself. Life magic could heal severe wounds, but it wasn't painless.

Damon led Ashlyn to the middle of the room. Kym hung back as they knelt on either side of a short table. Ashlyn rested her forearms on the wooden surface, and Damon slowly ran his hands over their blackened cracks.

"This would be easier with plants," Damon whispered, more to himself than to anyone else.

"You can heal her without plants?" Tomark asked, his brows forming one long line.

Kym's eyes narrowed. She knew why Tomark was confused. When Zara healed them, she used the life from various plants to replace what was lost. How could Damon heal Ashlyn without pulling life from something? What would he use? And if he wasn't using life, could he really be a Life Favored?

"I can," Damon said, his voice dark. "But it won't be fun for either of us."

Damon took a deep breath, and his pure white Marks burst into life on his dark skin. Kym squinted against the intense light, her heart racing in her chest, unable to look away. A cloud of shimmering white mist appeared, swirling gently around Ashlyn.

Kym couldn't breathe. The sight was all too familiar. The world around her faded, and suddenly she was outside the throne room in Crystal Palace, watching the same cloud of energy appear around Ashlyn's body as the Rulers ripped the magic from her. Kym wanted to turn away but stopped when she saw Ashlyn's face. Her pale green eyes were wide, and her frail shoulders shook violently. She, like Kym, was terrified.

Kym moved without thinking. She rushed across the room and knelt beside Ashlyn. Kym pressed her forehead into Ashlyn's shoulder, which shook more violently than before. Kym closed her eyes, but that didn't stop the glow of Ashlyn's life energy from penetrating her eyelids.

"It's alright," Kym whispered into Ashlyn's shoulder. "You're alright."

"It's not too bad."

Kym shook her head. Ashlyn wasn't fooling anyone as she trembled against Kym's forehead. Why was Damon drawing it out like this? When Zara healed their wounds in the past, she always put her hands on them, but Damon hadn't touched Ashlyn. What was he waiting for?

"What's that?"

Kym's eyes snapped open at Kat's voice. She sounded almost surprised. Kat's eyes were wide, and her mouth hung open as she stared at the glittering white mist surrounding Ashlyn. Kym's eyes darted around, taking in Ashlyn's life energy. Every so often, Kym saw a speck of yellow glimmer amid the white. It twinkled like a star and vanished as quickly as it appeared.

"Impossible," Kym heard Damon whisper.

Kym tore her eyes from the life energy to look at Damon. He, too, was staring at the flashes of yellow in Ashlyn's life energy. But unlike Kat, Damon didn't look surprised. He looked confused.

The life energy concentrated around Ashlyn's arms. She screamed, and Kym tried her best not to cry out. Kym pressed her forehead into Ashlyn's shoulder, trying to offer her some comfort. The glittering cloud vanished, and Ashlyn stopped screaming.

"You okay?" Tomark asked, kneeling beside Ashlyn and Kym.

Kym watched Ashlyn, her eyes locked on her hands, her fingers moving slowly up and down. The bottom fell out of Kym's stomach. Even though Ashlyn's Marks still looked like black cracks in her skin, her hands were moving. Damon had done it.

"How do you feel?" Kat asked.

"I…" Ashlyn tore her eyes from her hands to look at Damon. "I feel good. You said something was impossible. What did you see?"

"You still have magic."

"No, we don't," Kat said bluntly. "The Rulers ripped it out of us."

"She does," Damon nodded to Ashlyn. "It's faint, but it's there. That must be why you survived. The Rulers didn't take all of your magic."

Kym stared at Damon. How could they have magic left? The Rulers wouldn't let them keep it on purpose. Damon had to be wrong. The Rulers wouldn't mess up that badly. Besides, Kym didn't care if she had magic or not. She was done with it either way.

"Ash, try and do something," Tomark said.

Ashlyn held out her hand, staring at the space above her palm, her eyes narrowed in concentration. Kym didn't want to look, but she couldn't help herself. She held her breath, staring at the space above Ashlyn's fingers, waiting for something to happen. Nothing did.

"So much for that theory," Kat mumbled.

"Give me a minute," Ashlyn snapped.

Kym shook her head. Why was Ashlyn trying so hard? They all agreed they didn't want to be Favored anymore after the Calling. That included having magic. Kym walked to the window and nudged open the curtains with her elbow. Bright afternoon light stung her eyes as she looked outside. The vast front yard, covered in small, perfectly round bushes, was deserted. But how long would that last?

"Look!" Tomark shouted, his voice tense.

Kym spun around, expecting Protectorate to burst into the room. But there were no spear-wielding priests there—just Damon, Kat, and Tomark staring at Ashlyn. The Marks on her arms flickered between their blackened, burned state and a faint yellow. Ashlyn's face contorted in pain as she focused on the small sphere of light floating above her hand.

Kym stepped forward, dropping the curtains and plunging the room into shadow. Ashlyn's Marks faded, and her ball of light vanished. Ashlyn collapsed to the floor, clutching her forearms as she gasped with pain. Kat and Damon rushed toward her, their faces alight with excitement.

"See," Damon said excitedly. "I knew you still had magic."

"Barely," Ashlyn grimaced, pushing herself up. "It felt like my insides were burning."

"It's better than nothing," Kat said excitedly. "Do me next."

Kym retreated to the edge of the room while the others gathered around Damon and Kat. Even from the other side of the room, Kym saw the glimmers of green in Kat's life energy. But what was the point? What were they going to do after Damon healed them? The magic Ashlyn displayed was minuscule compared to what Kym knew she could do. Why did the others want their magic back if they couldn't do anything with it, especially if it was as painful as Ashlyn said?

The white mist around Kat faded, and Ashlyn and Tomark helped her to her feet. Kym watched Kat stare at her hands, several lines forming across her forehead. Her green Marks flickered on her arms, but Kym thought they looked fainter than Ashlyn's. A triumphant smile spread across Kat's face, and there was a twinkle in her light brown eyes. It was like her birthday had come early.

"Do something," Ashlyn said, sounding just as excited as Kat looked.

Kat ran from the room faster than Kym thought possible. The

others rushed after her, but Kym walked along at her own pace. Her insides squirmed uncomfortably. Once Damon healed Tomark, the others would want her to go next. There was just one problem with that. She didn't want him to heal her.

She knew she needed her hands to survive out in the world. And the thought of using her hands again, to once again be whole, was very tempting. But if the cost was getting her magic back, she didn't want Damon to heal her. Magic had brought her nothing but misery. Why would she want it back?

Kym found the others standing around Kat in the middle of the deserted garden. Kat's hands were pointed at the ground, and sweat dripped down her beet-red face. Kym stared at the ground. It was perfectly flat, with not a blade of grass out of place.

"Why…isn't…it…working?" Kat panted, not taking her eyes off the ground.

Kym's eyes darted between Kat and the grass-covered ground she was trying to control. Why wasn't it working? Ashlyn had controlled a small amount of light, so why was Kat struggling? Had Damon been wrong about all of them retaining magic? Kym had seen the flashes of green in Kat's life energy, but was it not enough for her to use magic after all?

"It's your energy," Damon said, his eyes narrowing as he stepped closer to Kat. "You don't have enough."

"There was just as much magic in my life energy as Ash's," Kat snarled. "And she did it."

"Only after light hit her," Tomark said.

"Of course," Ashlyn said, hitting herself in the forehead. "The planal Favored are at their most powerful when they are in contact with their element. That must be why I could only do magic when there was light hitting me."

"So," Kat retorted, finally lowering her arms. "I'm standing on earth. Why can't I move it?"

"The planal elements are different from the physical," Tomark said. "That's why we got the charms during the Calling. To level the playing field between the planal and physical elements."

"So you need the charms to do magic?" Damon said. "How're we gonna get them?"

"We don't know where they are."

Kym must have missed something. Why were they talking about stealing the charms? Kym saw so many problems with this plan, starting with it sounding absolutely crazy. Breaking out of Tenbatter was bad enough. Now Damon wanted to find and steal the charms from the Rulers? How did he even know what they were? Kym hadn't heard of them until halfway through the Calling.

Kym walked back inside while the others talked in excited voices. She sat on one of the couches, not even bothering to remove the dust-covered sheet. The silence pressed in on her, and Kym's body relaxed. After being alone for so long, hearing so many voices at once was a lot. Not to mention they were discussing something entirely insane. Finding the charms, getting their magic back, and fighting Thed sounded like a Ruler plan. Yet another reason why she didn't want to go along with it.

The door opened, and Tomark walked in. He pushed his long, wavy hair from his face, running his fingers through the tangled mess. Kym watched him walk closer, her insides twisting uncomfortably. Damon clearly healed him while they were outside. They must want her to go next.

"What?" Kym asked defensively.

"Just wanted to talk," Tomark said gently.

"What about?" Kym demanded, her voice a little harsher than she meant it.

"What's wrong with you?" Tomark asked. His voice was soft, but there was a bite there Kym wasn't expecting.

"Nothing's wrong with me," Kym snapped, anger boiling like lava inside her.

"There is," Tomark retorted. "You're not acting like yourself."

"Gee, I wonder why?" Kym shot back at him.

"Don't bite my head off," Tomark said. "I know you've been to Nothingness and back. We all have. But you...you're acting like Zara asking us to help save our home means nothing to you."

"Because it doesn't, Tomark."

"You don't mean that."

"Yes, I do!" The words exploded out of Kym as her anger reached its peak. "The Rulers tried to kill us! Why would we help them clean up this mess? They made it! They'd never help us if the roles were reversed. I said I didn't want to be part of this anymore when we tried to leave, and I meant it. I thought you died in front of me. Why would I help the people who did that to you? To our friends?"

Tomark stared at Kym, and she could see the shock on his face. She wasn't surprised. Tomark was a genuinely good person. That's why he won the Calling. Hearing Kym say she didn't want to help save Princirum must be a shock. But could he blame her? The Rulers ruined her life.

"What happened to helping people who couldn't help themselves?"

Kym stared at Tomark. Was he really throwing her words back at her? When Kym said that to Melana, the Ruler of Darkness, she'd been talking about protecting the cities from death demons. This was entirely different.

"The Rulers made this mess," Kym retorted. "They can clean it up."

"What about the people?" Tomark snapped, his dark hair flying around him. "They didn't ask for this, Kym! You promised to protect them!"

Kym opened her mouth to retort, but no sound came out. Her fiery anger waned, and Kym felt oddly empty. Tomark was right. She'd promised to keep the people of Princirum safe—and not just from Thed. She'd protect them from any threat, including the Rulers. How could she have forgotten about them?

"It won't be like last time," Tomark said, pressing on before Kym could speak. "We were stupid—trusting the Rulers would let us leave when we asked. We thought they wouldn't fall into Thed's arms. This time will be different."

"How do you know?" Kym asked. How could he be so sure?

"Because," Tomark said, his voice lightening ever so slightly. "The gods told me."

"Seriously?" Kym snorted. She couldn't help herself. "The gods are a joke."

"They're not, Kym," Tomark said. "I saw them. When I won the Calling, I got to speak with them, remember?"

"It kinda got eclipsed by other things," Kym said darkly. So many things happened after the Calling, she'd forgotten that Tomark's reward for winning was an audience with the gods where they'd grant him one request. She'd never even considered what he'd asked for.

"When I was with them, I was so confused," Tomark said. "The Rulers just told us the Calling didn't test our magic, but our character. I felt lied to, and even though I was the winner, I didn't feel like it. I didn't know who I could trust anymore."

"Did you see them?" Kym asked, her voice no more than a whisper. "What did they look like?"

"I don't really know," Tomark said. "They kinda looked like beings of pure element, if that makes any sense."

Kym fought hard to keep herself from laughing. It didn't make sense. She knew Tomark believed he'd seen the gods, but Kym wasn't convinced. If the gods had come to see him, why hadn't they done something about Thed taking over the Rulers in the next room? Kym didn't understand why they'd grant Tomark's request but not get rid of their eternal enemy.

"What did you ask for?" Kym asked.

"I asked them to answer a question," Tomark said. "I asked who I could trust."

"What did they say?" Kym shook her head. To her, the answer to Tomark's question was obvious.

"They said to trust the people who choose me, and not those who demand blind loyalty."

"Is that why you trust Damon?" Kym asked, raising her eyebrows as her anger mounted once again. "You're trusting a stranger on the words of gods who've never helped us. Do you trust

Zara too? According to all of you, Damon's here on her orders, following her horribly thought-out plan."

"No," Tomark said, his voice dark once again. "I don't trust Zara, and I don't know if I trust Damon. But I know who I do trust."

"Who?"

"I trust you. And Kat. And Ash. From now on, we only trust each other."

Relief spread through Kym. She'd been wrong. Tomark didn't blindly trust the plan created by people who tried to kill them. He was also reserving judgment on Damon, which made Kym's anger subside even more. Tomark was right. From now on, the only people Kym could trust were Tomark, Kat, and Ashlyn. They'd given Damon a chance, so Kym guessed it was worth a shot.

"Fine."

Kym followed Tomark out of the sitting room into the massive entryway. Damon stood alone in the shadows, his glittering white clothes shining like a beacon in the darkness. As Kym drew nearer, she noticed the deep lines on his forehead as he twisted the hem of his shirt around his slender fingers. Kym's eyes narrowed. What was wrong with Damon?

"So," he said, staring expectantly at Kym.

Kym shifted uncomfortably as his eyes raked over her. Did he need to stare all of the time?

"She's in," Tomark said, nudging Kym forward with his elbow. "You can heal her arms."

"Of course," Damon nodded.

He rushed forward, and his foot caught on something. Damon toppled to the ground, and Kym couldn't help but smile. She took a breath as Tomark helped Damon back to his feet, trying to calm her nerves. Damon invoked his white Marks, and Kym's insides turned to ice as her breath caught in her throat. Sweat coated her forehead as she tried to make herself calm down. It didn't work.

Tomark stepped between Kym and Damon. He wrapped his arms around her, and Kym shuddered. She couldn't remember the last time someone had hugged her or even put their hands on her gently. Tomark's long, slender arms wrapped around her, and a strange sense of calm washed over her. She buried her face in his chest. She didn't want to watch Damon do his work. It was bad enough watching him do it to Kat and Ashlyn.

"Breathe," Tomark's voice whispered right beside her. "You're gonna be okay."

Kym tried her best to breathe, but it was harder than Tomark made it sound. Even with her eyes closed and her face pressed into Tomark, she still saw the shimmering white light of her life energy through her eyelids. But even more than that, she felt it.

The aches and pains she'd grown accustomed to over the past year faded. But as the exterior of her body felt rejuvenated, something deep inside her grew heavy. It was like getting a massage after starving herself for a week. It was unlike anytime Zara had healed her in the past.

"Hold tight," Damon said, and his voice sounded just as strained as Kym's insides.

Kym braced herself. She knew what was coming, and there was no way to prepare herself. Damon's fingers slipped over her forearms, and that's when they exploded. It was like Damon filled her arms with white-hot fire. Her fingers burst into life, feeling every instance of pain as the life energy surged through her. Kym shook as the pain spread from her arms, filling her until it was all she knew. Kym pressed her face into Tomark's chest, her teeth bared against the pain, which was far worse than any time Zara healed her. She just had to get through this agony, then she'd have her hands back.

The pain faded as quickly as it came. Tentatively, Kym pulled away from Tomark, and she felt his arms slide down hers. Kym shuddered as Tomark's rough fingers met hers. Kym's eyes snapped open. Her fingers no longer hung limp and lifeless from the ends of her hands. She closed her hands into fists, and they did so without complaint.

"There," Damon panted.

Kym tore her eyes away from her hands to look at Damon. Sweat coated his forehead, and he swayed slightly where he stood. Tomark stepped forward and slipped his long arm under Damon's, catching him before he hit the floor. Kym reached out to offer him her hand, and she couldn't stop herself from smiling. She had her hands back.

"Where are Kat and Ash?" she asked.

"Out in the garden," Damon breathed, wiping the sweat from his forehead. "Deciding the best way to get the charms."

"Seriously?" Kym looked from Damon to Tomark. "What good will the charms do?"

"Well, if we get them, we could actually do magic," Tomark said.

"You're gonna need magic to save Princirum," Damon added.

Kym tried her best to hide her annoyance. What exactly was their plan? To save Princirum, or steal the charms from the Rulers? Kym had no idea how to do either. But Damon was right about one thing. They needed the charms, but not for the reason Damon or Tomark thought. No matter what they did, Kym knew the Rulers would find them sooner or later, and they'd need the charms to protect themselves when that happened.

"Alright." Kym looked at Damon, who stood a little taller as she addressed him. "Let's look for the charms."

Damon's smooth face seemed to burst with light.

"But," Kym said quickly, and Damon's face fell. "If anything goes wrong, or if any of us get hurt, I'm done. I meant what I said. I'm not a Favored anymore. You'll have to find someone else to fix the Rulers' mess. Deal?"

Damon opened his mouth to speak, but no sound came out. Kym's insides swelled. She knew she'd been harsh, but she needed to be realistic. She couldn't let her friends get hurt because of her, not again. She'd keep them safe, even if that meant dragging them away from a fight.

The front doors burst open. Light flooded the room as a gust of wind disturbed the layer of dust covering the furniture. Kym spun around, her heart racing. Kat and Ashlyn stood in the vast entryway, a tall woman dressed in dark, form-fitting robes slumped between them.

"What the Thed?" Tomark rushed forward, Damon right behind him.

"We have no idea where the charms are," Kat started.

"So we found someone who might," Ashlyn finished.

Kym stared at the Pro. She turned her head this way and that, blinking over and over again. Her eyes darted around, but never fixed on Kym or the others. Kym took a step closer. The Pro's eyes looked oddly colorless, and her face was blotchy and pink.

"What did you do?"

"Ash blinded her," Kat said flatly.

"You what?" Damon demanded. He sounded terrified.

"It was an accident," Ashlyn said, her ordinarily light voice dark.

Kym bit her lip. She knew she should feel bad for her. But she didn't. Kym recognized her as one of the Pros from Tenbatter. She'd kept Kym, Kat, Tomark, and Ashlyn locked up for over a year. Personally, Kym felt she deserved it.

"How is she gonna tell us where the charms are?" Damon asked, his voice trembling slightly.

"I'm gonna ask."

Kat let go of the Pro and stepped in front of her. Kym stared at Kat, her hands already balled into fists. She knew what was coming before it happened. Kat's fist disappeared in the woman's side, causing her to cry out in pain. Kym winced at the sound, fighting to keep her face calm.

"What are you doing?" Damon demanded, stepping forward.

"She's getting answers," Tomark said darkly, grabbing Damon's wrist.

Kym bit her lip as Kat crouched in front of the Pro. Kym's first impulse was to protect the Pro, but why would she? The Pros did worse to her when she was in Tenbatter. They didn't care about Kym, so why should she care about this Pro?

"Where are the charms?" Kat asked, her fist at the ready.

"You will pay for this," the Pro hissed.

"Wrong answer," Ashlyn said, shaking the Pro's shoulders.

Kat punched the Pro's stomach again, and Kym winced as the Pro cried out in pain. Kym shook her head. This was what the Pro deserved. Why did Kym feel bad for her?

"I don't know where the charms are," the Pro said frantically, a note of panic in her voice. "If they're with the Favored, they'd be at The Great Fortress."

"What?" Kym knelt beside Kat in front of the blind Pro. "Why would they be at the Fortress?"

The Great Fortress, the Palace of Darkness, was home to Lady Melana and her three Darkness Pupils. Why would the Favored, and the charms, be there? There wasn't even a darkness charm. There had to be something Kym was missing.

"As a reward for her loyalty, Lord Phillip, declared all Favored would train at the Fortress," the Pro said darkly.

T H E   P A L A C E
O F   D A R K N E S S

"This is a horrible plan," Kym said.

"I know," Damon said. "But—"

"What if it goes wrong?"

"Probably will," Kat muttered under her breath.

"It won't," Ashlyn said, although she didn't sound too confident.

"It can't," Tomark added, his voice dark.

Gravel crunched beneath Kym's feet as she walked down the front drive. Behind her, the estate looked just like it had when they arrived, except for the blind Pro tied up in the living room. Kym doubted she'd be alone for too long. The Tenbatter Pros were probably combing the forest for Kym, Kat, Ashlyn, and Tomark. Kym would be surprised if she was there for more than a day.

She and the others followed Kat down the front drive to the nearest clump of trees. After a few more persuasive hits, the Pro said they were half a day from the Great Fortress if they traveled on foot. Kym's legs ached after the first few minutes walking beneath the tall, silent trees. After months of inactivity in her cell, running for her life, and Damon's odd healing of her hands, all Kym wanted was to sleep for at least a week. Sweat poured down her face, stinging her sore eyes. The trees provided some shade, but it was so hot out Kym didn't think they made much difference.

The hairs on Kym's arms stood on end as the sun sank lower behind her. They'd arrive at the Fortress before nightfall, but then what? Kat suggested a plan before they left, but Kym thought it was more of a general idea. They'd wait until dark, then sneak in and steal the charms...if they were even there.

Kym's stomach twisted at the thought. If the Pro was telling the truth, the Favored and Masters were at the Fortress. It made sense to Kym; Melana had been the first Ruler to side with Thed when she tried to steal the Conduit and start this war by herself. But just because the Favored were at the Fortress didn't mean the charms were. When Nila gave Kym the water charm, she said the Favored only used them during the Calling. Why would Phillip, the Ruler of Death, give Melana the charms along with the Favored? The thought made Kym's stomach squirm again.

"Quiet," Kat hissed, making Kym jump.

Kym's eyes widened, her blood pounding in her ears. Had Kat seen something? This section of trees looked identical to the others Kym had seen.

"What is it?" Ashlyn asked, and she too spoke in a whisper.

"I think we're close," Kat said, her head moving slowly this way and that.

Kym peered sideways at Kat. As far as she knew, Kat had never seen the Great Fortress in her life. None of them had. She looked around, but saw no sign of the glittering, purple palace anywhere.

"How do you know?" Tomark asked.

"He...Xander showed me once," Kat said, her voice dark. "After fighting a death demon, I said I wanted to see the Fortress. It's just past those trees there."

Anger roared in Kym as she stared at Kat. Why was she talking about Xander? She hadn't given Xander, or Amber and Jazin, a second thought since the Rulers ripped her magic from her. They'd betrayed them, and did nothing when the Rulers tried to kill them. Kym hoped she'd never see Xander, Amber, or Jazin again. If she did, she knew there was no way she could keep her anger in check.

"She's right," Damon said. "I've been to the Fortress with Lady Zara."

"What should we do?" Ashlyn asked. "It's still light out."

Everyone looked expectantly at Kym, and she wanted to throw

her hands in the air. She'd been against this plan from the start. If she'd had it her way, they'd be running as far away from Melana as possible. Sneaking into her palace was the last thing she wanted to do.

"We should rest," Tomark said. "Stay behind the trees. That way, no one at the Fortress sees us."

Kym walked over to a tree. She slid down the rough bark, finally stopping when she hit the ground. She pressed her forehead into her knees, trying not to think about their ridiculous plan. She wished they'd stayed at the estate. There, they could hide if someone came looking for them. Here, out in the open, they were completely exposed. Kym didn't like it.

The sound of someone sitting on the hard ground reached Kym's ears. Kym heard their heavy breathing, but she didn't look up. Even after a year apart, Kym knew Kat's huffing breaths anywhere. Maybe, if she stayed still, Kat would leave her alone?

"What the Thed is up with you?" Kat demanded.

"Me?" Kym looked up, unable to keep her tone casual. "What the Thed's wrong with all of you?"

"We're not the ones who don't give a crap."

"I care."

"So why are you acting like this is a waste of time?"

"Because it is."

Kym bit her lip. Didn't Kat see they were making a huge mistake? Walking up to Melana's front door would've been risky when they had magic. But in their current condition, they were asking to get killed. They couldn't fight, and the only member of their group who could didn't know a thing about combat magic.

"Where's your faith?" Kat demanded. "We're still here, after all. There has to be a reason."

Kym stared at Kat, her mouth hanging open. She couldn't believe her ears. Kat was the last person Kym expected to put stock in the gods' plan. She was always the one who said the gods' plan was a pile of crap. But now, she sounded like she actually believed. Why?

"There is no reason," Kym said coolly. "The Rulers messed up. That's it. We should've died—"

"But we didn't," Kat cut across Kym. "Why didn't they kill us after?"

"I…I don't know," Kym stammered. The thought had crossed her mind several times, but she never could come up with an answer. "What I do know is for the past year, I thought you guys were dead. I wanted to do the right thing, and the Rulers tried to kill us for it."

"But they didn't," Kat insisted.

"Nothingness! Because they messed up!" Kym threw her hands up in the air. Why didn't Kat understand? "There's no special explanation. The Rulers got cocky and screwed up murdering us. Now we're walking up to Melana's front door; she hated us even before this whole Thed thing started."

"Fine," Kat snapped. "Still doesn't explain why you haven't made a decision since Damon broke us out."

Kym wanted to hit something. Did Kat really need her to spell it out? It didn't take an expert to know why Kym didn't want to make a choice. The last time Kym decided something, her friends almost died. She almost died. She wasn't eager to relive the experience.

"You heard the Rulers," Kym said finally.

"When?"

"When they ripped us. They said it was my fault. And they were right."

"This mess isn't your fault." Kat rolled her eyes. "If you think that, you're delusional."

"I know this whole thing isn't my fault," Kym snapped. "But what happened to you—to us—is. I'm the one who said we should leave. They tried to kill us because of me."

She turned from Kat, her eyes burning with tears. She didn't want Kat to see her cry. Kym wasn't sure why. Kat had seen Kym ball her eyes out plenty of times. But somehow, this time felt different.

"Look," Kat said, her voice flat and cold. "You may have said it first, but us leaving wasn't your fault. We all wanted to leave—for our own reasons. And you only thought we were dead because the sick and twisted Rulers made you watch us get ripped. I'd be worried if you weren't a mess right now. But you were right about one thing."

Kym turned to Kat, her arms wrapped around her knees. Kat never admitted when someone other than her was right. Kym wiped the tears from her eyes. What was Kat talking about?

"Right about what?"

"You're choices did cause this."

"You just said—"

"Let me finish, brainless. When you spoke out at that first Summit a million years ago, you showed us it was our duty to protect Princirum. And we're doing that now, magic or no magic."

Kym remembered that day. Melana had called the people who lived in the cities the detested, and something snapped inside her. Kym broke every rule she needed to follow and told Melana off for not caring about the people. Wasn't that what Tomark, Damon, Ashlyn, and Kat wanted to do? Protect the people? They didn't care about cleaning up the Rulers' mess. They wanted to help those who needed it, even if they didn't have magic to do it. So why didn't Kym?

"Something to think about." Kat pushed herself up and walked off, leaving Kym to sit alone with her thoughts.

DARK WALLS SURROUNDED KYM. She didn't remember getting there, but there was something familiar about this place. Fog swirled around her, its tendrils reaching forward like long, slender fingers, trying to pull her deeper into the maze. There was no light, and all around her, a faint rumbling filled her ears.

Kym shook her head, unsure where to go. Every time she tried to find her way out, she wound up back at the same spot. More than anything, Kym wanted to see light. She'd known darkness for so long. A glimmer of light would mean she was on the right path.

Kym took a step, and something wrapped around her ankles. She tumbled forward, her arms stretched out in front of her to break her fall. A shudder surged through her as her hands made contact with the wriggling ground. Wriggling? Kym's heart froze as the ground continued to slither beneath her. Why was it moving, and how? And that's when she heard the hissing.

Snakes slithered along the ground as far as Kym could see, at least ten feet long and jet black. Her breath caught in her throat as the scaly, muscular bodies twisted around her. Her heart raced as she tried to stand. But the snakes' powerful grip prevented her from moving an inch.

"Ssstay with usss, Kym."

The snakes' hissing filled Kym's brain as one coiled around her neck. Kym fought, trying to breathe the cool, damp air, but the snake was strong. Stars burst in her eyes as her vision blurred. She couldn't think. These snakes were killing her. She'd never escape this maze for the rest of time.

"Thisss isss where you will ssstay."

"No!"

Kym sat bolt upright, covered in sweat, as the last red rays of sunlight streaked the purple sky. Panting, Kym wrapped her arms around her knees. She didn't remember falling asleep, but she must have. How long had it been? It couldn't have been more than an hour.

"You alright?" Ashlyn asked, crouching beside Kym. "You were thrashing around."

"I'm fine," Kym panted.

"Good," Tomark said. He, too, knelt beside Kym, and his face was a faint green color. "'It's almost time."

"Really?"

Kym's insides turned to lead. Her eyes darted around, searching for something to take her mind off of her dream and what they were about to do. It was then that she noticed who wasn't there.

"Where are Kat and Damon?"

"Looking around," Ashlyn said, offering Kym her hand. "Kat said it was dark enough to sneak around without being spotted."

"So Kat's in charge?"

Kym knew Kat had many great qualities. She was smart, quick on her feet, and an exceptional fighter. But Kat was also extremely loud, abrasive, and rushed into things without considering the consequences. Leading a stealth mission didn't seem like something she'd excel at.

"I know," Tomark said. "I thought the same thing. But she and Damon have been here before. They might be able to tell if Melana upgraded her security with all the Favored training here."

"When'd they leave?" Kym didn't like the idea of them splitting up any longer than they needed to.

"Not sure," Ashlyn said, tucking her long, red hair behind her ears. "Maybe thirty minutes."

"They'll return soon."

Kat and Damon bloomed out of the shadows ten minutes later, joining Kym, Tomark, and Ashlyn in their small clearing. Kym wouldn't have known they were there if she hadn't watched them walk out of the trees. Seeing Kat move so quietly made the hairs on Kym's arms stand on end. Since when could Kat be quiet?

"What did you see?" Ashlyn asked, her voice shaking slightly.

"It's weird," Kat shook her head, her brows knit.

"Weird?" Kym didn't like the sound of that.

"Yeah, it was," Damon nodded. "There were some Pros outside, standing beside the door like they do. But that was it. Only a handful of guards."

Kym shook her head. Something was wrong. Before the Rulers locked them up, they'd called nearly all the Protectorate from the temples to the palaces. The Rulers, even with all of their magic, were so paranoid that they thought they needed an army of warrior priests to defend their strongholds, on top of the Favored who already lived there. Why would Melana only have a handful of Pros guarding her home, especially if the Favored were now training there? There had to be something Kat and Damon missed. The thought made Kym's insides writhe like a snake.

"But that wasn't the weirdest part," Kat added. "At sunset, they all went inside."

"What?" Tomark asked.

"Yup," Kat nodded. "The outside of the palace is deserted."

Kym glanced sideways at Ashlyn, expecting to see her fear reflected in those pale, green eyes. Instead, Kym saw relief.

"This may be easier than we thought," Ashlyn sighed.

"Now we just sneak in and find the charms before anyone wakes up," Damon said.

Tomark, Kat, and Ashlyn nodded. Kym, on the other hand, stopped herself from shaking her head. Something squirmed deep in her stomach. This couldn't be that easy. Melana wasn't stupid. Kym knew she wouldn't leave her palace unguarded for any reason. Had Thed's hold on the Rulers grown so strong they didn't feel the need to protect themselves anymore? The thought made Kym's insides squirm.

Kym followed the others as they crept forward under the moon's dim light. The Great Fortress was an enormous building, with many floors and even more towers protruding from its top. Vast, sweeping steps led to the huge double doors. Long, purple banners emblazoned with the symbol for darkness, the shadow, rippled on either side of the front doors in the gentle breeze.

Goosebumps rose over Kym's arms as she walked up the palace steps. She'd never been there before, but the violet palace looked strangely familiar. The solidified darkness walls, which looked like glittering purple stone in the moonlight, were identical to the palace Kym lived in for nearly a year. But now, her time at Wadita felt like someone else's life.

Tomark and Damon pushed on the massive front doors, which opened silently at their touch. Kym followed them into the grand, round entrance hall. Countless doors lined the far wall, illuminated by the light from the long, slender windows on either side of the front door. Torches sat in brackets on the purple walls, but none were lit.

"So," Ashlyn whispered. "Where should we look?"

Kym shook her head. She had no idea where Melana would keep the charms, or anything valuable. She still wasn't convinced the charms were there. Why would the Rulers even give them to her? And if the other Rulers gave Melana the charms, she'd keep them well hidden. Melana was smart. She'd keep the charms in a place only a few could access—those she trusted the most.

"The training rooms," Kym breathed.

"What?" Kat hissed.

"What if she's keeping the charms in one of the training rooms?"

Kym's heart fell as she said the words. A series of training rooms were located beneath each palace. They were accessed when a Ruler, or an extremely powerful Favored, magically opened the concealed staircase in the entrance hall floor. The Great Fortress was made of solidified darkness. Only Melana, or one of her Darkness Pupils, were powerful enough to open it.

"Nothingness," Tomark spat. "Why didn't we think of that?"

"It's perfect," Damon grunted, kicking the floor. "This way, only those truly loyal to Melana can access the charms."

"If they're even here," Kym said. If she was right about the charms being in the training rooms, there was no way they could get them. "Either way, we need to leave. Now."

"No," Kat said, her eyes narrowed at Kym in the moonlight. "I don't think they're down there."

"Where else could they be?" Ashlyn asked.

"I wanna poke around," Kat said, her eyes scanning the deserted entrance hall. "Hiding the charms in the training rooms is the obvious move. You thought of it in two seconds. Melana's not an idiot. The Rulers never trusted each other, no matter how much

Thed is influencing them. It makes more sense to hide them some-where unexpected, so no one could find them."

"Shh," Tomark hushed Kat, flapping his hands at her.

Kym whipped around, her insides rigid and cold. Had Tomark seen something? But the entrance hall was as deserted as ever. She turned back to the others, and she saw her tension reflected in their eyes.

"Kym," Damon said, his eyes wide. "It's your call whether we bail or not. What's your choice?"

"I…"

Kym's first impulse was to get as far from the Fortress as possi-ble. They'd already spent more time there than she wanted. But as she thought of leaving, something twinged in her stomach. They'd put themselves in great danger sneaking into the Fortress. If they left empty-handed, it would all be for nothing.

"You get twenty minutes," Kym said slowly. "If you don't find the charms, we leave. And we stick together."

The others nodded, and relief spread through Kym like a warm drink. At least this whole excursion wouldn't be a complete waste of time. Kat walked to one of the doors and pushed it soundlessly open. Kym's head never stopped moving as they climbed the stair-case in silence. She didn't understand where Kat was going. The top floors of the palaces were for the Favored's bedchambers. She couldn't think the charms were up there, could she?

After several minutes of climbing, Kat opened a door and led them through more hallways and staircases. Kym's irritation grew as Kat turned down more halls, always at the last possible moment. Kym was sure Kat had no idea where she was going. She'd never been inside the Great Fortress as far as Kym knew. So where was she taking them?

"How much farther?" Tomark panted after they'd spent five minutes climbing a tightly wound staircase.

"We're nearly there," Kat said between heavy breaths.

Kym clutched the stitch in her side. She didn't care where they were going at this point. All she cared about was sitting down and taking a break. This was more work than Kym had done in a long time. She was half tempted to sit and wait for the others to come back for her. It wouldn't be a big deal. They hadn't seen another soul since they'd stepped inside the palace.

Finally, the winding stairs stopped on a tiny landing with a small, wooden door. Kym, panting, stared at the door. Why, in a palace where everything was larger than life, was this door so tiny? She'd need to stoop down to walk through it. Even Kat, who was at least a head shorter than Kym, would need to duck.

"Where are we?" Ashlyn panted.

"One of the towers," Damon said, looking around.

"The tallest tower," Kat nodded, her hands pressed against her knees. "I figured this was the best place to keep something you'd want to hide."

"How'd you know how to get here?" Tomark asked.

"Oh c'mon." Kat rolled her eyes. "The palaces are all the same. I'd go up to Terradon's towers all the time when I was bored."

Kat pressed her hand against the door. It didn't move. Kym's heart pounded as Tomark and Ashlyn stepped forward and pushed with Kat. But still, the door didn't budge. Kym shook her head. Why would Melana lock a door at the top of her tallest tower? It didn't look big enough to hold anything important.

"Move," Damon said, his voice suddenly serious.

Kat, Ashlyn, and Tomark backed away. Damon stepped forward, took a deep breath, and invoked his Marks, filling the dark landing with light. He extended his hands to the door, and Kym held her breath, waiting for something to happen. Nothing did.

"The door's reinforced," Damon grunted. "I can't pull the life out of it."

Kym bit her lip. First, they find a door that's locked, and then it turns out to be magically protected. There had to be something Melana didn't want people to see behind it. But if they couldn't open it…

"Okay," Kat said quickly, her head turning wildly before she faced Damon. "Crash-course time. Blow the door open."

"What?" Damon's dark brown eyes grew wide. "But I…Zara never taught…"

"You're learning now," Kat said.

"Someone will hear us," Kym hissed, her pulse racing.

"Not if we're quick," Kat said.

Kym's breathing quickened. This idea was going from bad to worse. They couldn't risk taking the time to teach Damon to form a life bolt. It was a miracle no one had heard them already. But if Damon used magic to blast open the door, someone would definitely find them. And what would happen then?

"Let your energy flow into the life you're controlling," Kat said quickly, bringing Kym back to her surroundings. "Then throw it and push it through the air with your energy."

Damon focused on the space above his hand, and a small cloud of glittering life appeared. Kym couldn't take her eyes off the glowing mist. Where had it come from? Zara always pulled life energy from a source first. Where was Damon getting his life energy from? Kym watched Damon's dark brown eyes narrow, and the white light emanating from the mist intensified. The cloud condensed above his trembling hand, forming a smooth, white orb. Kym sighed as some of the tension inside her melted. Damon had done it. He'd made his first life bolt.

Damon threw the life bolt, and it collided with the worn wood in a blinding flash of white light. An echoing crash shook the air, filling every part of Kym's skull. Her insides felt like they were vibrating. If Melana didn't know they were there already, she knew now.

Kat kicked away the broken remains of the door and ran into the room. Kym hurried after her, blood pounding in her ears. What was so important that Melana wanted to keep it locked up? The room was small, with only a square table covered in purple cloth. A glittering red ring, a green armband, a silver bracelet, and a blue necklace sat on top of the shimmering fabric.

Kym's mouth fell open. This couldn't be possible. There they were—the four physical charms. She couldn't believe they'd actually found them. Kat had been right, and she'd been wrong.

"Let's get 'em and—ah!"

Kat's scream stopped Kym dead in her tracks. Kym whipped around, and terror coursed through her as several shapes materialized from the shadows. Kym's first thought was of people, but they couldn't be. Their arms and legs were overly long, and their heads hung limply to one side. They wore overlarge, ripped clothes, making the creatures look more disproportionate.

Kym's insides turned cold as the creatures stepped closer. It was a feeling she knew well from her time as the Vanquisher of Water. Death was radiating from the creatures in waves. These creatures were death demons.

"Stay back!"

Damon rushed past Kym, life energy floating in his hands. He raised them above his head, and the energy exploded outward. Kym covered her face, tears stinging her eyes in the sudden, white light as her long hair whipped around her. High-pitched screeches and hisses filled the air, followed by loud thuds.

Kym lowered her hands. The death demons lay slumped against the walls, their thin arms raised against the bright light. The table holding the charms flew across the room and crashed into the opposite wall in an explosion of broken wood and fabric. Kym glimpsed the charms glittering in the white light, then she lost sight of them in the wreckage.

"We're leaving," Kym said as shrieks filtered in from the landing. More creatures were on their way.

Tomark and Ashlyn hurried out the door, Damon right on their heels. Kym was about to follow them when she stopped. Kat wasn't running for the door. She was running for the remains of the table.

"Kat! What the Nothingness!"

"The charms!"

Kat skidded knee-first into the wreckage. Kym raced after her, the creatures staggering to their feet. The pounding in Kym's head intensified, as did the numbing cold. Kym grabbed Kat's arm and pulled with all of her might, lifting Kat to her feet as one of the creatures lunged for them. Kym needed to get Kat out of there, and she needed to do it now.

"What are you doing?" Kat demanded as Kym half led, half pushed Kat out of the room. "I only grabbed two of them."

"I don't care," Kym said, and she meant it. They'd agreed Kym could decide when they left. It was well past time. "We need to leave."

"But—"

"Kym's right," Ashlyn called from outside the room. "We need to go. Now!"

Out on the landing, Damon and Ashlyn were trying to force their way down the stairs. Kat tossed a silver bracelet to Tomark while shoving the green armband onto her upper arm. Kym's heart raced as more creatures crawled up the stairs. Damon tried to throw another life bolt, but collapsed before it left his hand, his face covered in sweat. Kym shook her head in disbelief. What was wrong with him?

"You guys gotta help," Kat shouted to Ashlyn and Tomark. "I couldn't get Kym's charm, and there's no earth in here for me—"

"I can't help either!" Ashlyn cut across Kat as she dropped to the floor to avoid one of the creatures' long arms. "There's no natural light in here for me to use."

"Move."

Tomark pushed past Kat and Kym to join Damon. He raised his hands, and his silver Marks flickered on his thin arms as the air charm glowed on his wrist. He shoved his hands forward, and two gusts of wind issued from his fingers. Kym's hair flew wildly around as the creatures in front of them toppled backward.

"Ah!"

Tomark collapsed to his knees, his face alight with pain as he clawed at his forearms. All thought of fear and escape vanished from Kym's mind. She ran forward, falling to her knees beside him. She lifted him into a sitting position, and her heart froze. Sweat covered Tomark's face, and his skin was ashen.

"What's wrong?" she asked as she helped him down the now-clear steps.

"It hurts," Tomark grimaced. "Like fire in my veins."

"Duck!"

Kym did as Damon instructed. She leaned over Tomark, covering his shining face with her chest. Damon's life bolt filled the dark stairwell with brilliant white light as it flew up the stairs. It exploded in the middle of the horde of creatures gathering behind them. Kym hadn't noticed them arrive. They were so quiet.

"We need to go!" Kym shouted, pulling Tomark to his feet.

They ran down the stairs three at a time. Damon threw life bolts to clear their paths, while Tomark sent gusts of wind at the creatures, keeping them at a safe distance. Kym held Tomark's arm over her shoulder whenever he wasn't attacking. Even that little bit of magic had him on the verge of passing out. If they didn't get out soon…

Kym burst after Kat into the moonlit entrance hall, and the bottom fell out of her stomach. More creatures than she could count crawled across the violet floor, their dark eyes flashing ominously. Kym tried to bury her fear as the creatures surged toward her. They were unlike any death demon she'd fought in the past.

Damon threw another bolt into the crowd of creatures. They scattered, running for the farthest corners of the room. Kym followed Kat and Ashlyn through the front door, Tomark still supported across her shoulders. They were nearly there. They just needed to reach the trees, then they'd be safe.

Bright purple light filled the night as the ground around them exploded. Kym looked over her shoulder, and every thought vanished from her mind as terror coursed through her like ice. A tall figure stood on a balcony several floors up, her vast dress billowing around her. Glowing purple orbs floated around her, illuminating her like odd moons.

"You dare steal from me? Soon, you will crumble beneath your fears. They will sort you out at Inferon with the rest."

Melana's voice jolted Kym's brain back into action. She needed to run, to get away from this place as fast as possible. Blasts erupted from the bolts floating around Melana, turning the night purple. One blast hit the ground a few feet from Kym, and chunks of earth and dust flew through the air.

Kat raised her arms beside Kym, her green Marks flickering faintly. The pieces of earth swerved away from Kym and the others as Kat cried out in pain. Kym watched, horrified, as Kat sank to her knees, clawing at her forearms. Kym didn't understand. First, Tomark's magic hurt him, and now Kat's. What was going on?

"We need cover," Damon said, diving to the side to avoid another of Melana's blasts. "Before she gets more help."

Kym couldn't think. Every bit of magic Tomark and Kat used, which had been basic at best, caused them intense pain. Nothing Kat or Tomark did could help them escape Melana. Damon could do some damage, but he'd used so much energy getting them out Kym feared what would happen if he pushed himself too far. Kym didn't see how they were getting out of there.

Ashlyn ran past Kym. She looked toward the moon, her arms outstretched like she was welcoming something. Ashlyn screamed as pale moonlight soared into her hands. She lifted the light over her head, and Kym closed her eyes, burying her face in Tomark's shoulder.

Kym saw the intense flash through her eyelids. She opened her eyes a fraction, and watched Ashlyn collapse as the world turned unnaturally dark. Kym looked to Tomark, who nodded and pulled his arm from Kym's shoulders. She ran to Ashlyn, who was barely stirring on the ground, Damon right behind her. They hoisted Ashlyn to her feet while Tomark helped Kat. Kym sprinted into the trees as more violet bolts exploded around her, not daring to look back at the Palace of Darkness.

CHAPTER FIVE

NOT WORTH THE COST

SWEAT RAN THICK AND FAST DOWN KYM'S BACK AS THE SUN slowly rose behind her. She had no idea where she was or where she was going, but she kept running, Ashlyn's arm around her trembling shoulders. Anger raged like a storm inside her, ready to erupt at any moment. She'd known going to the Great Fortress would be a disaster. Now, they'd stolen from the Rulers, who would surely punish her friends, or worse, if they ever found them. Why had she agreed to go? This whole mess was her fault.

"Hurry!" Damon yelled from Kym's other side. They still had Ashlyn supported between them.

"To where?" Kat asked thickly from somewhere behind Kym.

"Anywhere," Kym panted.

Kym's eyes darted around, trying to find somewhere, anywhere, for them to hide. But there were only trees as far as she could see. A shudder ran down Kym's spine that had nothing to do with her exhaustion. She knew Melana—she'd never let them get away after breaking into her palace and stealing from her. However, there was a glimmer of hope. Melana would never chase them herself. She'd send her Pros after them.

"There!" Tomark shouted, his voice strained.

Kym's head whipped around, the knot in her chest lessening slightly. She was running so fast she almost missed the vast estate, hidden by lines of perfectly manicured hedges. She doubled her pace, her insides searing as she dragged Ashlyn beside her. Kym gritted her teeth, ignoring her stinging legs as she willed herself to move faster. All that mattered was getting inside.

Kym burst through the massive front doors and found the inside deserted. Sheets covered the furniture, just like the last estate they'd taken refuge in. However, that wasn't what worried Kym. This estate was only a short run from the Great Fortress. None of the Water Master estates were this close to Wadita, the Palace of Water. After what happened, Kym wanted to put as much distance between herself and Melana as possible. But with Ashlyn, Tomark, and Kat hurt, it would do for the moment.

"We need to block the door," Kym said quickly, setting Ashlyn as gently as she could on a sheet-covered couch.

Damon nodded. They ran back into the foyer, leaving Tomark, Kat, and Ashlyn in the living room. Kym's eyes darted around the large room—there had to be something she could use to block the door. Damon ran to the windows and started pulling the curtains over the panes of glass. Kym's eyes fell on a large chest of drawers beneath one of the windows. It would have to do.

Kym pushed the drawers with all the strength she had, and it barely moved an inch. She took a deep breath and pushed again, and this time it moved even less. Kym's frustration raged inside her as her face grew hot. There was no way a set of drawers was this heavy. How had she gotten so weak?

"Help me!" Kym snapped through gritted teeth.

Together, she and Damon inched the drawers in front of the main doors, then ran around the rest of the estate, pulling every drape they found over the windows. Kym wiped the sweat from her forehead as she staggered back into the foyer. At least Melana's guards wouldn't see them inside. They were safe, but for how long?

Kat, Tomark, and Ashlyn were still lying in the living room when Kym returned. Luckily, they were still conscious, although Ashlyn looked like she was about to throw up. Kym knelt beside her and placed her hand gently on Ashlyn's back. Kym felt her shudder as Ashlyn stared pointedly at the patterned, purple rug.

"What's wrong?"

"It…it feels like…" Ashlyn stammered.

"Our insides have burned away," Kat finished.

Damon crouched beside Tomark. Out of all of them, Kym thought he looked the best. Damon invoked his Marks and ran his hands over Tomark's arms. Kym watched the lines on Damon's forehead deepen with every pass of his fingers. Kym's pulse quickened as she looked from Tomark to Damon. Something was wrong.

"What is it?" Tomark grimaced.

Damon didn't answer but moved to examine Kat. Kym's eyes narrowed as she stared at Damon, her stomach twisting around itself. He'd healed their hands when Kym thought they'd never work again. She could tell from the look on Damon's face that he was keeping something back. And whatever it was, Kym had a feeling it couldn't be good. But what was it?

"I think it's your magic," Damon finally said after looking over Ashlyn.

"What about it?" Kat asked.

"Well, it's…not yours," Damon said. "And I think that's the problem."

"What?" Ashlyn asked thickly.

Clearly, she was just as confused as Kym. What was Damon talking about? What did he mean that it wasn't their magic? That was impossible. Kym saw it glimmering in their life energies. Had Damon lied to them after all? Was Kym right to not trust him?

"The trace magic left inside you," Damon pressed on. "There's not enough for you to do magic on your own."

"We know," Tomark said. "That's why Ash needs direct light, and we need the charms. It amplifies what little magic we have."

"But maybe you don't have enough of your own magic to guide those energies safely."

"Dumb it down," Kat demanded, her eyes still shut.

"The magic from the charms…it comes from the Conduit. The Rulers caused a lot of damage when they ripped you. I think… forcing all of that pure magic through your damaged bodies is making things worse."

Kym looked at Kat, Ashlyn, and Tomark. Damon couldn't be right. When they'd used magic again, they'd said it felt like their insides were burning. Kym had assumed it was because of their lack of training over the past year. But if using magic was hurting them, as Damon thought, should they even be using it? Kym knew the answer in an instant. Of course they shouldn't. Why would they use magic if it was hurting them?

"Well, it doesn't matter right now," Ashlyn said, pushing herself into a sitting position. "You can still heal us, right?"

"I can't."

Anger raged inside Kym like fire as the world around her vanished. What did Damon mean, he couldn't heal them? He healed them when he broke them out of Tenbatter. What kind of Life Favored couldn't heal people? Kym wanted to throw something across the room. They were in pain because he convinced them they could do magic with the charms. This whole mess was his fault.

"Why not?" Tomark demanded angrily.

"You healed us before," Kat said.

"That was before," Damon said evasively. "I need to rest… before I do anything like that again."

Kym stormed across the room, not taking her eyes off Damon, who practically shrank under her gaze. He wasn't telling them something, and Kym was sick of not knowing things. Kym stood so close to Damon she could see the different shades of brown in his wide eyes. Up close, Kym saw dark circles under his eyes, and his cheeks looked sunken and hollow. If Kym didn't know any better, she'd say he was sick. But regardless of whether he was sick or not, that didn't explain his refusal to heal them.

"I brought these."

Damon plunged his hand into his pocket and pulled out several small vials full of clear liquid. Kym, taken aback, stared at the vials. They looked like the oils her maids used to put in her baths at Wadita. But what good would oils do them here? Her friends needed proper healing.

"They're Zara's healing oils," Damon said, passing one bottle to each of them. "She gave me these before I left. You've used them before?"

Kym and the others nodded. The Rulers gave them the oils to use during the Calling. Kym remembered her aches and pains fading into the background when she bathed in them after the Trials. But they always returned whenever she exited the water. But Kym didn't understand why Zara gave these oils to Damon. He was a Life Favored who could already heal himself and others. Zara giving these oils to Damon seemed like a waste.

"These don't heal," Ashlyn said, holding the vial close to her face. "They only help with the pain."

"When diluted with water," Damon said. "When used directly on injuries, they greatly speed up the healing process."

Kym looked closer at the tiny bottle. There wasn't a lot of it. Would there be enough to heal the damage from magically burning their insides? Kym looked from the bottle to Damon, her eyes narrowing. Why hadn't Damon handed these out earlier? The whole thing made Kym's insides squirm.

Kat, Tomark, and Ashlyn applied several drops to their forearms. Kym held her breath as they rubbed the oil over their blackened Marks. Their faces softened, and Kym's insides relaxed slightly. They weren't healed, but at least they weren't in pain anymore.

Kym plopped down on one of the couches, not even bothering to pull off the dusty sheet. Her brain felt like someone had pounded it with a hammer. The past twenty-four hours felt like a dream. How could so many things go wrong so quickly?

"Well," Kat sighed, her voice less strained. "That was a disaster."

"Completely," Ashlyn agreed.

"Totally," Tomark sighed.

"At least we'd been right about the charms being there," Damon said.

"Some good that did us," Kat grunted, leaning back in her seat. "We were wrong about everything else. The Favored weren't at the Fortress. That Pro lied to us, and we barely got out of there."

Kym couldn't help but agree with Kat. Sure, they had gotten the charms, but at what cost? Tomark, Kat, and Ashlyn, were hurt, and there was still something about Damon that made Kym feel uneasy. Melana almost caught them, and her guards were probably combing the forest for them as they sat there. Kym rubbed her throbbing forehead. How'd it all go so wrong?

"So what now?" Tomark asked. "What's next?"

"I vote for not getting caught," Kat said.

"You're not helping," Ashlyn snapped. "We should lie low for a while. Melana's probably told the other Rulers what happened by now. Could we hide in one of the cities?"

"No," Damon said firmly. "That's not what we're supposed to do. We need to break Thed's anchors to the land of the living. And the cities are all following what the Rulers say."

"Damon," Kym snapped, fighting to keep her anger in check. "How are we supposed to do that? I can't do magic. Kat, Tomark, and Ash can, but it's burning their insides, and you haven't learned any combat magic. How can the five of us fight an all-powerful god?"

Kym could see the hurt on Damon's face, but she didn't care. It was clear to Kym that Damon really had no idea what he was doing. The plan she'd thought he'd been keeping from her didn't exist. All he had was an idea, and Kym wasn't going to put her friends in danger for that.

"She's got a point," Kat mumbled. "I'm all for a good fight, but we need to be smart. We're not gonna save anyone if we get caught."

"Which could happen if we stay here too long," Ashlyn pressed on. "I don't care if we go to the cities or not. But we need to get out of Termubra."

"Agreed," Tomark said. "Any ideas?"

Kym stared at the blackened scars on her forearms. No matter where they went, these were a dead giveaway. They needed to go somewhere the Rulers wouldn't expect them to go, where they could lay low and devise a real plan.

Melana's words as they left the Fortress swam to the front of

Kym's mind. *They will sort you out at Inferon with the rest.* Why would Melana say that? Kym didn't think Melana knew they were the ones who broke into the Fortress. If she knew it was Kym and the others, she'd have killed them on sight. She must think they were other Favored. But why would other Favored want to break into the Fortress, and why would they need to be 'sorted out' at Inferon?

In Zara's message, she said the Rulers forced the Favored into compliance. Kym hadn't given it a second thought, but after what Melana said, she couldn't ignore it. If Favored needed sorting out, that meant not all of them wanted to follow the Rulers. And that gave Kym an idea.

"Maybe the mountains of Contellus?" Kat was saying. "Hide in our valley?"

"We should go to Inferon," Kym said, her voice no louder than a whisper.

"Could we make it to the mountains without being seen?" Damon asked, clearly not listening to Kym.

"We should go to Inferon," Kym said more loudly this time.

Kat, Damon, Tomark, and Ashlyn stared at her. Kat's mouth hung open, and Ashlyn blinked several times like she was having trouble focusing. Kym shifted in her seat. She never liked it when people stared at her. Kym knew her idea was crazy. If any of the others had suggested it, she'd think they were crazy too.

"You want to go where?" Tomark asked.

"Kym, we barely made it out of the Fortress alive," Ashlyn said.

"And now you wanna walk up to the Palace of Fire?" Kat asked, not even bothering to hide her disbelief.

"Look," Kym breathed, fighting to keep her voice calm. She needed to choose her words carefully. "Didn't you hear what Melana said when we left?"

"Not really," Damon said.

"My insides were too busy burning, in case you didn't notice," Kat mumbled.

"She said they'd 'sort us out' at Inferon," Kym pressed on, ignoring Kat's comment.

"So?" Tomark asked.

"Why would they have a designated spot for 'sorting Favored out'? I think the other Favored are there. And if some of them need sorting out, maybe they'd be willing to help us."

Kym waited for the others to respond. She knew her plan was crazy, but what other choice did they have? They needed help, and Damon already said they couldn't get it in the cities. If Favored were trying to fight back, Kym wanted to help them do it. They wanted to resist the Rulers, just like Kym, Kat, Tomark, and Ashlyn did before the Rulers tried to kill them.

"That sounds—" Ashlyn began.

"Like a great plan," Kat cut across her. Ashlyn shot Kat a dirty look, but Kat stared at Kym like she hadn't seen her before. "You're right. We're in no condition to fight a god. But those other Favored…they are."

"But…Lady Zara said…"

Kym watched Damon's dark brown eyes dart between her and the others. He looked like they'd taken away his favorite toy. She fought hard to keep the annoyance from her face. Why was he so determined to follow Zara's instructions to the letter? In case he hadn't noticed, her version of the plan ended the moment they left Tenbatter.

"Zara's not the one calling the shots," Tomark said to Damon, placing a hand gently on his shoulder. "But Kym, how do you know we can trust them?"

Tomark's words swirled around Kym's exhausted mind. She knew he was thinking about the warning the gods gave him. But Kym wasn't worried. If the Favored needed sorting out, then they weren't on the Rulers' side, just like Kym and the others. They'd broken free of the Rulers, but what had they done with their freedom? Ever since they'd escaped Tenbatter, they'd run blindly from one disaster to the next. They had an idea of a plan at best, and they couldn't agree on the best way to handle things.

Kat stood so abruptly it made Kym jump. Kat ran around the room, grabbing the most random assortment of objects Kym had ever seen: an old sheet from over the coffee table, several large cushions, a wooden chair, and three large, fragile-looking urns. Kym shook her head. What was Kat doing? They'd been talking about making a plan. How was her pile of junk going to help?

Kat marched out of the room, her odd collection of things threatening to spill out from her arms. Kym exchanged looks with Tomark and Ashlyn. They, like Kym, looked like they were trying to piece together what Kat was up to. On the other hand, Damon looked like someone had hit him over the head with a stick.

"Well, c'mon!" Kat's impatient voice called from the hall.

Kym looked warily at Tomark. What was Kat doing? Slowly, Kym stood and led the others after Kat into the hall. The dark corridor was deserted, but Kym saw an open door at the other side. Panic coursed through Kym like ice. What was Kat doing? They were supposed to be hiding from Melana's Pros. Why was she going outside?

Kym found Kat standing with her assortment of items in the back garden. Tall hedges, at least twenty feet high, surrounded the grassy lawn, which could have easily held Kym's childhood home. Towering trees sat grouped on one side of the yard, blanketing the bright green grass in shadow.

"Took you long enough," Kat huffed, dumping her objects on the ground.

"You didn't tell us what you're doing," Damon said.

"Isn't it obvious?" Kat gestured to the items piled around her feet.

Kym shook her head. Of course, Kat would think her plan was obvious. But Kym didn't understand why she brought all of those items with her. Or why they needed to be outside when they were supposed to be hiding.

"We're training," Kat said when the silence stretched on too long.

"What?" Kym asked, taken aback.

Kym knew that Kat didn't think things through all of the time, but this was on a whole other level. Training? How could they train? Kym couldn't even do magic, it hurt Tomark, Kat, and Ashlyn whenever they used it, and Damon didn't know how to fight. What good would training do?

"We're training?" Ashlyn asked tentatively. Kym saw her glance warily at the black scars wrapping around her arms.

"Yes," Kat said, her voice uncharacteristically serious. "If going to the Fortress taught us one thing, it's that we're horribly outgunned."

"That was your takeaway?" Tomark asked, his eyebrows raised.

"It was," Kat nodded. "If we're supposed to save Princirum—"

"It's your destiny," Kym heard Damon mutter under his breath.

"Whatever," Kat said impatiently. "We need to fight. So, Ash, Tomark, and I are gonna figure out how much magic we can do without setting our insides on fire. And Damon"—she shot Damon a look—"will get a real combat magic lesson. You need to do more than flash bright lights."

Kym shifted from side to side. What was she supposed to do while the others were training? Training had always been Kym's way of clearing her head, and she needed that now more than ever. But she couldn't go through the motions with them. At least if she had the water charm, she could suffer through training with the rest of them. For the first time since losing her magic, she actually wanted it back.

"Kym," Tomark said, nudging Kym with his elbow. "You take Damon. You can walk him through combat magic."

"What?" Kym had been about to walk inside.

Why was Tomark suggesting she teach Damon combat magic? She couldn't demonstrate how to do any of it. Besides, she still had a funny feeling that Damon was keeping something from her, and the last thing she wanted to do was spend time with him.

"I was gonna do that," Kat said.

"Kat, no offense, but your teaching style is…" Ashlyn trailed off, apparently trying to find the right words.

"C'mon," Kym huffed, waving to Damon.

Kym led Damon to the opposite side of the garden, her palms growing sweatier with every step. How was she going to do this? She'd never taught magic before, an honor Nila only entrusted to her most loyal Favored. She'd always been the one getting the instruction. And her teachers hadn't been the best instructors. Most of the time, she'd figure it out on her own while they glared at her.

Kym turned to Damon. In the bright morning light, he didn't look well at all. The circles under his eyes looked darker, and somehow, he looked thinner than he had inside. Kym's eyes narrowed. What was wrong with him?

"So," Kym began, her voice trembling slightly. "Combat magic. You already know how to manipulate your element, and you muddled your way through a few bolts at the Fortress. But you'll need more than that in a real fight. Right now, you're the best Favored we've got. Get yourself some life energy, and we'll get started."

Damon held out his hand, his white Marks shining on his dark skin. A glittering cloud of white mist appeared around Damon's fingers, which started to tremble violently. Kym narrowed her eyes. Why was he shaking? They hadn't done anything yet. And where had that life energy come from? Kym's eyes raked over Damon's fragile frame, and her mouth fell open as the realization dawned on her. Damon wasn't drawing from an external source. He was the source.

"Stop," Kym said abruptly, running forward.

Damon did as Kym instructed, a look of shock on his face. He lowered his hand, and Kym saw the sweat glistening on his forehead.

"Damon," Kym said, her voice stern. "Where are you drawing that life energy from?"

"What?" Damon asked. His eyes darted from side to side, like he was searching for an answer.

"Where are you getting the life energy you've been using?" Kym demanded, although she feared she knew the answer.

"Well," Damon said, his head falling slightly. "There hasn't been a lot for me to draw from. So…I've been using… my own."

Kym had feared this was the answer, but hearing Damon say it was worse than thinking it. He lifted his white shirt, and Kym had to stop herself from gasping. Dark veins covered Damon's torso, and Kym could count every one of his ribs. Anger and confusion swirled inside her. Not using your life energy to do magic was one of the first things she learned as a Favored. Surely Zara had taught him that. Why would Damon do this to himself?

"Why?" was all Kym could bring herself to whisper.

"Zara said I needed to help you guys complete the gods' plan," Damon said sheepishly. "Zara said I could use my life energy in an emergency, and I didn't want to let you down. "

White-hot anger filled Kym's heavy heart. This was all Zara's fault. She'd sent a wide-eyed fourteen-year-old boy to save the people who had once saved him. He believed in them, and he was putting his life on the line for them. But Zara hadn't remotely prepared him for the world he was entering. How could she do this?

"You are letting me down," Kym said slowly, placing a hand on Damon's shoulder, "by killing yourself with your magic. Your energy is finite. If you keep using your life energy, you will run out, sooner or later. From now on, you draw life from anything other than yourself. Agreed?"

"Agreed," Damon said, his eyes trained on the ground between them.

"Good."

Kym waited while Damon pulled life energy from the grass. The glittering white mist flew into his hands, turning the green blades under their feet black. Strangely, the sight made Kym relax a little. Dead grass was better than a dying Damon. Kym might think he was a little overbearing, but she couldn't bear the idea of him killing himself.

"Okay," Kym said awkwardly, staring at the life energy swirling above Damon's hands. "Magic…it's about intent. Having power and forcing it into your element isn't enough. Know what you want to happen. Let your intent become one with your energy."

Damon nodded, his eyes alight with excitement. Kym racked her brain. How had she been taught how to fight? It had been so long, Kym could barely remember. She'd been in her room with Kenna, another Water Favored who'd taken pity on her. She'd told Kym to throw a water bolt at her but failed to tell her how to make it reach her.

"So," Kym said, walking several feet away from Damon. "Remember how to make a bolt?"

"Yeah," Damon said in a quavering voice.

"Good. Make one and throw it at me." Kym paused, remembering how her attacks never made it to Kenna on her first try. "Push the attack toward me with your energy. Just throwing it won't be enough."

"You want me to attack you?" Damon asked.

"Yes," Kym said impatiently. "You have to learn somehow."

Kym took a deep breath. She used to practice evasive maneuvers every day before training at Wadita. This wasn't any different. Damon's bright white bolt flew out of his hands, and Kym moved without thinking. She lunged, and the bolt missed her by a foot. It exploded in a flash of white, burning a small hole in the brush behind her.

"Good," Kym panted, her heart racing slightly. Across the garden, she saw the smile growing on Damon's lips. "Again."

Kym spent the next hour showing Damon how to throw bolts, shoot blasts, and swipes. She even showed him how to make a shield. Kym couldn't stop herself from smiling. Damon was a quick study. And it gave Kym the opportunity to work on her rusty evasive skills. Luckily, Damon was still new to combat magic, and his attacks never actually hit her, although a few got close.

Kym stopped dodging when her face felt like a furnace. She ran over to Kat's pile of junk and grabbed two urns. Kym tossed them into the air, hoping to give Damon a bit more of a challenge. She knew immediately this was the right call. He struggled to hit moving targets, but his shield held well enough as Kym hurled broken pieces of urn at him. At least he could put up a fight if it came to it. Overall, Kym thought it was good for a few hours of work.

Kym called it when arms and legs felt like lead. Her muscles ached, and her throat felt like sandpaper, but for the first time in a long time, she felt like her old self. Damon didn't look much better with his sunken face covered in sweat, squinting in the bright afternoon light. Kym remembered how exhausted she'd felt after her first combat lesson. In fact, she had nearly passed out. Her insides squirmed uncomfortably. Maybe she should have given Damon a few more breaks.

"How'd it go?" Tomark asked as Kym and Damon joined the others.

"Good," Kym smiled, looking sideways at Damon. "I mean, he's not Vanquisher level yet, but he'll get there."

"You really think so?" Damon asked, his eyes wide.

"I do," Kym said, and she meant it. "How'd training go for you guys?"

"Well, long story about a short girl," Kat groaned. "Everything we tried hurts."

"Everything? Even after practicing—"

"That only made it worse," Ashlyn sighed. "And we only managed elemental manipulation."

"That's it?"

Kym suppressed a sigh. She'd hoped they'd manage to do more. How were they supposed to fight advanced magic if they could only manipulate elements in their natural states?

"Yup," Tomark said. "Even large-scale manipulation made the pain worse."

"The oil helps," Kat shrugged, rubbing a few more drops into her forearms. "The pain's tolerable now."

Kym eyed the bottle. She wasn't sure about applying it so often. Damon said it was for emergencies only. And even if it dulled the pain their magic caused, wasn't the damage still there? How were they going to save the rebelling Favored if their magic kept hurting them?

With their training over, they decided to leave for Inferon at nightfall. Kym had never been to Inferon, or Igmontis. But Tomark had. Igmontis and Silvaura were neighbors, so Tomark spent a lot of time there fighting death demons. But they needed to get out of Termubra and travel through Silvaura before they reached Igmontis. From there, they'd need to find Inferon and the other Favored. Luckily, Tomark knew where most of the Air Masters' estates were, so they could find places to rest along the way. It was going to be a long trip.

Kym and the others wandered around the estate, looking for anything they could find to take with them. Kat found some loaves of bread and fruit in the kitchen, while Kym discovered a hall closet full of purple cloaks. She wanted to find them other clothes as well —she, Tomark, Kat, and Ashlyn were still in the same tattered clothes they'd worn in Tenbatter. But aside from the cloaks, all the other closets were surprisingly bare.

As night fell, Kym led the others into the back garden. There was a small gate in the hedge, which Kat had discovered while they were training. Behind the hedge was a large stable. Horses roamed freely between the stable and surrounding fields, which looked very picked over. Kym stared at the horses walking lazily over the ground. How long had it been since someone came to check on them?

"The Servitude come check on them every few days," Damon said when Kym voiced her concerns. "They need to be ready just in case the gods' chosen show up in need of a horse. Even though Zara never leaves Crystal Palace anymore, she still had us make sure her carriages and horses were ready."

Damon found saddles in the stables. Kym lifted one of the saddles off the rack, and three different horses raced over to her. Kym smiled. Whoever's estate this was must have been good with horses. Damon took the lead, expertly placing pads and saddles on all the horses.

Kym climbed onto the back of a dark brown horse, her stomach twisting into knots. She peered over her shoulder at Tomark, who looked just as uncomfortable as Kym. They'd agreed to go to Inferon, but now Kym wasn't sure. It felt like they were walking right into an even bigger mess than the one they were leaving behind.

CHAPTER SIX

INFERON

MUCH TO KYM'S ASTONISHMENT, THE JOURNEY TO IGMONTIS WAS surprisingly uneventful. She'd ridden horses a few times before—on those days at Wadita when she couldn't stand being in the palace with the other Water Favored. She'd mostly just walk with the horses the stable master let graze on the beach, but actually climbed up one or two times for a little trot. This was nothing like that.

They rode through the night before resting at an Air Master's estate in Silvaura, and Kym felt like her muscles were splitting. There, they found another stable of perfectly trained horses. Kym worried they'd find a Servitude there tending the animals, but she needn't have bothered. They searched the estate and found it just as barren as the other two they'd seen. So, after a few hours of sleep, they set off for Igmontis with fresh horses.

Kym's unease grew as the forests of Silvaura dwindled, replaced by vast expanses of dark red sand. The temperature rose as sweat drenched Kym's clothes, and her tongue felt like sandpaper in her mouth. More than anything, Kym wanted a drink. But they already drank the water Damon put in their saddlebags. Secretly, Kym wished she had her magic back. At least then she could increase the water they had like she'd done so many times in the past.

Inferon, the Palace of Fire, glittered red in the distance. Kym could hardly miss it—it was the only structure for miles. Kym saw some mountains smoking way off behind the palace, but they were too far away to offer shelter. But that wasn't what worried Kym. Even from this far away, Kym heard the unmistakable sounds of people rising from the palace.

The others must have heard the noise, too. They stopped their horses at the same time as Kym. They dismounted, and Kym saw the tension in their faces as their eyes darted around the barren, red sand stretching before them. Kym took a shaky breath, trying to slow her pounding heart. It didn't work.

"Alright," Ashlyn said, and Kym wasn't surprised to hear her whispering. "What's the plan?"

"Plan?" Kat huffed. She pulled a saddlebag off her horse and filled it with dirt before slinging it over her slender shoulders. "We have a plan. We're gonna see if any Favored can help us clean up this mess."

"Kat, that's not a plan. It's barely an idea," Tomark said.

"Well, you come up with something," Kat snapped.

"This isn't going to be like the Fortress," Damon said, craning his neck to get a better look at Inferon. "I can see at least fifty Pros outside. And who knows how many are inside."

"Or what Favored are here," Tomark added.

"It doesn't matter," Kym said. Somehow, hearing them talk it through made her confidence rise. "We're not here to start a fight we can't win."

"But—" Kat started.

"We're not gonna fight them," Kym said pointedly. "Not if we can help it."

"What are you thinking?" Ashlyn asked.

Kym opened her mouth but closed it again. They needed to get inside without being spotted. Her eyes landed on their horses. The purple cloak she'd taken from the Termubra estate hung half stuffed in the saddlebag. Kym hurried over to the horses, their noses sniffing the sandy ground, and pulled the cloaks off the other horses.

"We use disguises." Kym threw the cloaks at the others.

"That's it?' Damon asked, his eyebrows raised.

"That's it," Kym said.

Kym fished in the pockets of her cloak, and her fingers brushed against something smooth. Kym pulled out the shimmering fabric and saw a pair of elbow-length gloves. Kym gazed at the black scars twisting around her arms. If anyone spotted them, they'd be discovered in seconds. Kym sighed and pulled the gloves on, along with the floor-length cloak.

"Look in your pockets," she said to Tomark, Kat, and Ashlyn. "If you have any gloves, put them on."

"By Pheil, Kym," Kat groaned as the others shoved their hands into their pockets. "It's a million degrees. Why do we need gloves?"

"Our scars are a dead giveaway," Tomark said, pulling on his gloves. "We're the only people in Princirum with them."

"If anyone recognizes us," Ashlyn said, and Kym heard the fear in her voice.

"Alright. Alright," Kat huffed. "But when I burst into flames, I'm gonna kill you."

"Fair enough," Kym nodded. "Remember, we're not wasting time in there. If anything goes wrong, we leave. Deal?"

Kym's eyes moved over the group, her insides writhing uncomfortably. She was asking a lot of them. This was her idea, after all. But she wasn't going to let anything happen to them. Not if she could help it. Slowly, the others nodded.

"Okay," Kym huffed. She turned to Tomark, and she could see the worry in his eyes. "If you see anyone you think we can trust…"

"I'll let you know," Tomark said, smiling faintly.

They left the horses concealed behind a group of boulders. Kym would've preferred bringing them along, but the others thought it may be too conspicuous. Kym hoped they'd still be there when they got back. Sweat poured down Kym's back as they crept forward, but she ignored it. The last thing she needed was Kat gloating about being right.

"I'm already melting," Kat hissed behind her.

Kym suppressed a shudder as Inferon loomed before her. The front grounds were expansive—the green lawn dotted with several crystal-clear ponds looked very out of place surrounded by the stretches of sand. At least fifty Pros stood in lines in front of the vast front stairs, and even more stood on either side of the massive front doors. Now that they were closer, Kym wished they'd taken the time to look around more before showing up.

But the Pros weren't the only ones on the grounds. Favored walked among the Pros like they owned the place in their fine red, yellow, green, blue, silver, and purple clothes. Kym knew the demeanor from a mile away. Her heart pounded in her chest as she walked among the Favored. This wasn't just some of them. By the look of it, this was all of the Favored and Masters. But why would they be at Inferon? A shudder ran over Kym's skin as she fought to keep her breathing steady. What would happen if any of the Favored or Masters recognized her or the others?

The Pros faced Kym and the others as they moved across the front lawn. Luckily, Kym had plenty of practice acting superior to Pros. After she discovered the Pros hunted down her aunt and uncle, she'd hated being anywhere near them. Ignoring them as she stepped onto the green grass was easy.

Kym tried to catch the eye of the Favored she passed, but they were focused on the direction they were walking. None of them acknowledged Kym and the others, but Kym didn't mind. They were probably just acting like this for the Pros. Maybe, once they were inside, they'd drop the façade.

Kym inclined her head to the front door as subtly as she could. A sigh behind her told Kym that at least Ashlyn understood. They hurried up the glittering red steps, the Pros moving to the side to let them pass. Kym noticed odd curves etched into the walls of the red palace, which looked like a combination of red, yellow, and orange in the bright sunlight. Kym couldn't stop herself from sighing. Solid fire was beautiful. If it was strange seeing the Favored and Masters together, watching Favored from different elements walk side-by-side was downright weird. They were supposed to hate each other, although Kym knew they only did to make the Rulers happy. So why were they together now?

Kym walked right past the Pros and stepped inside the palace. Kym's first impression was that she'd been stuck inside a giant ruby. Her eyes watered as she scanned the round entrance hall, which was full of Favored. An opening in the middle of the floor revealed stairs that descended deep below the palace. Favored emerged silently from the training room steps, all looking straight ahead.

Kym stared at them, her mouth hanging open slightly. She suspected they were coming from training, so why weren't they talking? Or even panting? Kym peered around the hall. Every single Favored shared the same blank expression. A shiver ran down Kym's back. Something was going on, and she didn't like it.

"Um…" Kym said to a passing Air Favored dressed in silver training clothes. She didn't even blink as she swept past Kym.

Kym turned to the others, desperate for a new idea. They looked just as confused as Kym. Why wasn't anyone in this palace reacting to them? It was like they couldn't even see them.

"Get off me!"

The shout echoed around the entrance hall, making the hairs on the back of Kym's neck stand on end. Reason told Kym to keep her head down, but the pain in the voice was too much, and she spun around. A group of Favored was walking in from outside. Four of them looked bored, just like the Favored in Inferon, but the one in the middle looked positively terrified. Rips covered his red clothes and there was an angry red burn across his left cheek. Two of the other Favored held his arms—a tall girl dressed in green, and a pale, thin eighteen-year-old boy in all black. Jazin.

Kym fought every impulse she had not to run forward. What was Jazin doing? Kym's legs trembled as Jazin led the screaming Fire Favored across the entrance hall and through a door on the curved wall. The boy's screams rang in Kym's ears as the door closed behind him and Jazin. He looked no older than twelve. Why was he so frightened? Kym needed to make sure he was okay. He'd resisted the other Favored, which meant he was exactly why Kym was there.

"Kym…" Tomark hissed, but he was too late.

She was across the entrance hall when she heard the others catch up to her. She placed her hand on the door Jazin had taken the

Favored through and paused. Would she be able to go inside? Back at Wadita, some of the doors required magic to open. But Kym didn't care. She needed to know what was happening. Kym pushed, and the door swung silently inward. Kym sighed. Finally, something was going her way.

The next room was dark except for a small fire crackling in a basin in the middle of the room. Kym's heart beat so loudly she was sure someone could hear it. She took a few tentative steps, then ducked behind one of the pillars supporting the domed ceiling. Slowly, barely daring to breathe, Kym peered around the pillar.

The screaming boy lay strapped to a table in the middle of the room. Three Favored stood over him, their red, yellow, and purple Marks shining like neon strings. The Fire Favored, who looked no older than eighteen, placed her pale, slender fingertips on the boy's shaking chest.

"Let me go!" the boy shrieked.

"You may begin," a sweet voice said from the dark edge of the room, making tiny bumps appear on Kym's arms.

"Do not worry," the Fire Favored holding the boy said. Her cool, flat voice sent chills down Kym's spine. "After today, you will fear nothing."

Kym stared at the Fire Favored's silky black hair as her hand tensed. The boy's screams cut through Kym like a knife. Kym saw the boy trembling as the girl dug her fingers into his chest. Kym didn't understand. What was she doing?

The boy's chest jutted forward, and fire exploded around the girl's fingers. She raised her hand, and the fire followed, resting above her palm. Kym's mouth fell open as the fire grew larger in the girl's hand, illuminating her face. A mixture of fear and anger swelled in Kym. She'd know those golden eyes anywhere. It was Amber.

Amber closed her hands around the fire. Tongues of flame burst from between her fingers as the boy screamed louder. Kym saw Amber's eyes narrow, just like Kym's did when she was concentrating. Her hands stopped shaking, fire stopped seeping between her fingers, and the room became oddly quiet.

Kym looked from Amber and to the screaming boy. But he wasn't screaming. He lay on the table, staring up at the domed ceiling, his face oddly blank. Kym shook her head. What had Amber done to him?

Kym looked back at Amber. Her hands were open, but the fire that had been there was gone. Instead, a single ember floated above Amber's palm. Amber waved her hand, and the ember floated to the boy's chest, where it vanished.

Kym's stomach lurched, and she clamped her mouth shut. She knew Fire Favored could control a person's emotions by manipulating the natural fire inside them. It was one of the Cladium—vile magic used by Light, Darkness, Fire, Air, Water, and Earth Favored to control some part of human existence.

Amber had used the fire Cladium on herself during the Calling so her emotions wouldn't stop her from winning. Kym never imagined what smothering her emotions looked like. Seeing it in person was worse than she could have imagined.

"That was disgusting," Kat hissed behind Kym.

"Why would Amber do that?" Tomark whispered.

"There," Amber said flatly. She stepped to the side, and the Light Favored took her place. "He will be easier to manage now."

The Light Favored reached out and placed his thumb and middle finger on the young boy's forehead. He stared at the spot, and so did Kym, as a light flickered like a star on his forehead. The Light Favored raised his fingers, and a glittering thread of yellow light stretched from the boy's head. Beside her, Kym felt Ashlyn's body tense.

"No," Ashlyn hissed, her voice full of anger. "Put that back."

Kym watched the glittering thread of yellow light, which was at least a foot long. Kym didn't know what the Light Favored was doing, but she knew it couldn't be good. He had to be using the light Cladium. Why else would Ashlyn sound so disgusted? But what part of a human was light?

The thread of light broke free from the boy's head when it was over a yard long. It drifted through the air like a fine hair caught in a breeze. The Light Favored released his grip on the strand, and it hung in the air, drifting eerily through the gloom. Then the string of light exploded.

Kym raised her hand, shielding her watering eyes. The light was so intense, it made her eyes burn, but she didn't look away. Shimmering, yellow light of different brightness and intensities filled the air above the boy. Kym stared, transfixed, at the swirling yellow mass. What was it?

"I understand," the boy said flatly from the table.

A section of the light above the boy glowed brighter as he spoke. Kym eyes darted to the light that had lit up with the boy's understanding. Kym's mouth fell open. Of course. How could she be so stupid? Thilg, the goddess of light, was also the goddess of wisdom. Kym looked back at the glittering light. These were the boy's thoughts.

"They will not trouble you for long," Amber said to the boy, her voice just as flat.

Kym's eyes darted between Amber and the boy. What did Amber mean? What was Amber going to do to the boy's thoughts? She'd already taken his emotions. Why would they take his thoughts? Kym wanted to hit Amber but stopped herself as the Darkness Favored, a large seventeen-year-old, stepped forward. Kym's insides did a summersault. She knew that muscular frame anywhere.

Xander placed his fingers on the boy's forehead, his purple Marks glowing, his face blank. Xander pulled, and a strand of purple light much smaller than the one the Light Favored summoned stretched from the boy's head. Xander released his grip on the purple strand, and it pulsed violently, quite at odds with the peaceful yellow thought. The Light Favored raised his hands again, and the boy's thoughts swirled around them like clouds.

Odd sounds reached Kym's ears; a dog barking, kids laughing, a woman screaming. A shudder ran down Kym's spine as the boy's thoughts grew smaller under the Light Favored's direction. The shining yellow light pulsed and flashed, but it wasn't as potent as the purple mist Xander created. When the boy's thoughts were no larger than a grain of rice, the purple cloud engulfed it, and the boy's thoughts vanished.

Kym shifted around her pillar, and she felt someone's nails scratch the top of her hand. She didn't care. She needed to see what Xander and Amber were doing. Kym saw the boy lying on his back, his face just as blank as the other Favored they'd encountered at Inferon.

"Connect him," the sweet voice said behind Amber. "He's ready to serve his purpose."

The Light Favored pointed his hand at a large stone full of glittering yellow light on a table beside the boy. Kym had been so focused on the boy that she hadn't noticed the enormous rock. What was it? What did the voice mean about connecting him?

A string of light rose out of the stone, drifted through the air, and touched the boy's forehead. There was a flash of yellow light, and the strand of light vanished. Kym watched boy's face, but it looked as impassive as ever.

Anger raged inside Kym like fire. This was what the Rulers had wanted for centuries. This was what Melana meant when she talked about 'sorting out' the Favored. Somehow, they found a way to force the Favored into submission once and for all. They had their magical army at last. It was something the Favored had talked about ever since Kym arrived at Wadita. Kym always thought it would never happen, but now, her worst fears had come true.

Kym's anger carried her to her feet as she glared at Amber, Jazin, and Xander's blank faces. How could they do this to a screaming kid? She thought she knew them, but she was wrong. She didn't know them at all.

Kym needed to do something. She needed to stop them before they did this to anyone else. Her eyes fell on the shining yellow stone. Smashing that felt like a good place to start. Kym had no idea what it did, but it had to be important.

"Kym," Kat hissed, her hand wrapping around Kym's wrist. "No."

"They can't," Kym said, her voice trembling with anger.

"We need to get out of here," Ashlyn whispered, also grabbing Kym.

Their hands only made Kym want to fight harder. Why didn't they want to stop this? Didn't they want to stop Amber, Xander, and Jazin? They betrayed them. They did nothing when the Rulers tried to kill them, and now they were doing their dirty work. If Kym and the others hadn't left, it could be them on that table. But more than anything, Kym wanted them to pay for what they just did to a little boy.

"Ash is right," Tomark said, also trying to push Kym back. "We gotta go."

More hands grabbed Kym's shoulders. No doubt Damon was trying to pull her back as well. Why were they so determined to stop her from helping? The whole reason Kym wanted to go to Inferon was to help the Favored trying to resist. She could've helped that boy. But now Kym was too late.

"Over here."

Kym heard the Pros before she saw them. The hands holding Kym vanished, and the unmistakable sounds of scuffling filled the air. Icy fear instantly replaced Kym's raging anger as someone yanked her hands behind her. How could she have been so stupid? She'd completely forgotten there were other people in the room.

Someone forced Kym out of the shadows. They led her to the center of the room, where Amber, Xander, and the Light Favored all stared blankly. Kym tried to worm her way out of the Pro's grip, but it was too strong. A scuffling behind her told Kym that the others were having just as much luck freeing themselves.

"Where'd—"

"—they—"

"—come from?"

Amber, Xander, and the Light Favored spoke one right after the other. A shiver ran down Kym's spine at how perfectly timed it was.

They didn't miss a beat as one stopped speaking and another picked up where the previous left off.

They stared at Kym, their heads cocked to one side. Kym bowed her head and prayed the others would do the same. Had Amber or Xander recognized her?

"Bring them here," the calm, sweet voice said from the shadows. "They will join the fold like the rest."

Kym chanced a glance up, fear coursing through her like fire. Amber, Xander, and the Light Favored stared impassively at Kym while someone stepped out from the shadows. She was tall, wearing a flowing red dress that complemented her dark complexion. The woman smiled sweetly at Kym, her face perfectly calm as a shiver ran down Kym's spine. Who was she?

"You will submit," the woman smiled, her brown eyes widening.

There was a scuffle behind Kym, followed by a cry of pain. Kym looked over her shoulder, and a mixture of fear and excitement raged inside her. Kat stood a little ways apart from the others, her eyes wide and her arms free. A Pro lay beside her, groaning as he clutched his stomach.

"Fat chance," Kat panted.

Kat swung her arm, and a stream of earth flew out of the large saddlebag on her back. It hit Amber in the chest, and she flew into the opposite wall, where she slid motionless to the floor. Kat jerked her arm back, and the earth she'd thrown returned to her bag.

Kym, Tomark, Ashlyn, and Damon all moved at once. Kym spun on the spot, and the Pro holding her lost his grip on her slick cloak. Kym stepped back as Kat ran forward. She slid to the ground, kicked a Pro's feet out from under him, and he fell to the ground with a thud. Several flashes of white light filled the air, along with a howling gust of wind.

Kym looked to Xander and the Light Favored, waiting for them to attack. But their faces were blank, and they watched the scene before them like it wasn't happening. Kym's fear momentarily faded as she stared at Xander. The Favored were trained to fight, so why weren't they?

The Fire Favored walked slowly to the glowing yellow stone. She placed her long, slender fingers on its surface, and the gem glowed like the sun. Shining yellow lines spread from the Favored's temples, covering their foreheads. The Favored all moved at once, their eyes locking on Kym as terror surged through her.

"Run!"

Kym didn't need Tomark to tell her twice. She turned and sprinted from the room as fast as she could. She didn't know what that woman was doing to the rest of the Favored, and she didn't want to know. All that mattered was getting out in one piece. How could Kym have let this happen? She was the reason they had gotten caught.

The entrance hall was full of Favored. However, unlike when they arrived, they were all looking at Kym and the others. Kym reacted without thinking. She dropped to the ground as bolts and blasts filled the air. Damon landed beside Kym as Ashlyn hurtled out in front of them. She stood in the light from one of the tall windows, her arms raised above her head.

Beams of light streaked from Ashlyn's hands, making Kym's eyes water. She squeezed her eyes shut, but even through her eyelids, she saw the multicolored flashes around her. Kym wanted to move, but fear rooted her to the spot as the sound of explosions filled her ears. If she was going to make it out of there, she needed to move.

Kym lifted her head, and a stream of earth flew past her. It soared across the room and hit one of the attacking Favored in the shoulder. He flew through the air, his blue clothes billowing around him. Kym stared at the muscular Water Favored as he rose mechanically to his feet. He didn't run, as Kym expected him to, but walked calmly forward. It was like the battle raging around him meant nothing. He didn't even bother pushing his golden hair out of his striking blue eyes.

Kym shook her head as Lance drew nearer. Lance? She hadn't

seen him since before the Fifth Trial of the Calling, and he'd been so angry Kym made it farther than him. But now, there was nothing behind his blue eyes. They were blank, and that scared Kym even more.

Kym jumped to her feet as Lance raised his hands. His blue Marks burst into life on his thick arms, as did a delicate chain draped around his neck. Kym's mouth fell open. Lance had the water charm. But how? She'd just seen it at the Great Fortress not two days before.

Something rushed past Kym, knocking her to the floor. Pain radiated from her back and side, and even though she opened and closed her mouth, she had trouble drawing breath. What hit her? Kym pushed her blond hair out of her face, and her insides turned to ice. Tomark and Damon were running at Lance, who had two water bolts glowing above his hands.

"What are you doing?" Kym cried out, pushing herself to her feet.

Neither Tomark nor Damon acknowledged her. They kept running, jumping this way and that to avoid Lance's attacks. Kym rushed forward, trying to avoid the bolts raining around her. What were Tomark and Damon thinking? There was no way they could beat Lance. He was one of the best Water Favored who ever lived.

Kym's hair billowed around her as a gust of air blasted Lance off his feet. He soared backward and crashed into the wall behind him. He slid to the ground and Kym held her breath as Tomark's silver Marks flickered feebly, his face full of pain. Had his attack been enough? Kym turned back to Lance, who was pushing himself up, his face still blank.

Kym's blood pounded in her ears. How was Lance already on his feet, and why was he only using basic attacks? Lance's magical knowledge was second only to Amber's. So why was he, and all the other Masters, limiting themselves to basic combat magic? Kym stared into Lance's blank face, which was just as impassive as that of the boy in the other room, and it was like a light going off in Kym's mind. Lance wasn't in control anymore.

A pure-white blast shot from Damon's hands. Kym stopped dead in her tracks as Lance flew back and crashed into the wall for a second time. Kym expected him to get up as he'd done before. But as Kym forced herself to take the last few steps toward him, Lance didn't move a muscle.

Damon bent over Lance but jerked back, staring at his fingers. Kym stopped beside Damon and saw his eyes dart from his hand to the water charm around Lance's neck. Had Damon tried to take it? Kym remembered when Lance tried to steal the water charm from her, he couldn't even touch it. But could Kym?

Kym knelt beside Lance and extended a trembling hand. Electricity coursed through Kym's veins the moment she touched the charm, but it didn't force her back like it had Damon. On the contrary, she felt almost drawn to the glowing necklace around Lance's neck. Kym lifted the delicate crystal chain from Lance, and a shudder ran down Kym's skin as the fine crystal thread touched her skin. She'd taken the water charm from him, but she had no idea how.

"At least this wasn't a total waste!" Damon shouted as he ran past Kym toward the door.

"Let's go," Tomark said, also running past her.

Kym hurried after them, slipping the water charm around her neck. Kat and Ashlyn were already at the door, their skin shining with sweat and their faces alight with pain. Kym doubled her pace, running as fast as she could as bolts exploded around her.

"We need to go!" Ashlyn shouted, ducking as an earth bolt soared over her head. "Before whoever's pulling their strings has them use stronger attacks."

Kym wanted to know what Ashlyn meant, but she pushed it from her mind. This wasn't the time for questions. She followed Kat through the vast front doors and out onto the grassy lawn. Kym expected to find more Favored and the Pros they'd seen earlier. But the grounds were deserted. Kym's insides turned cold as she thundered over the green grass. She didn't care why the grounds were clear. They needed to get out of there. Now.

"Running is pointless."

Kym skidded to a stop and spun around. At least ten Favored stood on the top of Inferon's front steps. They held their hands behind their backs and stared blankly down at Kym and the others.

"We know you, Ashlyn, Tomark, Kymbralyn, and Katarein," they said, their voices perfectly in synch. "What one sees, we all see."

Kym's legs trembled as her eyes darted between the Favored's impassive faces. Kym didn't know how they all knew what one saw, but one thing was clear. They knew Kym and the others. All of the Favored knew they were out of Tenbatter and fighting against the Rulers. Now, there was nowhere Kym and the others could hide.

"And we saw you." They raised their hands and pointed at Damon. "There is no stopping the inevitable. The time of Pheil has passed. This is the eternity of Thed."

The ground beneath Kym's feet trembled. The feeling of cold inside her intensified, and her stomach felt hollow and numb. Kym's eyes raked over the ground between her and the front steps. Cracks spread through the earth like spider webs which blackened as the ground gave another, more violent shudder.

A loud boom echoed in Kym's ears as chunks of rock and dust filled the air. She covered her face with her arms, trying to shield herself from the debris. She needed to run, but fear rooted her to the spot. Kym's eyes widened as something massive coiled out of the blackening ground, turning her insides numb.

The creature was at least one hundred feet long and as thick as a tree. It was unlike any snake Kym had ever seen, with jet black skin and matching eyes. But she knew better. No snake had fangs the length of her arm. No natural creature had a mouth full of jet-black flames. This was no snake. It was a death demon.

T H E
C H A S E

"SCATTER!"

Kym dove to the side, her heart thundering in her chest as brilliant black flames poured from the snake's mouth. The ground shook beneath her while crackling explosions filled her ears. Kym's arms and legs trembled as the snake's vicious hissing flooded her brain. Kym tried to move, but something stronger than fear rooted her to the spot.

Kym raised her trembling head. The snake opened its massive mouth, which could have easily swallowed Kym whole, revealing its murderous fangs. She saw more flames billowing in the snake's throat. The ground beneath the demon blackened and cracked, as did the patch of ground scorched by its fire.

Kym's hair whipped around her as a gust of wind rushed past her. The snake reeled back, the wind smacking its massive underside. Kym turned around. Tomark was on his feet with a pained look on his face, his silver Marks flickering.

Kat stood beside him. She raised her hands, and a chunk of earth rose out of the ground. Kat swung her arm, her eyes wide with pain, and the boulder rocketed forward. It hit the reeling snake in the jaw, and its shriek made Kym shudder.

"You okay?" Ashlyn yelled, running to join Kat and Tomark.

"I'm fine," Kym said, her voice oddly calm as she pushed herself up. Seeing her friends standing there jolted her sluggish mind into action. "We need to stop it before it hurts anyone."

"What?" Damon yelled, and Kym heard the fear in his voice. "We don't know how!"

"You don't," Kym said as the snake reared its head. Somehow, she thought its black eyes seemed angrier. "We do."

Kym gritted her teeth and ran right toward the snake. She heard the thundering of feet behind her, and her insides swelled. She didn't need to look back to know the others were there. This was what they'd trained to do.

Kym extended her arm to one of the ponds, and for the first time in over a year, let her magic flow through her. Energy surged from the charm around her neck, and Kym gasped. This wasn't the limitless energy that made her feel like anything was possible. It was like a million tiny pins pricking her veins. Kym shook her head, trying to ignore her discomfort. She'd felt worse.

A jet of water sloshed from the pond. It wobbled through the air and into Kym's outstretched hand, streams of water cascading off it. Kym stared at the giant snake, its mouth once again full of black flames. Trying to focus through the pain, Kym swung her arm, and her water flew forward with the force of a cannon. It exploded against the snake's muscular body, droplets of green, sludgy water flying in every direction.

Kym's arms exploded. She collapsed, clutching her stinging flesh as the world spun around her. The pinpricks from lifting the water were gone. Now, it was like white-hot razors were slicing through her blood. Lights popped in her eyes as her throat closed, and Kym trembled as the pain coursed up her arms and into her shoulders.

The edges of Kym's vision darkened as the world whirled around her. She ripped the purple gloves off her trembling hands. Her blue Marks flickered on her forearms, never staying as bright as she remembered them. There was no sign of the pain radiating inside her. On the outside, her arms looked perfectly normal.

"Stings like Heirraph, doesn't it?"

Ashlyn appeared beside Kym. She offered Kym her hand, who took it gratefully. Given the pain pulsating in her arms and head, Kym was surprised she could even stand. Stars flashed once again in her eyes, but at least the world wasn't spinning.

"Stings? How're you—"

"Damon's healing oil," Ashlyn said quickly. She uncorked her bottle and rubbed several drops into her forearms. "You'll get four or five moves before you need to—Duck!"

Ashlyn tackled Kym around her middle. They fell to the ground, and Kym gasped as the air was knocked from her lungs. More black flames flew through the air, right where they'd stood. Kym's stomach lurched, but she kept her mouth clamped shut. Being sick wasn't an option.

Kym staggered up, shoving her shaking hand into her cloak pocket as she ran. She pulled out the tiny vile Damon gave her, uncorked it with her teeth, and dribbled two drops on her stinging arms. She massaged the oil into her pulsing skin, and the pain decreased slightly. It was still there, like an odd throbbing beneath her skin, but was bearable enough for Kym to ignore—at least for a little while.

Kym hurried to join the others, throwing another jet of water at the snake. It hit the demon at the same time as a rock from Kat, which blackened and cracked as Kym's water once again turned a foul green color. The snake turned this way and that, hissing angrily as black sparks flew from its mouth. Her insides no longer scream- ing, Kym looked more closely at the death demon. She, Kat, Ashlyn, and Tomark had thrown several attacks at it, but Kym saw no sign of damage on its scaly body. Their attacks only made the demon angrier.

"This isn't working," Tomark shouted, his long hair billowing around him as another gust of air left his hands. "We're just pushing it around."

"I'm open to ideas," Kat snarled, throwing another large boulder at the snake. She fell to the ground, clutching her arms, her pain visible on her face.

All thought of fighting left Kym as she saw the pain in Kat's light brown eyes. She needed to get her friends out of danger, but what could she do? Usually, they'd use high-energy attacks to bring down a demon like this. But how could she do that? That type of magic was well beyond her capabilities, and her current attacks were dying the moment they touched the death-filled snake.

A white bolt flew over Kym's head and exploded in the death demon's face in a burst of brilliant light. Inky smoke bloomed from the place where Damon's life bolt hit. Kym stared at the spot, and her mouth fell open. A hole, at least as long as Kym's arm, was burned in the demon's face. But even as Kym stared, the hole repaired itself.

"Of course," Kym hit herself in the forehead. Why hadn't she thought of it before? Kym's water may be useless against the demon, but Damon's pure life magic wasn't. "Damon can kill it."

"He got lucky," Kat said.

"Then he needs to be again," Tomark said. "The four of us need to attack together. That should stun it long enough for Damon—"

"To finish it off," Ashlyn finished.

Kym ran toward one of the ponds, sweat dripping down her face, while the others took their positions. Her head throbbed but she ignored it as she rubbed another drop of healing oil on her arms. She couldn't be the reason they didn't pull this off. This plan had to work.

By the time Kym reached the nearest pond, the hole in the snake's face was nearly healed. She could see the glittering black flames building behind its massive fangs as her hands trembled beside her. Kat and Ashlyn were on either side of Kym while Tomark stood behind the snake as it whipped its head around, its great black tongue tasting the air.

Kym raised her hand, and more water rose from the pond as the prickling pain filled her arms. The ground to her left trembled, while to her right, light shone so brightly it made her eyes water. Kym didn't look away from the snake as her pounding heart filled her ears. Her hair whipped around her face as the wind howled around her. Kym's arms and legs shook with the strain of keeping her water aloft. But still, she didn't attack. Their timing needed to be perfect.

"Now!" Tomark and Ashlyn shouted as the blemish vanished from the snake's face.

Kym swung her arm, and it felt like she was throwing a sack of rocks through the air. Her water shot forward and splashed against the snake's scaly body with Tomark's gust of air, Ashlyn's beam of light, and Kat's boulder. The snake shuddered, its eyes popping wildly as green sludge, smoke, and chunks of blackened earth filled the air.

Kym collapsed, pain searing her arms as lights popped in her eyes. She watched, almost in slow motion, as Damon's life swipe flew from his hand. It hit the death demon's middle and sliced it cleanly in two. The two halves of the enormous snake slammed to the ground with an almighty shudder. Kym sighed and let her face fall onto the soft grass. They'd done it. They'd vanquished the death demon.

"Let's go!" Tomark shouted through the clouds of debris.

Even though every part of Kym wanted to sleep for days, she pushed herself awkwardly to her feet. She ran toward Damon and Tomark, sweat pouring down her face, and chanced a glance over her shoulder. The Favored who'd stood on the front steps were gone. Aside from the smoking remains of the death demon, the grounds were empty.

"Where's everyone?" Kym panted as they ran from Inferon.

"Who cares?" Kat demanded. "We need to put as much distance between us and them as possible."

"Agreed," Ashlyn panted.

"Let's find the horses," Damon said, overtaking Kym and taking the lead. "Hopefully, the Pros didn't find them."

Fear coursed through Kym like electricity. If the horses were gone, how were they going to get out of there? But she needn't have worried. They found the horses right where they left them, nestled behind the cluster of boulders. Kym mounted her horse, her head throbbing as sweat stung her eyes. She didn't want to walk for at least a year.

"Where to?" Tomark panted from atop his horse.

"Anywhere but here," Kat huffed as Damon, who was a good foot taller than her, gave her a leg up.

"And fast," Ashlyn added.

Kym's horse pawed at the ground as Damon mounted his. Kym bent forward, her hand outstretched, but her horse jerked its head before she reached it. Kym pulled back, holding tight to the reins as her horse stepped around, its ears darting this way and that. Kym's stomach twisted uncomfortably. What was going on with her horse? Maybe Damon would know? Kym turned to ask him, and her insides turned to ice.

Two snake death demons were slithering toward them across the sand. Each had a distinctive scar across its middle and were half the size of the previous snake. Terror coursed through Kym like fire. They hadn't killed the death demon. They'd split it in two.

"Go!"

Kym whipped her reins, and her horse galloped off. The others followed, the thundering of hooves filling the air. But the speed of their horses was nothing compared to the demons'. Every time Kym turned back the snakes were closer to them. Soon, they'd be near enough to spit fire at them again. But that wasn't even the worst part. Away from Inferon's glittering pools, Kym had no water to use, and no way to defend herself.

"How the Thed is that thing not dead?" Ashlyn shouted over the thundering of their horses.

"Thilg knows," Tomark said.

"Damon!" Kat shrieked. "You suck at killing death demons!"

Even with fear clouding her mind, Kym thought that was a low blow. Damon had only had one combat magic lesson. How was he supposed to defeat a death demon singlehandedly? Even with all of their training, Kym and the others never managed to kill demons on their own.

"It doesn't matter," Kym shouted. "But we need to kill them before they kill us."

"Then we'd better hurry," Tomark said.

The icy numbness inside Kym intensified, and she looked

behind her. The snakes were closer than before. One reared its head, and Kym saw the billowing black flames in its jaw. Kym gave her reins a good shake, and her horse picked up speed.

The ground shuddered, and a rock column shot out of the sandy soil. It slammed into one of the snakes, which flopped onto its back. The other snake, however, kept slithering toward Kym and the others. Kym turned around and saw Damon staring at the death demon, his eyes narrowed.

"Damon, no!" Kym shouted, but she was too late.

Damon raised his hands, and life energy swirled around his fingers. Kym saw his arms shake as Damon threw a swipe at the snake, which sliced through its neck. The snake's head toppled backward, and its body skidded across the sandy ground.

"Damon!" Kym shouted, unable to control her anger. "We talked about that."

Rage swirled inside Kym as she stared at Damon. He slumped over his saddle, and even from her moving horse, Kym saw the dark bags under his eyes. Kym wanted to slap him. Killing himself to defeat a death demon wasn't what they agreed.

"What's goin' on?" Tomark asked, his voice full of concern as his horse drew level with Kym's.

"It's Damon," Kym said. "He's been using his life energy to do magic, and it's making him…sick." She couldn't think of a better word.

"What?" Tomark's horrified expression reflected exactly how Kym felt. "Didn't he know—"

"He knows," Kym cut across him, her voice dark.

Kym kept her eyes on Damon as they rode, and he didn't look good. His dark skin was ashen, and he could barely keep his eyes open. Kym feared what would happen if he kept this up. How could Damon be so stupid? She'd told him what could happen if he used his life energy to fuel his magic. Why hadn't he listened?

Hissing rose behind Kym like a chorus, the icy cold of death growing even stronger inside her. She had a sinking suspicion there was more than one snake behind her. Kym glanced over her shoulder and wished she hadn't. The snake Kat had knocked down was back, as were two smaller ones. Each of the smaller snakes, about twenty feet long, had scars on their middle and beneath their necks.

Kym urged her horse to run faster. Why did the death demons keep coming back? None of the demons she'd fought in the past could do that. Damon couldn't keep cutting them in half—that just made more of them and worsened Damon's condition. Why couldn't they kill them? If they kept this up, there'd be too many snakes for them to fight. At least the smaller ones didn't move as quickly as the bigger one.

They rode as long as they could before the snakes got too close. Once the snakes were in range, Kat, Tomark, or Ashlyn would distract the nearest snake while Damon attacked. With no water and no way to help, Kym stayed at Damon's side, making sure he drew his life energy from something other than himself. Luckily, there were several small desert plants Damon could use. Once Damon finished one demon off, they'd move to the next one.

Kym sighed as she climbed back on her horse for what felt like the hundredth time. It took the snakes at least ten minutes to regenerate, and now they were so small the horses could walk at a leisurely pace, and they still stayed ahead of them. Kym knew the horses needed it. They'd given them plenty of breaks while they fought the snakes, but Kym knew they were exhausted. How long would it take before they needed a real rest?

Luckily, the snakes finally started to run out of steam. They kept getting smaller as they regenerated, and once they were about a foot long, Damon's attacks completely vaporized them. However, there was a small problem. By the time the snakes were small enough for Damon to destroy, there were nearly two hundred of them slithering after Kym and the others, who were all exhausted.

"I think the worst is over," Damon panted, sweat covering his dark face as the final snake vanished in a puff of black smoke.

"Anyone have a clue where we are?" Kat gasped as the sun sank on the horizon.

The barren deserts of Igmontis had slowly faded around Kym and the others as they rode, giving rise to large, grassy fields. Kym preferred these new surroundings, as they were much cooler. But she had absolutely no idea where they were. Green fields could mean Zara and Phillip's realm, or they could be in Luxmont or somewhere in Silvaura before the forest started.

Kym yawned but shook her head, determined to keep herself awake. They needed to find somewhere safe to hide for the night. She hadn't seen any Master's estates as they rode. But how could Kym find one if she didn't know where in Princirum they were?

"I think…" Ashlyn said after a while, jolting Kym's mind out of its daze. "I think I know where we are."

"You sure?" Tomark asked groggily.

"Yeah…" Ashlyn trailed off.

Kym watched her look around like she was searching for something she recognized. Kym held her breath. If Ashlyn knew where they were, they could find somewhere to sleep. Maybe she even knew somewhere they could lay low and come up with a new plan? Because after what happened at Inferon, they needed a new one.

How were they supposed to fight Thed and the Rulers when they had an army of Favored at their command? Forget about not having real magic; there was no way five teenagers, four of whom had spent the last year in prison, could fight an army of Favored. Not to mention the death demons. No matter what way Kym looked at it, they were entirely outmatched.

"We're in Luxmont," Ashlyn said finally.

"Okay…?" Damon said tentatively.

"I think we're near the City of Luxmont," Ashlyn said quickly.

"And that helps us because…?" Kat groaned.

"Could we hide in the city?" Kym asked Damon.

"I…I think so," Damon panted. He still looked winded after fighting the snakes for hours. "The Rulers have complete control of the cities. They haven't questioned them as far as I know."

"The cities are huge," Tomark said. "Surely we can find somewhere to hide and rest. At least for a little while."

Kym nodded. Ashlyn moved her horse to take the lead, and the others followed her as the sun sank lower in the sky. Relief spread through Kym as the enormous city walls peaked over the horizon. They'd made it. They were safe.

They found an excellent field full of tall, lush grass and a stream to leave the horses. Tomark didn't want to take them into the city. No one there rode horses, and it would be best if they didn't draw attention to themselves. Kym and the others agreed and walked to the city on foot under the darkening sky.

Kym had been to the City of Luxmont one time. As one of the final six Prized in the Calling, Kym toured the cities in a sick display of the Rulers' power. She'd seen the people's disappointment with the Rulers and magic during the Parade of Glory. They'd booed and rioted as Kym and the others paraded through the streets. So why were they following the Rulers now? A shiver ran down Kym's spine. To keep the Favored in line, the Rulers took over their minds. What had they done to the cities?

Kym followed the others through the city gates and onto the massive, deserted avenue. Hover cars lined the wide main streets, some parked at odd angles. Several shops were boarded up, and many of the buildings and roads had large pieces missing from them. Kym, sadly, expected that. With no Favored to protect the cities from the death demons, the damage wasn't a shock. It didn't stop the pang of guilt inside Kym as she walked past the boarded-up shops.

Protecting these people had been her job. She'd been the Vanquisher of Water; it was her duty to protect the cities from the power of death. But now, with signs of death's destructive touch everywhere, that seemed impossible. Kym still hadn't shaken the numbness the death snakes brought on. It felt like death was all around her.

"What should we do?" Ashlyn asked, looking around at the deserted streets.

"We could crash in one of those," Tomark jerked his head toward one of the abandoned shops.

"In there?" Damon asked, sounding a little disgusted.

"Well, do you have any suggestions, oh great life sucker?" Kat snapped.

"It'll at least be a place to rest for a while," Kym said quickly before Damon could retort. She squinted up the deserted street. "Where is everyone? It can't be too late."

"Don't question it," Ashlyn sighed, leading the way to the nearest boarded-up shop. "We've had enough bad luck lately."

Kym agreed, but she couldn't drive the thought from her mind. It was the beginning of summer, and the sun had barely set. The streets should be full of people going about their lives. Where were they?

The boards covering the door to the bookshop, Thilg's Bounty, were secured tightly. Damon, Kat, and Tomark pulled on a board for several minutes before it splintered and fell to the ground with a clatter. Kym spun around, her heart racing, sure someone had heard them. But the street was just as empty as before.

"Our turn," Ashlyn said, nodding to Kym.

Kym and Ashlyn grabbed another board and pulled. Kym's arms shook as she put all her weight behind her, the board cracking beneath her fingers. How long had these boards been up? It had to be a very long time, given how dry and brittle they were.

A long, withered hand shot out of the gap in the planks. Kym's arms went numb, and she jumped back. Ashlyn did the same, squealing as she flapped her hands rapidly.

"What in Nothingness is that?" Kym asked.

More hands, pale and thin, appeared in the opening they'd made. The boards cracked and splintered at their touch, then fell away in a cloud of black ash. Kym staggered back as the opening grew, and a figure emerged from the depths of the shop. Clothes hung loosely around its emaciated frame as the creature took slow, uneven steps into the night.

Kym froze, not daring to move. It was one of the death demons from the Great Fortress. However, unlike at the Fortress, this creature didn't swarm them. Kym stared at the solitary creature, its head moving slowly from side to side. It was like it had never been outside before. Kym narrowed her eyes. Could it even see?

A gust of wind shot past Kym, making her hair fly around her. It hit the creature in the chest, and it flew back into the depths of the shop. A chorus of high-pitched screeching emanated from the darkness, and more shapes moved into the opening, their black eyes glittering like the night. Kym spun around. Tomark had his hands outstretched, his face a mixture of pain and horror.

"Run!"

Kym and the others sprinted down the street, the horde of creatures shrieking behind them. Kym's heart pounded as anger raged inside her. Why'd Tomark attack the creature? It hadn't even attacked them.

"Good going, idiot," Kat hissed as they ran, anger dripping from every syllable.

"I didn't know there were that many," Tomark shot back.

"It doesn't matter," Kym said, although she agreed with Kat. "We need to get away."

"Where?" Damon asked.

"There!" Ashlyn shouted, pointing in front of her.

Kym saw where Ashlyn was pointing and ran as fast as she could. The old, grey truck was small, but its front window was open. Kym got there first and shoved her hand through the open window as the screeching behind her grew louder. She waved her hand over the sensor on the inside handle, and the door popped open. Kym jumped inside, and the others piled in after her. Ashlyn slammed the door behind her while Tomark, Damon, and Kat squeezed into the tiny back seat.

"What now?" Kat asked as the truck shook around them.

The truck gave an ominous creak, and several large cracks spread in the windows as Kym shuddered. Those creatures, like all death demons, killed everything they touched. Kym's stomach twisted into a knot. The demons were going to destroy the car, along with everything inside it.

"Drive!" Tomark shouted from the back of the truck.

"Um…"

Ashlyn held her hands over the two circular holo controls on either side of the driver seat. Nothing happened.

"You need to turn it on!" Kat said as something slammed into the truck again, and the creaking grew louder.

"How?" Ashlyn asked, looking wildly around.

"There!" Kym jammed the start button with her palm, and the engine revved to life. "Now drive!"

"I…I don't know…" Ashlyn stammered.

"How the Thed do you not know how to drive?" Kym shrieked as the truck tipped to one side before slamming back to the ground with an ominous creak. Even Kym's mom started giving her lessons before she discovered her magic.

"You're older than all of us!" Kat yelled. "Didn't your parents teach you anything?"

"I've been a Favored since I was eleven!" Ashlyn yelled hysterically. "My parents never taught me."

"Move."

Tomark clambered over the seat as Kym scooted over to make room for Ashlyn. Tomark placed his hands on the holo controls, which glowed pale blue at his touch. He raised his hands, the engine roared, and the truck hurtled forward. Kym slid down her seat, slamming her head on the dashboard while Kat and Damon yelled behind her.

"Car! Watch the cars!" Ashlyn shouted.

"I know!" Tomark barked. Kym watched him rotate his hands, and they veered to the side.

"Are they still behind us?" Kym asked groggily as she tried to pull herself back onto the seat.

"Yeah," Damon said. "And they're getting closer!"

Kym tuned to Tomark, whose eyes narrowed as lines creased his forehead. He lifted his hands higher, and the truck picked up speed. Ashlyn climbed into the back seat, and Kym gratefully pushed herself back into a sitting position. She stared out the cracked windshield, dark buildings zooming past them. Several blocks away, Kym spotted a building glowing in the distance.

Kym's heart jumped at the sight of it. This was the first building she'd seen that had power. If the lights were on, that meant someone had to be there. Maybe whoever it was could help Kym and the others?

"Go there," Kym said, pointing at the building.

Tomark sped them toward the building. But as they drew nearer, Kym realized it wasn't a building at all. It was a massive complex surrounded by enormous ring lights. Kym heard the creatures' shrieks growing louder as they neared the circle of lights.

The truck zoomed between two lights, and Kym's head split open. She cried out and pressed her hands to her temples. It was like someone had driven an ax into her head. Gasps of pain from the others filled Kym's ears, and the truck jerked to the side. Kym's insides lurched as she felt the world spin around. There was a crash and a shudder, and Kym flew into the dashboard. Then, the truck became quiet and still.

The pain in her head subsided, and Kym reached blindly for her door handle. She toppled out onto the hard ground, a high ringing in her ears. Ten yards away, the creatures stood at the edge of the ring of lights. Kym stared at the creatures, who stared back at her like skeletal statues. Kym shook her head. Why'd they stop chasing them?

Gruff, unfamiliar voices filled the air. Kym raised her head and saw several dark boots running across the ground. One of the pairs stopped in front of her face. Hands closed around her upper arm, and someone lifted Kym off the ground. Her heart racing even faster, Kym looked wildly around. More people dressed in dark clothes pulled the others out of the car. Who were all of these people? Clearly, the city wasn't as deserted as she thought.

"You're coming with us," said a rough, worn voice from behind Kym. "You're going to answer for your crimes against the gods and Princirum."

CHAPTER EIGHT

THE THILG INSTITUTE OF HIGHER LEARNING

"What?"

Kym struggled to free her arm from the man's grasp. She had absolutely no idea what he was talking about. Kym hadn't committed any crimes against the gods. The only crimes—and Kym used that word loosely—she or her friends committed were against the Rulers. If anything, their attempts to get away from the Rulers proved their devotion to the gods.

"Get them inside!" a different, female voice barked.

Kym pulled as hard as she could against the hands holding her. Guards held Kat, Tomark, Ashlyn, and Damon's hands behind their backs. The guards wore bulky, black clothes and had a long baton strapped to their belts. Kym recognized the uniform. But why was the city patrol accusing them of crimes against the gods? That was the Protectorate's territory. And anyway, Kym thought the city was deserted, given the level of destruction she saw when they arrived. How were these guards still here when the rest of the city was in ruins?

"Hands off, creeper!"

Kym failed to stifle her groan as Kat's voice rose over the chaos. Kat really picked the worst moments. The ground trembled, followed by a cry of pain and the sound of Kat's fist hitting someone. Kym tried to wriggle free as people cried in alarm, but her guard tightened his grip.

"Stop the traitor!" the female voice shouted again.

"Traitor?" This time it was Ashlyn's voice that Kym heard. "We haven't betrayed anyone!"

"Lies," the female voice said again.

Kym's guard attempted to push her forward, but she dug in her heels, letting her weight shift forward. Her guard lost his footing, and they both slammed to the ground. Kym, her side aching, rolled across the cobblestones before the guard could grab her again. She stood, pulling against the bands around her wrist as she looked desperately for a way out.

Tomark, Ashlyn, and Damon were still bound and held by guards. Tomark had a large cut down the side of his face, and dust coated all three of them. Kat stood several feet away, her hands extended toward the five guards in front of her. Kym sprinted between the Patrolmen and stopped at Kat's side.

"You'll fall off the edge of the world for your crimes." The female guard stood in the middle of the line, her voice full of anger. "You failed your sacred duty!"

"What the Nothingness are you talking about?" Tomark spluttered. His guard had him in a headlock.

"We're here to save you!" Damon shouted.

Kym fought the impulse to roll her eyes. Why did Damon need to shout that at the top of his lungs? They had no idea who these people were. For all Kym knew, these Patrolmen could work for the Rulers. Why else would they call them traitors? Besides, Kym wasn't entirely convinced that saving Princirum was her destiny. She barely survived a fight with one death demon. Damon was really overselling it.

"Declaring war on the gods' greatest creation is not saving us," the female guard spat. "You follow a vile path!"

Now Kym was lost. What was this woman talking about? Kym's eyes darted over the group of guards. What war were they talking about? Thed was using the Rulers to claim Princirum as his. Did they think Kym and the others were with the Rulers? They must, given the fear she saw in their eyes.

Slowly, Kym lowered her hands. These guards clearly thought the Rulers sent Kym and the others, a thought that clearly terrified them. These people weren't following the Rulers. But that didn't make sense. Damon said the cities were following the Rulers because they didn't know what was really going on.

"We aren't here to hurt you," Kym said slowly, taking a step toward the guards in front of her. "We're running from the Rulers."

Kym saw some of the guards in front of her relax slightly. The woman in the middle, however, didn't look convinced.

"Don't listen to her," she said. "I know who you are. You rode through our city in a chariot while the priests forced us to bow to you. You're Kymbralyn: Water Favored and Prized of Reta."

A bitter taste filled Kym's mouth. She remembered that day; the people in the city rioted when the high priest presented the Prized during the Parade of Glory. Kym hated every second of it. She'd wanted to help the people, but Nila's threat against her mother's life kept Kym from doing anything.

"The Rulers, and the Favored—you failed Princirum. You declared war on the gods and decimated the cities as you claimed power. You allied yourselves with the god of death, the only god who'd pity you. The Favored terrorized us with death demons until we accepted the Rulers as our new gods. But we are strong—we resist them and follow the true path of the gods."

Anger, sadness, and confusion swirled inside Kym like a storm as the woman's words washed over her. She was angry and had every right to be. The Rulers and Favored had failed her—and the rest of Princirum. Kym knew the feeling well. It was why she tried to leave in the first place.

But everything the guard said about the Rulers becoming gods and declaring war on Princirum made absolutely no sense. Why would the Rulers destroy the very land they wanted for themselves? And why were they talking about Thed as an afterthought? He was responsible for all of this happening, not the Rulers. Kym needed to know more. But she wouldn't learn anything if these people didn't trust her.

"I understand," Kym said slowly. "The Parade wasn't our idea. We didn't want any of this."

"So why do you follow the Rulers?" one of the guards asked, his voice trembling.

"We don't," Kym said, her voice shaking slightly. "We haven't for a long time."

Kym stepped up to the lead guard. She held out her arms, and the light from the glowing ring illuminated her forearms. The guards recoiled as they saw the blackened scars on Kym's trembling arms. She didn't want to show them. Somehow, the scars felt like something she wanted to keep private. But thanks to the Calling, all of Princirum knew Kym hadn't had the scars a year ago. They were proof that something had happened to her. Only the female guard didn't move, several lines creasing her forehead.

"What's that?" she asked, her voice slightly softer.

"We tried to leave," Kym said, lowering her arms. "We didn't want to be Favored anymore. The Rulers tried to kill us."

"How are you here?"

"Because the stupid Rulers messed up," Kat huffed.

The lead guard's face relaxed, and she nodded to the others. They removed Damon, Tomark, and Ashlyn's restraints, and Kym sighed. She hurried over to Tomark. His forehead was still bleeding, and his skin was tinged green.

"You okay?"

"I'm alright," he panted.

"If you're here to save us," the lead guard said, "why'd it take you so long? We've resisted the Rulers as the new gods for over a year."

"We..." Kym trailed off.

What could she say? They hadn't come to save them because they were locked in the Rulers secret prison didn't seem right. She doubted the people in the cities knew Tenbatter existed. Would they believe her if she told them the truth?

"How are you still here?" Damon asked. "I thought there was no resistance to the Rulers in the cities."

"It wasn't easy," the guard said evasively. "It was touch and go at the beginning, but we managed to hold on. Each of the cities resisted at first. As far as I know, we're the last one."

Kym's heart fell as she fought back tears. The cities had been through Nothingness since Thed's takeover, which Kym now suspected the people knew nothing about. And what had the Favored done? Nothing. They'd helped the Rulers do it. Kym tried to remind herself the Favored weren't in their right minds; they were being controlled. The thought didn't help much.

"So," said one of the other guards, stepping forward. "You said you're here to save us?"

Kym shifted on the cobblestone ground. If she was honest with herself, she wasn't sure why they were there. Sure, Damon broke them out because Zara had a change of heart, but what had they done since then? They'd wandered around Princirum, barely making it from one fight to the next. They were injured, tired, and had no idea how to break Thed's hold on Princirum.

"Yes," Damon said importantly, puffing out his chest. "We're going to free Princirum from Thed's control and send him back to Nothingness where death belongs."

Kym wanted to slap Damon. Why'd he tell these people that? It was clear to Kym that they didn't know Thed was the one behind the war they'd been fighting. Kym had wanted to find out more before telling them that.

"Oh." The lead guard raised an eyebrow. "So you're not here to fight the Rulers with us?"

"We'll save all of you when we put Thed back where he belongs," Damon said confidently.

Kym sighed, shaking her head as pain built in her forehead. This wasn't going well. She could see the little confidence the lead guard had in them vanish. She probably thought Damon was crazy. Kym would have, too, if she hadn't seen Thed possess the Rulers before they tried to kill her. Why couldn't Damon keep his mouth shut?

"We…should get you inside," the lead guard said slowly. "No telling when the morgar will return."

"The what?" Ashlyn asked.

"The morgar," the lead guard said. "The death demons that chased you here. Haven't you seen them before?"

"We saw them at The Great Fortress," Tomark said.

"Why were you at the Fortress?" The lead guard's eyes narrowed.

"We stole the—"

Kat stomped hard on Damon's foot, and he thankfully stopped talking. Kym shook her head. What was he thinking? Just because these people weren't attacking them didn't necessarily mean they trusted them. The lead guard was clearly suspicious, and so was Kym. She wanted to know more about the Rulers declaring themselves gods, and why these people knew nothing about Thed's involvement.

"We tried taking shelter there when we escaped from the Rulers' prison, Tenbatter," Ashlyn said quickly.

Kym couldn't help but be impressed. Of all of them, Kat was the liar. But Ashlyn didn't falter as the lead guard's eyes narrowed even more. She seemed to buy it though. Kym saw her face relax slightly, and Kym sighed.

"Hmm. I see. Well, you'd better come with me. The Council will want to speak with you. Our intel from outside the city is very limited."

Kym followed the lead guard while the other guards stayed behind. It was the first time since she got out of the car that Kym noticed her surroundings. The buildings around them were old—not as old as the massive stone Temple in the middle of the city, but close. And they were in bad condition. There were holes in the worn, discolored walls, and many of the grassy courtyards were yellowed and brittle. Strange, abstract statues lay on the cobbled path, along with signs. Kym read one of the signs as they walked past.

Wave Hall.

Second-Year Students.

"What is this place?" Tomark asked, also looking at the sign.

"Thilg Institute of Higher Learning," the guard said.

Kym's eyes widened as understanding washed over her. She'd heard of this place. Each of Princirum's cities, while identical, contained one unique feature. The City of Luxmont housed Princirum's university. In another life, one where magic hadn't stolen her from her home, Kym would've come here to earn her degree before getting a job. Her teachers talked about it all the time, saying only the best of the best were ever accepted.

They followed the lead guard to the center of the campus, where Kym saw an enormous building. To Kym, it looked like a cross between the Temple and a high-rise building. The bottom floors were made of stone, with pillars supporting the large roof hanging over the front steps. After the first few floors, a much sleeker structure stretched into the sky. Kym guessed it was a recent addition, given its glass walls and perfect corners.

The guard waved her wrist over a panel beside the door, there was a click, and the door swung open.

"In here," she said, holding the door open as Kym and the others walked inside.

Kym wrinkled her nose. The place smelled musty, while the bright lights hanging from the ceiling made Kym's eyes water. She couldn't remember the last time she'd been somewhere that hadn't been lit by torches. The artificial, almost blue light seemed very foreign. Countless rows of bookshelves stretched farther than she could see.

"The Council's on the thirty-fifth floor," the guard said, pointing at a pair of metal doors a little way down one of the rows.

"The Council?" Tomark asked.

"Our leaders," the guard clarified, waving her wrist over another sensor to open the elevator doors. "We needed to find a way to govern ourselves with no Rulers to guide us."

Kym stood beside Kat in the cramped elevator. Her hands shook slightly at her side, and her palms grew sweatier the longer they rode. Kym tried wiping her hands on her purple cloak. Who could these Council members be? Probably a collection of super-smart professors. They were hiding in a university, after all.

The elevator doors opened, and Kym followed the guard into the bright, white passageway. Compared to the rows of books on the first floor, this new hall looked barren. Several tall doors lined the walls, and Kym's steps echoed around her as she walked. The guard led them to the end of the corridor and a pair of white double doors.

Kym took a deep breath, trying to stop her shaking hands. This had to be where the Council was. What would they want to know? And how could Kym and the others be any help to them? They'd barely survived since breaking out of Tenbatter. But these people, they'd made it a whole year. Maybe they could help Kym and the others if they let them stay?

The double doors opened, and Kym and the others walked into the next room. It was large, with floor-to-ceiling glass windows along the far wall. Holoprojectors sat along the other two walls, filling the room with faint, multicolored light. A large, oval table sat in the middle of the room, surrounded by five large chairs.

"Lieutenant Parker," a very familiar voice said from one of the chairs. "What is the meaning of—"

The sound of the voice melted all the fear inside Kym. She sprinted across the room, tears streaming down her cheeks as she flung her arms around the speaker's neck. Cries of alarm rose around her, but Kym didn't care. She buried her face in his chest, barely daring to breathe. Kym had so many questions, but none of them mattered. For the first time in over a year, she truly felt safe.

"Kym?" Marek Collin's shaking hands wrapped around Kym. "What...how...?"

"Sir, you shouldn't—" Lieutenant Parker said.

"It's alright, Parker," Marek said, gently stroking Kym's hair with shaking hands. "This is my daughter."

A murmur of recognition surged around the room, but Kym didn't care. Her father was there. But Kym didn't understand? She had so many questions. Her parents lived in the City of Contellus. How'd he end up at the university, and why was he giving orders to a lead guard? And if he was here, where was ...?

"Where's Mom?"

Kym felt Marek's grip slacken. His body trembled against hers, and Kym had a hard time keeping her own from falling apart. Emptiness descended over her, and she felt hollow as white-hot tears burned her cheeks. If she was honest with herself, Kym accepted her mother was gone a long time ago. She'd failed to win the Calling for Nila, after all. But her dad's inability to say the words aloud made the pain ten times more excruciating. Yet another thing she was responsible for.

"Mrs. Mizel?" Kat's voice sounded a million miles away.

Slowly, Kym pulled her face from her father's chest. Kat was on the other side of the round table. The woman beside her was small, only a few inches taller than Kat. Her clothes had a worn look, but there was something about her that Kym recognized. She'd seen her before, but she couldn't place her. Mrs. Mizel's narrow, golden eyes locked on Kym, and a shudder ran through Kym's body.

Kym let go of her father. She walked around the table and was at Kat's side in seconds. She stared at Mrs. Mizel's golden eyes, and Kym knew she hadn't made a mistake.

"You're Amber's mom, aren't you?"

Mrs. Mizel's face fell. Kym had seen this woman before. She'd accompanied Amber during the Parade of Glory, just like Marek did for Kym. She'd know those eyes anywhere. They looked just like Amber's. Kym knew why Kat gravitated toward her. Mrs. Mizel had been Kat's teacher when she was little. That's where Amber and Kat first met—when the little Fire Princess screamed at Kat for not knowing any better.

"I am," Mrs. Mizel said. Her voice was soft but firm. "I…I'm sorry for my daughter's actions toward you during the Calling. Her conduct tainted her victory."

A mixture of rage and disgust boiled up in Kym's stomach. She was sorry for the way Amber treated Kym? How could she excuse her daughter's actions? What Amber did in the Calling, snuffing out her emotions to make sure she won, was inexcusable. A dark thought crept into Kym's mind. Should she tell Mrs. Mizel what

Amber had done to herself, and what she was doing to the rest of the Favored now?

Kym took in Mrs. Mizel's slight frame. She didn't look like she could handle a hard wind, let alone the devastating realization of her daughter's actions. Kym wasn't going to let Amber's actions hurt anyone else. But why did she think Amber won the Calling when Tomark won?

"It's alright," Tomark said quickly before Kym could speak. "She was…we all wanted to win."

Kym shook her head. Why was Tomark covering for Amber? He didn't owe her anything. She was the one everyone thought won the Calling, not Tomark. Amber nearly killed Tomark in the Fifth Trial and turned on them when they needed her the most. Tomark had more reason than Kym to hate Amber. But if Tomark didn't want to tell these people he won, Kym knew he must have a reason. Was it that he didn't trust them? After what the gods told Tomark, she knew he wasn't going to blindly trust that others would do the right thing anymore. So, Kym held her tongue.

Kym didn't want to look at Mrs. Mizel, so she turned to see the others standing around the table. Aside from Marek and Mrs. Mizel, there were three others. A man with a long beard that almost reached his vast stomach squinted at Kym from across the table. A woman with a worn face and shoulder-length black hair sat beside him, her uniform identical to Lieutenant Parker's. Kym's eyes locked on the third person, who sat between Mrs. Mizel and the man with the beard. Kym took one look at her tightly fitted robes and knew exactly who she was.

Fear coursed through Kym as she staggered back. What was a Pro doing here? They were loyal to the Rulers and Thed. Why would her father and the rest of this Council be so stupid?

"You needn't fear me," the Pro said gently, clearly sensing Kym's distrust.

Kym glanced sideways at the others. They all wore similar expressions of disgust and fear. They, like Kym, didn't trust anyone dressed in those fitted robes.

"Kym," Marek said, his voice stern, "where are your manners. Show High Priest Perla respect."

"Respect?" Kym breathed, shaking her head. Why would she respect anyone dressed in Protectorate robes?

"High Priest?" Kat asked. "She's a Protectorate."

"You must have many questions," the man with the beard said, his voice low and gravely.

"Sit," the woman in the officer uniform ordered. "We have questions for you."

"Commander Hale," Mrs. Mizel snapped, and Kym heard the teacher in her voice. "These kids look like they've been to Nothingness and back. They deserve compassion."

"Bring in some chairs," Marek said to Lieutenant Parker, who left the room without saying a word.

Parker returned less than a minute later with two other officers. They placed chairs between the Councilors before stepping back to the edge of the room. Kym took the seat between her father and the man with the beard, her body shaking slightly as she took a few breaths to calm herself. The Councilors stared at Kym, who shifted uncomfortably in her seat. Did they really need to stare?

"So," the bearded man said once the others had taken their seats. "I supposed the most pressing question is how the five of you came to be here. It's our understanding that the Favored's loyalty to the Rulers is unwavering."

Kym shook her head. Across the table, Kat snorted so loudly Mrs. Mizel and High Priest Perla shot her disapproving looks. Luckily, Tomark, Ashlyn, and Damon were better at hiding their surprise. But of course, Kym couldn't blame the Council for not knowing what was going on with the Favored.

"Is something funny?" Commander Hale asked.

"Well, the Favored aren't exactly loyal to the Rulers," Tomark said slowly.

"At least not willingly," Ashlyn added.

The Councilors exchanged looks with one another. Kym could tell by how her father's eyebrows contracted that he had no idea what Tomark and Ashlyn were talking about. How could they? To the people in the cities, magic was a mysterious gift from the gods that only the Favored and Rulers understood. They'd probably never heard of the Cladium before.

"Well," Kym said, choosing her words carefully. "Magic is… complicated. The planal and physical elements—"

"The what?" the bearded man cut across Kym.

"Let her finish, Professor Anderson," Marek said quietly.

"Light, darkness, fire, air, water, and earth," Kym clarified. "They can control some aspect of human existence. For example, Water Favored can control a person's body by manipulating the water inside of it."

Kym paused, giving the Council time to react, and they didn't disappoint. Looks of disgust flashed across their faces, and Perla's hands flew to her mouth.

"The Rulers are using this vile magic, the Cladium, to keep the Favored entirely under their control."

"How do you know this?" Mrs. Mizel asked.

Kym bit her tongue. She wanted to say she saw Mrs. Mizel's daughter snuffing out the emotions of a Favored the previous day. She deserved to know what her daughter had become.

"We saw it," Ashlyn said quickly before Kym could open her mouth. "At Inferon."

"When were you at Inferon?" Perla asked.

"Yesterday," Kat huffed.

"Is that where you've been all this time?" Marek asked, turning to look at Kym, who shifted uncomfortably in her chair. "And if that's true, and the Rulers have complete control over the Favored, how are you free?"

Kym closed her eyes. Why didn't they believe them? They clearly weren't under the Rulers' control. If they were, they'd have attacked the moment Lieutenant Parker showed up. The last thing she wanted was to relive her time since the Calling ended. But if Kym wanted these people's help, she needed to make them trust her.

"After the Calling," Kym began, "Tomark, Kat, Ashlyn, and I

didn't want to be Favored anymore. We tried to leave, and the Rulers didn't like that. They tried to rip our magic from us. It should have killed us."

"Tried?" Professor Anderson asked, his eyebrows raised.

"They messed up," Kat snorted. She raised her arms to show everyone the black scars of her Marks. "We survived, so they threw us in Tenbatter."

"Tenbatter?" Marek asked.

"The Rulers' secret prison," Ashlyn said, and Kym heard no lightness in her voice. "They built it after Melana tried to steal the Conduit during the Festival of Creation a few years ago."

"What?" Officer Hale slammed her fist on the table.

Kym sighed. This was going to take a lot more explaining. She and the others told the Council how Melana wanted to overthrow the gods, and when the other Rulers wouldn't help her, she agreed to Thed's possession. Kym watched the Council's severe expressions grow darker as they explained how they stopped the theft of the Conduit and how Melana was responsible for Thed's growing presence in Princirum.

"Very well," Mrs. Mizel said. "So the Rulers imprisoned you for wanting to leave. How'd you escape?"

"Damon," Tomark said, pointing at Damon.

"I'm a Life Favored," Damon said importantly. Kym wished he'd drop the superior tone. "Lady Zara found me when I was eight, and has trained me ever since. To keep my identity secret from the other Rulers, she had me pose as a Servitude at Crystal Palace. She's been fighting Thed's possession, and sent me to break them out of Tenbatter to fulfill the gods' plan."

"Thed's possession?" Hale asked, her thin eyebrows sliding up her head.

"Thed forced himself on the Rulers after the Calling," Kym said. "He's the one influencing their actions. The war you're fighting, it's all because of death. Thed wants to destroy the gods' creation, and he's using the Rulers to do it for him."

Kym knew this was the most challenging piece of information

for the Council to swallow. It meant they weren't just at war with the Rulers, but the god of death himself. Kym held her breath, waiting for them to deny her claims. After all, she had no proof other than her word.

"You spoke of the gods' plan," Perla asked slowly, sitting up a little straighter in her chair. "How can you know their intentions for us?"

"We do," Damon nodded. "Thed's hold on Princirum must be broken, and we are the ones who must do it."

Silence followed Damon's words. Kym tried to look confident at their supposed mission, but how could she? What had they done to break Thed's anchors to Princirum? They didn't even know how to do it. Sure, they knew his connection with the Rulers was his main foothold in Princirum, but how could they break it? And that didn't even count the people he was passively connected to like he'd been to Kym's mother. His power was literally every-where. How could they drive it back? How could they fight death itself?

"How would you do this?" Marek asked. For the first time, Kym heard concern in his voice. "The Rulers' power and reach is every-where. Nearly everyone in the cities views the Rulers as their chosen gods. Those who've resisted have gone missing."

"You're really the only resistance left?" Ashlyn asked, and Kym could hear the plea in her voice. "Aren't the other cities—"

"My dear, the other cities were not equipped to withstand a long-term magical assault," Professor Anderson cut across Ashlyn. "Luckily for us, the university has always been at the forefront of technological advancement. But even we're…"

"Starting to feel the strain," Commander Hale finished. "It's becoming harder to maintain what little order we have while also trying to bring in whatever refugees we find."

"There are refugees?" Tomark asked.

A tiny glimmer of hope flickered inside Kym at Tomark's ques-tion. So not everyone in the cities had fallen to the Rulers' power as Damon had thought. There were still people outside this little bubble trying to resist. A small voice pushed its way to the front of Kym's mind as though from a million miles away.

I will help those who cannot help themselves.

Kym remembered when she said those words at her first-ever Rulers' Summit. But how could she help people now? Her magic was so weak she could barely lift a ball of water without passing out. She couldn't even properly fight a death demon. Only Damon's life magic had any effect on the demon, but Kym wasn't too surprised by that. After all, life was death's opposite. Of course, Damon's magic affected the death more than…

"It's Damon," Kym said quietly. Every face turned to look at her, and Kym wasn't surprised to see the shock in their eyes. "Damon's the answer."

"No, Kym," Damon shook his head. "I was sent to—"

"On our way here," Kym said, barreling over Damon, "we were chased by a death demon."

"What?" Commander Hale snapped. "You brought that thing—"

"Our magic is weak," Kym pressed on. "We can barely control our elements, and when we do, we're in agony. We're forcing our bodies to do something they're no longer equipped to do. But Damon's magic affected the demon."

Kym shook her head, almost dazed. Why hadn't she seen this before? Zara didn't send Damon to break them out so they could stop Thed. She wanted them to teach Damon how to do it. And luckily for Damon, no one had more experience fighting death than Kym, Kat, Tomark, and Ashlyn.

"We," Kym gestured at Kat, Ashlyn, and Tomark, "were Vanquishers. We spent our time as Favored battling death demons."

"We were in the Calling," Ashlyn said. She locked eyes with Kym, and Kym knew she was thinking the same thing as she was. "We all made it to the Fourth Trial. We know magic."

"We can teach it to Damon," Tomark said. "Zara didn't teach him to fight. We can."

"And when he's ready," Kat said quickly, her eyes bright, "he can destroy death once and for all."

Kym's eyes darted between the Councilors. Just like before, they all wore concerned expressions, but Kym didn't care. For the first time since breaking out of Tenbatter, Kym knew what they were supposed to do. Of course, they needed to teach Damon how to fight death. Why else would Zara have Damon break them out when for all she knew, their magic was gone forever? This had to be the gods' plan.

Professor Anderson rose slowly to his feet. Kym stared unblinkingly at him, waiting for him to say something. Clearly, he was in charge of the Council. His puffy eyes narrowed as he looked at Kym, Kat, Tomark, Ashlyn, and Damon. Kym's heart raced in her chest while her palms filled with sweat. What was he going to say?

"Absolutely not."

C H A P T E R N I N E

T H E T R U E
D I S C I P L E S

"What the Thed?"

Kym must have misheard Professor Anderson. How could he tell them no after everything Kym and the others had said? It made no sense. Damon's magic was the key to fighting death—Kym was sure of it. Life was death's opposite. Why was Anderson refusing to help the people he was supposed to be leading? That was the job of a leader.

"Why not?" Kym demanded. "It's the best—"

"Enough," Professor Anderson said, his deep, gravelly voice stern. "We will not engage in that kind of thinking here."

"What?" Ashlyn asked, her red hair flying around her face.

"Magic caused this crisis," Marek said darkly, his eyes falling momentarily on Kym. "If you're right, the Rulers' ignorance let Thed into Princirum. We can't use magic to try and push him out. Magic has already caused too much damage to Princirum. We need to protect this last sanctuary for the True Disciples."

"The university's technology has kept us safe," Anderson continued. "And it will continue to do so."

"Forgive me, Professor," Perla said. Kym looked hopefully at Perla. She may not like the Pros, but Kym needed an ally. "These Blessed Ones claim to follow the gods' chosen path. We cannot hinder their progress. How can we claim the title of the gods' True Disciples if we deny their chosen champions?"

Kym sighed as her tense muscles relaxed slightly. Finally, one of the Councilors was on their side. Sure, Kym didn't like that Perla was a Pro acting the part of a high priest, but Kym needed to get over it. Perla wasn't so short-sighted that she'd refuse them for no real reason, and she was their only ally on the Council. Kym watched Anderson, whose cheeks were a pale pink color. Several lines crossed his heavily wrinkled forehead, and his long beard quivered in front of his vast stomach.

"High Priest Perla," Anderson said slowly. "I am sorry, but your argument is—"

"We're losing ground, Anderson," Commander Hale cut across him. "Our last three scouting parties haven't returned. It's been days now. I agree with the Priestess. Let them train the boy. While they do, our soldiers can study how the Favored fight firsthand. It's a win-win."

Kym held her breath, not daring to believe her luck. That was two Council members on their side. And she agreed with Hale. The soldiers should watch Damon train. They needed to learn to fight magic, and what better opportunity was there than watching Favored train in person? Kym looked back at Anderson. Kym doubted he'd say it aloud, but she had a feeling Anderson wanted his fighters prepared just as badly as Hale.

"Commander," Anderson said, his voice trembling with anger, "you must wait—"

"We can't wait any longer, Anderson," Mrs. Mizel said quietly. "We're out of options. We are losing. These five may be our last chance."

Joy coursed through Kym like electricity. With Mrs. Mizel on their side, it was three against two. Kym peered sideways and saw the disappointment on Marek's face. All the joy inside Kym vanished in an instant. Why was he against them using magic to fight magic? He saw what Kym could do during the Calling. Kym didn't care what technology they had—it wouldn't stand a chance against magic.

"It appears," Marek said slowly, "we're outvoted, Professor. Welcome to the True Disciples."

"So it does. Officer Short!" Anderson snapped.

One of the guards Lieutenant Parker brought with her rushed

forward. He, too, wore the black body armor of the city patrol, had closely trimmed light brown hair, and a lot of dried blood on his face. He didn't look at Kym or the others as he stepped forward, although Kym thought she saw his eyes dart toward Kat, who was about his height. Kym shook her head as understanding washed over her. This was the guard who'd held Kat outside. She must have hit him in the nose.

"Take our guests to medical," Anderson said to Short. "If they're going to train our soldiers in the morning, I want their injuries tended to."

The smile fell off Kym's lips. Was Anderson really giving them a babysitter? She looked from Anderson to her father, but Marek was staring deliberately at the holoprojector on his wrist. Kym shook her head. Anderson didn't care about Kym and the others training Damon. He wanted them to teach his people to fight magic. And by assigning a guard to watch them, it was clear Anderson didn't trust them. But Kym knew better than anyone that trust was a two-way street. She'd blindly trusted people before, and she wasn't going to make that mistake again. And wasn't that what the gods told Tomark? Even if Tomark imagined the whole thing, Kym knew she shouldn't trust these people…at least not right away.

Kym and the others followed Officer Short silently out of the conference room. Short waved his wrist over the sensor by the elevator, and the doors slid open. Kym and the others followed him inside, and Kym stood beside Kat as the elevator slid downward. In such a confined space, Kat's snorts were anything but discreet. Kym groaned as she glared at Kat, who she saw was fighting back tears.

"What?" Kym demanded. She didn't see anything funny about their current situation.

The others turned to Kat, and Kym saw her confusion in their eyes. What was wrong with her?

"The gods," Kat stammered, barely able to hold herself together, "really do have a plan."

"What?" Tomark asked.

Kym looked more closely at Kat. She didn't look injured, but she wasn't acting like herself. Tears slid down her face, and her cheeks were red and blotchy. Had the crash and struggle outside caused more damage than Kym thought?

"His name is Short," Kat wheezed, jerking her head at Officer Short. He stared at Kat, his eyes as wide as plates. "And he's one of the tiniest people I've ever seen."

Kat collapsed to the floor in a fit of laughter. Kym rolled her eyes, her annoyance bubbling beneath the surface. She shouldn't expect anything more from Kat. Kym looked at Short, and even with his perfect posture, Kym could tell he was at least a few inches shorter than Kat.

Kym couldn't stop herself from laughing a little. The sensation felt oddly foreign. Kym couldn't remember the last time she laughed. All around her, she heard the others chuckle as the doors opened and they followed a red-faced Short out of the cramped elevator.

Short took them down three hallways before stopping at a massive glass door. He waved his wrist over another scanner, and the door swung open. People dressed in white coats ran in every direction, projections floating in front of their faces from the mini holoprojectors on their wrists.

"Dr. Gwin!" Officer Short yelled.

Kym craned her neck, trying to see around Tomark and Ashlyn. One of the doctors broke away from the crowd and hurried toward them. She tapped her holoprojector, and the golden image of a leg she was studying faded away.

"Short," she said curtly, and Kym could tell this was someone she didn't want to get on the wrong side of. "I'm busy. What is it?"

"These five…" Short paused, looking back at Kym and the others. His eyes were narrow, and his nose was wrinkled like he'd smelled something foul. A shiver ran over Kym's skin. Why was he looking at them like that?

"Refugees," Short said slowly. "Need a full checkup."

"All of them?" Dr. Gwin asked, raising a thin eyebrow. "Now?"

"Yes," Short said, and Kym saw him stand up a little taller. "Professor Anderson sent us."

Dr. Gwin nodded. She tapped the holoprojector on her wrist. Kym's hands flew to her ears as a high-pitched beeping issued from every holoprojector. Five of the closest doctors rushed over to Dr. Gwin.

"Process them," Gwin said, waving a thin hand at Kym, Tomark, Kat, Damon, and Ashlyn. "Quick as you can."

A hand closed around Kym's upper arm and pulled. Kym reacted instinctively, her heart thundering in her ears. She reached out, her insides stinging as her energy coursed through her. Water shot out of the vases beside the door and hit the doctor holding her. The pressure on her arm vanished as air whirled around her and lights flashed.

Kym spun around, panting, her pounding heart filling her brain. Tomark, Kat, and Ashlyn all wore the same panicked looks. Why'd the doctors grab them like that? Kym glared at them, and their eyes widened as they scrambled back. Kym's anger vanished, leaving her feeling empty. They were afraid of them, and how couldn't they be? They'd been fighting the Favored for over a year.

"What is the meaning of this, Short?" Dr. Gwin demanded.

"They're on our side," Short said, although Kym could hear his confidence failing. "They've been through a lot."

"I won't put my doctors in harm's way."

Dr. Gwin helped another doctor to his feet and led him away from Kym and the others. Kym stared at the floor, her insides squirming uncomfortably. Why wouldn't they stay? Sure, Kym, Ashlyn, and Tomark overreacted, but after what they'd suffered, people grabbing them out of nowhere was an easy way to set them off. Kym wanted to explain, but the terrified looks on the doctors' faces stopped the words from forming.

"Short."

Kym raised her head, and saw a woman dressed in pale orange clothes, waving at Short from the other side of the room. She was older than Kym, maybe in her thirties, had a kind face, and lots of thick brown hair pulled up on the top of her head.

"Bring 'em in here," she said, jerking her head at the door behind her.

"C'mon," Short mumbled.

Kym and the others followed Short and the woman into the room, which was very small. A large table sat in the middle of the room, while medical equipment covered the tiny counter. By the time they were all inside, Kym and the others barely had a place to stand. The woman closed the door behind Tomark, and the room became oddly quiet.

"So, wassup?" the woman asked Short.

"These five need a full workup," Short said before turning to Kym and the others. "I'll be reporting you for this."

"Whatever," Kat shrugged.

"Kat," Ashlyn hissed.

"We're sorry," Tomark said, and Kym could hear the remorse in his voice. "We're just not used to…"

"Being touched," Kym finished. She couldn't remember the last time someone other than Tomark, Kat, Ashlyn, or Damon touched her.

"That doesn't mean you can attack people," Short snapped, his face turning red again. "We have rules here."

"Short, stop," the woman said abruptly. She was staring at a string of text floating above her holoprojector. Kym watched her eyes zoom back and forth, and the lines of her face softened. "The Council released the brief on their conversation with them."

"They what?" Damon asked.

"Why?" Tomark and Ashlyn demanded.

"The contents of all Council meetings are public," Short said. "Our leaders don't keep secrets."

"That's right, and this says these kids have been to Nothingness and back."

"Jamie—"

"It's Nurse Byrd, Jeren. It's no wonder they're out of sorts."

Nurse Byrd stepped forward, and there was a kindness in her eyes that made Kym's heartrate slow. She couldn't put her finger on it, but Kym felt like she could trust this woman. She stopped a few feet in front of Kat, and unlike the doctors outside, she didn't look afraid.

"You've been locked up and abused," she said gently. "You've every right to react defensively when you feel threatened. I'm going to examine you here. Together."

"Nurse Byrd," Short repeated.

"You can wait outside if you need to, Officer Short," Nurse Byrd snapped. "I'm going to take care of these kids."

The pounding in Kym's ears lessened as Short retreated into the corner of the room. She didn't know what it was, but something about Nurse Byrd made Kym feel at ease. She may not be in charge like Gwin, but Kym had a feeling none of the other doctors would get in Nurse Byrd's way. For the first time since arriving at the university, Kym felt like she could trust someone.

When Nurse Byrd asked for one of them to go first, Kym was as still as the rest of them. Kym balled her hands into fists, trying to stop them from shaking. She bit her lip and walked forward, and it felt like her legs were going to fall off with every step. Kym laid down on the table, and Nurse Byrd held a long, curved scanner over her chest.

She moved the scanner, which emitted a faint, lilac light all around Kym. It would beep, and Nurse Byrd would look at the holoprojector on the counter before moving on. She didn't say a word as she helped Kym into a sitting position, her hands covered in sweat as she took several deep breaths.

"You're malnourished," Nurse Byrd said. "You've experienced tremendous muscle loss, but other than that, everything seems to be okay."

Kym sighed. That wasn't too bad after all. After being in a cell for over a year, it could've been much worse.

"Now, if you're okay with it, I wanna take a look at those," Nurse Byrd nodded to Kym's forearms.

Kym's chest tightened as she stared at her black scars. She didn't need Byrd to tell her that her arms were a mess. They still throbbed after pushing the other doctor off of her. What would Nurse Byrd find if she examined them? Reluctantly, Kym held out her arms.

The holoprojector beeped the whole time Nurse Byrd moved the sensor over Kym's arms. Kym focused on her shoes, not wanting to look at the projection. When Byrd finished her exam, Kym looked at Kat. She was staring at the golden projection Nurse Byrd was studying. Why was Kat looking at it? It wasn't like she could see what was wrong with them.

"You weren't able to use your hands."

It was a statement, not a question. Bracing herself for the worst, Kym looked up. An arm made of shimmering golden light floated in the air. Nurse Byrd's eyebrows formed one long line as she turned the image around in midair. To Kym, it looked just like an arm.

"There's extensive nerve damage from your elbow to your fingers," Nurse Byrd continued. "Most of it looks partially healed. But there are places where the damage looks almost new. What happened?"

Kym looked to Kat, Ashlyn, and Tomark. They, like Kym, were looking at their blackened scars, their faces downcast. Finally, after trying to ignore it for days, they couldn't deny what Nurse Byrd said. Their magic wasn't just painful—it was damaging them.

"It can't be," Damon said. "I healed them myself. They should be fine."

"It seems," Nurse Byrd said, her voice gentle, "you didn't do as good of a job as you thought. Your continued use of magic seems to be causing new damage to the nerves. How are you coping? With this much nerve damage, the pain should be excruciating."

Kym had to agree. The pain was excruciating. Her arms still stung after what happened in the hall. She shoved her hand into her pocket and fished out her bottle of healing oil. There was nearly three-quarters of it left. She hadn't realized how much of it she'd used. She'd only had her magic for a day.

"What's that?" Nurse Byrd asked as Kym rubbed the oil into her arms.

Kym handed her the bottle, sighing as the pain in her arms subsided. She watched Nurse Byrd hold the oil up to the light, and her eyes grew as big as dinner plates. She leaped across the room and held the bottle under a new scanner. It beeped several times before Byrd stepped back from the scanner. She was smiling so broadly it was like they'd given her the best present ever.

"This is Lady Zara's healing oil," she said, her voice trembling slightly.

"Yeah," Damon said. "She gave it to me. How do you know about it? I thought it was a secret."

"I read about it in medical school," Byrd said eagerly. "I wanted to study its properties, but Lady Zara only permitted its use in the cities once—when a death demon destroyed half of the City of Termubra nearly two thousand years ago. So this is how you've kept going?" she asked, looking at Tomark, Ashlyn, Kat, and Kym. They all nodded.

"Zara's healing oils are extraordinary, but they're no replacement for proper rest and treatment. I'd suggest you refrain from using magic," she held up her hand, silencing Kym and the others before they could object. "But I know you won't. So, let me offer an alternative."

Nurse Byrd examined Kat, Ashlyn, and Tomark, whose nerve damage was far worse than Kym's. When she finished patching up Damon, Nurse Byrd told them her plan. Kym, Kat, Ashlyn, and Tomark were to apply the healing oil before, during, and after magic use, which they should limit to the bare minimum. That should give their bodies enough support not to make things worse.

To treat the damage that was already there, Nurse Byrd said she was going to administer a steroid that would encourage their damaged nerves to heal naturally. Kym tried not to look when Byrd pulled out the very large needle she needed to administer the injection. But Kym needn't have worried. The pain of the injection was nothing compared to the sting of her magic. When Byrd finished,

Kym's forearms felt oddly warm and stiff, which she felt was actually an improvement.

Nurse Byrd gave them each a hug as they followed Officer Short out of the examination room. Kym had to admit that she would miss her, although she doubted this would be the last time she'd see her. Short led them to the elevator, where they got off on a floor right above the library. There were no glass walls or massive windows. Just narrow halls with small, wooden doors every few yards, each marked with a number.

"Here," Officer Short said, holding open a door marked 233.

Kym followed the others inside, unsure what to expect. The first thing she noticed was the smell; clearly, the room had been vacant for a long time. The room was small, with a sagging couch pushed against the far wall and a bare shelf. The left wall had two doors on it, while the right had three, and there was a tiny window over the couch.

"What is this place?" Ashlyn asked.

"Converted dorms," Short huffed. "The Disciples moved to these floors after the other buildings were destroyed. I'll be by to check on you later, and I'll pick you up in the morning for your training."

"What a tall order," Kat smirked, and Kym couldn't help but roll her eyes.

"There's two beds per room," Short continued, his ears turning red as he pointed at the doors. "Bathroom's there. Training starts at seven. Until then, stay here and rest. It looks like you need it."

Kym tried to ignore his comment as Short marched out of the room. Sure, Tomark's wavy hair was in tangles, scrapes covered Kat's arms, Ashlyn looked like she hadn't eaten for days, and Damon looked like he'd been sick for months. But they'd honestly looked worse. At least they were all alive. And for the first time since leaving Tenbatter, Kym felt safe.

They took turns cleaning up in the tiny bathroom, which had a small shower, sink, and toilet. Kym didn't take too long. She scrubbed the layer of dirt, sweat, and grime that had accumulated during her time in Tenbatter, but she still didn't recognize the stranger staring at her in the dusty mirror. Kym tried not to look at her sunken face as she tied her long, blond hair behind her head. She didn't see the point in dwelling on it.

Unsure what else to do while she waited, Kym wandered into one of the bedrooms. The beds were small—like everything else in the dorm—but Kym found a surprise in the drawers by one of the beds. It was full of clothes. They looked secondhand, with several holes and worn spots, but Kym didn't care. They were better than the tattered remains of the dress she'd worn for over a year. Kym plunged her hand into the drawer and pulled on a light shirt and a pair of tight running pants.

"So," Kat said once they were all washed, dressed, and sitting in the tiny common room. "What's the plan?"

"Plan?" Tomark yawned. "What plan?"

Kym agreed with Tomark. As far as she was aware, they had a plan. They were going to teach Damon to fight and figure out how to break Thed's anchors to Princirum. How much more of a plan did Kat need? She hated planning.

"We have a plan," Ashlyn said. "We're teaching Damon to—"

"I'm not talking about that." Kat waved her hand at Ashlyn, silencing her. "I mean, what's the plan for lookin' around."

"What?" Damon asked.

"Short told us to stay here until tomorrow," Kym said.

"Since when do we listen to rules?"

"What's there to look at?" Tomark asked.

"Aren't you curious about this place?" Kat asked, running her hands through her light brown hair.

"Not enough to look around right now," Ashlyn yawned.

"C'mon!" Kat threw her hands up in the air. "This place is a freak show. The boss people wanted to know everything about us but didn't say anything about this place. Didn't you notice?"

Kym hadn't thought of that. The Council, the guards, and even Nurse Byrd were all so interested in them but hadn't told them anything about the Disciples. Kym still didn't understand how this place even existed. With the other cities and resistances fallen, how had this place survived?

Kym glanced at Tomark and saw his eyes narrow. She knew he was thinking about what the gods told him after he won the Calling. But Kym couldn't help but agree with Kat. The Disciples were keeping things from them, and that made them untrustworthy. But it wasn't Kym's opinion that mattered when it came to trust.

"What do you think?" Kym asked, looking expectantly at Tomark. "It's your call. Do we trust them?"

"I…" Tomark trailed off, several lines creasing his forehead. "I want to. They seem to be trying to do the right thing here."

"But?" Ashlyn asked, her pale green eyes widening.

"But they aren't telling us everything," Tomark said, his face downcast. "So, no. I don't trust them."

"Clearly," Kat snorted. "Since you didn't tell them it was you and not Amber who won the Calling."

That was all Kym needed to hear. She stood up and walked to the door. As quietly as she could, she opened it a crack. The hallway was deserted.

"No one's out there," she breathed.

Kym stepped into the hall. Now that Kat said it, it was like an itch in Kym's brain. She wanted to know what was going on. She heard several pairs of feet walking behind her, and Kat and Tomark appeared on either side of Kym.

"Where to?" Kat asked, the faintest trace of excitement in her voice.

"This place is enormous," Ashlyn said. "Where would we even start?"

"What're we even looking for?" Damon asked.

Kym tried to think of something, but her mind was blank. If she was honest, she didn't know if she wanted to find anything in particular. All she knew was she wanted to know more about this place. And poking around sounded like a good place to start.

"I guess we'll know it when we find it," Tomark said.

They didn't have a holowatch to access the elevator, but Tomark found the stairs quickly enough. Kym was ready to stop after about ten minutes. Her muscles felt like they were on fire, but she stopped at every door on the dorm floors. They peered into empty class-rooms, a kitchen, a laundry, and what looked like some sort of lab. Kym's confidence waned the more empty rooms they found. She didn't know what she expected to find. Short said all of the people lived on these floors.

"Kat," Kym sighed as they exited yet another stairwell. "I don't think we're gonna find anything."

Kym rubbed the butt of her hand against her forehead. There was a throbbing in her temples, and there was a faint ringing in her ears. She wanted answers, but it was getting late. They still had to get back to their room, and Kym doubted they'd find their way back easily. And they needed rest if they were going to train Damon in the morning.

"I wanna try one more door," Kat huffed, clearly frustrated with the lack of useful discoveries.

Kym grudgingly followed Kat down the hall. The only thing there was a set of large metal doors, a stark contrast to the wooden ones they'd seen previously. Kym read the sign above the door. *Department of Etheric and Alternative Energy.* Kym shook her head; the throbbing was getting worse. What were etheric and alter-native energies? Kym hadn't heard of them before.

"Kat," Tomark groaned as Kat grabbed the hefty door handle. "I think they're studying better energy sources in there."

"Kym's right," Ashlyn said. "We're not gonna find anything in there."

"Fine," Kat grunted, still facing the door.

"Good," Damon sighed, clearly happy this little excursion was over.

Damon started to walk back the way they'd come, Kym, Tomark, and Ashlyn behind him. It took Kym a moment to realize Kat wasn't with them. She looked over her shoulder and suppressed a groan. Kat was still at the metal door. Kym shook her head, and the pain inside her skull doubled as she hurried back to Kat.

"What're you doing?" she demanded.

"It—won't—open," Kat said through gritted teeth.

"What?"

Kym examined the door. Why wouldn't it open? All the other doors they'd tried weren't locked. The hairs on the back of Kym's neck stood on end as she pulled the door handle with Kat. But no matter how hard they pulled, the door wouldn't budge. Kym's eyes narrowed as she stared at the thick, metal doors. Why would the Disciples lock an alternative energy lab?

"What are you doing?" a stern voice called.

Kym spun around, the inside of her skull pounding just as quickly as her heart. Short ran toward them, his face beet-red. His eyes were so narrow Kym thought they were closed. Kym let go of the handle, but Kat kept pulling it as if she hadn't heard Short.

"Stop," he hissed, his voice cracking slightly.

"Why?" Kat asked, finally letting go of the handle. "Whatever's in there must be important."

"Why are you out of your dorm?" Short asked, ignoring Kat's question.

"We wanted to look around," Ashlyn said, crossing her arms as she glared at Short. "Was that wrong?"

"You can't be up here." Short started shepherding them back down the hall.

"Clearly," Kym said.

Kym glanced sideways at Kat as the elevator doors closed. So, Kat had been right after all. There was something the Disciples didn't want Kym and the others to know, and it was behind those metal doors. But what could it be?

Kym racked her brain to think of a reason why the Council, and her father, would lie. But no matter how hard she tried, she could only focus on one thing. After all of this time, nothing had changed. She was trapped in a place where she didn't know what was going on, where there were rules she needed to follow, and with leaders who demanded she listen without question or explanation. It was like living at the palaces all over again.

CHAPTER TEN

CONSTANT OVERSIGHT

KYM OPENED HER EYES, AND ALL WAS BLACKNESS. A VEIL OF DENSE mist engulfed her as the tall walls blanketed her in unnatural shadows. Kym turned slowly on the spot. Everything around her was the same. Which way would she go this time? She'd tried so many paths but never managed to find her way out.

Tentatively, Kym stepped forward, bracing herself for the worst. Nothing happened. Relief washed over her, and she took a few more steps. This wasn't so bad. After walking for a little while, or maybe an eternity, Kym's path diverged into six new routes.

Kym peered down the different aisles. Which way should she go? All of the paths seemed identical. Same tall walls. Same mist. Same soul-sucking numbness. Could she go back? At least she knew the way behind her was clear. But what if the exit, which she'd never found, was down one of the new paths?

This way.

Kym's hair stood on end. She spun around, her arms raised, desperate to see through the blackness pressing in on her. The voice was so close, like someone whispering in her ear. But the path behind Kym was empty. She narrowed her eyes, trying to peer into the blackness beyond. This didn't make any sense. More than anything, Kym wished she had some source of light.

Come with us.

This time, the voice was to Kym's left. She turned, expecting to see the speaker beside her. Again, all she saw was mist. Kym's heart thudded against her chest. Where could they be? There weren't any places to hide in this maze.

We need you.

Kym felt the speaker's cold breath on her neck She whipped around, her heart racing, expecting to see someone. However, no one was there. Kym stepped back on trembling legs. She'd been wrong. She shouldn't have come this way.

Something cool and clammy slid around Kym's wrist. She jerked her arm back, but whatever was holding her tightened its grip. Kym looked down, her heart thundering even faster. Black bands extended from the dark walls, where they twisted around her wrists. Kym pulled, desperate to break free, but the bands didn't budge. What was going on? Why was she being tied up?

We will help you.

The voice came from Kym's left. The band around her left wrist tightened and pulled Kym toward the voice. She dug her heels into the ground, trying to stop herself, but the glittering black stone was too slick. Kym didn't want to go there. She wanted to go back.

Trust us.

Something pulled the band on Kym's right, and she fell. Pain radiated through Kym's arms as the bands yanked her in different directions. She closed her eyes, trying to block out the agony as her arms stretched further. She couldn't take this. Why wouldn't it end?

KYM SAT UP. Sweat covered her skin, and she shook from a combination of terror and cold. Kym bit the inside of her cheek, fighting to keep her scream trapped in her chest. The room was dark, with no sign of daylight through the thin curtains over the singular window. Kat and Ashlyn's heavy breathing filled the darkness as Kym settled back on her thin pillow. The last thing she wanted was to wake them.

After Short brought them back to their dorm, they'd decided to call it a night. Kym, Kat, and Ashlyn decided to sleep in the same room, although they never really discussed it. Kym was glad they were there. She found the sound of their breathing soothing in the darkness.

Kym stayed under the blankets until the first rays of sunlight peeked through the curtains. She climbed quietly out of bed, walked around Kat, who was sleeping on a nest of pillows on the floor, and into the common room. Kym showered, taking more care than she'd done the previous night. She couldn't remember the last time she'd cleaned herself. Of course, cleaning herself wasn't an option at Tenbatter—they'd been too afraid to give her water. Kym's fingers drifted to the water charm around her neck. The Warden had been right after all.

Kym didn't have to wait long for the others to wake. They wandered out of their rooms, their hair unkempt and their eyes half-closed. Kym stayed on the lumpy sofa while the others got ready. The longer she waited, the more her insides felt like they were vibrating. But why? She wasn't the one having their first real magic lesson. So why was she nervous?

There was a knock on the front door, and Kym jumped a little in her seat. Who could be knocking so early in the morning? She stood up, taking a few breaths to calm herself. Kym opened the door, and annoyance replaced her curiosity.

"You ready?" Officer Short asked. He stepped around Kym and into their dorm.

Kym closed the door, not taking her eyes off Short. He seemed normal, but that didn't mean anything. Kym barely knew him. Short didn't mention the previous night, so their sneaking out mustn't have been too bad. The next chance she got, Kym wanted to find that department again. What was so special about it that the doors had to be locked?

When Kat was finally dressed, Kym and the others followed Short into the hall. He took them to the elevator, and Kym expected him to hit the button for the ground floor. Instead, he pressed one near the very top. The elevator rocketed upward, spitting them out on one of the top floors.

Unlike the floors Kym explored the previous night, there were no halls on this level. Just a large expanse of open space, surrounded by windows on all sides. Above them, a balcony wrapped around the square room. There were several people already leaning over the railings. Even twenty feet above them, Kym saw the nerves on their faces.

Kym exhaled, her hands shaking slightly. She couldn't worry about the people watching. Today, her job was to teach Damon. Teaching him magic was all that mattered. Kym glanced at Damon, who looked oddly small as he followed Tomark and Short to the middle of the room. His usually broad shoulders were hunched, and he wouldn't look up from the floor. Kym smiled. She wasn't the only one with nerves.

"This is where you're gonna train," Short said. "They used to use it for testing experimental machinery, so the walls, floor, and ceiling are blast-proof."

"Good," Tomark said, pulling his long wavy hair into a bun at the back of his head.

"Who're they?" Kat demanded, jerking her thumb at the people watching from the balcony.

"Our Lieutenants, squad leaders, and senior department heads," Short said. "They're observing today. They'll jump in after a few sessions."

"Great," Ashlyn said. "Can we get started?"

"We'll need supplies," Kym said, looking around the empty room. "Water, earth, and lots of plants. The larger, the better."

Short nodded and hurried out of the room. Kym turned to Damon, whose dark skin was tinged with green. Kym sighed as she took a step toward him. Kym knew how nervous he must be. She couldn't sleep the night before her first combat lesson with Kenna.

"Okay," Kym said, smiling at Damon. "We should start by reviewing what I taught you earlier. Remember, don't use your life energy. Got it?"

Damon nodded. Short returned a few minutes later, along with two other guards. They placed the four large barrels of water and earth and several large potted plants around the room before hurrying to join the other spectators on the balcony. As Nurse Byrd suggested, Kym, Kat, Tomark, and Ashlyn applied their healing oil, and walked to different sides of the room, leaving Damon standing in the middle.

"Start with life bolts," Tomark shouted. "Throw them at us one at a time."

"And don't tell us who you're aiming for," Ashlyn added, tying her fiery hair behind her head. "We need the evasion practice."

"Speak for yourself," Kat smirked. "I'm an expert at avoiding trouble."

Kym shifted her feet as Damon pulled life from one of the plants. She watched the glittering white mist glow and condense into a sphere, her pulse racing in her ears. She waited, and the room fell silent. Damon raised his hand, but Kym was already three steps ahead of him.

She dove to the side before Damon's bolt left his hand. It flew past the spot where she'd stood and exploded in a flash of white against the glass wall. Kym sprang to her feet, smiling as Damon's dark brown eyes narrowed. Kym looked behind her and saw a massive black scorch mark along with several large cracks in the glass wall. Kym smiled. The room may be blast-proof, but there was nothing stronger than life. She shifted her weight back and forth as Damon made another bolt. After all of this time, sparring was like riding a bike.

Damon spent the next twenty minutes throwing bolts, blasts, and swipes at Kym, Kat, Tomark, and Ashlyn. Not one of them hit Kym, and her insides swelled with pride as she leaped around the room. They exploded on the blast-proof walls, leaving more black scorch marks in their wake. Damon telegraphed his attacks like he was holding a sign, always squaring up his feet toward whoever he was attacking. But Kym had to admit, Damon was a quick study. His last few attacks were closer to hitting her than the others.

"Really good," Tomark smiled, wiping the sweat shining on his forehead. "You nearly got me that time."

"Thanks," Damon panted, his hands on his knees.

"Ten-minute break," Ashlyn nodded, her eyes narrowing at Damon's sweat-covered face. "You'll be doing a lot of magic today. We can't have you pushing yourself too far."

"Tell us if you feel lightheaded, shaky, or if the room starts spinning," Kym added, remembering how she almost blacked out the first time she learned combat magic. "We'd rather you take breaks than pass out."

"But don't be a wimp," Kat huffed impatiently. "We got a lot of work to do."

Next, they decided to test Damon's reaction times. Kym and the others walked to the edge of the room while Damon stayed in the center. Damon formed his bolts and threw them one right after the other. The first zoomed toward Tomark while the other flew straight at Kym. She leaped to the side, invoking her Marks as she landed. She swung her arm, and a jet of water flew out of the nearest barrel as the insides of her arms burned. She focused on the water, forcing the energy out of her fingers, and pushed it to Damon.

The water slammed into Damon's chest, and he flew back. He landed in a heap on the floor, his clothes soaked. Damon scrambled to his feet, but Kym knew he wasn't fast enough. Kat's earth knocked Damon's feet out from under him, and he tumbled back to the ground.

"C'mon," Ashlyn said, her voice strained as a shining orb of light floated above her fingers. "Don't let us pile on you like that."

"How?" Damon panted, pushing himself gingerly to his feet.

"You're standing in one place," Kym said, sighing as she rubbed healing oil into her arms. "Move around. It's harder to hit a moving target."

"But, I thought the Favored—" Damon began.

"You're not learning to be a Favored," Kat panted. "You're learning to fight like a Vanquisher. Get your head in the game."

This, it turned out, was harder for Damon than Kym thought. He was getting faster at forming attacks, but getting knocked down completely killed his momentum. He was fine as long as he was on the offensive. Once Kym, Kat, Tomark, or Ashlyn tripped him up, they had him pinned until they finally stopped attacking.

Kym applied a drop of healing oil every two or three attacks, and it seemed to be helping. It kept her pain at a minimum, which was a good thing. With the pain no longer clouding her mind, her control over the water improved. Droplets no longer beaded off the streams of water she threw at Damon, and when they finally stopped as the sky turned pink outside, the water didn't feel as heavy as a bag of bricks.

"Good job," Tomark panted, patting Damon on the back.

They were sitting in the middle of the training room. Kym surveyed the balcony, which she'd completely forgotten about. There were more people there than when they arrived. Kym scanned the watching people and stopped halfway around the room. Her father stared back at her, his brows knit, and there were several lines along his shining forehead. If Kym didn't know any better, she'd say he looked mad. But why? What had happened to the kind, gentle father Kym knew to make him so angry?

Kym was surprised how easily she and the others fell into their new routine. They'd train for several hours each morning, eat something, then do it again in the afternoons. They always had an audience for their morning training sessions, which they did on their own. The afternoon sessions, on the other hand, were a different story. After a week of observation, guards started joining them after lunch. They stood to the side, watching as Kym and the others drilled Damon on basic combat magic. It took them a couple more days before they joined in.

"The Favored fighting style is actually really simple," Ashlyn said to the guards clustered around her one afternoon. "They will try and overwhelm you."

Different groups of guards joined them for training under the watchful eye of Lieutenant Parker. For this, the goal was always the same. The guards needed to reach Kym or one of the others while they tried to hold them back. Kym could only describe their first attempt as pathetic. First, it was clear to Kym that these soldiers had very little experience with the Pro spears. They didn't wield the weapons with the experience only a lifetime of dedication and training could provide. Even after not using the spears for years, Kym's lady's maids, Veronica and Isabel, still wielded the weapons with ease. On top of that, nearly all the guards had little to no combat experience, and joined the Disciple guard as volunteers—and Kym could tell. The two guards trying to reach Kym ran right at her, not even trying to avoid her jets of water.

"You need to move!" Kat shouted at a group of five guards one day. "Running at me is going to get you killed!"

"We made it to you," one of the guards retorted, his face coated in dirt.

"Because Kat was playing with you," Tomark said slowly, and Kym could see the frustration in his face.

"I don't see what the problem is," Lieutenant Parker said. "We've studied the combat tactics of the winner of the Calling. Amber's attacks are calculated, and lack any aggression. The same is true for the other Favored we've seen. Their attacks are controlled and minimal at best. I believe this squad did an adequate job—"

"Because they're being controlled!" Kym snapped, the throbbing in her head doubling as her anger mounted.

She bit her lip. No matter how many times they told them, the people in this place never remembered the Favored weren't controlling their actions. Their fighting was limited because the Rulers wanted it that way. But Kym knew what would happen when the Rulers finally let the Favored off of their leash. If these soldiers weren't ready, they'd all be screwed.

"Maybe," Officer Short said quickly, "you could show us what you mean?"

Kym nodded. She and Kat walked to opposite sides of the room. Kym took a shaky breath as she faced Kat, quickly rubbing a few drops of healing oil into her arms. So far, they'd focused entirely on Damon's combat training. Kym, Kat, Ashlyn, and Tomark were so tired at the end of each day that they didn't get much practice themselves. Sure, Kym's control over water had improved, but that was only for a few moves at a time. Was she ready for a full-on sparring match that could last minutes?

A light flashed from Ashlyn's fingers, and Kym sprang into action. She ran forward, throwing a jet of water at Kat's feet. Kat leaped to the side, cartwheeling away from Kym's attack, which exploded in a shower of droplets beside her. Kat shoved her arm, and a stream of earth flew through the air toward Kym. But Kym was ready for her.

Kym's water collided with the earth, blowing it apart as mud flew in every direction. Kym spun on the spot, swinging her arms as she pulled water from the barrels around her. Streams of water flew at Kat, colliding with the hardpacked earth wall that rose to shield Kat. Panting, her insides burning, Kym lowered her shaking arms. The column of earth shot forward with a crack. Kym dove to the side, her heart racing, as pieces of earth and dust exploded around her.

Kym threw her arms in a circle, and another stream of water flew at Kat. It encircled her, forming a ring of water in the air. Kat reached for the earth beside her, but Kym was faster. Her head pounding, her arms searing, she pushed her hands forward.

The ring of water exploded inward. Kat spun like a top as water knocked her feet out from under her. Kym bent down, her hands on her knees, the edges of her vision growing blurry. But even her exhaustion couldn't keep the smile from Kym's face. She'd beat Kat in their first sparring match in over a year. She would've been proud, except her legs felt like jelly while her arms were on fire.

"Kym!"

Tomark's hands slipped under Kym's arms as her legs gave way. Her limbs were heavy, and her head felt like someone was banging on the inside of her skull with a hammer. Tomark pulled out his healing oil and rubbed several drops into Kym's stinging arms. Kym sighed as the pain subsided slightly.

"That," Kym heard Ashlyn say, her voice oddly distant and echoey, "is how Favored fight. We do whatever it takes to bring our opponents down. Do you understand?"

The training sessions improved as the weeks wore on. Damon progressed from basic combat magic to slightly more advanced skills. He couldn't form a compact bolt after two weeks of practice, so Kym and the others spent a lot of time running for cover as massive amounts of life energy exploded wildly from Damon's hands. However, Kym noticed he had a talent for defensive magic. His shields were already good, but his defenses were incredible when put on a larger scale. Nothing Kym or the others did affected his shield domes. Granted, their attacks weren't energized, but Kym was still very impressed.

Kym and the others spent most of their time in their dorm when they weren't training. It was small, especially with the five of them only using two of the four bedrooms, but none of them minded. Kym certainly didn't. She'd been alone for so long she was happy for the closeness. She relished having people she trusted within arm's reach.

However, something she hadn't anticipated was people watching her every move. Sure, soldiers were always there during their training sessions, and Kym didn't mind that. That was the point of them, after all. The guards needed to learn to fight magic. But Kym hadn't expected Officer Short to never leave them alone.

Kym was starting to get really annoyed with it. He was always there—collecting them in the mornings, helping them in training, sitting with them in the large dining hall on the ground floor. He even stayed with them during their treatments with Nurse Byrd at the start and end of every week. Kym was happy when Byrd said their nerve damage was improving, although she reminded them it would get better faster if they used less magic.

After a couple of weeks, Kym and the others stopped going to medical for their treatments. Many soldiers needed to be patched up during training, so Byrd started attending the afternoon sessions with them. Kym preferred this, even if she found Byrd's slightly overprotective presence a little annoying. She always made sure Kym and the others used their healing oil, and made them take breaks whenever she thought they looked a little winded.

"Don't you have a life, Shorty?" Kat asked Short when he turned up at their door one night.

Kym shook her head. She and Kat had been trying to sneak off and find that science lab for weeks. But every time they had enough energy to leave the dorm, Short was there. He never looked too happy to be there. Kym felt the same way.

"It's my job to make sure you're—"

"Looked after," Ashlyn groaned. It was the response he always gave.

Kym started to doubt if she'd ever find out what was behind the locked door. She didn't even know if they could find it again. They'd happened on it by accident the first time, and they'd been delirious as well. Short's constant babysitting wasn't helping her search. How could she find the lab if she could only train and eat?

But the locked door wouldn't leave Kym's thoughts. At this point, she really didn't care what was behind it. She was sick of always being kept in the dark. She'd spent her time at Wadita being told what to do or entirely helpless. She wasn't going to let that happen to her ever again.

"I don't know what to do," Kym said to Kat and Ashlyn as they sat on the floor in their bedroom. "There's something going on here they're not telling us about. It's driving me crazy."

"What can we do?" Ashlyn asked. "Short won't leave us alone. He even followed me to the bathroom today during training."

"What?" Kym asked. She hadn't even noticed Ashlyn leave. She'd been focused on breaking Damon's shield dome with Tomark.

"Yeah," Ashlyn shrugged. "He waited outside until I was done and walked me back. It was weird. Something is definitely off about this place."

"In related news," Kat smiled, rolling her eyes, "the sky is blue."

"Shut up," Ashlyn smiled, shaking her head. "But seriously, we're not gonna figure anything out if all we do is train all day."

"I know." Kym shook her head.

The more she thought about it, the more the answer seemed

obvious. They needed to find a way to leave the True Disciples. Sure, the past several weeks of training in the safety of the Disciples' tower was refreshing. Damon's magic was progressing nicely, and Kym and the others were finally starting to heal, but how long could that last? It was only a matter of time before the Rulers sent the Favored to snuff out this last pocket of resistance. And Kym didn't want to be anywhere near when that happened. There had to be a way out of there.

"Why don't you ask your dad?"

"What?" Kym looked at Ashlyn, whose pale green eyes bored into her.

"Talk to your dad," Ashlyn said. "He can tell you what's goin' on here. He's on the Council."

"The Council we haven't seen or heard from since we got here," Kat mumbled.

Kym stared at her bare feet, her insides squirming uncomfortably. She hadn't seen her father up close since the first night, and whenever she saw him observing a training session, he looked so upset. Kym wanted to go to him the first couple of days, but he always vanished before she could reach him. He clearly had other things to worry about.

"Could you ask Mrs. Mizel?" Kym asked Kat. "She was your teacher. You know her."

"I thought we agreed talking to Amber's mom wasn't a good idea?" Kat said. "Like, a really stupid idea."

"We can't tell her about Amber," Ashlyn nodded. "She looks too fragile as it is. We agreed she couldn't handle it."

"I can't handle it," Kat mumbled.

"But," Ashlyn pressed on, "she's on the Council too. She could help."

Anger bubbled inside of Kym at the mention of Amber's name. They'd barely mentioned Amber, Xander, or Jazin since they saw them at Inferon. One of them always became too angry and stormed off before the conversation started. Kym knew talking to Mrs. Mizel wasn't an option. Personally, Kym didn't want to think about

Amber for the rest of her life. She, Xander, and Jazin did nothing to stop the Rulers from trying to kill Kym and the others. But if they couldn't talk to Mrs. Mizel, that left Kym with only one option.

"Fine," Kym said finally, not taking her eyes off the floor. "I'll talk to my dad."

Kym didn't have to wait long for a chance to speak to her father. Marek walked onto the viewing balcony as Kym slipped on her water pack the following day for afternoon training. It was a neat little pack used for taking water on long hikes. One of the guards suggested it so Kym could always have water with her, which she appreciated.

Kym sighed, and she felt the water slosh around on her back. Her heart raced as she watched her father, who was looking out the windows on the opposite wall. Why wouldn't he look at her?

"Hey," Tomark said, slipping his hand into Kym's shaking one.

Kym's pulse slowed at the sight of his soft, green eyes. She smiled, and for the first time in weeks, she felt relaxed. Kym stepped closer to Tomark, and the room faded into silence around them.

"Hey," Kym smiled.

"You good?" Tomark asked, pulling his wavy hair out of his face with his free hand. "Kat told me what you're gonna do."

"Nope," Kym shook her head. Why was talking to her father such a hard thing? "He's barely looked at me since that first night."

"I know," Tomark said, squeezing Kym's hand. "But your dad loves you. Heirraph's flame for Thray didn't burn as bright as his love for you."

Kym smiled. Tomark was right. No matter what happened, Kym knew her dad loved her. She was probably tired and reading into things too much. After all, Marek was trying to keep the last outpost of life in Princirum going. He had enough on his plate.

Kym walked up to the balcony, the shadow of Short a few steps behind her. Kym rolled her eyes as she worked her way through the crowd of eager watchers. She expected Short to stop her—he'd done so every other time she tried to deviate from the schedule the

Council gave her. But much to Kym's surprise and delight, he stayed silent as Kym reached her father.

"Hey," Kym said, trying her best to make her voice light.

"Aren't you supposed to be training?" Marek asked, watching Damon, Ashlyn, and Tomark practice evasive maneuvers.

"Dad, I wanted to see you," Kym said, trying to keep the disappointment from her voice. "We've barely spoke since I got here. I miss you."

"I miss my baby girl too," Marek said slowly. He still wouldn't look at Kym.

"I'm right here," Kym burst.

Kym fought to keep her anger in check. Why wouldn't he look her in the eye if he missed her so much? This didn't make any sense. And how could he miss her if she was right there?

"Are you?" Marek finally tore his gaze from the fighting below. He turned to Kym, his eyes narrow and his brows knit.

"What are you talking about?"

"You're not the Kym I knew," Marek said. "And I don't think you've been for a very long time."

It was like he'd punched Kym in the gut. She couldn't breathe. His words echoed around her mind, boring into the deepest parts, and each felt like a knife in her heart. How could Marek say something like that about his daughter? She was the only family he had left.

"You've threatened doctors."

"That was an acci—"

"Was it?" Marek cut across Kym. "During the Calling, I was so proud when you fought as Reta's champion. But I see that fighting is all you are now."

"Dad." Kym shook her head. "Fighting isn't—"

"You've been here for weeks, and I've only seen you use magic for violence. It may be the gods' gift to you, but magic has destroyed the kindhearted girl I raised."

Tears burned Kym's eyes as she stared into Marek's worn face. Why was he saying these things about her? Kym wanted to leave and forget this whole thing. She didn't care what the Disciples were hiding. All she wanted was to be as far away from Marek as possible.

A siren blared over the loudspeakers. Kym jumped, the harsh noise jarring her out of her sorrow. She'd only heard the loud-speakers go off once, and that was to announce a lockdown on one of the medical levels for a flu outbreak. But it wasn't the curt voice of Dr. Gwin that issued from the speakers this time.

"Favored attack incoming," Commander Hale's voice rang through the silent training room. "Civilians, return to your dorms. Soldiers, prepare for immediate departure."

Kym looked sideways at her father, who was busy reading something from his holowatch. She wanted to say something, but after their conversation, she stopped herself. He'd clearly said all he needed to, and Kym was happy to avoid the argument. Kym turned on her heel and ran along the balcony, Short panting behind her. She found the others waiting for her at the bottom of the stairs, looks of excitement in their eyes.

"Finally," Kat said, bouncing slightly on the balls of her feet. "Let's get outta here."

"Where's the attack?" Ashlyn asked Short as they followed him to the elevator. "It must be close if people need to wait in their rooms."

"It's close," Short huffed, leading them back out of the elevator and down a hall. "A few miles outside the city walls."

Kym shook her head, trying to clear it. They were finally going to fight the Favored. This was what she'd been training Damon for. So why couldn't she stop thinking about Marek? Anger boiled inside Kym as her father's words swam around her. She couldn't think about what Marek said. She needed to blow off some steam, and fighting some mind-controlled Favored sounded like the perfect opportunity.

"Get in," Short said, holding open the door to their dorm.

Kym stared at the door. Why were they at their dorm instead of going to the ground floor with the rest of the soldiers?

"What the Thed?" Tomark demanded.

"What're we doing here?" Damon asked as Short shepherded them inside.

"You're not members of the Disciple guard," Short said, his voice oddly cold. "You're civilians. And like the rest of the civilians, you're confined to your room until the battle is over."

Before Kym or the others could say a word, Officer Short backed out of the room and closed the door with a snap.

CHAPTER ELEVEN

A REAL
FIGHT

"Well, this is great," Kat scoffed, plopping down on the sofa.

Kym wanted to hit something. Her fury at being locked in her room, combined with her anger toward her father, raged inside her like a storm. Why weren't they going to the battle? Kym, Tomark, Kat, and Ashlyn had more experience fighting Favored than all of the Disciples combined. They needed them. Why wouldn't they want their help?

Kym paced back and forth, trying to burn off some of her anger. Tomark and Kat looked just as upset as Kym, and Ashlyn looked like she wanted to break something. Damon, on the other hand, just looked disappointed.

"What're we gonna do?" Damon asked, his eyes locked on Kym.

"How the Thed should I know?" Kym snapped, her anger exploding out of her. "We're trapped here, and there's nothing we can do about it!"

"Kym," Tomark said, stepping in front of her, his hands raised. "You need to calm down."

"What's up with you?" Kat asked. "You're acting crazier than usual."

Kym ran her hands through her long hair. What was she supposed to tell them? She couldn't say that her dad wanted nothing to do with her. To say it out loud would make it real. If she kept it inside, at least then no one would know.

"It was your dad, wasn't it?" Ashlyn asked.

"No, it was…" Kym stared into Ashlyn's kind face, and her resolve melted. "He hates me."

"What?" Tomark's voice cracked through the air like a whip. "He said that?"

"Not those words," Kym said, tears sliding down her cheeks. "But it's what he meant. He said after seeing us train here, he doesn't know who I am anymore."

Silence pressed in on them. Kym slumped to the floor, wrapping her arms around her knees. She knew telling them was the right thing. During the Calling, Kym learned the hard way that keeping her friends in the dark was a bad thing. She just wanted the pain, which was like a thousand knives in her heart, to go away.

"What do you wanna do?" Kat asked, kneeling beside Kym.

"Wh-what?"

"What do you want to do?" Damon asked. "What would make you feel better?"

Kym wiped the tears from her eyes. What would make her feel better? She knew the answer in an instant. No matter what it took, she needed to get as far away from the tower as possible.

Kym marched across the room and wrenched open the door. Officer Short stood out in the hall, illuminated by the faint orange glow of his holowatch. He held his arms out when he saw Kym, blocking her access to the hallway. Kym stared at him, her anger bubbling just beneath the surface. Did he really think he could stop her from leaving?

"What're you doing here?" Kym asked as the others joined her at the door. "Why aren't you at the battle?"

"My orders are to keep an eye on you," Short said, his hand drifting to the long, black baton on his belt. "The Council thought you might try and leave."

"Of course they did."

Kym's anger raged inside her like a tornado. Short said the Council, but Kym knew the orders came from one member. Why would her father want to lock her in her room? He must know how being locked up would affect her. She'd been locked up, in one way or another, for the better part of two years. That was why she left the Favored. She wasn't going to let anyone control her again.

"You need to move," Kym said, and she was surprised at how calm her voice was.

Kym raised her hands, her Marks flickering as her arms stung. Short's eyes darted from Kym's hands to the straps of her water pack. They'd left training in such a hurry Kym hadn't taken it off. She was happy she hadn't.

Short reached for his baton, but Kym was faster. Her jet of water flew from her pack and hit Short in the chest. He flew back and slammed into the opposite wall with a thud. He slumped to the floor, soaked to the skin, and didn't move a muscle.

"Kym?" Damon asked, his eyes wide. "What did you…?"

"We're gonna pay for that," Tomark said.

Kym knew Tomark was right, of course. She felt bad for attacking Short, but her anger quickly consumed her regret. She didn't care what the Council thought. She walked over to Short and ripped the holowatch off his wrist. Kym ran down the hall, the others thundering behind her. She waved Short's holowatch over the sensor, and the elevator doors slid open. They piled inside, and Kym jammed the number one button with her thumb.

"Do we have a plan?" Kat asked. "I'm all for winging it, but…"

"We're going to that battle."

The elevator doors opened, and Kym led the others into the library. They didn't meet anyone as they walked out onto the vast front steps. Kym saw what she was looking for almost immediately, and had to suppress a snort. A line of jeeps sat parked in a row in front of the steps. She climbed into the first one and pressed her thumb on the ignition button. The engine roared to life as the others climbed in.

"What're we doing?" Tomark asked, sitting in the seat beside Kym.

"I told you," Kym said hotly. She slid her hands back over the holopanels, and the jeep jerked back. "We're going to—"

"That's not what I meant," Tomark said. "Are you sure this is what you want?"

Kym raised her hands, and the jeep lurched forward. She kept her eyes on the road, not wanting to look at Tomark. She knew what he was trying to do, and she didn't want him to talk her out of this. She was fed up with always being told what to do and lied to. Didn't he understand that?

"I…I want us to make the decisions," Kym said. "The gods told you to trust people who choose you, Tomark. The Council barely tolerates us. They've told us what to do ever since we arrived, but they don't tell us what's going on or what the plan is. Isn't that why we left the Favored?"

"It is," Tomark said calmly. "And you're right. I still don't trust them. But remember, they are trying to do good here."

Kym shook her head. She hadn't once seen any of the good work these people were doing since they arrived. Sure, they said they took in the odd refugee here and there, and they were fighting the Rulers, but what did they have to show for it? Whatever they were doing, it wasn't enough for Kym.

"Look!"

Kat's face appeared between Kym and Tomark. She pointed out the windshield to something in the distance. Kym followed her finger, and her insides quivered as she raised her hands higher. The jeep accelerated, hurtling them toward the city walls. The sky was dark with clouds, and beyond the city walls, Kym saw faint flashes of multicolored light.

"Any idea what they're fighting?" Damon asked.

"No," Ashlyn said slowly. "But it doesn't look like there's a lot of magic happening for a battle."

Kym agreed. If the Favored really were part of the battle, there would be more than the occasional flash of light. They must be using something else as part of their attack. But what? Kym's first thought was death demons, but it couldn't be that. If it was, she'd feel their cold presence already. But if it wasn't death demons, what could it be?

Their jeep passed through the city gates and out onto the road. After about a mile, Kym veered off and drove them through an open field. The jeep bumped and shuddered over the uneven ground, but she didn't slow down as the flashes of light drew nearer.

Kym stopped at the bottom of a tall hill beside a line of empty jeeps. She climbed out, and the unmistakable sounds of battle filled her ears—voices shouting orders, grunts of pain, and weapons discharging. Kym ran up the side of the hill and crouched on her stomach as she reached the top. She peered down the other side, and she understood why there weren't many signs of magic.

Constructs, elements shaped into the form of animals and given a single purpose, ran around the small valley. Soldiers charged the constructs, their long spears held at the ready, but their weapons made no mark on the glowing creatures. Another group of soldiers stood behind the first, running this way and that like ants caught under a bowl. Some launched explosives into the hoard of constructs, but they had as little effect as the other weapons.

"Well," Kat said, cracking her knuckles, "this should be fun."

"We really should have a plan," Tomark said, pulling his wavy hair out of his face.

"I doubt our limited magic will do much good," Ashlyn said, also tying her hair back.

"Mine could," Damon said, his voice quivering slightly.

"Damon, we haven't taught you to fight constructs."

Kym could've kicked herself. Why hadn't they thought to teach Damon to fight constructs? Favored always used them when they didn't want to engage in battle. Kym stared down into the valley as the constructs bore down on the soldiers. They, like Damon, had no idea what they were doing. If Kym and the others didn't do something soon, they'd lose.

Several red and blue constructs rose into the air, sand flying in every direction as they beat their massive wings. They swooped down, their long talons poised to grab the struggling soldiers. Kym leaped forward, her mind blank. She swung her arm, and a jet of water flew from her water pack. It exploded against the nearest construct, which staggered back as droplets filled the air.

Kym spun on the spot, swinging her stinging arms each time she faced a construct. Streams of water flew from her pack, colliding with the constructs, which turned from the soldiers to face her. But Kym didn't care. Her head throbbing, her arms on fire, she kept attacking. This was what she needed. This was the perfect way to blow off steam.

"Fall back!" Kym panted, sweat running down her stinging arms as she pushed two constructs away from the line of guards with a jet of water.

The ground beneath Kym shuddered, and a wall of earth rose between Kym and the constructs. Kym turned around, squinting through the dusty air. Kat was sliding down the hill, her arms outstretched, the others right behind her.

"Great plan," Kat smiled, sending a chunk of earth at one of the flying constructs. "I approve."

"What are you doing here?"

Kym turned toward the voice. Lieutenant Parker rushed toward them. Her face was bright red, and her eyes were so narrow they almost looked closed.

"We're here to help," Tomark said, a gust of air flying from his hand and into a massive hawk construct.

"I have this under control," Parker said. "I'll be informing the Council of—"

The sound of crumbling earth filled the air. Dust exploded behind them as constructs broke through Kat's wall. Kym stepped in front of Parker as a massive lizard construct raced toward her. Kym threw her hand forward, and she focused all of her energy on her water. It pierced the construct's body, leaving a hole the size of a coin. But the construct didn't stop. Kym dove to the side, wrapping her arms around Parker's middle. They fell to the ground as the lizard construct leaped over their heads.

"Get off me," Parker grunted, pushing Kym off her.

Kym struggled to her feet. The insides of her arms were on fire, and lights popped in her eyes. She'd forgotten to apply her healing oil before fighting, and she was paying for it now. She blinked several times, trying to clear her vision. But as she looked up, the edges of her vision were fuzzy and out of focus.

"Damon," Ashlyn's voice reached Kym over all the noise. "We don't have enough energy to destroy the constructs. Throw attacks at them, and try to hit them in the center."

Kym pushed herself up, her ears ringing as her muscles ached. A large construct rushed toward her, and she didn't wait for it to attack. Kym swung her arm, and a jet of water pushed the construct back. A gust of wind shot past Kym, lifting her construct into the air. It crashed to the ground, and a stalagmite burst from the earth, piercing the construct's middle.

Kym spun around, throwing another jet of water at a large snake construct. It flew into a pillar of light, where it writhed under the intense heat. The construct slithered toward the edge of the light, and Kym squared up her feet, ready to attack again. A bright white bolt streaked past her head, blowing her hair back. It hit the writhing construct, which vanished in a red and white flash.

"This isn't working," Kat yelled, throwing a rock at another construct. "There are too many!"

"We're pushing them around," Ashlyn agreed. Her bright beams of light fell on the constructs, which hissed as the brilliant light burned their glowing exteriors.

Kym tried to get her exhausted mind working. What could they do? Kat and Ashlyn were right. She hadn't managed to destroy a single construct. Clearly, someone created these constructs with the intent to overpower and overwhelm. But that didn't help Kym stop them. Their attacks didn't have enough energy, and Damon could only do so much.

A shimmering white blast flew past Kym, making her hair fly around her. The life blast ripped through three constructs, which vanished in yellow, blue, and green flashes. Kym whipped around, struggling to catch her breath. Damon stood a few feet behind her, two more life bolts ready in his hands. He threw them, one right after the other, into the mass of constructs. The first one hit its target, but the second missed as the intended construct leaped out of the way.

It was like a switch flipped in Kym's head. She knew what they needed to do. Kym ran forward, pulling most of the remaining water from her pack. She extended her arm, and the water mirrored her actions, stretching into one long strand. She swung her arm, and the water arced around, forcing back the constructs at the edge of the horde.

"We need to contain them," Kym said through gritted teeth, her arms shaking.

Tomark swung his arm, and a gust of wind billowed around Kym, filling the air with dust. Light filled the air as Ashlyn sent a beam of burning light over the constructs, preventing those with wings from taking to the skies.

"Kat," Kym muttered, her voice strained. She couldn't keep this up much longer. "We need…"

"Walls," Ashlyn finished.

Kat nodded. She pushed her arms into the air, and the ground beneath Kym trembled. Earth walls rose around the constructs, fencing them in. Kat dropped to her knees, clutching her arms as she trembled in pain.

"Damon," Kym panted, pulling her remaining water back into her pack, "have fun."

Kym fell to her knees beside Kat, and Damon ran forward, the air alight with brilliant white light. Sweat poured down her face, and her blood felt like razors in her veins. Kym shoved her hand into her pocket and withdrew her vial of healing oil with trembling fingers. After over a month of near-constant use, the vial was nearly empty.

Kym poured one drop on her forearms as Damon's pure white attacks exploded against the constructs, and her pain faded slightly. It wasn't enough to stop her arms from shaking, but Kym didn't dare use more. She'd need it if Damon didn't pull this off.

"I can't believe a pack of constructs kicked our butts," Kat moaned, cradling her shaking arms.

"I know," Ashlyn said. "I never realized they were so hard to fight."

"Damon's doin' alright," Tomark said.

Kym turned, and her muscles relaxed slightly. Only a few constructs remained in the pen. Damon swung his arm, and a pure white arc shot from his fingers. The life swipe cut the remaining constructs in half, which faded away. Cheers issued from the soldiers, and Kym smiled as she stood on trembling legs. They'd won.

Lieutenant Parker hurried toward them, looking a little worse for wear. There was a long cut down one of her legs, but other than that, she looked okay. Kym braced herself, ready for the explosion. Even if they were the reason the battle was over, Parker didn't seem like the type to forgive easily. They'd broken the rules after all.

"Everyone okay?" she asked.

"We're fine," Kat said forcefully, although ruining it by swaying on the spot.

Parker's eyes flashed over Kym, who shifted uncomfortably. Kym could almost see the anger behind Parker's eyes. She was mad they were there, and she was clearly unhappy her troops weren't enough to win the battle. Kym fought hard to keep her face calm. Why did it even matter who won? Why did Parker care that Kym and the others were the reason that happened?

"Thank you," Parker said slowly, like each word was causing her pain, "for your assistance. I will be sure to include your contributions to tonight's victory when informing the Council of your disobedience."

If Kym wasn't so exhausted, she'd have punched Parker. Was she really going to report them to the Council? Why? They'd helped her win the battle. It was just like being back at the palaces, where the Water Favored told Nila every little thing she did—right or wrong.

"Is that necessary?" Ashlyn asked.

"Absolutely," Parker said. "I'll recommend the least-possible punishment. Your contribution tonight won't go unnoticed.

Alright," Parker turned from Kym to face her soldiers. "Pack it up. We're headin'—"

Boom!

Kym flew through the air, her ears ringing, her eyes full of bright red light. She slammed into something hard, and her back exploded with pain. Her vision was foggy, and the screams around her sounded oddly distant. Kym gazed above her. Massive red, silver, and purple bolts soared over her head, filling the sky with light.

Kym pushed herself up as the world exploded around her. Soldiers lay motionless on the ground as attacks rained down on them. Every other thought vanished from Kym's mind. Her anger with Parker and the Council didn't matter. She needed to get out of there in one piece.

Kym stood as another bright red bolt exploded in front of her. Kym covered her face, shielding it from the flying debris. Screams assaulted her ears as reality slammed in around her. She sprinted forward, her arms held over her head, to where Parker sat crouched on the ground, her holowatch glowing.

"Rear squad, return fire! Forward squad, prepare to advance!"

"Pull your people out," Kym said. Why was Parker getting her soldiers ready to fight?

"We aren't backing down," Parker shouted, diving to the side as another bolt exploded a few feet away. "It's about time they showed their faces."

Kym looked up, and her insides froze. Even from the bottom of the valley, Kym saw the vacant expressions of the Favored on the top of the hill. Glowing elemental orbs floated between every two Favored, spitting attacks down into the little valley.

"Wait," Kat's voice brought Kym crashing back to her surroundings. "You've never actually fought the Favored before?"

"It's always been those glowing animals," Parker said. "Why show themselves now, of all nights?"

"Because you finally won." Kat shook her head. "And they're gonna blow you to Nothingness for it."

Kym looked this way and that, but she couldn't see Ashlyn, Tomark, or Damon anywhere. How could she get everyone out of there safely on her own? She could barely move. The Favored had them pinned down, and nothing the soldiers did made any difference. She needed to do something.

Kym sprinted toward the Favored, ignoring Kat's and Parker's yells. She reached up, and all her remaining water flew out of her pack. She swung her arm as hard as she could at the Light Favored ahead of her. Her water flew through the air, hitting the Light Favored in the chest. He flew back, and the Favored dropped their hands as they stared blankly at Kym.

Kym froze and stared at the watching Favored. They were waiting for something, but Kym had no idea what. Faint, yellow lines glittered on the Favored's foreheads, starting from their temples and working toward their eyes. The glowing yellow lines faded, and the Favored all stepped forward.

"We've been waiting for you, Kymbralyn," they said in unison.

The Favored raised their hands, bolts floating above their fingers. They shoved their hands forward, and blasts of light, darkness, water, earth, fire, and air streaked toward Kym. She stayed rooted to the spot, bracing herself for the impact. She couldn't avoid twenty attacks at once. There was nothing she could do.

A wall of earth erupted out of the ground. Chunks of dirt and stone flew in every direction as the Favored's blasts exploded against it. Kym turned away from the explosion, but she wasn't fast enough. Something large and dense smashed into Kym's right temple, and she crumpled, her ears ringing.

Kym tried to sit up, but the world was spinning too fast. Her stomach lurched, and she couldn't stop the bile from spilling from her mouth. Kym tried to make out where she was, but her vision was too blurred and the air was so dusty that she saw nothing. All she knew was that her head felt like it had been split open.

"You alright?" Kat's voice reached Kym from a lifetime away. "What happened up there?"

Three Kats wavered above Kym, several large cuts on their foreheads. Kym shook her head. How'd Kat get there, and why was she covered in dirt? Kat slipped her arm around Kym, hoisting her to her feet, but her legs felt nonexistent.

"We need to get to the jeep," Kat grimaced as bolts and blasts exploded around them.

"What's jeep?" Kym's head was swimming. What was Kat talking about."

"For Pheil's sake," Kat spat. "The others are heading there now."

Kym stumbled along, Kat supporting most of her weight. Luckily, Kym didn't need to know where they were going. Kat led the way, leaving Kym free to witness the horrors around her. Soldiers lay on the ground, their bodies motionless. Screams and shouts worked their way into Kym's mind, sounding oddly distant as more attacks flew around her.

Kym's mind started to clear when she and Kat reached the jeep. Kat shoved Kym inside, and she fell into someone's lap. The jeep lurched forward, and Kym rolled around uncomfortably. Gentle hands found the throbbing spot on Kym's head. Above her, Tomark's kind face swam into focus.

"You alright?"

Kym nodded, although she wasn't too sure. "Everyone here?"

"We're here," Ashlyn's voice came from somewhere near Kym's feet.

Kym's muscles relaxed slightly. She stared out of the top of the jeep, watching the sky grow darker above her. This had been too close. Lieutenant Parker said the Favored never attacked in person, having always sent constructs in their place. She understood them escalating when the constructs lost, but why'd they change targets to Kym?

Something must have happened when they saw her. But what? They were attacking, those yellow lights appeared on their foreheads, and then they all stopped and spoke to her. The answer came to Kym like a bag of bricks falling on her brain. The Favored were being controlled, so someone must have changed their instructions mid-battle. But who could do that?

Two large shapes zoomed through the sky above them, illuminated by the silver Marks on their arms. Kym's heart froze as air bolts formed in the flying Favored's hands.

"Air Favored," Kym said, pointing at the sky.

The jeep swerved to the side, narrowly avoiding the attacks as they exploded against the ground. Kym sat up, trying to keep herself steady as the jeep rumbled over the uneven ground. She looked wildly around for the Air Favored, but saw no sign of them in the darkening sky.

"Where'd they go?" Kat demanded from the driver's seat.

"I dunno," Damon said, peering around from the seat beside her.

"They're not gonna give up," Tomark said, pressing his sleeve to Kym's stinging forehead. "Where're the others?"

"Parker and her crew left before we did," Kat said. "I think they made it—Ah!"

Bright red and green light assaulted Kym's vision. The jeep lurched, and Kym felt momentarily weightless. The world whirred around her as the jeep spun like a top. Then, the jeep slammed onto the ground, pieces of metal and glass flying in every direction. There was so much dust and smoke Kym couldn't tell where she was. All she knew were Tomark's and Ashlyn's bodies pressed tightly around her.

A hand closed around Kym's wrist and pulled. Pain seared through her back as whoever held her dragged her over the busted remains of the jeep. Kym dug her heels into the ground and pulled, trying to free herself. But her captor's hand didn't budge. Panic coursed through Kym like ice. Where were the others?

"Bind them."

Kym's fear doubled as her capture lifted her to her feet. She knew that voice, and all too well. The Favored holding her, a Light Favored, waved her hand over Kym's arms. A shimmering yellow band appeared around Kym's wrists. Her panic rising, Kym tried to run, but the Light Favored's grip on her was too tight. The others appeared on either side of her, their hands magically bound like Kym's. But that wasn't what made her breath catch in her throat.

Kym stared at the Fire Favored in front of her, her blue eyes drawn to the blank golden ones staring back at her. Amber glided forward, as did the Favored on either side of her. They moved as one, their motions perfectly matching each other. Amber stopped in front of Kym, staring impassively into Kym's face. Kym wanted to be angry, but her fear drove her anger from her mind. It was like Amber didn't even recognize her. Was Amber even in there?

"Kymbralyn Collins," Amber and three of the others said in unison. "We have questions for you."

CHAPTER TWELVE

LUCIA

All the air vanished from Kym's lungs. She stared into Amber's vacant, golden eyes, trying to catch a glimpse of the girl she knew. But Kym saw no fire there, no proud determination. Amber's eyes were as blank as the rest of her face.

"We have…"

"…questions…"

"…for you," Amber and two others said, one right after the other.

Questions? Kym had questions too, but fear drove them from her pounding mind. How was Amber there? The last time Kym saw Amber, she'd been smothering emotions at Inferon. Why was she at a battle with the True Disciples? And what could the Favored want to ask Kym? Thanks to Short's constant babysitting, she knew nothing about the Disciples.

Amber and the other Favored looked to the right, faint yellow lines glittering on their foreheads. Kym followed their gaze, her heart racing. What were they looking at? But Kym saw nothing but a vast, open field. Amber looked back at Kym, her face as frigid as ever.

"She's eager to see you again," Amber said.

Amber held out her arm. The Light Favored holding Kym took Amber's hand, while those restraining Kat, Tomark, Ashlyn, and Damon did the same. Kym's quivering muscles relaxed a little at the sight of them. They weren't in good shape, covered with cuts, blood, and dirt, but at least they were alive. Given the circumstances, that was more than Kym could ask for.

Amber twisted on the spot, and the Light Favored's grip on Kym tightened. She hurtled forward, the crackle of flames filling her ears. The world pressed in around Kym as she was simultaneously pulled apart and compressed. Kym closed her eyes, but it made no difference as Amber warped them through space. Where was Amber taking them?

Kym's feet slammed into solid ground. Her knees buckled, and her legs gave way as she fell to the cool ground. Ashlyn lay sprawled a few feet away, her face illuminated by the glowing blue bands around her wrists. Kym closed her eyes, trying to stop her heart from hammering. She had no way to know where Amber warped them, or who wanted to see them. She needed to think of a way out of this, and fast.

"Get up," the Favored said in unison.

Hands grabbed Kym before she tried to stand. They hoisted her to her feet and forced her forward on trembling legs. A massive building stood before her, surrounded by trees and perfectly groomed hedges. Confusion momentarily overrode Kym's terror. She'd thought Amber was taking them to one of the palaces. Why were they at a Master's estate? Damon had said the Masters and Favored didn't use them anymore.

Kym didn't resist as the Favored forced her and the others inside. The foyer was massive, with floor-to-ceiling windows lining the walls. A large basin stood in the middle of the room, a fire crackling inside it. Torches set in brackets on the walls provided even more light, making the already-warm room stifling. An Earth Favored opened a door at the other end of the room, and pushed Kym and the others inside.

"We need a plan," Kat hissed the moment the door closed behind them. She struggled against her bands, but like Kym's, they weren't budging.

"We need a plan?" Ashlyn said, her voice trembling. "I'm more worried about what they're planning for us."

Kym pushed herself into a sitting position, her eyes flashing around the dark room. There had to be something in there that could help them. But the room was bare. No furniture. No windows. The only way in was the door they'd entered through.

"We need to think of something," Damon groaned. "This isn't good."

"Really? No kiddin'?" Kat mocked. "I thought we wanted emotionless, mind-controlled Favored to capture us. Thilg really blessed you with her wisdom. "

"Kat," Tomark snapped. "Not the time."

"But he—"

"Shut up!" Kym hissed. Why was Kat trying to start a fight? "I need to think."

Kym racked her brain. She wanted to call for help, but how could she? Kym's eyes fell to her wrist, and her heart skipped a beat. She was still wearing Short's holowatch. Kym lifted her hands to her face. The glass front of the holowatch was shattered, but could it still work?

Kym shook her head. Calling the Disciples for help was a long shot at best. She didn't even know where she was. This was a problem they needed to get out of themselves. But how? Their hands were bound, and even if they managed to free themselves, their magic was incredibly weak. The Favored would wipe the floor with them in a second. No matter how hard Kym and the others fought, they'd never win.

Kym strained against the glowing yellow bands around her hands. She looked to the others and was sad to see them also struggling to break their bonds. Kym stopped struggling, her heart growing heavy. How were they going to get out of there? Then it dawned on Kym. They weren't.

"Damon," Kym said slowly. "You're going to run."

It was the most obvious plan. Kym, Kat, Tomark, and Ashlyn couldn't fight their way out. But they could buy Damon some time. After all, Damon was the one who needed to stop death. Kym wasn't going to let the Favored get ahold of him. So, Kym and the others would fight the Favored, giving Damon enough time to slip away.

"No," Damon said, his eyes wide. "No way."

"You have to," Kym said. "You're the only one who—"

"I'm not leaving you behind," Damon cut across Kym.

"Kym's right," Tomark said, his eyes widening. "We don't have any other choice."

"We're getting out of here together." Damon shook his head.

"No, brainless," Kat said. "You're getting out of here."

"We'll buy you as much time as we can," Ashlyn nodded. "But we need to get rid of these bands."

Kym pulled against her yellow bands, but the harder she pulled, the tighter they became. The others were having just as much luck freeing themselves. Could they fight with their hands bound? They could, but Kym doubted they'd buy Damon enough time to escape. To give Damon his best chance, Kym needed to free herself.

"How…do they," Kat panted, pressing her foot between her hands to try and break her bond, "know…how to make…these things?"

"I don't know," Ashlyn sighed, also failing to make any progress. "I don't even know how I did it the first time. And I never told anyone how to do it."

Kym stopped trying to break her bands. Kat's question stirred something in Kym's mind. These magical bands weren't common knowledge among the Favored. How'd they learn how to do it? Ashlyn invented it when they fought Xander during the Festival of Creation. Melana said she'd never seen anything like it. Kym had only used them once before—when she'd fought Lance in the Calling. But how had she done it?

"Damon," Tomark said, bringing Kym back to her surroundings. "Have you tried overpowering yours?"

"What?" Damon asked.

"Of course."

Kym wanted to smack herself. It was so simple. When she'd bound Lance, she'd wanted him not to move, and the bands appeared around him. These restraints were just like constructs, and constructs could be destroyed. Melana broke the bands they'd used to restrain Xander during the festival. She'd overpowered them somehow, and the bands exploded. If Melana destroyed them, Kym knew Damon could too.

"Hit it with an attack," Ashlyn said quickly. "Any attack. It may be enough to break—"

The door behind them burst open. Kym spun around, her heart pounding in her chest. Two Favored walked inside, their faces blank as they stared at Kym and the others on the floor.

"She's ready for you," they said in unison.

Kym glanced at the others, who all looked ready to fight. Kym liked their chances—they could easily fight two Favored, especially when they weren't expecting it. But what then? She wanted to get Damon as close to the exit as possible before things went crazy. If the fight started and more Favored showed up before Damon got out, they'd be trapped.

Slowly, Kym pushed herself up. She walked to the Favored, her hands held limply in front of her, her head bowed. She needed to look as unthreatening as possible. Kym glanced back and saw the others following her lead. Kym took a shaky breath. They needed to work together to pull this off.

Kym followed the Favored into the foyer. Someone had extinguished the fire basin, making the massive room much darker. The Favored opened another door, then stood like statues on either side of it. Her legs trembling, Kym bit her lip and walked inside.

The room was huge, with a massive chandelier hanging from the ceiling and bright red tapestries over the windowless walls. The only light in the room came from the fire in the enormous fireplace. A wooden table, at least fifty feet long, sat in the middle of the room. Favored stood like statues around the table, turning their heads in unison to follow Kym and the others as they walked.

Kym lost all feeling in her legs, and her mouth fell open. Amber stood near the head of the table, but hers wasn't the only face Kym recognized. Xander and Jazin were there, seated on Amber's right. Kenna, Kym's former instructor and fellow Water Favored, sat at the end of the table nearest Kym. Lennax, an Earth Master with an arm made entirely of earth, sat across from Kenna.

Kym couldn't breathe. The more she looked down the table, the more faces stood out to her. But Kym didn't understand why they were all there? Nearly every Favored and Master in the room had participated in the Calling. They were the best of the best. How could Kym and the others possibly fight all of them so Damon could escape?

"Ah," a silky, sweet voice rose from the other side of the room.

A shudder ran down Kym's spine. She craned her neck, trying to see who was speaking. A woman dressed in red emerged from the shadows, the whisper of a smile on her lips. Her dark eyes were the same color as her skin, and her even darker, braided hair swayed around her face as she glided forward. Kym's heart raced even faster. She'd seen this woman before. She'd been at Inferon, directing the Favored as they used the Cladium on that boy.

"Welcome," the woman smiled. "I've been looking forward to speaking with you."

"Who the Thed are you?" Kat demanded.

"Silence," Kenna, Amber, and Lennax said flatly.

"It's alright," the woman smiled coldly, waving away Amber, Kenna, and Lennax's objection. "Where are my manners? We weren't properly introduced when we last met. Call me Lucia."

Sweat pooled in Kym's hands, and it wasn't because she hadn't ever heard of Lucia before. Lucia had smiled. Her emotions weren't smothered like the other Favored. But why? Kym thought all of the Favored didn't have their emotions. And why wasn't Lucia speaking in unison with the others? Why would the Rulers let her think for herself?

"As I said," Lucia continued, strolling around the table toward Kym and the others. "I've wanted to speak with you."

As Lucia drew nearer, something inside Kym told her it was time. They weren't likely to get another chance to get Damon out, and this was as good as any. The Favored in the room weren't paying them any attention. It was only Lucia. Surely Kym, Kat, Tomark, and Ashlyn could keep her busy while Damon ran for it.

Kym subtly shifted her feet into a fighting stance while trying to look meek. She hung her head, and saw Kat and Ashlyn also preparing for a fight out of the corner of her eye. They all knew what was coming.

The glittering hem of Lucia's red dress drifted in front of Kym. Lucia placed her long, slender finger under Kym's chin and forced her head up. Kym tried to stay calm, but Lucia's touch sent her anger skyrocketing. She didn't want those cold, long fingers anywhere near her.

"Now," Lucia said, smiling down at Kym. "We will deal with your treason momentarily. There is something far more pressing I require of you. Kymbralyn, where is the resistance hiding?"

Kym didn't know if it was Lucia calling her actions treasonous, her sickly sweet demeanor, or the fact that Lucia used Kym's full name. Every worry fled her brain as she stared up into Lucia's chocolate eyes. Anger raged through Kym like fire, and it exploded out of her before she could stop herself.

"Go to Nothingness!"

Kym swung her bound arms at Lucia's head. Kym's muscles seized, and her hands froze an inch from Lucia's dark braids. Panic coursed through Kym as she tried to move her arms. Her muscles convulsed painfully, and she stood where she was—immovable as stone.

"Thank you, Kenna," Lucia smiled, not taking her eyes off Kym's frozen hands as Kenna stepped out from around the table, her blue Marks glittering on her outstretched arms.

Kym tried to move, but her arms wouldn't respond no matter how hard she willed herself. Kym's heart pounded in her ears as she stared at Kenna's blank face. This wasn't the first time a Water Favored had controlled the water inside of her. The discomfort and pain of no longer having control of her muscles and veins wasn't something she'd forget.

"Let go of her!"

A scuffle followed Tomark's words, and even though Kym couldn't move she knew what was happening behind her. Kat no doubt tried to punch whoever was holding her in the face, while Tomark, Ashlyn, and Damon all fought to free themselves. Their struggles turned to cries of pain as Lucia continued to stare at Kym, her smile still firmly in place.

"Ryland."

A tall boy with broad shoulders stepped out from around the table. Kym's surprise at the sight of her old training partner momentarily drove her fear from her mind. Ryland raised his hands, his blue Marks glowing. Behind Kym, the others cried out as the sounds of their struggling instantly stopped.

"Much better," Lucia smiled. "How can we have our little chat with all of that noise?"

"What do you want?" Kym spat, her voice shaking with suppressed anger.

"Kenna."

Kym's muscles lurched inside her. Her body flew through the air and slammed into the wall. Pain exploded in Kym's shoulder, but that wasn't the worst of it. Kym hurtled around the room, bouncing off more walls before stopping in front of Lucia. Kenna now stood beside Lucia, her face blank, her arms raised as she held Kym aloft.

"I'm asking the questions," Lucia said sweetly, sending a shudder through Kym's aching, rigid body. "Where's the resistance? You were attempting to flee from the aftermath of a battle. These people threaten the balance and peace the Rulers strive to provide as our new gods. Tell me where they are, and your punishment may be lessened."

Kym's mind raced. Why would Lucia, and the rest of the Favored, want to know where the Disciples were? They should know they were in the Thilg Institute of Higher Learning tower. Clearly, Kym had been wrong about that, and she wasn't about to tell Lucia what she wanted to know.

"I don't know."

For the first time, Lucia's smile faltered. She glared at Kym, who stared resolutely back at her, not that she had much choice. Kenna was still controlling her, forcing Kym to look into Lucia's face. Lucia, who was at least a head taller than Kym, leaned down until her nose was an inch from Kym's.

"I don't believe you."

Lucia swung her hand, striking Kym across her face. Pain bloomed in Kym's cheek, and she wanted to cry out. But she bit her tongue, staring into Lucia's dark eyes as tears streamed down her frozen face. Lucia's smile returned, and she looked even more terrifying than before.

"You filthy little traitor," Lucia whispered, her voice still soft and gentle. "Your treachery really is limitless. You will spend the rest of your days in agony, locked up in Tenbatter. But you will tell me what I need to know. One way or another. Lennax."

Lennax joined Kenna and Lucia. All the swagger Kym knew he had was gone as he raised his hands, his Marks glowing on his regular arm, while green light shone through the cracks in his earth one. Kenna waved her hands, and Kym's body moved against her will. The glowing band around her wrist vanished while one of her hands jerked down to her side. The other extended in front of her, trembling slightly as her rigid muscles shook.

Lennax held his hands over Kym's arm. Kym held her breath, her heart pounding in her chest. What was Lennax doing? It couldn't be anything good. Lennax ran his fingers over Kym's skin before stopping halfway down her forearm. Lennax raised his hands, then flicked his wrist.

"Ah!"

Pain exploded inside Kym as a loud crack emitted from her arm. This time, she couldn't keep her mouth shut. Kym's scream reverberated through the vast room as tears welled up in her eyes. Kym looked at her arm and her stomach lurched. It hung loosely in the air, jutting out at an odd angle.

"That looks painful," Lucia smiled, tracing the black scars on Kym's broken arm with a slender finger.

"Ghah!" Kym cried out, pain erupting beneath Lucia's fingers.

She couldn't think straight. How'd Lennax break her arm? He hadn't touched her.

"I will ask once again," Lucia said. "Where is the resistance hiding?"

"I…I don't…" was all Kym could say.

The pain in her arm was too intense. The room swam around her as she tried to keep Lucia in her line of vision. She was fuzzy, but Kym could still see the smile on her lips. Was she enjoying this? Kym didn't know how much more pain she could take.

"You're lying," Lucia smiled.

She wrapped her long fingers around Kym's forearm, and pain flooded Kym's mind. She didn't know if she screamed. Kym must have because in some faraway place, she heard Tomark. The fear in his voice was even worse than Kym's pain.

"Stop!" he pleaded.

Lucia's fingers tightened, and Kym couldn't take anymore. She closed her eyes, letting the pain take over. What else could she do? Kenna had her held there like a statue while Ryland kept the others in their place. She couldn't use her magic. Things couldn't get worse than they already were.

"Ryland," Lucia snapped, her voice uncharacteristically crisp. "Bring Tomark here."

Kym's eyes snapped open. She watched Tomark approach from the edges of her vision. His limbs moved strangely, jerking back and forth under Ryland's blank stare. Tomark froze beside Kym. She looked into his green eyes and knew the words he couldn't utter.

"Kneel," Lucia commanded, not taking her eyes off Kym as Ryland forced Tomark to his knees. "Now, Kymbralyn. I will ask you once more. Where is the resistance?"

Kym's eyes darted to Tomark before looking back at Lucia. Why was she asking her again, and why was Tomark there? She'd already refused to answer after Lennax broke her arm. What else could Lucia do to her?

"Your will is strong," Lucia smiled. "No wonder Lady Nila valued you so much before the Great Union. But you will break."

Lucia stepped closer to Kym, and Kym felt her warm breath on her ear as she spoke.

"And so will he."

Kym's eyes flashed to the side. Lennax's hands were over Tomark's leg, which was stuck out in front of him. All reason left Kym as she fought to break Kenna's hold on her, but her struggle was fruitless. Lennax flicked his wrist, and a loud crack issued from Tomark's leg as it jutted in the wrong direction. Tomark's scream of pain bored into Kym, burning away every part of her until there was nothing left.

Kym glared at Lucia, rage billowing in her like fire. Lucia smiled at Kym, a triumphant look on her face. She grabbed Kym's face, forcing her to look at Tomark. He was writhing on the ground, Ryland no longer holding him in place.

"Tell me where the resistance is," Lucia whispered, "or, one by one, your friends will break."

"I…they're…"

Tears swam in Kym's eyes, clouding her vision. It was just like the throne room antechamber at Crystal Palace. It was Kym's idea to quit being Favored, and the Rulers made her watch them rip the magic from her friends. And now, because she wanted to fight in a battle, she was watching Lennax break Tomark's bones. Once again, everything was her fault.

"Don't, Kym!"

Ashlyn's voice reached Kym even in her despair. The world flew back into focus, assaulting her as a tidal wave of pain, grief, and anger flooded her mind. Tomark wasn't moving, but she saw his chest rise and fall rapidly as he lay on the ground.

"We'll be fine," Kat's voice rang through the room. "Don't worry 'bout us!"

"Oh. I see."

Lucia's fingers fell from Kym's face. She walked out of Kym's line of vision, no doubt to the spot where Damon, Kat, and Ashlyn stood, frozen under Ryland's control. Kym needed to stop Lucia before anyone else got hurt. Kym tried with all her might to move something—a toe, a finger, an eyelid. But nothing she did made any difference.

"I see the fire billowing in you," Lucia said, and Kym's heart froze. Who was she talking to? "I will enjoy watching Amber reduce it to nothing but embers."

"Whatever, lady," Kat's retort echoed through the nearly silent room. "I'd rather wander Nothingness."

"Oh no," Lucia's voice was silkier than before. "It's not your time to wander, little one. I have other plans for you. Ryland."

Kym's heart race as Ryland raised a hand, the other still pointed at Tomark on the floor. He pulled his free hand toward him, and Kat's cry of discomfort was unmistakable. She jerked into Kym's line of vision, her limbs moving mechanically under Ryland's command. However, unlike Tomark, Kat remained standing as Lucia rejoined them in the middle of the room.

"Kymbralyn," Lucia said, once again grabbing Kym's face. "There's no point trying to resist. Sooner or later, I will get the information I require. Where is the resistance?"

Kym's soft blue eyes locked with Kat's brown ones, and understanding passed between them. Kym knew what Kat wanted—for Kym to stay silent, no matter what happened to Kat. Kym tried to remember that, but her instinct overrode her reason. She needed to keep Kat safe. She couldn't let her choices put her friends in danger again.

"Ryland."

Ryland raised his hand before Kym could speak. Kat's arms extended out to her sides, her eyes narrowed as she stared determinedly at the floor. Ryland twirled his hands, and Kat's arms twisted around like someone was pulling them behind her. Kat's face contorted with pain as she cried out.

"Stop," Kym pleaded, looking into Lucia's cruel face. "Stop it."

"That was not the answer to my question," Lucia smiled. "Lennax."

"No!"

Kym barely heard her screams as the sound of both of Kat's

arms breaking reverberated in her skull. Tears streamed down Kym's face while Lucia continued to smile. Lucia didn't want answers. If she did, she'd give Kym a chance to respond. Now Kym understood why the Rulers didn't need to control her. She enjoyed seeing Kat, Kym, and Tomark in pain. She was evil, and thrived on lording her power over others. She was just like the Rulers.

Anger collided with the sorrow swirling inside Kym. She didn't care that her magic was weak. She didn't care how powerful Lucia was, or how many Favored she had under her control. Kym was going to make Lucia pay for hurting her friends. Her rage was more powerful than any magic Lucia could summon.

"This is your last warning," Lucia said smoothly, her silky voice unfazed by the horrors around her. "Tell me where the resistance is, or Katarein will break."

Lucia waved her hand to Lennax and Ryland. They raised their hands, and Kat rose into the air. Ryland contorted her body, twisting her limbs into awkward positions while Lennax reached for her legs.

"Let go of me!" Kat shrieked, and for the first time, Kym heard fear in Kat's voice.

"I'll tell you!" Kym shouted desperately. Keeping the Disciples safe wasn't worth Kat's life. "I'll tell you whatever you want. Just stop."

"You will tell me now," Lucia said, the light of victory flashing in her chocolate eyes. "Where's the resistance hiding?"

"Let Kat go," Kym pleaded.

"Stupid girl." Lucia nodded to Lennax, who stepped forward, his hands held above Kat's legs. "End her."

There was a deafening crack and Kat's scream of pain drove every thought from Kym's mind. Helpless, unable to move, Kym stared at Kat, her little body floating in the air, her limbs jutting out at odd angles. How could she have let this happen? Her friends were paying the price for her actions once again. The pain in her arm was nothing compared to the pain in her heart.

A glowing red orb streaked past Kym's face, its high-pitched ringing filling her ears. The fire bolt exploded against Lennax's chest, filling the room with red light as he flailed through the air. He slammed against the opposite wall and fell to the ground in a crumpled heap.

Kym's muscles relaxed, and she collapsed. Kat lay a few feet in front of her, and she was barely stirring. Kym struggle to lift her aching neck. She didn't understand. Who threw the fire bolt at Lennax?

Amber stood a little ways away from the other Favored, her hand outstretched, her red Marks glowing on her slender arms. And her face wasn't blank. On the contrary, there was a fury in her eyes Kym thought she'd never see again, and she was looking right at Kym, Kat, and Tomark.

"What is this?" Lucia demanded.

"You," Amber's voice trembled with rage as she stepped toward Lucia. The other Favored invoked their Marks, pointing their hands at Amber. "Will not...hurt...my friends."

Amber spun on the spot, and a ring of fire appeared around her, sending waves of heat through the room. She threw her hands out, and the ring exploded outward. Flickering red flames knocked the Favored and Lucia off their feet, sending them into walls and over the table. Amber ran through the debris, pushing people aside as she sprinted toward Kym.

"Come...c'mon!" Amber stammered, offering Kym her hand.

Kym stared at Amber, unable to process what she was seeing. Amber's face contorted, and she kept looking this way and that, like there were people all around her fighting for her attention. It was so far from the composed face she knew.

Kym didn't believe it. She must be in shock—overcome with pain and guilt. She blinked several times, determined to remove Amber from her sight. But Amber didn't disappear, and questions flooded Kym's mind. What was Amber doing? How was she free from Lucia's control? And why was she so angry?

"A—Ash," Amber stammered like every word was causing her pain. "Get...Kat..."

"What's going on?" Ashlyn demanded, appearing beside Kym with Damon. They looked just as confused as Kym.

"I'm…getting you…out."

"Stop them!" Lucia's voice rang through the room.

Attacks flew around Kym, exploding against the walls and ceiling. Amber raised her hands, and a bright red shield appeared. Bolts bounced off it as cracks spread through the red dome like spider webs. A light bolt hit the shield, and it exploded in a flash of red. Amber raised her arms, but she wasn't fast enough to stop an earth bolt from hitting her chest.

"I never would have guessed this," Lucia's sweet voice rang through the chaos. "The Fire Princess, a traitor. End her with the rest."

"No!"

Kym didn't know what shocked her more: the sound of Jazin's voice or the bright purple dome that appeared around her as attacks flew from the Favored's hands. Kym pushed herself up, fighting to ignore the screaming pain in her arm. It was nothing compared to Kat, who lay half slumped in Ashlyn's lap.

Damon ran forward, a life blast exploding from his trembling hands. The Favored scattered, avoiding the white blast as Jazin and Xander raced toward them. They threw bolts over their shoulders, the pained looks on their faces identical to Amber's. Kym shook her head, trying to clear it. How were they acting like themselves while the other Favored still followed Lucia's commands? What changed?

"Are…okay?" Jazin stammered, pulling Amber to her feet.

"I'm fine," Amber hissed, her golden eyes darting around her.

"We need to go!" Damon shouted, throwing a life swipe at the approaching Favored.

"Any…ideas?" Xander grunted. His dark blue eyes were wide and his muscular frame trembled as he scooped the the barely conscious Kat into his massive arms.

Every fiber of her being told Kym not to trust Amber, Xander, or Jazin. They had betrayed Kym, Kat, Tomark, and Ashlyn by letting the Rulers try to kill them. But she couldn't let her anger get the better of her. Kym needed to get the others to safety, and the only way she could do that was with Amber, Xander, and Jazin.

"Away from here," Kym spat, not wanting to look at any of them.

"Quick…my hand…"

Kym didn't need Amber to tell her twice. She grabbed Amber's slender fingers, which trembled beneath her own. Tomark, Ashlyn, and Xander's hands wrapped around Kym's and Amber's while Jazin and Damon threw attacks at the approaching Favored.

"Hurry!" Tomark groaned.

Damon and Jazin threw swipes and sprinted for the others huddled around Kat. They shoved their hands into the middle of the bunch, and Kym cried out as they hit her broken arm. She closed her eyes, trying to force the pain away. She felt Amber's hand twist in hers, heard Lucia's scream of fury, and then all she knew was flames.

C H A P T E R   T H I R T E E N

A   S T O R M   O F   F E A R
A N D   A N G E R

KYM'S BACK SLAMMED INTO SOMETHING HARD. SHE SQUEEZED HER
eyes shut, determined to ignore the world around her. Her scream of
pain started somewhere in her stomach, burning through her until it
finally burst out. Everything hurt, from her broken arm to her fried
muscles to her pounding head. Something stirred beside her, and
Kym knew she couldn't hide any longer.

Kym opened her eyes and saw a sea of green. The large bushes
and red and blue wildflowers that peppered the ground almost
glowed in the darkening night. Trees rose all around her, and the
unmistakable rush of a river hit her ears. Grass tickled her nose as
she lifted her face from the cool ground. Where was she?

"Damon!"

Ashlyn's horrified scream sent a jolt through Kym's spine. She
pushed herself up, ignoring the pain coursing through her. Tomark
and Kat were lying on the ground, their bodies nothing more than
crumpled messes. Ashlyn sat between them, her face as white as a
sheet. Jazin and Xander were also on the ground, their heads held
between their hands. Amber paced back and forth, hitting herself
repeatedly in the forehead with her fist. Damon stood in the middle
of the chaos, his mouth hanging open, his eyes wide with terror.

"Heal Kat," Kym grunted, fighting to keep the pain from her
face. "She got the worst of it."

"The Thed she did," Ashlyn said, brushing Kat's brown hair
from her pale face. "She didn't deserve that."

"None of us did," Tomark grimaced.

Silent tears slid down Kym's cheek as Damon raised his hands.

Life energy rose from the grass, which crumbled to ash as the glittering white mist floated above Damon's fingers. Kym closed her eyes as Damon placed his hands on one of Kat's broken arms. That didn't stop Kat's screams from piercing Kym's heart.

"Shut…her up…"

Kym's eyes snapped open. They fell on Amber, who was still pounding her forehead with her fist. Disgust filled Kym's mouth like bile. Was Amber really telling Kat to be quiet when she'd just broken both of her arms and legs?

Kym moved without thinking. She lunged forward, wrapped her good arm around Amber's waist, and tackled her. They fell to the ground, nothing more than a mess of limbs. Kym's shattered arm exploded with pain, and her head felt like there was an axe in it, but she didn't care. How could Amber say that to Kat?

"Get off," Amber yelled, her words clearer.

"What the Thed's wrong with you?" Kym demanded, pushing Amber onto the grass.

"She's gonna…get us caught…" Amber stammered, her speech once again fractured as she sat up, her silky black hair hanging in her pale face.

"Her legs and arms are broken!" Kym yelled, pushing Amber back to the ground. How could Amber be so insensitive?

"I…know…that…" Amber growled.

Kym stared at Amber, and for the first time since she'd gotten out of Tenbatter, Amber looked back. Her golden eyes darted in every direction, and there were several lines on her forehead. It was like she was in pain. Kym shook her head. Kat, Tomark, and Kym were the ones with broken bones. Amber just stood there and watched it happen.

"Wha's goin' on?" Tomark grimaced cautiously.

Kym's anger faded at the pain in Tomark's voice. She hurried to his side, and fresh tears welled in her eyes. Tomark was pale, his eyes shut against the pain caused by his broken leg sticking out at an odd angle. She wanted to make it better, but there was nothing she could do. She was the reason he and Kat were in terrible pain.

"I'm sorry," Kym breathed. "I'm…"

"Don't worry," Tomark said, squeezing Kym's fingers. He pushed himself into a sitting position, and Kym saw no kindness in his eyes. "Why are you helping us?"

"What did…you expect…us to do?" Xander stammered.

"You didn't do anything when the Rulers tried to kill us," Ashlyn said darkly, still kneeling beside Kat. "Thought you wouldn't mind torture after that."

"What choice… did we have?" Jazin said.

"You could've helped us," Kym spat. Every negative thought she'd had about the three of them exploded out of her. "You could've told them to stop. You could've fought with us when Thed showed up. You could've done something other than watch the Rulers rip the magic out of us."

Kym stared at Amber, Xander, and Jazin, daring them to respond. She knew they wouldn't. Their actions were inexcusable. Besides, it looked like they were having enough trouble stringing two words together. Kym smiled at the pained looks on their faces. Whatever pain they were feeling, it was nothing compared to what Kym and the others had endured. Kym knew they deserved whatever discomfort they were feeling.

"What's wrong with you?" Kat asked.

Kym turned so fast she nearly lost her footing. Kat was sitting with her back against Ashlyn's knees. Her face was a faint green color, and she looked like she was on the verge of vomiting. Kym's eyes raked over her arms and legs, which looked perfectly normal. Relief coursed through Kym as she walked over to Kat.

"You alright?" Kym asked gently, kneeling beside Damon.

"I couldn't heal her entirely," Damon panted, sweat shining on his forehead. "The damage is complex, and I need to save my strength for you guys."

"How'd you break free?" Kat asked, clearly not listening to Damon. She glared at Amber, who looked like she'd seen a ghost.

"We…I don't…" Jazin stammered, his thin, pale frame trembling as his grey eyes widened.

"I didn't ask you, death boy," Kat snapped, and Jazin buried his face in his hands.

"Lay off him!" Amber yelled, once again sounding like her old self.

"Can someone explain what the Nothingness is going on?" Tomark grimaced as Damon examined his broken leg.

"I...I can't..." Xander stammered, his muscular body looking oddly small as he curled up in a ball.

Kym shook her head as she stared at Xander. She didn't know what to expect, but it hadn't been this. If she didn't know any better, she'd have said he looked terrified. Some of Kym's anger faded as Xander crumpled, his muscular body trembling like a leaf. Why did he look so afraid? What did he have to be scared of?

"It's...long story," Amber said, her eyes darting around again.

"We have time," Ashlyn said. "Unless your new friends already know where we are?"

"They...can't hear," Jazin stammered. "Too much...noise."

"Noise?" Kat scoffed. "The Fire Princess just yelled at me for being too loud."

"Not you," Amber snapped. "There's too much...it's inside."

Kym's eyes narrowed as she looked from Amber, to Xander, to Jazin. They all had their heads in their hands, their palms pressed against their temples. Inside? What did Amber mean? When they were at Inferon, that Light Favored put light from a crystal in the little boy's head. Was the same thing inside Amber, Jazin, and Xander? And if it was, what was it?

"How're you even here?" Tomark asked. "You didn't recognize us before. What changed."

"Kat," Amber spat. She stared at Kat so intently Kym was surprised Kat didn't flinch.

"How the Thed is this my fault, Fire Princess?" Kat demanded.

"After you tried to leave," Amber snarled, still glaring at Kat. "The Rulers couldn't risk any other Favored following you. So, we used the Cladium to obliterate their free will."

"We saw," Kym said, her anger boiling inside her.

"We smothered their emotions and used their fear to bury their conscious minds."

"What?" Ashlyn snapped.

"The darkness Cladium," Xander said quickly, sounding almost disgusted. "The light Cladium controls conscious thought. Well, the darkness Cladium controls a person's fear. To keep the Favored from their own thoughts, we trapped their consciousness in a storm of their fears."

"Then," Amber continued, still glaring at Kat like her life depended on it, "the Favored were connected to a single, artificial consciousness. That way, what one saw, they all saw. We became the Rulers' Unity—a perfectly in sync, never-questioning army."

Anger raged in Kym like a wild beast, ripping through her insides. She wanted to vomit. The Rulers were so afraid the other Favored would try to leave they obliterated their free will. They smothered their emotions and buried the Favored under a mountain of fear, and Xander and Amber were the ones who did it. Kym wanted to hit them. How could they have done that to the other Favored? To their friends? But there was something that didn't make sense.

"So, how'd you break free?" Ashlyn asked, her voice shaking with suppressed anger.

"Like I said," Amber snarled through gritted teeth. "Kat."

"Oh, Nothingness," Kat said. "I don't buy it. You saw me plenty of times before then, and you did nothing."

"You weren't in pain," Amber burst out.

"What?" Kym shook her head. What was Amber talking about? They'd been in a constant state of pain ever since they'd gotten out of Tenbatter.

"Seeing you in pain," Amber said, "was too much. It…it ignited…"

Amber trailed off, her eyes widening as her breathing quickened. Kym turned to Xander and Jazin, but they were lying on the ground, muttering to themselves. Kym raised her good hand toward Amber, who scurried back, her eyes wide. Kym shook her head.

What was going on? Why did they look terrified? Kym knew the answer in an instant. They looked terrified because they were.

Kym's anger subsided as she saw Amber's, Xander's, and Jazin's fearful faces in a new light. Amber said the Favored's minds were buried by their fears, and Kym had a feeling she was watching that happen again. They were like the other Favored—the Rulers took their free will from them, then forced them to do it to the others. They'd suffered just as long as Kym had.

Kym's first impulse was to step back, but something Amber said stirred in her mind. Seeing Kat in pain ignited something inside her. Was it her emotions? Amber sounded more coherent when Kat provoked her. But why now? Kym knew Kat and Amber had a long history, but how'd seeing Kat in pain reach the humanity the Rulers tried to bury inside Amber? She'd seen Kat in pain plenty of times before the Rulers took over her mind: during the Calling, when they tried to leave, and when the Rulers ripped Kat's magic from her. Why was this time different?

Going against every instinct she had, Kym stepped forward. She walked past Amber as she wandered in circles, her eyes fixed on the ground. Instead, Kym knelt beside Xander. She placed her good hand on his wide, trembling shoulders. His head jerked up, his dark blue eyes wide, and Kym fought the urge to recoil.

"Xander," Kym said, struggling to keep her voice calm.

"No." Xander closed his eyes, shaking his head as he tried to bury his face in his hands.

"Xan," Kym said, grabbing one of his hands. "You're okay. Your fear…it's not real."

"It is," Xander said. "That's the only way it can keep our minds at bay. The fears are ours."

"But they're not happening." Kym hadn't noticed Kat beside her. She grabbed Xander's other hand, wincing as she squeezed his fingers.

"You're okay?" Xander asked, his eyes widening as his face softened slightly.

"I'm stronger than you, Muscle Man," Kat said, the ghost of a smile on her lips. "Tell me what you see?"

"I'm alone," Xander said, his voice shaking. "I have nowhere to go. I failed."

"Welcome to the club," Kat said, and Kym couldn't help but smile a little. "The stupid Rulers chucked us out, and we're still here, Xan."

Kym stepped back as Xander buried his face in Kat's shoulder. Kym wanted to say she was surprised, but deep down, she wasn't. She'd suspected something was going on between Kat and Xander for a while. Xander even helped Kat sneak into Kym's room one time. He'd risked everything to help her. Kym wasn't surprised to see Kat doing the same. Was their connection what woke Xander's emotions?

"Xander," Tomark groaned, appearing beside Kym. "You were the one doing the fear thing."

"The darkness Cladium," Amber snapped, sounding much like her old self.

"Right," Tomark rolled his eyes. "You can undo it."

"I...I don't..."

"Don't be a wimp, Xan," Kat snapped, punching him softly on the shoulder. "You got this."

Kym stepped back as Xander screwed up his face. Was this really the best idea? If Xander's fears were strong enough to suppress his mind, could Xander put them back in their place? To Kym, he didn't look like he was up to standing, let alone advanced, vile magic. What if something went wrong? What if Xander's darkest fears got out of control?

Kym looked to Tomark, and saw none of her concern in his eyes. In fact, given the circumstances, Kym thought Tomark looked perfectly calm. Kym shook her head. Did Tomark actually trust Xander?

"Wait," Kym said as Xander pressed his shaking hands into his forehead, his purple Marks shining like neon strings.

"Kym," Kat whispered, her usually harsh voice calm. "Not now."

"But," Kym said, kneeling beside Xander, "aren't they still connected to the other Favored? Won't they know what's goin' on?"

"Does it matter?" Kat asked.

"Yes," Kym said.

How could Kat not see the danger Amber, Jazin, and Xander posed. If they were still connected to the Unity, the Favored could be there at any moment. The longer they stayed together, the easier it would be for the Unity to find them.

"Of course, we're connected to the Unity," Jazin said. "But I don't think they can hear us."

"Why?" Tomark asked.

"Too much…noise," Amber struggled to say. "Our partial emotions and free minds are creating interference. They hear that; our emotional, illogical thoughts, not what we're saying at the moment."

"How long do we have?" Ashlyn asked.

"I can already feel my emotions waning," Amber said. "Seeing Kat in pain reignited my anger. This caused a chain reaction with some of my other emotions. But they're already starting to die. Once they go out, and my fears bury me again, the Unity will know where we are."

Kym turned to Xander. She didn't like it, but if their free thoughts were the only thing keeping the Unity from finding them, they had no other choice. Kym knelt beside Xander and placed her good hand on his shoulder. He was shaking so violently Kym had to focus to keep her hand from falling off him. She knew his fears drove him more than anyone. He didn't deserve that.

"Do it."

Xander screwed up his face, took a deep breath, and pulled his hands away from his forehead. A great, purple cloud of glittering light burst from his skull, making Kym's hair fly around her. It thrashed around them, encasing them until Kym couldn't see the stars. Kym saw the tiniest strands of yellow, flickering and dying among the violent purple storm as Xander's fear swirled around it. Kym's hair stood on end as whispers filled her ears—whispers of a voice she knew well.

"*You are a failure,*" Lady Melana's voice echoed through the purple cloud. "*You are worthless. You are powerless. You are nothing. No one will ever want you.*"

"Don't listen to her," Kym heard Kat's voice ring out through the cloud. "She's lying."

"We want you," Ashlyn called out. "You have a place, and it's right here with us."

"*Why would anyone want someone as weak as you,*" Melana's voice hissed.

"We need you." Tomark's voice was soft, but Kym heard it as though he stood right beside her.

Kym stepped forward, pushing her way through Xander's fears. She knelt beside him and found Ashlyn, Kat, and Tomark there. Tears welled up in her eyes as she gripped Xander's hand. This was Xander's greatest fear. After everything he'd done to prove himself, he was still afraid of being worthless.

"No matter what happens," Kym whispered, squeezing Xander's hand. "No matter what we've done to each other, we will always be here for you. We will never turn our backs on you."

The thrashing purple cloud slowed around Kym, and the glimmer of yellow exploded. It swirled gently around Kym as the violet mist subsided. Kym felt Xander stop shaking, and he raised his head. Kym saw tears in his eyes, which no longer darted in every direction. He pointed his hands at the thrashing cloud and brought them closer together. The cloud shrank, condensing while the glimmers of yellow grew stronger. Xander brought his hands to his forehead, and his fear receded inside his head.

Kym slumped into Tomark's chest. Even though they hadn't been her fears, she still felt shaken. What would her greatest fears be? What could keep her mind constantly bogged down, unable to think? Kym's stomach twisted uncomfortably. She didn't want to know.

"How do you feel?" Ashlyn asked Xander, who stared at his own hands like he hadn't seen them before.

"Good," Xander said flatly. "I'm not afraid anymore."

"Um…" Kym exchanged looks with Kat and Ashlyn. "Why are you—"

"My emotions are dwindling," Xander said flatly. "With my fear under control, there isn't much left to keep them going. They will die out soon."

Xander walked over to Jazin, who sat on the ground with his head between his legs. He placed a large hand on Jazin's forehead and pulled. A long purple thread extended from Jazin's forehead, the tiniest trace of yellow flickering inside it.

"Now that I'm in my right mind," Xander droned. "I'll be able to reduce the amplified fear myself. It won't take long."

And Xander was right. In no time, he'd released Jazin and Amber from their fear. It didn't explode outward as Xander's did, so Kym didn't experience their fears with them. Personally, Kym was relieved. She wasn't sure about Jazin's fear, but she knew she didn't want to get anywhere near what scared Amber.

Jazin adopted the same calm demeanor as Xander when his mind was restored. He stood there, looking almost bored while occasionally staring off in random directions. Amber, on the other hand, continued to stare at Kat. Her nostrils flared, and she looked like she was on the verge of smacking someone.

"We don't have much time," Jazin said mechanically. "With our emotions dying, and with no more fear to cloud our consciousness, the Unity will be able to interact with our minds again."

"Can they control you?" Damon asked.

"No," Xander said. "The Unity is artificial and cannot overpower a true mind. But they will have full access to our thoughts, and we theirs."

"There has to be some way to block them out," Kym said.

Kym waited for Amber to say something, but she was still staring daggers at Kat. She knew more about magic than any of them. There had to be some trick she knew to keep their minds safe.

But Amber didn't seem to want to offer up any suggestions. All that interested her was staring at Kat.

"Amber," Ashlyn asked. "Any ideas?"

"I need a minute."

Amber turned on her heel and walked off toward a nearby clump of trees. Kym watched her leave with her mouth hanging open. Why was Amber walking out on them? Anything Amber needed to do, Kym wanted her to do with all of them. Why'd she need time alone?

Kym ran after her while the others stayed back. She caught up with Amber as she slipped between two vast trees. Amber sat on a stump, her hands clutched to her chest. Kym stood in front of her, and Amber looked as angry as ever.

"What gives?" Kym demanded. "Why'd you walk off?"

"I said," Amber's voice shook with every word. "I need a—"

"Not good enough," Kym cut across her. "You're gonna tell me what's going on."

Amber closed her eyes, shaking her head. Kym opened her mouth to retort but stopped as Amber's red Marks glowed on her forearms. Amber jerked her hands away from her chest, and a minuscule ember glowed above her fingers. Tongues of flame burst out of the ember at random, filling the air with heat and blowing Kym's hair back.

"Is that…?" Kym asked, staring at the flames exploding in the air.

"My emotions," Amber said through gritted teeth as another jet of flame burst from the ember.

"What's wrong with them?" Kym asked, backing away from the erratic flames.

"They're trying to restore themselves," Amber said as more flames burst forth. "What I did, during the Calling, was extreme. Smothering emotions isn't natural. It took so much magic to force them down to a point where I couldn't experience them. But they're still there, even if I couldn't feel them.

"My emotional connection to Kat is deeper than it is with any of you. Seeing Kat tortured pushed me over the edge," Amber pressed on. "And now, my emotions are breaking free."

"Isn't that good?" Kym asked. "Don't you want to feel again?"

"Don't be stupid," Amber snapped. "Of course I do. But…not all at once."

"What?"

"Right now, I'm focusing on my anger. Letting it out in spurts. I'm feeling all of the anger I should've felt over the past year and a half. If I let them all out, I'd feel it all."

Amber's head drooped as she stared at the ember glowing above her hand. Kym wanted to be angry at her. She had every right to be. Amber turned on her, and tortured Kym to make her watch the Rulers rip the magic from her friends. Amber had done so many terrible things without her emotions. Didn't she deserve to feel the consequences of her actions? She couldn't hide from them forever.

"I'm an idiot," Amber spat, shaking her head. "What the Thed is wrong with me? How'd I let this happen?"

Cautiously, Kym stepped forward. Avoiding the fiery anger blasting from Amber's ember, she sat beside her. She put her good hand on Amber's shoulder, which shook with suppressed rage. Kym took a deep breath. She needed to keep her cool if this was going to work. Kym wanted to be angry at Amber, but after seeing how angry Amber was, especially with herself, Kym's anger faded.

"You can do it."

"Can I?" Amber shook her head. "After everything I've done, I don't know if I can take it."

"You can," Kym said, and she meant it. "You're the strongest person I know. And I'm here. I'm not leaving."

"You sure?" Amber asked. "You may not like what you see."

"I'm sure."

Amber nodded, and Kym stepped back. Kym braced herself, staring at the flames bursting from the ember. If that was Amber trying to rein her emotions in, what was it going to look like when she let them out? Amber closed her hands around the ember, which shook as warm firelight shone between her fingers.

Fire exploded from Amber's hands. Kym fell back, and her broken arm screamed with pain as heat from the flames stung her face. She held her good hand over her eyes, shielding them as she stared at Amber. The flames swirled around Amber, a tornado with her at its center. It grew higher and higher, taller than any of the trees. The fire surged to the ground, engulfing Amber in a ball of flames. Kym held out her hand, wanting to help Amber, but the flames and the world became still and silent.

Kym locked eyes with Amber's golden ones, which were full of tears. Kym stepped forward and caught Amber as she collapsed to the ground. Amber shook in Kym's arms as she held her, her breaths coming in odd, rasping intervals. Kym held her close, not knowing what else to do. This was the first time since she met Amber that she'd seen her composure truely break. Sure, it cracked on occasion, but she always left before it went too far. Now, there was no were for her to go.

"I'm…so sorry," Amber sobbed into Kym's chest, "for everything I…why does it hurt so much?"

"I…" Kym trailed off. What was she supposed to say to that?

"I can't take this," Amber gasped, clawing at her chest. She sounded hysterical. "Make it stop."

Kym wrapped her good arm as tightly as she could around Amber's slender shoulders. Seeing her like this, her eyes swollen and bloodshot, snot dripping from her nose, was the final straw. Even though she couldn't feel it at the time, Kym knew better now. Amber regretted the horrible things she'd done in the past. Kym had held onto her anger at Amber for so long, but now was the time to let it go.

"Like I told Xander," Kym said, tears streaming down her face as well, "no matter what happens, I won't turn my back on you."

It took Amber a long time to calm down. She cried for at least ten minutes, muttering, 'I'm sorry' or 'what have I done' over and over. Kym didn't say a word, not wanting to interrupt her. Amber was processing all the things she should have felt for over a year all at once. If she needed Kym, she'd ask, and Kym would be there.

When Amber was finally calm enough to walk, she and Kym rejoined the others. Amber reignited Xander and Jazin's emotions while Damon healed Kym's broken arm. Kym didn't know what was more painful, having white-hot life forced into her arm or watching Jazin and Xander work through the emotions they hadn't felt for a year.

"Okay," Kat said once Jazin and Xander had stopped sobbing. "We need a plan."

"We have a plan," Jazin sniffed, his head resting on Amber's slim shoulder. "With our emotions back, the other Favored will have a harder time accessing our thoughts."

"That's not a plan," Ashlyn said. "It's a temporary solution."

"Ashlyn's right," Amber added, her face turning dark. "Right now, we're experiencing a year's worth of emotions at once. We've worked through the worst bits, but we're still—"

"A wreck?" Kat suggested.

"Overwhelmed," Amber said coolly, although Kym saw the corners of her mouth twitch. "Once those die down and our emotions are back to a baseline, it won't take long before Lucia sends the Unity after us."

"Who is she?" Kym asked. "You've never mentioned her before."

"Because I've tried to forget her," Amber said, shaking her head. "She's Lord James's Master of Masters, like Lance is for Lady Nila. Lucia took over my training when the Ruler of Fire thought my father was taking it easy on me. I was five. She's who you have to thank for the Fire Princess."

A chill ran over Kym's skin, making her hair stand on end. No wonder Lucia walked around like she owned the place. Kym wanted to get as far away from her as possible. But where? Amber was right. Once she, Xander, and Jazin got their emotions under control, the Unity would find them in seconds. They needed to hide somewhere until they found a way to free the others from the mind link.

"Can they hear us now?" Damon asked.

"Who are you?" Xander asked. "Aren't you a servant at Crystal Palace?"

"He's a Life Favored," Ashlyn said. "He's gonna break Thed's anchors to Princirum and end this whole nightmare."

"That sounds insane," Jazin said.

"The gods told Lady Zara—"

"Damon," Kym said, cutting him off.

She didn't care what Amber said. Kym didn't think it was the best idea to lay out their whole mission while Amber, Xander, and Jazin had the Unity in their heads.

"So where should we go?" Amber asked, her eyes darting between Kym and Damon.

"Um…"

Kym thought hard. Her first impulse was to go back to the True Disciples. But would they take them in? Amber's mom was on the Council, but Kym knew having a parent on the Council didn't equate to a warm reception. After the frosty welcome she and the others got, Kym wasn't sure how the Disciples would react to three Favored who were still connected to the Unity. Would they throw them out, or worse?

Kym and the others could vouch for them, but would it be enough? They weren't exactly on the best terms with the Disciples. They'd attacked a guard, stolen a car, participated in a battle without permission, and got captured. But if they didn't go back to the Disciples, where could they go? Aside from the Disciples, nowhere else in Princirum was safe.

"Amber," Kym said, standing up. "You good to warp us somewhere?"

"Yes, so long as I know where it is," Amber said. Her eyes fell on Kym's black scars. "I don't think you can guide me. Your energy…"

Kym couldn't tell Amber exactly where the Disciples were. She needed Amber to take them somewhere close enough to the tower that they could walk the rest of the way before it was too late. Kym racked her brain. What was close to the university that Amber knew?

"That's fine," Kat said as the others gathered around Amber. "You've been there before."

"Where're we going?" Xander asked as he took Kat's hand.

"Home," Kat said simply, looking up at Amber.

Realization dawned on Amber's face. She invoked her Marks, and Kym braced herself, staring at their joined hands. Of course, Amber knew what Kat meant. Amber's mother had been Kat's teacher. There was only one place home could be. Amber spun on the spot, and Kym exploded into a million pieces as flames consumed her once again.

A   S I M P L E
S O L U T I O N

Kym opened her eyes, and relief spread through her as her muscles relaxed. The City of Luxmont's main avenue was deserted, just like it had been when Kym and the others first arrived. Kym pulled her hand from the others, shielding her eyes from the bright, morning light. The university tower rose off in the distance. It was less than a ten-minute walk away.

"Where to now?" Xander asked, looking around.

"Um…" Tomark trailed off, his eyes darting between Xander, Amber, and Jazin. "Should we—"

"For Pheil's sake." Amber rolled her eyes. "Are you really not gonna tell us?"

"What if the Unity hears?" Ashlyn asked.

"We told you, we're good," Xander said. "All they're getting from me is a constant flow of disgust."

"But when that wears off," Kym said, looking at Amber, "what happens then?"

"I'm not sure," Amber said.

Kym rubbed her eyes with the heel of her palm. What were they supposed to do? They couldn't tell them the Disciples were at the university. Lucia wanted information, and Kym was keen to keep it from her. But how could they get them there without telling them?

The sound of ripping fabric reached Kym's ears. She spun around, her heart racing, expecting an attack. Kat was on the ground, her coat hanging from her mouth. She pulled, and pieces of fabric easily ripped from the worn garment. She threw a piece to

Xander, Amber, and Jazin, who eyed the strips of cloth with disbelief.

"You're not serious?" Jazin asked.

"You have a better idea?" Damon asked.

"C'mon," Kat said, wincing as she pushed herself up. "We don't got all day."

Amber, Jazin, and Xander tied the strips of cloth over their eyes. Kym glanced at Tomark, who looked just as skeptical as Amber. Sure, they wouldn't be able to see, but would it be enough? They could still hear everything around them, and Amber knew exactly where there were. Kym hoped it was enough.

Kat led the way, taking Xander's hand and moving slowly down the long avenue. Ashlyn acted as Amber's guide, while Tomark led Jazin by the shoulders. This left Kym and Damon to bring up the rear. Kym kept glancing over her shoulder, half expecting a horde of morgar to appear and chase them down the street. But all was quiet.

"What's gonna happen when we get there?" Damon whispered.

"I don't know," Kym said honestly. "They may not want Amber, Xander, and Jazin there. And we have our own mountain of trouble to deal with."

"Trouble?" Damon asked, looking puzzled.

"Everything we did last night," Kym said. "Parker said she'd report us, and I doubt the Council will give us a free pass."

"But we won the battle," Damon said confidently. "They'll be happy we've returned."

Kym shook her head. How could Damon believe that? For one thing, they didn't exactly win the battle. Once again, Damon was paying the price for all the time he'd spent with Zara. The Council wasn't going to forgive them because they were Favored on a mission from the gods. The real world didn't work like that. And the sooner Damon realized that, the better.

It didn't take them long to reach the university perimeter. Kym's head started aching as they approached the grounds, as did her arms, legs, and chest. Amber, Xander, and Jazin cried out, and Kym watched helplessly as they fell to their knees. They'd worked through the worst of their emotions in the forest, but Kym knew they still had a lot to process. Kym wished there was something she could do to help, but she knew this was something they needed to work through on their own.

More than anything else, Kym wanted to crawl into bed and sleep for five weeks. As they approached the tower, her stomach growled loudly. When was the last time she ate? Maybe she would eat something before going to bed.

"Stop right there!"

Kym stopped dead in her tracks. Lieutenant Parker stood on the library steps, and she wasn't alone. Guards flanked her on either side, and Commander Hale stood behind them. She glared down at Kym and the others, who couldn't help but shake where they stood. If Kym was honest, this type of reception wasn't too far from what she'd expected.

"What is the meaning of this?" Hale said, her eyes glued to Amber, Jazin, and Xander's opulent clothes.

Kym could've kicked herself. There was no mistaking who Kym brought back with her, their clothes covered in jewels and metallic thread. Why didn't they find them something else to wear? And the fact that they were blindfolded probably didn't help.

"Where'd you go?" Parker demanded, hurrying down the library steps. "We searched but couldn't find you anywhere."

"Um…" Kym didn't know what to say. She should tell them what happened. It wasn't like Kym could keep it a secret for long. "We were captured."

"I figured," Parker said, her eyebrows raised as she took in Kym's ragged, bloody clothes. "What happened? And who are they?"

"Well, we—"

"She does know we can hear her?" Amber sneered, and Kym knew she was rolling her eyes beneath her blindfold.

"Cool it," Kat hissed through gritted teeth.

"Your kind are not welcome here," Commander Hale thundered

from the top of the steps. "Why would you bring Favored into this sanctuary?"

"Excuse me?" Amber's indignant tone cracked through the air like a whip. "You will show the gods' chosen the respect we—"

Wham! Parker's hand struck the side of Amber's face. Kym held her breath, waiting for the bomb to go off. Amber may have her mind and emotions, but she was still the Fire Princess. Kat, clearly sensing danger, stepped between Amber and Parker.

"What the Thed, Parker?"

"She spoke out of—"

Wham!

Kat's fist disappeared into Parker's stomach. Kym stood as still as a statue, her mouth hanging open as Kat's light brown eyes widened with pain. Parker fell to the ground, coughing and sputtering insults at Kat, who was cradling her half-healed arms. The guards rushed down the stairs, their batons ready in their hands. Kym's first instinct was to attack, but she'd emptied her water pack at the battle, and her broken arm still wasn't completely healed. She doubted she could fight anyone in her current condition.

"Take the Favored to the cells," Hale ordered, her voice booming like a cannon in the quiet air. "They will answer for their crimes against Princirum and the gods."

Cells? Kym had never heard any of the Disciples mention cells. Where could they be? The tower used to be a school after all. It wasn't built to hold prisoners. Why hadn't anyone told Kym about the cells before?

"You can't do that," Ashlyn said, stepping between Xander, Jazin, and two guards.

"You'll find I can," Hale said. "These three are traitors to their country and their faith. They must be punished."

"It wasn't their fault," Tomark said. "They weren't in—"

"Control?" Hale said. "We know about the Favored and the link their minds share. How could you bring these three here? Because of you, the Favored know exactly where we are!"

"They saved us!" Damon said. "They want to help."

"This whole mess is their fault," Hale said. "Take them."

Guards pulled Amber, Xander, and Jazin away from the others. Kym expected them to fight, but they didn't resist as the soldiers dragged them off. Kym put her hand on Kat's shoulder and felt her shaking.

"Cool it," Kym whispered.

"As for the five of you," Hale continued, taking a step toward them. "You're confined to your dorm until further notice."

"What?" Kat shrieked, not even trying to mask her outrage. "Why?"

"Where should I begin?" Hale asked. "You left your dorm during a lockdown. You attacked a guard, stole a vehicle, and engaged in combat when you weren't authorized to. You brought enemy combatants into our home and attacked Lieutenant Parker. Thank the gods I don't throw you in the cells with the others."

Both Kat and Tomark stepped forward, their mouths open, no doubt ready to retort. Luckily, Ashlyn and Kym grabbed them before they could say anything. Kym pulled Kat back, who wrenched her arm out of Kym's grip. She glared up at Kym, who shook her head the smallest amount. Kym knew Kat wanted to help, but they were in enough trouble as it was. They'd be no help to the others if they got thrown in the cells with them.

Kym didn't like Hale, but she was right about one thing. If they didn't get with the program, they'd be locked in the cells with Amber, Xander, and Jazin. If Kym wanted to help their friends, they needed to play nice.

Parker typed something on her holowatch, and Short showed up a few moments later. Kym bit her lip at the sight of him. Several bruises covered the side of his face, and his arm was bandaged, but other than that, he looked alright. She hadn't meant to hit him that hard when they left.

"C'mon," Short huffed, jerking his head toward the main doors. "Nurse Byrd's waiting in your dorm. Looks gnarly," he added, pointing to the large bruises covering Kat's, Tomark's, and Kym's arms.

"Only a little, Officer Tiny," Kat winced, pushing past Short as they made their way inside.

Kym sighed as she followed Short. At least he wasn't too mad at them for attacking him. Nurse Byrd stood waiting for them in their common room, which was cleaner than when Kym and the others left. The random clothes that usually littered the floor and backs of chairs were gone. The furniture, which Kym and Ashlyn had moved into the middle of the room one restless night, now sat in its original places.

Kym froze in the doorway. Why did it look like Kym and the others hadn't lived there for a month? Had the Council thought they weren't coming back? Why else would they restore the room to its original layout?

"What happened?" Nurse Byrd asked as Kym sat on the lumpy couch.

"We got beat up," Tomark groaned, sitting beside Kym.

"I can see that," Byrd said, waving one of her scanners over Tomark's leg while examining a projection of his bone. "Short, run to medical. Tell them I need bone thread accelerant."

"Sure," Short said and hurried out of the door.

"I healed them the best I could," Damon said, looking crestfallen.

"I know," Nurse Byrd said, patting Damon gently on the arm. "But it looks like your magic…needed a bit longer. See there," she pointed at the scan of Tomark's leg.

Kym squinted at the golden image floating in the air. She saw Tomark's bone, and a line was clearly visible across the middle of it. However, the line was faint, with no space between the pieces that Kym could see. In Kym's opinion, Damon actually did a good job.

"The break's partially healed," Byrd said. "And the stress you've put on it since Damon tended to the injury has irritated it."

"Can you do something about it?" Kat groaned from the old armchair. "I'm slipping into Nothingness over here."

"Drama queen," Byrd smiled.

Byrd scanned Kat's and Kym's injuries and concluded they were no worse than Tomark's. Kym smiled as she tentatively placed her arm on the armrest. From the others getting tortured to the escape and reunion with her friends, Kym had barely noticed how sore she was. But now that she was back with the Disciples and off her feet, the pain hit her like a ton of bricks.

"What happened to your head?" Byrd prodded Kym's temple gently with her fingers, but that didn't stop her from wincing.

"I hit it?" Kym couldn't even remember what happened to her head at this point.

"When those Favored tried to blow you up," Kat said. "A rock hit your head."

"Oh yeah."

"Is that how this happened?" Byrd asked as she tended to Damon and Ashlyn, who luckily only had a few cuts and bruises. "At the battle you weren't supposed to be at?"

"Not exactly," Tomark groaned. "We kinda got captured by the Favored."

"What?" Byrd asked, her voice an octave higher than usual.

"Yeah, they found us after the battle," Damon said. "They took us to an estate."

"And this crazy Fire Favored had an Earth Favored break our bones," Kym said.

"How'd he do that anyway?" Ashlyn asked, looking at Kat.

"Search me," Kat shrugged.

Kym sighed. She'd hoped Kat would know something about what Lennax did. She'd trained with him for months when they'd been partners in the Calling. If anyone knew his tricks, it was Kat. But clearly, there were things about Lennax that Kat didn't know.

"Was it the Cladium?" Damon asked.

"I don't like the sound of that," Byrd said.

"It's vile magic to control parts of human existence," Kym explained, trying to ignore the disgusted look on Byrd's face. "Water Favored can control the water inside of a person. They can move you around or keep you still."

"It didn't feel too great," Tomark nodded, and Kym felt him shudder beside her.

"Breaking bones can't be one of the Cladium," Kat said. "Bones aren't earth."

"Emotions aren't fire," Ashlyn retorted. "Thoughts aren't light and fear isn't darkness. Maybe it's not as literal as the water Cladium?"

"Well, whatever it was, it sucked," Kym sighed.

Short arrived a few minutes later. He handed Nurse Byrd several thin tubes and a large syringe. Kym stared at the long needle, and a shiver ran down her back as Byrd inserted it into one of the vials.

"This," Byrd said, kneeling beside Kat, "will help accelerate your bone's healing."

"Like the healing oil," Damon asked, sounding almost excited.

"Not quite," Byrd smiled. "This accelerant only affects bone cells. And it will hurt."

"Great," Kat sighed, looking up at the ceiling. "Let's get it over with."

"Kat, you have a major break in each of your limbs. I don't think—"

"Just do it," Kym said, shaking her head. She knew better than anyone how pointless it was to try and talk Kat out of something.

Nurse Byrd was right; the bone thread accelerant did hurt. Kym thought Kat put on a brave face, only grunting slightly as Byrd inserted the long needle into her arms and legs. Kym, however, had a hard time not screaming. She tried to keep it together; she was used to pain in her arms after all. But this was something else altogether. Byrd injected each break site multiple times, using her scanner to guide her to the correct spot. When she finished, it felt like fire ants were crawling along Kym's bone. Secretly, Kym preferred the pain of the broken arm.

"Well, that sucked," Tomark grimaced once Byrd finished with his leg.

"What part?" Short asked.

"Getting tortured, our friends getting locked up, us being locked in here," Kat said, waving her hand lazily. "Take your pick."

"You're not locked up here," Byrd said as she packed up her scanner.

"Oh?" Ashlyn walked over to the door and opened it. "Hey there!"

Ashlyn closed the door quickly before returning to her seat. Kym couldn't help but laugh. She didn't know what Ashlyn was expecting. After all the trouble they'd gotten in, guards standing outside their door wasn't exactly a shock.

"Guards out there?" Damon asked.

"Yup," Ashlyn smiled.

Kym rolled her eyes. Of course, the Council sent guards to watch their room. But Kym didn't see why they were there. It wasn't like Kym and the others were in any fit state to sneak out again. And Short was there. Why did they need more guards?

"I bet they're waiting for an excuse to throw us in the cells," Kat said.

"The cells?" Short's eyes narrowed as he shot a glance at Nurse Byrd. "Who's in the cells?"

"You didn't hear?" Ashlyn said. "We brought some other Favored back with us, so Hale locked them up."

"You what?" Byrd asked, her voice much higher than usual.

"Didn't you tell us they were mind-controlled?" Short asked. "Why'd you bring them here?"

"They kinda broke free," Kym said slowly. "We knew them before, and when they saw us getting tortured, they snapped out of it enough to help us."

"And to repay them, we got them locked up," Tomark said darkly. "We'll be next if we're not careful."

"Don't be silly, Tomark," Byrd said. "The Council wouldn't lock you up. You're here to help us banish Thed from Princirum. And Kym's dad's on the Council. He'd never let them lock you up."

Kym couldn't stop herself from laughing. If it had been any other time in her life, she might have agreed with Byrd. But after the conversation she'd had with her father before the battle, she wasn't so sure. There was something off between Marek and Kym, and she wouldn't be surprised if he locked her up. He implied he'd do as much when they were talking.

"What's so funny?" Short asked.

"Having a Council member as a parent isn't protection," Ashlyn said. "It didn't help Amber."

"Who?" Byrd asked.

"Mrs. Mizel's daughter."

"The Fire Princess?" Short asked, his eyes narrowing even more.

"Don't call her that," Kym, Kat, Tomark, and Ashlyn said.

Kym pushed her hair out of her face. She wanted to see Amber and the others. What were Hale and the guards going to do to them? Hale didn't seem to care that they weren't part of the Unity. But Kym had no idea where the cells were, and doubted Hale would let her within ten feet of them if she did.

"You said they broke free of the mind control?" Short said.

"Well," Damon said, "They did, and they didn't."

They explained how Amber, Xander, and Jazin temporarily broke free from the Unity. Short didn't say a word during the whole explanation, while Nurse Byrd's eyes widened as she listened. Kym's heart grew heavier as they spoke. Tomark was right. Amber, Xander, and Jazin risked so much to save them, and now they were locked up.

"Well, can't you fix them?" Nurse Byrd asked, looking at Ashlyn.

"Me?" Ashlyn asked. "What could I do?"

"You said Light Favored control thoughts. You're a Light Favored. You could be the answer your friends need."

"I'm not a Light Favored," Ashlyn said, holding up her arms so Byrd could see the black scars on her forearms and hands. "Not anymore."

"You can still do magic," Short said.

"I can barely turn on the lights." Ashlyn shook her head.

"There's barely any magic left in any of us. And the magic required to use the Cladium is immense."

"Well, can't you get more?" Short asked, pointing at Kym, Kat, and Tomark. "They have those charm things. Can't you use those?"

Kym stifled a laugh. Byrd and Short may be experts in their fields, but they didn't know magic. Kym knew they were trying to help, but magic was out of their realm of expertise. Even if they could give Ashlyn the charms, Kym doubted it would give her enough energy to use the Cladium, not to mention the pain that much magic would cause her.

"The charms are element-specific," Tomark said. "They can only amplify the element they were made for."

"Well, can't you make Ashlyn one?" Byrd asked.

"The Rulers spun the charms out of the Conduit," Damon said. "We'd never have the power to do that, even if they were at full strength."

"I'm sorry," Short said, rubbing his eyebrows like he had a headache. "The Conduit? What's—"

"The source of Princirum's magic," Ashlyn said. "The Rulers refill it with their magic every year."

Kym leaned back in her chair. This conversation was getting them nowhere. They should be trying to find a way to go down and see Amber, Xander, and Jazin. Why were they talking about charms and magic and the Conduit? It wasn't going to help them.

"That's it," Byrd said quietly.

"That's what?" Kat asked.

"That's your answer."

Kym stared at Byrd, who looked almost excited. But why? She paced back and forth, pushing her hair out of her eyes. She had that look on her face that she always wore when presented with a problem that needed solving.

"So, hear me out," Byrd began. "You are naturally meant to have magic, but the Rulers forcibly took yours from you. Why can't you use this Conduit to replace what the Rulers took?"

Kym stared at Byrd, her mouth hanging open. What was Byrd

even talking about? The Rulers ripped their magic from them, and there was no way they could get it back. And even if what Byrd said was true, how could they even get to the Conduit? It was at Crystal Palace, which was where Damon said the Rulers were. They'd be walking right into the Rulers' arms.

"I'm sorry," Kat said, a dumbstruck look on her face. "But what?"

"When a patient loses blood, we give them a blood transfusion to replace what was lost," Byrd said. "Why can't the same rules apply to magic?"

"Because..." Kat trailed off, clearly unable to think of an answer.

Kym's heart raced as Byrd's explanation filled her mind. If they could get their magic back, they could free Amber, Xander, and Jazin. They wouldn't need to be locked up anymore. They'd be able to fight the Favored in a fair fight. If they got their magic back, they'd actually stand a chance of breaking Thed's anchors and driving death from Princirum once and for all.

"We've been idiots," Ashlyn said, slowly shaking her head. "Why didn't we think of this?"

"Because it's crazy, Ash," Tomark said. "We'd need to break into Crystal Palace to pull this off. We were barely able to steal the charms when they weren't expecting us."

"They wouldn't expect us to walk right up to Crystal Palace," Kat said. "It's so stupid it just might work."

"But what if other Favored are there?" Kym asked. "We won't be able to fight them."

"We take Amber, Xander, and Jazin with us."

"You're not serious," Damon said. "The Council locked them up so the Unity won't know what we're doing. Now you wanna bring them along?"

"If the other Favored are already there, it won't make a difference if they know our plan or not," Ashlyn said. "I say we take them."

"When did we agree to do this?" Tomark asked.

"Like four seconds ago," Kat said. "Keep up."

Excitement coursed through Kym like electricity. Could this really work? At best, it sounded like a long shot. But if it worked, they wouldn't need to worry about the Rulers knowing what they were up to anymore.

Ever since the Rulers ripped her magic from her, Kym never thought she'd get it back. Even when they discovered the charms could let them use some magic again, Kym thought that would be the end of it. But if their plan worked, she'd get her magic back. She couldn't even remember what magic without pain felt like.

Kat stood so abruptly it made Kym jump. She ran over to the door and wrenched it open. Kym gawked at her as she stuck her head into the hall. What was she doing? They already knew there were guards outside.

"Get back inside," Kym heard a guard say from the hallway.

"I am. Jeez," Kat said, backing into the room.

"What was that about?" Kym asked, her eyebrows raised.

"There's two of them out there," Kat said. "If we're gonna do this, tonight's our best bet."

"What?" Byrd said, her voice trembling. "You can't go tonight. You don't have a plan."

"This is our best chance," Kym said, almost reading Kat's mind. "Amber, Jazin, and Xander's heightened emotions are masking their thoughts from the Unity. But we don't know how long that will last. It's now or never."

Kym, Tomark, Ashlyn, and Damon all stood. Nurse Byrd backed into a corner of the room while Short stepped in front of the door. He crossed his arms, and his eyes were so narrow they looked like slits. Kym squared up her feet. Sure, she and the others weren't in good shape, but it was five against one. Surely, they could take on Short with no real problems. But if they made too much noise, they'd alert the guards in the hall. Kym wasn't sure if they could get Amber, Jazin, and Xander out of the tower with the Disciples chasing after them.

Short held up his wrist, and Kym saw a new holowatch glowing on it. Kym's body tensed. Was he going to call for backup? Kym's hand drifted slightly to her side. She hadn't taken off her water pack. As subtly as she could, she prodded her pack, and her heart fell. She hadn't refilled it since the battle.

"Jeren," Nurse Byrd's voice rose from her corner.

Kym glanced over her shoulder. Who was Nurse Byrd talking to? She also had a holowatch. Had she called for backup while Short kept their attention? However, Byrd was looking at Short, her face surprisingly soft.

"Jeren," Nurse Byrd repeated, stepping between Kym and Short. "Let them go. It's what's right."

"Jamie…" Short said, his voice quiet. His stern exterior faded under Nurse Byrd's gaze. If Kym didn't know any better, she'd have guessed there was more between the two of them than she'd originally thought. "I have my orders. I have to—"

"I know you do, Jeren," Nurse Byrd said just as quietly, her wide eyes full of understanding. "But you also know this is the right thing."

Kym stared determinedly at Short. His eyes darted from his holowatch to Kym and the others. Kym glanced at Kat, who nodded her head the smallest amount. Kym took a breath. If they both dove at once, they could tackle him before he called for help.

"Alright," Short said and unfastened his holowatch. "Don't break this one."

He stepped forward, closing the space between himself and Kym in two strides. He grabbed her hand and slipped his holowatch into her palm. Kym stared at it, opening and closing her mouth several times. She couldn't believe it. Was Short actually going to help them?

Kym turned to Tomark, her question burning in her mind. Could they actually trust Short? Tomark smiled, nodding his head as he took in Short's determined expression. Kym didn't need Tomark to answer. She knew what he was thinking. Tomark trusted Short, and that was good enough for Kym.

"Wait two minutes," Short said, his hand already on the door. "Then go. Good luck."

"Thank you," Kym said, her voice no louder than a whisper.

"Don't screw it up. Jamie, show them the way out." Short took a deep breath, then walked out of the room.

No one spoke while they waited the eternity for the two minutes to pass. Kym slipped on the holowatch, which lit up every time she touched it. Her heart pounded in her chest, and her skin felt like it was on fire as she refilled her water pack at the little sink. If they did this, there was no turning back. But Kym knew that there was no other choice as she watched the time draw nearer. She wasn't going to leave her friends alone if she could help it.

"It's time," Nurse Byrd said.

Kym walked up to the door and put her hand on the worn knob. She took one last look over her shoulder at the room the Council already decided they didn't need anymore. They'd given up on Kym and her friends. Kym wouldn't give up on Amber, Xander, and Jazin. As calmly as she could, Kym opened the door.

The hallway was empty. Byrd swept past them, leading them to the elevator. Kym couldn't help but wonder where the guards went? What had Short done to make them leave their posts?

"The cells are in the basement," Nurse Byrd said as they climbed into the elevator. "It's a restricted area. You'll need Jeren's holowatch to access it."

Kym waved Short's holowatch over the sensor, then pressed the button closest to the bottom with her thumb. The panel beeped, and the elevator doors slid silently shut. They rocketed downward, and Kym watched the numbers flash on the panel above the doors. *Six.* Kym shook out her arms, hoping to work off some of her nervous energy. *Two.* Kym closed her eyes and tried to remind herself this was for the best. Kym opened her eyes as a large letter B appeared on the panel, and the doors slid open.

"They should be the only ones down here," Nurse Byrd whispered, staying in the elevator as Kym led the others into the dark hall.

"Thank you," Ashlyn said. "For everything."

"Good luck." Byrd nodded, pressing another button. "May the gods watch and guide you."

Kym stepped forward. The hall was dark and looked like no one ever went down there. Her hair stood on end as she led the way down the corridor. There were very few lights, and even fewer doors, and no guards.

"Where do we go?" Damon asked in a whisper.

"Um…"

Kym had absolutely no idea where to go. Short hadn't said where in the basement the cells were. They could be behind any one of these doors. She didn't want to waste their time searching. She wasn't even sure how long they had. Surely, Short was the reason there were no guards on this floor. But sooner or later, they'd return.

"Let's just hurry and find them," Ashlyn said, rushing past Kym and pulling open doors.

They split up, opening every door they walked past. All of the doors were unmarked and opened with the slightest touch. But just like the hallway, every room Kym tried was empty. Her heart raced as she moved from empty room to empty room. If they didn't find them and got caught, Kym was sure getting confined to their dorm would be the least of their worries.

"Guys," Tomark's whisper echoed through the dark hall.

He was standing at a door halfway down the hall. Kym hurried over to him, her heart pounding in her throat. She looked at Tomark, who hadn't opened the door. Kym's eyes narrowed. Why hadn't he opened it? Kym pushed on it, but the heavy metal door wouldn't budge.

"This has to be it," Kat said, appearing on Kym's other side. "It's the only locked door down here."

"How're we gonna get in?" Ashlyn asked, bending to examine the handle. "There's no lock or scanner thing to use Short's holowatch."

"We could bust it open," Kat suggested, raising her arms.

"And cause a scene?" Damon asked. "Good thinking."

"Could you drain the life out of it?" Tomark asked. "You know, reduce it to dust?"

"That's just as bad as breaking the door down," Ashlyn said. "We need a better—Ah!"

Kym swung her arm, and Ashlyn jumped out of the way just in time. The jet of water collided with the center of the metal door, and droplets of water flew in every direction as the others held their arms over their heads. Kym smiled at the massive two-foot dent in the middle of the door.

Panting, her arms stinging, Kym threw another jet of water before the others could open their mouths. She focused on the water, willing it through the air with all her might. The water slammed into the door, which burst from its hinges with an almighty crash. The door fell to the floor, filling the dark corridor with deep, clanging booms.

"What the Thed?" Kat asked, her eyes wide as she stared at Kym.

"So much for being subtle," Tomark said, pushing himself up.

Kym shook her head as she stepped onto the door and into the next room. She knew they didn't want to draw attention to themselves while they broke probably ten Disciple laws. But Kym didn't care. Short and Byrd risked their positions to help them. They needed to get Amber, Xander, and Jazin out of there while they still had a chance.

The room was empty, except for three small beds in the very center. Large bags filled with liquid hung from poles beside each bed. Tubes connected to each bag were inserted into small ports in Xander, Amber, and Jazin's arms. Strange hoods sat on their motionless heads, covering their eyes, ears, and mouths.

Kym wanted to vomit. She didn't know what she'd expected, but it wasn't this. Kym didn't understand why they were drugged, or why they were blindfolded, gagged, and had their ears covered. How could the Council, Amber's own mother, be okay with this? They knew Amber, Xander, and Jazin weren't a threat. Why would they treat them like this?

"Why'd you…" Kat trailed off, stopping beside Kym as her mouth hung open.

"Oh, Pheil," Ashlyn sighed. "They're…"

"We need to unhook them."

Tomark and Damon ran forward. They moved down the line, pulling the needles from Amber, Xander, and Jazin's arms with surprising speed. Kym stared, transfixed, as they worked. How'd they know how to do that?

"Nice skills," Kat said, sounding almost impressed.

"Thanks," Tomark shrugged. "My grandpa got sick when I was little. We couldn't afford a nurse, so I learned how to do it."

Kym's heart swelled as she smiled at Tomark. He didn't talk about his life before becoming a Favored often, and Kym knew it was because it was painful. After all, death demons killed his parents, leaving him in the care of his grandparents. Kym wouldn't want to talk about that either.

"Leave those on," Kym said, stepping forward as Tomark started to remove the strange blindfold covering Xander's eyes and ears.

"What? Why?"

"I don't know," Kym said quickly. "It's just a feeling."

She didn't know why, but she thought having their eyes and ears covered would be useful. They'd done the same thing when they brought them to the tower, after all. The fewer clues they gave the Unity, the better.

"It'll take them a while to come round," Damon said, his eyes narrowed as he lifted Jazin's limp arm. "Whatever sedative they gave them is strong. The Council clearly doesn't want them waking up."

"Well, let's go then," Ashlyn said. "We're wasting time."

Kym ran out the door while Tomark, Damon, Kat, and Ashlyn carried Amber, Xander, and Jazin between them. The hallway was just as deserted as it had been five minutes before. Kym hurried back to the elevator, waving the holowatch over the sensor. The doors slid open by the time the others got there, and they climbed inside.

"Now what do we do?" Kat asked in a strained voice as she held Jazin's feet.

"We go to Crystal Palace," Kym said, pummeling the number one button with her thumb.

"And how're we gonna get there?" Tomark groaned, hunching under Xander's massive form.

Kym's mind raced. How were they going to get to Crystal Palace? If Amber or Xander were awake, warping to the Palace of Life would be an option. But Kym doubted either of them would be in a fit state to help for a while. They needed to get out of the tower on their own, and before the Council realized what they were up to.

"We stole a jeep once," Kym said, her confidence rising as the elevator doors slid silently open. "Let's do it again."

W I T H I N
C R Y S T A L

"THIS JUST GETS BETTER AND BETTER," DAMON GROANED AS KYM stepped out of the elevator.

Kym tried to ignore Damon's comment as she led the others through the library on shaking legs. The last thing she needed was for someone to notice them. They looked conspicuous enough as it was, carrying three unconscious teenagers through the library. But Kym saw no one as they walked through the towering shelves.

They hurried down the front steps under the red-tinged sky. Kym looked every which way as they walked around the building, ready to encounter someone at any moment. But they didn't. What had Short done to distract all the guards in the True Disciples. Whatever it was, Kym knew it had a heavy cost. She hoped she'd be able to make it up to him someday.

They found the jeeps parked along the side of the building. They lifted Amber, Xander, and Jazin in the back of the largest one, which Kym had to admit was difficult. Once they were safely buckled in, Kat, Ashlyn, and Damon took the middle row while Kym and Tomark sat in the front.

"Do we know where we're going?" Kym asked, as Tomark pressed the ignition button on the front dash.

"I think so," Ashlyn said, pulling her long red hair out of her face. "We'd always pass the city when Evanna took me to the Summits."

"What if there are morgar?" Damon asked, his voice full of worry.

"Then you'll finally get to use your training," Kat snorted.

Kym nodded as Tomark slid his hands back over the holo controls and the car reversed. Kym closed her eyes, taking several deep breaths. Now that she was still, she realized her hands were shaking. Kym focused on the hum of the engine, trying to ignore her mounting nerves. Worrying wasn't going to help her now, not when they were about to break into the most secure place in Princirum—Crystal Palace.

KYM STARED down the black path. She'd been wandering for hours and hadn't seen a single soul for days, or maybe years. More than anything, she wanted to find someone, anyone. Maybe she would finally figure out how to escape the maze if she did. But to do that, she needed to keep going. If she'd learned anything, it was not to stay still for long.

Kym followed the new path, the vast, stone walls disappearing into the blackness above. Unlike the other paths she'd tried, she saw the darkness lighten ahead of her. Kym's pulse quickened, as did her stride. This path didn't stretch on for an eternity—it had an end. Maybe she didn't need to find help after all. Finally, she was going to get out of here. She didn't even know how long she'd been here.

Kym rushed forward, and the ground gave way beneath her. She fell, her hands plunging into the soft ground. Panic coursed through her like electricity as something crept up her legs. She squinted against the blackness, and her heart froze. The path wasn't made of solid black stone but glittering sand. Kym spun around, determined to go back, and sank several more inches into the path. She clawed at the ground, desperately trying to pull her way out of the shifting sand.

There is no escape.

Kym ignored the voice. She struggled more viciously through the black sand, which was now to her waist. It was wrong. She wasn't going to let it end like this. She could see the end of the path. She was going to get out of there. Kym reached up, trying to let her energy flow through her. But no matter how hard she tried, her Marks wouldn't glow on her skin. The sand shifted again, and Kym sank up to her chin.

Fighting only causes pain.

"Ah!"

~

KYM SCREAMED as her eyes snapped open. She jerked forward and her seatbelt dug into her neck. Kym held her head in her hands, taking several deep breaths as her pounding heart slowed. She was okay. It was just another nightmare.

"Wha's goin' on?" Xander asked groggily from behind Kym.

"Can't you recognize a nightmare-induced scream?" Kat asked. "How you doin'?"

"I'm fine," Kym lied. The last thing she needed was to worry the others.

"Where are we?" Kym heard Amber ask, a hint of confusion in her cool voice.

Kym swiveled around. Amber, Xander, and Jazin were turning their heads, no doubt trying to see something through their blindfolds. Kym wanted to remove them, but she knew better. If the Unity found out what they were doing, they'd be done for. They needed to stick to the plan.

"Who's there?" Jazin asked, turning his head this way and that, apparently trying to see.

"Why am I strapped in?" Amber asked, her long fingers running over the seatbelt across her chest. "Where are you taking us?"

Kym wanted to take Amber's hand, but Kat was faster. She reached across Jazin and punched Amber on the arm. Kym saw Amber jump, but the little of her face Kym could see relaxed as the corners of her mouth twitched. Amber knew who punched people like that. She leaned back, her arms folded across her chest.

"Whatever you're doing," Amber said to the car at large. "You better have a good plan."

Kym sighed and settled into her seat, watching the countryside flash by as the pit in her stomach deepened. She tried to shake it off, but Amber's words bounced around her head. For the first time in a long time, they actually did have a plan. Damon knew Crystal Palace like the back of his hand, and they knew where the Conduit was. They just needed to get there without being spotted, and everything would be fine.

The black mountain bloomed out of the horizon sooner than Kym expected. A shudder ran down Kym's skin as she squinted up the mountainside. She could just make out Crystal Palace twinkling on its peak. Kym took a deep breath, trying to stop herself from shaking. She hadn't seen the Palace of Life since the Rulers tried to kill her. She'd never thought she'd return, especially of her own free will.

"Stop here," Damon said when they were at least a mile from the mountain's base.

Tomark lowered his hands, and the jeep slowed to a stop. Kym climbed out, stretching her sore limbs after being cramped in the car for so long. She followed Damon and Ashlyn a little ways from the jeep, leaving Amber, Xander, and Jazin safely strapped inside.

"Why'd we stop?" Kat asked. "We're nearly there."

"We can't show up in a car," Damon said, rolling his eyes. "It's a dead giveaway."

"And," Tomark added, placing a hand on Kat's shoulder. "We'd have to drive past the entrance to Obsidian."

"Is anyone even there?" Ashlyn asked. "I thought the Rulers were at Crystal Palace."

"Better safe than sorry," Kym said, glancing at the mountain. She'd never been to Obsidian, the Palace of Death, and she really wanted to keep it that way. "So, how are we getting up there?"

It took them a few minutes to get Amber, Jazin, and Xander out of the jeep. Damon took the lead, guiding them around the mountain's base, while Kym, Ashlyn, and Tomark led the blind and deaf Amber, Xander, and Jazin, and Kat brought up the rear. Kym spotted a small, winding path snaking up the mountainside. She craned her neck, trying to see up the mountain. The path was wide and could easily fit two people standing side by side.

"It's for bringing in supplies," Damon said, panting as they started to climb upward. "Zara said the front entrance is only for Rulers and Favored. No one should see us coming this way."

Sweat covered Kym's face as she started up the path, which wasn't particularly difficult. On the contrary, Kym would have found it enjoyable under different circumstances. The problem was Amber. Kym tried her best to guide her safely up the path, but Amber made that nearly impossible. She turned or sped up at random moments, forcing Kym to keep a constant grip on her shoulders to stop her from wandering off the trail.

"Where are we?" Amber, Xander, and Jazin asked on an almost constant loop.

Kym rolled her eyes, focusing on not letting Amber fall. Why did they keep asking? They knew Kym wouldn't tell them anything, no matter how many times they asked. Kat punched each of them on the arm when they got out of the car, so they knew they were with their friends. Kym thought that was plenty of information given the circumstances.

Sweat drenched Kym's shirt when she finally reached the mountaintop. Panting, her body shaking, Kym set Amber down on a large boulder beside Xander and Jazin. She put Amber's hand on Jazin's knee, hoping they'd keep each other from falling over. She collapsed under the shade of a large clump of trees. Ashlyn plopped down next to her while Kat, Tomark, and Damon crept forward to see what was going on at the palace.

"It's a ghost town," Kat said when they returned.

"No one's there?" Kym asked, her eyebrows raised.

"Other than servants, there's no one," Damon nodded. "There are fewer Servitude than there were when I left, and even then, we weren't fully staffed."

"Oh, Pheil. How many servants does Zara need? She's one lady," Kat asked, rolling her eyes.

"She's the Ruler of Life," Damon said, puffing out his chest. "She can have—"

"Are we really talking about this?" Kym hissed. Why, when they were about to break into yet another palace, were they talking about Zara's staffing habits?

"Kym's right," Tomark smiled gently. "What's the plan?"

Kym, Kat, Tomark, and Ashlyn stared expectantly at Damon. All the confidence he exuded moments before vanished as they stared expectantly at him. Kym tried not to laugh. She knew he put up a good front, but Damon was still a fourteen-year-old boy. Kym never really considered how this was affecting him. If Kym was his age, she'd have had at least twenty breakdowns at this point.

"We," Damon began, his voice cracking. "We should be able to get inside from the garden. Zara hardly goes out there, and the servants only work outside early in the mornings."

"Should be?" Kat said, raising her eyebrows. "Sounds like my kind of plan."

"Once we're inside," Tomark said, "it shouldn't take us long to get to the tunnels. We've been there before."

"We're assuming Zara doesn't have the Conduit guarded," Ashlyn said. "What if she does?"

"Why would she?" Kat asked. "The Rulers and Favored are the only people who know about the stupid thing. And with Thed influencing the Rulers and the Favored part of the Unity, there's no one left to steal it."

"She's right," Damon said. "Zara never had guards down there, even after Xander and Melana tried to steal it."

"Okay," Kym said, her heart rate growing faster by the second. "Just remember, we're not here to fight. As soon as we get our magic back—"

"If it even works," Tomark added, cutting across Kym.

"As soon as we get our magic back," Kym repeated, "and we unlink Amber, Xander, and Jazin from the Unity, we leave. No hanging around."

The others nodded. Kym sighed, pulling the straps of her water pack a little more tightly on her shoulders. She hurried over to Amber, who sat where Kym left her beside Jazin and Xander. Slowly, Kym placed her hands on the headphones covering Amber's ears. She lifted them off, trying to keep her shaking hands steady. There was no going back now.

"Amber," Kym whispered, throwing the headphones to the side.

"Finally," Amber scoffed. She held out her arm, and Kym reluctantly helped her up. "Kym, what the Thed is going on? Where are we?"

"No time to explain," Kym said.

Kym grabbed Amber's strange blindfold but stopped herself before pulling it free. It was one thing to uncover Amber's ears, but her eyes as well? If her emotional storm had passed, the Unity would know exactly where they were. Could she take that risk? But what if something went wrong? They'd need Amber, Jazin, and Xander if a fight broke out.

"I know what you're thinking," Amber said, squeezing Kym's fingers. "And you're right. My emotions are stabilizing. It won't be long before they're completely under control. Whatever drug they gave me really calmed me down."

"Then what do you suggest, Princess?" Kat said; she was undoing Xander's headphones beside Kym and Amber.

"Hey," Amber snapped, her head turning toward Kat's voice. "It's not my fault. I'm just telling you what's—"

"So helpful," Kat said, rolling her eyes.

"You're infuriating," Amber said, her voice reaching danger zone.

Kym's eyes darted between Kat and Amber's bickering. They needed to keep Amber, Xander, and Jazin in a heightened emotional state until they reached the Conduit. And Kat and Amber acting like themselves gave Kym an idea. It was crazy and risky, but it could buy them some time if it worked.

Kym squared herself in front of Amber, raised her hand, and swung with all her might. The sound of Kym's hand hitting Amber's face echoed around them. Her hand stinging, Kym pulled the blindfold off Amber's face. Amber's golden eyes flashed dangerously as her hand shot to the bright red welt on her cheek.

"What the Thed was that for?" Amber demanded.

"You angry?" Kym asked, taking a step back to make sure she was out of Amber's reach.

"Of course I am," Amber said, rubbing her face.

"Good," Kym smiled. "That should buy us some time."

"What's going on?" Jazin asked, still wearing his blindfold beside Amber.

"Oh, nothing," Kat smiled.

Kym knew she should try and stop Kat, but they needed to get Jazin, Amber, and Xander emotional, so she really didn't see the point. Kym took several steps back, giving Kat enough space to run down the line. She punched Amber, Xander, and Jazin hard in the stomach, who all gasped and spluttered in pain. Kym and Ashlyn ran forward and removed Jazin's and Xander's blindfolds.

"What was that for?" Xander wheezed, clutching his stomach.

"Are you insane?" Jazin asked, his eyes darting in every direction as tears streamed down his face.

"Maybe," Kat shrugged.

"Sorry," Kym said quickly, offering Amber her hand. "But we needed more time."

"Time?" Amber asked, her eyes widening as they fell on the glittering white palace behind Kym. "You're not serious?"

"What the Nothingness?" Jazin asked. "Why'd you bring us here?"

"We've…" Kym trailed off. What could she say without telling them the plan?

"We've got stuff to do," Kat said lamely. "You in?"

"Why not?" Xander said, getting slowly to his feet. "Beats being drugged."

"Could be fun," Amber said, her voice about an octave higher than usual. "What could go wrong?"

"About a million things," Jazin sighed. "But I'm in too."

"Good," Tomark said. "Follow our lead."

With no other reason to wait, Damon led them into Crystal Palace's back garden. It looked just as it did in Kym's memories, a large expanse of grass surrounded by large trees and bushes overlooking the mountain edge. A small stream wound its way through the garden, forming a pond at the far edge. Kym remembered, as though from another life, playing games out here with Amber, Kat, Tomark, Ashlyn, and Xander after they first met.

Crystal Palace was larger than the other palaces, with an extra wing on either side of the main building. Made of solidified life, Kym thought it looked like pristine white marble coated in diamond dust, twinkling every time she moved her head. Damon opened the large back door, and Kym took a deep breath before following him inside.

Like the garden, the entrance hall was just as Kym remembered. Two curved staircases led to the overhanging balcony, which ringed the curved wall covered with doors. However, unlike almost every time she'd visited the palace, the entrance hall was deserted. They stuck to the shadows, walking along the glittering walls until they reached the right door. Damon pushed it open, revealing a set of dark stone steps.

Kym shuddered as they walked down the torch-lit passage. Something wasn't right. Why hadn't they seen a single person since they'd arrived? She knew the Favored were probably at Inferon or one of the other palaces, but to not see a single person. Where were Zara's servants or Protectorate? Surely they should have seen someone.

Kym's pulse quickened when they reached the bottom of the stairs. The passage was large, and like the stairs, it was carved out of the dark stone of the mountain and not the glittering solid life of Zara's palace. Dew glistened on the walls as they walked down the winding tunnels, lit by torches in brackets on the wall. Kym held her breath as they traveled down the dark tunnel. They were so close.

"Why are we down here?" Jazin asked as they rounded a corner.

A large, circular stone door sat at the other end of the tunnel.

Torches sat in brackets on either side of the door as they drew nearer, and Kym's heart pounded in her throat as sweat filled her palms. She couldn't believe they'd actually made it. Kym pressed her hands against the round door, the flicker of flames from the torches filling her ears. Once they were through the door, she'd be able to save her friends.

"You guys really are crazy," Amber hissed, anger dripping from every word. "Why would you bring us here?"

"That," a soft, sweet voice rang out from behind them, "is precisely what I want to know."

Kym spun around, her every muscle tensing as fear coursed through her. Lucia stood at the other end of the tunnel, flanked on either side by three Favored. Kym saw Kenna and Aidan, her instructors from Wadita, among them. Kym shook her head. How'd Lucia and the other Favored find them, and just appear out of nowhere? She'd been so careful.

"You are foolish," Lucia said, venom dripping from her sweet voice.

"Oh yeah," Kym shouted, her voice shaking with suppressed fear. If she could keep Lucia talking, they stood a chance.

"Did you think," Lucia said, taking a step forward, "we wouldn't know where you were the moment Amber, Xander, and Jazin could see? Your arrogance..."

"We move," Kym whispered, praying the Unity couldn't hear her. "When I say."

"...will return to the fold soon enough," Lucia continued, who clearly hadn't noticed Kym speak.

"Not interested," Kat shouted.

"The five of you," Lucia said, her voice even more venomously quiet than before, "will return to your cells at Tenbatter. The Warden tells me she cannot wait to see you again. So many happy reunions."

"Now!"

Amber threw her arms forward. Flames exploded from her fingertips, filling the tunnel with waves of heat as fire rushed toward Lucia and the Favored. Kym ducked, covering her head with her arms as Jazin and Xander joined Amber.

"Whatever you're gonna do, do it fast." Amber waved her hands, and five fire bolts orbited around her like red moons.

Kym turned on her heel, not waiting to see Lucia or the others emerge. She needed to get the door open. The last time they were down there, Xander was trying to steal the Conduit for Melana and Thed, and it took him a while to force the door open. Kym's heart fell. Did they need magic to open it? Kym prayed they didn't.

Kym put both her hands on the door and pushed with all of her might. It didn't budge. Kat and Ashlyn appeared on either side of her, but the door still didn't budge with all three of them pushing on it. But Kym kept on pushing, trying to block out the high-pitched ringing of magic as multicolored lights flashed around her. Lucia and her Favored were getting close.

"Xan!" Kat yelled in a strained voice. "We need you."

Xander appeared at Kat's side. Sweat covered his sun-kissed forehead, and Kym saw a cut on his left arm.

"What's up?" he panted. "Lucia's not playing around."

"How'd you open the door?" Kym asked, ducking as a water bolt flew over her head and exploded against the door in a flash of blue.

"I forced it open," Xander said. "With darkness."

"Do that now," Ashlyn said. "We'll cover you."

Kym whipped around, throwing a jet of water from her pack in Lucia's general direction. She lost sight of it in the cloud of smoke and debris, but it didn't matter. She threw another one, her arms stinging as if they were splintering apart. There was the sound of water hitting something solid, followed by a loud grunt and a thud. Kym sank to her knees, lights bursting in her eyes.

"Good shot," Amber said. She stood a few feet away from Kym, thin blasts firing from the bolts floating around her.

"How much longer?" Tomark asked, throwing a gust of wind into the cloud of dust and smoke.

"Nearly…there," Xander panted.

"You'll never reach the Conduit," Lucia's voice cut through the chaos like a knife. "The Rulers' sacred vessel will remain in their care."

"Good thing we're not taking it," Kat grunted, her hands held over her head.

She yanked them down and cracks spread through the tunnel around them with an ominous shudder. Kym dove to the side, pushing Tomark out of the way as chunks of stone rained down on them. Cries of pain filled the tunnel as more pieces of rock covered Lucia and her Favored. Amber raised her hand, a small bolt quivering above her fingers. She looked at Kat, who Kym saw nod as she scurried toward the Conduit chamber door.

"Xander!" Kym said as Amber raised the compact bolt over her head. "Open the door now!"

Amber threw her compact bolt, and the world slowed around Kym. She saw Lucia, her face full of determination, emerge from the cloud of smoke. Kym watched Lucia's face fall as Amber's attack flew right at her, and Kym knew there was nothing Lucia could do. Lucia held up her hands, her red Marks glowing on her arms.

"Kym!"

Tomark pulled on Kym's arm as Amber's compact bolt exploded. Waves of red energy filled the narrow tunnel. Pieces of rock, loosened by Kat, crashed around them as Xander yelled in triumph. Kym tore her eyes away from Lucia and her insides swelled as she looked to the other end of the tunnel. The Conduit chamber was open.

"Let's go!" Damon yelled.

Kym ran as fast as she could, her arms held above her head as the tunnel continued to collapse behind them. She hurtled into the Conduit chamber, not stopping as she ran down the steps and onto the dark stone walkway lined with deep pools of water. Panting, her heart racing, Kym turned to the stairs. Tomark, Xander, and Damon had their hands on the round stone door. Kym wiped the sweat from her forehead and ran back up the stairs. Together, the four of them pushed the chamber door shut.

"What…was…that?" Tomark panted, his eyes darting between Amber and Kat.

"What?" they both said at the same time.

"Trapping us in here wasn't part of the plan," Damon said darkly.

"Speaking of," Kym said, tearing her eyes away from the door. "We should get moving."

Kym half walked, half ran, to the other end of the chamber. A small, simple box sat atop a pedestal illuminated by a shaft of pure-white light. Kym ran up the stairs to the altar, the others hurrying behind her. Kym picked up the surprisingly heavy box with trembling hands. She took it down the stairs and placed the box on the dark stone floor. Unsure what to do next, Kym stared at the unopened box.

"Anyone mind telling us what the plan is?" Amber asked.

"Well," Tomark said, kneeling beside the little box. "We're getting our magic back."

"What?" Xander asked.

"How?" Jazin said, his voice full of doubt.

"We'll fill you in if it works," Kat said, also kneeling by the box.

"Pheil, please let this work," Ashlyn sighed as she knelt as well.

Kym sank silently to her knees. Now that she was there, and after caving in a tunnel in the process, she was starting to have some doubts. She didn't even know if this was going to work. If it didn't, they were in for the fight of their lives when Lucia made it through the door.

"May the Great Mother protect you," Damon said. He reached out, his white Marks glowing, and tapped the lid.

A rainbow of glittering light spilled out of the box, filling the dark, torch-lit chamber. Kym stared, almost transfixed, as the massive crystal rose silently into the air. She'd only seen the Conduit once before—during the opening ceremony of the Festival of Creation. It looked just as it had that night. An enormous, clear crystal full of glittering, white, yellow, purple, silver, blue, red, and green light. However, there was another light there that Kym didn't remember. Black mist swirled peacefully among the other colors. As odd as it was to see, Kym didn't think it looked out of place.

Kym saw her calm reflected on Tomark, Kat, and Ashlyn's faces. What should they do now? She'd been so focused on getting there, she never considered what they'd do if they finally reached the Conduit. Kym looked down at her hands, at the blackened, burned scars of her Marks. They showed the path Kym's magic used to follow; the magic that was causing her so much pain.

Kym stretched out her hand to the Conduit, which floated level with her chest. The swirling magic inside the crystal moved faster, as though something inside it had woken. Kym stopped, her fingers an inch from the ridged surface. The glittering blue light inside the stone concentrated, gathering at the spot nearest her trembling fingers.

Kym's heart beat like a drum in her chest. She breathed rapidly, although she didn't feel like she was getting any air. Her fingers shook as she focused on the blue light. A faint ringing filled her ears, and Kym's body relaxed. The world faded, leaving only the soft, blue light. Kym knew what she needed to do. She leaned forward and placed a finger on the crystal's smooth surface.

Brilliant blue light burst from the Conduit, flooding Kym's senses. The blue mist descended on Kym. It enveloped her, obscuring everything until there was only blue. The ringing in her ears intensified as warmth seeped up Kym's arms. But Kym didn't panic. In fact, she felt perfectly calm. Kym's feet left solid ground, and she closed her eyes, letting the magic take her.

The blue light vanished, Kym's eyes snapped open, and she fell to the ground in a heap. Pain radiated from her arms and legs as she pushed herself into a sitting position. She examined her arms, looking for injuries, and her heart stopped.

Her black scars, the constant reminder of her failures, were gone. Only the faintest line remained, and Kym had to squint in the torchlight to make it out. It was still a scar, but it looked several years, even decades, old. Tears welled up in Kym's eyes as she looked to the others. They too were examining their arms, and Kym could barely see the black scars she'd grow used to seeing. Had it worked?

Boom!

Fear coursed through Kym like fire, burning away her joy. Lucia stood at the top of the stairs, her eyes wide with fury. Dirt and blood covered her clothes, and there was a large gash across her forehead, but that wasn't what scared Kym. Lucia smiled down at them, several bolts flying around her like moons.

"Now you wander Nothingness!" Lucia raised her hands, and the ten bolts swirling around her shot forward.

"No!"

Kym jumped to her feet, her arms held wide, shielding the others behind her. Energy surged through her like electricity, and Kym's arms shuddered with the power coursing through her. There was a flash of blue light, and a massive dome formed around Kym and the others. Lucia's attacks collided with the blue dome, ricocheting and flying into the walls.

Kym's mouth fell open. Tentatively, not daring to believe it was real, she looked at her arms. Her blue Marks shone brightly on her fair skin, no longer flickering or fading. She felt the energy flow down her spiraling Marks and into the protective dome around them. She smiled as she raised her arms, which no longer stung or burned. Kym's magic was back.

"This," Kat said, pushing herself to her feet, her eyes trained on the stairs, "is gonna be fun."

"How's this possible?" Amber asked, her golden eyes wide as Tomark, Ashlyn, Kat, and Kym admired their Marks.

"Later," Tomark said, his tone urgent. "Ash, fix them up."

"I will," Ashlyn nodded.

"Let's go," Kat said to Tomark and Kym. "I want a word with Master Lucia."

Kym lowered her hands, and her water dome vanished. She,

Kat, and Tomark sprinted toward the steps, where Lucia stood, her mouth hanging open. Lucia's sickly smile was gone, replaced by a look of pure disgust. She pointed at Kym, her finger shaking with rage.

"Blasphemous!" she screeched. "You dare touch the Rulers' sacred vessel?"

"We dare," Kym and Kat said at once.

Kym raised her hands, the energy from the water charm surging through her. Two water bolts appeared above her hands, and she threw them, one right after the other, at Lucia. Lucia screamed, diving to the side to avoid Kym's attacks. But Kat and Tomark were ready for her. Kat's green earth blast hit the ground where Lucia landed, blasting her back. Tomark's silver air swipe caught her in the chest, and Lucia hurtled through the round doorway, her screams filling the air.

A flash of yellow light behind Kym made her stop. She spun around, looking wildly for the source, expecting to see one of Lucia's Favored. She was wrong. Amber, Xander, and Jazin were on the ground, strings of pure yellow light extending from their foreheads to Ashlyn's hand. She pulled, and the yellow strands broke from Amber, Xander, and Jazin's heads. Ashlyn threw these strands out over one of the pools, where they drifted through the air. Ashlyn's light bolts left her hand before Kym could blink. They hit the strands of thought, which exploded in a burst of yellow light.

"Where's Lucia?" Xander asked, jumping to his feet.

"Running scared," Kat snorted, jerking her head toward the door.

"Lucia doesn't run from a fight," Amber said, her long, black hair flying around her face. "She'll be back."

The vast, stone ceiling above them trembled. Kym's heart raced as dust swirled around them. The water in the pools on either side of the stone path quivered, while the flaming torches flickered ominously. She didn't know where Lucia had gone, but she knew one thing. Something was happening outside.

"Let's go," Ashlyn said.

Ashlyn sprinted for the door, Xander, Jazin, and Damon right on her heels. Kym lifted the Conduit box off the ground. The floating crystal, still full of multicolored light, sank silently inside. Kym slammed the lid shut and ran back toward the altar. They weren't there to steal the Conduit. She needed to put it back where it belonged.

"Kat!" Xander's voice rang over the rumbling sound of shifting stone. "Can you clean up your mess?"

The tunnel was a disaster. Kym doubted she could see the others, even if it wasn't full of smoke, dust, and drifting debris. Amber and Kat did a great job making sure no one could follow them. But their destruction now blocked their way out.

Kat swept her arms to the side, her green Marks shining. The rocks and stone filling the path flew through the air, crashing into the tunnel walls. It wasn't perfect, but there was enough room for Kym and the others to crawl through one at a time.

They didn't see anyone as they ran up the stairs, and Kym's sense of foreboding grew. The stone walls quivered the higher they climbed, and Kym's mind raced. Something big had to be happening outside to draw Lucia away from Kym and the others. Lucia didn't strike Kym as the type to stop something halfway. But what could lure her away?

The entrance hall was empty, but Kym saw flashes of multicolored light through the high windows. Kym's heart jumped into her throat, and she took one final breath to calm herself before rushing outside. Favored stood in lines on the sweeping front steps, throwing bolts and firing blasts down into the crowd gathered on the lawn. They wore heavy, black uniforms and wielded long batons and staffs.

"What the Thed are they doing here?" Kat demanded, elbowing her way through the attacking Favored. "They're gonna get creamed!"

Kym ran after Kat, her mind racing as she jumped this way and that to avoid the attacks raining down around her. They didn't pay Kym or the others any attention. They only had eyes for the small band of Disciple soldiers. Kym's heart froze, her mind full of questions. What were the Disciples doing there?

"There they are!" a voice shouted from the small group of fighters.

Kym scanned the group, looking for the source of the voice. Her eyes fell on the tall woman standing in the middle of the fighters, and Kym bit her lip. Parker's face was white as a sheet, and her eyes were so narrow it looked like they weren't open at all. The Disciple soldiers parted as Kym and the others drew nearer. Kym didn't stop, her hands held over their heads as more attacks fell around her.

"You idiots!" Parker shouted over the crashes around them. "If you'd been caught—"

"Well, we weren't," Amber snapped. She spun on the spot, throwing two fire bolts toward the palace stairs.

"Get ready," Tomark said, invoking his silver Marks. "This might get messy."

"They're all accounted for," Parker said into her holowatch. "Show them what we got."

Several soldiers ran forward, pulling small cloth bags from their belts. Kym froze, her arms raised, ready to fight, as the soldiers emptied their bags into their hands. Each bag held a small collection of what looked like marbles. Kym couldn't believe it. What were marbles supposed to do? How was this Parker's big rescue plan?

The soldiers closed their hands around the marbles, and when they opened them, bright orange lines glowed on their surface. The soldiers threw the marbles onto the steps, which bounced around the Favored's feet. Nothing happened.

Kym stepped forward, her heart racing. She needed to do something. A hand closed tightly around her upper arm. Kym whipped around, and saw Parker behind her. Kym shook her head. Why didn't Parker want her to help?

Multiple flashes of bright orange light erupted on the palace steps. The Favored screamed as the bolts floating above their hands withered and faded away. Some fell to the ground as more flashes of orange light burst from the little marbles. The Favored backed up the steps, withdrawing to Crystal Palace's entrance hall.

"Let's move out!"

A soldier grabbed Kym's arm and pulled her down the massive front drive, but she barely noticed. She couldn't think straight. She had no idea what she witnessed, but one thing was clear. Whatever those marbles were, they stopped the Favored's magic, and all of the soldiers knew how to use them. But Kym had never seen anything like them before.

Anger swirled inside Kym like a tornado as the soldier holding her led her down the front drive. She'd been right all along. The Disciples were hiding things from them, and now she had proof.

"You have a lot of explaining to do," Parker said to Kym as they hurried down the steep mountain path to the jeeps parked at the base.

"Maybe," Kym panted, her voice dark. "But so do you."

THE DEPARTMENT OF ETHERIC AND ALTERNATIVE ENERGY

"What do you mean we can't leave?"

"Miss Mizel, my orders were very—"

"You can't keep us here!"

"I'm sorry, but you must stay put until the Council has reached its decision."

The guard backed out of the dorm, closing the door behind him. Amber threw her hands in the air, and Kym saw the frustration on her pale face. Amber stomped around the common room, which Kym felt was overly crowded with eight of them there. Everyone tried their best to move out of Amber's path, not daring to stop her.

Kym leaned back on the couch, trying not to roll her eyes. She didn't know why Amber bothered trying to talk to the guard in the first place. Parker had been specific when they returned to the tower. Kym and the others were to stay in their dorm until she and the Council decided the best way to handle the situation.

But Kym didn't care—she already knew what the Council would say. They were going to punish Kym and the others for releasing three prisoners and walking into the heart of the enemy camp. But Kym had other, more important things to worry about. She wanted to know what weapons Parker's soldiers used at Crystal Palace. She'd been with the Disciples for weeks and never saw anything like them. How could they stop the Favored from using magic? The Rulers were the only people who could stop the Favored's energy flow like that. How had the Disciples done it?

"Give it a rest, Fire Princess," Kat said, lying flat on her back in the middle of the floor. "These people don't give in to scary eyes and insults."

"Shut up," Amber snapped. She stopped her pacing and sat on the arm of the old chair in the corner.

"Hey," Jazin said quietly, taking Amber's hand. "She's only teasing."

"The guards here are useless," Damon sighed. "They never tell us anything."

"Short helped us," Ashlyn said defensively. "I wonder what happened to him?"

Kym crossed her arms. She hadn't seen Short or Nurse Byrd since they got back. Parker took Short's holowatch from Kym the moment they got into the jeep at the black mountain. That was how Parker found them. Kym didn't know the holowatches were trackable. Kym hoped Short was alright. She'd thought he hated them ever since they arrived, but after helping them escape, Kym wasn't so sure. She may have misjudged Short.

"Who's Short?" Xander asked, sitting cross-legged beside Kat.

"He's a guard here," Tomark said, "assigned to watch us. He helped us break you out."

"So he's not all bad?" Jazin asked.

"Nope," Kat smiled. "Just short."

"I can remember his name," Jazin said quietly. "It's not exactly difficult."

"Kat means he's physically short," Kym groaned, kicking Kat softly.

"Poor guy," Amber said, the faintest trace of a smile on her lip. "How'd he survive this long with the short one?"

"Hey! I'm vertically challenged. And," Kat added, a dark note to her voice, "being locked up for over a year stunted my growth."

Silence fell over the room. Kym sighed and buried her face in her hands. Why'd Kat need to do that? They'd just gotten Amber, Xander, and Jazin back. Starting an argument was the last thing they needed, especially after what happened at Crystal Palace. Kym didn't trust the Disciples, but she trusted Amber, Xander, and Jazin. She needed them if she was going to find out what was happening.

"So," Xander said tentatively into the silence. "What're you guys doing here anyway?"

"Well, for a while, we were hiding from you," Ashlyn said.

"That's not what I meant," Xander said, his eyes narrowing. "I mean, why are you even out of Tenbatter? Lucia never told us what was happening. She just told us what we needed to do and when to do it."

Kym stared at the others. So much had happened since they'd broken out. She didn't know where to start. She didn't want to relive it all again, but if they were going to save Princirum, they needed to fill the others in.

"Well," Kym began. "We got a message from Zara."

"What?"

"No."

"How?"

"She said," Kym pressed on. "that we're destined to save Princirum. She sent Damon to break us out, and Zara told him that we needed to break Thed's anchors to Princirum to destroy death once and for all."

"Destroy death?" Jazin said, his pale eyes widening. "Why would you do that?"

"Because, Death boy, death is evil," Kat said. "Look at what it's done?"

"Death isn't evil," Jazin said quietly, shaking his head. "It's just like life or earth or water. It's part of the world."

"It's destroying Princirum," Damon said, puffing out his chest. "Death is the enemy of life."

"No it's not."

Kym sighed. She didn't know what to believe. She wanted to trust Jazin. She'd seen how many people flocked to him during the Calling. Princirum saw him as a sign of things changing. Kym racked her brain, trying to remember what he'd told those who supported him. He'd said something about his brother and sister dying, and death not being bad, but how could death be good?

"I've been dying since I was born," Jazin said quietly. "My brother, sister and I were born with cancer, and Thed claimed my brother and sister an hour after we were born. I was about to wander Nothingness when I got my magic. Now, I use my own death as a source for my magic, and it's…healed me. I use death, but I haven't left a path of destruction behind me.

"Death isn't evil—people are; gods are. Thed wants to use death to destroy the gods' creation. I don't. Thed is the evil one, not death itself. When people wander Nothingness, they find peace. That isn't a bad thing."

Kym couldn't stop the smile from spreading on her lips. She'd never heard Jazin talk about death like that. Kym always thought Jazin looked sickly, and she was right, in a way. And Jazin was right, too. Not one element could be bad—they were the building blocks of the world. It was how people used them that made them bad. The Favored created the Cladium because they wanted to control people. They made magic vile, just like Thed made death evil.

"You said something about Thed's anchors?" Amber asked, clearly trying to change the subject.

"The things keeping Thed bound to Princirum," Damon said importantly. Kym tried not to laugh. "Thed can't remain here because death wasn't present during Princirum's creation. So, he bound himself to living things to stay here."

"He said that after the Calling," Xander said, sitting up a little straighter. "He used the people first, and that made them sick. Then, once his power was strong enough, he took over the Rulers."

"Yup," Tomark said. "So it's our job to break Thed's anchors to free Princirum."

"And how's that gone?" Jazin asked.

Kym shifted uncomfortably in her seat. Sure, they'd done a lot since breaking out of Tenbatter, but when it came to their mission, what had they actually accomplished? It had been months, and they'd done nothing to break Thed's anchors. Kym's insides deflated as Amber, Xander, and Jazin looked at her.

"We…"Ashlyn said, her voice slightly higher than usual. "Some things got in the way."

"We couldn't do magic," Kat said bluntly. "And our bodies were shot. We needed to find a way to fight before even getting started."

"We got the charms, which let us use a limited amount of magic," Kym said.

"That was smart, especially since the charms already bonded with you," Amber said.

"What?" Kat asked.

Amber looked from Kym, to Kat, to Tomark. "You didn't know? I thought Lords Kai and Stailin and Lady Nila told you how the charms work?"

"They did," Tomark said. "But they never said anything about them bonding with us."

"Well, they do," Amber said. "The charms bind with the life energy of the Favored wearing it until their death. That connection stopped Lance from taking the charm from you during the Calling. Remember?"

Kym remembered. Whenever Lance tried to take, or even touch, the water charm, he couldn't. It always forced him back. And, Kym remembered with a pang, the same thing happened when Damon tried to take the charm from Lance. Kym was the only one who could touch it.

"How'd you end up here?" Jazin asked.

"After Inferon," Kym said. "We've been training Damon to fight ever since we arrived."

"Why him?" Amber asked, her eyes narrowing at Damon.

"He's a Life Favored," Kym said. "His magic is the opposite of death. He's the one who can beat Thed back."

"Then why break you four out?" Xander said. "Why wouldn't Zara have him break Thed's connection to her, and then the two of them could free the other Rulers? If Damon's the answer, why break the four of you out in the first place?"

Kym opened her mouth to answer but stopped. Hearing Xander say the words made Kym feel like an idiot. When he said it like that, it all made sense. Damon wasn't the secret weapon they thought he was. They'd told the Council Damon was the answer when they took them in, but now, Kym wasn't so sure.

"And this place?" Jazin asked. "What can you tell us about it?"

"What's there to tell?" Kat shrugged. "It's just the stuffy university."

"And the only resistance left in Princirum," Amber said impatiently. "I wanna know how they did it."

"Search me," Ashlyn said. "They don't tell us anything."

"Are you telling me," Amber said, her eyebrows raised, "that you've been here for months and haven't poked around?"

"We tried," Kym said defensively. "When we first arrived. They caught us, and Short wouldn't let us out of his sight after that."

"What? Why?" Xander asked.

"We don't know," Tomark said. "After we went looking around the first night, they had us focusing on training Damon and their soldiers."

Kym stood up, shaking her head. What was the point in going over all of this? It didn't matter. What mattered to Kym was finding whatever weapons the soldiers used at Crystal Palace. She wanted to know how the Disciples stopped the Favored from using magic.

"You must have stumbled onto something you shouldn't have," Jazin said. "Where'd this Short guy find you?"

"A couple of floors up," Ashlyn shrugged. "At some old department entrance."

"What was in there?" Xander asked.

"We don't know," Damon said. "Short caught us before we could get inside."

Kym stopped so abruptly she nearly tripped over her own feet. How could she be so stupid? She'd wanted to find out what was behind that locked door for weeks. She'd thought the Council was keeping things from her the moment Short started following them. Could those weapons be behind the locked door?

"We need to go," Kym said, walking over to the door.

"Wha'?" Kat said, not getting up from the floor. "I thought we were supposed to wait until the high and mighty Council decided our fate?"

"I'm not," Kym said. "We thought the Council was keeping things from us, and we were right. They have weapons that stop magic. Have you," she turned to Amber, Xander, and Jazin, "seen anything like that?"

"No." They all shook their heads.

"And like Xan said," Kym pressed on, "we must've been near something important when Short found us that night. What if it was those weapons?"

"Why don't we ask Short?" Ashlyn said. "Or Nurse Byrd? I bet they'll help us."

"We haven't seen them since we got back hours ago," Tomark said. "Besides, they've gotten into enough trouble on our behalf. Kym's right. We need answers. I want to know what's going on here."

"Finally," Amber said, smiling down at them. "You're starting to sound like yourselves."

"How do we do this?" Kat asked. "I doubt those guards outside will let us go. We could…" she trailed off, raising her eyebrows significantly.

"We're not attacking the guards," Ashlyn said pointedly. "We're in enough trouble as it is for doing that."

"You attacked guards?" Jazin asked, his eyebrows raised.

"Long story," Kym shrugged.

"So, how do we get out?" Damon asked.

"Everyone hold hands," Xander said.

They did as Xander instructed. Kym stood between Kat and Tomark, grasping their hands while Xander took Ashlyn's at the front of the line. Kym saw him inhale, and his violet Marks glowed on his skin. Kym braced herself, ready for Xander to warp them out of the room. But how could he? He didn't know where to go.

A cold, clammy sensation seeped up Kym's right arm. She shuddered as though someone dumped ice water all over her. She closed her eyes, trying to ward off the strange feeling, but it only grew more intense. Kym opened her eyes, but there was something wrong with her vision. The lamp beside her, which she knew was on, looked black as night, while light shone from under the couch and through the gaps in doorways.

"What's happening?" Amber asked, her voice clipped.

"Welcome to the plane of darkness," Xander said. "We can move freely here."

"This is what you see when you become a shadow?" Tomark asked.

"Yup," Xander said. "Just make sure to keep holding hands. If you let go, you'll shift back into the plane of light."

Kym redoubled her grip on Tomark and Kat, her heart racing slightly. They stepped forward, linked together like some strange creature. They reached the door, and Xander placed his foot right up against the dark strip between the door and the floor. Kat tugged on Kym's arm, pulled along by the others in front of her. Kym focused on her hands, determined to hold on as darkness and light streaked past her.

The distorted world slammed back into place around them. Kym blinked, trying to get her eyes to adjust to the strange, dark light. But no matter how hard she tried, her strange surroundings never settled around her. She didn't know how Xander could stand it. Kym's stomach lurched as they walked along the hall, their feet glued to the bright strip of shadow where the floor met the ceiling.

"Where is this place you couldn't get into?" Xander whispered from the front of the line.

"Six floors up," Ashlyn hissed. "But we can't go that way?"

"Why not?" Jazin asked from somewhere behind Kym. "The guards aren't following us, and there's no one coming."

"We don't have access," Tomark breathed. "None of us can run the elevator."

"Really?" Amber hissed, the disbelief evident in her voice. "So they watch you all the time, *and* you're not allowed to go anywhere? What the Nothingness! This place has creepy written all over it."

"We had other things on our minds," Kym said defensively as they approached the elevator. "Like not dying."

"Well, what do we do?" Xander asked.

"Take the stairs," Kat said. "And shut the Thed up. We're lucky no one's heard us already."

Kym wanted to retort, but she knew Kat was right. If they wanted to find that lab, getting caught wasn't the way to do it. Luckily for them, the door to the stairwell was unlocked and deserted. They wound their way up the stairs in silence, not daring to make a sound in case they met someone. But they didn't see a single soul.

Kym's head throbbed as Xander pulled them under the stairwell door. She bit her tongue, trying not to cry out. It was like someone was banging a mallet on the inside of her skull. Kym redoubled her grip on Tomark's hand. She wasn't going to let a headache be the reason they got caught. She needed to keep it together.

"Where are we going?" Amber asked in a strained voice.

"Up there," Ashlyn groaned.

Kym saw the heavy, metal door ahead of them, the worn sign reading *Department of Etheric and Alternative Energy* still on the wall. They approached the door, the pounding in Kym's head growing with every step. She grit her teeth. What was wrong with her? She'd never had a headache like this before.

"It won't open," Xander said, his hand on the doorknob.

"We know," Kat snapped. "That's what locked means."

"How do we get in?" Jazin asked.

"Could you do the slide under the door thing?" Kym asked, the tension in her head growing.

"There's no gap," Xander said, looking around the door. "It's sealed tight."

"Something is definitely going on here," Amber said. "I want to know what's in there."

"How, Princess?" Kat snapped. "We can't exactly blast the door down."

"Why not?"

"So much for not drawing attention to ourselves," Kat groaned.

Kym shut her eyes, trying to soothe her throbbing temples. But instead of seeing the darkness behind her eyelids, all she saw was blinding light. She opened her eyes, and the strange world wobbled slightly around her. The sooner they got this over with and were out of the plane of darkness, the better. But how could they get in if they couldn't open the door?

"Xan," Kym hissed over Kat and Amber's bickering. "How'd you open the Conduit Chamber?"

"What?"

"You forced the door to the Conduit Chamber open," Kym said quickly. "You could do that here."

"Maybe…" Xander stepped toward the door, pulling everyone with him. "The door looks like it slides. But I don't think I could do that and keep us all here."

"Works for me," Tomark said. "Being here is giving me a headache."

"Same," Ashlyn, Damon, and Jazin said.

They let go of each other, and it was like a switch flipped in Kym's eyes. Everything that had been dark became light, and she felt like she'd been doused in warm water. Kym breathed a sigh of relief as the world returned to normal. Her head was still pounding, but at least the world made sense.

Xander extended his hands, and a cloud of shadow flew from his fingers. It enveloped the door, shrouding it in darkness. Kym held her breath, watching Xander's large arms twitch as his eyes narrowed. The shadow covering the door glowed violet, and the sound of straining metal filled the hall.

"Keep it down," Kat hissed. "Someone's gonna hear us."

"I'll do that, Queen Subtle," Xander groaned. "This thing weighs a ton."

The door slid open a few inches, but not enough for any of them to fit through. The pain inside Kym's head increased. How could it be so hard to force open a door? Xander opened the door to the Conduit Chamber, and Kym was sure Zara enchanted that door so it wouldn't open. How was this lab door harder?

"It's like it's fighting me," Xander panted, his arms shaking. "I don't think I can…"

"How're you doing that?" Tomark said, running up to stand beside Xander.

"I cover it in a…skin of darkness," Xander grunted. "Then I energize it."

Tomark invoked his silver Marks. He extended his hands, and the unmistakable roar of wind filled the hall. Patches of silver bloomed among the purple, making Kym's eyes water. Tomark and Xander moved in unison, their outstretched arms sliding like snails through the air. Kym watched their arms shake as the metal door in front of them screeched open.

Xander and Tomark dropped their arms as soon as the door was open enough for them to fit through. The patchwork of silver and purple energy on the door vanished, leaving it looking very plain and dull. Kym rushed forward, placing her hand on Tomark's back, who was bent over, his hands on his knees.

"You okay?"

"Yeah," he panted, wiping sweat from his forehead. "That was harder than I thought."

"Let's hope it was worth it," Damon said, sliding through the doorway and into the next room.

Kym followed Damon inside, her excitement and headache growing. The room was massive. Large cables as thick as Kym's arm ran over the floor. Workstations sat around the edge of the room, except for the far wall, which was glass. Kym saw flashes of orange light through the window, making the oddly dark room feel like it was full of sunlight.

"What do they study here?" Amber asked as she glided silently around the room.

"Energy," Kym said. "At least that's what it said above the door."

"Then why do they need Pro spears?" Jazin asked.

Kym and the others ran over to the workstation Jazin was standing by. Several long, slender spears sat on the smooth work surface. One was split open, revealing an intricate network of wires running up and down the weapon. Kym stared at the tangle of cables. She knew Pro spears discharged an electric shock from either end. This must be how they did it. But why was a weapon sitting in an alternative energy lab?

"What're those?" Tomark asked.

Kym looked away from the spear and rubbed her fingers over her temples, trying to alleviate the throbbing. Tomark was staring at the thick cables crisscrossing over the lab floor. One of the cables was plugged into the station with the spears on it. Kym followed the cable along the ground, trying not to trip as the cable wound its way along the floor. What was it connected to?

"I'm sure it's just for power," Ashlyn said, her voice strained.

"I'm sorry," Amber sneered, "I know I haven't lived in the cities, but what power cable is that thick?"

"Maybe they need a lot of it?" Xander asked lamely.

"For a Pro spear?" Amber retorted.

Kym rolled her eyes, and pain shot through her temples. She followed the cable until she found its other end, which was attached to a large port beneath the wall of windows. The flashing orange light filled Kym's eyes, making them water. Kym raised her hand, trying to see the source of the bright light in the next room.

Kym squinted through the windows, which were at least a foot thick. A glass dome, large enough for fifty people to fit comfortably inside of, sat in the next room. The dome was full of swirling, bright orange light that flashed and pulsated like a lightning storm. Kym's mouth fell open. Cables were hooked into ports at the dome's base, siphoning off the swirling orange cloud. But no matter how much energy the cables took, the cloud never vanished.

"What's that?"

Kym jumped. She hadn't noticed Damon standing beside her. His eyes were narrowed in concentration, and his mouth hung open slightly. Kym looked back at the swirling orange light, trying to ignore the throbbing in her head. She didn't know what it was, but she did know one thing. She'd seen that light before.

"It's like those things Parker's soldiers threw at Crystal Palace," Kym said. "The ones that made the Favored's magic stop."

"But what is it?" Ashlyn said, appearing beside Kym.

"And how the Thed did it get here?" Kat asked.

"It," Damon said, placing his hands on the thick glass. "It looks like pure energy."

"But that doesn't explain—"

"What are you doing in here?"

Kym spun around. Mrs. Mizel, Amber's mother, stood in the now completely open doorway. She held her hands behind her back, and the kind face that Kym knew she had was gone. Her eyes were narrow, and even though she was almost as tall as Kat, Kym felt small under her gaze. For the first time since meeting her, Kym saw a flicker of Amber in her mother.

"Mom?"

Kym had never heard Amber speak so softly. All of the poise and determination melted from Amber's face. Her golden eyes widened as tears slipped down her cheeks. Kym took a step back, pulling Kat and Ashlyn with her. Amber hadn't seen her mother in a long time. Sure, Mrs. Mizel had been there during the Calling, but Amber's emotions had been smothered. Amber hadn't been herself. But now she was.

"What are you doing here?" Mrs. Mizel repeated, not dropping her stern tone. She didn't look at Amber. Instead, her eyes darted around the room, finally landing on Kat. "This area is restricted."

"We figured after we forced the door open," Kat said. She stepped up beside Amber, and Kym saw her elbow Amber in the ribs.

"Mom," Amber said quietly, taking a step forward. "What is this place? What is that?"

"It's nothing," Mrs. Mizel said. "You need to return to your dorm."

Anger swirled inside Kym like the orange energy in the next room. Why was everyone in this place determined to keep things from her? Kym thought they were supposed to be working together. That was the deal they made when they first arrived. But keeping them in the dark wasn't helping. Kym needed answers. She was done trusting these people.

"No," Kym said firmly but politely.

"Miss Collins," Mrs. Mizel said, her voice cracking like a whip. "You don't—"

"Her name is Miss Kym," Amber said, the softness in her voice vanishing. She glided toward her mother, who she towered over by at least a foot. "She is a Favored. Show her the respect she deserves."

"Amber," Mrs. Mizel snapped, and the Fire Princess deflated under her mother's stern gaze.

"We want to know what's going on," Tomark said gently. "We have a right to know."

"And," Kat added, "if you don't tell us, we'll just have to find out what's in here ourselves."

Mrs. Mizel gave them a scathing look that made Kym flinch. She'd never seen her angry before. Mrs. Mizel raised her wrist and tapped her holowatch twice. A beam of orange light burst into the air, and Kym's mouth fell open. A tiny head made of orange light floated above Mrs. Mizel's wrist, and it wasn't a head Kym wanted to see.

"Lieutenant Parker, please come to the Department of Etheric and Alternative Energy immediately and escort the Favored to the Council room."

"Of course, Councilor Mizel," Parker's head said, her voice stern.

Mrs. Mizel tapped her holowatch again, and the hologram of Parker's head vanished. Kym stared at Mrs. Mizel, whose face softened slightly as she lowered her hand. Why'd she need Parker to come get them, and why were they going to the Council room? They hadn't been up there since they arrived.

"What is that energy?" Xander asked. "We know it affects magic."

"I promise, the Council will answer all of your questions," Mrs. Mizel said. "It's time you knew the truth."

Kym suppressed a snort. The truth? Kym doubted the Council would tell them the truth if their lives depended on it. Mrs. Mizel was probably trying to get them out of there without causing a scene. But why? What was so special about the orange energy that they needed to hide it?

Parker arrived in no time, her face bright red and covered in sweat. Kym led the others out of the room, not wanting to start a fight. It was better for everyone if they did what Mrs. Mizel asked. Amber glanced over her shoulder every few feet, and Kym grasped her slender fingers. Kym looked back, but Mrs. Mizel, was looking pointedly away from her daughter. Kym pretended not to see the tears in Amber's eyes. Kym knew better than anyone what it was like to disappoint a parent.

They piled into the elevator, the pounding in Kym's head receding, and before she knew it, they were on the Council's floor. Parker led them down the hall and into the large, windowed room. Professor Anderson, Marek, Commander Hale, and High Priest Perla sat around the large table. They fell silent as Parker led Kym and the others inside, all looking equally shocked.

"Parker, explain this," Hale ordered.

"We're in a meeting, Blessed Ones," Perla said. "This is most irregular."

"Councilor Mizel discovered these eight in the Department of Etheric and Alternative Energy," Parker said, her tone flat.

"What?" Anderson snapped, his cheeks flushing pink.

"How'd—"

"We broke in," Kat said matter-of-factly. "Why's no one grasping this?"

"That area is off-limits to civilians," Hale said. "Why'd you go there?"

"Because none of you will tell us the truth!"

The words burst from Kym before she could stop them. She stepped forward, carried by the anger and frustration raging inside of her. She wanted to hit something. Why wouldn't she want to know what was going on? The Council had kept them in the dark ever since they arrived. But she wasn't going to let anyone manipulate her or her friends again.

"Kymbralyn." Marek stood so quickly his chair toppled over. "You cannot—"

"Yes, I can," Kym said, cutting across her dad, ignoring the appalled look on his face. "We're all trying to save Princirum from Thed. We want things to go back to the way they were. But we can't work together if you won't tell us what you're doing."

"What we're doing?" Anderson said. "It's not us who haven't been honest. You've attacked guards, engaged in combat when not cleared, released prisoners, sneaked behind enemy lines, and broke into secure facilities."

"Only because you wouldn't listen to us," Ashlyn said. "We want to help, but you—"

"But nothing," Anderson cut across Ashlyn. "Just because you are Favored doesn't mean you have the right to know our plans. You're children."

"Children who the gods picked to save you all," Damon said. "We are not—"

"What is that thing in the Department of Energies?" Kym asked. "We deserve to know what that is."

"That's classified," Hale said.

"We saw Parker use it at Crystal Palace," Tomark said.

"We know it disrupts magic," Amber said coolly, her eyes narrowed in full Fire Princess mode. "You will tell us how."

Kym held her breath. Usually, she didn't approve of Amber intimidating people, but Kym needed answers. She was going to get them whatever it took. Anderson's puffy eyes narrowed as his vast stomach swelled, but Amber didn't back down. She drifted forward, looking down her nose at the old man.

"You don't give the orders here, Miss Mizel," Anderson huffed, his long beard quivering. "Just because you won the Calling doesn't give you the right to—"

"What the Nothingness are you talking about?" Amber demanded. She scanned the room, her golden eyes reduced to mere slits. "I didn't win the Calling."

"You won the Calling," Hale said. "The Rulers paraded you through the streets after your victory in the Fifth Trial."

"And you believed them?" Amber asked.

"Amber—" Kym began, but she was too late.

"Tomark won."

Silence followed Amber's words. Kym looked to Tomark, whose eyes were glued to his shoes. She knew Tomark didn't want to tell the Council the truth until he was sure he could trust them. But thanks to Amber, that was impossible now.

"Blessed One," Perla said, her voice shaking as she rose from her chair. "All of this time, we've been in the presence of the gods' chosen. It was you who answered the gods' call?"

"Why didn't you say anything?" Marek's eyes narrowed as he stared at Tomark, who seemed to shrink under the collective gaze of the Council. "You had plenty of opportunities to tell us."

"I—"

The Council room door banged open, cutting Tomark off. Kym spun around, her heart pounding in her chest. Mrs. Mizel walked into the room, her arms full of objects. She placed them on the Council table before taking her empty seat. Kym stared at the items and couldn't believe her eyes. A guard's baton, more of the beads from Crystal Palace, a Pro spear, and what looked like a long, metal arm cuff.

"We need to tell them."

"You're not serious? I want them to help, but their magic—"

"I am serious, Marek," Mrs. Mizel cut across Marek. "If we want to move forward, they deserve to know."

A shudder ran over Kym's skin as Marek slowly sat down. Kym tried to ignore Marek's comment about her magic. She had more important things to worry about. What did Mrs. Mizel mean by move forward? And why did she bring the weapons with her?

"Very well," Anderson said, his voice trembling slightly. "The storm is our gift from the gods."

"The storm?" Kym asked, crossing her arms.

"The orange energy you saw," Anderson clarified. "When the Favored first attacked the cities, they destroyed our energy grid. It was only a matter of time before we depleted what little resources we had. This university has researched alternative energy for decades, and the attacks caused the need for this energy to become immediate."

"But what is it?" Jazin asked.

"We began searching," Anderson pressed on as though he couldn't hear them, "for an energy source that could sustain the university. We thought all hope was lost when the influx of people seeking refuge here caused the energy centrifuge to overload. I went in to assess the damage, and as I touched the fried circuitry, there was a flash of light, and the storm appeared."

Kym shook her head. She didn't care how Anderson discovered the storm. All that mattered to her was how it affected magic. She could tell that Anderson was proud of his discovery, but if the storm was so incredible, why were they determined to keep it a secret?

"The storm is a limitless supply of energy," Anderson said. "Completely self-sustaining. It is the gods' gift to us, for not straying from their true path. And its effect on magical energies was extraordinary."

Kym shifted her feet, her skin practically vibrating. They were getting to the answers she wanted at last.

"The storm's energy frequency, being artificially produced, is the opposite of the magical energies you naturally use. We discovered that, when the two energies meet, they negate each other."

Kym nodded. Finally, Anderson confirmed what she'd suspected all along. Somehow, they discovered energy that negated magical energy. Sure, it was an interesting and important discovery, but it didn't explain why they kept it a secret.

"And you decided to weaponize it?" Tomark asked, his voice full of shock.

Kym's eyes fell again to the weapons on the table, and her mouth fell open. She could've kicked herself. The spears in the lab and the marbles the soldiers used at Crystal Palace all made sense. Somehow, Anderson found a way to put the storm energy inside weapons.

"You don't understand," Hale said. "We were under attack. We needed to protect ourselves."

"Still doesn't explain why you didn't tell us," Ashlyn said. "We were teaching you how to fight the Favored. Would've been nice to know about these weapons."

"We weren't sure we could trust you," Anderson said.

"Good. At least we were on the same page," Kat snorted.

Kym turned away, the arguing growing more incoherent as more people talked on top of each other. She wandered toward the wall of windows, pushing her long hair out of her face. This was too much. She needed time to sit and process what she'd heard. She still had so many questions, but she'd solve none of them in a screaming match. Maybe, after a night's sleep to cool off, they could talk about this in the morning. However, that would require the Council agreeing to see them again.

Bright, red light filled the sky outside. Kym squinted, shielding her eyes with her hand as she looked out the window. Her body froze, fear rooting her to the spot. A fire bolt, at least twenty feet tall and just as wide, soared through the darkening sky. Kym knew it could only have one target, and she was standing in it.

F L I G H T   A N D   F I G H T

"Hold on!"

The bolt exploded against the tower in a flash of brilliant red light. The floor lurched, and Kym flew back, her body screaming as chunks of stone, metal, and glass rained down around her. She curled into a ball, desperately trying to keep some part of herself safe. She closed her eyes, her heart pounding in her ears, and hoped the crashing would stop.

It never did. Through the gap in her arms, Kym glimpsed massive bolts streak past the tower, which shuddered and swayed ominously. Dust filled the air, and Kym could only see a few feet in front of her. Cries and moans rose around her like a dark chorus, making her insides shudder.

"Everyone okay?" Kym coughed, pushing herself up on all fours.

The Council room was in ruins. The glass walls were shattered, and large chunks of the ceiling lay in heaps on the floor. Kym crawled over the debris, her heart racing. She needed to find someone, anyone. Panic coursed through her like ice. They had to be okay. They couldn't be...

"Kym?"

"Tomark?" Kym called, her heart skipping a beat. "Where are you?"

"Here!"

Tomark lay a few feet away. Dust coated his long wavy hair, and he had a long scrape down his arm. Kym's insides relaxed slightly as she crawled toward him. Tomark was okay. But what about the others?

"What happened?" Kym heard Professor Anderson cough through the dust.

Kym grabbed Tomark's hand and dragged him to the wall of windows, or at least where they used to be. The force of the explosion had blown them out, and a light breeze drifted in through the opening. Kym leaned over the edge, squeezing Tomark's hand even tighter. Off in the distance, just outside the university grounds, Kym saw bright flashes of multicolored light. Kym swallowed, and she couldn't stop herself from shaking. The Favored were here.

"Sound a general call," Hale yelled behind Kym. "Anderson, relinquish control to me."

"Fine. Just get this done."

Kym turned to face the room. Besides being covered in a lot of dust and a few scratches, Hale and Anderson looked alright. Hale stood at the table, typing something into the glowing panel on the surface. Kym was surprised it still worked as the tower gave another shudder.

Flashes of green light erupted around the room. Massive earth columns appeared out of thin air, and slammed into the crumbling ceiling. Kym spun on the spot, her head throbbing. Kat was on her knees, her arms trembling above her head. Xander, Ashlyn, and Jazin were on the floor, and Kym's heart skipped a beat. They weren't moving.

"We need to do something," Kat said in a strained voice. "Lucia's gonna tear this place apart."

"No," Marek said, taking a step toward the door. "We're not fighting them with magic."

"But we can help," Kym said. She couldn't believe what Marek was saying. Why was he being so childish?

"He's right," Mrs. Mizel said. "Commander Hale's troops have this under control. Right?"

"Right," Hale said, not looking up from her keyboard.

Kym stifled a groan. Why, after all that talk about helping them train, weren't they allowed to fight? Kym and the others were the best chance they had against Lucia. If the Council didn't let them help, their arrogance was going to get them killed.

"We're going," Kym said, stepping toward the door.

"Stay put," Hale barked, not looking up from the projections over the table. "Professor, report on the trunk line."

"It's still operational," Anderson said, looking at something on his holowatch. "Output holding at twenty-five percent."

"Increase it to fifty," Hale said before turning to Parker. "You're sure the test wasn't a fluke."

"Yes," Parker nodded. "All weapons used at Crystal Palace functioned as Professor Anderson predicted."

"Good," Hale said, shaking her head like she was going against her better judgment. "Get the soldiers ready."

Parker nodded and ran from the crumbling room. Kym tried to follow her, but Marek and Mrs. Mizel stepped into the doorway. Kym turned back in a huff. Why didn't they want them to help? Parker was going to get the troops ready, and that's where Kym needed to be.

"Trunk line output increased to fifty percent," Anderson said, typing furiously on the glowing table.

"What's the trunk line?" Amber demanded. Dust covered her face, but other than that, she looked unhurt.

"It's a massive power line encircling the campus," Hale said, still examining her panel. "After discovering the storm's magic-negating properties, feeding the energy through it seemed like a sound defensive strategy. It's prevented several magical attacks."

Kym's mouth fell open as her fingers flew to her temples. She'd had a headache when they first arrived at the university. She'd thought the crash caused it, but now she wasn't so sure. Whenever she was on the floor with the storm or near the campus boundary, her head hurt. And it wasn't just her. Amber, Xander, and Jazin had all clutched their heads when they first arrived. She'd thought it was because of their emotional turmoil, but had it been the storm?

"What good will that do?" Kat panted.

"See for yourself," Anderson said.

Kym ran to the window. More massive bolts flew through the air, but as they approached campus, they shuddered. Energy surged off of them as they soared over the boundary, and the bolts grew smaller. Kym's mouth fell open. She couldn't believe it was working.

"It's not enough," Hale said. "Attacks are still getting through."

"How?" Anderson asked. "These three were almost unconscious when they crossed the barrier at ten percent."

"Glad we could help," Amber huffed.

"Why isn't the storm neutralizing their attacks?" Hale demanded. "It's weakening them, but it's not enough."

"Because it's more than one Favored," Amber said.

"More than one, Blessed One?" Perla asked.

"They're working together," Tomark said. "Combining energy into one attack."

"You never said they could do that during training," Hale said.

"You never asked," Kat spat. "Can someone do something? I'm kinda holding up a building here."

"They're gonna crush you if you don't let us help," Kym said, walking up to the table.

More bolts collided with the tower. Kym flung her arms out, trying not to fall as more chunks of concrete fell around them. Kat's labored cry drove all other thoughts from Kym's mind. She may not be able to help Kat, but she could do something. She invoked her Marks, waved her hands, and a large, blue disk appeared over their heads, deflecting some of the smaller debris. Marek, Mrs. Mizel, and Perla huddled beneath it while Damon crouched over Ashlyn, Xander, and Jazin.

"Increase output to seventy-five percent," Hale said, typing something into her panel. "Parker, deploy now!"

"By your command," Parker's voice rang out from speakers in the table.

Kym looked to the blown-out windows. Deploy? Hale wasn't going to send soldiers to fight the Favored, was she? Kym knew they weren't ready. Most of them hadn't beat Damon during training, and he wasn't even ready for a proper fight himself. But these Favored—fighting was all they knew. They did whatever Lucia told them, and Kym had a feeling Lucia wouldn't have them hold back this time.

Below them, Kym saw the soldiers running toward the campus boundary. They moved slowly and were obviously wearing heavy body armor. But Kym didn't see what good armor would do against magic. Bolts still flew through the air, but withered as they passed over the trunk line. They didn't reach the tower, but exploded against the other smaller buildings on the campus.

"Civilian report?" Hale barked, still not taking her eyes off her screen.

Kym's heart froze. Why was Hale calling for a civilian report? Were people out on the grounds? They couldn't be. It was late, and the Disciples barely left the tower as far as Kym knew.

"Eighty-seven percent accounted for," Marek said, his eyes glued to his holowatch.

"Dr. Gwin reports multiple casualties arriving at medical," Mrs. Mizel said, also reading from her holowatch.

Kym saw her fear reflected in Tomark's eyes. People were getting hurt, and Kym couldn't help but feel responsible. If Kym hadn't taken the others to Crystal Palace, Parker wouldn't have come to get them. Kym was sure that was the reason for this attack. The Disciples showed Lucia the weapons they had, and she was striking back.

"Attacks are still incoming," Anderson said. "Trunk line holding steady at seventy-seven percent."

"Why are they attacking?" Perla asked. "They've never acted with such aggression before."

"Gee, let's think?" Kat burst, her frustration evident. "Why would the Favored attack now?"

"If you have something to say, spit it out," Hale snapped.

"You made weapons to fight magic and used them against the Favored," Kym said darkly. "What did you think would happen?"

"Crossing the trunk line now," Parker's voice rang out from the table speakers.

Kym turned to the window, squinting through the darkness and flashing bolts. It didn't take her long to pick out Parker and her squad as they hurried down the main road. Kym held her breath, standing as close to the edge as she dared. She saw several soldiers duck behind cars and pieces of rubble as they neared a group of Favored.

"Deploy concussive beads," Hale said.

On the street, Kym saw several soldiers throw something toward the Favored. Kym bit her lip, waiting for something to happen. Flashes of orange light burst around the Favored, and Kym heard the deep hum of the energy. The Favored clutched their arms, chests, and heads, and a few even fell to the ground. Kym looked away. She didn't need to see the Favored in pain.

"Magic neutralized," Parker's voice rang around the room like a gong.

"Engage," Hale ordered.

Kym narrowed her eyes as a trio of soldiers rushed forward. Over the speakers, she heard the clink of expanding metal, meaning they'd pulled out their spears. They surrounded the fallen Favored, and grunts of pain issued from the table speakers. Kym closed her eyes. The Favored weren't in control. They didn't deserve this.

"Commander!" a new, familiar voice cried from the speakers.

Kym tore her eyes away from the window, her heart pounding in her chest. She waited for Hale to respond, but she kept typing on her console. Anger boiled inside Kym like lava. Why was Hale ignoring the call? Short sounded like he was in trouble.

"Commander!" Short yelled again, more desperate this time. "I have people trapped in a collapsed building. Send reinforcements."

"I can spare a few," Parker's voice rang out as more orange flashes erupted in the distance.

"Negative," Hale said, continuing to type. "All troops reinforce the trunk line."

Kym fought every impulse she had not to smack Hale. Why

wasn't she saving the people in a collapsing building? Their lives weren't less important than winning a fight. If Hale wouldn't let her guards do it, Kym would.

Kym turned to Tomark, staring into his dark, green eyes, willing him to read her thoughts. He knew Kym well enough to know what she was thinking. Tomark always counseled her against acting impulsively in the past. How could he not know what she wanted to do?

Tomark's nod was so subtle Kym barely noticed it. He turned, locked eyes with Amber, and winked. Kym glanced around, searching for a way out of the room. Marek and Mrs. Mizel still stood in the doorway, which was the only entrance. How was Kym going to get out of there?

Amber raised her hand, and Kym reacted just in time. She buried her eyes in the crook of her elbow as a ring of flames burst from Amber's fingers. They lapped around Kym, who thought they felt like a warm blanket. There was a thud, a cry of pain, and Kym knew someone had fallen. Slowly, Kym lowered her arms. Marek and Mrs. Mizel were lying on the ground, while Amber sprinted away from them, her hand outstretched.

"Catch!" Amber yelled, tossing something to Kym. "I've got up here."

Kym caught the holowatch and slipped it on her wrist while the rest of the Council struggled to their feet, trying to recover from Amber's burst of fire.

"Let's go." Tomark invoked his Marks and stepped out of the broken window. There he stayed, suspended in midair, his long, wavy hair blowing around him.

Kym peered at the water charm resting on her chest. In addition to elevating her magic to its peak, the water charm let Kym swim through the air like water. But Kym hadn't done that for over a year. Would she be able to do it again?

Trembling slightly, Kym invoked her Marks. Power rushed through her from the water charm, making her skin vibrate. It was a great feeling—like there was no feat she couldn't accomplish. Kym closed her eyes, imagining herself under the water—weightless, powerful, and free. Under the water was where she felt most at home. That was her place.

Kym opened her eyes. She was floating several inches off the floor, her blond hair swirling oddly around her like she was underwater. Unlike Tomark, who stayed in one place as he flew, Kym bobbed slightly up and down. Kym sighed, letting the warm, dry air fill her lungs as she drifted out of the window. Even though she hadn't swum through the air for over a year, the hot, dry air still didn't feel right. She longed for the cool touch of real water.

"Kymbralyn!" Marek's disapproving tone cut through the air like a knife.

Kym focused her energy on herself, and she shot forward, Tomark right on her heels. She didn't care what her father, or any of the Councilors, thought. She wasn't going to leave people out there while a battle raged around them. She was fed up with other people telling her what was best. She knew what the right thing was, and she was going to do it.

"Short?" Kym said tentatively into the holowatch.

"Councilor Collins?" Short's voice rang out from Kym's wrist.

"It's Kym."

"How'd you get Councilor Collins's holowatch?" he asked, a slight edge to his voice.

"I…um… It doesn't matter. Where are you?"

"Where are you?"

"Look up."

Kym drifted to a stop, her hair floating around her face. The number of bolts crashing into buildings was dwindling, but that didn't mean people were out of danger. Short needed to see where she and Tomark were. It would be easier for him to see them. Kym just hoped they weren't too late.

"Down here!"

Kym looked down, and relief spread through her as her pounding heart slowed. A cloud of bright pink smoke billowed around the remains of a building. That had to be where Short was.

"Let's go," Tomark said.

They dove down, flying this way and that to avoid the bolts still flying through the air. Kym flipped around when she reached the pink cloud, and her feet slammed into the hard ground as she landed. Pain exploded up her leg muscles, but she didn't care. Short stood at the base of a large pile of rubble, covered in a good deal of dust and blood.

"Where are they?" Kym asked.

"In there." Short pointed to the building, which looked on the verge of collapse. "Thanks for coming."

"Of course," Kym said, smiling faintly. Short wasn't telling her to leave, or calling the Council. Kym had been right about trusting Short after all.

Kym scanned the building. She had no idea how to get the people out. She and Tomark couldn't move concrete as effortlessly as Kat, and if people were trapped inside, blasting it wasn't an option either. Why hadn't Kym thought to bring Kat along?

"How many are in there?" Tomark asked, peering through a gap in the rubble.

"Five, I think," Short panted.

Kym invoked her Marks, rising into the air again. She flew around the building, looking for something, anything, they could use as an escape route. Rubble lay in piles around the entrances, and there were several fires in the windows.

"It's all blocked," Kym shouted as she landed beside Tomark.

"We need to move fast," Tomark said. He threw an air bolt above them, which collided with a light bolt in an explosion of yellow and silver.

Kym's eyes narrowed as she examined the large pile of rubble in front of her. She needed to move it. If Kym could, the people inside would have a clear path out. But how could she lift the stone?

Kym had an idea, but it was risky. She held out her hands, and an orb of water appeared over her trembling fingers. Kym shoved her arms forward, and the ball of water shot toward the building, but it didn't stop at the rubble. It wrapped itself around the massive chunk of stone, looking like a strange, rippling skin. Kym took a breath and focused all her energy on what she wanted to do.

The water around the rubble glowed bright blue and tightened around the large piece of stone. It was like she'd wrapped the debris in blue light. She felt the water, weirdly shaped and hollow, but she had no sense of the stone inside. Kym braced herself. When Xander and Tomark opened the door at the energy lab, they looked like they were going to pass out. Kym hoped this was easier.

Kym raised her hands, and it was like chains were pulling her wrists while she lifted a boulder with a piece of wet paper. She felt the stone pressing against her water, fighting to break free. Kym gritted her teeth, channeling more of her energy into the water. The debris was already off the ground. If she stopped now, she'd have wasted all her energy for nothing.

"Good," Tomark said, running forward into the small space Kym made. "You're nearly there. Keep going."

"You're not helping," Kym panted, sweat pouring down her face as her arms shook with the strain of lifting the stone. The last thing she needed was a pep talk. "Get them out. Now!"

Short ran forward and dove through the small gap Kym made, disappearing in a cloud of dust. Kym stared at the spot where he vanished. It was about the size of a garbage lid, and Kym wasn't going to let it get smaller. She lifted her hands even higher, and it felt like her muscles were shredding in her arms. Lights popped in her eyes, and the edges of her vision blurred as her head began to pound.

"Tomark…"

"They're coming," he shouted.

Kym didn't relax as Short's dust-covered face reappeared in the gap. The last thing she needed was to drop a ton of stone on him. He wriggled through the opening, then he and Tomark helped the others out. Kym sank to her knees as the sixth person climbed out. Kym sighed and dropped her shaking arms to her sides.

The blue skin around the rubble vanished, and it fell to the ground with a crash. Dust flew in every direction as Kym collapsed, her arms shaking as her muscles seized with pain. She lay on the ground, the world swirling around her, as she tried and failed to catch her breath. She watched the bolts flying overhead like oddly colored stars. There were fewer than before, and these were even smaller. Had Parker and her soldiers defeated enough Favored to force Lucia to retreat?

Slowly, Kym pushed herself into a sitting position. Tomark stood a few feet away, smiling weakly at her. Kym smiled back, warmth growing in her chest. She didn't care how much trouble they'd get in. They'd gotten those people out, and that was what mattered.

"Where's Short?" Kym panted.

"Took the civilians to find shelter," Tomark said, offering Kym his hand. "He said he'd return soon."

"I wonder what's going on out there?" Kym said, taking Tomark's hand.

"Wanna take a look?"

They invoked their Marks. Kym, her body still a little shaky, didn't let go of Tomark's hand as they rose into the air. She scanned the distant buildings for signs of magic or the resistance weapons, but there were no flashes of light anywhere. Kym sighed. Parker must have beaten them back after all. Kym focused on the campus boundary. Parker and her soldiers should be there if they hadn't already returned.

Flames burst from out of nowhere, right in front of the border. Kym narrowed her eyes, her heart racing, as seven figures appeared outside the barrier. Six raised their hands, and a silver sphere appeared around the seventh. Kym drifted toward the sphere, unable to believe it. The sphere was moving—the Favored were pushing it over the boundary.

"They're trying to get in!"

Tomark flew forward, and Kym reeled back, momentarily unsteadied by Tomark's burst of speed. Kym flung out her arms, trying to right herself, and directed herself downward. She rocketed toward the border, stopping beside Tomark, who floated about a block from the boundary line. The silver sphere was halfway across the trunk line, arks of silver energy bursting off it. But, for every piece of energy the storm negated, more flew from the Favored's hands to repair the cracks in the shield.

"Um…Hale…we have a problem," Kym said into her holowatch.

"Hale's…busy," Amber's cool voice rang out from Kym's holowatch. "What's happening?"

"Someone's crossing the trunk line!" Tomark said, and Kym heard the panic in his voice. "We could use some help."

"Where?" Amber asked.

Kym looked at Tomark. If she didn't know any better, she'd have thought Amber was directing the Disciple troops. But how was that possible?

"East side," Tomark said quickly.

"Thed," Amber snapped. "We thought the Favored moved to the west side. Lieutenant, halt your attack. Send all troops to the east side."

"Hold your position, Lieutenant Parker!" Hale's groggy voice barked in the background.

"Hang on," Short's voice shouted. "Be there soon."

"Short," Hale said. "You're not cleared to—"

Kym switched off the holowatch. Beside her Tomark nodded, his face set. Kym didn't need to tell Tomark what she was thinking. He already knew. And Kym knew he wouldn't leave her. Kym took a deep breath, trying to calm the fluttering in her stomach. It had been so long since she'd been in a proper fight. Hopefully, this wouldn't go too badly.

Kym and Tomark landed as the silver sphere crossed over the barrier. It burst apart, and Kym threw up her arms. Her bright blue shield stopped the arks of energy from hitting her and Tomark, but the force of the explosion pushed her back several feet. Cautiously, Kym lowered her shield.

Lucia stood before them, her long, dark braids tied behind her head. She smiled sweetly at Kym and Tomark like they were long-lost friends finally reunited. Kym's eyes fell to Lucia's hands, and anger swirled inside her like a tornado. Lucia's Marks were invoked, glowing like red strings on her slender arms, as did the delicate red ring on her finger. Lucia had the fire charm.

"You never answered my question," Lucia said, her sweet voice cutting through the night like a knife. "Where is the resistance?"

Kym's water bolt flew from her hand, exploding in front of Lucia. She jumped back, her red dress billowing around her. She landed silently, still smiling at them, but Kym thought she saw Lucia's dark eyes narrow.

"Your treasonous actions show your true colors," Lucia said quietly. "Not even Reta could wash your sins away. You will fail, and the Rulers will restore order."

A fire blast exploded from Lucia's fingers. Kym launched herself into the air, arching sideways to avoid the attack. She spun in midair, throwing two bolts at Lucia, one right after the other. But Lucia was fast. She jumped from side to side, easily evading Kym's bolts and Tomark's silver blast as even more bolts flew from her fingers. Lucia waved her hands, and a bright red ring appeared in front of her. She jerked her arms apart, and the ring splintered, reforming into several small bolts.

Kym threw her hands up, and her arms trembled as she struggle to maintain the shield as it blocked multiple blasts firing from the bolts floating around Lucia. Tomark zoomed past Kym, flying right toward Lucia, an air bolt ready in his hand. Lucia's orbiting bolts changed target, and all six fired at Tomark. He flew back, landing in a heap on the ground behind Kym.

Kym dropped her hands, and her shield vanished in a flash of blue. All thought of fighting faded from her mind as panic coursed through her. She ran to Tomark, skidding to the ground beside him. He couldn't be hurt. Not now.

"Don't worry," Lucia said, oddly illuminated by the light of her orbiting bolts. "You will both wander soon enough."

Kym stared at Lucia, her eyes burning with tears. She stood up, two bolts appearing above her trembling hands. She wasn't going to let it end this way. She couldn't let Lucia win.

A Protectorate spear flew past Kym's face. It pierced the ground in front of Lucia, the intricate lines on its surface glowing orange. Orange energy burst from the spear, and Lucia's bolts vanished as she fell to the ground, clutching her arms as a low hum filled Kym's ears.

Kym staggered back, not wanting to get anywhere near the orange energy as her head pounded. She looked over her shoulder. Short stood atop a pile of rubble, his face set. He jumped down and ran to stand beside Kym.

"Friend of yours?" he asked, detaching his baton from his belt, which also glowed orange.

"Not really," Kym said. "We need to get her out of here."

"Got it."

Kym and Short ran forward. Kym threw two bolts at Lucia, who was struggling to stand, a pained look on her face. She jumped to avoid the first, but the second hit her in the chest. She flew back, landing on the ground as dust flew around her.

Short closed the space between them in two strides. He swung his baton at the bolt above Lucia's hand. Orange energy burst from his baton when it hit the bolt, which faded away. Kym smiled at the utter shock on Lucia's face.

"Heads up!"

Kym stepped to the side as several strands of shimmering silver light streaked past her. They wrapped around Lucia, binding her arms to her sides. Lucia's eyes flashed as she wriggled on the spot, trying to break free from Tomark's bands. But Kym knew better. There was no way she was getting out of that.

"How dare you," Lucia spat, her eyes narrowing at Short. "You defile me with your perverse weapons. The Rulers will strike you down for this vile display."

"She seems nice," Short panted, pointing his baton at Lucia. "What're we gonna do with her?"

Kym stepped forward as Lucia struggled against Tomark's

bands. Her eyes fell to the fire charm glowing on Lucia's slender finger. Kym knew they couldn't keep Lucia there. She'd attack them the instant she was free and probably burn the whole place down for good measure. Lucia needed to leave, but Kym had a question for her first.

"How'd you get that?" Kym asked, nodding to the fire charm. "The fire charm's bound to Amber's energy. How'd you get it?"

"The great Unity doesn't question me," Lucia smiled. "I asked Amber for it, and she complied. Not that she had a choice."

"Take it off." Kym shook her head. She knew Amber wouldn't hand over the fire charm willingly.

"You dare command me?" Lucia said, her voice quiet and silky.

"Take the charm off," Kym said, her voice just as calm.

"If you want it so bad, take it." Lucia smiled, her eyes glinting maliciously. And she spat in Kym's face.

Kym staggered back as Tomark and Short cried out in alarm. Kym held up her hand, silencing them. She wiped her face with her sleeve, trying not to look too disgusted. Kym wished she could take the fire charm from Lucia and be done with it. But that wouldn't work. Only Amber could physically take it from her. So, if Kym wanted the fire charm, Lucia would have to take it off herself.

"Short," Kym said, turning to him. "You got any of those bead things?"

Short shoved his hand into his pocket and pulled out a small cloth bag. He handed it to Kym, who poured the contents onto her palm. Several tiny, dark grey beads rolled across her hand, intricate lines carved into their surface. Kym was pleased to see that Lucia was no longer smiling.

"Take the charm off."

"I will never betray my divine duty," Lucia said, her voice shaking slightly.

"Screw this. Tomark, back up."

Kym took several steps back, as did Tomark and Short. She'd only seen the beads used once, but they didn't seem to have a wide range. Kym took one of the beads and squeezed it. The lines covering its surface glowed orange as the bead emitted a low, deep hum, making Kym's head throb. Her heart pounding, Kym rolled the bead across the ground, where it stopped at Lucia's feet.

Orange energy burst from the bead. Tomark's silver bands vanished as Lucia clutched her arms, her face alight with pain. Kym nodded at Tomark. He waved his hands, and new silver bands appeared around Lucia before she could stand. She glared at Kym, who saw the fire glinting in her eyes.

"You sin against the new gods," she spat. "Your suffering will be—"

"Take the charm off, Lucia," Kym said, walking forward and kneeling in front of her.

Lucia's eyes darted from Kym to the others behind her, but Kym didn't take her eyes off Lucia. She knew better. Lucia was looking for a sign of weakness, but Kym knew it was pointless. They had plenty of storm weapons to keep her at bay. Kym held another bead in Lucia's face. Lucia's eyes fell on the little ball, and her face fell.

Lucia slipped the fire charm off her middle finger. She tipped her awkwardly bound hands, and the fire charm fell silently to the ground. Kym stared at the charm, her blood pounding in her ears. She couldn't believe her luck. Kym wanted to take the charm and run. But she knew Lucia wouldn't make it that easy.

"You want it?" Lucia asked silkily. "Take it."

Kym inched forward until she was almost nose to nose with Lucia. Barely daring to breathe, not taking her eyes off Lucia, Kym reached forward. She lifted the fire charm from the ground, a smile growing on her lips. She'd done it. She'd got the fire charm.

Wham!

Lucia's forehead slammed into Kym's face. Pain bloomed in Kym's nose as she reeled back. She fell to the ground, the metallic taste of blood filling her mouth, lights popping in her eyes. Around her, someone yelled, and there was a flash of silver light. Kym pushed herself up just in time to see Lucia fly back over the barrier. She slammed into the ground, and the Favored on the other side of the trunk line gathered around her. There was a whirl of silver wind, and Lucia and the Favored vanished.

"Kym! You okay?"

Tomark bent over Kym, his eyes wide with worry as he helped her into a sitting position. Kym wiped her nose, and the pain in her face doubled. But she didn't care. She closed her hand around the small, weightless ring on her palm. They'd beat Lucia and got the fire charm all at once. For the first time in a long time, Kym finally felt like she'd done something right.

C H A P T E R   E I G H T E E N

T H E   S T O R M
C A G E S

"You're bleeding."

Tomark gingerly wiped Kym's face with his sleeve, his eyes full of concern. But Kym couldn't help but smile. She didn't care about her throbbing nose or pounding head. They'd beaten Lucia—really beat her. And thanks to them, they'd gotten those people to safety. That was all that Kym cared about.

"I'm fine," Kym shrugged. She thought Tomark looked worse—his clothes and hair were covered in dirt, and there was a lot of dried blood on the side of his face. "You?"

"I'm good," Tomark smiled. He wrapped his arm around Kym's shoulders, making her insides feel warm.

"Well, that was something," Short grunted, pulling his spear out of the ground.

"You did good," Tomark nodded. "I'm impressed."

"Thanks," Short said, standing up a little taller. "You two weren't bad either."

Gratitude swelled inside Kym. Short was the only soldier who had helped her and Tomark. But that wasn't all. He didn't care about fighting the Favored like all the others. He'd been more concerned with saving the people caught in the crossfire. He reminded Kym a bit of herself. He wasn't just a Disciple guard. He was one of them.

Kym walked to the tower in silence. She passed rubble and demolished buildings, and some of the lightness inside her faded. She knew the Disciples lived in the tower, but seeing the campus demolished made her heart fall. The university had felt like a safe haven—a small pocket the Rulers' destruction hadn't touched. But now, even that was gone.

Kym led the way into the library, which was full of people. Doctors dressed in white coats ran in every direction, yelling orders at one another. People lay on benches and the ground, cuts, bruises, and burns covering their bodies. Kym's throat closed as the horror in front of her made her insides implode.

"Jamie!"

Short ran forward, and Kym and Tomark hurried after him. Nurse Byrd lay on a low wooden bench, her face tense with pain. She clutched her left arm, and Kym knew from the look on her face that it was broken. Kym knelt down, placing her hand gently on Byrd's shoulder.

"What happened?" Short asked.

"Part of the wall exploded," Byrd grimaced. "I threw myself in the way to stop it hitting a patient. But…oh hun…your face."

"I'm fine," Kym lied, trying to ignore the throbbing in her nose. "We need to get you a doctor."

"They're busy," Byrd winced, waving her good hand. "They'll get to me when they can."

"Kym!" a familiar voice shouted from behind her.

Kym spun around. Amber, Xander, Jazin, and Damon were running toward her, Professor Anderson and Commander Hale right behind them. Kym's muscles relaxed as they drew nearer, and she sighed. Aside from being covered in dirt, they looked just fine.

"What happened?" Jazin asked, his eyes wide with concern.

"Not much," Kym said, and her eyes widened as she noticed who wasn't there. "Kat and Ash?"

"They're fine," Xander said. "Ash came round, and Kat's restabilizing the building. You're a wreck."

"I'm okay," Kym said. She grabbed Damon and pulled him toward her. "Byrd broke her arm."

Damon's dark eyes narrowed as he looked at Byrd. He slipped his hand out of Kym's and began running his fingers up and down Byrd's broken arm. Kym held Byrd's hand, who gasped as Damon's fingers traveled up and down her arm. Damon may be a healer, but like Zara, he didn't have a gentle touch.

"I need plants," Damon said, turning to Short, Amber, and Xander. "Lots of them."

Short, Amber, and Xander ran off and returned not a minute later, a large potted tree held between the three of them. They placed it beside Damon, who invoked his white Marks. Pure, white life seeped from the tree, reducing it to a crumbled, blackened heap. Damon let the energy drift around Byrd, whose face relaxed as the glittering white mist swirled around her.

Kym's aches and pains vanished as the mist engulfed her. She sighed and relaxed as she held Byrd's hand. She smiled at Byrd, who grinned weakly back.

"There," Damon said, his hands hovering at a point above Byrd's forearm. "You ready?"

"Remember," Byrd said, and Kym was surprised at how calm she sounded, "you're not just putting the bones back together. You need to encourage new growth between the bone fragments."

Kym redoubled her grip on Byrd's hand as Damon grasped Byrd's arm. The cloud of life energy floating around them condensed, forcing its way between Damon's fingers and into Byrd's arm. Byrd screamed, and her hand trembled in Kym's as the white mist disappeared.

"Okay," Damon panted, removing his hands from Byrd's arm. "That should do it."

Kym let go of Byrd as she sat up. Byrd tentatively moved her formerly broken arm, testing its range of motion. To Kym, it looked and moved perfectly fine. Professor Anderson and Commander Hale, who'd stood off to the side, stepped forward, their mouths slightly open.

"Thank you, Miss Kym and Mister Tomark," Commander Hale said, inclining her head to them.

A shudder ran down Kym's spine. Ever since their arrival, the Disciples never addressed Kym or the others with the proper title. Personally, it never bothered Kym. She didn't like people treating her differently because she was a Favored. But why was Hale addressing them properly now? She'd never done that before.

"Without your help," Hale continued, her eyes darting to Amber, "that woman could have done some real damage. You saved lives."

"Yes," Anderson said, his voice clipped. "We may not have survived this assault without your interference."

"That's why we're here," Tomark said kindly. "We want to help."

"Now that Lucia knows your capabilities," Amber said, her voice dark, "and that your fighters are competent, she'll be back."

"Oh!"

Kym jumped up, shoving her hand into her pocket. Seeing Byrd hurt and worrying about the others had driven everything else from her mind. She hurried to Amber and held out her hand. For a moment, Amber stared at Kym, her eyebrows knit. Then, Amber's golden eyes fell to the delicate, red ring on Kym's palm, and her face softened.

"What…how…?"

"Lucia gave it to me," Kym said truthfully, slipping the fire charm on Amber's finger.

"She gave it to you?" Amber said, her eyebrows raised. "Just like that?"

"Well," Kym smiled at the look on Amber's face as she stared at the fire charm. "I asked once or twice."

Xander laughed, so did Jazin and Damon. Tears slid down Kym's cheeks as she smiled. She turned to Short, who stood a little off to the side, and saw the corners of his mouth twitch.

"So, what now?" Jazin asked. "Do we have a plan?"

"I think we can relax for the rest of the day," Tomark said. "We've earned it."

"I agree," Commander Hale said. "Aside from the unfortunate injuries and the damage to tertiary buildings, I'd say today was a victory."

"The storm weapons performed well," Anderson nodded. "This

was a very promising test drive. After all of our research, I never expected this type of result."

Kym turned to Anderson. All the joy and happiness inside her vanished as she stared at the old man, his worn eyes narrowed. What did he mean by research? There were still things she didn't know about the Disciples. They'd kept her in the dark for too long. From now on, she wanted to know everything.

"Research?" Kym asked, stepping toward Anderson. "What research?"

"That's classified," Anderson said, his long, grey beard swaying in front of his vast stomach. "You don't have the clearance."

"Show us," Kym said, fighting to keep her anger at bay. "We helped you. We want the same thing. But we need to trust each other."

"I'm sorry, but the protocols are—"

"She's right, Anderson," Commander Hale cut across him. "They proved themselves tonight. Without their insight or intervention, we'd have lost more than a few buildings. I'm clearing them."

Hale raised her holowatch and quickly typed something on the screen. Kym turned to Hale, her insides feeling lighter. Finally, someone here was starting to see them as allies. And she was clearing them for something. But what?

"Dr. Gwin," Hale said into her holowatch, "The Favored are on their way up to the medical level with Professor Anderson. Show them what you've been working on."

Hale lowered her wrist and nodded to Kym, who smiled back. On the other hand, Anderson looked like he'd swallowed something sour. He stood still as a statue, glaring at Hale. Kym expected Hale to respond, but she turned on the spot and walked into the crowd of doctors, nurses, and patients.

"Follow me," Anderson said, his voice shaking slightly.

Kym, Tomark, Xander, Amber, and Jazin followed Anderson to the elevator, while Damon and Short stayed with Nurse Byrd. It didn't take them long to reach the medical floor. Kym hadn't been there since that first night. Since Nurse Byrd treated Kym and the others during training, and because the other doctors didn't like having them around, Kym hadn't been to medical for weeks. Unlike the last time she'd visited, the medical floor was nearly empty.

Dr. Gwin stood waiting for them as they stepped out of the elevator. She, like Professor Anderson, looked like there was something vile under her nose. Kym didn't care if the Council didn't want her to know what was happening. Hale said they'd proven themselves. Kym deserved to know what the Council was up to.

Dr. Gwin led Anderson, Kym, and the others down several halls, not speaking until she reached a heavy metal door. She waved her holowatch in front of a panel, which flashed green. Kym expected Dr. Gwin to open the door, but instead, she placed her thumb on the panel.

"Identity confirmed: Dr. Gwin—chief medical officer," a stiff, automated voice said.

Metal grinding filled Kym's ears as the door slid to the side, revealing a dimly lit corridor. Kym stared into the darkness. This door had more security than the Department of Etheric and Alternative Energy. Kym shifted from side to side, the hairs on her arms standing on end as her pulse raced. What could be down there?

"Watch your step," Dr. Gwin said, gesturing for Kym to lead the others inside.

Kym glanced at Tomark, Amber, Xander, and Jazin, who looked just as nervous as she felt. She couldn't put her finger on it, but there was something off about this place. But Kym's curiosity outweighed her discomfort. She needed to know what was going on.

Slowly, Kym stepped over the threshold. The hall was freezing —a cold that bored deep into Kym's soul. A light flickered overhead, apparently activated by her presence. Kym shuddered, and a cloud of mist burst from her lips. The walls were glass, revealing small rooms on the other side. There wasn't much in the rooms— just a bed, a small counter, a heater, and...

Kym's mouth fell open. A person, their skin ghostly pale, their face sunken and gaunt, lay on the bed. Tubes and wires ran off them, plugged into ports in the back wall. The person twitched, their arms and legs jerking every few seconds.

"What is this?" Kym asked, turning to look at Dr. Gwin.

"This," Dr. Gwin said, gesturing down the hall, "this is what we've spent the last year working on."

"But what is it?" Amber asked, her voice dark. "Who are they?"

"Before the Rulers began their war with the gods," Professor Anderson said, "people all over Princirum fell ill. We didn't know what this sickness was, only that it rendered its victims unresponsive to the outside world."

The bottom fell out of Kym's stomach. She knew exactly what Anderson was talking about. Kym's mother had been a victim of the sickness, which hadn't been a sickness at all. These people were Thed's first attempts to anchor himself to Princirum. But, they weren't strong enough to keep him here indefinitely. He needed stronger anchors, which was why he turned to the Rulers.

"They aren't sick," Jazin said, his eyes narrowing at the person lying on the bed. "They're overrun with death."

"Yes," Dr. Gwin said, her eyebrows contracting at Jazin. "We deduced as much. We thought Lord Phillip caused it until you told the Council of Thed's influence on the Rulers."

"But why are they acting like that?" Xander asked, looking from the person on the bed to Kym. "Wasn't your mom…asleep?"

"She…" Kym trembled, fighting to keep her voice calm. "I don't think she knew what was happening."

"So, what are you doing?" Tomark asked. He wasn't looking at the person but the strange heater hanging from the ceiling. "What is that thing?"

"It's a storm emitter," Anderson said. "We found that exposing the inflicted to the storm…it didn't make things worse."

"But it didn't make it better?" Jazin said, shaking his head.

"No," Dr. Gwin confirmed. "It only stops their condition from worsening."

"Worsening?" Tomark asked. "What's worse than this?"

"You've seen them out there," Anderson said. "They followed you here when you first arrived."

Kym's heart fell. The morgar. She thought they were another type of death demon. She'd been wrong. They weren't death demons at all, but people overrun by death. Kym wanted to kick herself. Why hadn't she thought of that? Over a year ago, before the Calling started, she'd fought one of these people—a little girl. She'd been so overrun with death that it exploded out of her. The Rulers locked the little girl in Tenbatter, claiming she was a traitor for falling under Thed's influence.

"This isn't safe," Xander said, clearly thinking along the same lines as Kym. "These people, death can explode out of them at any moment."

"That happened when we first captured these morgar," Dr. Gwin nodded. "However, prolonged storm exposure seems to have fixed—"

"Kym!"

Startled, Kym tore her eyes from the man lying on the bed. Marek stood down the dark corridor, a look of utter shock on his face. Kym stared at her father. He hardly ever raised his voice to her. Even from this far away, Kym saw his face turn red, and his eyes widen.

"You can't be here!" Marek shouted. "Get them out! I don't want them here!"

"Marek," Anderson said, his gruff voice much softer than usual. "Hale gave them clearance. They deserve to see what we've accomp—"

"Get them out!"

Kym moved without thinking. She sprinted down the hall, the others thundering behind her. Dread filled Kym's heart as other rooms flashed past her, all full of silently writhing people. This couldn't be happening, but why else would Marek want her to leave?

Marek tried to block Kym, but she was too fast. She slipped under his outstretched arms and faced the window. She was so close her breath fogged the glass. A woman lay on the bed, her hair the same blond color as Kym's. She was so thin she looked like a skeleton, but Kym would know that face anywhere. It was her mother, Elena.

Kym couldn't think. This couldn't be her mother. Marek told Kym Elena died, or at least heavily implied it. And Kym believed him. But Elena wasn't dead. She was in the next room, her body jerking in pain under the light of the storm generators.

"Stop it," Kym said, her hands shaking against the glass.

Every thought, every question she'd had about this place vanished as Kym watched her mom in the next room. She'd thought Elena was wandering Nothingness. At least there, she'd find the peace she deserved. But this? Kym knew the pain the storm energy caused. But that still didn't explain how Elena was here.

"Let me in," Kym whispered, her head pressed against the glass wall.

"What's goin' on?" Jazin asked, clearly not hearing Kym. "Who is that?"

"This is Elena Collins," Professor Anderson said. "Elena was one of the first—"

"That's Kym's mom?" Tomark demanded, his voice full of fury. "We thought she was…"

The sound of their conversation faded away as Kym watched her mother, anger swirling like fire in her stomach. Yes, she'd thought her mom was dead. And yes, she'd blamed herself for it. But her mom was alive, and Kym wasn't going to let anything happen to her again. She wasn't going to let the Disciples cause her any more pain.

"Let me in," Kym repeated, more loudly this time, not taking her eyes off her mother.

"Absolutely not," Marek said.

"No?" Kym's voice shook with suppressed rage. "You're hurting her."

"We're not hurting her," Anderson said flatly. "This is for her protection."

Kym's body trembled so badly she felt like she was going to explode. How were they protecting her mom? Elena was in pain. They were experimenting on her. Kym knew her mom couldn't speak or probably even think, but she knew what her mom would want. And this wasn't it.

Kym closed her eyes, tears streaming silently down her face. She stopped fighting her anger and let the storm raging inside her burst out. There was a high-pitched ring and a flash of blue light as energy surged down Kym's arms. The glass separating her from her mom shattered, tinkling to the ground in a million pieces.

Voices rose in alarm behind Kym, but she ignored them as she stepped over the threshold. Her insides turned to ice as the death radiating from Elena Collins washed over her. Kym raised her hand to the storm generator suspended from the ceiling. Her water bolt exploded against it, and the orange glow emitting from the box faded as the room grew quiet.

Kym knelt at her mom's bedside, taking her ghostly, pale hand in her own. It was cold as ice. Slowly, Elena stopped her thrashing and became still. This was how she'd been when Kym last saw her —when Kym had no idea Thed's power was making her sick. She, and the doctors, had no idea how to help her then. But now, Kym did.

Kym turned, and the most bizarre sight met her eyes. Amber, Xander, and Tomark had their hands directed at Dr. Gwin, Professor Anderson, Marek, and four guards. Their Marks were invoked, and the guards held their batons, bright orange energy glowing from the lines on them. Kym looked into her father's beet-red face and saw him shake his head. He was angry, but Kym didn't care. He'd lied to Kym about her mom ever since she'd arrived. He'd had her mom locked up here for who knows how long. Elena needed help, and Kym knew just who to ask.

"Jazin," Kym said, and she was surprised to hear her voice wasn't shaking. "Jazin, help her. Please."

"What?" Jazin asked. His pale face was even paler than usual, and his grey eyes were wide. "What could I do?"

"Help her," Kym repeated. "Like you did with the death girl."

The death girl had been the first death demon Jazin fought with them. Kym and the others couldn't get anywhere near her as death exploded out of her, but Jazin could. Jazin pulled the death energy from the girl, and Kym knew he could do the same for her mom.

"Kym," Jazin said softly, "I don't know—"

"Just try," Kym cut across him. "Please."

"No, Kym," Amber snapped. "He said he can't—"

"It's okay," Jazin said, smiling at Amber. "I can at least try."

Jazin nodded. He stepped into the room, shattered glass crunching under his feet. He gave Kym a significant look, and Kym knew she couldn't stay. She gave her mom's hand one last squeeze, then backed out of the room. She stood beside Tomark and Amber, but they weren't watching Jazin and Elena. They pointed their arms at the Councilors and the guards, their Marks still glowing.

"This is ridiculous," Dr. Gwin said. "What can that boy do?"

"You'd be surprised," Amber said coldly.

Jazin raised his hands, his black Marks glittering on his slender forearms. A cloud of black mist appeared around Elena, and Kym heard the others gasp. But she didn't take her eyes off of her mom as the glittering mist drifted into Jazin's hands. It seeped out of Elena's skin, floating around her like a black cloud. And as more death oozed out of Kym's mother, Elena's hand twitched.

Kym didn't dare to breathe. It was working. Finally, after thinking she'd failed for so long, she was going to save her mother. She hadn't failed her after all.

"It just…keeps coming," Jazin said, his voice strained.

Kym shook her head, not wanting to believe it. But even she could see the cloud of death seeping out of Elena wasn't stopping. She'd seen Phillip, the Ruler of Death, pull death from a fallen tree to prove himself. The cloud of blackness eventually stopped seeping from the tree, which looked good as new. But there was no end to the death pouring out of Elena. Jazin was right.

"Jazin," Amber said, her voice full of concern "Shut it down."

"No," Jazin said, his voice shaking more than before. "I can do this."

Every part of Kym wanted to tell Jazin to keep going. But she could tell from the way Jazin's arms shook that he couldn't do it for much longer. He'd pulled so much death from Elena that it filled the entire room. Soon, they wouldn't be able to see him at all. Jazin needed to stop.

"Jazin," Kym called into the blackness, "It isn't working. Stop! Now!"

Kym could just make out Jazin through the death. He dropped his arms, and the inky black cloud surged toward Elena. It disappeared into her as her skin grew paler, and her feebly stirring limbs grew still once more. Jazin collapsed, and Tomark and Amber rushed to his side while Kym stepped past him to her mother.

"I'm sorry, Kym," Jazin panted, his pale grey eyes locking on Kym. "It just… it didn't have an end."

"At least you tried," Amber said, her arms wrapped around Jazin's neck. "And you're still alright."

"You need to leave," Professor Anderson said. "It was a valiant effort, but we need to reseal the room. We can't have death seeping through the halls."

Amber helped Jazin up, but Kym stayed where she was. She examined her mother's blank face, the death seeping back inside of her, while Kym's heart to ice. But it wasn't the death that made Kym's insides writhe with pain. She looked at Marek Collins, and her hands balled into fists.

"Kym, c'mon."

Tomark stepped in front of Kym, his pale green eyes wide. Kym tried to hide her anger, but as she watched Tomark's face stiffen, she knew she'd done a lousy job. Tomark looked over his shoulder at Marek, and realization dawned on his face.

"You heard him," Amber said, her voice unusually soft as she grabbed Kym's hand. "We need to…"

Amber trailed off. Her golden eyes narrowed as they darted between Kym and her father. Kym expected Amber to drag her out, so she was shocked when Amber's slender fingers slid from her wrist.

"Let's go," Amber said, her tone once again brisk.

Amber took Jazin's hand and led him and Xander down the hall while Kym stayed where she was. Tomark stepped to her side, and his fingers found their way into Kym's. She held on tight, anger thrashing inside her as she looked into Marek's eyes. She clenched her fist so tightly she felt blood throbbing in her fingers.

Kym tried to think of something to say, but no words escaped her lips. Marek told her Elena was gone. But she wasn't gone. She'd been there this whole time, suffering while Anderson, Hale, and Gwin experimented on her. But Kym didn't care about them. Right now, she only had eyes for Marek. He'd lied to her, and she wanted to know why.

"You should leave," Marek said, his voice no more than a whisper.

"What?" Kym asked, her voice trembling.

"Leave, Kym," Marek said darkly. "Just go with your friends."

Kym's rage flared. Everything inside of her told her to lunge forward. Instead, Kym doubled her grip on Tomark. Why was Marek saying this?

"Why didn't you tell me she was here?" Kym said, fighting to keep her voice somewhat calm. "I deserved to know."

"You deserved?" Marek said. "Great Pheil, Kymbralyn! You deserved nothing after what you did to her."

"She's my mother!" Kym was shouting now, but she didn't care. "And I never—"

"Magic is the reason she's like this," Marek said, taking a step toward Kym and Tomark. "Magic is the reason my wife is gone. First magic took her sister, then you, and now, it's taken her."

Every word Marek said felt like a million knives stabbing Kym's soul. How could he say these things? Kym always hated what magic did to her family, but that didn't mean she was responsible for her mother's fate. Kym became the first Vanquisher of Water to protect her mother and the cities. She fought in the Calling so Nila would keep providing doctors to care for Elena. This wasn't her fault, no matter what Marek said.

"We're here to save her," Kym said in a tremulous voice. "We're here to save you all. And I'm not gone!"

"From where I'm standing, you've only brought Thed closer to us," Marek said. "Because of you, the Rulers and Favored have escalated their attacks on us."

"But…we never…the gods sent us—"

"Nothingness, Kymbralyn! Have you ever considered that you, the Favored, and magic are, in fact, the problem?"

Kym opened her mouth, but no sound came out. Of course, Kym thought the Rulers, and Favored, and magic, were a problem for most of her life. They'd caused her so much pain, but she'd seen the good they could do. Magic did extraordinary things in the right hands, even if Marek refused to see that.

"We can help Mom," Kym said, and she was surprised to hear her voice was calm. "If you let us. Please."

Kym stared into her father's face and saw the pain radiating from his eyes. He was hurting, but Kym knew she and her friends could help her mother. All Marek had to do was let them.

"No," Marek said, and his word pierced Kym's heart like a knife. "When the doctors left after the Calling was over, I brought your mother here so Professor Anderson and Dr. Gwin could help her. Their technology and dedication has made it so your mother is not a threat to anyone. And I'm not going to have them stop now.

"None of you are permitted on this level again. I'm having storm emitters placed all through the hall. No magic, not yours or that of the gods, will torture these people again. Now, please leave, Kym. I need to clean up the mess you made."

Marek turned on his heel and walked down the corridor, leaving Kym frozen where she was, Tomark's fingers still held in her own. She opened her mouth, but closed it. How could her father say those things about her? This wasn't her fault. It couldn't be. If she'd just done what Nila wanted and won the Calling, her mother may not be like this. So was this really her fault?

Kym didn't remember walking down the hall, or letting go of Tomark. All she knew was that she was at the elevator, pummeling the buttons, desperate to leave this place. Kym's body shook, white-hot tears swelling in her eyes as she stared at the metal doors. Voices rose around her, but she couldn't make out who they belonged to. It didn't matter. All that mattered was escaping the grief threatening to take her over.

But the elevator never came. Kym hit the button again and again, each time with more force. Why wasn't the elevator coming? Tears slid down her face as her knuckles screamed in pain. If she didn't get out of there, she was going to explode.

"Kym," a voice said very close to her ear.

Kym ignored Jazin and continued to punch the button. But it wasn't enough. The pain inside of her mounted. It was too much. She couldn't take it anymore. Kym pounded her fists on the elevator button, the wall, and anything she could reach. The world around her drifted away as sorrow claimed her.

"Kym. What are you doing?"

"Please stop."

Hands tried to hold Kym back, but their presence triggered something inside her. She wrenched her hands free, her Marks flashing. The hands withdrew, and Kym continued to thrash out like some feral animal. But no matter how hard she swung her fists or how badly her heart ached, it was nothing compared to the pain radiating through her soul.

Kym's legs gave way, and she collapsed under the weight of her sorrow. She crumpled, no longer able to take it. This pain, like red-hot needles forcing their way through every part of her, was worse than anything she'd ever felt. Worse than thinking her mother was dead. Worse than thinking she'd caused her friends' deaths. Worse than having her magic ripped from her. Nothing compared to this pain.

A face swam into focus in Kym's tear-filled eyes. Amber's usually impassive face was soft, her narrow eyes shining with tears. She reached forward to grab Kym, but Kym yanked her hands back.

Amber reached forward again, and her slender fingers wrapped tightly around Kym's shaking ones.

"Kym," Amber said, her voice shaking slightly. "It's gonna be okay. We'll save her. We'll save all of them."

"I can't," Kym gasped between her sobs. "It hurts too much."

"I know," Amber whispered, and even in her state, Kym heard the understanding in Amber's voice. "It does hurt."

Kym looked into Amber's narrow eyes. She knew how this felt. When she watched Amber reignite her emotions, it had been almost too much for Amber to bear. That was what Kym needed. To make this pain go away.

"Make it stop." Kym's voice was no more than a whisper. "Please. I can't feel this anymore."

"No," Amber said, and the understanding in her voice was unmistakable. "It won't do what you want. We need to feel, Kym. You may not see it now, but you need this. I don't know how, but it will help you."

Kym buried her face in Amber's slender shoulder, her tears falling thick and fast. Of course, she knew Amber was right. Running from her feelings wasn't the answer. But how could pain this horrible help her?

Somewhere, the elevator beeped, and light spilled into the hall. Kym's body relaxed slightly as she lifted her head. Finally, she was getting out of this place.

"C'mon," Amber said, helping Kym to her feet. "Let's find the others."

It didn't take them long to return to their dorm. They didn't see anyone as they walked through the halls. When Kym reached the door, Tomark stepped in front of her and Amber, who hadn't let go of Kym since the elevator arrived. But as Tomark opened the door, something caught Kym's eye.

"Where'd Jazin go?" she asked thickly. Even though he failed, she wanted to thank him for trying to save her mom.

"With Xander getting the others," Tomark said gently, stepping aside to let Amber and Kym inside. "He went when—"

"He went when you lost it," Amber said briskly. "You need your friends right now."

Kym expected to see Jazin, Kat, Ashlyn, Damon, and Xander waiting for them when she stepped inside. However, Xander was the only one there. He paced back and forth, wringing his hands while his eyes darted this way and that. The strange sight momentarily drove Kym's sorrow from her mind. Why did Xander look so worried? And where were the others?

"Xander," Tomark said, clearly seeing the same look on Xander's face. "What happened?"

"Where's Jazin?" Amber asked, finally letting go of Kym. "And everyone else?"

"It's not my fault," Xander said, clearly not listening to them. "I told her it was a stupid idea, but you know what she's like. Once she gets an idea in her head, there's no stopping her. I told her it was a mistake, that we needed to wait and talk it through but…"

"What?" Kym wiped her face with shaking hands. Xander was starting to scare her. "Xander, you're not making sense."

"Of course, the others told her it was a great idea, and after that she wouldn't listen to me," Xander pressed on quickly. "They went with her, and I couldn't stop them."

Fear pierced Kym's sadness. Clearly, Xander was talking about Kat, Ashlyn, Jazin, and Damon. Who else wouldn't let go of an idea, even if it was a bad one? But what were they doing that frightened Xander so much? Where did Kat take them?

"Slow down," Tomark said, grabbing Xander by his broad shoulders. "What are you talking about?"

"When Jazin told Kat about Kym's mom, she flipped," Xander said, speaking more slowly. "She couldn't believe they were experimenting on her. She kept saying they were idiots, then she took Ashlyn, Damon, and Jazin with her."

"But where's Jazin?" Amber asked, and Kym heard the panic in her voice. "What exactly is Kat up to?"

"They're outside the trunk line," Xander said. "Kat wants to capture a morgar and free it from Thed."

CHAPTER NINETEEN

THE ENSNARED ANCHOR

"OF ALL THE STUPID, IDIOTIC, BRAINLESS THINGS, THIS IS THE worst!" Amber hissed, sprinting a little ahead of the others.

"What was she thinking?" Tomark panted.

Kym didn't answer. The stitch in her side throbbed as she raced through the rubble-covered campus behind Amber and Xander. Kym gritted her teeth and pushed forward, not wanting to fall behind. She didn't care that she was a wreck. She needed to get to Kat before she did something that couldn't be undone.

Kym racked her brain, trying to come up with some explanation for Kat's actions. Why would she take Jazin, Ashlyn, and Damon beyond the trunk line? They didn't even know if Lucia was still in the city. If the Unity caught them because they wanted to save Kym's mom, Kym would never forgive herself.

Kym's head pounded as she sprinted over the trunk line. Her insides burned, and her stomach lurched uncomfortably, but still, she didn't stop. Neither did Tomark, Amber, and Xander. Kym didn't care how she felt. All that mattered was finding Kat.

"Did she tell you where they were going?" Tomark asked Xander, who turned down the closest street.

"No," Xander said. "But I don't think finding them will be hard."

A large cloud of smoke rose over the buildings a few streets away. Kym felt the ground shudder beneath her as panes of glass fell from the high windows. Kym willed herself to move faster as she raced toward the crashes and booms erupting around the cloud of smoke. Kat and the others had to be there. Kat was many things, but subtle wasn't one of them.

Kym rounded the corner and skidded to a stop. An enormous sphere of earth sat on the middle of the street, its surface blackened and cracked. Damon and Jazin stood on either side of it, clouds of shimmering life and death floating above them, while brilliant yellow light flashed behind the sphere. Kat stood in the middle of the road, her arms shaking in front of her.

"You morons said you got this," she shouted in a strained voice.

"Lay off," Jazin shouted. He pulled his arms toward him, and black mist flew out of the sphere, restoring the decayed sections to their natural brown color. "We're doing the best we can."

"Well, do better!" Kat shouted as black cracks spread across the sphere's smooth surface. "We can't let it get out again."

"What the Thed are you doing?" Kym demanded.

Kat didn't take her eyes off the sphere, but Kym saw her face relax slightly. The knot in Kym's chest didn't ease as quickly. She looked from the sphere to Damon and Jazin and back to Kat. Sweat covered their faces, and Kat's arms were trembling.

A massive black spot bloomed on the sphere's surface. The blackened pieces of earth fell away, and Kym's insides turned to ice. There was a man inside the sphere. He looked only a few years older than Jazin, and his ghostly skin hung loosely from his limbs.

A flash of yellow streaked past Kym. It flew into the hole, exploding against the morgar. Kym spun around, anger raging inside of her. Thanks to Anderson and Dr. Gwin, they knew the morgar weren't death demons like Kym initially thought. They were people. Why would Ashlyn attack it?

"What the Nothingness!" Kat shouted in a strained voice. "Are you trying to make it mad?"

"It was getting out," Ashlyn said defensively, her yellow Marks glowing as she stared at the morgar.

"We've got it," Damon said through gritted teeth.

"Clearly," Kym said, fighting the urge to roll her eyes. "Please tell me you have a plan."

"You're lookin' at it," Kat grimaced. She waved her arms, and more earth filled the hole in the sphere.

"What?" Tomark asked. "This is your plan?"

"Yup," Kat said. "We catch one, and then we free it ourselves."

"Catch one?" Xander asked, his voice full of concern. "You're barely containing it. You're gonna hurt yourself, Kat."

"I am fine," Kat said pointedly.

Kym couldn't help but agree with Xander. Capturing and curing a morgar sounded like a good plan, but Kym didn't know if it was even possible. How could they capture something that killed everything it touched? Kym's insides already felt numb and lifeless. There was no way they were going to get close enough to help it.

"We need to knock it out," Ashlyn said. "Like we did with that girl before the Calling."

"This guy's more powerful than she was," Jazin said, the glittering cloud of death above him growing larger. "I don't think—"

"We didn't have Damon then," Kym said, her mind jolting into action.

When they escaped Inferon, Damon's magic was the only thing that hurt the death demon. If Kym was right, his magic might stop the morgar, at least for a few minutes. At the very least, it would buy them some time.

"Jazin," Kym said, her eyes darting around the abandoned street, "keep doing what you're doing. The rest of us are going to attack."

"It won't work," Amber said, her eyes narrowed at the crumbling sphere. "Jazin's right. This guy's—"

"Tomark and I will attack from above while you, Ash, Kat, and Xan attack from the ground," Kym cut across Amber.

"What good will that…?" Kat trailed off, another hole appearing in the sphere.

"We're not stopping it," Kym said, looking up at Tomark. "We're stunning it."

"Of course," he said. His eyes widened as he turned to Damon, and understanding shone on his face. "Once we've stunned it…"

"Damon can finish it off," Kym finished his thought.

Kym invoked her Marks and rose into the air, Tomark right behind her. They soared over the sphere, stopping when they were directly above it. Amber, Xander, and Ashlyn ran to their positions while Kat lowered her arms. Icy numbness filled Kym as the remaining portions of the sphere crumbled, revealing the morgar.

Kym took a deep breath, bobbing up and down slightly. She needed to focus, but something gnawed at her brain. Her mom and the other morgar in the tower looked like they were in pain. Did that mean they could feel? If so, what would this man feel when they hit him with six simultaneous attacks. Kym stopped, her hands partially raised. Was she doing the right thing?

"It's now or never!" Amber shouted.

Kym shook her head. She couldn't worry about what she didn't know. Kym waved her arms in circular motions, and streams of glowing water flew from her fingertips as energy surged through her. She brought her hands together, compressing the enormous amount of water to the size of an apple. The compact bolt quivered above her palm, pushing against her like a million tiny hands as the energy fought to escape the small space.

"Everyone ready?" Kym heard Ashlyn shout. "One! Two! Three!"

Kym and Tomark moved at the same time. Their compact bolts flew from their hands, no more than silver and blue blurs. Below her, Amber, Kat, Ashlyn, and Xander's attacks streaked toward the morgar. Kym pushed her bolt forward with her energy, willing it to hit the morgar at the same time as the others.

The six compact bolts collided with the morgar in a multicolored explosion. Kym raised her hands, shielding her face as the force of the explosion blew her back. She tensed her muscles, fighting to keep herself upright as she looked down. A massive plume of smoke rose from the spot where the morgar stood. Kym flew down several yards, her heart racing, her eyes narrowed against the smoke and dust. But she didn't need to see to know the morgar was there. Her insides were just as numb as ever.

"Damon!" Kym heard Kat shout. "Do it now!"

Kym pushed herself higher as Damon's life blast left his hands. The beam flew through the smoke, and exploded against the morgar, filling the air with white light. A horrible, pained scream filled the air, and Kym's heart ached as she watched the morgar collapse as the cold inside her subsided. He may be overrun with death, but the morgar was still a person.

Kym landed, unable to take her eyes off the motionless man on the ground. If Kym didn't know any better, she'd have thought he was sleeping. She wanted to help him—to make sure he was alright. But as Kym drew nearer, the cold numbness in her stomach intensified.

"Stay back," Jazin shouted at Amber, her face full of concern. Jazin knelt beside the morgar, who was already stirring. "We need somewhere to hide him."

"Hide him?" Kat asked.

"Yeah," Tomark said, shooting Kat a look. "Or did your master plan involve sneaking him into our dorm?"

"Fine," Kat shot back.

Kym's eyes darted around, taking in her surroundings. Concrete buildings lined the street, which weren't as tall as the hundred-story glass towers of the main avenues. But these smaller ones had held up well enough, considering they'd been attacked two hours earlier.

Kym looked down at the man. He was still stirring, even as dark black mist seeped from his body into Jazin's hands. Kym doubted they'd be able to move him very far, if at all. And what would happen if the Disciples came looking for them? Surely, someone had noticed their absence or saw the explosions.

"This way," Ashlyn said, running toward the nearest building.

Kym ran after her, the others right on her heels. Together, she and Ashlyn pushed open the door, and the others hurried in after them. When Jazin and the man were inside, Kym and Ashlyn slammed the door behind them. They were standing in what Kym guessed used to be an office building. Tiny cubicles filled the space, and loose paper and supplies littered the floor.

"Good thinking," Kat said, smiling as she plopped down on top of a table. "So, what do we do now?"

Rage roared inside Kym like a lion. This horribly thought-out mess had been her idea. If they hadn't shown up to help, Kym wasn't sure what would have happened. Why was it so hard for Kat to think things through?

"Seriously?" Amber drawled, glaring down at Kat. "This disaster is your baby. You figure it out."

"You must have a plan," Xander said, and Kym heard the desperation in his voice.

"Not really," Kat shrugged. "I figured we'd come up with something once we caught one."

"Well, you caught one," Tomark said, his brows furrowed. "Now we need to do something."

They lapsed into silence. Kym rubbed her hands over her face, pushing her hair out of her eyes. Now that they had a morgar, she had no idea what they should do with it. When Jazin tried to sever the Thed's link with her mom, he'd said it was endless. How could they help this man if they couldn't sever his link to Thed?

"What are we gonna do?" Ashlyn finally asked, her voice no more than a whisper.

"I don't know," Tomark said. "Jazin tried to help Kym's mom, but it didn't…"

Tomark trailed off. He glanced at Kym, who turned quickly away. Hot tears stung her eyes, and she fought to keep them from falling down her face. She didn't want to cry. She'd already shed too many tears for her liking. Besides, crying wouldn't help her mom or the man they just captured.

"Can't Jazin just, y'know, pull it out?" Kat asked, her expression softening at the look on Kym's face. "He did it with the death demon girl."

"She wasn't a death demon," Amber reminded Kat, her voice dark. "And Jazin couldn't completely free her either."

"Amber's right," Jazin nodded, his grey eyes trained on the man lying in the middle of the room. "I couldn't free her or Kym's mom.

How are we supposed to free this guy when we have no idea what we're doing?"

"Because we have to." Kym's voice was no more than a whisper, but everyone fell silent her as she spoke. "Damon told us we needed to break Thed's anchors. This man, and my mom, and that girl…they're his anchors. We need to free them."

"But how?" Ashlyn asked. "We have no idea what we're doing. We could ask the Council—"

"The Council won't agree to this," Xander cut across her. "Not after tonight."

"They don't trust us," Amber agreed, nodding her head. "And I don't trust them."

"They did tell us the truth," Tomark said, shooting a look at Amber. "Maybe we should trust them."

Kym shook her head. Of course, after the Council did one good thing, he was willing to trust them. But Kym wasn't so sure. What had the Council really done to earn their trust? They'd tried to stop Kym and Tomark from saving people, and only told them the truth when they had no other choice. Kym agreed with Amber—she didn't trust the Council.

"After we forced them to," Amber sneered. "The Council didn't tell you they were making weapons to fight magic. They didn't tell Kym her mother was still alive and essentially being held against her will. Why should we tell them anything? Like Kym said, destroying Thed's anchors is our job. We need to do this ourselves."

"I'm all for keeping them out of it," Kat said, jumping back to the ground. "But they'll notice we're missing. We're supposed to train their soldiers to fight magic."

"So we don't tell them."

Silence followed Kym's words. She stepped forward, and a shiver ran down her spine. Had her nerves caused it, or the unconscious man lying on the floor? It really could have come from either.

"You want to lie to them?" Ashlyn asked, her eyes wide. "To your father?"

Kym's anger and rage at Kat's plan reared its head at the mention of her father. Her cheeks grew hot, and her hands shook at her sides. Some of her anger must have shown on her face, because Tomark's fingers found their way into her hand. She squeezed them tight, fighting the urge to scream.

She didn't want to lie to her father, but his anger toward magic was clouding his judgement. Kym knew he'd try and stop them if he ever found out they were trying to save a morgar with magic. If they wanted to free the morgar from Thed, Marek and the rest of the Council couldn't know what they were up to.

"Yes," Kym said, her voice shaky but determined. "We're not telling them what we're doing here. Not until we've saved him."

"You want to do it here?" Amber asked, her eyes narrowing as she glared around the partially destroyed building. "This place is a wreck."

"It's the best place," Kym nodded. "They won't look for us here."

"But Kym," Damon said. "They'll notice when we don't show up for training in the morning."

"No, they won't," Kym assured Damon, stepping forward and letting go of Tomark. "They're not gonna know we're gone."

THE TRAINING ROOM was full of people when Kym led Amber, Ashlyn, and Kat in the following day. Soldiers, more than had ever shown up for training in the past, ringed the edge of the room. Most were covered in bandages, but Kym could see the determination in their eyes. The balcony was full as well. Kym looked up, and anger swirled inside of her. Her father was there, along with the rest of the Council. Her heart racing, Kym tore her eyes from the balcony as she reached the middle of the room. At least during training, she could let off some steam.

"Where are the others?" Parker barked, stepping in front of her troops. "The deal is you'd all—"

"They're resting," Amber snapped, cutting Parker off. She

glided forward, her hands behind her back, her head held high. "Recovering after last night's events. I assure you; you will have your hands full with us."

Kym fought to keep the smile from her lips. Of course, she knew Damon, Jazin, Xander, and Tomark weren't resting. It was all part of their plan. By now, they should be beyond the trunk line and with the morgar. Kym, Ashlyn, Amber, and Kat's job was to keep everyone focused on training. That's where the Fire Princess came in.

"This isn't Inferon," Parker glared up at Amber, who towered over Parker by several inches. "You're not in charge here."

"Of course," Amber said, her voice silky. "This is training. I'm told you've yet to train against Favored with full access to their magic. Shall we begin, Lieutenant?"

Parker nodded. Beside Kym, Kat's shoulders shook with suppressed laughter. Kym stamped hard on Kat's foot, who gasped as she stopped her silent fit. They couldn't let anyone think anything was going on. They needed to give the boys time to find a solution to the morgar.

Kym had only trained with Amber a handful of times, and nearly every instance had been sparring matches. Kym had never actually seen Amber teach. She started Parker's soldiers out with basic evasive drills—jumping from side to side while Kym, Kat, and Ashlyn threw bolts at them. Amber walked among the soldiers, pointing out every little mistake as she gracefully avoided the attacks herself. She saw every hesitation; every misstep; every weakness. In Amber's training room, there was no tolerance for errors.

"Again," Amber drawled, sounding almost bored as she glared at a soldier who Kat knocked back with an earth bolt. "It's a miracle you've survived this long."

"We haven't engaged in actual combat with the Favored until recently," Parker pointed out, her eyes narrow as she glared up at Amber.

"Yeah, and you're still barely scraping by," Kat snorted. "Good thing you've got your weapons, or you'd be—"

Kat stopped at the look Kym shot her. Kym stepped forward, trying to make her face look concerned as she observed the soldiers in front of her. Even with Amber's nagging, they'd done reasonably well.

"You did okay," Kym said, shooting Amber a look. "Energized magic moves much faster than what you're used to practicing with."

"We noticed," Parker scowled.

"You need more practice," Ashlyn smiled. "It takes time."

"We don't have time," Parker said before turning back to her troops. "Back in formation. We're going again."

They worked on evasion the rest of the morning. Taking a page from Amber's book, Parker moved through the crowd, barking at her soldiers whenever they made a mistake. It reminded Kym of Aidan and Kenna training the other Water Favored for the Festival of Creation. Like Amber, they yelled at Kym for every mistake she made. Kym bet the soldiers were doing everything they could to make Parker shut up.

When Parker released them for lunch, Kym, Kat, Amber, and Ashlyn left the room as calmly as possible. Parker said they had one hour before they needed to return, which wasn't a lot of time. Kym ducked into the nearest stairwell and waited for it to get quiet. Amber held out her hands, and Kym, Ashlyn, and Kat took them. Amber turned on the spot, pulling the others with her through the flames.

Kym tried to close her eyes, but it was over before she could blink. They were standing behind a particularly large piece of rubble. After looking around the previous night, they decided it was the best place to warp in and out of the tower. Initially, they considered warping right into the building where they were keeping the morgar, but Amber fought against it. She didn't know how warping over the trunk line would work, and she didn't want to risk it.

Once they stepped over the trunk line and the throbbing in Kym's head subsided, it didn't take them long to reach their building. Kym strained her ears, listening for any sign of something happening inside. But it was completely silent.

Tomark, Xander, Jazin, and Damon sat on tables near the door, their faces shining with sweat. Kym saw the morgar on the other side of the room as she hurried toward the others. He lay on a long table, and he wasn't moving. Kym's eyes darted from the man to Tomark and the others. The icy death radiating through Kym meant one thing—they hadn't freed him.

"No luck?" Ashlyn asked, sitting beside Jazin.

"Nope," Xander shook his head. "Every time we tried taking the death out of him, he'd go crazy. We'd have to stop and blast him to knock him out again."

Kym looked at the man, her heart heavy. She knew they were doing the right thing, but it sounded like they were hurting more than helping. Were they doing more harm than good? Kym's stomach twisted around itself. She hoped this was worth it.

"How was training?" Tomark asked as Kym sat beside him.

"These people," Amber began, shaking her head, "have a long way to go if they want to stand a chance against Lucia."

"The screaming Fire Princess didn't help," Kym said.

"I didn't scream," Amber shot back. "And I thought you wanted the Fire Princess?"

"You did fine, Amber," Kat said, rolling her eyes. "With you there, they didn't even notice these guys were gone."

"Parker noticed," Kym reminded her.

"And we planned for that," Ashlyn said, her voice wary.

"Speaking of," Damon said, stretching his arms in front of him, "who's covering what this afternoon."

"I'm staying," Jazin said, glancing back at the man. "Until we know he's safe, I don't think I should leave him."

"You're gonna need to show up to train at some point," Amber said, placing a hand on his shoulder. "And you'll need to rest."

Personally, Kym agreed with Jazin. The morgar was calm, but for how long? What would happen if he woke and death exploded out of him? At least with Jazin there, he could contain things if they got out of hand.

With their hour break nearly over, Kym, Tomark, Damon, and Xander returned to their warping spot while Ashlyn, Jazin, Kat, and Amber stayed behind. This time, Xander warped them to their dorm room, where they simply walked out and made it to the training room with a minute to spare.

"Busy lunch?" Short asked, raising an eyebrow at Kym as she hurried into the training room.

"Not really," Kym shrugged, trying to look innocent. "Just relaxed for a bit."

Kym walked passed Short and into the training room. The viewing balcony was just as full as it had been that morning, with the onlookers pointing and whispering excitedly as Tomark walked beside Kym. Kym suppressed a groan. No doubt word had gotten out that Tomark was the real victor of the Calling. Kym just wished people would stop pointing.

They spent the afternoon letting Parker's soldiers practice with their storm weapons. Kym, Tomark, Damon, and Xander stood back while the soldiers used the weapons on darkness constructs Xander created. The soldiers beat them every time, but Kym didn't think it was much of a challenge. Xander's constructs only attacked when the soldiers got close. However, Kym still found it odd seeing Protectorate spears pierce the constructs, the strange orange light of the storm shining from the grooves in the metal. And the constructs never lasted long, always vanishing after two or three hits from the storm weapons.

"Well," Parker said, triumph shining in her eyes as her soldiers destroyed Xander's final constructs. "I'd say that was a good day of training. Rest up. Report at the same time tomorrow morning."

Kym sighed with relief as she turned to leave. This had been one of the longest, most stressful days she'd endured. More than anything, she wanted to sleep. Kym's thoughts turned to Ashlyn, Amber, Kat, and Jazin. Had they made any progress with the morgar? She wouldn't need to wait long to find out, since they were supposed to return at sunset. However, when she reached the training room door, she found someone blocking her path.

"Must have been some nap," Short said, leaning against the door frame.

"What?" Kym asked as Damon, Xander, and Tomark caught up with her.

"The nap you took," Short said, taking a step toward Kym. "But, it's funny. I went to check your dorm halfway through lunch. It was empty."

The bottom fell out of Kym's stomach. She'd completely forgotten Short. Even after the attack on the tower, he was still assigned to watch them. Kym could have kicked herself. Why hadn't she thought of Short coming to check on them? He'd done so every day for over a month.

"Don't worry," Short said, a smile flashing on his lips. "I'll cover for you, but if someone else catches you, they'll report it to the Council. You're on thin ice as it is. Just…watch your back."

"Thin ice?" Tomark asked.

Kym looked from Tomark to Short, who could be talking about any number of things. She defied the Council all the time; she broke rules, attacked guards, crossed the trunk line, and was trying to unlink a morgar from Thed. Of course, the Council was unaware of Kym's most recent actions. And she was determined to keep it that way.

"People here blame you for the attack," Short said.

"What?" Xander demanded.

"Short, that's crazy," Damon said, crossing his arms.

"Is it?" Short asked, raising an eyebrow. "Look, I don't blame you for helping your friends. But going to Crystal Palace brought the Favored here. And," he added before Kym could respond, "you blew up a cell in the experimental medical wing. Of course, not everyone knows about that, but the people in charge do. Watch yourselves."

"Thanks," Kym nodded. "We will."

Tomark grabbed Kym's hand and led her out the door. She

couldn't believe it. How could the people not see they were trying to help them? Sure, a few bad things happened, but it wasn't much worse than the way things had been. But with Kym and the others there with their magic, they were a constant reminder of what waited outside the trunk line. No wonder the people didn't trust them.

"Hey, Kym!"

Kym glanced over her shoulder. Short closed the space between them in three long strides. He was so close to her his lips almost touched her ear.

"I don't know what you're up to. But, if you need help, just ask."

Short stepped around Kym so quickly he disappeared down the stairs before she could blink. Kym stared after him, her chest lighter than it had been all day. Ever since they decided to free the morgar, she'd felt so alone. But she'd been wrong. Even though it didn't always feel like it, there were Disciples she could trust.

Kym led the others back to the dorm. No one spoke while they ate their dinner—a mixed assortment of supplement powders and dried fruit. The kitchen had been damaged during the attack, as had the dining hall on the ground floor. So, the Council was limiting food consumption to things that could be easily replaced. Kym wolfed down her food, her eyes trained on the window, watching the sun sink toward the horizon. Any minute now, Ashlyn, Jazin, Kat, and Amber would return, hopefully with good news.

Sunset came and went. Xander paced back and forth while Damon stood so close to the window his breath fogged it up. Kym sat beside Tomark on the small sofa, her hands clasped tightly in her lap. What was taking them so long? Surely they'd know if something terrible happened. But if something had happened, why hadn't the others come to get them?

Bright red flames swirled through the air, and Kym jerked back reflexively. There was a loud thud as something heavy hit the ground, and the flames vanished. Kat, Amber, and Ashlyn stood in the middle of the room, their faces shining with sweat. Kat and Ashlyn fell to the floor, but Amber stayed where she was.

"What's wrong?" Kym asked, taking in the concerned look on Amber's face. "Where's Jazin?"

"He wouldn't leave the morgar," Amber said, her voice higher than usual.

"What? Why?" Xander asked.

"Because we couldn't fix him," Kat said, her voice dark.

"Nothing we did worked," Ashlyn said. "Jazin pulled the death out of him, we attacked it, but more just kept coming. It was endless."

"And the more we attacked, the more it fought back," Amber said in a rush. "I tried to make him come, but he wouldn't listen."

"It fought back?" Tomark asked, sounding shocked.

"It destroyed half the building."

Kym's mouth fell open. She'd been sure they'd figure out how to save the morgar by now. At the very least, she'd expected them to make some progress. But by the sound of it, they'd made things worse.

"But why'd Jazin stay?" Tomark asked.

"He's being noble," Kat said, rolling her eyes as she dumped protein and vitamin powder into a glass of water. "He said he could keep it under control if it got loose."

"He's not an it!"

The words exploded from Kym before she could stop them. The others stared at her, and there was too much understanding in their eyes for Kym's liking. They'd been in this situation before, after all. With the first morgar they faced, before the Calling, everyone kept calling her "thing" or "it." Kym nearly attacked the Warden when they took her to Tenbatter.

"We know," Tomark said gently, placing a hand on Kym's shoulder.

Kym closed her eyes, breathing deeply through her nose. The pounding in her head subsided, but only by a little. She needed to get it together. She couldn't lose her cool now.

"But Jazin's right," Ashlyn said. "We can't leave that guy there without someone to watch him."

"Agreed," Damon said, squaring his shoulders. "I'll go switch him out."

"Are you crazy?" Kat asked. "Your combat skills are basic at best. If he wakes and attacks you, you're wandering Nothingness."

"I'll go with him," Xander said. "I'll warp us there, and we'll send Jazin back. We'll watch him tonight. Take it in shifts."

Kym nodded. She didn't like the idea of them being alone with the morgar at night. But she knew Jazin was right; the morgar needed to be watched. Before Kym knew it, Xander and Damon were gone in a swirl of shadow. Kym barely had time to put her cup in the sink before Jazin appeared in a flash of icy blackness. He collapsed to the floor, and Kym saw the dark circles under his sunken eyes. Kym's breath caught in her chest as Amber fell to her knees beside him. He really didn't look good.

Tomark helped Jazin into the boys' room while Kym, Kat, Amber, and Ashlyn walked silently into theirs. They changed in less than a minute, and crawled into bed in even less time. Kym pulled the thin sheets over her head, sleep already starting to cloud her mind. How could they break Thed's anchors if they couldn't free one man? Thed said the non-magical people were the easiest to corrupt. If releasing one man was this hard, how were they supposed to free the Rulers?

Chapter Twenty

Tethered Death

Kym was frozen. She wanted to move, but every time she tried, she couldn't bring her limbs to respond. She tried to fight the cold seeping through her soul, but eventually, it was easier to give in. Why was she fighting? What good was struggling when she didn't even know what she wanted anymore? She had nowhere to go. This blackness was all there was.

You are lost.

Kym sighed as the words consumed her. She knew she was lost, but that didn't matter to her anymore. Kym looked at the vast walls rising into the blackness above her. She doubted she'd ever get out of the maze, so why was she bothering to fight? She had nothing left to give. It was easier to lay there and let the cold take her.

Very good.

It was dark when Kym woke, the air full of Kat, Amber, and Ashlyn's breathing. Kym lay there, staring at the dark ceiling, not wanting to move. Her stomach was a twisted knot, fluttering every time she tried to sit up. She wished she could spend the day in bed, wrapped in the warmth of her blankets, not worrying about what might happen.

The silence was short-lived. Ashlyn sat up, then walked silently into the common room a few minutes later. Kym stifled a groan and climbed reluctantly out of bed. There was no point staying there now—not when Kat and Amber would wake soon. She opened a drawer at random and grabbed the first sweater she could find. It was a little small, but the neck was worn and it fit well enough.

Jazin and Tomark were on the couch in the dark common room when Kym walked out. They looked tired, with dark circles under their eyes and their heads hung. She flipped the switch by the sink, her eyes stinging in the bright, artificial light. Ashlyn sat on the ground, her fiery hair hanging loosely around her face, her back pressed against the coffee table.

"You sleep?" Kym asked Jazin, sitting beside Ashlyn.

"Barely," Jazin said, his voice rough. "I kept thinking about the guy."

"Nothing happened," Ashlyn said gently. "Damon and Xander would've gotten us if it had."

"She's right," Tomark said, patting Jazin gently on the back. "Everything's fine."

Kat and Amber to join them a few minutes later, neither looking particularly happy as they stumbled into the room. Kat's short brown hair was stuck up at odd angles as she wandered around with her eyes half open. Amber didn't look much better, with her usually sleek black hair hanging in front of her face. Kym stifled a laugh. They weren't morning people.

"So," Kat yawned, stretching her arms. "What's the plan?"

"The plan?" Tomark asked. "Isn't it the same as yesterday?"

"I mean," Kat said, "who's doin' what?"

"Jazin should train this morning," Kym said.

"No," Jazin said, his grey eyes widening. "I need to go to the morgar."

"Jazin," Amber said, her voice much softer than usual. "You need to rest."

"And you need to train," Kym said firmly. "You're the only one of us who didn't yesterday. We need to show up to stop Parker asking questions."

"Or Short," Tomark added.

"What's Captain Small-Stuff want now?" Kat asked, rolling her eyes.

"He came to check on us during lunch yesterday," Kym said. "You know. When we weren't in the building."

"Oh," Kat said.

"He said he wouldn't turn us in, though."

"And you believe him?" Amber asked, her golden eyes no more than slits.

"I do."

Kym tried not to sound defensive, but it was hard. Amber hadn't been there as long as Kym and the others. After spending nearly every day with him for over a month, Kym felt like she knew Short. Kym trusted him, and that should be enough for Amber.

"So, Jazin's training," Ashlyn said quickly before anyone else could speak. "Who else is going?"

Kym and Ashlyn stayed in the common room while Amber led Tomark, Jazin, and Kat out the door for morning training. Secretly, Kym was happy for the break. At least with the morgar, her father wouldn't be glaring at her. A bitter taste filled Kym's mouth; did she really prefer being around death to her own father?

Kym took Ashlyn's hand, and dazzling yellow light filled her eyes, warming her skin. Ashlyn pulled on her arm, and Kym lurched forward. She hurtled through space and closed her eyes, bracing for the impact. Her feet slammed into solid ground, and the warm glow faded. She opened her eyes, and the world looked oddly dark. She blinked several times, forcing her eyes to adjust to the pale grey light that preceded sunrise.

It didn't take Kym and Ashlyn long to reach the office building. They found Xander sitting in a chair, his chin held awkwardly on his palm. Damon was curled up on what looked like the remains of an old sofa. They'd even managed to find a tattered blanket.

"How was the night?" Kym asked, offering Xander some water from the thermos she'd brought.

"Quiet as Nothingness," Xander said thickly. "He didn't move once."

"I'm not surprised," Ashlyn said, gently shaking Damon's

shoulder. "He probably won't wake until we start working on him again."

While Xander and Damon ate the food Ashlyn gave them, Kym walked to the other side of the room. The morgar was still on the table, his body as thin and pale as ever. Every now and again, she'd see him move, but it wasn't the uncontrollable twitch of someone who was sleeping. His movements were much slower—like something was stirring deep inside him. Luckily for Kym, that something was also too weak to move.

"Okay," Xander said when Kym returned to the others. "Any ideas?"

"What did you try yesterday?" Kym asked. She was the only one who hadn't been there.

"Well, in the morning, we tried pulling the death out of him and attacking it," Xander said. "Damon's attacks had some effect, but it wasn't much. The death just kept coming."

"That's what we tried in the afternoon," Ashlyn said. "Jazin pulled out as little death as possible, but once he started, it was hard to keep it contained. It kinda exploded when Amber attacked it."

"It exploded?" Kym asked, her mouth hanging open.

Ashlyn pointed at the other side of the room. Kym shifted around and saw a gaping hole that certainly hadn't been there the day before. Kym stared at the blackened pile of sand that used to be the wall, trying to think of something, anything. What were they supposed to do? She thought back to the death demons she'd fought. They, too, killed everything they touched as death radiated from them. But, when Kym defeated them, the death emitting from them always faded away. She couldn't wait for the death to fade away on its own, if that was even possible. If she wanted to break this man's link with death, doing it by force seemed like the only option.

"What if," Kym said slowly, "instead of taking the death out, we put life in."

"What?" Ashlyn and Xander said.

"I don't know," Damon said. "Offsetting that much death will take a lot of life energy."

"Think about it," Kym said, her mind racing. "The morgar are like this because there is too much death around, right? So we need to restore balance. We do that by adding more life."

Kym smiled as she looked at the others. She thought it sounded like a good plan. Why hadn't they thought of it before? They'd been so focused on fighting death they forgot the gods wanted them to restore balance. And if they couldn't take out what was causing the problem, they needed to add more of the solution.

Kym stayed with Damon while Ashlyn and Xander warped to get what he needed. When they returned, it looked like they'd raided a greenhouse. Kym had to admit she was impressed. She hadn't paid any attention to things like potted plants since they arrived, given how little time she'd spent outside the tower. However, Damon had noticed. Kym guessed it made sense. He needed living things to fuel his magic after all.

Ashlyn, Xander, and Kym arranged the plants around the morgar, still lying like a statue on the table. Kym stepped back once the plants were in place, her heart racing in her numb chest. She turned to face the table, bouncing slightly on the balls of her feet. If this didn't go well, she'd need to attack at a moment's notice. Ashlyn and Xander took similar stances, their Marks filling the dim space with yellow and purple light.

Kym nodded, and Damon turned to face the morgar, a determined look on his face. He raised his hands, his white Marks glittering. Pure white mist rose from the plants surrounding the morgar, which crumbled into black dust as Damon ripped the life from them. The glittering cloud of life filled the room, sweeping over Kym. Her aches and pains faded as the cloud engulfed her, as did her worry. With this much life energy, Kym's doubts seemed almost laughable.

Damon pushed his arms forward, and the cloud of life descended on the morgar. Kym held her breath, blood thundering in her ears. Would the morgar return to normal instantly, or would it take time? Whenever Zara healed her wounds, it was almost instantaneous. But this, this was essentially healing someone from death. Kym figured that would take more time than the brain damage she sustained in the Calling.

A swirling storm of black death exploded from the morgar. Kym held up her hands, but her hastily made shield shattered as the force of the explosion knocked her back. She flew through the air, her muscles throbbing and achy. She crashed into the wall, and stars popped in her eyes as she slid to the floor.

"Ah!"

Kym's eyes snapped open as Xander's scream filled her ears. She didn't care that her limbs were on fire or her head was aching. She needed to make sure her friends were okay. Using all the strength she could muster, Kym pushed herself to her knees.

A shimmering cloud swirled around the morgar, but it wasn't the gentle, white one Damon created. Death whirled around him like a tornado, while pieces thrashed and jutted out of the black mass. Kym couldn't find Ashlyn, Xander, or Damon anywhere. What had happened to them? Kym feared the worst. Had that black cloud… Kym shook her head. She couldn't think that. She needed to get this mess under control.

Kym sprinted forward, and her water bolt flew from her hand. It soared into the black cloud and exploded in a flash of blue light. The small section of swirling death her bolt hit vanished, but it was nothing compared to what remained. The blackness spun faster as more pieces branched off from the main storm.

"Is everyone okay?" Kym heard Damon call, but she still couldn't see him.

"Yeah!" she heard Xander yell.

"All good," came Ashlyn's voice.

"Yup!" Kym called, her panic subsiding slightly.

"What do we do?" Ashlyn asked.

Kym's mind raced. If she didn't think of something soon, the cyclone of death would bring the building down. But that was the least of her worries. She didn't care about saving the building. She needed to make sure she and her friends made it out in one piece. But with a literal storm of death swirling around her, Kym saw no way out.

"Should we attack?" Kym heard Damon shout.

Kym saw a glimmer of white light through the swirling cloud of death. No doubt Damon was getting ready to fight. Kym raised her arms, her blue Marks glowing, ready to join him. But as the energy from the water charm surge through her, Kym lowered her hands. The tendrils of death were lashing out, destroying everything ten feet around the morgar. However, the tendrils never extended beyond that point. It was like a light went off in Kym's head. It wasn't attacking Kym or the others. It was making sure nothing got close.

"Stop!" Kym shouted, her heart pounding in her ears.

"What?" Xander's voice rang out from somewhere on Kym's left.

"Kym, we need to do something!" Ashlyn's high voice yelled.

"We need to stop!" Kym shouted again.

She backed up several feet and took a deep breath. She relaxed, and she felt her energy stop flowing. Her Marks faded from her arms as she stumbled backward, trying not to trip over the piles of debris. Maybe they were going about this all wrong. Was attacking it really the only way to free the morgar?

"What are you doing?" Damon's voice reached Kym's ears.

"We can't attack," Kym said calmly, continuing to back up.

"Why not?"

"Because," Kym said, "look at it. It's not attacking us. It's defending him."

Kym watched the swirling mass of black death above them. The whole time they'd been talking, it hadn't expanded beyond the man lying motionless on the table. It had only lashed out when they attacked, then returned to normal when they stepped back. Kym didn't know how to get rid of it, but one thing was clear. They couldn't attack it out of him.

The others must have done as Kym said. The swirling mass

slowed, looking more like black silk sheets drifting in the wind. Kym continued to retreat, hoping the others would do the same. Her feet ran into the wall, and Kym stumbled. She slid down the rough concrete, landing hard on the ground. Her tailbone throbbing, Kym watched the death continue to recede. It seeped back into the man, leaving the room oddly quiet.

Kym sighed and pushed herself back up. The others stood at the far edges of the room, a mixture of surprise and relief on their faces. Kym crossed to the far side of the room, giving the morgar as much space as she could. The others joined her, sitting on the odd assortment of chairs and tables in the corner.

"Well, that was a bust," Ashlyn said, pushing her hair out of her face.

"Completely," Xander said, shaking his head and covering his face with his massive hands.

"C'mon," Kym said, a little crestfallen. "It wasn't a total waste."

"How?" Damon asked, raising his eyebrows. "We failed to free him. He's still anchoring Thed to Princirum."

"But we learned something," Kym said, unable to keep the excitement from her voice. "We know the death inside him is protecting him. We can use that."

"How?" Xander asked.

Kym opened her mouth but shut it just as quickly. She had no idea how to use what they'd learned, but it was something. At least now she knew attacking the morgar wouldn't work. They'd taken a step forward, and Kym thought that counted for something. Maybe now they could make some progress.

NEARLY TWO WEEKS PASSED, and Kym was starting to think they'd never free the morgar. Maybe Dr. Gwin was right. Nothing they'd tried had any effect on the nearly endless death trapped inside the morgar. Was Thed's connection to Princirum so strong that there was no way to break it? Every day they tried something new, but no matter how hard they tried or how creatively they thought, they couldn't sever death's connection to the man.

"We need to keep trying," Damon would say whenever they voiced their doubts. "The gods chose us for this. Stopping Thed is their plan for us."

Kym bit her tongue every time Damon said something like that. She'd been on the wrong end of the gods' plan one too many times to blindly trust it—if it even existed. The gods knew Thed's power was growing but did nothing to stop him before it was too late. And now their master plan was having a group of teenagers fix it? Kym knew Damon was a believer, but it took all of her willpower not to tell him how crazy he sounded. She was already having a hard time with the Disciples staring at Tomark now that they knew he'd won the Calling.

And on top of trying to help their morgar, who Kat nicknamed Theddie, they still had training with the Disciples. And that was getting more difficult as well. Commander Hale's fighters were improving under Parker's watchful eye, but that wasn't what Kym found difficult. They used so much energy trying to free Theddie that Kym barely had enough left for training. Parker also insisted Kym spar at least twice a session while her soldiers and everyone on the viewing balcony watched.

"It's as much for our benefit as it is yours," Parker snapped when Kat complained about training one afternoon. "If you're going to help us fight, you need to be in fighting shape."

Kym hated to admit it, but she wasn't anywhere near what Parker called "fighting shape." She was fine demonstrating attacks, but any type of prolonged magic use left her winded, with a throbbing headache. In the past, Kym spent her evenings honing her skills to make sure she was the best, but those nights were a thing of the past. If it wasn't her turn to help with Theddie, Kym barely kept her eyes open before collapsing in bed.

And if that wasn't hard enough, Amber took it upon herself to further Kym's and the other's magical training.

"How are you gonna stand a chance against the Unity if you

don't know more advanced combat magic?" she demanded when Xander asked why she was teaching them. "The Unity knows the most advanced forms of combat, and you will too."

Amber started teaching them satellite magic—a form of combat Kym had seen the Rulers and Masters use. It involved creating bolts that orbited around Kym, which would attack or defend her without her needing to move. At first, Kym thought this wouldn't be too hard. Satellite magic sounded a lot like construct magic. But then Kym remembered the only proper construct she'd made had been during the Calling, which Xander had easily destroyed. Kym's satellite bolts drifted halfheartedly around her before finally exploding, leaving Kym feeling drained and angry, not to mention the ringing in her ears.

They also practiced Xander's door-opening technique, which Ashlyn named "sheathing." Kym found sheathing far easier than satellite magic, mostly because she already managed it when helping Short during the attack. Sure, it was more exhausting than satellite magic, but Kym preferred feeling exhausted to having her attacks blow up in her face every time she tried.

"You look like crap," Short whispered to Kym as she walked into the training room behind Damon, Kat, and Tomark.

Kym couldn't bring herself to fake a smile. She'd been on guard duty with Jazin until midnight and barely slept after. She would've told Short, if the training room wasn't packed with people.

"Full house today," Tomark said, and Kym saw his eyes darting around the overlooking balcony.

"New storm tech demonstration. That's all I know," he added as Kym opened her mouth.

Kym's mind slowly ground into action as Short disappeared among the other officers. New storm tech? A shiver ran down her spine as she joined the others in the middle of the training room. They'd seen the soldiers practicing with the spears, batons, and pulse beads in training plenty of times. Kym hated to admit it, but they worked really well. Why would Anderson make a new weapon if there were no problems with the old ones?

"Thank you," Professor Anderson said from the balcony, his hand raised, calling for quiet. "Today, we celebrate the hard work of those working in the Department of Etheric and Alternative Energy. Their dedication keeps us alive, thwarting the death that threatens us every day."

The crowd broke into polite applause, and Kym joined them, but only halfheartedly. She doubted these people knew these advancements came from subjecting trapped morgar to untold pain and suffering. She knew the Disciples weren't fond of magic, but they wouldn't be okay with Anderson torturing people, would they? Kym had a sinking feeling they wouldn't be, not if they knew there was a chance to save the morgar.

"After the Favored attacked," Anderson pressed on, and silence fell over the room, "we realized our soldiers, while equipped with means of offense, needed protection. Lieutenant Parker."

The soldiers parted, and Parker stepped forward, her face impassive. Kym's eyes flashed over Parker, but her City Patrol uniform looked perfectly normal. Where was the new defense tech Anderson gave her? Kym doubted it was small. She knew the storm was effective against magic, but something to defend the soldiers couldn't be so small that Kym couldn't see it.

"We will, of course, need a volunteer," Anderson said, bringing Kym back to her surroundings.

Everyone stared at Kym, Kat, Tomark, and Damon, making her skin crawl. She stared at Anderson, and saw the other Councilors standing around him. The sight of Marek made Kym's insides scream. Her hands balled into fists, and she fought hard to keep her face calm. After they freed the morgar, Kym's father would realize she was helping all along. Kym stepped forward. She hoped for Parker's sake that Anderson's new defense worked. If not, Parker was in for a world of hurt.

Kat, Tomark, Damon, and the other soldiers backed away while Kym faced Parker in the middle of the room. Kym raised her hand, her Marks glowing as a water bolt appeared above her fingers. She expected Parker to do something—pull an item from her pocket or take up a fighting stance. But to Kym's surprise, Parker just stood there, her dark eyes locked on Kym.

"Thank you, Miss Kym," Anderson's voice rang out. "You may begin."

Kym raised her hands, taken aback. What were Anderson and Parker playing at? From what Kym could see, Parker had no way to defend herself. If Kym attacked, she'd hurt Parker. And no matter how much Kym wanted to blow off steam, she drew the line at attacking a defenseless person. She looked at Parker, whose lips twitched in the faintest trace of a smile. Kym relaxed slightly. Parker must know what Kym was thinking, and if she was smiling, Parker knew what was going to happen.

Kym's water bolt flew through the air in a flash. Kym pushed with all her might, willing the bolt to hit Parker in the chest. It flew right at Parker, who didn't take a step, her face calm. Kym saw her hand fall to her waist, where she slammed her palm onto her large belt buckle.

Bright orange lines, thin as hair, crisscrossed Parker's uniform like an eerie web. A low, deep hum filled the air, and Kym's head throbbed. Kym ignored the pain, focusing even harder on her bolt as it collided with Parker. It exploded in a flash of blue, but Parker's cry of pain never reached Kym's ears. When the blue light faded, Kym's mouth fell open. Parker stood only a foot from where she'd been. Kym shook her head. Her bolt should've knocked Parker on her back, at the very least. Applause filled the training hall as Parker hit her belt buckle again. The orange lines in her clothes faded, as did Kym's headache.

"Well done," Anderson called over the roar of the crowd. "This new storm mesh will ensure our soldiers' protection against the Favored."

The crowd cheered, and Kym shook her head as she rejoined the others. She knew she should be happy. Anderson was right. The storm mesh meant Parker and her soldiers stood a chance against the Favored and death demons. But at what cost? The Disciples' time would be better spent trying to free those trapped by Thed instead of making weapons.

"Lieutenant Parker's suit is one of two prototypes," Anderson pressed on as the cheering crowd quieted. "We don't know the full extent of its capabilities. Lieutenant, power up the suit again. Miss Kym, you and your fellows may do your worst. Let's see what the suit can handle."

Kym glared at Anderson, unable to keep the look of disgust from her face. He really wanted Kym, Kat, Tomark, and Damon to attack Parker and not hold back? She understood making sure the suit worked, but she'd done that. Kym saw no point in all of them attacking Parker. She didn't care if Parker's storm mesh worked. Without weapons, Parker didn't stand a chance.

Kym stayed back with Tomark while Damon and Kat stepped forward. Kym shook her head as they raised their hands and Parker reactivated her suit. The throbbing in Kym's head returned, and she pinched the bridge of her nose, trying to alleviate it. All she did was make her nose hurt.

After nearly three minutes, Kym had to hand it to the scientists in the Department of Etheric and Alternative Energy. They'd done well. Damon and Kat's bolts, blasts, and swipes knocked Parker off balance, like someone was punching her. Paired with Parker's masterful evasion skills, the suit kept Parker on her feet. Even though Kym didn't like why they made it, this new suit may make a difference. Parker was holding her own in a fight with magic.

A hand appeared on Kym's shoulder, which felt like someone had dumped ice water all over it. Kym glanced to the side, a shiver running down her spine, expecting to see someone. But there was no one there. Instantly, Kym's eyes drifted to the ground, and she shook her head. Thanks to the vast glass walls, Kym's shadow stretched several feet behind her. Tomark's shadow was on her right, and the shadow of a muscular teen was on her left, its hand on the shadow of Kym's shoulder.

"What?" Kym hissed, trying not to move her lips.

"Something's happening," Xander whispered in Kym's ear. "Jazin thinks he did it. But he needs Damon."

"He's busy," Kym mumbled.

Kym's heartbeat quickened. Had Jazin really managed to free Theddie at last? If that was true, she needed to get Damon out of the training room. But how could she do that with everyone watching the storm mesh demonstration?

"We need a distraction," Tomark whispered, clearly listening to Kym and Xander's conversation. "We can't let them know what's going on until we know for sure."

"I'm open to ideas," Xander said, and Kym heard the urgency in his voice.

Kym nodded. They needed to do something, and they needed to do it fast. Kym tried to think, but Parker jumped closer to her, and the throbbing in her head intensified. She groaned, rubbing her forehead with her fingers. How was she supposed to think with this headache? If she stepped into the stairwell for some peace…Kym had to stop herself from crying out. It was so simple.

"Wait at the stairs," Kym whispered to Xander. The clammy feeling left her shoulder as she turned to Tomark. "Keep them busy."

Tomark nodded, his eyebrows contracting. Kym knew she should tell him her plan, but there was no time. Kym took a breath and braced herself. This was really going to hurt.

Without warning, Kym closed her eyes and let her legs give way. She fell to the floor, crumpling in a heap as gasps filled the air. Kym fought to keep her face blank as pain radiated through her back. She couldn't let anyone know she hadn't passed out.

"What happened?" Kym heard Parker's concerned voice.

"Damon," Tomark said, not missing a beat. "Take her back to the room. I'll keep going here."

"Are you sure?" Kym heard Damon ask, his voice full of concern. "She doesn't look—"

"Go," Tomark ordered.

Kym didn't move a muscle as indistinct murmurs swirled

around her. She tried not to react as Damon slipped his hands under her knees and back. Kym let her body go limp, her limbs dangling around her as Damon carried her out of the training room.

Kym opened her eyes the moment she heard the training room door shut. She sat up, startling Damon, but luckily he had enough sense not to cry out. Kym swung her feet to the ground, scanning every surface for the shadow she knew would be there.

"What's goin' on?" Damon asked, his eyes wide with confusion.

"No time," Kym said, spotting Xander's shadow near the bottom of the first set of stairs.

She sprinted down the steps, Damon's hand held in hers. She felt Xander's clammy touch, which consumed her as Xander's hand twisted in hers. Kym flew through space, Damon's fingers held tightly in her own. Her feet hit solid ground, and she was at their usual warp spot.

Xander, no longer a shadow, broke into a run. Kym raced after him, her heart thundering in her throat. She barely noticed the head-splitting pain as she leaped over the trunk line. Off in the distance, she heard the unmistakable sound of crumbling stone. Kym quickened her pace, ignoring the growing discomfort in her side as her muscles tensed. Were they too late?

Kym burst into the office building, Xander and Damon right on her heels. Jazin stood beside Theddie, his arms held up, while the usual mass of death swirled above him. Ashlyn and Amber also had their hands in the air, but they weren't directed at Theddie, or even Jazin. Their hands were pointed at the crumbling walls, which glowed red and yellow as cracks spread through them.

"What the Thed—"

"Shh," Xander hissed, cutting Kym off.

Kym couldn't think straight. She didn't understand what was going on. To her, it looked like every other time they'd tried ripping the death out of Theddie. This was why they stopped trying that strategy. It never ended well.

"C'mon," Xander whispered, jerking his head toward Jazin.

Kym and Damon followed, Kym's insides turning to ice the

closer she got. The cloud of death Jazin summoned was larger than any she'd ever seen. A shiver ran down Kym's spine. How were the others managing the numbing cold? It had only been a few seconds, and Kym already felt miserable.

A low, almost nonexistent moan issued from the middle of the cloud. Kym froze, not daring to move a muscle. She stared at Theddie, unable to believe her ears. His eyes were still closed, but his body was moving. Moving? Theddie had barely twitched since they started working on him.

"We think he's waking," Xander said so quietly Kym could barely hear him. "Can you sense any life in him?"

Damon raised his hands, his white Marks shining. Kym held her breath. If there was life in Theddie, there might be hope for her mom after all. This could be her chance to save everyone.

"It's faint," Damon said, his eyes narrowed in concentration. "But it's there. He's alive!"

Damon rushed forward. Kym held out a hand to stop him, but he was already out of her reach. Kym couldn't understand what his plan was. They knew attacking the death wouldn't work. It may make a piece of it vanish, but the remaining cloud always defended itself. How'd Jazin removed it so peacefully?

The rumbling around Kym intensified as more cracks spread through the walls and ceiling. Kym raised her hands, and an energized mass of water appeared above her fingers in a flash of blue. She sent it upward, where it sheathed the cracking roof. Kym's knees buckled as the weight of the ceiling pressed strangely on her palm. She focused her energy, letting it flow from the water charm and around the crumbling concrete. It barely made a difference.

"Hurry up," Amber snarled. "The building's comin' down."

Stars burst in Kym's eyes as her arms and legs shook violently. Somewhere beside her, there was a flash of purple light, and she felt an odd sense of determination spread warmly through her energy. Kym chanced a shaky glance up. The ceiling was a patchwork of blue and purple light. Kym sighed. At least Xander bought them a few more moments.

"We need to sever it," Kym heard Jazin say, his normally quiet voice no more than a whisper. "But gently."

"How?" Damon asked, and Kym heard her confusion in his tone. How could they sever death gently?

"No sudden moves," Jazin said, his voice still oddly calm. "Don't try and hurt it."

Now Kym was really confused. She wasn't sure if it was the strain of holding up the building or the creeping cold of death, but she must've misheard Jazin. To Kym, it almost sounded like Jazin wanted to protect the death he'd removed from Theddie. But why? The whole reason they wanted to take it out was to destroy it. Death was evil after all.

"Nobody move!"

Kym's heart nearly stopped. She wasn't facing the entryway, but she didn't need to turn to know who the voice belonged to. Professor Anderson and Commander Hale swept past Kym, Kat, Tomark, and Short right behind them. Confusion drove away Kym's panic. What were Anderson and Hale doing there, and why were Tomark and Kat with them? And why did Short look like he was in trouble?

"No problem," Ashlyn groaned.

Kym gritted her teeth, determined not to move a muscle, but not because it was what Anderson ordered. If she, Ashlyn, Amber, or Xander moved, the whole building would collapse on top of them.

"What do you think you're doing?" Anderson demanded, stopping a few feet from the cloud of death.

"We told you," Tomark said. "We're saving him."

"You've doomed us all!" Anderson said, his voice full of panic. "I order you to stop."

"I'm sorry," Jazin said. His voice was still calm, but there was an edge to it Kym hadn't heard a moment before. "We're doing this."

"Stop them!"

Kym watched, frozen like a statue, as Hale ran forward, a storm spear in her hands. Damon swung his arm calmly in front of him, and a pure-white arc flew from his fingers. It glided forward, not toward the mass swirling above Theddie but at the few remaining tendrils still oozing from his chest. Kym saw Hale lunge, her spear poised to strike, as the ground rumbled beneath her feet. A wall of earth rose in front of Hale, separating her from Jazin, Damon, and Theddie.

There was a flash of blinding white light, and Kym's hair whipped behind her as she slid several feet. Kym focused harder than she'd ever focused before, pushing the sheathed ceiling over them as her muscles tore. Smoke and dust filled Kym's lungs, momentarily obscuring her vision. The sound of crumbling stone filled her ears, and Kym knew Kat's wall of earth was no more.

Slowly, the smoke and dust fell. Kym squinted through the gloom, her head throbbing as more stars popped in her eyes. The swirling black cloud floated peacefully above Jazin and Damon, no longer tethered to Theddie. Kym sighed, and warmth spread through her as her insides swelled with pride. They'd done what Anderson and his scientists failed to do. They freed Theddie from Thed. He was no longer a morgar, or an anchor for the god of death.

W H I S P E R S   I N
T H E   D A R K

"We win," Kat said, her voice full of triumph.

Kym couldn't believe it. After all of this time, they'd freed Theddie. Now, Damon's constant reminders that they were following the gods' plan didn't seem too far-fetched. They could actually save Princirum. But that wasn't what made Kym's heart soar. Finally, after over a year, Kym could save her mother.

"I doubt that," Anderson said, his voice icy. "You eight have a lot of explaining—."

"Could we do that later?" Amber demanded, her voice strained.

"Yeah, as much fun as holding up a building is…" Ashlyn trailed off.

Kym's arms shook with the strain of keeping the ceiling from collapsing. The death from Theddie hung in the air like a delicate black sheet, no longer causing damage to the building. But that didn't undo the destruction it had already caused.

"They're right," Hale said in a curt voice. "This isn't the place. Short, call Dr. Gwin. Tell him—"

"I've relieved Officer Short of duty," Anderson snapped. "He knew these Favored were up to something, but didn't inform his superiors."

"Technically, Officer Tiptoes only knew we were sneaking around," Kat said in an offhand voice.

Kym wanted to smack Kat. This wasn't the time to pick a fight with Anderson. The weight in Kym's hands doubled, and she groaned with the strain. She glanced up, and saw cracks spreading through the layer of water and darkness holding the ceiling. Kym pushed with all her strength, determined to keep the ceiling above them. But as she fed more energy into the sheath, she felt it fracture even more.

"We need to go," Tomark said, stepping into Kym's limited line of vision.

He swept past Anderson and Hale and scooped Theddie into his arms. Even from several yards away, Kym thought Theddie looked better. He was still thin, and his eyes were closed, but his skin was no longer ghostly white. And as he lay in Tomark's arms, Kym saw his hand twitch.

"We need to hurry," Hale said as the crumbling intensified.

"Not gonna happen," Kym groaned. The weight of the ceiling was becoming unbearable. "If we move, this whole thing's coming down."

Xander, Ashlyn, and Amber all grimaced in agreement. Kym's body shook with the strain of keeping the ceiling intact. She didn't know how much longer they could keep this up. But what could they do? She couldn't move without the building collapsing. But Kym didn't care about getting herself out. All that mattered was Tomark getting Theddie to safety.

"We're not going anywhere with that thing," Kym heard Anderson say.

Anger raged inside Kym. What was Anderson talking about? What thing? Surely, he didn't mean Theddie. He had a whole floor of morgar in the tower, and Theddie wasn't even a morgar anymore. But if he wasn't talking about Theddie, what was he talking about?

"Hale, get rid of it," Anderson barked, his voice shaking.

"Professor, we don't—"

"You can't!"

Kym didn't know what was more shocking—Hale questioning Anderson or Jazin speaking up. Kym tried to turn and see what was happening, but the weight of the building was too much. She was rooted to the spot.

"You don't give the orders here," Anderson snapped, clearly talking to Jazin. "Hale, now!"

The sound of scuffling feet filled the air, as did bright white and green flashes. Kym's mind raced. Whatever Anderson wanted Hale to do, Kat and Damon were trying to stop it. Kym wanted to help, to leap to their sides. Instead, she fell to her knees, her trembling legs finally giving way.

Kym heard sliding metal, a low hum, and her head felt like it was going to split open. Somewhere, she heard Kat cry out as a green orb streaked past her line of vision. A long, slender metal shaft flew through the air, its intricate markings glowing bright orange. Kym's heart stopped as the spear nearly missed Jazin, its tip piercing the ground beneath the peacefully floating death. Kym opened her mouth to speak, to yell, to do something. But she was too late.

Bright orange energy erupted from the spear, filling the collapsing building with a low hum. Kym's head split open, and her hands flew to her temples as the pain in her skull mounted. She couldn't think. She couldn't see. All around her, she heard odd swishing sounds as chunks of ceiling rained down around her. But even through the chaos, Kym could still hear the screams.

Kym remained still for a long time—she was so exhausted she doubted she could move more than a few inches. Fingers wrapped around Kym's ankle, and an eerie chill engulfed her. She hurtled through space, and the strain of the building vanished from her hands. Someone was warping her, but who?

Pain erupted in every particle of Kym's body. She opened her mouth, desperate to scream, but no sound came out as she surged through space. Suddenly, the world exploded back into existence. She slammed into something hard, and the fingers around her ankle fell away.

Dazed, Kym pushed herself up. She was in the middle of the library, which was full of people running in the dark. Kym blinked several times, trying to force her eyes to adjust. But they never did. Why was it so dark? Kym looked to the ceiling and found her answer. All of the lights were out.

"Way to go, Professor Stupid."

Kym's muscles relaxed slightly. Kat was on the floor a few feet away, Short kneeling beside her. She was glaring at Anderson, who stood beside Jazin and looked murderous. Kym pushed herself up, her arms and legs shaking dangerously.

"Why'd you attack it?" Amber demanded, her eyes narrow. She marched up to Anderson, glaring down her nose at him.

"It's my duty to protect the True Disciples," Anderson said, not backing down from Amber's intense gaze. "I'm not letting death anywhere near our sanctuary."

"It wasn't hurting you," Jazin said, shaking his head. "It wasn't hurting anyone!"

"It did disappear," Commander Hale said, her voice dark.

"After you attacked it," Damon retorted. "We had it under control before you—"

"What's wrong with the power?" Anderson interrupted, staring at his wrist.

Kym stepped forward, and goosebumps rose on her arms. The screen of Anderson's holowatch was dark. Kym's eyes narrowed as she offered Short her hand. He took it, and as she helped him up, she glanced at his holowatch. It was off too.

"It went out a couple of minutes ago," someone in the crowd shouted. "The building shook, and everything went black."

Kym spotted Kat's face, and saw her fear mirrored in Kat's eyes. That was when Hale attacked the death cloud. Could it have caused the power outage? Kym knew the storm powered the tower. If the power was out, that meant…

"We're not safe," Tomark said, clearly thinking along the same lines as Kym. He stepped forward, Theddie still held in his arms. "If the storm's down…"

"Agreed," Hale said, her voice stern. "Return to your designated quarters," she barked, and the room fell silent around her. "Wait there for further instructions."

Everyone moved at once. They ran to the stairwells, forming large crowds as people fought their way through the doors. Kym turned to Tomark, and saw Theddie stir in his arms. They needed to get him to the medical level.

"He needs a doctor," Kym said to Short.

"Byrd will see him," Short nodded. "She's on duty."

Kym hurried to Tomark's other side and draped Theddie's thin arm over her shoulders. Even with the death out of him, Theddie still looked incredibly thin and weak. She hoped Byrd could help him.

"Where are you taking that man?" Anderson's voice cracked.

Kym fought to keep her anger in check. She and Tomark turned as Anderson and Hale rushed toward them. Why were they still treating Kym and the others like they'd done something wrong? Thanks to Kym and the others, they knew how to free the morgar from Thed. Why was Anderson being so difficult? He should be grateful.

"Ma'am, this man needs medical attention," Short said, addressing Commander Hale.

"Officer," Hale said slowly, "that man is—"

"He's hurt!" Kym yelled. Anger coursed through her like lightning, and her Marks flashed blue. "We're taking him to medical."

Kym didn't wait for Anderson or Hale to respond. She turned on her heel and marched toward the stairwell with Tomark. She heard several feet behind her, but she didn't care. She glanced at Tomark, expecting to see a disapproving look on his face. Instead, she found his eyes narrow and his brows nearly touching.

"You good?" Kym asked, raising an eyebrow as they mounted the steps.

"Yeah," Tomark said, shaking his head. "I…I was just thinking."

"About…?"

"The storm is down."

Kym nodded, waiting for him to say more, but Tomark didn't elaborate. Kym didn't understand what Tomark was so focused on. Sure, the storm being down meant the tower was vulnerable, but they already knew that. There had to be something more. Personally, Kym didn't mind the break from the near-constant headaches.

"We'll know if an attack is coming," Short said behind Kym. "You can see the city walls from the top of the tower. There's always a couple of guards stationed there. If the Favored arrive, we'll be ready."

"It's…it's not that," Tomark said slowly.

"By the gods, Tomark! Spit it out!"

Kym glanced over her shoulder. Kat, Amber, Ashlyn, Xander, Damon, and Jazin were all behind them. Kat's nostrils were flared, and she looked like she was on the verge of punching Ashlyn, who was in front of her.

"If the storm's down," Tomark said, turning to face the others, "what's keeping the morgar sedated on the research level?"

The bottom fell out of Kym's stomach. She'd completely forgotten about the morgar in the tower. An icy chill rippled over Kym, making the hairs on her arm stand on end. She looked from Tomark to the others. Was her worry making her skin crawl, or was it something more sinister? Had they felt it too?

"Short, get him to medical," Kym said, handing Theddie over to him. "Are the morgar still there?"

"No," Short said, his eyes growing wide as comprehension dawned on him. "They moved them after the attack. They're on a new research level; eight floors up."

"Stay with Theddie," Kat said, grabbing Jazin and Ashlyn's hands as she pushed past the others. "Make sure he's okay."

Kym didn't wait for the others to respond. She sprinted up the stairs behind Kat, Ashlyn, and Jazin. Sweat poured down her face, and it felt like her side was going to split open, but she didn't stop. She kept going, counting the floors until Kat burst onto the research level.

Kym's body felt like it had been filled with ice. A numb throbbing radiated from her stomach, and as she exhaled, pearly white clouds of breath burst from her lips. Kym squinted through the dark but saw no more than a few feet in front of her.

"Ash," Kat whispered.

Pure bright light filled the dark hall. Three little suns, each as large as an apple, floated down the corridor, lighting their way. Kym suppressed a shudder. The whole place was deserted.

"What are we supposed to do?" Jazin asked. "Attack them if we see them?"

"No," Kat said firmly. "We need to keep them from getting out."

"We can't do anything if they're running around in a pack."

Kym knew Ashlyn was right. Taking on one morgar was hard enough. How were they supposed to handle a whole floor of them? There was one thing Kym could think of.

"Even with the storm down, they should still be in their cells," Kym whispered, stepping down the hall. "When we found the morgar in the city, they only swarmed when we provoked them. If we can keep them in their cells, we should be okay until they get the storm back up."

"If they can," Kat said, her eyebrows raised.

They crept down the hall, Ashlyn's little suns floating ahead of them. Kym tried to keep her breathing steady, but it was difficult. She didn't know if it was the ever-growing presence of death or her nerves, but she couldn't stop her hands from shaking. How long would it take for Anderson to get the storm working again? Hadn't he said it couldn't go out?

They slowed as they reached the first cell. Her heart racing, Kym stepped toward the glass wall. She couldn't see anything inside it. Breathing quickly, Kym swallowed before taking another step, placing her hand on the glass.

A ghostly thin hand flew out of the darkness. It slammed into the thick glass, and Kym jumped back as cracks spread through the surface. She panted, her hand freezing and numb, her heart thundering in her ears. She tried to catch her breath, but the frozen air felt like razors in her lungs.

"We need to split up," Ashlyn said as Kym's heart slowed. "Station ourselves down the corridor. Just in case."

Kym didn't like the idea of splitting up. She already felt uneasy about being there in the first place. It had taken all eight of them to get Theddie under control. How could the four of them handle a horde of morgar if they split up?

The others didn't give Kym time to voice her concerns. Jazin and Kat moved down the hall, two of Ashlyn's little suns lighting their way. The third remained with Ashlyn and Kym, who stayed by the first cells. Before Kym knew it, the dark corridor swallowed Jazin and Kat, and all she could see was blackness.

Kym shifted uncomfortably while Ashlyn went to look at the five nearest cells. Kym couldn't take her eyes off the other end of the hall. Her mother's cell was down there. What would happen if she got out? Kym's heart fell. She couldn't attack her mom. She knew Jazin and Ashlyn wouldn't. Ashlyn never hurt innocent people, and Jazin was determined not to attack the morgar. But what about Kat? Would her love of fighting stop if she saw Kym's mom?

"They better get the storm running soon," Ashlyn whispered, pulling her long hair out of her face.

"Yeah," Kym said, turning so Ashlyn wouldn't see the worry in her eyes.

"Don't worry," Ashlyn said gently, placing a hand on Kym's shoulder. "They'd never hurt your mom."

Kym actually laughed. Was she that easy to read? She shouldn't be surprised. Ashlyn could always tell when Kym was worried about something. Even during the Calling, when they were all focused on other things, she knew Kym was miserable. Of course, she'd sense it now.

"What if, after everything with Theddie, we can't save them?' Kym asked, a tear slipping down her cheek.

"Of course, we'll save them," Ashlyn said. "It's why we're here."

"C'mon Ash," Kym sighed. "We saved one, and when we did, we broke the magic-resistant battery."

"We don't know if that was us," Ashlyn said, stepping in front of Kym. "And Anderson will fix it. If he hadn't…"

Ashlyn trailed off, and Kym saw her cheeks flush in the light of their little sun. Kym couldn't stop the smile from appearing on her lips. It was nice to feel like she wasn't alone in her hatred of Anderson. For one of the smartest people in Princirum, he really was stupid.

Kym walked a few paces down the hall, stopping at the next cell. The morgar inside stood beside the glass wall; his head drooped forward. Kym tried to shake off the creeping emptiness inside her, but it only intensified as she watched the morgar's shoulders slowly rise and fall.

"Why aren't they doing anything?" Kym whispered, turning to face Ashlyn.

"You want them to do something?" Ashlyn asked. "Hopefully, Anderson will have the storm working again, and then—"

Fools.

The hairs on the back of Kym's neck stood on end. A shiver ran down her spine as the soft hiss filled her brain. It was no more than a whisper, but she heard it. A thin, raspy voice, like someone who hadn't spoken in a long time. But where had it come from?

Kym's eyes drifted over her shoulder. The morgar stood in his cell, his head still drooped. Kym approached the glass, her breath fogging the smooth surface. It couldn't have been him that spoke. Kym had only ever heard morgar scream. But if it wasn't him, who was it?

You are fools.

Kym jumped, her hands shaking uncontrollably. This time, the voice came from behind her. She spun around, searching wildly for the source of the strange voice. But the only person behind her was Ashlyn, her eyes wide with concern. Kym ignored her and hurried to examine the cell on the other side of the hall. The morgar kept to herself, staying near the back of the room.

"Kym, what's going on?" Ashlyn asked, her voice trembling.

"Don't you hear it?" Kym asked, peering into the cell.

"Hear what?" Ashlyn's voice rose an octave. "Kym, you're scaring—Ah!"

Ashlyn whipped around, and Kym reacted instinctively. She raised her hands, and the faint blue glow from her Marks and the water charm filled the dark corridor. Ashlyn was staring into one of the cells; her arms wrapped tightly around herself. Slowly, Kym drew nearer.

"What?" Kym breathed in her ear.

"A voice," Ashlyn said, her voice still shaking. "In there."

Kym took several breaths to calm herself, but she shook even more violently. She squinted through the gloom, trying to see the morgar in the cell. What was going on? Why were she and Ashlyn hearing things? And why couldn't they hear what the other one could?

Your fight is pointless.

This time, both Kym and Ashlyn jumped. Kym reached down, her trembling fingers desperate for something to hold onto. She found Ashlyn's hand and wasn't surprised to feel her shaking too. Kym stared at Ashlyn, and the terror in her eyes told her all she needed to know. This time they'd both heard the voice.

The morgar appeared so quickly Kym didn't have time to think. The numbing cold inside Kym was so intense she could barely feel her feet. One second, the cell looked empty, then the morgar stood beside the glass, her long, thin hair hanging over her face. The morgar lifted her head, her black eyes glittering strangely in the darkness.

"Did you really think you could force me out?"

Kym's breath caught in her chest. She'd heard that voice before. How many nights had she woken, screaming from what it said? It was the voice that filled her nightmares. It was the voice of death.

"Why do you resist?" the morgar asked, her head hanging limply to the side.

"You cannot stop death." This time, the voice of Thed came from the cell behind Kym.

Slowly, Kym turned, not daring to let go of Ashlyn's hand. The morgar stood at the edge of the cell, its black eyes shining in the faint light from Ashlyn's little sun. Kym opened her mouth, but no sound came out. Kym didn't understand. How were the morgar talking, and how was Thed speaking through them? He'd never done that before.

"Why would you deny Princirum my gift?" the morgar wheezed, stepping so close to the glass her nose almost touched it.

"G-gift?" Kym stammered, her voice much higher than usual. "What gift?"

"My gift," the morgar in the next cell said. *"The gift I was denied to share with humankind millennia ago."*

Kym glanced at Ashlyn, the icy numbness in her stomach growing stronger. She knew what Thed was talking about. She'd heard it all before. Before the gods created Princirum, they banished Thed to Nothingness because he tried to destroy life every time Pheil, the goddess of life, created it. Death was never a part of Princirum's creation, which was why Thed needed his anchors to stay there. Thed's gift to Princirum was death.

"The time is near," the morgar continued. *"Soon, my gift will be all that Princirum knows."*

"We…we'll stop you," Ashlyn said, her voice trembling almost as bad as the hand still clutching Kym's.

"You will try," the morgar said. It straightened up and raised a withered hand. *"But first, you will accept my gift."*

The morgar placed its hand on the glass. Cracks instantly spread through the thick pane, which turned yellow and wavy. Kym stepped back, letting go of Ashlyn as two water bolts appeared above her fingers. The glass shattered, and the morgar stepped into the corridor.

Kym's water bolt flew from her hand. It exploded against the morgar's chest, filling the dark hall with blue light. Its frail body flew through the air, landing with a muffled thud in its cell. Kym waved her hand, and a shimmering blue shield rose from the ground. It filled the empty doorway, sealing the morgar in its cell.

"Kym!" Ashlyn called as the sound of more shattering glass filled the corridor.

Kym turned around, and her insides froze. At least six morgar were in the hallway, the glass walls of their cells reduced to sand.

Deep inside her, Kym felt her shield crack as something icy pressed against it. She turned to Ashlyn, her eyes wide with terror. They were officially outnumbered.

The morgar lunged forward, their arms outstretched. Kym swung her arm, and her bright blue swipe hit three of them in the chest. They flew back, falling to the ground in crumpled heaps. But that didn't stop the others from stepping on them as they drew nearer to Kym and Ashlyn.

"Any ideas?" Kym asked, her mind blank.

"We need to keep them here," Ashlyn said. "If they leave the floor…"

Kym didn't need Ashlyn to finish her thought. She knew what would happen if the morgar made it into the rest of the tower. She wasn't going to put anyone else in danger. All they needed to do was keep the morgar busy until Anderson fixed the storm. But how long would that take?

Two more morgar reached out. The tips of one's fingers brushed the hem of Kym's shirt. The material withered and blackened, drifting like ash to the ground. Kym scurried back, her thundering heart filling her ears, and shoved her arms forward. The water blast filled the corridor with blue light, exploding against the nearest morgar and sending him hurtling through the air. Kym threw two more water bolts, which hit the nearest morgar, but it was no use. There were too many of them, and the ones she attacked kept getting back up.

"Run!"

Kym turned on her heel and sprinted as fast as she could, Ashlyn thundering behind her. A chorus of snarling followed them, and Kym breathed a small sigh. If the morgar were following them, they weren't trying to get to another level. Kym threw bolts randomly over her shoulder, not even bothering to see if they made contact. All that mattered was keeping the morgar far enough away from them.

Wham!

Kym collided with something very small and solid. Her feet

flew out from beneath her, and Kym slammed into the hard floor. Barely able to breathe, lights popping in her eyes, Kym pushed herself up. Kat lay sprawled on the floor, slightly cross-eyed, rubbing her temples with her fists.

"Where'd you come from?" Kat asked thickly.

"You didn't see us coming?" Ashlyn demanded, offering Kym her hand.

Kym took it, her mind full of questions. But as she took in the scene before her, all her questions vanished. Kat and Jazin were already on the attack, facing the hoard of morgar at the other end of the corridor. Kym saw the remains of the glass walls glittering on the floor in the light from Ashlyn's two suns.

"They broke out," Kat yelled, throwing a bright green bolt into the morgar.

"Ours too," Kym said, not missing a beat and following Kat's attack with one of her own.

"Try not to hurt them," Jazin said, raising his arms. "Remember, they're not in control."

Kym, Kat, Ashlyn, and Jazin attacked, standing back to back in the middle of the hall. Kym threw bolts and swipes, fired blasts, and conjured shields, but nothing she did made a difference to the morgar. They just kept coming. But Kym knew she couldn't stop.

Kym wasn't sure how much time passed. All she knew was that her arms shook, her temples pounded, and stars flashed in her eyes. If Kym didn't rest soon, she'd pass out, or worse. Instead, she gritted her teeth and pushed forward, focusing her energy on hitting every morgar she targeted. But she knew it couldn't last. How long could she keep this up?

There was a flash of green light, and a massive green dome appeared around Kym and the others. Kym collapsed to her knees, panting, barely able to see straight. Kat stood in the middle of the dome, her hands extended to her sides, an intense look on her face. Kym couldn't believe it. She doubted Kat could keep the shield dome up for long.

Morgar threw themselves into the shield, and cracks spread

across the glittering green surface. Kym tried to raise her hands, but they felt like useless lumps. How was Kat's shield still intact?

"A…little…help," Kat snarled through gritted teeth as more cracks appeared in the dome.

Kym pushed herself up with all the strength she had left. There had to be some solution she hadn't thought of. She could fill the corridor with water. She didn't know if morgar could swim. They weren't very coordinated. At the very least, it would buy them time to come up with a real plan.

Light burst from the ceiling and tears filled Kym's eyes as the sudden change burned her retinas. But it wasn't the soft, pulsating light from Ashlyn's suns. This was artificial—from the long panels in the ceiling. Kym sighed as relief washed over her. If the power was back on, that meant the storm was running again.

Small, metallic balls rolled across the floor, and bright orange energy filled the hallway. Kym pressed her hands to her temples, her stomach lurching. Her exhaustion, along with the headache from the storm, had her on the verge of being sick. Kym clamped her mouth shut, breathing deeply through her nose as she fought the urge to vomit. Two figures ran toward them, their clothes glowing with the same bright orange energy.

"What're you doing here?" Kym moaned, more stunned than anything else.

"Isn't it obvious? We're here to help," Short said, offering Kym his hand. She took it, smiling feebly.

"You are?" Jazin panted his hands on his knees.

"Of course we are," Parker snapped. "Anderson has the storm running again. He wanted to activate the emergency hallway generators to subdue the morgar. We convinced him to give you a chance."

"Thanks," Kat said, feigning gratitude while she pressed the heels of her palms into her eye sockets. "I appreciate not having my head split open for the tenth time today."

Kym fought the urge to roll her eyes. She was grateful Short and Parker were there to help. Kym's gaze fell on Parker and Short's clothes. They were both wearing the storm mesh and had several collapsed spears, batons, and beads attached to their belts. Kym had never seen a Disciple with that much weaponry before. How'd Parker and Short get ahold of it? Had Hale helped them? Kym thought it was possible. She'd been against attacking the death cloud.

"I hope you have a plan," Kym said quickly as the morgar started getting to their feet. "Because we've got nothin'."

"Now that the power's back on, we can seal them in their cells," Short said quickly. "There's a manual override beside each door. Anderson will activate the cell generators when the emergency doors are secure. Get them inside, and we'll do the rest."

Kym nodded, her pulse slowing. With the lights on, the corridor didn't seem so endless. In fact, it looked crowded with all the morgar pressed against the walls. But that was a good thing. That meant they were right where Kym wanted them—by their cells.

Kym rushed forward, two bolts appearing in her hands. She threw the first at the closest morgar, and used her second bolt to fire a blast. Her bolt caught the morgar in the side, and it staggered back. It raised its drooped head, and Kym's water blast exploded against its chest.

The morgar flew into the cell, crashing against the opposite wall. Parker ran forward and waved her holowatch over a small, glowing panel. A thick, metal door slammed into place, securing the opening with an ominous thunk.

Smiling, Kym ran back into the fray. Kat threw a green swipe at the ground near a group of four morgar, and Kym moved instinctively. She waved her hands through the air, and four bolts appeared in front of her. She cleared her mind, focusing on the morgar staggering from Kat's attack, and flicked her wrist. The tracking bolts arched upward, hitting each morgar in the chest. Two flew back into adjoining cells, which Short quickly closed with a wave of his holowatch.

It didn't take long for them to get the rest of the morgar back in their cells. Parker and Short took different sides of the hall, throwing storm beads at the morgar if they grew too aggressive. Personally, Kym didn't see the point. The hard part of reducing the morgar's numbers had passed. She didn't see why Parker and Short needed to keep weakening them. They weren't trying to hurt the morgar after all.

Kym sank to the floor as Parker closed the cell on the last morgar. The others fell around her, red-faced and sweaty, but Kym couldn't stop herself from smiling. They'd prevented the morgar from getting out or hurting anyone else. Now, all Kym wanted was to check on the others and Theddie before going to their dorm. After the day she'd had, the peace of her little bed sounded beyond perfect.

"Where're the others?" Parker asked. She pressed her belt buckle, and the orange lines faded on her suit.

"Others?" Kym asked, her tired brain moving like a slug. "They're in medical with Theddie."

"You didn't see anyone else here?" Short said, the color draining from his cheeks.

"Nope," Kat shrugged. "What's the big deal, Little Man?"

"There were at least ten scientists and guards on this floor when the power went out." Short said, standing as his eyes widened. "And there's an empty cell."

The bottom fell out of Kym's stomach. They hadn't seen anyone since they'd arrived. Kym hadn't even registered that people would be there. How could she have forgotten? Now that Parker said it, Kym felt like an idiot. Of course guards and scientists were supervising the floor full of morgar. But if people were on the floor, where were they now? And where was the missing morgar?

Kym pushed herself to her feet as her fried muscles screamed in protest. She walked down the hall, away from the exit and the stairs. The guards and scientists couldn't have gone too far. There weren't that many places for them to hide. Kym hoped they knew it was safe to come out with the power back on.

Kym's insides turned to ice as she approached the end of the hall. A thin figure stood beside what Kym assumed had been a door.

What was left of it sat in a blackened, sandy heap on the slick floor. Kym froze, her Marks glowing, ready for the morgar to attack. Slowly, the morgar lifted its thin head, and sheets of blond hair slid out of its face.

"No."

Kym fell to her knees as Elena Collins stepped toward her. In all the chaos of the other morgar getting out, Kym had forgotten about her mother. But there she was, standing beside the blackened remains of a door. Dread coursed through Kym as the cold death bored deeper into her soul. What had her mother done?

Kym didn't move as Parker's storm bead rolled toward Elena. She barely even noticed the pounding headache as Jazin scooped Elena gently into his arms. All Kym could do was stare at the opening to the next room. She felt more icy death seeping out of the doorway. Swallowing her fear, Kym took a deep breath and stepped into the next room.

The guards and scientists were lying on the floor, their chests barely rising. Their skin was pale, like they hadn't seen the sun for months, and they stared blankly at the ceiling. None of them moved as Kym drew closer, her heart as heavy as a boulder.

"Great Pheil," Ashlyn whispered.

Kym fell to her knees, and it was like someone had ripped her in two. She'd been an idiot. Getting the morgar back in their cells hadn't mattered. Her mom, one morgar, was enough to cause untold damage. Kym went to that level to keep people safe. And because of her mother, she failed.

CHAPTER TWENTY-TWO

A PERFECTLY RISKY PLAN

"SEE ANYTHING?"

"Nothing! Just like all the others we've checked."

"Amber, c'mon. We need to keep going."

"We need to do something important," Amber groaned.

"This is important," Kym said heavily.

"Let's go. We don't want Short to leave us behind."

Kym followed Tomark and Amber to Short, who stood in the middle of the street. He yawned and glanced down at his holowatch with heavy eyes. Kym fought the urge to yawn herself. They'd been beyond the trunk line all night, checking the closest buildings for signs of morgar activity. They hadn't found a single one.

Kym wasn't complaining. After what her mother did to those doctors and guards, she didn't want to see the experimental floor again. That was why she volunteered to check buildings with Short instead of morgar duty with Parker. That was where Kat and Jazin were. The others were going to join them until Byrd came looking for help with medical stuff. Damon went with her, of course, but Ashlyn and Xander also offered to help. That left Amber checking buildings with Kym, Tomark, and Short. Amber wasted no time letting them know she'd rather be anywhere else.

Kym found it easier to ignore her. She had enough to worry about without Amber's bitter mood for having the "boring job." For Kym, their job was anything but boring. The trunk line had been down for almost an hour after the death cloud exploded. She wanted to make sure nothing got inside the line. The tower was already on high alert after what happened.

They worked from building to building, checking everything within a block of the trunk line. But just like all the others they'd checked, these too were empty. Kym's insides relaxed as they exited the final one. At least they weren't under threat of another attack. She still couldn't shake the strange, eerie cold from the previous night.

Short stepped over the trunk line, and Kym braced herself as she did the same. Her head split as she stepped across, and she bit her tongue, fighting the urge to cry out. The headache was worse than it used to be. Had Anderson increased the power in the trunk line? Given what happened, Kym wouldn't be surprised.

"Alright," Short said, rechecking his holowatch. "Let's do one last sweep of campus. Then we're in the clear."

"Seriously?" Amber groaned. "If anything got inside, we'd have seen it."

Kym's anger bubbled near the surface. Why did Amber need to make such a big deal about everything? Kym knew checking buildings they already knew were empty was beneath the Fire Princess, but Amber volunteered to help. Why was she complaining?

"We'll check from above," Tomark said, his fingers sliding into Kym's.

The pressure of his hand on hers was enough to make Kym's heartbeat slow. Kym invoked her Marks, and power from the water charm surged through her like electricity. She shot upward, Tomark's hand still held in hers, and didn't let go until they were one hundred feet in the air.

"Thanks," Kym said sheepishly, her hair drifting dreamlike around her face.

"It's fine," Tomark smiled, his own long, wavy hair flying back in the wind.

"She just...she could be nicer," Kym spat out, scanning the ground below for anything out of the ordinary. She couldn't see anything.

"This is an adjustment for her," Tomark said calmly. "Remember, she's been a Favored her whole life."

"That's no excuse for her to be mean," Kym retorted. "And we stuck her with Short."

"Short can handle the Fire Princess. She's just mad she's not calling the shots."

"Because everything went perfectly the last time we did that," Kym said, feeling suddenly heavy.

How'd everything go so wrong? Every time she tried to help, it blew up in her face—freeing Theddie, getting their magic back, stealing the charms, breaking out of Tenbatter, trying to leave the Rulers. Every time she tried to do the right thing, it made things worse. Was fighting Thed out of Princirum really the right thing? If she were honest with herself, Kym didn't know the answer anymore.

Kym had gone to see the scientists and guards her mother attacked that morning, hoping things had improved. She'd been wrong. They were all in beds on the experimental floor, staring blankly up into space while Dr. Gwin and her team ran around them, scanning things and taking vitals. Kym doubted they knew people were trying to help them. They didn't respond when Dr. Gwin tested them. They were dead to the world.

Kym focused her energy and shot forward, the wind howling in her ears. She heard Tomark behind her, but she didn't look back. Instead, she focused on the ground, trying to catch any sign of something out of the ordinary. But just like before, everything looked fine.

After circling campus several times, Kym and Tomark returned to the ground. Amber and Short stood waiting for them on the tower steps. Even from one hundred feet in the air, she could tell Amber's mood hadn't improved. Kym landed gently beside Amber, her skin feeling oddly warm as the water charm's energy faded.

"Anything?" Tomark asked, appearing silently beside Kym.

"Nothing," Short said. "No sign of anything that shouldn't be here anyway. There's damage to some of the buildings, but nothing we can't fix."

Kym stared at the tower. Several pieces of the tan stone were discolored, and there were dark cracks in the glass walls. Kym sighed. At least the damage wasn't worse. The death energy they removed from Theddie could have destroyed six Disciple towers. They were lucky.

"There are signs of decay everywhere," Amber said. "It seems the trunk line stopped most of it before it reached campus."

"But it must have been too much for the generator to handle," Short added, his voice dark. "Since it didn't stop all of it."

"If you thought that thing could stop pure death, you're delusional," Amber said, rolling her eyes.

"Hey, it stopped magic before," Tomark said defensively.

"Yes, magic," Amber said. "But the death wave wasn't magic. Sure, Jazin used magic to remove it, but the death itself wasn't magical. It's just like when you control air. Your energy surrounds and moves it, nothing more. The trunk line neutralized Jazin's magic. After that, it was free to drift through space and damage whatever it touched."

Kym opened her mouth, ready to retort, but stopped herself. There was no point arguing with Amber, especially when she was right. Amber may be a snob who treated most people like they were beneath her, but her magical knowledge was second only to the Rulers. And it didn't help that her explanation also made total sense.

Kym wondered what Amber would do if she were ever wrong about something? Probably burn the place down out of anger. Kym stifled a laugh at the thought.

Kym followed Short and Tomark up the tower stairs, Amber gliding silently beside her. Kym expected the library to be empty, so she was shocked to find it full of people. The long benches that usually surrounded the tables sat in the normally open space. At least three people sat on each bench, their skin pale beneath their thin blankets. Doctors and nurses ran around, yelling instructions to one another in panicked voices.

Kym's heart froze as a cold wave rushed over her. Why weren't these people being treated on the medical level? And why were the doctors panicking? Kym's mind went to the worst-case scenario—had something happened with the morgar again?

Kym scanned the room, looking for something to explain what was going on. She spotted Nurse Byrd and Ashlyn kneeling beside a bench, examining a patient. Kym ran toward them, her heart pounding in her chest.

"What's going on? I thought you were helping on medical?"

"We were," Ashlyn said in a rush.

"Were?" Tomark asked.

"It's strange," Byrd said, not looking up as she waved a scanner over the woman lying in front of her. "People started showing up a few hours ago. We took as many as we could, but they just kept coming."

Kym took a closer look at the woman Byrd was examining. She didn't look good at all. Her hair was thin and discolored, and her skin was ashen. Her eyes drifted around, never focusing on anything for too long. Kym knew nothing about medicine, but she knew sick people when she saw them.

Byrd's scanner beeped, and Kym stepped beside her, eager to see the results. But no matter how closely Kym studied the projection floating above the disk in Byrd's hand, she couldn't make heads or tails of it. Byrd, of course, knew what it meant, and it couldn't be good. Why else would her face turn white?

"She's like the others," Byrd said to Ashlyn, pushing past Kym to kneel by the woman.

"Again?" Ashlyn said, and the fear in her voice made Kym's heart race.

"Their symptoms are the same?" Short asked. "Can you treat them?"

"I…it's really," Byrd stammered, as she draped a blanket over the woman.

"Get to the point," Amber said coolly, her eyes narrowed at Byrd.

Kym wanted to slap Amber. Why was compassion so hard for

her to understand? First Short, and now Byrd? They'd helped Kym and the others since they arrived. Kym wasn't going to let Amber walk all over them. The next time they were alone, Kym needed to talk to her.

"My dear," Byrd said, her normally warm voice uncharacteristically dark, "all the people we've seen are presenting with physical and mental deterioration."

Kym shook her head. She didn't know what deterioration meant, but it didn't sound like a sickness. And how could multiple people have it? Kym knelt beside the woman, her chest barely moving as she drew thin, raspy breaths. She looked like a good wind could knock her over. It was just like when Kym's mom was first…

Kym's mouth fell open. No. It couldn't be. She stood up, her eyes flashing over the room, looking for some sign that she was wrong. Every person she saw looked like they were on the brink of death. The cold she'd felt when she walked into the building made sense. Why hadn't she realized what was happening? Like the scientists and guards from the previous night, these people were infected with death.

But that was impossible. These people had been in their rooms or other parts of the tower while Kym and the others fought to keep the morgar on the experimental level. Had all of her hard work been for nothing? Death couldn't have infected them all, could it? Kym needed to figure this out. But with doctors, nurses, and helpers running this way and that, she could barely hear herself think.

Kym started walking, not really sure what she was looking for. Most of the activity in the library was in the lobby, nearest the front doors and elevators. That gave Kym an idea. She turned down the nearest aisle and walked away from all the noise. The sound of shuffling feet told her the others weren't far behind.

The buzz of activity faded the more bookshelves Kym walked through. After a few minutes, Kym spotted a dark corner where several old, worn armchairs sat out of sight. Kym smiled. This was perfect.

"Hey," Tomark said, his green eyes narrowed. "Why'd you walk off?"

"I didn't want to be overheard," Kym whispered even though there was no one around. The last thing she wanted to do was start a panic.

"Kym, spit it out," Amber snapped, gliding up with Short and Byrd.

"Where's Ash?" Kym asked, noticing the absence of the smiling redhead.

"She said something about getting the others," Amber huffed. "I'm sure she'll find us."

"Kym," Short said. "What's goin' on?"

"I think," she said slowly, "that all of these people are turning into morgar."

A shiver ran over her arms as the thought sunk in. Saying it out loud somehow made it worse, but that wasn't even the worst part. Kym didn't know how long it took for sick people to become morgar like those locked several floors above. A few weeks? A month? How many of them would be left when it was all said and done?

"That's what we theorized," Byrd said. "We gave Damon a room to conduct an examination."

"You let him do that alone?" Tomark asked.

"Don't worry," Byrd said calmly. "Xander's with him. None of these people are as bad as the morgar on the experimental level. Damon should be safe."

Kym's breath caught in her throat. That's what Dr. Gwin and Anderson said about the morgar when they first saw them, and that turned out to be a disaster. The sound of hurrying feet reached Kym's ears. Ashlyn appeared a moment later, Damon and Xander right behind her.

"Finally," Amber said impatiently.

"We…it took us…just shut up, Amber," Ashlyn panted, her hands on her knees.

"What did you learn?" Kym asked Damon. There was no point avoiding the topic.

"It's…weird," Damon said slowly.

"Weird?" Tomark asked.

"Yeah. I examined three people, and on the surface, it looks like they're turning into morgar. But…" Damon trailed off, his eyes darting around as he wrung his fingers.

Kym leaned in, the hairs on her arms standing on end. What had Damon found? Had he, somehow, found a way to save the morgar? These people weren't as bad as Theddie had been. Could they save them after all?

"The death in them…it's not growing."

"Growing?" Byrd asked.

"I don't really know," Damon said. "But the other morgar I've seen, the death in them was always growing, while their life faded away. But for these people, the death is just…there."

Kym shook her head. Damon wasn't making any sense. Death was a parasite. How could it not flourish inside a living being? Clearly, the others felt the same way, given the nearly uniform looks of shock on their faces. The only person who didn't look entirely confused was Amber. Her golden eyes narrowed, and her mouth hung open slightly.

"Of course," Amber whispered, more to herself than to anyone else. "With its connection severed, its ability to spread would be compromised. It makes sense, really."

Kym groaned as a light throbbing bloomed around her temples. Now Amber and Damon weren't making sense. What was she even talking about?

"Care to share with the rest of us?" Xander asked.

"The death we pulled from Theddie," Amber snapped like it was the obvious answer.

"What about Theddie?" Kym asked. What did this have to do with him?

"Don't you see?" Amber groaned, rolling her eyes. "We severed his connection to Thed."

"Amber, we know," Tomark said. "We were there."

"When Hale attacked the death we removed, it exploded, right?" Amber asked, turning to Short.

"Yeah," Short said slowly, his eyes narrowing at Amber. "We saw the damage it caused outside."

"Exactly. It damaged the buildings. The death wave must've affected the people too."

"That's why the death inside them isn't getting worse," Damon said excitedly. "They're not connected to Thed. They're just…dying."

Kym's insides grew numb as Damon's words washed over her. Yet another thing to add to the list of things she caused. But not on her own. This wouldn't have happened if Anderson hadn't ordered Hale to attack the death cloud. All of this—the morgar getting out, the affected scientists and guards, and now the sick people and building damage—it was all his fault.

But Kym knew blaming Anderson wouldn't solve anything. And did it matter who was responsible? For Kym, it didn't. All that mattered was finding a way to fix it. She owed everyone there that much.

"We need to fix this," Kym said.

"How?" Tomark asked. "Last time we tried to fix things it didn't go that well, remember?"

"Kym, remember what Thed said?" Ashlyn said quietly. "Ripping him out of people won't work. His other anchors will keep him here."

"Would taking the death out of the affected people work?" Byrd asked. "Like you said, its connection to Thed has been severed. We could—"

"Where would we put it?" Amber cut across Byrd. "Disposing of death isn't like throwing out the trash. It has to go somewhere."

"I wish we could send it back to Nothingness," Xander huffed. "At least there, the death wouldn't bother us here."

Kym laughed, as did Short and Damon. She couldn't help herself. Xander's whole idea was ridiculous. And how would they send the death to Nothingness? Nothingness was the land of the dead. Last she checked, there was only one way to get there. And what would happen if they did? Nothingness was Thed's domain, and Kym doubted he'd welcome them there with open arms. It's not like they could fight him there and come home after.

Kym smiled at the thought. If it were possible, it would be a perfect solution. If they defeated Thed in Nothingness, all their problems would disappear. They'd disconnect Thed, and there'd be no danger of death destroying Princirum. It would stay in Nothingness where it belonged. It was a perfect plan. There was only one problem; Kym had no idea how to get to Nothingness.

For the first time in her life, Kym wished she'd paid more attention in religious studies class in school. Her teachers discussed Nothingness several times, but Kym hadn't bothered to listen. Now, Kym wished she had. Kym racked her brain. Who could she ask? Her first thought was the Rulers. They knew more than anyone about this stuff, but they weren't an option. So who else was there?

The answer came to her in an instant—High Priest Perla. Kym ran off, her heart pounding, her skin feeling like it was vibrating. The others yelled after her, but Kym ignored them. It would take too long to explain. Besides, she knew they'd say she was crazy. Kym didn't want to give them a chance before she knew for sure.

Kym stopped in the library lobby, a stitch blooming in her side. She scanned the room, searching for the long, billowing robes she knew well. She spotted Perla bending over a young man on a makeshift bed, her hands held over his chest. Kym ran over to her, stumbling over her feet in her excitement.

"Blessed One!" Perla gasped, catching Kym by the shoulders. "You honor me with you—"

"Tell me about Nothingness," Kym said in a rush.

Kym expected Perla to look shocked. What she didn't expect was for her mouth to actually fall open in surprise. Clearly, the others shared Perla's feelings. Tomark, Byrd, and Amber stared at Kym, while Damon, Ashlyn, Xander, and Short looked like Kym knocked the wind out of them. Kym didn't care. She stared at Perla, determined not to miss a word.

"Forgive me, Blessed One," Perla said slowly. "I'm not sure what you're asking."

"Kym, what're you thinking?" Amber asked, her voice clipped.

Kym took a deep breath, trying to calm her excited nerves. Xander said it as a joke, but it really was the best plan. Death in Princirum caused too much damage. Death wasn't supposed to be with the living. They needed to fight death in a place where it couldn't hurt anyone. Kym didn't know why she hadn't thought of it sooner. They needed to fight death in Nothingness. All she needed to do was get there.

"How do you get to Nothingness?"

"Kym," Perla said slowly, her face full of concern, "Nothingness is a land where death runs wild. Where our souls wander when they've reached the end of the gods' path. It's where we search for peace."

"I know that," Kym said quickly, unable to keep the impatience from her voice. "But it's…it's a real place, right?"

The others groaned audibly around Kym. The sound brought Kym's irritation itching to the surface. She knew she sounded crazy. Just two minutes before, she would've laughed at the idea. But now…she didn't need their negativity. They didn't see what she was trying to do. They couldn't understand.

"Why would you want to go to Nothingness?" Perla asked. "You are living, blessed to be among the Great Mother's creation. Your time to wander hasn't come."

This time, it was Kym who stifled a groan. Why was this so hard for them to understand? She didn't want to die and go to Nothingness. She wanted to go there, cut the god of death off from the land of the living, and come back.

"There may be a way," Perla said defensively. "You wouldn't be the first to try. Devout Favored have ventured there, determined to end the reign of the gods' sworn enemy."

"So, it's possible?" Tomark said, and Kym heard the shock in his voice.

"I'm not sure. All Favored who embarked on such quests never returned."

Kym's mouth fell open as she stared at Perla, her eyes growing wide. So, not only could she get to Nothingness, but other Favored had gone there before. Kym's breathing quickened as her heart fluttered. This was how she could end it—the way to stop Thed was from the realm of the dead. But Kym still had no idea how to get there.

Perla bowed to Tomark, inclined her head to Kym and the others, and hurried off to the bedside of another patient. Kym didn't mind. She had a feeling Perla told her all she knew. After all, Perla was a Pro acting the part of a High Priest. Kym turned to the others, eager to discuss what they learned, and but stopped herself. Their skepticism was unmistakable on their faces.

Kym shook her head. Clearly, they all thought she'd lost her mind. She needed to talk about this, but who could she talk to? Tomark, Ashlyn, Xander, Amber, and Damon already thought she was nuts. There had to be someone in the tower who wouldn't reject her idea the first time they heard it.

Kym's feet moved automatically. Before she knew what was happening, she was pummeling the elevator button with her fist. She stepped inside, and everyone but Byrd followed her. Kym didn't say a word as the elevator shot upward, watching the numbers flash by on the screen until the doors slid open.

The experimental floor was a wreck. Decayed piles of glass and wall littered the floor, and several lights flickered halfheartedly. Kat, Parker, and Jazin stood huddled in the center of the corridor, each looking in a different direction. Parker and Jazin both wore serious expressions, while Kat looked like she'd rather be anywhere else.

"Finally!" Kat yelled, throwing her hands in the air as Kym approached. "I thought I was gonna die of boredom! Let's…"

Kat trailed off, her eyes narrowing as Kym drew nearer. Clearly, she could tell there was something on Kym's mind. Kym took a deep breath. How could she tell Kat she wanted to go to Nothingness? It would be easiest just to say it. Kat wasn't one for sugarcoating things anyway.

"I'm going to Nothingness to fight Thed. Wanna come?"

Kym heard the others groan for what felt like the millionth time. She ignored them, not taking her eyes off of Kat while she forced her irritation down. The others could think whatever they wanted, but Kym knew she could do anything if Kat was with her. Kat stared at Kym, her brown eyes narrowing as she cocked her head to the side.

"Did she lose it or somethin'?" Kat asked, peering around Kym to look at the others.

"Kym, what the Nothingness are you talking about?" Tomark stepped in front of Kym, and she saw the concern in his eyes.

"I want to fight Thed," Kym said firmly.

"Just to be clear, you want to go to the land of the dead and fight the literal god of death?" Xander asked, his deep voice full of disbelief.

"Are you sure she didn't hit her head?" Kat murmured.

Kym pressed her hands over her eyes. Why didn't they see this was the way to end everything? They were the Vanquishers. They'd spent their time training to fight death demons. Wasn't this the next logical step? To stop all of it—the death demons, the morgar, the sickness, Thed's control of the Rulers. This was how they used their magic to do better. But Kym couldn't do it alone. For her plan to work, she needed her friends.

"Look," Kym said, lowering her hands. "Fighting death isn't working. We've done it for years, and Thed is on the verge of destroying the land of the living. Look what happened last night. Too many people are getting hurt, even when we try to keep them safe. We need to stop Thed before he causes any more damage, and the way we do that is by fighting him in Nothingness."

Kym paused. Kat, Ashlyn, and Short's eyes were wide, while

the others still looked like Kym was speaking another language. But that didn't stop Kym's insides from swelling like a balloon.

"Whether we believe the gods chose us to end this or not, we're losing. We're standing in the last pocket of true life in Princirum, and because of us and the choices we made, that life is in danger. I'm not putting people in danger anymore. We need to do better. Fighting the Favored, or the morgar, or the death demons isn't enough. We need to fight Thed."

Kym lapsed into silence. She waited, hoping someone would say something. What would she do if they said no? They all looked either shocked, stunned, or confused. Could she go to Nothingness and fight Thed on her own? Finally, Parker broke the silence.

"It's a sound battle strategy, Kym. It keeps the risk of unnecessary casualties low. But your plan…it's insane. How're you gonna reach the land of the dead?"

"Perla said Favored have gone there," Kym said excitedly, happy someone was finally on her side.

"She also said none of them ever came back," Amber countered.

"How would we get there?" Damon asked, taking a step toward Kym. "Don't you have to…you know…die?"

"Not necessarily."

Kym spun around so fast she nearly lost her balance. She stared at Jazin, who was looking at her with an odd expression on his face. His eyes were wide, and his dark eyebrows had disappeared under the black strands that hung over his pale forehead. Kym's heart rate quickened. This was what she'd wanted. What did Jazin know?

"What the Thed are you talking about?" Ashlyn asked, her voice full of disbelief.

"When I warp, I harness the energy from a death site to open a gateway to move instantly from one place to the next."

"That's like darkness warping," Xander said. "When I warp, I travel through the plane of darkness."

"Exactly," Jazin said.

"I think…I think I'm traveling through Nothingness when I warp."

Kym's hands shook at her sides. This was it—the answer she'd been searching for. Jazin was the key to getting them to Nothingness. All they needed to do was find a death site, and they could end this horrible nightmare once and for all.

"Hold up," Short said, bringing Kym's excitement screeching to a halt. "You can't just go to Nothingness and fight the god of death on your own."

"Why not?" Kat shrugged. "Parker said it was a good plan."

Kym stared at Parker. She'd been the first to agree with Kym. Kym knew she wanted this war over just as much as she did. So why wasn't she telling them to go?

"Short's right," Tomark said, stepping in front of Kym. "We need a better plan than 'go there and fight.' The last time we had a half-formed plan, it blew up in our faces. Literally."

Kym bit her lip. Why wasn't Tomark siding with her on this? She knew fighting wasn't his first impulse, and that he was worried for everyone's safety, but they were out of options. Why did he want to wait? Kym knew this was the right thing to do.

"Kym, Tomark's right," Parker said. "We'll need proper planning and resources to pull this off."

Kym blinked several times. We? Who was Parker talking about? Kym stared at Parker. She didn't think she was going, did she?

"I'll take it to the Council," Parker said, walking past Kym to the elevator. "They have a meeting in an hour. In the meantime, wait in your dorm. And I beg you," she added as the elevator door closed, "don't do anything until I get back."

Kym wanted to leave right then. While Parker was off wasting time with the Council, they could be out finding a death site for Jazin to use. However, Kym was officially outnumbered, and Tomark and Amber dragged her back to the dorm. Kym paced back and forth while the others took turns staring at her like she'd lost her mind. She didn't know why they bothered. Parker said her plan wasn't crazy. And if Jazin said he could do it, then Kym didn't see why they were so skeptical.

Kym started to worry after several hours had passed. What was taking Parker so long? She didn't care whether the Council accepted the plan. Kym was going to go through with it. It was too important not to. But would the others join her if the Council said they couldn't go? Kym knew Kat would join her, permission or not, so at least Kym wouldn't be alone.

The common room door swung open, and Kym finally stopped her pacing. Parker walked inside, dressed in storm mesh, a slight smile on her face. Commander Hale, Perla, Mrs. Mizel and Marek followed Parker inside. Kym's insides tensed as she stared open-mouthed at her father. What was he doing there? Had the Council voted to not let them go, and Marek was there to talk Kym out of going alone? Kym shifted her feet as subtly as she could into a fighting stance. Not even Marek could talk her out of going.

"Kym." Marek wrapped his arms around Kym. Taken aback, she tried to pull away, but stopped when she felt him shaking. "I was wrong."

Kym didn't move a muscle. Her father hadn't hugged her since she first arrived, and they'd been at odds ever since. If she were honest with herself, she'd thought he'd never hug her again. What changed?

"I thought by keeping your mother here, I was helping her. I thought Anderson, Gwin, and the storm were making her better. But after she...those guards...I was wrong. I'm so sorry for not believing in you."

"Thank you."

Kym closed her eyes and rested her head on Marek's chest. It was as if the last few months hadn't happened. She let her father's arm's take her, and all of her worry melted away. She'd been driven by her anger toward him for so long she'd forgotten how small her problems seemed when he was there. But no matter how much love passed between them, Kym couldn't forget that the only reason he was there was because her mom finally lost control.

"You need to go do what's right. I trust you."

Kym pulled away from her father, not daring to breathe. What did he mean? Kym looked over Marek's shoulder to Parker. She was smiling, as were Hale, Perla, and Mrs. Mizel. Kym still didn't understand why they were all there.

"The Council approved your plan," Parker nodded, no doubt seeing the confusion on Kym's face. "We're all cleared to go. A team of seven volunteers will join us. Let's go fight the god of death."

CHAPTER TWENTY-THREE

THROUGH THE
TEAR

KYM STARED OUT THE JEEP WINDOW, WATCHING THE RUINED CITY
buildings flash by. She took a deep breath, trying to stop her hands
from shaking. She couldn't believe this was actually happening. In a
few hours, they'll have defeated Thed, her mom would be better,
and everything would go back to normal. This was going to fix
everything.

"How much farther?" Parker asked from the driver's seat.

"A little ways outside the city," Jazin breathed. He sat beside
Kym with his eyes closed, his black Marks glittering on his thin,
pale arms.

"Good," Parker said. She pressed a button on the dashboard.
"Alright, people. Stay close. The last thing we need is to get
separated."

Kym twisted in her seat. Two other jeeps sped behind them,
their bumpers less than a foot from each other. Kym swallowed as
they hurtled under the city walls. She hadn't left the city since
getting her magic back. It felt strange, like she was leaving home
for the first time all over again. Kym shook her head. She couldn't
let doubt get to her now. She needed to leave—it was the right
thing. All that mattered was fighting Thed. Gods' plan or not,
fighting Thed was her responsibility.

"We're close," Jazin said a short while later, his eyes
fluttering.

"Finally," Xander said. Kym looked across Jazin at Xander, who
was twisting the hem of his shirt around his fingers.

"Hey," Kym whispered, leaning across Jazin. "You good?"

"Yeah," Xander said, nodding his head. "I just…what if this doesn't work? What if we fail?"

"We won't," Kym said pointedly, grabbing Xander's hand. She knew Xander was afraid of failing. That was how Melana manipulated him into stealing the Conduit for her.

"How do you know?" Xander asked.

"Because we're doing this together," Kym smiled. "And I know we can do it."

When the jeep finally stopped, Kym flung open the door with shaking hands. She climbed out, Jazin and Xander right behind her. They were in the middle of a vast, grassy field. Little bushes and flowers peppered the surface, but other than that, it was green as far as Kym could see. Kym couldn't remember the last time she'd been anywhere so peaceful. It reminded her of the mountain valley she used to sneak to when she needed a break from Wadita. The thought made her heart ache. Would she ever see that place again?

"Unload the gear," Parker ordered.

Kym did as Parker instructed. She hurried to the back of their jeep and grabbed one of the supply packs. Kym slung it over her shoulder, and her knees nearly buckled under the weight. What was in them? Kym hadn't bothered to look before they left.

Kym stepped aside so the others could get their gear. While Tomark, Jazin, Xander, Kat, Damon, Amber, and Ashlyn got their packs, Parker's soldiers double-checked all the gear they'd brought. They were dressed in storm mesh and had spears, batons, and beads hanging from their thick belts. Kym only knew one of the volunteers, aside from Parker. She wasn't surprised that Short volunteered.

"We're at the site," Parker said into her holowatch.

"Good," Hale's voice rang out from Parker's wrist. "We've located you. We'll monitor the surrounding area from here. May Kensrad's bravery flow through you. Good luck."

Kym fought the urge to roll her eyes. She knew she should be grateful. The Council agreed to let them try her idea after all. Well, almost agreed. Anderson was the only Councilor who voted against the plan. Kym's excitement deflated slightly. Did Anderson think the plan would fail? Kym pushed the idea from her mind. It didn't matter what Anderson thought. All the other Councilors believed in her plan. So did Parker and her soldiers. And that was all Kym cared about.

"Jazin," Parker said, bringing Kym back to the group. "Whenever you're ready."

Jazin stepped forward, and Kym saw his hands shaking. His face, which was always pale, looked white as a sheet. She knew he was nervous. After all, opening a portal to the land of the dead wasn't something you did every day. But Kym knew it was worth it, and she knew he could do it. She'd seen Jazin do incredible things in the past.

"I know I'm the last person to ask this question," Kat whispered beside Kym. "But do we have a plan?"

"I..." Jazin said, his voice trembling. "I'm gonna try and open a portal."

"Try?" Parker's voice cracked through the air like a whip. "I thought you could do this?"

"I will," Jazin corrected. Kym saw his eyes dart toward Amber, who smiled gently. "I don't know how long I can keep it open. So, whatever you're gonna do in there, do it fast."

Kym's veins pulsated with electricity as she bounced on the balls of her feet. Once Jazin opened the portal, they'd fight Thed and end this. How long would it take for things to return to normal? Kym doubted it would happen overnight. But maybe, with Thed's anchors severed, the morgar would regain their humanity. Finally, after all this time, she'd get her mom back.

Jazin raised his trembling arms, his black Marks glittering. He waved his hand through the air, and Kym held her breath, waiting for something to happen. A sound like a cannon blast filled Kym's ears as the air in front of her ripped open. Kym's insides froze as her heart thudded in her throat. She staggered back, knocked off balance by the force radiating from the tear. She'd seen a tear like that before. When Thed possessed Melana during the Festival of

Creation, she summoned a death demon from Nothingness by opening a rip in space. This was it. Jazin had done it.

The bright green grass beneath the rip blackened and withered. Kym scurried back, her heart racing as the cold inside her intensified. The circle of dead grass spread, consuming everything around it. Kym squared up her feet, ready to fight the source of death, but there was nothing. How were they supposed to go to Nothingness if they couldn't get near the portal?

Damon sprinted past Kym, his white Marks shining. He jerked his arms up, and clouds of white mist rose from the green grass around the rip. However, it didn't blacken or wither the way plants normally did when Damon pulled life from them. The grass was yellow and dry, but it wasn't dead. Damon raised his hands, and the cloud of life drifted gently around himself, Jazin, and the rip.

Kym sighed as the cold throbbing of death lessened in her stomach. Relieved, she looked at the ground. The grass nearest the rip was still blackened and dead, but it was no longer spreading.

"Everyone okay?" Parker asked. Everyone nodded. "Jazin, what the Thed was that?"

"Death's seeping out of the opening," Jazin said through clenched teeth. "If I keep the portal open, I don't know what will—"

"Keep going," Damon cut across Jazin, sounding just as strained. "I can keep the death contained."

"You guys go," Jazin said. "You're wasting time."

Kym shook her head. This was all wrong. She needed Damon and Jazin in Nothingness to fight Thed. Kym, Kat, Amber, Tomark, Ashlyn, Xander, Parker, Short, and the other soldiers were good fighters, but they didn't stand a chance against Thed without Jazin and Damon. They were their best weapons against him. Leaving them behind wasn't part of Kym's plan.

"What? No," Amber said, her golden eyes wide.

"We can't leave you alone here," Short said.

"Out of the question," Parker nodded. "Two others will stay to help secure our retreat."

Kym bit her lip. She didn't like the idea of leaving more people behind, but she knew Parker was right. Jazin and Damon already looked like they were ready to pass out, and they were only keeping the portal open. What would happen if morgar showed up? Or a death demon? Or the Unity and Lucia? Would Kym and the others be stranded in Nothingness if something happened to Jazin or Damon?

"I'll stay with them," Ashlyn said, stepping away from the group.

"Me too," Xander said, joining Ashlyn.

"Absolutely not," Parker said, and Kym couldn't help but agree. They couldn't go to Nothingness with half of their Favored. "We need you in Nothingness. Two of my soldiers will—"

"They need us here," Ashlyn cut across Parker, her tone uncharacteristically stern. "Your soldiers are good, Parker, but they don't have the battle experience we do. We know how to fight death demons…and Favored."

"You guys need to go. Now," Xander said, handing his and Ashlyn's packs to Short and Tomark. "Don't worry. We'll keep them safe."

They exchanged hurried good-byes. Kym wrapped her arms tightly around Ashlyn's and Xander's necks, wishing each of them luck. She nodded to Jazin and Damon, not daring to do more as they struggled to keep the tear open.

Kym's stomach twisted into a knot. Things were already going wrong, and they weren't even in Nothingness yet. How could they defeat Thed when only half of them were going? Kym needed her friends for this plan to work. She stared at the black tear in the air, and a shiver ran down her spine. She couldn't turn back now.

Kym took a deep breath, and energy from the water charm surge through her. Her blue Marks appeared on her arms as she stepped toward the rip. The icy numbness inside her intensified with each step until she felt nothing else. Kym glanced over her shoulder and saw the others right behind her. Mustering her courage, Kym closed her eyes and took the final step.

Emptiness consumed her. Every thought and feeling Kym ever

experienced faded away, leaving her hollow, empty, and alone. The hopelessness was so heavy it made her body ache. It was too much. She couldn't bear one more step into this agony. But strangely, this despair wasn't unfamiliar to Kym. It was like something from another life. Somehow, she knew she was strong enough to handle it.

Kym opened her eyes, and all around her was blackness. Tall, black walls rose around her, disappearing into the void above. The walls extended ahead of her, stretching on as far as she could see. Kym shook her head. This place stirred something deep in her memory. Where had she seen it before? Kym turned to ask the others, and her heart stopped. Everyone but Tomark was on the ground, their hands at their throats, their faces slowly turning blue.

Kym ran forward, her heart pounding in her ears. What was going on? Why couldn't they breathe? She and Tomark weren't having any issues breathing. Kym fell to her knees beside Kat, who opened and closed her mouth, her eyes flashing wildly. Kym racked her brain. She needed to save them, but she had no idea how.

There was a flash of silver, and a gust of cool wind swept over Kym. Kym's hair whipped around her as tears filled her eyes. Tomark held his hands over his head, his silver Marks and the air charm on his wrist glowing as a dome of air swirled around them. Kym sighed as Kat gasped, spit flying from her lips. A chorus of coughs filled Kym's ears, and she relaxed, patting Kat gently on the back.

"You okay?" Kym breathed.

"What the Thed?" Kat sputtered.

"It's like there's no air here," Short panted.

Small bumps rose over Kym's skin as Short's words washed over her that had nothing to do with the chilling numbness. How could there be no air? She and Tomark didn't have any trouble breathing. But why could they breathe when everyone else couldn't?

Beside Kym, Parker shoved her hand inside her pack. She pulled it out, revealing a small, flat disk that Kym didn't recognize.

Parker pressed a button on the disk's rim and threw it outside Tomark's air bubble. It landed silently on the black ground, and Kym stared at Parker's holowatch.

"This can't be right," Parker breathed, although Kym caught every word. "It says there's nothing out there."

"Are you surprised?" Kat snorted. "It's Nothingness."

"But that's impossible," Parker retorted. "There can't be nothing out there. I can see the hundred foot walls right in front of me."

Kym's head started to hurt. First, some of them couldn't breathe when they arrived, and now Parker's scanner thing said there wasn't anything out there. Even in the strange blackness, Kym saw the vast, black walls stretching ahead of her. How could Parker's scanner not see them when she could?

"Is it broken?" Tomark asked, his voice slightly strained as he held his hands over his head. "I mean, we're standing on something."

Kym eyes flashed down. The ground was like the walls—made of some shimmering, black stone. It was unlike anything she'd ever seen. But, she could see it. It existed. So what was it?

Kat's finger's closed tightly around Kym's wrist. She pulled herself up, and Kym's shoulder felt like it was going to pop out of its socket. Kym gasped, but Kat didn't seem to hear her. Kat focused on black ground, her brown eyes narrowed. She raised her arm, invoking her green Marks and the earth charm on her upper arm, and waved her hand. Kym braced herself, ready for the ground to split open. Nothing happened.

"Any time, Kat," Kym said.

"It. Won't. Move." Kat punctuated each word with a wave, but the black ground remained still. "It's not earth."

"Of course!" Amber said. "Kym, hold this."

Kym barely had time to blink before Amber slipped the delicate, red ring in her palm. Kym stared at it, her mouth hanging open. Why would Amber take off the fire charm? Kym couldn't use it, and it made Amber the most powerful Fire Favored. What was Amber doing?

Amber waved her hand, and just like when Kat tried, nothing happened. Kym shook her head. She'd seen Amber make fire out of thin air countless times. She didn't need the fire charm to do that. Kym's pulse quickened as she looked from Kat to Amber. Something was wrong with their magic. But what?

"Nothingness isn't part of Princirum," Amber said quickly, slipping the fire charm back on her finger. "The elements the gods created don't exist here. Skilled Fire Favored use heat from the sun to create a spark that we increase into a flame. But there's no sun here. There's just…"

"Nothing," Parker said, her eyes growing wide as she looked back at her holowatch.

Kym wanted to smack herself in the forehead. How could she have been so stupid? Of course, their magic wouldn't work here. Magic came from the gods and was part of Princirum itself. But if Amber was right, how'd Tomark make air for them to breathe? And why hadn't Kym been affected at all?

"If you can't do magic," Short said, "should we go—"

"We can still do magic," Amber said. She waved her hand, and flames appeared above her palm as the fire charm glowed on her middle finger. "The charms provide a direct connection to the Conduit. So long as we have them on, we should be able to do magic here."

Kym's hand flew to the delicate, crystal thread around her neck. Now she understood why she could breathe when she first arrived. The water charm granted Kym all the abilities she had under the water, including breathing water. The water charm had kept her alive.

"Good thing we left Ashlyn and Xander behind," Kat whispered so only Kym could hear. "They'd be useless here."

"Alright," Parker said, stepping into the middle of the air dome by Tomark.

"We stay together. Tomark, can this thing move with us?"

"Yeah," Tomark nodded. "If we go slow."

"Good. Kym and Amber, you're in the front with me. Kat, take the back with Short and Ezark. The rest of you, cover Tomark. The last thing we need is to suffocate here."

They moved forward, their footsteps oddly silent on the black stone. Kym turned her head this way and that, looking for any sign of trouble in the light cast by Amber's fire. But all she could see were the black walls—stretching on for eternity. Kym shivered as she looked down the endless path. Something about the walls seemed very familiar, but Kym couldn't place them. She knew she'd seen them before, but she couldn't imagine where.

After walking for nearly fifteen minutes, they reached a fork in the path. Kym peered down the new paths, which looked identical. She had no idea which one to take. If she picked the wrong path, would they wander around forever? She turned to Parker and Amber, desperately wanting one of them to take the lead. But they looked just as confused as she did.

"Any ideas?" Amber asked.

Kym watched Amber's golden eyes flicker in the light of the fire above her hands. There was something in Amber's eyes that Kym hadn't seen very often. Fear. She was scared. If Kym was honest with herself, she was terrified. But she couldn't be. This plan was her idea. She wasn't going to let fear get in her way, not anymore.

Kym examined the paths again. They really did look identical. How was she supposed to pick? Whatever she did, she needed to do it fast. She wasn't sure how much longer Jazin and Damon could keep the tear open. For some reason, she felt like the right path looked better. Kym couldn't explain why—it was like a tug deep in her gut. She knew it was the way to go.

"I think…" Kym said, taking a step.

"We should go right," Kym, Kat, and Tomark said.

Kym glanced at Kat and Tomark. She didn't know which path she was going to choose until the words left her lips. How'd they know which one she'd pick?

"How do you know?" Parker asked, and Kym saw her hands tighten around her Pro spear.

"I…I'm not sure," Kym said honestly.

They stepped silently down the new path. It was just like the one they'd left, with endlessly tall walls of the strange black stone. Soon, they reached another split in the path. However, there were at least ten paths for Kym to choose this time. Kym's stomach twisted in a knot. How was she supposed to pick now? After a moment's hesitation, Kym walked down the center path. She prayed it was the right one.

The new path was just as deserted as the previous two. Kym walked a little faster, her confidence growing. Nothing bad had happened yet. Was she choosing right after all? Kym shook her head. Just because nothing was happening didn't mean she chose the right way.

The sound of crumbling stone filled the path, oddly magnified in the silence. Kym flung out her arms to stop the others, who stumbled back. Kym squinted through the blackness, hoping to see something to stop the fear surging through her. She couldn't see the stone, but she knew it was there, just out of sight. She'd dreamt of this—a nightmare in Tenbatter when she'd lost all hope. How could it come true? Was this place turning her nightmares into reality?

"Look!" Short's voice rang out over the rumbling. Kym spun around and saw him pointing at the ground. "It's breaking!"

Kym didn't need to move to examine Short's claim. She knew he was right as the ground shuddered beneath her. The same thing happened in her dream. Kym's breath caught in her throat. How could she stop the world from literally crumbling around them?

"Don't look down," Kat snapped, punching Short in the arm.

"We need to retreat," Parker said. "Find a new path."

"No," Tomark said. His voice shook, but Kym heard his determination. "We need to keep going."

"How?" Amber demanded. "There's barely any ground left."

"Just…trust us."

Kym grabbed Parker and Amber's hands, and going against every instinct she had, stepped forward. She didn't look at the ground, but her foot found something to rest on. Kym sighed. She closed her eyes, fighting the impulse to look down.

"Wow!" someone yelled behind Kym as the ground shuddered again.

"What did we say?' Kat shouted. "Stop looking down, moron!"

The crumbling stopped. It was like someone flipped a switch. Kym let go of Parker and Amber, her eyes snapping open as her heart pounded. What happened? Why'd it stop?

There was a flash of red, and the crackle of flames filled the air. Kym looked to the side. Amber's hands were over her head, flames dancing around her fingers. Kym peered at the ground, grateful for the additional light. She expected to see a giant chasm, but it looked just as smooth and perfect as ever.

"Look alive," Parker's voice rang out.

Kym froze as thick, glittering smoke filled the path. She didn't know how, but she knew it was dangerous somehow. It pressed in on them, right up to Tomark's bubble. Kym's stomach lurched. Would the mist stay outside of their air bubble? Kym feared what would happen if it got inside.

Kym barely heard it at first. It wasn't even a whisper—more like a thought. The murmurs grew louder, and Kym took another step back. There was a cry of pain and a sharp intake of breath. Kym whipped around so quickly she stepped on a soldier's foot. But the soldier didn't look at Kym. She gazed into the mist, which obscured everything outside their little bubble.

"You didn't protect me."

Kym looked wildly around, her hair hitting her in the face. The voice had come from the mist, like some long-forgotten friend from her childhood. But Kym couldn't place it. More voices echoed around her, these just as unfamiliar to Kym as the first.

"I'm so cold."

"You're nothing without me."

"You're a failure."

"Don't listen," Tomark called, his voice oddly distant.

Kym shook her head. What did everyone say about Nothingness? People wandered to find peace, facing their demons along the way. This was just like the crumbling path. It wasn't real.

"You left me behind," Jazin's voice rang out from the mist.

"You didn't save me," Elena's voice called from the darkness.

Kym closed her eyes, focusing on her breathing. It wasn't real. Jazin wasn't in Nothingness. He was back home with Ashlyn, and Xander, and Damon. He was safe. Her mom was with the other morgar in the tower. They were all safe. She needed to hold onto that.

Several people rushed past Kym, bumping into her shoulder. Kym's eyes snapped open, and her insides froze. Amber was sprinting toward the edge of the dome, her arms outstretched. Parker was beside her, her weapons nowhere to be seen.

"No!" Kym screamed, but she was too late.

Parker and Amber stepped outside the bubble. Kym ran forward as they collapsed, their hands clawing at their throats. She reached out for them; her mind blank except for one thought: to pull them back. Bright blue water shot from Kym's fingertips. It soared out of the bubble and enveloped Amber and Parker, who lay motionless in the thick mist.

Kym pulled, focusing with all her might on bringing them back. Amber and Parker, their bodies sheathed in glowing blue water, rose into the air. They flew back, breaking through the bubble and into breathable air. Kym dropped her arms, sweat pouring down her forehead. The blue sheathing around Parker and Amber faded, and they fell to the ground.

Panting, her heart racing, Kym rushed forward. Amber was already on her feet and walking back to the chorus of voices outside the air bubble. Kym lunged forward and wrapped her arms around Amber's slender waist. They fell to the ground, and Kym's shoulder stung with pain, but she ignored it.

"Let me go!" Amber demanded, throwing her arm back and hitting Kym in the chin.

"No!" Kym spluttered. She wrapped her legs around Amber, who toppled back to the ground in a heap. "Amber, it's not real."

"I can hear him!" Amber snapped. "He needs help."

"Amber…that's not …"

Kym couldn't tell Amber they were there to fight Thed. She knew it wouldn't change a thing. Nothing Kym could say would make a difference. If Amber thought Jazin was in danger, Kym knew Amber would do anything to help him. She shook her head. How were they supposed to defeat Thed if they couldn't find him? They had enough trouble just walking around.

"How are you so calm? All of you?" Short said in a tremulous voice. "This place is…"

Kym shook her head. If she was honest with herself, she didn't know why she was calm. Was it her dreams? She'd dreamt about the crumbling path and voices of people she'd failed countless times. Kym had always blamed her guilty conscience for her nightmares, but everything she'd dreamed about had happened. Why was that?

"I don't know," Tomark said. "It feels like…this place is familiar."

"Like I know what's coming," Kat added. "But that's crazy. How would we know what the land of the dead is like?"

"I'm not surprised you know what's coming," Amber said, no longer struggling against Kym. "You did die, after all."

CHAPTER TWENTY-FOUR

THE GIFT OF DEATH

IT WAS LIKE AMBER HAD KICKED KYM IN THE STOMACH. SHE couldn't breathe. She couldn't think. Kym stared at Amber, the words washing over her sluggish mind. How could she have died? That was impossible. Amber had to be wrong.

"What…what're you talking about?" Tomark asked.

"C'mon…you know when…" Amber said, her narrow eyes widening as her stony expression softened. "You…you didn't know?"

"Know what?" Kat demanded, walking right up to Amber, who towered over Kat.

"When you tried to leave, and the Rulers…" Amber trailed off, her voice much softer than usual. "Your hearts stopped."

Kym shook her head. Her body felt like lead, and her legs gave out beneath her. She collapsed, but she barely noticed the pain in her knees. It was nothing compared to the pain in her heart. She couldn't believe what Amber was saying. She wouldn't. Kym would've known if she'd died. And if she'd died, how was she alive?

"No," Tomark trembled, shaking his head. "You're—"

"I'm not wrong, Tomark," Amber said, and the pain in her voice was unmistakable. "I checked your pulses myself. You, Kym, Kat, and Ashlyn…you all died. I thought you knew."

Tears flooded Kym's eyes as she stared at the faint scars still visible on her forearms. She hadn't known. Was that why the Warden was so afraid of her? It wasn't because she was a Favored, or betrayed the Rulers. Now everything at Tenbatter made sense—

being chained and confined for over a year; the water restriction; the beatings. It was because she died…and somehow came back.

Kym stood, ignoring Amber's outstretched hand. With Amber's revelation swimming around her head, Kym saw the vast maze in a new light. Her dreams hadn't been nightmares brought on by guilt. They'd been memories. She'd wandered Nothingness before.

White-hot tears slid down Kym's face, and she wiped them away with trembling fingers. Anger unlike any she'd experienced rose inside her, ripping through her like a wild animal. The Rulers, under the influence of Thed, had killed her. She didn't know how or why she had come back, but she didn't care. It didn't matter. All that mattered to Kym was making things right. And beating the crap out of the god of death sounded like a good place to start.

The others followed Kym, not saying a word as they turned down countless new paths. Kym, along with Tomark and Kat, always knew which way to turn, but she wasn't shocked anymore. She'd died, after all. It was helpful, knowing what dangers lurked around corners before they appeared. They passed by the floor of snakes, the pit of their mistakes, and the faceless men tying up people with no real issue.

The blackness lightened the deeper they traveled in the maze. After a while, she could see without Amber's ring of fire or the light prisms Parker brought. The persistent numbness inside Kym faded, and she started to feel like herself again. But with the cold of death fading, there was nothing to quell Kym's anger.

Outside the air bubble, Kym started to see what she could only describe as ghosts. They weren't the black, formless specters that tormented them before, but distinct human shapes, their heads slowly turning this way and that as they drifted along. Kym wanted to give these souls a wide berth. The last thing she wanted was to disturb their wanderings for peace. Besides, Kym wasn't even sure they knew Kym and the rest of them were there.

However, that didn't stop Kym from watching them. Was that what she looked like when she died? Had she been reduced to a formless specter, wandering blindly, searching for peace? Did she deserve peace after everything she'd done?

But these souls weren't the only things on Kym's path. Kym first saw them on the walls. They looked like vines—clinging to the walls, wriggling and pulsing as they inched upward. These vines stirred something in Kym's memory. She'd seen these before too. They looked just like the death Jazin pulled from Theddie.

Kym increased her speed, and the vines became more numerous the farther into Nothingness they traveled. Kym's heart raced in her chest. Could these vines be Thed's anchors, clinging to the substance of Nothingness? What would happen if Kym attacked them? Kym didn't dare try. Breaking a few small anchors wasn't why they were there. She needed to find Thed.

Kym rounded another corner and stopped dead in her tracks, her hands trembling at her sides. Twenty yards ahead was another inter-section—the largest she'd seen. At least twenty different paths converged there, but that wasn't what made Kym's heart pound like a drum. A massive, black throne sat in the middle of the intersec-tion. The blackness she'd grown accustomed to faded behind the throne, and Kym saw majestic fields and rolling streams. Voices met Kym's ears from the field—happy voices, talking and laughing.

Kym stepped forward, and her insides felt lighter. Was that peace? After wandering Nothingness, the souls of the dead were supposed to find peace. She always thought it was a state of being, but was peace an actual place? Kym didn't think it looked so bad. In fact, she thought it look almost tranquil.

"Where is he?" Short's whisper brought Kym back to herself.

The others were staring at the massive, empty throne. Kym's muscles tensed as she shifted her feet into a fighting stance. Where could Thed be? More vines than Kym had seen crept up the throne, extending off the back and reaching into the black abyss above.

"Be ready," Parker whispered, and Kym saw her hands drift to her weapons. "Don't hesi—"

Parker fell silent, and terror coursed through Kym's body like fire. A massive, black form bloomed from the throne's gleaming surface. It was featureless—a blank, humanoid shape. The millions of black vines extended from its back, looking like odd, veiny wings. The eyeless face tilted down, and Kym's breath caught in her throat. There was no question who this could be. She was standing at the feet of the god of death.

"Attack!"

Kym invoked her Marks at Parker's command. She shot into the air, anger coursing through her like fire. Two bolts appeared above her hands, as energy coursed through Kym. Thed was the reason everything had gone wrong, and Kym was going to make him pay.

She threw her bolts, one after the other, at Thed. They exploded against his inky body in flashes of bright blue. Kat's and Amber's bolts did the same, filling the strange twilight with green and red. Spears flew past Kym, piercing Thed's body. Kym dropped to the ground and threw her hands over her face as bright orange light burst from the spears.

Thick, black smoke filled the air as the low storm hum subsided. Kym squinted through the gloom, her head pounding as stars flashed in her eyes. She bit her lip, barely daring to breathe. Had it worked?

"*You dare attack a god in his domain?*" The dark, worn voice filled the space around them, making the hairs on Kym's neck stand on end. "*I thought Thilg gifted wisdom to Pheil's creation. Clearly not.*"

Kym's mouth fell open. Thed emerged from the smoke, the soldiers' spears nowhere to be seen. The glistening surface of Thed's body looked perfect, his anchors swaying gently from his back.

"*Why do you resist?*" Thed asked, his formless face gazing down at them. "*Soon, all of Princirum will embrace my gift, unlike some of you.*"

A shiver ran down Kym's spine. After what Amber told her, she now understood what Thed was talking about. Kym's hands balled into fists as she stared into Thed's face. She'd refused his gift— she'd died and had come back. It wasn't like she chose not to die.

She still had no idea how she'd come back to life in the first place. But apparently, so did Thed.

"*You three,*" Thed waved his hand toward them, and Kym held her breath, "*were stolen from me, along with one other. But now, you will be mine again—all of you. You wandered well. It is time you receive the gift of death.*"

The ground beneath Kym shuddered as Thed waved his massive hand above her. She and the others toppled forward, the rumbling of stone filling her ears. Kym pushed herself up, her arms raised, ready for a fight, as an icy numbness flooded her insides. She squinted through the blackness as things—many things—emerged from the towering stone walls.

"Death demons!"

Kym shot into the air. Her blast hit the closest death demon, a beast with the body of a massive cat and the head of a serpent. It flew back, but more death demons rushed to take its place. Kym threw two more bolts, her heart racing, not even bothering to aim. They exploded against the nearest demons but did little to slow their advance. Behind the death demons, Kym watched Thed vanish in a ripple of blackness.

The demons burst through Tomark's air bubble. Kym dove down, but a massive, winged construct rose in front of her, turning her insides to ice. Kym shoved her arms forward, her heart racing, and her blast exploded against the demon's massive underside. The demon fell, landing silently on the black path. Kym turned back to the bubble, and her heart froze. Two death demons had their jaws clamped around two of Parker's soldiers and were dragging them out of the air bubble.

"No!"

Kym swung her hand, and a massive water swipe soared from her fingers. It exploded in front of the bubble, blowing the closest demons back. But the ones holding Parker's soldiers had reached the glittering black walls. They melted back into the stone, dragging the soldiers along with them.

"Get back to the tear," Parker shouted below Kym.

"We need to save them!" Kym yelled.

Kym soared over the demons to the maze wall, but they were as smooth as ever. Her panic rising, Kym spun like a top. She needed to find the soldiers. She wasn't going to leave them to Thed and his death demons.

"It's too late, Kym," Parker yelled, and Kym heard the pain in her voice. "You're the only one of us who can leave the bubble. Clear us a path out of here. We're pinned down."

Kym nodded, her insides writhing. She didn't want to leave the soldiers, but deep down she knew they were beyond her reach. She flew over the bubble, throwing bolts and firing blasts as fast as she could. Behind her, the unmistakable sounds of magic and storm weapons filled the air, as did screams. Kym forced her sadness down, burying it in a deep part of her mind. Parker was right. If she didn't get the others out of there, they'd lose more than two people in Nothingness. Kym's anger swirled in her like a tornado. She failed to stop Thed, but she could get these people out of Nothingness.

Kym spun in a circle, letting her anger spill out of her as a blue ring appeared around her. She jerked her hands apart, and the ring splintered, forming several apple-sized bolts. They orbited her like tiny moons as three skeletal death demons materialized from the walls. Kym flew forward, throwing bolts one right after the other at the demons. They exploded against the skeletons, which flew back into the walls. Kym felt two of the bolts orbiting her fly off, and more blue light filled the blackness as they found their targets. Kym didn't dare check where they went. She had enough to deal with in front of her.

Kym saw the portal ahead of her—a massive white tear in the near-constant blackness. Relief flooded Kym's frozen body. They made it back. They were safe.

"You will receive the gift," Thed's voice echoed around the maze, boring into Kym's brain.

The black walls and floor rumbled. Kym stopped in midair, a new bolt ready in her hand, her head pounding as sweat poured down her face. She expected to see more death demons flooding the path below her. Instead, she watched open-mouthed as they melted back into the maze.

Spikes grew from the walls and ground. Horror coursed through Kym as the pieces of stone swept across the ground like a strange, spiky wave. Countless spikes spread inside the bubble before Kym could lift a finger. They grew faster than anyone could react, and screams filled the silent air as the points of the black stone pierced flesh. One stabbed Kat's leg; she wasn't fast enough to move out of the way. Another pierced Tomark's chest, and his gasp of pain froze Kym's heart as the bubble of air around him faltered.

"No!"

Kym's mind went blank. All thought of leaving, fighting, and anger vanished in a flash. None of it mattered. Kym flew down, flipping around at the last minute. Her feet slammed into the ground, and pain erupted through her leg like fire as something wet trickled down her calf. Kym gritted her teeth, trying to ignore the pain.

"Let's go!" Kym yelled.

Kym threw a bolt at the ground and let her energy explode out of it. The nearest spikes crumbled, as did the ones nearest the storm beads thrown by Short. The soldier beside Amber screamed, and Kym's heart stopped as she watched the spike emerge from her chest. The spike lifted the soldier off her feet like a doll, and Kym saw the light fade from her eyes.

"You heard her!" Parker yelled, throwing more storm beads into the spikes ahead of them. The black stone crumbled, clearing the path to the tear. "Retreat! Get out now!"

Kym grabbed Kat's arm. She hoisted Kat to her feet, ignoring her cries of pain. All that mattered was getting Kat and the rest of them out alive. She struggled toward the tear, Kat limping beside her. Her head split open as more storm beads exploded around her. She stared at the tear, focusing on that as she leaped with all the strength she had left.

Warmth flooded Kym's body as she landed on something solid.

Bright, intense light filled her eyes as her muscles screamed in pain. Something dripped down her leg, but she didn't dare look at it. She had more important things to worry about.

Kym sat up, and the tightness in her chest lessened. Tomark was on the ground, his face alight with pain, while Parker and Amber leaned over him, their hands pressed against the bright red spot on his shirt. A mixture of relief and anguish flooded Kym's brain. She crawled toward Tomark and slipped her fingers into his. He was okay. They'd all made it out.

"I can't keep this up!"

Kym forced herself to lift her head. Jazin was on his knees, his face tinged green, and he looked like he was on the verge of passing out.

"Where are the others?" Ashlyn asked, and Kym heard the terror in her voice.

Others? Kym tore her eyes away from Tomark, and she forced herself to her feet. What was Ashlyn talking about? Aside from Kat, Amber, Tomark, and Parker, Kym saw only three soldiers crouched around her. The bottom fell out of Kym's stomach.

"Where's Short?"

Kym gazed through the black tear in the air, which was starting to close. Short stood twenty feet from the tear, throwing storm beads in every direction. Kym's heart skipped a beat as she spotted a massive spike sticking out of Short's leg. He turned to the portal, and his caramel eyes locked with Kym's blue ones. He nodded, and Kym saw the faintest trace of a smile flash across his lips as he threw more storm beads toward the tear. He was staying.

Kym reached to Short, wanting to pull him to her with every ounce of her being. A cloud of blue energy burst from her fingers. It flew through the portal and sheathed Short's slight frame. She didn't care that he was being noble. She wasn't going to leave anyone else behind. They'd already lost too many people in Nothingness.

Kym pulled Short toward her with trembling arms, and Short flew through the air. Kym jerked her hand this way and that, guiding Short between the erupting spikes as stars burst in her eyes.

Kym narrowed her gaze, focusing everything she had on bringing Short to her. She felt him within her energy—felt his heart racing against the water sheath she'd placed around him.

Short was only a few feet away, and Kym pulled with all the willpower she had left. A massive spike appeared right in front of the tear, piercing Short directly in the chest. Kym felt the black stone rip through her sheath, which vanished in a flash of blue. Kym fell, her hand still outstretched as the world darkened. She glimpsed Short, his body suspended on the spike, as the tear sealed and Short vanished. Then everything was black.

T H E   T R U E
F A V O R E D

"The embarkment will begin at sundown," Perla said thickly.

"I'll issue a community alert. If we relieve everyone an hour beforehand, they should have enough time."

"Thank you, Marek," Hale nodded. "But I'd still like to discuss the possibility of a retaliatory attack. We should be—"

"After," Mrs. Mizel said. "First, we honor those who gave their lives."

Kym sat on the ground, her back pressed against the new window in the Council room. They'd been talking for hours, but Kym hadn't said much. Parker gave her report, her voice oddly clipped, and Kym couldn't think of anything else to add. They'd failed to defeat Thed and lost four people in the process. To the Council, the mission was a failure. But to Kym, it was so much more.

Kym hadn't said a word since Short died. She still felt the spike piercing her sheath as it ripped through his chest. Every time she closed her eyes, she saw the tear closing on him, and it was all her fault. They were planning embarkments because going to Nothingness was her idea. She'd been so sure she could stop Thed. She couldn't have been more wrong.

"Twenty minutes should be sufficient," Anderson croaked. "No sense dragging things out."

Kym looked up. Only twenty minutes to honor the heroes who went to Nothingness to end the eternity of Thed? Only a brief moment to celebrate Short, who stayed behind to ensure the others escaped? Short and the other soldiers were heroes who battled death. Why wouldn't the Council honor their actions? Kym felt they deserved much more.

"I'll inform the families," Perla said, getting to her feet. "Give them enough time to provide a personal effect."

Another pang. Kym fought to keep the tears from spilling down her face. Normally, the dead were displayed in the Temples for the living to honor during the embarkment. But that was impossible. Short and the other soldiers were in Nothingness, so Perla needed something connected to the fallen to display. Yet another reminder of Kym's many mistakes.

"Anderson," Hale said, also getting to her feet, "We should check the trunk line. I'll have my men do a sweep of the perimeter."

Everyone stood, but Kym couldn't bring herself to move. Her legs felt oddly distant—like they weren't attached to the rest of her. Tomark appeared in front of her, looking perfectly normal. Parker patched him up before they returned, and Damon healed him after he'd recovered from containing the tear to Nothingness. Kat and Amber too. They were fine, but Kym had a hard time looking at them. They were reminders of the faces she'd never see again.

Tomark offered Kym his hand, and she took it. They walked into the hall, Ashlyn and Amber behind them. Jazin and Damon were, of course, exhausted, and Kat hadn't said a word since leaving Nothingness. Xander offered to stay with her in their dorm, and Kym hadn't objected. Kat may have made fun of Short every chance she got, but Kym knew better.

Parker stood with Perla beside the elevator, her face blank with dark circles beneath her eyes. Kym wanted to say something— Parker had lost four soldiers. She'd vouched for Kym's idea with the Council, and it was her soldiers who volunteered to go. Parker hadn't spoken to Kym since they got back. Kym didn't know if she could feel any worse.

"Anything would be helpful," Perla said, placing her hand gently on Parker's shoulder. "To guide him on his wandering."

Parker nodded as Perla walked off. She turned and locked eyes with Kym, who shifted uncomfortably, her skin crawling. She didn't want to be there. Tomark, however, had other ideas. He walked up to Parker, dragging Kym along with him.

"Everything okay?" he asked.

"What?" Parker asked like she hadn't heard Tomark. She kept blinking, like she was having trouble focusing. "Yes."

"What did Perla want?" Amber asked.

"She wants me to represent Jeren at the embarkment," Parker said thickly.

Kym looked from Parker to Perla as the elevator doors closed on her. Why would Parker represent Short at the embarkment? That task was reserved for family members. Surely someone from Short's family would represent him. Why wouldn't Perla ask one of them?

The answer hit Kym like a ton of bricks. Perla asked Parker because Short had no one else to ask. How could she not know that Short was alone? After all the time they'd spent together, Kym never once asked him one thing about himself. Kym didn't think it was possible, but the thought made her feel even worse. Why hadn't she bothered to ask him?

"I'm sure he'd appreciate that," Tomark said.

Parker nodded, her lips pressed tightly together. She walked off, and Tomark started to follow her. Kym tightened her grip on his hand. He turned, but all Kym could do was shake her head. He probably hadn't noticed the tears in Parker's eyes, but Kym had. Parker needed time, and Kym saw no point in chasing after her. They'd see her at sundown.

"Kym."

Kym took a deep breath. If she was honest with herself, she'd been expecting this since they'd gotten back. Slowly, Kym turned away from the elevator. Marek was walking toward her, his face downcast.

"Could I have a moment?" Marek asked.

Kym nodded. She let go of Tomark, trying her best to smile. It felt wrong. She followed her father into the closest room, which was deserted. It looked like the Disciples used it for storage.

"Kym," Marek said, wrapping his arms around her.

"I know," Kym croaked. Not even her father's arms could drive away the sorrow inside her. "I messed up. This is all…"

"It's not your fault," Marek said.

"Yes it is," Kym said, pulling away from her father as tears burned her eyes. "Going to Nothingness was my idea. If I had just kept my mouth shut, we wouldn't be having four embarkments today."

"Maybe," Marek nodded, his eyes full of tears. "But the soldiers —they knew the risks. The idea may have been yours, but going was their choice."

Tears spilled from Kym's eyes. They slid down her face, burning like fire. "Dad…they deserve so much more than this."

"They do," Marek nodded, and placed his hand gently on Kym's shoulder. "But the other Councilors…they've made up their minds."

Kym ran her fingers through her hair. She knew her dad voted for not shortening the embarkments, but why hadn't he done more? Kym wanted to talk with Perla. She'd been on Kym's side since she arrived. Maybe, if she would just listen…

"Kym," Marek said, wiping the tears from Kym's cheeks, "you don't need to fight…not today."

"But-but I…" Kym stammered. Marek was wrong. Kym could help Short and the others if the Council would just listen.

"Kym," Marek repeated, and there was a little too much understanding in his voice. "You're not responsible for saving everyone."

Kym walked back to her dorm in a daze, her father's words swirling around her. How could she stop fighting to protect people? When she became a Favored, protecting people had become her purpose. Fighting death was what she'd trained to do ever since she discovered her magic. If she stopped fighting now, she'd have nothing left.

The dorm seemed oddly dark, even with the lights on. Kym

found Kat lying on the couch, Xander sitting beside her on the floor. Tomark looked to Kym when she walked in, and she tried to wipe the tears from her face. She knew he wanted to know what Marek said, but she saw no point in repeating it since Tomark probably agreed with him. Besides, she had more important things to worry about.

They sat in silence for a long time, but Kym didn't mind. She tried to find something to distract her, but everything reminded her of Short. When he'd first shown them their new home. Helping them sneak out to free Amber, Xander, and Jazin. Covering for them when they were trying to free Theddie. Short filled every inch of the dorm. He deserved more than a quick service at sunset—all of the soldiers did.

"We should get ready," Amber said, lifting her head from Jazin's shoulder as the light from the window shifted from yellow to orange.

Kym sighed. She was still wearing the clothes she'd worn to Nothingness. They were ripped in several places, and dried blood covered her left leg. In a distant part of her mind, she heard the voices of her lady's maids, Veronica and Isabel, as they dressed her to honor the dead during the Festival of Creation. *It's not a day for happy colors.* Somehow, the thought made Kym smile.

She followed Amber into their room, Kat and Ashlyn behind her. She pulled open her drawers and stared at the clothes. What should she wear? Not what her maids called 'happy colors.' But what?

She'd never been to an embarkment before. The only people she knew who'd died were her aunt and uncle, but that didn't help her. The Protectorate killed them for speaking out against the Rulers and the gods, and the priests refused to give them a proper embarkment. According to them, her aunt and uncle's treason made them unworthy of the gods' final blessings.

"We should put in some effort," Ashlyn said, rifling through her drawers beside Kym.

"How?" Amber sneered. "The selection's nonexistent."

Kym wanted to punch Amber. Was she really complaining about

their wardrobe selection? Ashlyn was right. They should put in as much effort as they could, for Short's sake. At least that was something Kym could do. And she needed to do something.

Kym turned to Amber, ready to tell her off, but stopped herself. Now that they were up close, Kym saw that Amber's golden eyes were bloodshot. Kym's anger evaporated as she looked at the ever-poised Fire Princess. Had she been crying?

In the bottom of her drawers, Kym found a blue blouse. Compared to the rest of the clothes in there, which were very secondhand, it looked like it had only been worn a few times. Kym held it up to her chest and was surprised it looked like it would fit. She'd avoided blue clothes since escaping Tenbatter, because blue was what Water Favored wore, and Kym wasn't one anymore. But something told her this was the time to wear it.

Kym slipped on the top, which fit well enough. If she was going to wear her elemental color, she might as well go all the way. There was only one problem; the only nice bottoms she had in her drawers was a skirt, and it was dark green. Even if Kym wanted to wear it, the skirt was way too small for her. But that gave Kym an idea.

"Here," Kym said, handing the skirt to Kat.

Kat took it, not taking her puffy eyes off of her drawers. Kym grabbed Kat's hand and squeezed her trembling fingers. She knew Kat liked to act tough, especially around Amber. But Kym wanted Kat to know she was there, and that she knew how Kat felt.

"Wear it," Kym said, and she actually smiled.

"Thanks," Kat croaked, wiping her eyes on her sleeve. "It's not horrible. The blue's nice."

Kym, Kat, Amber, and Ashlyn spent the next hour helping each other get ready. Kym hated to admit it, but Amber had been right about their clothing selection. There were enough clothes, but the problem was none of them were the right size, especially when Ashlyn and Amber decided to wear their elemental colors, too. Luckily, Ashlyn had experience in this department.

"When you grow up in clothes from several older sisters, you learn to make do," Ashlyn said, the ghost of a smile flashing on her lips.

Ashlyn set to work, emptying their drawers into the middle of the small room. Kym stepped back, not wanting to get in the way as Ashlyn ran around; she knew when she was outmatched. For the second time that day, she remembered her lady's maids. In addition to her blue blouse, which slipped off one of Kym's shoulders, Ashlyn gave Kym a blue skirt from Amber's drawers. It was a little big, but Ashlyn tied the excess fabric from the waistband into a knot, and it fit well enough. Finally, Kym ran an old brush through her blond hair, which she just left plain behind her back.

"It should hold up. Just don't move too much," Ashlyn smiled.

Kat wore the green skirt Kym gave her, along with an old, faded green button-up shirt. It didn't quite fit right, and Kym was pretty sure it was a men's shirt, but Kat didn't seem to care. Ashlyn tied it in the front and topped it off with the boots Kat insisted on wearing. It was an odd assortment, but Kym thought it was a very Kat thing to wear.

Amber, as Kym expected, was just as picky as ever. Ashlyn found a red tee-shirt in Kat's drawers that was long enough to be a short dress. Amber, however, refused to wear it until it was, in her words, 'more flattering.' Therefore, Ashlyn spent thirty minutes cutting and retying the sides back together. Finally, Ashlyn threw a long, yellow cardigan over a plain white shirt and yellow shorts.

Kym couldn't help but smile as she took in her friends' appearances. It wasn't much, but the effort they made was noticeable. Somehow, in these cobbled together outfits, Kym thought they looked more like themselves than they had in months. Kym certainly felt more like herself as she glimpsed her reflection in the small bathroom mirror.

Kym found the boys waiting for them in the common room. They, like the girls, had tried to dress in their elemental colors. Damon's white shirt and pants were fraying at the edges, Jazin's black shirt hung loosely off his thin frame, and Xander's purple sweater was several sizes too small, but Kym didn't care. She was impressed that they each managed to find shirts that were the right color.

Tomark, his wavy hair pulled back out of his face, smiled at Kym. She smiled back, but the warmth Tomark brought quickly faded as she remembered why he was dressed in his shiny, grey shirt. It wasn't for fun or to feel like themselves. It was because their friend stayed in the land of the dead so they could escape. It wasn't a day for smiling.

"It's time," Damon said, rolling up the sleeves of his white shirt.

Kym followed Amber and Jazin into the hall. She slipped her hand into Tomark's and was surprised to find it shaking. Kym looked into his green eyes and rested her head on his shoulder as they walked, unable to speak. She wanted to say something, but nothing seemed right.

The library was packed when they arrived. Kym looked over the crowd, and her heart swelled. They, like Kym and the others, had put some effort into their outfits. Most wore what Kym would've called Temple clothes. Heads turned toward Kym and the others as they walked through the crowd, and a shiver ran down Kym's spine. Why did they need to stare?

Kym knew they must blame her and her friends for what happened, and they were right. It didn't help that a few people inclined their heads as Kym walked by. Kym tried not to sigh. Not only did they blame them, but they also pitied them. Kym didn't think she could possibly feel worse.

Kym followed the crowd outside through the side doors she'd never used before. This struck Kym as odd. Why weren't they using the front entrance? Kym found her answer when they reached the grassy lawn, which had been cleared of most of the debris from the recent battles.

Pyres sat before the library doors, completely taking over the veranda. Kym's blood turned to ice as her eyes drifted over the wooden structures. Four pyres—one for each person they lost. But the pyres were bare. Kym saw no sign of the gods' statues or the elemental banners that should surround the pyres. Short and the others deserved more than empty pyres to honor them. They were heroes. Kym wanted to do more for them, but what else could she do?

The sun kissed the horizon, and Kym doubled her grip on Tomark's hand. The library doors slid open, and people dressed in black exited the building, their arms full of random objects—a book, a picture, an old sweater. The families and friends of the departed didn't look up as they placed these items on the pyres.

Parker walked out last, and tears burned Kym's eyes as she placed a folded guard uniform on the final pyre. White-hot blades tore at Kym's throat as she stared at the clothes. Short's uniform. That was all he had left—the thing that defined him most. He'd dedicated himself to protecting people, and this was all he got? Kym couldn't believe it.

Perla, dressed in dark, form-fitting robes, led the Council onto the veranda. The crowd didn't make a sound as Perla stepped in front of the others. She raised her hands, calling for silence, although Kym didn't see why. It was so quiet Kym heard everyone's collective breath.

"My children," Perla called over the crowd, her voice somber. "Today, we honor four of our brothers and sisters. It is always sad when a soul reaches the end of the gods' journey. The paths the gods laid before these four have ended. Now, they embark on a new path as they join our ancestors to wander Nothingness, searching for peace."

Kym rolled her eyes. Perla made wandering Nothingness sound so peaceful, but Kym knew firsthand how wrong she was. Short and the others would face every mistake they ever made before finding peace. How long would that take? Kym hoped, for their sakes, it was quick.

Another priest stepped forward, a tray covered in supplies in his arms. Perla raised the small, blue urn and approached the closest pyre. She looked to the sky and dribbled a few drops of water over Short's uniform.

"Cleanse this soul."

Kym's mouth fell open as Perla moved to the next pyre. Kym couldn't believe that was it. She'd asked Reta to cleanse her several times, and it sounded nothing like what Perla just said. She needed to call on Reta and ask her waters to wash Short clean. Why was Perla speeding through the last rites Short would ever receive? Kym's eyes fell on Anderson, who stood a little behind Perla as she hurried through the rites. Kym had her answer.

Kym's arms shook with suppressed fury. This wasn't right. Short and the other soldiers deserved more than a service shortened for Anderson's convenience. These people were warriors. Fighters. Perla should be honoring them like that.

Kym didn't remember letting go of Tomark. She stepped forward, carried by something stronger than anger as the crowd parted before her. Some made sounds, but the pounding in her ears drowned everything out. Before she knew it, she was running up the final steps to the veranda.

"Stop!"

Perla nearly dropped the flickering candle in her hands. She stared at Kym, her mouth slightly open. Kym couldn't believe it herself. She hadn't meant to yell.

"Kymbralyn," Marek stepped in front of the other Councilors. "What are you doing?"

Kym ignored him. Instead, she looked to Perla, whose eyes grew wide as she closed her mouth. Slowly, Perla stepped back and placed the candle on the golden tray. She inclined her head to Kym, and Kym knew Perla would hear her out. But what could Kym say?

A shudder ran over Kym's skin, and she turned to face the lawn. Every person in the crowd was staring at her, their faces oddly blank. Kym saw the others among them, their shock clearly evident. Kym took a shaky breath, trying to calm her nerves. She'd always hated being the center of attention, but she couldn't let that get to her. She needed to make a stand. For Short.

"I'm not a leader," Kym began, her voice shaking as she addressed the crowd. "I'm a Favored. A warrior. That's what the Rulers turned me into. These people, they're warriors too. They pledged their lives to keep you safe. They fought to keep death out of Princirum, just like the Favored are supposed to.

"To me," Kym turned to Short's pyre, tears sliding down her cheeks, "Jeren Short is…was a Favored. They all were. These soldiers deserve to be honored as Favored."

Kym watched the crowd, waiting for something to happen. She imagined the scathing look on Anderson's face but Kym didn't care. All that mattered was the crowd. Did they feel the same way she did?

Kym didn't notice it right away. First, one person fell to their knees. Then another, and another. A moment later, the whole crowd was kneeling, their heads bowed. The only people left standing were Tomark, Jazin, and the others, who looked equally shocked.

Kym felt like the wind had been knocked out of her. She didn't want them to kneel to her. She wanted to give Short and the others a proper embarkment. She turned to the Council and family members, but they too were on their knees. Kym walked up to Perla, who looked slightly shocked as Kym approached. Tears glistened in her eyes, and she was smiling.

The others joined Kym on the veranda. Based on their bewildered expressions, Kym knew they wanted an explanation. But how could Kym explain when she had no idea what was happening? She hadn't even known she was going to do it before she did it.

The kneeling crowd stared at Kym, who took a deep breath as she stepped forward. She opened her mouth to speak but quickly shut it. She knew there were specific words she needed to say, but she didn't know the right ones. Kym turned to Perla, who rose to her feet, a warm smile on her lips.

"Reta," Perla began, her voice shaky but firm, "goddess of water, bringer of purification, we beseech you. Cleanse these souls of their sins as the paths you laid before them end. Let your waters wash them clean as they depart the Great Mother's creation."

Perla looked at Kym and nodded. Kym raised her hands, invoked her Marks, and took a deep breath. Sheets of crystal clear water appeared over the pyres. Kym lowered her hands, and the water followed, drifting down and around the pyres like panes of molten glass. Kym closed her eyes and stopped her energy flow. The water cascaded over the pyres and spilled down the steps.

"Heirraph, god of fire, protector of love, we beseech you," Perla called over the crowd. "Let your fire bring the fallen comfort as they move from the lands of life. May their passions burn bright as they wander their new paths."

Amber stepped forward and waved her hand. Fires erupted on each of the pyres, engulfing the personal belongings. Kym opened her mouth, unable to believe what she was seeing. She wanted Amber to stop—to preserve the belongings of the fallen. But the fires went out before Kym made a sound, and the personal belongings looked perfectly normal.

When Amber was done, Kat encased the personal effects in earth while Perla called on Thray to grant them his strength. She then granted them Rai's insight while Tomark sent a soft breeze over the pyres. Ashlyn bathed the pyres in light while Perla bestowed Thilg's wisdom on the departed to help them find their peace. Then, Xander shrouded the pyres in darkness to grant the fallen the bravery of Kensrad. Damon stepped up next, pulling the life from the plants encircling the pyres. It drifted over them before expanding outward, making Kym's body feel as light as air while Perla called for Pheil's protection.

Finally, it was Jazin's turn to grant Thed's peace. He stepped up and pointed his hands at the newly dead plants. Black mist flew toward him as the plants bloomed back to life, and wound around the pyres. Kym saw cracks appear in the wood as the death seeped into the structures, but it wasn't enough to make the pyres fall apart.

Kym smiled as Perla handed torches to the family members. Kym glanced at Tomark, who smiled at her before pressing his lips to her forehead. She watched the pyres ignite, her stomach fluttering as everyone bowed their heads. This was what she wanted. This was what Short and the others deserved.

Crying for what felt like the hundredth time that day, Kym lifted her head to wipe her eyes but stopped with her hand halfway to her face. Amber stood at the top of the stairs, looking at her feet. Kym's eyes darted to the side, but none of the others had lifted their heads. Kym turned back to Amber. What was she doing?

You blessed us with your deeds, Favored of the gods.
Your strength and bravery, a passion born in flames.
Though many tears may fall, their source is pure and true.
The flames of Heirraph's love, burn bright because of you.
Your time has come, the path has reached its end.
And now you go, to wander Nothingness.

The land is cleansed, now guided by your fire.
It's time you go, to find your peace and rest.
Heirraph's chosen one, know you're not alone.
The flames you leave behind, shine bright with all your love.
Your time has come, the path has reached its end.
And now you go, to wander Nothingness.

Kym's mouth fell open. She'd never heard that song before, but clearly, it was one Amber knew well. She had no idea Amber could sing. Had she sung it at Favored embarkments in the past? It was possible. Amber had lived at Inferon her whole life. She'd probably attended more Favored embarkments than any other Favored. And it wasn't the fact that Amber could sing that Kym found so shocking. It was that, in front of all of the Disciples, Amber finally put the Fire Princess away.

Kym turned to Kat. Her mouth was hanging open while her head moved slowly from side to side. Clearly, she was more in shock than Kym. The others were a little better at hiding their surprise. At least they didn't look like fish out of water.

Kym turned to the families of the fallen. She hoped they didn't mind Kym and the others taking over the embarkment of their loved ones. Above anything, the last thing she wanted was for them to be angry. What had Parker thought? Kym hoped she'd done Short justice.

But the families weren't looking at Kym. They were on their knees again; their heads pressed to the ground. And they weren't the only ones. All the Councilors, including Anderson, were bowing. Kym saw tears shining in Perla and Mrs. Mizel's eyes, while Marek shook with silent sobs. Kym shook her head. Were they bowing to the pyres?

Kym looked over her shoulder and saw the crowd was in the same position. Tiny bumps rose all over Kym's arms as the truth dawned on her. These people weren't bowing to the departed—they were bowing to Kym and her friends.

But why? Less than a day ago, they blamed Kym and her friends for all the bad things that had happened since they arrived. Now they were acting like the servants used to when Kym lived at Wadita. But as Kym watched the bowing crowd, she realized that wasn't exactly true.

Servants never bowed like this to Kym. They only pressed their heads to the floor when a Ruler was near. Kym looked to Amber, Ashlyn, Kat, Tomark, Damon, Jazin, and Xander, who were just as bewildered as Kym.

Kym didn't know why, but for some reason, these people were treating them like Rulers. Kym looked back at her father, his forehead pressed to the ground. He'd been wrong. Fighting to save these people was Kym's responsibility. Even if she didn't believe in the gods' plan, protecting Princirum from death was her destiny. But how could she defend the people and save Princirum at the same time?

N O   M O R E
S A C R I F I C E

IT WAS DARK WHEN KYM OPENED HER EYES. SHE STARED AT THE ceiling, absentmindedly tracing the faint scars on her forearms, listening to Kat, Ashlyn, and Amber's heavy breathing. More than anything, she wanted to stay there—to burrow beneath the thin blankets and not face the world. But Kym knew that wasn't an option. Not after the embarkment.

She'd wanted to show Short the respect he deserved. It never crossed her mind that the Disciples would bow to her when it was all over. For one thing, she hated when people bowed to her. But there was no changing what happened. Somehow, the Disciples now looked to Kym and her friends as leaders. But how could Kym lead them in a war they couldn't win?

Kym sat up, her muscles quivering uncomfortably. She needed to move around and burn off some of her nervous energy. Kym climbed out of bed as quietly as she could, trying not to wake the others. She opened her drawers, put on the first things she found, and slowly pushed open the door.

Kym crossed the deserted common room and was out in the hall in seconds. She didn't meet a soul as she walked to the stairwell, but she wasn't surprised. The Council announced that all non-essential workers wouldn't start work until nine because of the embarkment. Kym doubted anyone would be up for hours.

When she reached the bottom of the stairs, Kym half walked, half ran through the dark library. She burst through the front door and stopped dead in her tracks. The blackened, crumbling remains of the pyres still sat on the veranda. Kym's breath caught in her throat as her eyes fell on the one that had been Short's. Why hadn't the Council cleared them away? They'd only wanted to spend twenty minutes on the service, after all.

Kym walked past the smoking pyres, staring determinedly ahead. She needed to relax. In another life, Kym would've gone to the water dome at Wadita and spent the morning swimming, training, and being alone. But there was nothing like that at the tower. She could try the training room on the top floor, but it was very limited. Kym wanted to be underwater—to let everything go. Even if it was only for a moment.

"Running away?"

Kym jumped, her heart racing in her chest. She spun around, her long hair whipping her in the face. Tomark stood behind her, smiling faintly. Kym shook her head. How long had he been following her? She hadn't heard him as she descended the tower.

"No," Kym said. "I just…I needed some time to think. After last night."

"I can go," Tomark smiled. "Take your space."

Kym laughed. She didn't want him to go. Sure, Kym was the one who started all of the craziness at the embarkment, but it happened to Tomark too. He wasn't like Amber or Kat or Xander, who liked having all eyes on them. At least with Tomark, Kym had someone who knew how she felt.

Kym invoked her Marks and looked to the sky. She drifted into the air, her hair floating dreamlike around her. She saw Tomark shake his head before rising into the air. Kym focused her energy, imagining the water swirling around her. She floated upward, trying to leave her worries on the ground as she rose higher.

Tomark shot past Kym, and she smiled. She refocused her energy, determined to catch him, but it was more complicated than it looked. Swimming through the air wasn't like flying. The air felt oddly thick and warm as it pressed against her skin. Tomark glanced over his shoulder, and Kym saw him smile as he veered to the side.

Kym followed, not really paying attention to where she was going. She flipped around at the last minute, and her feet slammed into the hard tower roof. Kym stumbled back, pain shooting through her legs like needles. Tomark's fingers wrapped around Kym's wrist, holding her steady.

"Thanks for the save," Kym panted, pulling herself back up.

"Always," Tomark smiled. He jerked his head to a large vent. "Wanna sit?"

Kym nodded. She followed Tomark, who sat on the large grate-covered box. It wasn't very comfortable, but Kym didn't care. She laid her head on Tomark's shoulder and watched the sun creep over the horizon. It was beautiful, and Kym lost herself staring at the molten sky. She could stay there forever.

"Wanna talk about it?" Tomark asked a lifetime later.

"About what?" Kym asked although she knew exactly what he meant.

"Last night," Tomark laughed, and she could hear him smiling. "What were you thinking?"

"I...I wasn't," Kym said, and she meant it. "I didn't mean for any of it to happen."

"I know," Tomark breathed. "But it did, and we can't take it back—us taking over, the crowd bowing, all of it."

Kym closed her eyes. Maybe, everything that happened was a one-time fluke? After all, most of the Disciples didn't like the Favored. Kym was sure they'd get over it soon. And the quicker things went back to normal, the better. She hoped Tomark was wrong.

Kym and Tomark lapsed into silence, just sitting together as the sun rose higher and higher. After a while, oddly distant voices reached Kym's ears. Kym sighed. How much longer could she and Tomark stay up here? No matter how long it lasted, she knew it wouldn't be enough.

The people on the ground grew louder. In fact, Kym didn't think they were talking—she heard them repeating the same thing over and over. Her curiosity piqued, Kym stood and walked to the edge of the tower. She saw the massive crowd on the lawn, which looked like a ring of ants gathered around two individuals from so high up.

Kym narrowed her eyes and smiled. She'd know that fiery mane in the middle of the crowd anywhere.

"Blessed ones!" the crowd shouted, closing in on the two in the center.

"Please." Kym heard Ashlyn's voice rise over the crowd. "That's not necessary."

"Blessed one!" the crowd continued.

"Don't you got anything better to do?"

Kym's smile widened. Even though she couldn't see her, she knew Kat's voice. But what were they doing in the middle of a crowd of Disciples? Kym knew the answer before the question formed in her mind. They were looking for her and Tomark. But how could they let them know where they were? Kym had no desire to enter that mob.

"I've got it," Tomark said beside Kym.

He raised his arm, his silver Marks glowing. A gust of wind burst from his fingers, blowing Kym's hair around her. Dust rose around the crowd, their clothes and hair flying around them. And while everyone else covered their faces, Kym saw Ashlyn and Kat look up.

Kym smiled and stepped back from the edge of the roof. She turned just in time to see the flash of yellow light fade around Kat and Ashlyn. Ashlyn smiled at Kym, but Kat looked downright annoyed.

"That was ridiculous!" Kat groaned, plopping down and crossing her legs.

"I'm sure it wasn't—"

"It was," Ashlyn nodded, cutting across Tomark. "They followed us through the tower while we looked for you."

"They wouldn't leave us alone!" Kat snapped.

Kym sat beside Kat, and she could feel Kat's annoyance at the crowd radiating off of her. Kym fought to keep herself from laughing. Kat and Kym usually agreed on most things, but where they differed was their delivery. And even though Kym wasn't as blunt, she still thought Kat was right…even if she was a little over-dramatic.

"Why were you looking for us?" Tomark said, sitting beside Kym.

"Because we need to talk," Ashlyn said, the smile falling from her lips.

All the happiness inside Kym vanished in a flash. She knew precisely what Ashlyn wanted to say. With losing Short and the others, and the embarkment after, they never had a chance to tell Ashlyn what they learned in Nothingness. It seemed Kat filled Ashlyn in.

"Is it true?" Ashlyn asked weakly.

Kym opened her mouth, but closed it. She couldn't bring herself to say the words aloud. Somehow, now that she was out of Nothingness, admitting that she'd died made it more real. But Kym knew she couldn't hide from this. Not when it was this big. Slowly, she nodded.

Ashlyn's face fell, tears streaming from her green eyes. Kym crawled over to her and wrapped her arms around Ashlyn. Her shoulders trembled, but Kym didn't let go. Kym felt two more pairs of arms appear around her, sending a shudder down her spine. She wasn't sure when she started to cry. But after a while, tears covered her face too.

"How'd this even happen?" Ashlyn asked after a while, her face still buried in Kym's shoulder. "How could we not know that we died?"

"I guess we always did," Tomark said thickly. "We've been dreaming about our time in Nothingness for over a year. We just didn't realize what it meant."

"But how are we still here?" Kat snapped, wiping her face with her sleeve. "Amber said we died, and Thed said we were snatched from him. What does that even mean? How could we die, then come back without the god of death knowing how?"

"It makes no sense," Ashlyn agreed.

"Murdered," Kym said, her voice dark. "We didn't just die, Kat. The Rulers intended to kill us when they ripped out our magic."

Kym felt sick. She didn't know what she found more confusing —the fact that the Rulers murdered them or that they somehow came back. How could the god of death not know why they'd come back to life? He was a god, after all. If Thed didn't know who saved them, who could?

"We should get going," Kat said, pulling away from the others and standing.

"Where?" Kym asked.

"We ran into Parker earlier," Ashlyn said, offering her hand to Tomark. "There's a Council meeting today. They want us there."

Kym stared at Ashlyn. Why would the Council want them at their meeting? They'd barely tolerated them at the best of times. Kym had a sinking feeling in her stomach. The Council hadn't done anything when Kym took over the embarkment. Was that because all of the Disciples were watching? Was Kym about to pay for stepping in?

The crowd of people on the lawn seemed even more excited to see Kym and Tomark. They reached out, trying to grab Kym and Tomark as they followed Ashlyn and Kat into the tower. Kym tried to shake off the discomfort rippling across her skin. She'd expected this type of reception for Tomark, but why her? She wasn't the one who answered the gods' call during the Calling.

In contrast to the front lawn, the library was a ghost town. Light filtered through the vast windows, catching the dust floating through the air. Kat waved a holowatch over the panel in the elevator and pressed the button for the Council's floor. Kym stared at the large device on Kat's wrist. Where'd she get it?

The elevator doors opened, and Kym was surprised to see the hall full of people. People dressed in lab coats, robes, business suits, and workmen's overalls lined the walls. Like the crowd outside, they descended on Kym and the others the second they stepped into the corridor. Kym stepped back, her heart pounding in her ears.

"Make way!" a clipped, familiar voice yelled over the crowd.

Kym relaxed as Parker pushed through the throng, four other soldiers behind her. She grabbed Kym's shoulder and steered her down the hall while her guards kept the jostling crowd at bay. Kym slipped her hand into Tomark's as they approached the Council's room, her heart racing again. It, like the hall, was full of people.

The Council room looked different than the last time Kym was there. More chairs than normal sat around the oval table and lined the walls, and there were several more holoprojectors. Kym instinctively looked to the outside chairs, but they were all occupied. This only left one place for Kym and the others to sit.

"Blessed Ones," Perla said, smiling widely as she bowed to Kym, Kat, Tomark, and Ashlyn. "You honor this room with your presence."

"Thanks," Kym said slowly, shifting uncomfortably.

"Please, join your fellows," Perla said, still bent with her back parallel to the floor.

Kym had been so focused on the number of people there she hadn't noticed Amber, Damon, Jazin, and Xander sitting on the slightly larger chairs around the table. Xander and Jazin looked just as uncomfortable as Kym felt, while Damon looked baffled. Amber, of course, looked right at home. Kym suppressed a snort. Amber thrived being the center of attention.

Kym took one of the larger chairs since she had a feeling Perla would explode if she tried to sit on one of the smaller ones. Tomark took the one beside her, while Ashlyn and Kat took the other two. Anderson, Hale, Perla, Marek, and Mrs. Mizel stepped forward, taking the remaining chairs around the table, and silence fell over the room.

"Welcome," Anderson said. "We are honored to welcome these eight brave heroes to this meeting, where we value their input."

Those standing around the edge of the room applauded, and Kym tried to keep her face calm. What was Anderson talking about? Last she checked, Anderson only let Kym and the others be there because he needed their magic to help win a war. Why was he acting like they were honored guests? And since when did Anderson welcome Kym's, or anyone's, input?

"As you know, Princirum stands at the precipice." Marek stood, and Kym saw his eyes were narrow. "Everything we've struggled to maintain here, following the paths set before us by the gods, hangs in the balance. Thed threatens everything we hold dear with his eternity of death. We mustn't let that come to pass."

"On that note," Hale said, her tone much more businesslike, "now that we've honored the fallen, we must discuss the possibility of a retaliatory attack from Thed's forces."

Hale stared at Kym and the others. Kym stared back, her mind blank. Why was Hale staring at her? They'd talked about this the previous day—they agreed Thed would influence the Rulers to attack after their failed mission in Nothingness. But why was Hale looking to her for confirmation? It wasn't like Kym or the others had any power here. Weren't they guests in this meeting like everyone else?

"The Rulers, under Thed's influence, will no doubt attack again," Hale said after no one spoke. "Our failed assault on Thed will not go unpunished. Therefore, we must ensure our forces are ready for whatever they throw at us."

Again, Hale looked across the table, her eyes wide. Now Kym was really confused. Even if Kym had any idea how the Rulers might retaliate, what right did she have to speak here? She'd already messed up by taking over the embarkment. She wasn't going to overstep again.

"Blessed Ones," Perla said, getting to her feet. "What insights do you have?"

"Um…" Kym, Kat, Jazin, and Damon all said.

Kym couldn't believe it. They actually wanted their input. But why? All they'd wanted for months was for Kym and the others to do what they were told. Kym shifted uncomfortably. Why the sudden change of heart?

"Well," Xander said, his deep voice shaking. "They will attack. And soon."

"What type of attack do you think we'll face?" Hale asked, typing something on the table so that a map of the tower burst into the air. "Something similar to the attack a month ago?"

"No," Amber said, and she too stood up. "The Favored share one mind. The Unity knows your defensive capabilities and that long-range attacks won't work. They also know it's nearly impossible to cross the trunk line when its output is maxed out. Lucia's smart and ruthless. She'll do whatever it takes to bring this place down."

Silence followed Amber's words. Goosebumps rose over Kym's arms, and she shifted in her seat. Amber was right, of course. The thought of the Unity laying siege to the tower was one thing, but Lucia was a whole other problem. With the Unity under her control, they'd never stop. Would Lucia send the Favored there and force them to cross the trunk line, even when she knew it wouldn't work? She'd tortured Kym and the others by breaking their bones. Lucia wouldn't think twice about sacrificing the Favored to win.

"Agreed," Hale nodded. "We are safest if we remain here, but that leaves us exposed and confined while leaving the Rulers and Thed free to make their move."

"We should start by increasing the trunk line output to one hundred percent from now on," Anderson said.

"But what if someone gets in?" Marek asked. "We'd still be vulnerable to attack, even if the trunk line greatly weakened them as they entered."

"Could we set up storm generators and beads to remote detonate?" Parker asked. "My soldiers could place them in rings between the line and the tower. If someone got in, we could activate them remotely. That way, we'd be in a better position to mount a counterattack."

There was a murmur of assent from the Council and gathered spectators. Kym's eyes narrowed as Parker's words sunk in. This didn't sound like a battle plan at all, but like they were fortifying the tower. But what good would that do? They couldn't stay there forever, no matter how prepared they were. Sooner or later, Kym knew Thed would find a way in. Death always found a way.

"It's possible," Anderson said. "However, the output from the storm to these defensive measures may have a negative impact on our power supply."

"We'll manage," Mrs. Mizel said. "What matters is keeping our people safe. We should take a look at our food stores and make sure we have enough to sustain the community for a long-term assault."

"The farms on the basement level are finally back to peak efficiency after suffering damage in the last attack," Marek said. "If we start storing food today, we should be able to survive a prolonged battle in about a month."

"Storm generators should be set up in the farm levels as well," Hale said, typing on her screen. "We don't want to leave our food vulnerable."

Kym couldn't believe what she was hearing. They weren't planning to fight at all. To Kym, it sounded like they were giving up. But how could they? No matter how prepared they were or how strong their defenses, Kym knew the Favored would break in sooner or later. This was what the Favored trained to do—attack and overwhelm their targets until they either surrendered or broke. This wasn't a defensive strategy. It was a slow death.

"What?" Damon asked, and Kym saw her shock in his eyes. "You're not gonna fight?"

"Mister Damon," Anderson said, inclining his head to Damon. "We're no longer in a position to make an offensive move."

"But—" Damon spluttered, looking around the room.

"We have the welfare of our citizens to consider," Mrs. Mizel said. "The safety of the Disciples must be our priority."

Kym wanted to say that they were wrong, but the words wouldn't form in her mouth. After all, Mrs. Mizel wasn't wrong. They needed to make sure the Disciples were safe. They'd already lost too many people in the war with Thed, and Kym wasn't going to lose any more if she could help it. However, Kym still thought they needed to be ready to fight when it came to it.

Kym remained silent for the rest of the meeting. The Council worked through the logistics of what would happen if, and when, an attack occurred. They divided the population into groups, which would gather and wait out the attack in the basement levels. They discussed food rationing, as well as weapons distribution. With every vote the Council made, they looked to Kym and the others for confirmation. Kym always nodded. What more could she do? She wasn't going to talk the Council out of giving up when they'd clearly made up their minds.

When the meeting finished, Kym left the room as fast as possible. The crowd in the hall had thinned, as the meeting had gone for nearly two hours. Those who remained bowed as Kym ran past, and she tried not to look at them. Did they know the Council had condemned them to live the rest of their lives trapped in this tower? They would when the Council released the brief of the meeting to the public.

Kym didn't know how she made it back to the dorm. One minute she was waiting for the elevator, the next she was on the old sofa in the common room, her arms wrapped around her knees. It was like a boulder was sitting on her shoulders. This was it. They'd done all they could, and now was the time to admit defeat. Kym didn't want to, but what choice did she have? She couldn't put any more people in danger to end this war with Thed.

The door opened, but Kym didn't look to see who it was. She didn't need to. Ashlyn sat beside her, while Tomark sat on her other side. Amber, Xander, Damon, Kat, Jazin, and Xander were there too, and they all looked just as miserable as Kym felt.

"This is a disaster," Xander said, running his fingers through his sandy hair.

"Thank you, Master Obvious," Kat huffed, punching Xander's massive shoulder. "I can't believe they're giving up."

"Can't you?" Tomark asked. "What else are they supposed to do, Kat?"

"They could fight!" Damon said, throwing his hands in the air.

"They have," Jazin said. "And they're losing."

"That's no excuse for giving up," Amber snapped.

"What choice do they have?" Ashlyn asked. "You heard them in there. They're preparing for the end."

"C'mon Ash," Kat snorted. "They're preparing for a battle they can't win, and you agree with them."

"I never said that," Ashlyn said quickly. "Of course I don't think they should give up. But I don't want them to fight either."

"If they don't fight," Damon started, "Thed will wipe them out."

Kym buried her face in her knees. She didn't want to listen to this anymore. Why were they having the same argument she'd spent the past two hours listening to? Like Amber, Kat, and Damon, Kym didn't want to give up. But she also saw where Tomark, Jazin, and Xander were coming from. The Council was right for not putting their people in unnecessary danger. Too many lives had been lost because Thed wanted to destroy the world the other gods built.

"What do you wanna do, Kat?" Tomark asked. "Go out and battle the Rulers and Favored and death demons ourselves?"

"Of course she doesn't." Kym shook her head, looking at Tomark. "That would be ridiculous. We couldn't fight them all on our own."

"Well, we need to think of something," Damon said. "The gods chose us to end this war, and we're not going to do that hiding here."

"Who said anything about hiding?" Xander asked, his eyes narrowing at Damon. "We don't run from a fight."

"Says the guy who's too scared of Melana to stand up to her," Amber murmured.

Kym shook her head. That was a low blow, even for Amber. Kym didn't see why Amber felt the need to fling insults. All it did was drive a wedge between them, and Kym knew that was something they couldn't afford. The Disciples were looking to them to lead, but they couldn't do that if they were at each other's throats. Kym needed to do something, even if the Council wouldn't. But what?

"What if we broke Thed's grip on the Rulers?" Ashlyn asked. "They're what's holding him here."

"We barely got Thed out of *one* morgar," Jazin said. "And it turned into a disaster afterward. Besides, we'd never get close enough to them."

"We could if Parker and her guys came with us," Kat said, lying back on the floor in the middle of the room.

"Their storm gear would give us an edge," Amber nodded. "And the Rulers wouldn't expect it."

"She wouldn't do it." Kym shook her head, even though she wished she was wrong. "Parker lost soldiers because she listened to us. She won't put her soldiers in danger for another one of our plans. Besides, the Council wouldn't approve it. And we're not going to steal the only fighters and weapons they have left."

Silence followed Kym's words. She wished she was wrong, because Kat and Amber had a point. With Parker's soldiers and their weapons, they'd stand a chance of beating the Rulers. But it was too risky. If they took Parker and her men, they'd leave the Disciples open for an attack. They needed a better plan.

"What if...taking the Rulers by surprise *is* the right play?" Tomark asked.

"What?" Kym asked.

"Like you said, we can't take them head-on. What if we surprise them?"

"How the Nothingness would we do that?" Kat asked. "They'd see us coming from a mile away."

"We could sneak in," Damon said excitedly. "Like we did to get your magic back. It's perfect!"

Kym's heart thudded a little faster. Why hadn't she thought of it before? It was so simple. If they snuck into Crystal Palace without being seen, they could take the Rulers by surprise. Damon had said only servants knew about the back path.

"No," Amber said, shaking her head. "It's not."

"Oh, c'mon," Ashlyn said, her disappointment apparent. "Why not?"

"Because we knew about the path when we were connected to the Unity," Jazin said darkly. "So all the Favored may know about it."

"May?" Kat asked, sitting up a little.

"Our emotions were still causing interference," Xander said. "But anyway, it's stupid to use a secret path that may or may not be secret."

Kym's heart fell. Xander and Jazin were right. They couldn't risk the mountain path, especially since they needed the element of surprise. But without the mountain path and not being able to attack the Rulers outright, Kym saw no other options.

"What else can we do?" Tomark asked, standing up and pacing around the room.

"We could kidnap Lucia," Amber said bitterly.

"And…what good would that do, exactly?" Ashlyn asked.

"It would make me feel better," Amber huffed. "And if we take her out, she wouldn't be able to control the Unity."

"C'mon, Amber. You know we can't do that," Kym sighed, even though the thought of kidnapping Lucia made her feel somehow lighter. "You just wanna fight her because she spent a year bossing you around."

"No," Amber bleated, but Kym saw right through her.

After everything that happened between them, the thought of fighting Kenna, or Aidan, or Lance was tempting. But Kym knew Ashlyn was right. No matter how Amber spun it, fighting Lucia wouldn't help them beat the Rulers.

"If we could just get the Rulers alone," Damon said, sitting down in a huff.

"We'd be lucky to be in the same realm as them," Xander sighed. "Either way, it's not gonna happen."

"I doubt they'd even show up if we attacked Crystal Palace," Jazin said. "Thed wouldn't risk losing his most powerful anchors to Princirum. He'd hide them somewhere until the attack was over."

Kym opened her mouth but closed it. Jazin was right. The Rulers were Thed's most valuable prize, and she knew he wouldn't put them in danger. That was why he kept them hidden away in Crystal Palace while Lucia controlled the Unity for them. If Kym and the others attacked the Rulers in any way, Thed wouldn't let them attack back. He'd probably have them hide on the other side of Princirum, or at the edge of the world where the ocean fell into the void. But if Kym and the others couldn't get close to the Rulers, they'd never be able to break Thed's connection.

Slowly, Kat sat up from her place on the floor. She looked at Kym, her eyes slightly glazed over, her mouth hanging open. Kym shifted uncomfortably as Kat stood, her head moving slowly from side to side like she was trying to take in the whole room. Kym watched the corners of Kat's lips turn upward, and a shiver ran down Kym's spine. What was Kat doing?

"Okay," Kat said, her voice uncharacteristically low. "I have a really, *really*, stupid idea."

CHAPTER TWENTY-SEVEN

ON BENDED KNEE

KYM TOOK SEVERAL SHAKY BREATHS AS THE SUN SLID OVER THE horizon, filling the sky with warm, red light. A light breeze tickled her face, her long blond hair flying back as she stepped forward. It was a peaceful moment, but Kym knew it wouldn't last. In her experience, nothing peaceful ever did. That didn't stop her from savoring the moment.

Kym's head split open as she crossed the trunk line, lights exploding in her eyes as tears streamed down her face. She gasped, rubbing her temples as she pressed on. The pain would pass. It always did. Kym just hoped the fluttering in her stomach would stop too.

"Well, that hurt," Kat groaned.

"And that's only fifty percent," Ashlyn said. "When they increase it to one hundred, it should stop any Favored who try to cross."

"For now," Damon murmured.

"Hopefully, it won't come to that," Tomark said.

A shiver ran down Kym's spine. She hadn't slept all night, even though she knew she needed to. She couldn't get her mind to turn off. How could she? There were so many things that could go wrong. If their plan failed, all they'd fought for would be for nothing.

Kym followed Amber and Xander away from the university. She glanced over her shoulder and saw the vast tower shining in the early morning light. People would be waking up soon. How long would it take before anyone realized they were gone? Kym hoped it would take a while. The last thing she needed was for the Council to try and stop them. They'd have a hard time talking her out of it. She could almost hear her father's voice telling her it was too risky, or dangerous, or stupid. She didn't care. She'd made up her mind the night before. This was her only chance to end the eternity of Thed.

"This is far enough," Xander said when they were several blocks from the trunk line.

Kym stopped, standing between Kat and Jazin while the others joined them. If Kym didn't know what they were up to, she'd have thought they were out for a morning stroll, all dressed in casual training clothes. But Kym knew better. And Ashlyn was right about their choice of clothes. The less threatening they looked, the better.

"So…" Jazin trembled, shifting from one foot to the next.

"Everyone clear on the plan?" Amber asked. She spoke in her usual confident tone, but Kym saw her slender shoulders shaking.

"Remember," Kat said, her voice higher than usual, "Wait until you're as close as you can get. We've only got one shot."

"And keep your cool," Xander said, looking knowingly at Kat. "Don't get cocky and give away the plan too early."

"But don't be stupid," Kym said, her voice shaking a little. "If things go wrong, just bail like we planned."

"Kym's right," Tomark said. "No matter what happens, don't trust a thing they say."

"We don't need to worry," Damon said, puffing out his chest. "It's gonna work. It's the gods' plan. We got this."

Kym nodded. She knew a million different things could make this idea a disaster, but she hoped it would work. They'd thought it all through the night before. After all, they knew the Rulers better than anyone. Their plan would work—they just needed to keep their heads until it was over.

"It's time," Ashlyn whispered.

Kym's stomach lurched as electricity jolted over her skin. She walked to Tomark, pressing her forehead into his chest. He wrapped his arms around her, and pulled her closer as he rested his chin on the top of her head. Like they had many times before, Kym's fears melted away in Tomark's arms. She wanted to stay there forever—together and out of danger. But she knew she couldn't.

"This is it," Kym whispered into Tomark's chest, not daring to look up.

"It is," Tomark answered, his usually calm voice trembling.

Kym's heart thundered against her ribs. That sound, Tomark's fear, was more frightening than anything. He trembled against her, and Kym wanted to do something to stop it. She wrapped her arms around Tomark's neck, and pressed her lips against his. Warmth spread through her as Tomark became very still, and the world faded around her until it was only them.

Even though Kym didn't want to stop, she knew she had to. She pulled away, opened her eyes, and saw Tomark staring at her. He was smiling, and the sight made Kym smile too. That smile was all she needed. It was what she was fighting for.

"I'll see you in a bit," Tomark said, tucking Kym's hair behind her ear.

"See you in a bit," Kym nodded, her face growing hot while her insides squirmed. She hoped Tomark was right.

Kym turned to the others. Jazin and Amber were still holding onto each other while Xander ruffled Damon's black hair. Ashlyn had one arm draped over Kat's shoulder, who elbowed Ashlyn in the ribs, the ghost of a smile on her lips. Kym fought to keep her tears from spilling down her face. She couldn't cry. If Kym let her fear get to her, she'd never go through with the plan. She needed to stay strong.

They all moved at once. Kym invoked her Marks, and her skin vibrated with the power radiating from the water charm. Kym closed her eyes, focusing all of her energy and willpower on her destination. The image formed easily in her mind, and Kym felt her magic pulling her toward it. Kym spun on the spot, and the rush of waves filled her ears.

Kym hurtled through space, her body everywhere and also nowhere. She redoubled her focus, not letting the image in her mind waver. The pieces of Kym collided back together, and the sound of the world assaulted her ears. Kym's feet slammed into solid ground, and she opened her eyes.

She was at the end of a long, dirt road lined with palm trees. Large, colorful birds flew above her, filling the air with their beautiful song. The sound of waves crashing on the sand rose off in the distance as salty air stung her nose. An enormous, glittering blue building sat at the end of the long drive, its base surrounded by golden sand.

Kym took a deep breath, trying to stop her hands from shaking. She moved toward the palace, not even bothering to conceal herself. She could've easily kept to the shadows, but that wasn't part of the plan. So, she strolled down the middle of the front drive, the massive blue palace growing larger with every step.

The building looked just as Kym remembered it. An enormous structure made of solidified water, it looked like a wave made solid. Its many levels and towers loomed ever larger as Kym drew nearer. The sight slowed the thudding in Kym's chest. She may have been miserable most of her time there, but it was still her home. It was a strange thing for her to admit, but she'd actually missed the Palace of Water.

Wadita loomed larger than Kym remembered as she drew nearer. Long, blue banners emblazoned with the symbol of water, the wave, flapped meekly in the sea breeze. But that wasn't why Kym's hands were shaking. Before the Rulers locked Kym in Tenbatter, Nila's growing paranoia resulted in her summoning a small army of Protectorate to the palace. But as Kym approached the sweeping blue stairs, she saw no one.

Kym stopped a few feet from the steps, her hair standing on end. Where was everyone? Kym knew Nila was at Crystal Palace, but Amber said the Favored always slept at their own palaces before warping to Inferon. That was why they decided to arrive at sunrise. Their plan wouldn't work if there was no at the palaces to receive them.

As calmly as she could, Kym sank to her knees. The hard earth of the front drive dug into her skin, but she ignored the pain. Kym raised her trembling hands to her shoulders and stared at the grand front doors, but they remained shut. Kym closed her eyes, steeling herself for one final moment, then opened her mouth.

"I am Kymbralyn Collins, the Vanquisher of Water and Prized of Reta. I am here to surrender to Lady Nila."

Kym braced herself, not taking her eyes off the door. After getting over her shock at hearing Kat's really stupid plan, Kym had to admit it was actually quite brilliant. They'd talked themselves in circles, trying to figure out how to fight the Rulers head-on. But they weren't going to do that. At least, not at first. Kym knew Nila —she couldn't resist Kym's surrender, no matter how loudly Thed whispered in her ear. This was how they'd get the Rulers in the open. Now all Kym needed to do was wait.

The front doors swung open, and Kym tried her best not to react. Acting frightened wouldn't get her close to Nila. Four people stepped out onto the front steps, and Kym's heart skipped a beat. Aidan, Kenna, Ryland, and Jean stared at Kym, their faces emotionless and empty.

"Lady Nila is away," they said in unison, their voices flat. "We accept your surrender."

Ryland and Jean descended the stairs, and Kym took a breath to calm herself. It was okay. Xander thought the Rulers wouldn't come out when they first asked. Kym had hoped he'd be wrong, but she didn't worry. They'd planned for this too.

Kym dropped her hands and turned on the spot. Two water bolts shot from her fingers before Ryland or Jean reached the bottom of the stairs. The bolts hit them in the chest, and they flew back, slamming into the wall on either side of the doors. Kenna and Aidan raised their hands, their Marks glowing, but they needn't have bothered. Kym was back on her knees, her hands once again raised.

"I am Kymbralyn Collins, the Vanquisher of Water and Prized of Reta. I've come to surrender to Lady Nila," Kym repeated, fighting to keep her voice calm.

Kym tried to force her face to be just as impassive as her former teachers'. It was harder than it looked. Kym's first impulse was to attack—too much training, she guessed. But she couldn't. That was Tomark's part of the plan. They'd only attack if anyone other than the Rulers tried to take them. This way, the Rulers had no choice but to appear. But how long would that take, and how many Favored would Kym need to fight before it was all over?

Faint yellow lines bloomed from Aidan and Kenna's temples, stretching to their blank eyes. Kym held her breath. They were getting their new orders from Lucia. Kym hoped she was telling them to back off. She didn't want to keep attacking them. Aidan and Kenna stepped forward, and Kym suppressed a sigh.

"Lady Nila accepts your surrender," they said together. "We will take you to her."

Kym invoked her Marks and shoved her hands forward. Her water blast streaked through the air and shattered Aidan's hastily made shield. He flew back and collided with Ryland, who'd just managed to get back to his feet. They slammed back into the wall as Kenna raised her hands, two water bolts at the ready, but Kym was back on the ground, her hands raised in surrender once again.

"I am Kymbralyn Collins, the Vanquisher of Water and Prized of Reta. I am here to surrender to Lady Nila," Kym said again, looking right into Kenna's blank face.

Anger boiled inside Kym as more yellow lines flashed on Kenna's forehead. What was taking Nila so long? Had Kat been wrong? Were the Rulers going to refuse their surrender after all? Kym's stomach squirmed uncomfortably at the thought.

Kym's eyes raked over the glittering blue palace. If Nila didn't come, she needed to run as soon as possible. Warping wasn't an option—she couldn't manage it if the Favored attacked her. She could fly away, but she doubted she'd make it far before something caught up with her. She needed to get back to the Disciples. Kym had a feeling they'd be the target of the Rulers' retaliation if things went wrong.

Kenna stepped down the stairs, her arms raised, ready to attack. The power from the water charm surged through Kym, and two bolts appeared above her fingers. Kym stood, her own hands raised as she planted her feet. It wouldn't take her long to beat Kenna, and then she'd make a break for it.

"Stop."

Kenna froze, her foot suspended in midair. Kym looked past her friend, and the air vanished from Kym's lungs. A tall, slender woman glided out the front doors, her shimmering blue dress floating around her. A towering, seven-pointed crown sat atop her dark hair, making the enormous woman look even taller. She glared down at Kym, and the delight in her cold eyes made Kym want to run in the opposite direction.

"Kymbralyn Collins," Nila said, her voice dripping with venom. "After all this time, you have returned home."

Kym fought every instinct she had not to blast Nila where she stood. She wanted Nila to pay for everything she'd put Kym through—the training, the isolation, the punishments, the attempted murder. But for Kat's plan to work, Kym couldn't let her anger get the better of her. For once, she needed to keep her emotions in check.

Kym sank to her knees, fighting to keep her anger under control as she raised her arms. Her water bolts vanished as she stared at Nila, daring her to approach. Kym couldn't attack Nila by surprise if she was too far away. But Nila stayed at the top of the steps, her thin lips stretching into a twisted smile.

"After months of searching, it seems you have come to your senses at last," Nila whispered, but Kym heard every word like Nila stood right next to her. "The loyalty of my Favored means everything to me, as you know, Kymbralyn. I do not know how you survived your previous…transgressions. But it does not matter. Not anymore."

Nila's face relaxed, and inky blackness flooded her eyes. Kym's breath caught in her throat. While Thed influenced her actions, Nila's guard was down. This was Kym's chance to attack. But Nila was still too far away. She'd stop Kym's assault before it reached her. Kym just needed to get a little closer.

"Kenna. Jean," Nila snapped, her eyes returning to their usual color. "Escort Kymbralyn to her bedchamber. A Favored of her status should not wear such…common clothes."

Yellow lines glowed on Kenna and Jean's foreheads as they stood on either side of Nila. They walked down the steps, their Marks no longer glowing. Kym didn't resist as they grabbed her upper arms and pulled her to her feet. Getting a makeover wasn't exactly what she'd had in mind when Kat suggested they surrender. But once she was dressed correctly, she'd see Nila again. She'd make her move then. For now, she needed to play along.

Kenna and Jean marched Kym up the front steps and into the palace. The massive, round entrance hall was just as Kym remembered it. Kym didn't say a word as Kenna and Jean dragged her through one of the doors along the curved wall. The stairs were empty, but Kym didn't expect anything less. No doubt Nila wanted the Water Favored to give her a wide birth. She wasn't dressed correctly after all.

They reached the floor where Kym's bedchamber had been a lot faster than she expected. They walked down the hall, morning light streaming through the tall windows. Somewhere outside, she heard the crash of the sea. She remembered the last time she was here like it was yesterday. She'd just finished the Third Trial of the Calling, and Tomark had snuck into her room while she worried about saving her mom. The whole thing seemed like a lifetime away.

Jean opened Kym's bedchamber door, and Kym stepped inside, unsure what to expect. The large room was spotless, with a large bed on one wall and the little sitting area beside it. Light from the glass balcony doors flooded the room, making it look oddly bright. It looked just like it had when Kym left. But how was that possible?

"Lady Nila wants her dressed," Kenna and Jean said in unison.

Kym's pulse quickened as Kenna closed the door behind Kym. Two women walked out of the closet, their eyes wide. They were older, in their fifties, and wore simple blue dresses. Kym's heart stopped at the sight of them, and for the first time since arriving at Wadita, she forgot her mission. How was this possible? She'd thought they were dead.

"My dear," Isabel said, her light, singsong voice no more than a whisper.

"What's the occasion?" Veronica asked. Her voice was stern, but Kym saw the tears glittering in her eyes.

"She is to be presented to her Ruler," Kenna and Jean said flatly.

"We will remain here…" Kenna said.

"…until she's ready," Jean continued without missing a beat.

"For your protection," they finished in unison.

"Of course, Miss Kenna and Miss Jean," Isabel said, inclining her head to each of them.

"We appreciate your protection," Veronica added.

Kenna and Jean released their hold on Kym, who found it hard to remain standing. This was impossible. How were Veronica and Isabel there? Kym stepped closer to them, taking in their sunken eyes, pale skin, and thin frames. Anger raged inside of Kym like a wild beast. What had Nila done to them? Kym clenched her jaw as her hands shook at her sides. She couldn't let her anger overtake her reason. Too much was at stake.

"Well, if she's to be presented to Lady Nila, she'll need a bath at least," Veronica started. She circled Kym, looking everywhere but in her eyes. "She's filthy."

"And she'll need a full workover," Isabel said, running her trembling fingers through Kym's hair.

"Get it done," Kenna and Jean said.

They raised their hands, and their Marks glowed on their forearms. "We control the water in this room, Kymbralyn. Any signs of disloyalty, and we attack the Servitude."

Kym spun around, her heart jumping in her throat. Were they really threatening Veronica and Isabel? They were the kindest, sweetest people Kym knew. Kym fought back her urge to water blast Kenna and Jean out of the room. She could take them both easily in a fight. It would be over before they knew what was happening. But Kym couldn't let her anger get the better of her. Someone else was pulling their strings, after all.

"Lucia," Kym said, staring into Kenna's blank face, "I surrendered, and I meant it. I'm not going to do anything."

"Perhaps," Kenna said. Her voice was no longer flat, and she spoke in Lucia's quiet, gentle cadence. "If you really mean it, hand over the water charm."

Kym shook her head and smiled. She knew this would happen. With the water charm, Kym was a threat, and Lucia knew she couldn't take the water charm from Kym. It was bound to Kym's magic, and the only way she'd get it was if Kym willingly handed it over, or if Kym died. But the charm was Kym's only leverage against the Favored. They'd listen to Kym so long as she still wore it.

"The charm will be yours…when I'm kneeling at Nila's feet."

"I look forward to it."

"Miss Kenna," Veronica said, her light, singsong voice higher than normal. "This girl needs a bath. Would you please fill the tub?"

The emotion vanished from Kenna's face as she raised her hand. The sound of splashing water drifted in from the next room, and Kym relaxed slightly. Kym turned and followed Isabel into the bathroom, trying to hide the smile on her face. If they were letting Veronica and Isabel wash her, they believed she was going to keep her word. But how long would that last?

Isabel flung her shaking arms around Kym the moment Veronica closed the door. Kym staggered back, her legs trembling as she held onto Isabel. Behind her, Kym felt Veronica's shaky breaths as her hands stroked Kym's hair.

"My dear," Veronica whispered, her voice shaking. "How is this possible?"

"We thought you'd left us to wander Nothingness," Isabel sighed.

"It didn't take," Kym said, laughing a little. She didn't know how to explain it. Besides, she knew her time was limited.

"Let me see you," Isabel said. She placed her hands on Kym's cheeks, brushing her hair out of her eyes. "You've endured a great deal."

"So have you," Kym said, looking from Isabel to Veronica sunken features. "What happened?"

"After the Calling, Lady Nila told us of your death and reassigned us to manual labor," Veronica said.

"What?" Kym shouted.

Veronica's hand flew to Kym's mouth while Isabel hurried to the door. They waited in silence, Kym's heart pounding in her chest. Had Kenna and Jean heard her? But after a few moments' silence, the door remained closed, and Veronica lowered her hand.

"Don't worry about us," Isabel said. "Our sole concern was your well-being."

"My well-being?" Kym shook her head. "It looks like you've been to Nothingness yourselves."

"We've endured worse," Veronica said, smiling at Kym. "But why did you return, my dear? After all this time—"

"Veronica," Isabel cut across her. She was staring at Kym, her eyes narrow. "Kym wouldn't return unless it was important."

Kym nodded, her eyes darting to the door. She wanted to tell them everything, but she couldn't risk Kenna and Jean overhearing. Kym grabbed Veronica and Isabel's hands, squeezing them so tightly they winced.

"I'm here to surrender," Kym said pointedly. "But only to Nila."

Kym watched Veronica and Isabel's eyes widen as her words washed over them. Aside from her friends, they were the people who knew her best. They'd dedicated their lives to caring for her, after all. They knew how much Kym disliked Nila. They knew she'd never willingly surrender to her, not if it wasn't for a good reason.

"Okay," Veronica said slowly, nodding her head. "Then we'll do our best to help."

"She'll need her best clothes," Isabel said quickly, unzipping Kym's running jacket. "Nila will expect nothing less."

It was like the past year and a half apart never happened. Veronica and Isabel sprang into action, no more than blue blurs as they ran around Kym. She was undressed and in the steaming tub in seconds. Kym sighed as Isabel poured sweet-smelling oils into the water while Veronica examined Kym's clothes.

"She's smaller in the hips and chest," Veronica said, and Kym tried not to laugh. How did she know that after just looking at her clothes?

Veronica left the room, no doubt to deal with the clothing situation, while Isabel let Kym soak. But it didn't last long. In no time, Isabel was handing Kym a shimmering blue robe. Kym climbed out of the tub and stood in front of the enormous wall of mirrors. The woman looking back at her, her forearms and body covered in scars, her hair an unkempt mess, looked so different from the strong, powerful warrior she used to see in this room.

Isabel set to work on Kym's hair, massaging oils and sprays into it before combing it through. When Isabel finished, she led Kym back into the bedchamber. Kenna and Jean were statues beside the door, their Marks still glowing. Behind her, Kym heard the water from the tub flow down the drain.

Veronica emerged from the closet, a shimmering blue gown in her arms. She slipped it over Kym, who stared in the dressing mirror as Veronica and Isabel circled her, making their final adjustments. The dress was sleeveless and fit perfectly around her chest and hips. The lightweight skirt flared slightly, and drifted around Kym's toes as Isabel fussed with it. The shoulder straps were a light, pale blue, and the fabric darkened gradually down the dress until it was a deep, sea blue. Glittering jewels covered the dress, making Kym think she was wearing shimmering water, while her blond hair drifted behind her in a silky sheet. Kym fought to keep her face impassive as she stared in the tall dressing mirror. In her maids' expert hands, Kym finally looked like the Water Favored from her memories.

"She's ready," Veronica said after Isabel slipped a pair of flat sandals on her feet.

"Good," Kenna and Jean said. "Join the other Servitude. Now."

Veronica and Isabel bowed and left the room, and Kym fought even harder not to attack Kenna and Jean. She didn't care that they weren't in control. No one spoke to her maids that way. They'd taken care of her, and she wanted to do the same. But she couldn't. She was so close to getting Nila. She needed to keep up the act for a little longer.

"Come with us," Kenna and Jean said, yellow lines of light flashing on their foreheads. "You're needed in the entrance hall."

Kym took a breath, trying to keep her nerves from showing on her face. This was it. Nila would be in the entrance hall to accept her surrender. She'd only have one shot, so she'd need to make it count. The other Favored would probably be there as well, so Kym's timing needed to be perfect.

Kym, Kenna, and Jean returned to the entrance hall less than five minutes later. The mass of people gathered there parted, creating a path to the middle of the room. Kym walked forward, her head held high, scanning the crowd. Some of the faces she recognized, but there were others she'd never seen before. Favored dressed in red, yellow, green, purple, and silver surrounded those dressed in blue near the center.

Kym shook her head as her muscles tensed. Something was very wrong. Favored from the other elements shouldn't be at Wadita. But as Kym reached the middle of the entrance hall, another thing crossed her mind. Someone was missing from the throng.

"Where's Nila?" Kym demanded, turning to stare at the blank faces surrounding her.

"You will join her momentarily."

Aidan, Ryland, Lance, Jean, Kenna, and Roetta, the oldest living Water Favored, emerged from the crowd. Kym's legs trembled as they drew nearer. She racked her brain for something to do, but what was there? She couldn't fight her way out—there were too many Favored. But where was Nila? Kym needed Nila to show up; otherwise, she'd turned herself in for nothing.

"My terms were clear," Kym said, her voice shaking. "I'll only surrender to Nila."

"And so you shall," the crowd said in unison, making Kym's hair stand on end. "All must see the surrender."

The Water Favored raised their arms, their Marks glowing. Pain radiated through Kym's legs as her muscles moved without her consent, forcing her to her knees. Kym's muscles quivered beneath her skin as her heart raced, held in place by the collective power of her former friends, mentors, and rivals. Kym focused her mind, trying to will herself to move, but her insides were stiff as stone.

Kenna and Aidan grabbed Kym's shoulders. Kym willed her frozen muscles to move, desperate to escape, but it was no use. Kenna and Aidan spun on the spot, and Kym's body exploded into a million frozen pieces as the rush of waves filled her ears.

T H E   W A R
B E G I N S

KYM HURTLED FORWARD, UNABLE TO MOVE, PULLED THROUGH SPACE by Kenna and Aidan. She felt like an idiot. Of course, Nila wouldn't keep her word. She threatened Kym's mom to make Kym do what she said. She was a horrible person who Kym should have expected would stab her in the back. But she had bigger problems than Nila's double-cross. Where were Aidan and Kenna taking her?

Kym slammed into solid ground. Bright, midday light filled her unblinking eyes, and tears streamed down her face. Kym tried to move, but her muscles and veins quivered under Aidan and Kenna's control. A massive, black shape loomed overhead, blanketing Kym in shadow as her pulse raced.

"Good," a sweet voice said, which sent Kym's heart hammering.

Lucia, her long, braided hair pulled back, drifted into Kym's limited line of vision. Her dark brown eyes were wide, and her slight smile made Kym's heart race even faster. What was Lucia doing here? This wasn't part of the plan.

"Raise her with the others," Lucia said, her sweet voice dripping with triumph. "All will see the traitors."

Kym's heart raced. *Traitors*? Kym had a sinking feeling in her stomach. Traitors meant multiple people. Who else was there?

Kym's muscles tensed under her skin. She gasped as she rose into the air like some strange puppet. Kym's eyes darted around searching for something, anything to help her. She was floating above a crowd of Favored and black-robed priests standing at the base of a black mountain. She was at Crystal Palace.

Other people floated in front of Kym, their bodies just as still as hers. She stared at the person in front of her, his wavy, brown hair drifting in the breeze. Dread flooded Kym's pounding heart as she took in the fitted silver vest and pants, and the dark, knee high boots. Tomark. She didn't need to see the others to know they were there. Kym's heart thudded in her chest. How'd their plan fall apart so fast? She needed to find a way to get them out of there.

Kym lurched forward, and so did Tomark. The crowd roared below her, clapping and cheering as they made their way up the mountain. More people lined the winding path and joined the procession as Kym and the others floated above them, adding their screams of delight to the ever-growing throng.

Kym's mind raced. The reason they surrendered at the different palaces was to separate the Rulers. How were they supposed to fight the Rulers and the Favored all at the same time? But to fight, Kym needed to escape, and she needed control over her body to do that. There was no way she could get out of this.

Crystal Palace glittered as Kym floated above the front drive. More people cheered on the lawn—a mix of Favored, priests, and what looked like regular citizens. Kym would've gasped if she could. How were so many people still following the Rulers after everything they'd done? And why were they even at Crystal Palace? Zara, and the other Rulers, never let regular people near their homes.

Kym jerked to a stop before the sweeping front steps. Out of the corner of her eye, she glimpsed the others as they formed a line to face the palace. Kym's heart pounded in her throat while she tried and failed to move some part of herself. She'd never felt so helpless.

Silence fell instantly over the crowd like someone turned off the volume. A shiver ran over Kym's tense skin as she continued to stare at the Palace of Life. What were the Rulers waiting for? Then, almost in answer to her question, the massive front doors swung silently open.

Thunderous applause filled Kym's ears as the Rulers glided onto the palace steps. Kym's muscles tensed and shifted, and she bent forward slightly. The Rulers looked just as she remembered them—all very tall, with their pointed crowns making them look even taller. Their elegant dresses and suits floated around them, the precious stones twinkling on them like stars.

The Rulers stopped at the top of the stairs, and their strange smiles made Kym's skin crawl. She hadn't seen them all together since they tried to kill her, Tomark, Kat, and Ashlyn. Every part of Kym wanted to attack them for what they did to her. But she knew it was pointless. Not only because that wasn't part of the plan, but because the Water Favored still had a firm grip on her every muscle.

Zara raised her hands, her glittering white dress floating around her. The crowd fell instantly silent again, and Kym wanted to vomit. This was what the Rulers always wanted—a perfectly loyal army of Favored. And that wasn't the worst part. The priests and other people there were playing along. But why? What did they gain by following the Rulers and Thed?

"Today," Zara began, her voice cutting through the air like a knife, "marks an auspicious day for Princirum. The eight traitors have been captured at last. Our struggle is finally over."

More cheers erupted as Zara paused. Kym would've screamed if she could've opened her mouth. Zara and the other Rulers were calling them traitors? She couldn't think of a more hypocritical statement. As far as Kym was concerned, she and her friends were the only ones who weren't traitors at this point. At least she was still trying to keep Princirum safe. The Rulers were the ones destroying her home.

"These eight tainted souls," Zara continued, "have returned the final weapons we require. With the power of the charms and the only life and death Favored in our custody, we are finally ready to take what has been denied to us for millennia.

"The gods abandoned you—they left us to fend for ourselves while they watched us struggle. It was us, your Rulers, who led, guided, and protected you. Princirum is no longer the land of the gods. It is ours. We are the gods now!"

Another shiver ran down Kym's spine as the crowd clapped and cheered. She knew this was the Rulers' plan—it's what they'd wanted for as long as she'd known them. But hearing Zara say the words herself was different from hearing Damon or the Council say them. Zara had always been against going to war with the gods. Was ultimate power really worth destroying Princirum?

Kym needed to stop this before it was too late, but she was still under Aidan and Kenna's control. She'd have her chance once they put her down. Kym took a deep breath. She needed to be patient. The Rulers were putting on a show, and Kym and the others were the honored guests. Her time to act would come.

"To accomplish our great goal, all of Princirum must be unified." Zara paused, and even from her height, Kym saw her eyes momentarily flash black. "Unity requires devotion, power, and loyalty. These traitors are not worthy of our divine crusade. However, they will still serve and further our cause. After much deliberation with my fellow Rulers, we have reached a decision. For the crimes of desertion, treason, theft, and attempted regicide, we sentence these Favored to death."

Kym would've laughed if she could open her mouth. Sure, Kym quit being a Favored, attacked the Rulers, and stole the charms, but she never tried to kill them. It was so ridiculous Kym thought she'd misheard Zara. It had been the Rulers who tried to kill her, not the other way around. But, Kym knew, Zara needed a reason to execute them. And now she had it. Who would question the new goddess of life?

"Master Lucia, bring them to their knees."

Kym felt like a million tiny strings were pulling her insides. She lurched downward, stopping a few inches from the graveled drive. The muscles in her legs pulled and tightened, and her knees bent beneath her. She slammed onto the ground, gravel digging painfully into her legs. Kym gasped, unable to hold it in any longer. On either side of her, she heard Amber and Tomark's cries of pain.

Lucia walked in front of Kym; her large, brown eyes narrowed as her lips curled into a sweet smile. She waved her hand, and several servants dressed in white togas rushed forward. Lucia pointed silently at the hem of Kym's glittering dress. A servant ran forward and gently pulled the crumpled heap free from beneath her frozen knees. He draped it delicately on the ground around Kym before moving on to fix Amber's.

Kym tried to move the whole time the servant adjusted her dress, but it was futile. She could barely move when one Water Favored used the Cladium on her. But now at least two of them were keeping her there. There was no way she could move with them holding her down. But how could Kym attack the Rulers if she was frozen? The answer dawned on her as the servants finished adjusting her friends' clothes. She couldn't.

The Rulers glided down the sweeping steps, Zara and Phillip, the Ruler of Death, leading the way. They formed a line in front of Kym, each Ruler facing their former Favored. Kym stared into Nila's cold face, her heart racing. If she could move, she knew she'd be shaking like a leaf. This was her chance; Nila was only a few feet away from her. But Kym could barely blink, let alone mount a surprise attack.

Kym watched helplessly as blackness flooded the Rulers' eyes. They raised their hands, their Marks glowing on their forearms, and pointed them at Kym and the others. Kym focused her energy, trying to reach the water charm's power or even her life energy. Energy surged through her, but it was nothing compared to the grip the Water Favored had on her. She was helplessly stuck.

Kym felt like an idiot. She'd convinced herself that the Rulers would walk willingly out to them when they surrendered. She never considered what would happen if the plan went horribly wrong. The Rulers weren't dumb, and Kym should have known better. The Rulers always knew when Kym and the others were up to something. Why did Kym think this time would be any different? Because she hadn't seen this coming, the Rulers were going to kill her again, and Kym had a feeling this time it would stick.

Small bolts appeared above the Rulers' long, slender fingers. Kym tried to close her eyes, but her eyelids were like stone. The Rulers were going to make her watch just like they did last time. But

Kym knew better now. This wasn't her fault. She and her friends were trying to do the right thing, even if their plan had been a giant risk. She hoped the Disciples would survive the war with the gods. Kym wondered what would be left when the dust finally settled. Maybe her dad would find some peace, knowing she tried her best.

"For Princirum!"

The Rulers' eyes flashed over Kym's and the other's heads. Kym wanted to turn around, her heart racing at the sound of the voice, which she knew well. Several dark grey beads flew over the Rulers. They landed on the ground, bouncing on the glittering palace steps. They rolled down the sweeping stairs, the intricate lines glowing orange as they stopped at the Rulers' feet.

The storm beads exploded in bursts of orange light, their low hum filling Kym's ears. Her head split open as her muscles relaxed all at once. Kym toppled forward, falling face-first into the gravel. The metallic taste of blood filled Kym's mouth as her chin throbbed painfully.

"Attack!" Lucia screamed.

Cries of pain rose around Kym as the low hum of storm explosions filled her ears. Kym tried to sit up, but the pain in her head was too much. How were the Disciples there? They didn't even know Kym and the others had left.

Feet flashed past Kym's face, but they weren't the elegant boots and heels of the Rulers or Favored. Kym watched the sturdy combat boots race past the Rulers, their hands pressed into their temples. The boots hurried up the palace steps and out of Kym's line of vision.

"Secure the palace!" the familiar voice shouted. "Cut off their retreat!"

Kym pushed herself up, trying to ignore her pounding head. Six resistance soldiers stood at the top of the steps, their black packs at their feet. They pulled out large, grey cubes, and set them up in the massive palace doorway. They stepped back, and Kym saw the swirling grooves on the cubes glow orange.

"Need a hand?"

Kym looked over her shoulder. Parker stood beside Kym, the lines of her Protectorate spear glowing orange. A bright green bolt flew at Parker, and Kym reached out, ready to stop it, but the pain in her head was too much. Parker spun around, twirling her spear in her hands. The glowing orange tip hit the earth bolt, which vanished in a flash.

"What? How?" was all Kym could bring herself to say.

"You didn't think I'd let you do this alone?" Parker asked, a smile flashing on her lips. "Duck!"

Kym dropped down while Parker ran forward, slapping her massive belt buckle. The threads of her uniform glowed orange as a darkness blast collided with her. She staggered back several feet, but didn't fall as the purple energy faded around her. Kym sighed as she pushed herself back up.

"What's the plan?" Parker asked, lobbing a storm bead over Kym's head.

"Um…" With all the flashing lights and her splitting headache, Kym was having trouble focusing.

"How are you here?" Tomark shouted, deflecting a fire bolt with a silvery air shield.

"The Rulers announced your surrender," Parker said. "I figured you were doing something noble."

"Not really," Kat snorted, throwing an earth bolt randomly into the crowd.

Kym turned to the stairs, expecting to see the Rulers. But they were gone. Anger raged through Kym like an inferno. She spun on the spot, invoking her Marks and throwing two bolts into the battle raging on the front lawn. She couldn't believe she'd lost her chance to face the Rulers. The element of surprise was long gone.

"Secure the stairs!" Parker ordered.

Several soldiers broke free from the fighting crowd. Tomark grabbed Kym's arm and pulled her after Parker as she raced up the steps. The soldiers stopped at the base of the palace stairs and pulled more grey cubes from their packs. They activated them, then ran back into the fight wielding storm spears and batons.

The Favored nearest the steps collapsed, their hands pressed to their temples. Kym stepped forward, her hand outstretched. She wanted to get them away from the generators. This wasn't their fault, after all. They didn't deserve to be in pain.

"I want this mountaintop secure," Parker said into her holowatch. "Status."

"Security team conducting internal sweep," a voice issued from Parker's wrist. "The palace is free of hostiles."

"Enemy forces are attempting to retreat down the main road," another voice said. "Preparing to deploy generators to prevent their return."

"The rear mountain path is secure, Lieutenant," a third voice said. "Generators deployed every ten feet. No one's getting up this way."

Kym couldn't believe her ears. Parker wasn't there to rescue them at all. She was there to take Crystal Palace. Questions flooded Kym's pounding brain. When did Hale and Parker plan this? The Disciples never once mentioned a plan to take Crystal Palace. As far as Kym knew, it had never happened in thousands of years.

"Lieutenant, we have a tentative hold on the mountaintop."

"Good," Parker said into her holowatch, her spear collapsing in her hand. "Lock it down."

"What's going on?" Kym asked, following Parker as she stood by the palace doors. "How is this possible?"

"I went to check on you this morning," Parker smiled. She hooked her collapsed spear to her belt and removed her baton. "It didn't take a genius to figure out where you went. Then a little after sunrise, this massive construct flew over the city. All of the Rulers voices came out of it, saying you'd surrendered and you were going to be executed."

"Well, it was nice of them to keep you informed," Xander huffed. "We had no idea what was going on."

"How'd you convince the Council to let you bring the army?" Ashlyn asked. "Yesterday, they didn't want to fight."

"Seeing you willing to sacrifice yourselves to save us made quite the impression," Parker shrugged. "The vote was unanimous."

Kym didn't know what was harder to believe; the Council agreeing to save them or that the vote was unanimous. Sure, the Council had been more on their side lately, but Kym had screwed up more times than she cared to admit. Someone must have pushed them to send Parker, but who? Kym's heart fluttered as the answer came to her. Marek must have convinced the Council to send their army. He sent them there to keep her safe.

"How many are with you?" Amber asked. She waved her hand, and her red shield deflected a blast from the crowd. "You've cut off their access from the ground, but more will come from the air."

"We've got that under control." Parker pressed her holowatch again. "Commander Hale, ground access is locked down. Requesting permission to secure the airspace."

"Confirmed and acknowledged," Hale's voice rang out from the holowatch.

Kym stared at Parker. She had so many questions, she didn't know where to start. Why was Parker ordering her soldiers to secure the airspace? Clearly, Parker's plan was far more thought-out than any plan Kym had ever devised.

"Deploy storm drones," Parker said into her holowatch.

Kym held her breath, waiting for something to happen. Nothing did. Her heart thudded in her chest as her eyes darted in every direction. Had something gone wrong? She stared at the still-fighting crowd in front of her. There were a lot of Favored left on the mountaintop, trapped inside Parker's storm perimeter.

"Deploy storm drones," Parker repeated, her voice tense.

"Rear team deployed," a voice said from her holowatch.

Kym watched, openmouthed, as several small machines rose into the air, their four turbines glowing orange. They stopped sporadically above the palace towers. Kym couldn't believe it. Parker wanted to dome off the palace with storm energy. But Kym knew the handful of drones wasn't enough to seal the palace off entirely. Where were the rest of them?

"Forward team's pinned down," a frantic voice yelled from Parker's holowatch. "We can't deploy."

"Hold position," Parker said quickly. "We'll get you out of there. Use storm beads to identify your location."

Kym's hands balled into fists, shaking at her sides as she waited for the flash of orange. She watched it appear, and her breath caught in her throat. It was in the middle of the front lawn—right in the center of the fight.

Kym ran forward, her glittering blue dress fluttering around her. She leaped over the storm generators at the foot of the steps, and it felt like her head had split open. She tumbled to the ground, ignoring the pain in her head and legs, rolled to her feet, and kept running. She needed to reach the soldiers before it was too late.

"Do we have a plan?"

Kym glanced sideways. Kat, Ashlyn, and Amber were there, sprinting beside her, their glittering green, yellow, and red dresses flying around them. Kym's heart swelled at the sight of them. Kym looked at the fight raging in front of her, her mind moving fast. The Favored outnumbered Parker's men four to one. The only reason they'd survived this long was because of their storm mesh uniforms.

"We need to get Parker's guys out of there," Kym said.

"Kat, clear a path," Amber huffed, throwing a fire bolt at an oncoming light blast, which exploded in a burst of yellow and red. "Ash, get Parker's soldiers out of there. Kym, Kat, and I will handle the rest."

Kym invoked her Marks and soared upward as Kat sank into the ground and Ashlyn vanished in a flash of yellow. A column of dust exploded into the air as green lights flashed near the middle of the fight. Even with the crashes of battle all around her, Kym heard the unmistakable sound of Kat's taunting among the Favored. But Kat's voice wasn't the only one Kym heard.

"Seize the traitors!" Lucia's sickly sweet voice rose above the chaos.

As the Favored faced Kat, Kym saw a flash of yellow in the middle of the Disciple soldiers. Then, less than a second later, another flash of light fifty yards away. A man dressed in storm mesh stood with a dazed look on his face, his baton raised, ready to fight. There were more flashes of yellow in and outside the battle as Ashlyn pulled more of Parker's people to safety.

Kym threw her bolts, one after the other, down into the fight. They exploded on the ground, blowing several Favored into those behind them. Fire appeared in the space Kym cleared, and Amber emerged from the bright red flames. Amber raised her hands, and glittering red flames bloomed around her. Kym shot into the air, her heart hammering as the explosion reached her ears.

"Lucia, I'd like a word!"

Kym wheeled around, her heart pounding. Amber stood in the middle of the Favored, protected by a circle of glowing red flames. The Favored tried to attack, but their attacks merely collided with Amber's energized fire as it rose to protect her. Lucia stood a little ways away from Amber, bright red bolts orbiting around her. Bright green circles glowed on either side of Lucia, and the resulting boom shook Kym's insides. The Favored surrounding Lucia flew back, and inside Amber's circle of flames, Kym saw Kat rise out of the ground. Kym smiled. This was the fight Amber and Kat were meant for. Lucia may have made the Fire Princess, but Kat was Amber's creation. Lucia didn't stand a chance.

Bright green light filled Kym's eyes as pain erupted in her side. She plummeted toward the ground, her mind blank as her limbs flailed around her. Kym focused her energy as she hurtled toward the ground, slowing herself just enough before she slammed into the hard earth. Dazed, her ears ringing, Kym pushed herself up. Kenna, Aidan, and Lennax towered over her, their faces blank as they raised their arms.

"Seize the traitor," they said in unison.

Kym flung her arms, energy surging through her like electricity. A massive water swipe burst from her fingers, knocking Lennax, Aidan, and Kenna back. Kym sprang to her feet, threw two bolts wildly in their direction, then rose into the air. Water bolts flew from Kenna and Aidan, and Kym spun on the spot. A bright blue sphere appeared around her, and cracks spread across its surface as the attacks exploded against it.

"Ah!"

Kym's shield burst apart as a bright green blast collided with it. She flew back, spinning like a top. Kym focused her energy, determined to stop herself. She slowed, and below her, she saw bolts glowing above Kenna and Lennax's hands. Kym gritted her teeth. She was done playing defense.

Kym dove down as Kenna and Lennax's bolts flew from their hands. Kym swerved this way and that, expertly avoiding the blue and green attacks exploding around her. She flipped around at the last possible moment, swinging her arms around herself. Long tendrils of glowing water grew from her hands, wriggling like tentacles. They smacked Kenna and Lennax in the chest, and they flew back into the battling crowd.

Kym turned to Aidan, and a bright red blast shot past her. Kym's eyes narrowed at the Fire Favored standing beside Aidan. Kensrix raised his hand, another fire bolt at the ready. Kym whipped her arms, and her tendrils of water pierced Kensrix's bolt. It exploded in a burst of red light, and he flew back, landing with a thud on the ground. Kym turned back to Aidan, ready to fight her old teacher, but his five tracking bolts had already left his hands.

"Ghah!"

Bright yellow light obscured Kym's vision as warmth enveloped her. Her feet slid across the ground as the sound of distant explosions filled her ears. The yellow light faded, and Kym stood a hundred feet from where she'd been. She could see the confusion on Aidan's blank face as he stared at the spot where she'd stood, a column of dust rising into the air. Aidan turned to Kym and water flew to his hands from the nearby streams.

There was another flash of yellow, and Ashlyn stood between Kym and Aidan. She yanked her hands down, and a massive disk of energized light fell above Aidan. It exploded around him in a flash of yellow, and Aidan crumpled. Kym rose back into the air, waving her arms in a circle as Aidan struggled to his feet, but Ashlyn was faster. She appeared behind Aidan in another flash of yellow, and her light blast hit him as light bands appeared around his hands and feet. He flew toward Kym, who shoved her hands forward. Thin, blue blasts burst from the water bolts orbiting around her, which exploded against Aidan and forced him to the ground.

A deep throbbing erupted in Kym's skull while the Favoreds' pained cries filled the air. She turned, bolts flashing above her fingers, ready to attack, but stopped. More storm drones rose into the air, controlled by the soldiers Ashlyn saved. Kym sighed as sweat trickled down her face. They'd done it.

Kym flew toward the soldiers, flipping around just in time. Her feet hit the ground as the storm generators positioned themselves in a dome above Crystal Palace, the Favored's cries fading around her. Kym turned her attention back to the fighting, and her mouth fell open. The Favored were standing there, their faces blank, not moving a muscle. A shiver ran down Kym's spine. Why'd they stop attacking?

There was a flash of yellow light, and Ashlyn stood beside Kym, her face shining with sweat. Kat rose out of the ground, while Amber appeared in a rush of flames, her glittering red tiara askew. Kym's excitement faded as she noticed Amber and Kat's dark faces. Something was wrong.

"What happened?" Ashlyn asked. "Did you beat Lucia?"

"We did," Amber nodded, and Kym saw the pride in her golden eyes. "Right before the generators went up."

"What?" Kym asked.

"Yup. That was when this lot stopped attacking," Kat said, jerking her head at the frozen Favored behind her.

Kym shook her head. With Lucia out of commission, there was no one to control the Unity. But Kym knew that wouldn't last long. The Rulers would pick a new Master to control them, or do it themselves. As soon as they did, the fight would resume.

"What should we do?" Amber asked. "We can't leave them here."

Kym nodded. She turned and walked up to Parker's soldiers. They were busy going through their packs but stopped as Kym approached. They bowed their heads to her, which made Kym's skin crawl. She tried to ignore her discomfort.

"I need your storm beads."

They obeyed at once. The four closest soldiers removed the small bags from their belts, and handed them to Kym. She smiled and walked back to Ashlyn, Amber, and Kat. Kym gave each of them a bag, then dumped the contents of hers into her palm.

"These should knock them out for a while," Kym said. She squeezed her hand around her beads, and orange light glowed from the gaps in her fingers. "That should buy us some time."

Kym lobbed the beads over Kat's head, the pounding in her head growing. She ran back, bracing herself for the headache she knew would come. Orange light filled the air as a deep hum shook her bones. She groaned, her head feeling like it was splitting in two. She fell to her knees, her hands pressed to her temples. She bit her lip, waiting for the pain to pass.

Her head no longer ringing, Kym pushed herself into a sitting position. At least fifty Favored lay on the ground, not moving a muscle. Kym sighed. It wasn't a perfect solution, but at least they couldn't attack for a while.

Kym found Parker at the foot of the palace steps. Tomark, Xander, Jazin, and Damon were there too, their vests and white shirts a little more disheveled than when Kym left. She walked up to Tomark and wrapped her arms around him. She sighed into his chest, her head throbbing slightly from all the storm generators.

"Did the Rulers give up?" Parker asked.

Kym pulled back from Tomark to look at Parker. Her eyes were narrow, and her eyebrows were so close together they looked like one long line. Kym shook her head. The Rulers were many things, but they weren't quitters. And Kym knew better. The Rulers just lost Crystal Palace—the seat of their power, their thrones. The Rulers weren't going to take that lightly.

"Lieutenant, the Favored trapped in our perimeter have ceased fighting. We've knocked them out with storm beads as an extra precaution," a guard said to Parker.

"It looks like Crystal Palace is ours," Parker nodded, although Kym could see the worry in her eyes.

"For now," Kym said darkly.

Kym turned to the front lawn. Unconscious bodies lay all over the grass. What was going to happen when they woke? Kym didn't want to think about it. But she did know one thing. This fight was far from over.

T H E   M I G H T   O F   R E S O L V E

"MY FEET ARE KILLING ME."

"Really, Kat? Your feet?"

"In this exact moment, yes. I've decided to focus on that."

Kym stifled a groan as she readjusted her grip on the Disciple soldier. They'd moved all of the injured Disciples and unconscious Favored into Crystal Palace. Kym knew the Council wouldn't approve of them sheltering the Favored, but she didn't care. The Favored needed saving just like the rest of Princirum. Parker didn't object, so Kym didn't dare push her luck. Besides, Parker's main concern was using the break in the action to devise a plan.

Kym and Kat deposited their soldier with the rest of the wounded in the entrance hall. Kym's heart fell as she took in their many cuts and bruises, while some had limbs sticking in odd directions. Kym didn't know how many people Parker brought with her, but Parker said at least half of them were injured taking the palace.

"Kym, give us a hand?"

Nurse Byrd was leaning over a soldier a little ways away from Kym, a bag of medical equipment and scanners slung over her back. Kym hurried to Byrd's side, her heart quivering. Once Parker was sure the palace was secure, she brought in the medical brigade. Unlike the soldiers, who the Council sent to fight, the medical brigade were volunteers. Kym wasn't surprised Byrd was there. She'd probably been one of the first to volunteer.

"What am I doing?" Kym asked, kneeling beside the screaming man.

"Just talk to him," Byrd said, shoving her hand into her bag. "The bones in his leg are shattered."

Kym took a shaky breath. Out of all the scenarios she'd imagined that day, comforting wounded soldiers hadn't been one of them. But she wasn't complaining. If Kym and the others hadn't run off, none of these soldiers would be hurt. They'd be safe at home, without the imminent threat of an attack from the Rulers looming over them. She was happy to help in whatever way she could.

"Hey," Kym said, taking his hand. "You're gonna be fine."

"Thanks, Miss," the soldier grimaced. "It's an honor to finally meet you."

"What?" Kym shook her head, stunned. "It's an honor to meet you. You're here fighting for your home. You're a hero."

"Not like you," he winced, squeezing Kym's fingers.

"Byrd!" Kym called, her heart racing. Byrd appeared at Kym's side, pulled a scanner out of her bag, and held it over the soldier.

"His heart's racing," Byrd said. "Damon! We need you here!"

Damon ran over, surrounded by white-clothed servants carrying potted plants. Kym stared at the servants, her mouth hanging open. Kym had assumed they'd fled the palace when Parker's soldiers cleared it. Why would Zara's servants help Damon heal the Disciples? Could it be that, until recently, Damon had been a servant at Crystal Palace too? Kym thought it was possible.

Damon sank to his knees, his fingers running like spiders over the soldier's leg. He screamed, and squeezed Kym's hand so tightly her fingers cracked. Kym bit her lip, trying not to let the pain show on her face. This soldier had enough to worry about.

"I need three large plants," Damon said, not taking his eyes off the soldier's leg.

The servants acted at once. They placed three large pots around Damon, who invoked his Marks. Glittering white mist seeped out of the plants, which withered and dulled as Kym doubled her grip on the soldier's hand. Damon was going to force the life energy into his leg, and Kym didn't want him to lose it.

"Look at me," Kym said to the soldier, her body feeling lighter than air as the life energy drifted around them. "I'm not gonna lie. This is gonna hurt. You need to stay still."

The soldier nodded, his hand trembling in Kym's. She looked to Damon and inclined her head. Kym placed her free hand on the soldier's shoulder as Damon wrapped his fingers around the man's shattered leg. Even though Kym knew what was coming, she wasn't ready for the screams. The soldier convulsed as bright white light filled Kym's eyes, and it took all of her strength to keep him lying flat. But Kym didn't let go.

The bright light faded, and the man's hand relaxed in Kym's. Kym sighed and stepped back, happy to let the others do their jobs. The soldier needed rest, and Byrd needed to properly examine him now that Damon healed his injuries. Kym turned to Damon, but he was already off healing another soldier.

"Kym."

Kym spun around. Tomark stood a few feet away, leaning against one of the glittering white pillars near the edge of the entrance hall. Kym smiled and walked over to him. She wrapped her arms around him and sighed into his chest.

"You did good," Tomark smiled.

"We've been healed loads of times," Kym smiled, looking up at Tomark. "These guys don't know how awful it is."

"They'll need it," Tomark said. "Hopefully, Damon and Jazin can fix everyone up before the Rulers attack again."

The warmth faded from Kym's chest. She pulled back from Tomark and glanced at the palace doors. It had been hours since the Rulers stopped their attack. Their absence made Kym's skin crawl. Kym knew they were off somewhere, making a plan. But what plan took this long to craft? She'd expected the Rulers to retaliate by now, throwing all the magic they could muster at the Disciples.

"C'mon," Tomark said, jerking his head in the other direction. "Parker wants to talk to us."

Kym took Tomark's hand and followed him across the entrance hall to the pair of curved staircases. Parker and Kat stood on the balcony, their lips moving quickly as they looked down at the injured below. Kym stared at them. She hoped they weren't talking about strategy. Kat was many things, but a strategist wasn't one of them. But if they were talking strategy, why wasn't Amber there? Kym hadn't seen Amber, Ashlyn, or Xander since they took refuge inside the palace.

"Good," Parker said, nodding as Kym and Tomark joined her and Kat. "You found her."

"The girl in a glittering blue dress isn't exactly hard to miss," Kat snorted.

"Says the girl in the bright green one," Kym smiled. She knew Kat hated the fancy clothes the Favored wore. She was surprised Kat hadn't found something else to wear.

"C'mon," Parker said. She turned and walked down the corridor behind her. "The Council wants a word."

A sinking feeling filled Kym's stomach as she followed Parker and Kat. If the Council needed to talk strategy, they could have spoken to Parker, or Tomark, or even Kat. But why did the Council want to talk to her specifically? They'd already agreed to fight the Rulers with Kym and the others. What else could they say? Were they going to tell her off for leaving in the first place? If they did, she didn't see the point in reprimanding her now. They had bigger problems at the moment than Kym and the others leaving without permission.

Four large holoprojectors sat on the glittering floor, partially transparent versions of Hale, Anderson, Perla, and Mrs. Mizel shining out of them. But the sight of so much technology inside Crystal Palace wasn't what made Kym's mouth fall open. Her father and Dr. Gwin were there in person, standing on either side of the holoprojectors. Kym shook her head. Marek wasn't a fighter like Parker or a doctor like Byrd or Dr. Gwin. Why would Parker let him come? He was in so much danger here.

"You're okay." Marek ran to Kym and wrapped his arms around her. Kym gasped, a little taken aback.

"Wh-what are you doing here?"

"I needed to know you were safe," Marek said, pulling away

from Kym. He placed his hands on her shoulder, and Kym felt him shaking. "And I wanted to help you make things right. I'm so proud of you."

"He convinced the Council to mount the attack. I tried to make him stay back," Parker added, "but he insisted."

"Dad," Kym said, shaking her head.

"Don't worry," Parker said. "He's staying with the medical brigade. And I've got two of my guys with him at all times. They'll keep him safe."

"Is this it?" Anderson huffed as Kat, Parker, Tomark, and Kym joined the circle. "Where are the other Vanquishers?"

"Damon and Jazin are assisting the medical brigade, sir," Dr. Gwin said.

"Very well," Anderson said.

"What about Amber?" Mrs. Mizel said quickly. Kym watched her narrow eyes dart back and forth, and Kym knew she was looking for her daughter. "And Xander and Ashlyn?"

Kym looked to Parker. She'd been wondering the same thing. She hadn't seen Amber, Xander, Ashlyn, or any of the other Favored since she'd been inside the palace. But that didn't make sense. She'd watched the Disciples bring the unconscious Favored inside. Where'd they go?

"They're coordinating the…confinement of the Unity," Parker said slowly.

Kym looked at Parker. Kym could tell Parker was choosing her words carefully. But why? What was Amber doing that Parker wanted to keep it from the Council?

"Good," Commander Hale said. "They'll need to be properly restrained. Are the storm cuffs functioning as expected?"

"They are," Parker nodded. "We have Master Lucia restrained with four guards on her."

"Lucky girl," Kat mumbled so only Kym could hear. She bit her lip to stop herself from laughing.

"Alright," Hale said. "Do you have enough cuffs for the rest of the Favored?"

"We're not locking them up," Tomark said.

"What?" Hale asked, her eyes narrowing.

"Amber, Ashlyn, and Xander are freeing the Favored from the Unity."

The floor trembled beneath Kym as the sound of an explosion hit her ears. Kym braced herself, ready to attack, but Tomark grabbed her arm. Kym turned to him, and he shook his head the tiniest amount. Kym's pounding heart slowed, and she understood. That wasn't the sound of an attack.

"What was that?" Perla asked.

"That is Amber reigniting the emotions a Favored should've felt for the past year and a half," Kat said. "Emotions are a little volatile."

"You're not locking them up?" Anderson demanded, his long beard quivering.

"Why would we?" Kym asked, her anger flaring up. "They can help us. Your storm weapons are powerful, but they're no match for an army of Favored. Freeing them helps us even the odds."

"If they join you," Hale said darkly.

"They will," Tomark said, stepping toward the holoprojectors. "I know they regret the things they've done as part of the Unity. They'll just need time to recover."

"We may not have time," Kat whispered so only Kym could hear.

Kym wanted to tell Kat she was wrong, but she knew better. It took Xander, Jazin, and Amber days to process their emotional baggage. Kym knew the Rulers wouldn't wait days to attack, not after Parker and her soldiers made them look bad. For all Kym knew, they could be on their way at that moment.

"Very well," Anderson said. "Parker, we expect hourly updates."

"Yes, sir," Parker nodded.

The holograms of Anderson, Perla, Hale, and Mrs. Mizel faded away. Kym sighed, trying to stop her hands from shaking. They didn't know if the Favored would join them or when the Rulers would attack. They didn't even know how long they could hold the palace once the fighting resumed.

"Please tell me we have a plan?" Kat asked, looking at Parker.

"We do," Parker nodded. "I have a team fortifying and patrolling the perimeter. Nothing's gonna get past them, at least for now. Damon, Jazin, and Dr. Gwin's team are patching up our guys, and they'll be good to go. I've also sent a team down to secure the Conduit chamber."

"What?" Tomark asked.

Kym's mouth fell open. She hadn't even thought about the Conduit. It was the source of all magic in Princirum, and that was something the Rulers would fight to the death to get back. It was the weapon they needed to wage their war on the gods.

"Why didn't you move it?" Kym asked.

"The chamber's protected, right?" Parker asked.

"Yeah," Tomark said. "After the Festival of Creation a few years ago, the Rulers made it so you can't use magic to get in."

"Then it's the safest place for it," Parker said. "My best close combat fighters are guarding the entrance. Don't worry."

But Kym couldn't help but worry. She knew the Rulers wanted the palace back, but she'd only considered their pride—their need to have the seat of their power under their control. But the Conduit was a whole other problem. They'd burn Princirum down to get it back.

"Of course, that's just our end of the battle," Parker said, her voice stern. "The point of holding the palace is to keep the Rulers' forces focused on us while you do whatever it is you came here to do."

"Why did you leave?" Marek asked, and Kym heard the pain in his voice. "We were safe. We had a plan."

"Dad…"

Kym didn't know where to start. How could she tell him their plan when she didn't even know what it was anymore? So much had gone wrong Kym wasn't even sure their plan existed. Saying they were going to break Thed's connection to the Rulers didn't sound good enough to Kym—not with so many lives on the line. But what else could she say? That was their end goal, after all.

"Marek, we're going to free Princirum from Thed," Tomark said. "All of this, the war with the gods, the parasitic death, it's happening because of Thed. If we break his connection, it all ends."

"But if Thed forced himself on the Rulers, how can they break free?" Marek asked.

Kym opened her mouth but closed it quickly. The truth was, she didn't know. Apart from attacking the Rulers, she had no idea what they could do to break his connection. Kym's heart grew heavy. Had her ignorance put people in danger again?

"Would the Rulers expect a direct attack on their person?" Parker said, her eyes narrow.

"I doubt it," Kat shrugged. "They think they're above everyone. In their eyes, no one would dare attack them."

"And they'd never risk their safety," Tomark added. "Not when they have the Unity to fight for them."

"They might," Kym said, an idea forming in her head. It was a risky idea, but it might work.

"How?" Parker asked.

"They'd come for us," Kym said. She knew she was right the moment she said it. "The Rulers hate us, no matter who's influencing them. They want us to pay for leaving. That was our original plan—use their hatred of us to draw them into the open."

"Then we use that," Parker said, her eyes growing wide. "My soldiers and I will draw the Favored from the Rulers, giving you a shot at taking them on."

Parker tapped her holowatch then raised it to her lips. "All team leaders converge on my location."

Kym's heart slowed. They weren't as ill-prepared as she thought. In fact, from the way Parker put it, it sounded like they may have a shot. All Kym needed to do was find a way to break Thed's seemingly unbreakable connection to the Rulers. But how could she do it? It took them weeks to break Theddie's connection, and they weren't in the middle of a battle then.

Bright green light filled Kym's eyes. The sound of breaking glass assaulted her ears as the glittering white floor trembled. Somewhere, someone screamed as Kym fell to the ground. She threw her hands over her head, her heart racing in her throat, as glass and wood flew around her.

Kym pushed herself up, her ears ringing as the world wavered around her. She crawled to the edge of the balcony, and her heart stopped. The front door was gone; so was the massive circular window above it. Debris lay all over the entrance hall as people ran around like ants, pulling the wounded out of the wreckage.

Red, yellow, and purple light filled the air as the palace rumbled. Through the blown-out windows, Kym saw plumes of dirt and smoke burst into the air. She sprang to her feet, barely daring to breathe. Their time for planning was over. The Rulers were attacking at last.

"Perimeter team! Report!" Parker shouted somewhere behind Kym. "What's going on?"

"Attacks are flying up from the mountain's base," a voice shouted from Parker's holowatch. "At least eight Favored per attack. The portable generators aren't strong enough!"

"Retreat!" Parker ordered. "Get inside! Now!"

Kym leaned over the banister, her blue Marks glowing. A bright blue shield appeared above the entrance hall, covering a good portion of the people as they ran for cover. More flashes of blue, green, and silver light filled the air as attacks exploded against the palace. The solid life walls blocked the attacks, but the empty doorways and windows didn't.

Remnants of energy streaked into the hall. They collided with Kym's shield, and cracks spread through the blue disk like spider webs. Kym skidded back, her hands shaking, sweat running down her face. She focused her energy, funneling it into the shield. The cracks sealed, but not before more attacks created new ones.

Kym's shield vanished in a flash of blue as yellow, red, and purple energy exploded against it. Kym's legs buckled, and she collapsed, knocked back by the force of the attacks. Panting, stars bursting in her eyes, Kym waved her hand again. Another shield appeared over the entrance hall, but it shattered seconds later.

"Take cover!" Tomark yelled.

The people below ran in every direction, pulling open the doors that lined the round room as more explosions filled the air. Kym racked her brain, her body shaking. Making shields over these people wasn't enough. Even with the water charm boosting her power, she needed more water to stop these attacks. To do that, she needed to be outside the palace.

Kym sprinted down the balcony stairs, ignoring Kat and Tomark's surprised yells. The remains of three more bolts burst through the palace windows as she reached the landing. Kym waved her hand wildly, but her shield didn't do much to stop the attacks. Kym skidded around, her feet slipping on the combination of dust and debris littering the ground. She saw the door she needed and sprinted forward, her heart pounding in her ears.

Kym burst out onto the back garden. It looked just as she remembered it—covered with bushes and trees with a large stream on one side. Kym ran for the stream, ignoring the multicolored flashes exploding around her. She stopped at the water's edge and held out her hands as energy surged through her from the water charm. Kym closed her eyes, imagining what she wanted to happen. She saw it clearly in her mind—a massive blue dome surrounding the palace. It was larger than any shield she'd ever dared make, but Kym knew it was the only way.

Kym shook her head—self-doubt would get her nowhere. She let her intent fill her whole being until it was all she knew. Her arms shook as energy surged from both the water charm and deep inside of her.

Kym opened her eyes, and the glowing blue light of the energized stream sent tears down her cheeks. Kym panted as the ground beneath her shook. She stared at the stream, focusing even harder on the shield in her mind. She needed to keep these people safe.

An orb of glowing blue water shot out of the stream. Kym watched it fly through the air before it stopped above the tallest tower. Energy surged through Kym again, and another orb launched out of the water. It rose to join the first, which had flattened and spread by the time the second one reached it.

Kym held her breath, her arms shaking as more glowing orbs rose from the stream. She couldn't believe it. The shield was forming. The question was, how long could she keep it up?

The shield was halfway formed when Kym heard footsteps behind her. She didn't take her eyes off her work as she felt attacks colliding against her shield. Kym gritted her teeth, forcing more energy into the stream to fix the partially formed shield. The edges of her vision started to blur, but she didn't care. If Kym didn't finish the shield before her energy ran out, all of this would be for nothing.

"What the Thed are you doing?" Kat's voice snapped at Kym.

"I'm…shield…" was all Kym could manage. The shield was almost at the ground. She was so close.

"We can see you're making a shield," Ashlyn's voice said. "It's gonna kill you."

More attacks exploded against the shield, and Kym's legs gave out. She fell to her knees, lights popping in her eyes. She heard the others cry in alarm, but she tuned them out. She kept her blurry eyes on the stream, and her arms felt like they were splintering. Having her bones exploded by Earth Favored was less painful.

"She's gonna pass out," Kym heard Xander say as though from a long way away.

"Kym!" Tomark's face swam in front of Kym, his voice oddly distorted. "Stop. Please."

But Kym couldn't stop. She didn't care what happened to her. All that mattered was keeping the people inside the palace safe. And her shield was working.

"Kym," Amber's sharp voice cut through the fog descending on Kym's mind. Kym saw her golden eyes, which were so narrow they looked like slits. "Let me help."

Help? How could Amber help Kym make a shield? Bright orange and red light filled Kym's blurry vision. Heat kissed her face, and the feeling jolted something awake in Kym's mind. Using all the energy she had left, Kym looked to the side. Amber stood beside Kym, a massive bonfire at her feet. Her hands were held out like Kym's, and her face was set.

"Kym, don't try and repair any of the damage to your shield," Amber said. "Just get it to the ground. I'll handle the rest."

Kym had no idea what Amber was talking about, but she didn't have time to think about it. Another massive bolt exploded against the shield. She felt it fracture, like someone stabbing a million needles into her skin. But Kym didn't repair the damage. Instead, she redoubled her focus on extending the shield to the ground. Beside Kym, four red orbs shot out of Amber's bonfire. They rose into the air, and expanded to fill the cracks in the shield.

Kym gasped as the glowing red energy met hers. She felt them pressing against her, a determined warmth full of power and intent. But instead of overtaking Kym's energy, it coexisted. It was a bizarre feeling.

More attacks exploded against the shield, but Amber quickly repaired the damage. Soon, the solid blue shield was a patchwork of blue and red, the shining energies bleeding into one another. Kym's arms and legs didn't shake as violently now that she wasn't responsible for repairing the damage. She just wished her vision would clear. Kym could barely make out Amber's trembling arms beside her as three more attacks exploded against the shield.

"You two are morons."

Kat appeared on Kym's other side. She pointed her hands at the hard ground, which cracked and loosened. Glowing green orbs rose from the earth, filling in the gaps Amber's magic missed. But even with Kat and Amber repairing the damage, Kym still felt the shield cracking. Slowly, Kym forced herself to her feet, determined to keep the world around her in focus.

"Let…me…help…" Kym panted.

"Absolutely not," Amber snapped. "You need to maintain the shield."

"The Fire Princess is right," Kat said, her voice strained. "You're barely keeping it together."

"But…you need…help."

Kym winced as two more attacks exploded against the shield. Her trembling legs buckled, and she fell back to the ground. Kym didn't want to admit it, but Kat and Amber were right. She could barely keep her arms up. How was she supposed to help them too?

"They have help."

Kym glanced from side to side. Ashlyn, Tomark, and Xander joined them, massive yellow, silver, and purple spheres in their hands. Orbs shot from the spheres, filling in the cracks spreading through Kym's initial shield. Kym felt their energies blend with hers in an odd patchwork. If she focused, Kym could pick out someone specific, but overall, she felt her friends' love, compassion, and determination mixed with her own desire to protect the palace.

More attacks exploded against the shield, but Kym didn't feel the full impact anymore. The shield was no longer her sole creation. The pounding in her head subsided, and Kym slowly made herself stand. Her stomach lurched, but she kept her mouth shut. Vomiting was the last thing she needed.

"They're not slowing down," Xander said.

"And Parker's perimeter sucks," Kat barked.

"She said it would keep people from physically entering," Tomark said. "The portable generators aren't strong enough to stop combined attacks."

"We just need to buy Parker some time," Kym panted, no longer feeling queasy. "Once Damon and Jazin heal her soldiers, we'll be ready."

"Will we?" Ashlyn asked pointedly.

"Tomark and Kat filled us in," Amber said. "We won't stand a chance against the Rulers if we use all our energy here."

Kym shook her head. Amber was right. Fighting the Rulers sounded like a challenge when she was rested and prepared. But now, with her arms and legs shaking as she tried to keep the shield up, it seemed almost impossible. How could she fight after using all her energy to protect everyone else?

"Can we help?"

Kym looked over her shoulder, unable to believe her ears. It couldn't be. Kym didn't even hear her arrive, but there she was. Kenna stood a few feet away from Kym and the others. Her face was puffy, and her eyes had a vacant, glassy look about them. And Kenna wasn't alone. Four other favored stood with her, and Kym thought they all looked on the verge of breaking down.

"What are you doing here?" Kym asked.

"We told you to rest," Amber snapped, not taking her eyes off of her fire.

"We're here to help," said Kensrix, a Fire Favored who'd been Amber's partner in the Calling.

"Why would you help us?" Kat snapped.

"Look, we don't have time to argue," Kenna said, stepping beside Kym. "You need to rest."

"We saw the shield from inside," Kensrix said. "It's gotta be taking a lot out of you."

"It is," Ashlyn said.

"Then let us take over," Kenna said.

Kym looked at Kenna, at the girl who made her life miserable during most of her time as a Favored. She'd spied on Kym for Nila, constantly critiqued Kym as her magic instructor, and pretended to be her friend when it suited her. All Kym wanted to do was punch her in the gut. But there was something in her eyes that made Kym stop.

"Why are you helping me?" Kym asked, and she genuinely meant it.

"Because I'm sorry," Kenna said, her brown eyes dropping to her shoes. "I followed Nila because I thought it was the right thing. But you were right about her. She never cared about me. I wished I'd seen it sooner."

Kym's heart swelled at Kenna's words. She almost couldn't believe she heard them. After all this time, Kenna finally saw what Kym did. Nila turned on Kenna, one of her most trusted Favored, when Kenna finally stood up for herself. And now, Kenna was going to help Kym stop the Rulers once and for all. Kym couldn't help but be proud of her.

"Tell me what to do," Kenna said, raising her arms and invoking her blue Marks.

"Well…" Kym trailed off. She didn't even know where to begin explaining what she was doing. "It's kinda…like a construct. I'm not really focusing on the shield itself, but on the water."

"Okay," Kenna said, narrowing her eyes at the stream. "What's your intent?"

Kym paused. What was her intent? There were so many things she was focusing on. Her friends. Her desire to keep everyone inside safe. Her determination not to fail again.

"Protecting everyone."

"What? Kensrix asked. "Your intent isn't maintaining the shield?"

"No," Amber shook her head. "Feelings are more powerful than a single thought. The Rulers didn't teach us everything. Focus your energy on keeping the people you care about safe."

Kenna, Kensrix, and the other Favored nodded. They raised their hands, and it was like a weight lifted off Kym's soul. She felt the energies of the new Favored intertwine with hers, along with their determination to make things right.

Panting, Kym dropped her hands and fell to the ground for what felt like the tenth time. Around her, she heard the others do the same. She lay on the grassy ground, waiting for the pounding in her head to subside. If the circumstance were different, she could have slept for days. She closed her eyes, trying to ease the pounding in her skull.

Screams ripped through the air, and Kym sat bolt upright, her heart racing. She looked wildly around, determined to find the source of the pained sound, but there was no one new in the garden. More screams reached Kym's ears, and her insides froze as her eyes locked on the glittering white building behind her. The screams were coming from inside the palace.

CHAPTER THIRTY

THE BATTLE OF LIFE

MORE SHRIEKS FILL THE AIR AS KYM FORCED HERSELF TO HER FEET on trembling legs. She shook her head, driving her pain into a deep corner of her mind. She didn't care that her insides were burning. Someone needed help, and she couldn't do anything lying on the grass in the garden.

Inside the palace was chaos. People ran screaming in every direction, their hands over their heads. Sounds of battle raged from the entrance hall—the deep hum of storm weapons, followed by the high-pitched wail of something more sinister. Kym doubled her pace, her insides turning to ice as she sprinted through the corridors. She knew that chilling numbness well. There was a death demon near.

The death demon was massive, with six feet and just as many eyes. Kym's first impulse was to call it a cat, but that didn't come close to describing it. Cats didn't look like they were made of rotting tree roots or have multiple tails that ended in sharp points. The death demon's tails whipped around, and the soldiers gathered around it scattered as the razor tips carved deep grooves into the glittering entrance hall floor.

Kym spun on the spot, fear coursing through her like ice. Her water bolts exploded against the demon's grey body, filling the entrance hall with blue light. The demon jerked around, its tails flying wildly. The tips pierced one soldier's chest while another grazed a soldier's leg. The demon lunged at the fallen soldier, its blackened teeth bared as it hissed menacingly.

"No!"

Kym reached out, her mind blank except for one thought—she needed to save the soldier. A cloud of blue energy burst from her fingers. It sheathed the soldier, and Kym pulled with all her willpower. The soldier flew back as the demon's jaw snapped on thin air. It snarled as Kym released the soldier, not daring to take her eyes off the demon. Any minute now, it was going to charge.

The demon let out a strange, otherworldly roar and lunged forward. Kym jumped to the side, another bolt forming in her hand as she floated into the air. She shoved her hands forward, and the blast hit one of the demon's back legs. It skidded across the glittering floor but righted itself quickly.

"Advance!"

Parker's command sent Kym's heart racing. What was she doing? Kym was fighting the demon so Parker's soldiers could get to safety. Why was she running into a fight?

Two of Parker's soldiers ran forward, spears expanding in their hands. The first threw a storm bead at the demon's feet, while the second hurled her spear, its fine grooves glowing orange. The bead exploded, and Kym's head split as the demon let out a shriek. The glowing spear tip lodged in the demon's front leg, and it collapsed.

"Lock it down!" Parker shouted, throwing another storm bead at the demon.

Kym closed her eyes as the storm beads detonated, fighting to keep herself airborne. She dragged her arms around, streams of energized water trailing from her fingertips. She brought her hands together, and the water condensed into a compact bolt no larger than an apple. Kym raised the bolt, her energy fighting to break free of the tiny space.

"Clear out!" Kym yelled.

The soldiers scattered, and Kym threw her compact bolt, willing it to hit the demon's middle. The compact bolt exploded, filling the entrance hall with blue light. Kym threw up her arms, her dress billowing around her from the force of the attack. Kym lowered her hands, and her muscles relaxed as the numbing cold inside her faded. All that remained of the demon was a pile of glittering ash.

"Everyone good?" Kym panted as she landed shakily among the soldiers lying on the ground.

Kym tried to put on a brave face as she examined their wounds. Black pus oozed from the deep cuts the demon's razor tail had made. The skin around the injuries didn't look much better as the color faded from the area. Kym felt like she wanted to vomit. Death demons killed everything they touched.

"You're gonna be fine," Kym lied, trying her best to smile. "We'll get you fixed up in no time."

"What happened?"

Damon and Jazin ran toward Kym, their faces shining with sweat. Jazin's eyes darted from the man lying on the floor and the pile of ash on the ground, and his face fell. He dropped to his knees beside Kym, holding his hand just above the soldier's wound. Kym bit her lip, praying he wouldn't say what she feared was inevitable.

"The death is spreading too fast," Jazin said, his black Marks glittering on his pale arms. "I don't know if I can stop it before it reaches his heart."

"Don't worry about me," the soldier said, his voice weak. His eyes drifted to Kym. "It was an honor to fight beside you, Vanquisher of Water."

"The honor was mine," Kym said, tears streaming down her cheeks. She reached down and brushed the soldier's light hair out of his face. "You fought the power of death. You're a Vanquisher too."

Kym forced herself to keep smiling as something faded deep in his eyes. His hand went slack, and it was like someone kicked Kym in the stomach. She wanted to leave—to run away where no one else would ever get hurt. But as attacks continued to explode against the shield outside, she knew she couldn't hide. These people were counting on her to protect them, and she was failing.

"What happened?" Kym asked thickly, wiping her tears on the back of her hand.

"It came from outside," Parker said shakily. Her uniform was ripped in several places, and there was a large cut on her forehead.

"We think it tunneled through the mountain. It burst inside and started attacking. So many people got hit before I ..."

Parker trailed off, and Kym didn't press her further. She didn't need to know any more. She'd fought enough death demons in her life to know what happened. Kym stared at the soldier lying before her. How many people would they lose before this battle was over? Kym couldn't let this go on any longer.

"Kym," Damon said, pulling Kym back to her surroundings.

Kym turned to Damon. His dark eyes were wide, and he was looking over Kym's head. He shifted from one foot to the other, playing with his fingers. Kym inched closer to him. There was something he wasn't telling her. But what could it be? Nothing could be worse than what Kym just witnessed.

"Kym," Damon said again, this time looking her in the face. "Your dad was in the entrance hall when the demon got in."

All the feeling drained from Kym. Sound faded away, and her frantic mind came to a screeching halt. Her legs trembled as Damon's words bored into her brain, where they echoed around until they were all she knew. But they couldn't be true. Kym's dad couldn't be hurt.

Damon led her through one of the doors on the ground floor. Moaning, crying people lay on the ornate benches in the middle of the room. Kym saw her father at once, and it was worse than she could've imagined. His shirt was ripped and decayed, and there was a long, oozing gash up his torso. Black veins spread across his chest, inching toward his heart. Nurse Byrd knelt next to him, wiping his sweaty brow with a cloth.

Kym sank to her knees, her sorrow too heavy to bear. She grabbed Marek's hand, ignoring the icy chill of death blooming in her fingers. She didn't care. She needed to be by his side. Nothing else mattered.

Marek's eyes fluttered open. Kym was happy to see they were their normal warm color. His eyes found Kym's blue ones, and the ghost of a smile flashed on his lips.

"Hey, Kym," he said, his voice weak and slow.

"Dad," Kym gasped, unable to keep it together. Tears streamed down her face, burning like acid against her skin.

"It looks worse than it feels," Marek coughed.

"No, it doesn't." Kym shook her head, her insides growing colder as the black veins crept closer to Marek's heart. "Don't worry. We'll fix you."

Kym turned to Jazin. This wasn't like the soldier out in the entrance hall—his wound had been right over his heart. Kym understood why Jazin couldn't save him. But her father—he still had a chance. Kym felt the death racing toward his heart and knew his time was limited. She needed Jazin to do this. Kym wasn't going to lose her father.

"Jazin…please…" was all Kym could say.

Jazin nodded. He knelt beside Kym, his hands tracing Marek's wound. Kym tried to breathe, but no air reached her lungs.

"He doesn't have a lot of time," Jazin said, "but I think—"

"Son."

Marek let go of Kym and grasped Jazin's hands. He pulled Jazin close, and whispered something that Kym couldn't hear. Kym's eyes darted between the two of them. Jazin said Marek didn't have a lot of time. Why was her dad not letting Jazin heal him?

Jazin stood and walked over to Damon, but Kym didn't move. She wasn't going to leave her father until he was better. After everything that happened between them, she owed him that much. He was her father. Nothing could change that.

"I'm sorry," Marek wheezed.

"For what?" Kym asked, unsure what else to say.

"For not trusting you," Marek said. "After the Calling, I lost my faith. But you brought it back. I'm so proud of you."

Kym's heart splintered into a million pieces. Why was her father saying this? He didn't need to make amends with Kym. Jazin was going to fix him, and he was going to be okay.

"Stop," Kym stammered. "Don't say—"

"I thought all hope was lost, but you brought it back to life. You believed there was a way to save everyone, including your mother, when I didn't."

Kym shook her head. She couldn't hear this. It hurt too much. She wanted to bury her face in her hands, but she couldn't tear her eyes from her dad. She didn't want to lose him. She'd already lost too much.

"Thank you, Jazin," Marek wheezed as Kym heard footsteps behind her.

Kym whipped around. What took Jazin so long? She needed him to pull the death from her father before it was too late. But it wasn't Jazin kneeling beside her. Tomark grabbed Kym's hand, his green eyes red with tears. Kym shook her head. Why had Jazin gotten Tomark? Is that what her father had whispered? But why? Tomark wasn't a healer.

"Tomark," Marek grimaced, sitting up a little. "Thank you for everything you've done for my daughter."

"Of course," Tomark said, his voice shaking.

"Promise me…you'll protect her."

"Always."

Kym shook uncontrollably as Marek pulled his hand from Kym's. She reached out to take it back, but Tomark wrapped his trembling arms around her. Kym thrashed around, tears running down her face, trying to break free from Tomark. But his grip was too strong.

"It's too late for me, Kym," Marek said, lying back on the bench and closing his eyes. "But not for everyone else."

"I don't care about anyone else," Kym sobbed. Why was he doing this? "I want to save you."

"You can't," Marek said, his voice no louder than a whisper. "My path has reached its end, sweetheart. But yours hasn't. Save Princirum. Save your mother. Make the most…"

Marek's eyes fluttered shut, and Kym turned into some kind of feral animal. She lunged forward, desperately trying to reach her father. Pain unlike anything she'd experienced exploded inside her, and it was like she was being ripped apart. He couldn't leave her, not when she'd just gotten him back.

Kym felt Tomark's arms tighten around her, but not even that could drive away her despair. Kym looked at Byrd through tear-filled eyes. She was still wiping the sweat from Marek's forehead, her eyes full of tears. The sorrow on her face knocked the wind from Kym's lungs. Luckily, Tomark knew what Kym wanted to say.

"Stay with him," Tomark said.

"Of course," Byrd croaked. "He'll… he won't be alone."

Tomark stood behind Kym, and she didn't fight as he half lifted her to her feet. He led her back into the entrance hall while soldiers and doctors ran around her, carrying injured people to safety. Kym heard them yelling, but their words made no impression on her. It was like she was sinking into deep water. The light faded around her as the world grew strangely quiet. Maybe, if she kept sinking, the pain would fade too?

Flashes of purple, blue, red, and green light filled Kym's eyes. She forced herself to look up, roused from her stupor. Through the nearest window, she saw cracks spreading through the shield, which didn't repair themselves. Terror surged through Kym, beating back her grief into some dark part of her heart. The shield was failing.

Kym ran forward, Tomark, Jazin, and Damon hurrying behind her. She burst into the garden, her heart pounding in her ears. Several people lay on the ground, their veins prominent on their thin, sunken arms. Kym whipped around, trying to find Amber, Kat, Ashlyn, and Xander, but they were nowhere to be seen.

"Kenna!"

Kym dropped to her knees as Kenna's legs gave out beneath her. She collapsed into Kym, her skeletal arms still held up as her Marks flickered feebly. Kym stared at Kenna's sunken, sweat-covered face as her body convulsed. She was exhausted. But Kym didn't understand. Why hadn't Kenna stopped?

"We did the best we could," Kenna wheezed. "Sorry, we couldn't buy you more time."

"Why'd you keep going?" Kym asked. "You could've switched with someone—"

"Your friends left to find swaps, but it doesn't matter," Kenna breathed weakly, her Marks barely visible as more attacks than ever exploded against the shield. "They're coming. Don't let her win, Kym. She can't..."

Kenna's eyes closed, and her arms finally fell. The fractured remains of the shield exploded around Kym, filling her eyes with blue light. Kym wrapped her arms around Kenna, shaking her head in disbelief. Kym's thoughts turned dark, but she refused to acknowledge them. Kym had already lost too much. As though he'd read her mind, Damon knelt beside Kym. He held his hands over Kenna, his white Marks glowing.

"She nearly used all her life energy keeping the shield going on her own," Damon said, looking at Kym.

"Will she be okay?" Kym asked. She lowered Kenna to the ground as gently as she could. The last thing she wanted to do was cause more damage.

"She has enough life energy to live," Damon nodded. "But I don't know anything beyond that."

Kym nodded, her arms shaking as she tried to get to her feet. Soldiers appeared around them, along with Kat, Amber, Ashlyn, and Xander. Someone said something about taking Kenna and the others inside, but Kym couldn't tell who. She looked to the sky, once again full of multicolored attacks as the Rulers continued to rain fire down on them.

The sight of soldiers carrying Kenna and the others off stirred something inside of Kym. Fire coursed through her veins, making her arms shake at her sides while her hands balled into fists. She rose to her feet, anger burning away her sorrow. She'd lost too many people she cared about. She wasn't going to lose anyone else.

"We need to move!"

Kat's voice penetrated the storm of anger swirling inside Kym. Ashlyn, Amber, and Tomark had their hands in the air, yellow, red, and silver shields floating above their heads. Attacks rained around them, growing in number by the second, and Kym didn't need to think hard for an explanation. It was time to fight.

Kym ran to the side, not bothering to use the back entrance. She didn't need to go through the palace. All that was inside were reminders of the people who'd gotten hurt because of her. She skirted the edge of the palace, running this way and that to avoid the bolts exploding around her.

Kym slowed when she reached the front of the palace. Parker's soldiers stood in rows on the vast steps, their storm mesh glowing as they held their spears and batons. Kym stopped beside Parker at the top of the stairs, looking out at the long front drive. Kym followed her gaze, and her heart skipped a beat.

The Favored stood at the edge of Parker's perimeter, bolts glowing above their hands. The Rulers hovered above the Favored like ghostly giants, their elegant clothes drifting around them. The sight of the Rulers sent Kym's rage into overdrive. All reason left her mind as she stared at the figures drifting gracefully through the air. Everything that happened, all the people she'd lost, was because of them. She wanted them to pay—to feel the pain that was ripping her heart into a million pieces. She wasn't going to let them get away with everything they'd done. Not this time.

Kym invoked her Marks, and energy surged through her, mixing with her anger until they were the same. She rose into the air, bolts appearing above her hands. Kym felt a gust of wind, and Tomark appeared beside her. His face was set, and glittering, silver air swirled around his fingers bolts. Kym glanced down. Kat, Amber, Ashlyn, Xander, Jazin, and Damon were looking to Kym, their Marks glowing on their arms.

"We need to draw them away from the palace," Ashlyn said as light bolts appeared above her fingers. "We can't fight them around all these people."

"Keep your heads," Amber said. "Remember, they're still the Rulers. They're stronger than us."

"But we know how to fight," Kat said. "Stay together, and don't be idiots."

Kym nodded. She turned to Tomark, his long, wavy hair billowing around him. His deep green eyes widened, and for a brief moment, the rage ravaging Kym's mind quieted. She wanted to say something to Tomark, but she couldn't think of anything. If they survived, maybe she'd find the right words. They had no plan other than not losing. Kym prayed that would be enough.

Energy surged through Kym from the water charm, and she shot forward. She heard the crowd below scream and cheer, but Kym wasn't really aware of them. All she cared about were the Rulers floating above the Favored. Her eyes locked on the one who'd caused her the most pain, and Kym's rage mounted.

Kym spun through the air, throwing bolts at the Rulers, who scattered. A silver blast shot past Kym, widening the gap between the Rulers. Kym smiled as she felt Tomark soaring behind her. She focused her energy on herself and hurtled forward with a burst of speed. She rocketed through the gap she and Tomark made, barely noticing the headache the storm generators at the perimeter brought on. Kym needed to draw the Rulers away from the palace, and she knew they wouldn't pass up the chance to have her in their clutches at last.

Bolts and blasts streaked past Kym, and she flew this way and that, trying to avoid the attacks exploding around her. Kym spun around, slowing slightly as she threw two more bolts behind her. Tomark was right on her heels, and he swerved to avoid her attacks. Kym glimpsed the Rulers behind Tomark, their elegant clothes glittering around them as they closed the distance between them.

"Down!"

Kym obeyed Tomark's order at once. She dove, the massive black mountain rising behind her. The Rulers' attacks exploded against the dark rock, and columns of smoke and dust rose into the air. Kym changed direction, once again flying away from the mountain. The wind of Tomark's flight roared behind her, but she didn't dare look back again. She needed to focus on flying quickly. If she didn't, the Rulers would catch her, and everything would be over.

"Cut them off!"

Kym had only heard Zara shout a few times in her life. The way her deep voice cut through the air made Kym's insides freeze. Kym focused all her energy on herself. She couldn't let the Rulers catch her or Tomark.

Red, yellow, and purple shields burst into existence directly in front of Kym. She flipped around, her heart racing, trying to stop, but she was moving too fast. Kym slammed into the darkness shield, and pain exploded in her legs and lower back. Purple tendrils grew from the shield and wrapped around Kym's arms and legs. Kym struggled against the bands, her heart pounding in her ears, but it was no use. She couldn't break free.

Tomark stopped a few inches from the fire shield. More tendrils bloomed from the red disk, and Kym's panic increased. The Rulers couldn't get Tomark too. But Tomark was one step ahead of them. He waved his hands through the air, and four bolts appeared in a line in front of him. Tomark's alignment blast ripped through the shield, which exploded in a burst of red and silver.

"Kym!"

Tomark flew to Kym, and she could see the terror on his face as the tendrils coiled around her. Kym opened her mouth to speak, to tell him to leave her behind and finish the mission. But no sound came out—a purple tendril had wrapped around her throat, stopping her from speaking…and breathing. Kym pulled harder than ever as lights flashed in her eyes and the edges of her vision blurred. Kym was going to pass out, and she was powerless to stop it.

The Rulers drifted to a stop a few yards from Kym and Tomark, and Kym's heart beat so fast it felt like it would explode. Tomark turned to face them, two bolts floating above his hands. Kym pulled with all her might. She couldn't let Tomark fight the Rulers on his own. She needed to help him.

"Look, Stailin," Nila said, drifting ahead of the other Rulers. "Our lost Favored have returned at last."

Anger raged inside Kym at the sight of Nila. Lost? She and Tomark weren't lost. They were the ones doing the right thing. The Rulers were the ones who were lost.

"Indeed, Nila," Stailin said, a strange smile stretching on his thin lips. "It is nice to have them back with us."

"Nila, Stailin," Melana said, her silky voice boring into Kym's ears, making her shake. "Stop playing with them."

"Get on with it," James snapped, his nostrils flaring. "We have our own traitors that need tending."

"Of course," Nila smiled, and the sight was even more unsettling than Stailin's. "I will go first, shall I?"

Kym struggled harder against the tendrils holding her. They tightened, and Kym lost feeling in her hands and legs, and her vision started to grow dark. But she didn't stop fighting. She wouldn't let it end this way.

There was a flash of red, and the shield holding Kym exploded in a burst of purple. White and black blasts shot up from the ground, while a green bolt exploded in the space between Kym, Tomark, and the Rulers. The force of the explosion blew the Rulers back and sent Tomark flying through the air.

No longer held up by the tentacles, Kym plummeted. She tried to focus her energy, but her mind was too foggy. Breathing on her own was a struggle. There was a flash of yellow light, and Kym felt arms wrap around her middle. She looked to see who it was, but there was another flash of yellow. Everything around Kym grew warm as she moved faster than ever. All she could see was glittering yellow light while she received the tightest hug of her life.

The yellow light vanished, and Kym's back hit something very solid. There was a gasp of pain around Kym's middle, and the arms holding her fell away. Kym coughed, gratefully gulping down mouthfuls of air. She rolled onto her side and saw a great deal of fiery red hair.

"You okay?" Ashlyn asked, pulling her arm out from beneath Kym.

"I...think..." Kym wheezed.

"You idiot."

Someone smacked Kym on the back of the head. She wheeled

around, her temper flaring. Kat stood over her, her eyes full of fiery anger.

"You were supposed to draw them away, not get caught."

"You try it next time," Kym panted.

Slowly, Kym pushed herself up. She was standing in the middle of a forest clearing surrounded by large, upright stone slabs. Amber, Jazin, and Damon stood with their backs together, their eyes trained on the sky. Xander and Tomark sat a few feet from Kym and Ashlyn, looking windswept but unhurt.

"Here they come," Amber said.

Kym looked to the sky. The Rulers flew through the air like comets and would reach the ground any second. Kym walked to the middle of their circle, standing with her back to the others. She took a deep breath, trying to calm her racing nerves. It didn't work.

James landed in front of Kym. She stepped forward, shooting a water blast between two earth walls. James spun to the side to avoid the attack, his red cape fluttering around him. He raised his arms, and fire bolts the size of marbles shot from his fingers. Kym dove to the ground, sliding behind a wall just in time. James's bolts collided with it, and the wall exploded.

Kym covered her head, expecting debris to rain down on her. But nothing did. She lowered her arms and saw the remains of the wall floating a few inches above her head, sheathed in glowing red energy.

"You dropped this, my lord."

Amber flung her arm across her chest. The chunks of earth hurtled through the air at James, and Kym saw the look of utter shock on his face. He dove to the side, narrowly avoiding the boulders as clouds of dirt and rock flew into the air.

Kym's mind raced a mile a minute. The Rulers didn't know that Kym and the others had learned new ways to use magic. They expected them to fight like normal Favored, but Kym had never fought like a normal Favored in her life.

Kym jumped to her feet as more Rulers drifted to the ground. She saw Melana on the other side of the clearing, three violet orbs floating around her head, blasts firing out of them. Kat dove behind an earth wall to avoid the attack as dust and smoke filled the air.

"Kat!" Kym yelled, taking cover behind another wall. "Launch her!"

Kat nodded. She held out her hands, and Kym saw the ground beneath Melana glow green. Kat flicked her wrists, and the earth under Melana exploded. She flew into the air in a cloud of dirt and dust, her arms and legs flailing around her.

Kym reached out, focusing all her energy on the woman flying through the air. A cloud of glittering blue energy shot from Kym's fingers. It sheathed Melana, catching her in midair. Kym felt Melana struggle against her energy, but Kym's focus was strong. Kym swung her arms and pushed with all her might. Melana flew backward and disappeared between the tall trees.

"Nice shot!" Kat shouted before running off.

Panting, Kym turned and saw two more Rulers hurtling away from the fight, their bodies enveloped in energy. Kym's body felt lighter as she ran forward, throwing bolts at Phillip and Kai's feet. They staggered backward as the ground beneath them split open at Kat's command. Clouds of yellow and white energy sheathed them, and they flew back like the other Rulers.

Kym's confidence rose even higher. This wasn't going to be as hard as she thought. The Rulers didn't fight like they did. They fought alone, trying to overwhelm Kym and the others with sheer force. But Kym and the others knew how to work together. Even with Thed influencing their actions, the Rulers still refused to fight as a unit. And that was what Kym and her friends excelled at.

Kym rose into the air as more attacks exploded around her. She waved her hands, and a glowing ring of blue water appeared in front of her. Kym jerked her hands apart, and the ring splintered as several of the Rulers emerged from the trees. Kym focused on the two nearest Rulers, and energy coursed through her like electricity. Blasts erupted from the bolts floating around her. They struck the ground with tremendous force, sending the Rulers flying while dust filled the air.

Kym arced around, easily avoiding the bolts and blasts flying around her. She spun around, two more bolts appearing above her hands. She threw them one right after the other in the general direction of another Ruler, and her insides warmed as a cry reached her ears. Kym swam higher into the sky, sweat pouring down her back as her pulse raced. There were so many attacks flying around her that she couldn't really see what was happening. From above the chaos, Kym saw Ashlyn standing between two earth walls, firing a blast at Kai. But Kym also saw Evanna behind Ashlyn, streams of glittering yellow light swirling around her slender arms.

Kym dove down, her heart pounding in her ears. Her feet slammed into the ground, and she skidded several feet as she threw her hands up. Kym's bright blue dome surrounded herself and Ashlyn just as Evanna's attacks reached them. Cracks spread through Kym's shield as her arms trembled, but the dome didn't shatter as Evanna's attacks faded.

"Thanks," Ashlyn panted.

"Don't mention it. Go," Kym panted, and she lowered her hands.

The bright blue dome vanished, and Ashlyn disappeared in a flash of yellow. Kym looked to where Evanna had been, but all she could see was a lot of fire. Kym focused her energy on herself again, and her feet left the ground. There was a flash of silver, and pain exploded in her side. Kym fell to the ground, flashing lights filling her eyes. Stailin floated in the air before her, his eyes narrowed as a glowing silver sphere appeared above his hands. Kym gritted her teeth, ignoring the pain as she fought to get to her feet. She couldn't let it end like this.

A glittering purple dome appeared around Kym as Stailin's air blast left his hands. It collided against the darkness shield, which cracked and shattered in a flash of silver and purple. Kym spun around, and she couldn't help but smile as the shadow of a muscular teen bloomed off the ground beside her. Kym looked back to Stailin, who was already readying another attack. Kym turned to Xander, who nodded before turning back into shadow. Xander slid across the grassy ground, reappearing behind the unsuspecting Stailin.

Xander's darkness blast hit Stailin in the back. He flew forward, his silver bolts vanishing as he spun wildly around. Kym took a deep breath, focusing on her energy holding Stailin. Bright blue energy shot from Kym's fingers. It sheathed Stailin, who froze in midair a foot from Kym's face. Kym swung her arm with all her might, which felt like it was made of lead. Stailin hurtled through the air and disappeared into the trees once again.

Kym turned, her face shining with sweat while her head throbbed. The others still fought behind her, always keeping the Rulers away from their circle of stone walls. But how long could they keep this up? Kym already felt exhausted, and the Rulers weren't going to give up. What would happen when Kym and the others needed to rest?

Kym shook her head. She couldn't think about that. Right now, all that mattered was fighting the Rulers. They had no other choice.

"Enough!"

Bright, white light erupted behind Kym. She spun on the spot, expecting to see Damon readying an attack. But Damon wasn't there. A pure white orb hovered between Kym and the others. Zara stood across the field, her fingers pointed at the orb, her white Marks glittering. Zara flicked her wrist, and Kym raised her hand, a water bolt at the ready. But she was too late. The life bolt exploded, flooding Kym's senses with white light and agony.

CHAPTER THIRTY-ONE

TO THE
SEA

PAIN OVERTOOK KYM. SHE FLEW BACK, HER EYES CLOSED, ODDLY weightless. She braced herself, ready for her body to slam into the hard ground. But it never did. It took some time, somewhere between a second and a lifetime, but Kym opened her eyes.

She was suspended in midair, almost where she'd been when Zara's bolt exploded. Above her, the sky was streaked with clouds. Zara's bolt still hovered in front of her, exploding like a pure white sun. Dirt swirled around the imploding life, but slowly. Kym saw individual grains of sand rise off the ground as the force of the explosion hit them.

Kym's heart raced. What was going on? An explosion like that should've knocked her back twenty feet. Why was she still in the air, and why was time moving so slow? Kym immediately jumped to the worst conclusion. Had the Rulers killed her again? But how? The last time she died, she remembered everything fading away. So why was she still in so much pain?

"We don't have much time."

Kym's eyes, the only part of her still able to move, darted to the side. A woman with a kind face stood beside her. She was tall, maybe a foot taller than Kym, with brown hair cascading down her back. She wore a simple blue dress belted at the waist and smiled warmly at Kym. She was vaguely familiar to Kym, but she couldn't place her.

The woman reached forward before Kym could breathe. She touched Kym's cheek, and a remarkable sense of calm washed over her. All of her fears and worries faded away, as did her pain. She sat up, and her feet drifted to the ground, her mind blissfully blank. It was a wonderful feeling.

"Come," the woman smiled, offering Kym her hand.

Kym reached out, but a quiet voice in her head told her to stop. She looked over her shoulder and saw herself still floating in the air, a pained look on her face. But how could that be? Kym was standing with the woman. She'd felt her touch her face. How could she also be in the middle of a fight? Something was going on, but Kym had no idea what.

"Don't worry," the woman said. "We won't be gone long."

Even though every fiber of her being told her not to, Kym took a deep breath, closed her eyes, and took the woman's hand. Kym braced herself for something to happen, but just like before, nothing did. She opened her eyes, and her mouth fell open. She was standing on a pristine beach. It wasn't the beach she knew from Wadita, but very similar. Kym turned to the side and saw the woman in the blue dress strolling across the sandy shore.

"Hey," Kym said, hurrying after the woman. "Where are we?"

"Somewhere we can talk," the woman said. "I have much to tell you and very little time, Kymbralyn. I'm so proud of you."

Kym shook her head. She'd never seen this woman in her life, yet she spoke to Kym like she'd known her for years. How could she be proud of Kym? Was she a Favored? She had to be. How else could she warp Kym to a beach?

"Who are you?"

"Forgive me." The woman stopped and knelt so that her face was level with Kym's. "Call me Reta."

It took every ounce of Kym's willpower not to fall over laughing. How could this woman be Reta, goddess of water? Kym had met a god, and Thed looked nothing like this woman. To Kym, the woman standing in front of her seemed perfectly normal. When Tomark told her about his meeting with the gods, he said they were being of pure element. There was no way this woman could be Reta.

Kym stared at the woman's kind face, and her eyes narrowed.

Something stirred in the deepest part of Kym's mind. She had seen this woman's face before, but not on a person. She looked just like the statues of Reta in the temples. Kym remembered looking into that kind face the day she discovered her magic.

"You…you're…" Kym stammered.

"I know you have questions," Reta said, resuming her walk on the beach as Kym hurried after her. "But as I said, our time is limited."

Kym agreed with Reta. With the shock of her identity fading, a million questions rose in Kym's mind. But so did anger. She'd wanted to ask the gods why they let Princirum descend into chaos for as long as she could remember. But now that Kym was face to face with a god, she had a hard time forming the words. Finally, she found them, and they poured out of her.

"You left us and let the Rulers run Princirum into the ground. Why haven't you done anything to stop them?"

Reta stopped, her hands clasped in front of her, looking out at the sea. Kym held her breath. Had she gone too far? What would Reta do if Kym upset her? Kym didn't even know where her body was or how to get back to it.

"The answer is…complicated," Reta said. "I suppose it begins with our choice to leave Pheil's great creation behind. After ruling humankind, we realized our time among Pheil's creation needed to end. We'd guided you as best we could, but it was time for you to venture forth on your own. We stepped back and left our children to lead you. I'm sorry to say they failed."

Kym stared at Reta, the strange sense of calm fighting with her raging insides. The gods stuck Princirum with the Rulers because they were bored? Kym couldn't believe it. How could the gods not see what the Rulers would become? Kym wanted to say something, but Reta pressed on.

"We left our children clear instructions—do as we did. We never imagined their lust for power and jealousy would cause such destruction. We hoped they'd grow in their positions and see the error of their ways, but we were mistaken."

"Yeah, you were."

The words flew from Kym's lips before she could stop them. For a moment, she was afraid she'd offended Reta, but Kym's anger quickly overrode her fear. Kym couldn't believe the gods were so blind. She stared at Reta, expecting her to be angry. Instead, she smiled.

"We were," Reta nodded. "And when it became apparent that our children wouldn't change their ways and were leading Princirum on a path of destruction, we took steps to correct it."

Kym couldn't stop herself from laughing this time. Reta sounded ridiculous. Kym had heard about the gods' plan her whole life. The priests, her parents, even the Rulers brought it up all the time. But Kym knew better. The gods' plan was a joke. They never did anything to fix the problems their absence caused in Princirum. So why would Reta say that? There had to be more to the story.

"Our interference and disagreements left Princirum on the brink of total destruction when we left Pheil's creation. So my fellow gods decided a different approach was needed to right the wrongs we saw among humankind. We watched, and only interfered when the need was absolutely dire."

"But you didn't," Kym fumed, unable to stop herself as waves crashed on the shore. "The Rulers have planned on going to war with you for years. Thed's been trying to worm his way out of Nothingness for even longer. You didn't do anything to stop those things from happening. You left us to fend for ourselves."

"But we didn't," Reta said. Her voice was still soft and gentle, but something flashed in her eyes that made Kym think she finally had stepped over the line. "We gave them you."

"What?" Kym asked, taken aback. "What do I have to do with any of this?"

"Everything that has come to pass has been because of you," Reta smiled.

Kym's stomach lurched. So, finally, Kym had divine confirmation that this whole mess was her fault. All the people she'd lost, and all the suffering she'd seen, was because of her. Kym didn't know how she could feel worse.

"So I'm to blame for all of this," Kym whispered.

"You misunderstand," Reta said, speaking faster as the waves grew louder. "We've known of the Rulers' desire to wage war for centuries. When it became clear that they would enact their war, we knew we needed to turn the tide in our favor. But the warriors already in possession of our gifts couldn't bring about that change. New voices were needed, voices who'd remain strong around the opulence and grandeur the Rulers surround themselves with.

"The Great Mother decided three would tip the scales in our favor. She instructed Rai, Thray, and myself to grant magic to those who would use it for the right reasons."

Kym's mind was whirring. Why was Reta telling her this? She didn't care about the gods' plan that they secretly had. Kym didn't even know if she'd call it a plan. How was giving three more people magic and watching what happened going to fix things? And what did it have to do with her?

"I found my champion in a river," Reta continued, smiling at Kym. "This girl had no trace of magic inside her, and had suffered enough hardships to last her a lifetime. But in her heart, I saw more compassion than any of the Rulers possessed. I knew if given the opportunity, she'd change Princirum's path. And I was right. You were the perfect choice, Kymbralyn."

The calm feeling Reta induced vanished as Kym's insides raged like fire. She stared at the goddess and had an uncontrollable urge to slap her. She remembered the girl Reta spoke of, as though from another life. She'd been clearing trash from the river grate, eager to glimpse the world outside. That was when the glowing wave swept her away. Kym had always thought that wave was the magic she never wanted finally showing itself. But it hadn't been her magic at all.

"You gave me magic?" Kym asked, her voice shaking with anger. "You're the reason Nila stole me from my family?"

"Yes," Reta said gently. "I knew your influence on the Favored would change the course of Princirum. And I was right."

Kym couldn't think straight. She wanted to run away—to hide where no one could hear her scream. Nila stole Kym from her home and pitted her against the other Favored. Kym risked her life learning magic to fight death, competed in the Calling against her will, and fought in a war against the Rulers. All this time, she thought that had been her destiny. She couldn't have been more wrong.

"You ruined my life," Kym said, her anger mounting. "I never wanted magic."

"I know," Reta nodded. "That was why I chose you. You didn't want it, so I knew you would use it for the right reasons."

"Did you ever think to ask what I wanted?"

"What you wanted didn't matter, Kym. All that mattered was saving Princirum. The gods' plan was working. Through no divine intervention, you found Thray and Rai's champions. Together, you encouraged other Favored to question the Rulers' motives and to consider their own actions. Everything was going perfectly until you tried to leave. Thed's influence on the Rulers ended your path before your work was done. That was why I pulled you from Nothingness."

Kym turned away from Reta. She wanted to leave, but Kym still had no idea where she was. She'd thought Reta was different from Thed, but Kym was wrong. Reta and the other gods didn't care about Kym. She only cared if her plan failed. And when it did, the gods didn't even let Kym, Kat, Tomark, and Ashlyn die in peace.

"You're angry," Reta said, appearing beside Kym. "But know, victory is nearly in your grasp. You're so close."

"Then you do it," Kym snapped. "You and the other gods can get your hands dirty. I'm done fighting Thed and the Rulers for you."

"If only we could," Reta said, and for the first time, Kym heard a hint of remorse in her voice. "Thed's presence in Princirum shifted the balance. It's taking all my power to maintain this moment with you."

"Then how are we supposed to stop him?" Kym asked, throwing up her hands. "If you can't do anything, how can we—"

"You are stronger than you believe," Reta said quickly. "Look at how far you've come. Not even death broke the strength of your spirit. Once Thed is back in Nothingness where he belongs, we will restore order once again."

"We can't fight Thed," Kym said. "We tried. We're not strong enough."

She didn't want to admit it, but she knew in her heart that she was right. They'd tried to fight Thed in Nothingness and failed miserably. Kym knew they needed the power of the gods to win. There was no other way to stop Thed. If Kym was going to succeed in fulfilling the gods' precious plan, they needed to help her.

"You're right," Reta said. She sounded strange, like she was speaking to Kym from a long way away. Beside Kym, the waves grew smaller and the sea became oddly still. "Once you draw Thed out, only the magic of the gods can put him in his place."

"Draw Thed out?" Kym asked, her mind racing.

"So long as he's bound to our children, his foothold in Princirum will be eternal. He must willingly break from the Rulers for our magic to send him to Nothingness."

"I don't have your magic," Kym said. "Could you give—"

"I am too weak to do what you ask of me," Reta said, and there was a real note of urgency in her voice as it grew fainter. "But there is another way."

Kym racked her brain. How could she use the power of the gods to fight Thed if they didn't give it to her? It made no sense.

"Our magic, our pure magic, resides within the children we created," Reta said, the edges of her body shifting out of focus.

"The Rulers won't help us fight Thed," Kym said.

"They won't," Reta agreed, now no more than a blue blur. "But the magic we gave them does reside within a vessel. You saw them put it there."

Kym's mouth fell open. Reta was right. She had seen the Rulers put their magic somewhere. Every year at the Festival Of Creation, the Rulers filled the Conduit with their magic, revitalizing the magical power in Princirum. That was why Melana tried to steal it —to use it as a weapon against the gods. The Conduit was full of the gods' magic.

"Our time is up," Reta said, her voice echoing through the darkness as the world around Kym disappeared. "I am so proud of everything you've done, Kym. Don't give in to the eternity of Thed. You are the Vanquisher of Water. Go vanquish death."

CHAPTER THIRTY-TWO

THE GOD OF DEATH

KYM FLEW BACK, HER INSIDES PUSHING AGAINST HER BY THE FORCE
of Zara's attack. She flailed her arms, trying to stop herself, but she
was too late. Kym slammed into the hard ground, her ears ringing as
white light filled her eyes.

"Ah!"

Pain burned through Kym like lightning as she slid across the
ground, and it was like dragging razors across her skin. All around
her, she heard the others cry out in pain. Kym tried to push herself
up, but her arms were worthless. What was going on? Why was she
in pain? Wasn't she at a beach?

Kym racked her brain, willing herself to think faster. Images
flashed in her mind—a woman in a blue dress, the waves crashing
around her, Kym's storm of anger. What had the woman said? It
was all too jumbled.

Kym looked to the sky and saw a man in glittering red clothes
hovering over her. He waved his arms, and tongues of flame flew
from his fingers. Fear coursed through Kym as she watched the
flames streak not toward her but Amber, who lay motionless a little
ways away.

The sight jolted Kym's mind into action. She jumped to her feet,
ignoring her screaming body, and clapped her hands together. She
jerked them apart and flicked her wrists, not taking her eyes off of
the jets of flame. Kym's tracking bolts shot through the air and
collided with James's attacks. They exploded in flashes of red and
blue, filling the air with smoke and dust.

"What happened?" Amber asked, pushing herself up.

"Zara knocked us back," Damon said, throwing two bolts randomly over his shoulder.

"I know that," Kat snapped. "But didn't you—"

"Duck!"

Kym dropped to the ground, as did Amber and Damon. A bright purple shield appeared over their heads, stopping four light and water constructs shaped like birds from grabbing them. Their long talons scratched the shield, and cracks spread across its surface like fractured glass.

Kym shoved her hands above her, and a blue water blast burst from her hands. It pierced Xander's shield and hit two of the constructs, forcing them away. Black and silver bolts exploded against the other two constructs, which reeled back. They flapped their wings, spraying dust and dirt in every direction as they flew higher above Kym.

"We need to draw Thed out of the Rulers!"

Kym didn't know what was more surprising—the fact that Kat said the words or that she saw Tomark nodding behind her. How could they know that? They hadn't been on the beach with Kym when Reta told her. Kym wasn't even sure the whole conversation actually happened. But it must have if Kat and Tomark knew what Reta said. But that begged the question, who told them?

"What?" Jazin waved his hands, and three black shields appeared around them. "Are you crazy?"

"We need to fight the Rulers," Damon said, jumping to one side before throwing another bolt.

"If we beat them and Thed's still connected, it won't work," Tomark said, dropping to the ground to avoid three black blasts. "We need to draw him out."

"How do we do that?" Ashlyn jerked her arms apart, and ten light bolts exploded from her hands, colliding with more oncoming attacks. "We barely pulled him out from Theddie."

"That's easy."

Kym glanced at Kat. Their eyes met, and Kym watched Kat's light brown eyes widen as her face split into the first genuine smile

Kym had seen there in a long time. Kym knew they couldn't magically pull Thed out of the Rulers—he was too strong. They needed to take another approach. If they couldn't pull him out, then they needed Thed to come out on his own. Luckily for Kym, and thanks to Reta and the other gods, Kym, Kat, Ashlyn, and Tomark were just what they needed.

"Cover me," Kym said, looking to Amber.

Kym ran off, Amber right on her heels, and darted around an earth wall. Smoking craters covered the flat, grassy expanse, and Kym saw her target instantly. She couldn't miss Nila's extremely tall frame as she stood beside James. Kym threw a bolt at Nila, intentionally hitting the ground a few feet to her right.

James and Nila's twisted smiles faltered as a cloud of red light shot past Kym's ear. It sheathed James, who rose into the air and flew forcefully into the trees. Kym silently thanked Amber. Drawing Thed out of Nila was going to be hard enough without James getting in the way.

"You want me?" Kym shouted, ignoring the explosions behind her. "Come and get me!"

Nila lunged forward, but Kym was ready. She threw her arm, and a jet of water shot from her fingers like a hose. It slammed into Nila, exploding in a shower of droplets in every direction. Nila staggered back, her dress soaked through, her eyes alight with anger, but Kym didn't care. She wasn't trying to beat Nila anymore.

"C'mon, Thed!" Kym shouted, and Nila's eyes flash black. "Reta told me the truth. She took me from you. You want me back? Well, here I am!"

"*Mine!*"

Nila raised her arms, and three bolts appeared above her head like moons. Blasts exploded out of them, but Kym didn't move a muscle. Amber gasped, and a glittering red dome encircled the two of them. Nila's attacks exploded against it, which cracked but remained intact.

"Take the shield down," Kym whispered, not taking her eyes off Nila.

"This better work," Amber huffed, and the shield vanished.

"You can do better than that," Kym shouted, stepping toward Nila as black veins appeared on her face. "Why's the god of death hiding behind a Ruler? Afraid to come get me?"

"*I fear nothing!*" Nila shouted, her voice a dark mixture of her own and Thed's. "*All of death is my domain.*"

"Really?" Amber said, stepping up beside Kym. "Why won't you fight two weak Favored?"

"*My power is limitless!*"

Nila ran forward, her skin as pale as snow while black veins spread across her arms like cracks. Kym's heart thudded in her chest as she spun on the spot. A massive blue dome appeared around Kym and Amber. Nila slammed into it, and fissures spread across the blue surface. Amber reached out, and bright red energy filled the cracks as Nila staggered back.

"I know why he won't fight," Amber sneered in full Fire Princess mode, and Kym faked a laugh. "He's too weak on his own. He needs the Rulers to take you back."

"You are the weakest god," Kym nodded, throwing caution to the wind. "You can't even stay here on your own."

"*I am not weak!*"

Thed's roar of fury completely overtook Nila's voice. Kym staggered back, her heart racing, not daring to breathe. Nila rose into the air, her arms stretched awkwardly at her sides as her head drooped. What looked like black ink seeped slowly out of her body. It swirled like a storm around Nila, and Kym's insides turned to ice. Thed was coming.

Kym turned to Amber, who nodded. Kym waved her hand, and the blue dome vanished around them. Kym spun around and was happy to see the others had been busy. Several of the Rulers floated in the air, clouds of black ink oozing from them as more clouds of ink rose into the air above the surrounding trees.

"What now?" Xander said quickly.

"He's coming," Jazin said, directing his hand toward Kai, who was the closest Ruler to them. "We may have two minutes."

"Okay, I'm lost," Damon said. "How are we supposed to fight him? We tried that, and it didn't work."

"We need the gods' magic to send him back to Nothingness," Tomark said.

"Cause the gods' magic is the only thing strong enough to work," Kat nodded. She waved her arms, and the earth walls she made to give them cover repaired themselves.

"The gods' magic?" Amber asked. "How're we gonna get—"

"It's in the Conduit," Kym said quickly as the black masses oozing from the Rulers grew denser. "The Rulers' magic comes from the gods, and they put their magic in the Conduit."

"How do you three know—?" Ashlyn began.

"We promise we'll explain everything," Kym cut across her. "But someone needs to get the Conduit. Now."

"I'll go," Damon said, his voice shaking slightly. "I know a shortcut."

"Go with him," Kat said, looking at Xander. "You've stolen the magic battery before."

Xander nodded. He grabbed Damon's thin arm, their bodies turned to shadow, and they slid off in a flash. Kym looked to the Rulers, and her heart sank. The Rulers were lying motionless on the ground, their skin and eyes returned to normal. The clouds of black death that oozed from the Rulers had combined, creating an enormous, human shaped figure at least one hundred feet tall.

"*You will pay for your insolence*," Thed said, raising his inky hands.

"Scatter!"

Kym didn't need Amber to tell her twice. She invoked her Marks and shot into the air, Tomark right behind her. Below her, Amber, Kat, Ashlyn, and Jazin ran in different directions as glittering black flames flew from Thed's hands. They danced across the earth, which blackened and cracked ominously.

Kym spun like a top, energy and fear surging through her like fire. Bolts flew from her hands, exploding against Thed's inky skin. Kym stopped, panting, her heart racing, and watched the ripples cascade over Thed's body. But other than that, Thed didn't indicate that he'd felt the attacks at all.

Red and green light filled the air on Thed's other side. Kym shoved her hands forward, and a bright blue blast shot from her fingers. She tensed her muscles, letting her energy flow into the blast as she pushed with all her might. But it did no better than the bolts. Three silver orbs flew past Kym, making her ghostly hair dance around her head.

"Do we have a plan?" Tomark swung his arm, and a shining silver arch soared into Thed's back.

"Buy time until Damon and Xander get back," Kym said as she threw another bolt. She had so many things she wanted to ask him, but she knew this wasn't the time. If they made it through the day, maybe she'd ask.

Kym's muscles tensed. For now, Thed was playing with them. The moment he decided to end things, he would. He was a god. But after everything that happened in Nothingness, Kym had a feeling that Thed liked to take his time. So, they were safe for the moment, but Kym feared it wouldn't last long. She needed to keep Thed occupied for as long as she could.

Kym spun like a top, her arms outstretched. Streams of glowing blue water trailed off her fingers until there was enough energized water to fill a small swimming pool. Kym brought her hands together, forcing the water into an orange-sized bolt above her palm. She threw the compact bolt, willing it to reach her intended target. The compact bolt exploded against the back of Thed's head with the force of a bomb, and Thed lurched forward.

Kym floated where she was, not daring to breathe. Slowly, Thed's enormous body turned toward her. His face was featureless, reminding Kym of a skull wrapped in fabric. The only distinct things were Thed's eyes, which were full of shining blue flames. Thed raised his arms, and more black fire flew from his fingers.

Kym dived, her heart racing, Tomark right behind her. She swerved this way and that, narrowly avoiding Thed's fire, which made her feel dull and empty rather than warm. Kym flipped over an inch from the ground. She slid across the grassy earth, stopping between Amber and Jazin.

Kym and Amber moved at the same time. Their bolts flew through the air as Thed turned, his black face looking this way and that. Kym and Amber's bolt's hit Thed's hand, knocking it to the side. More black flames spilled from Thed's fingers, scorching the ground, leaving it black, cracked, and empty.

"Ah!"

Beside Kym, Jazin threw out his arms like he was on the verge of falling over. A horrible low scream of pain filled the air, boring into Kym's soul. Kym scanned the ground, searching for the source of Thed's pain. Her eyes fell on the three massive stalagmites piercing Thed's foot, and Kym's heart raced. However, they crumbled into black dust as Kym watched, leaving three large holes in their wake.

Thed turned to where Kym knew Kat must be, and raised his inky hands. Kym's heart thudded like a drum. She couldn't let Thed hurt Kat. She shot into the air, tracing a large circle with her fingers. A ring of glowing blue water appeared in the air. Kym jerked her hands apart, and the ring splintered into four large bolts. Kym arranged the bolts in front of her and shoved her hands forward.

The alignment blast that burst from the fourth bolt was as thick as a tree. It hurtled through the air and slammed into Thed's inky shoulder. The force of the collision sent Kym flying back. She focused her energy, willing herself to stop while keeping the alignment blast going. Lights popped in Kym's eyes as her head throbbed, and she dropped her hands. The alignment blast faded, and Kym's heart stopped as she gazed at Thed. Her alignment blast had ripped an enormous hole all the way through Thed's shoulder, which Kym could have easily flown through

Kym's insides swelled with pride as she watched Thed stagger around. Had Reta been wrong? First, Kat hurt Thed, and now Kym had too. Maybe they didn't need the Conduit and the gods' magic after all. Maybe, they could actually do this themselves.

"Insect!"

Thed turned to Kym, the blue flames in his eyes growing brighter. He raised his arm, and Kym's body tensed, ready to evade his black fire. But there was no fire. The inky surface of Thed's arms rippled, and at least a hundred snakelike tendrils grew from his skin.

They extended from Thed like lightning, and Kym threw up her arms, her heart racing. The tips of the tendrils pierced the glittering blue surface of Kym's shield, which shattered like glass the instant they touched it. Kym shot backward, focusing all of her energy on herself, the numbing cold of the tendrils creeping up her legs. She threw up her hands again, but the tendrils broke her second shield like it wasn't even there.

There was a flash of yellow and a shriek of pain. Kym spun around, enveloped by warm light as something wrapped tightly around her waist. Kym's body slammed into something solid. The hands around her loosened as more gasps of pain filled Kym's ears.

Dazed, her stomach spinning, Kym pressed herself onto her elbows. Ashlyn was lying on the ground, clawing at her back, her face contorted in pain. The world faded away as Kym crawled toward her. There was a deep, black puncture at the small of Ashlyn's back. The area around the wound was pale, and black veins crept across her skin.

"Jazin!" Kym screamed, the sounds of battle around her no more than white noise.

Jazin appeared at Kym's side, and she saw her horror reflected in his pale eyes. He dropped to his knees and held his hand over Ashlyn's back. Ashlyn squeezed Kym's hand as she cried out in pain, tears streaming down her cheeks.

"It's progressing slowly," Jazin panted. "It won't reach anything vital for a while. But I can't heal her now."

Kym shook her head as she watched the black veins creep across Ashlyn's back. How was this slow? She needed Jazin to fix Ashlyn now. She wasn't going to lose another person she cared about.

"Heal her," Kym said, brushing Ashlyn's red hair out of her face. "Before it gets—"

"No," Ashlyn grimaced. She pushed herself up into a sitting position, squeezing Kym's fingers so hard they cracked. "There's no time."

"Ash, what're you doing?" Kym demanded.

"I'm fighting," Ashlyn said, staring determinedly at Jazin. "Use me as a death source."

"What?" Jazin asked, clearly just as confused as Kym.

"You can't take all the death out of me. Don't. Use me as a source for your magic."

Kym couldn't believe her ears. How was Ashlyn still willing to fight? But Kym knew the answer. Ashlyn would never leave her friends. She was going to fight until she physically couldn't. Kym's heart swelled with pride as she watched her friend stagger to her feet.

"It won't make it better," Jazin said. "But it will stop it from getting worse, like my cancer."

Ashlyn nodded. Jazin held out his hands, his black Marks glowing. Glittering black mist seeped from Ashlyn's back, forming a cloud above Jazin's fingers. As the death energy left her wound, Kym felt Ashlyn's hand stop shaking. Kym sighed with relief. Ashlyn was okay, for the moment.

Ashlyn disappeared in a flash of yellow, and Jazin ran off in the direction he came from. Kym shook her head, trying to clear it. She'd been stupid. Why'd she think they could beat Thed on their own? His touch was just as deadly as his magic. She needed Damon and Xander to get back with the Conduit. What was taking them so long?

A jet of black flames flew over Kym's head. She dropped to the ground, her chin slamming into the hard earth. Shaking, the world spinning around her, she rolled over. Thed's flames engulfed the trees behind her. She watched as they withered and blackened before collapsing in clouds of ash.

"*Insolent worms.*"

Thed's booming voice made Kym's skull vibrate. Her insides froze as he loomed over her. The hole she'd blasted in his shoulder was gone; so were the ones Kat had made in his foot.

"You dare strike a god? You reject the peace of my gift and attack me. I offered you freedom from the tyranny of my brothers and sisters. I freed you from the gods' watching eyes. You will bow before me."

"Fat chance!"

The red and green explosion was so bright Kym needed to shield her eyes. The ground trembled as Thed staggered back, and Kym rose into the air. She waved her hands, and six small bolts appeared around her. They orbited her like moons as she flew toward Thed, her heart racing. When she was as close as she dared, she threw two bolts at Thed's head.

More tendrils shot out of Thed's back, but Kym was ready for them this time. She spun in midair, an image of the ground in her mind. There was a flash of blue light and the rush of waves, and Kym's feet slammed into solid ground. Panting, she swung her arms out in front of her, sending two large water swipes at Thed's legs. They exploded against his calves, and he staggered backward, but he didn't fall.

"Your fight is futile," Thed said as thousands of tendrils bloomed from his inky body. *"After today, death will be all there is."*

Thed's tendrils shot outward, and Kym threw her arms up. She braced herself, waiting for them to reach her, but they never did. Kym opened her eyes. Thed's tendrils weren't flying toward her. They'd arced up and pierced the earth around him. Everything in a twenty-foot radius around Thed was dead, but that wasn't what made Kym's heart stop. The circle of death was growing.

Kym shot into the air. All around Thed, she saw flashes of red and yellow while Tomark flew through the air behind Kym. She smiled as he drew nearer, but her smile fell when she got a better look at him. He had puncture wounds in each of his arms from Thed's tendrils, which looked oddly thin and cracked as black veins spread across them.

"What happened?" Kym demanded, firing a blast at Thed.

"It's fine," Tomark said, and Kym heard the pain he was trying not to show on his face. "Let's find the others."

Kym knew where the others were at once. She saw several round stone walls separated by rings of fire almost two hundred feet away. Kym hurtled toward them, Tomark right behind her. She landed inside the walls, and her heart almost fell out of her chest. Kat was on the ground beside Ashlyn, a large tendril wound in her left calf. Jazin knelt beside her, pulling a glittering cloud of death from her leg, but he didn't look much better.

"We need a new plan," Amber said, raising her arms as a giant fire comet exploded out of the flames in front of her. "This isn't working."

"Damon and Xander need more time," Tomark winced, collapsing on the ground.

"We don't have time," Kat panted, her Marks invoked as she placed her hand on the ground. "He's killing everything."

"Should we move?" Ashlyn winced.

"Where?" Jazin panted. "Thed's literally killing the world right now. Where can we go?"

"Then we keep fighting."

The words flew from Kym's lips before she knew what was happening. What else were they supposed to do? They couldn't stop fighting Thed now. She knew things would turn around when Damon and Xander got here. They had to. But how much longer would that take? Kym stared at her injured friends, Jazin siphoning the death from them so they could keep fighting. They weren't giving up, and neither was she. She didn't care if this was Reta's plan or not. She and her friends all chose to fight, and she needed to see it through.

"We fight from here," Kym said, walking to stand beside Amber, who was the only other person besides Kym who was uninjured.

Kym invoked her Marks, the image of what she wanted clear in her mind. Her energy flowed from her fingertips, twisting itself into the shape in her mind's eye while she focused on a singular thought —rip tendrils. Kym opened her eyes, her brow covered in sweat, and smiled. Four glowing blue sharks floated in the air in front of her. She flicked her wrists, and the sharks swam over their protective walls and toward Thed.

"That won't work for long," Amber said, flicking her wrists and sending three fiery birds after Kym's constructs.

"Better the constructs than us," Kym said, glancing over her shoulder at her friends lying on the ground. "We can't do this on our own."

"I know," Amber whispered. She waved her hand, and a ring of fire appeared on the ground. "We need to hold on until Damon and Xan get back. And they need to conserve their strength."

Kym nodded. Amber was right. The point of stealing the Conduit was for them all to use the magic inside it to fight Thed. That wouldn't work if half of them were unconscious. In some distant part of her mind, Kym felt her connection to her constructs vanish. They were running out of time.

Jazin walked up beside Amber, and Kym thought he didn't look good. And it wasn't the massive sphere of death energy that worried her. There were dark circles under his eyes, and he panted every time he moved. Kym had never seen him looking this sick. Was this what he looked like before he got his magic?

"You okay?" Amber asked, her voice full of concern as she grabbed Jazin's arm.

"Uh-hum," Jazin said. "It's just…a lot of death."

"Well, we have a target," Kym said.

"I can't," Jazin panted. "He's too far."

"We'll get you closer," Amber said, straightening up a little. "Don't push yourself. I've got you."

"What about them?" Kym asked, looking back at Tomark, Kat, and Ashlyn.

"They'll be fine," Jazin said. "So long as they don't exert themselves."

"Good," Amber said. She grabbed Jazin and Kym's arms. "Let's keep the god of death busy."

Amber turned on the spot, pulling Kym with her through the flames. Kym's feet slammed into solid ground, and she invoked her Marks the moment Amber released her. She floated in the air, her insides cold as ice. She was at the edge of Thed's death circle, which was at least two hundred feet wide now. How could she attack Thed from so far away?

Jazin raised his arms, and the death he'd pulled from the others swirled above his hands. Amber ran around the edge of the circle, two fire bolts glowing in her hands while Kym rose higher into the air, unsure what to do. She needed to keep Thed busy, but the only attacks that hurt him required immense amounts of energy. How could she conserve herself and keep Thed distracted at the same time?

Kym soared across the barren wasteland, trying to stay as close to the ground as she could. But there was so much death radiating from the decaying ground that her insides lurched, and she clamped her mouth shut. When she was close enough to see the individual tendrils boring into the ground, Kym swung her arm. The water swipe soared through the cold air and severed multiple tendrils.

Thed raised his head, the blue fire glowing brighter in his eyes. Kym spun in midair, focusing on her friends inside the walls of stone. There was a flash of blue light, Kym's body surged through space, and she was back inside the walls. The sound of a massive explosion reached Kym's ears as the ground trembled. Kym threw out her arms to steady herself as a deep, ominous roar filled her brain.

Flames swirled in the air beside Kym, and Amber and Jazin appeared at her side. Kym's mouth fell open. Jazin looked a lot better than he had a few moments before. She guessed holding the death from the others did take a toll.

"Anything?" Kym asked.

"No," Amber shook her head. "More tendrils grew to replace the ones you and I cut, and Jazin's attack barely fazed him."

"Good thing we're here then."

CHAPTER THIRTY-THREE

THE POWER OF PRINCIRUM

KYM SPUN AROUND SO FAST SHE LOST HER FOOTING. SHE FELL TO her knees, but couldn't stop the smile from spreading on her face. Damon and Xander were on the other side of the circle, looking a little worse for wear. There was a massive cut down Xander's arm, and Damon looked like he'd crawled through a mud pit. Damon shifted his arms, and Kym saw the simple wooden box resting in his hands.

"You got it!" Kym shouted, unable to contain her excitement.

"Yeah," Xander said, kneeling beside Kat and taking her hand. "What happened?"

"Thed," Amber said, Jazin's thin arm draped over her slender shoulders. "We should be able to heal them when this is all over."

"Should?" Damon asked, raising his eyebrows.

"Don't worry about it," Kat said groggily, punching Xander in his good arm. "We were waiting for you to start the fun."

Damon set the wooden box on the ground. He invoked his Marks and tapped once on the smooth surface. Kym hoisted Tomark to his feet while Xander and Amber helped Kat and Ashlyn up. Kym led Tomark to the box, her insides shaking excitedly as the lid opened of its own accord. Bright, multicolored light flooded Kym's eyes, making them water and sting. The Conduit rose out of the box, turning slowly on the spot, its insides looking like a glittering, multicolored storm.

"We need a clear shot," Xander said, one of Kat's arms draped over his broad shoulders.

Kat raised her free hand, as did Amber. The walls surrounding

Kym crumbled while the rings of fire between them withered. Thed stood across the field, and he looked bigger than ever, as did the circle of death radiating from him. It had been hundreds of feet from them when Kym had last seen it, but it was so close she could see individual blades of grass blackening.

"So we got the Conduit," Ashlyn grimaced. "Now what?"

"Now, we blast him back to Nothingness where he belongs," Amber said.

Kym shifted herself and Tomark to face Thed, Tomark's arm shaking on her shoulders. She held out her hand, her blue Marks shining on her skin while energy surged through her from the water charm. But Kym had no idea what to do next. How was she supposed to use the Conduit to fight Thed? Kym still didn't understand how it restored her magic. How had she reached the magic inside of it?

"Let's surround it with our energy," Amber said, her hands outstretched. "Think of it like an alignment blast. Have our energy compound the gods' energy inside."

Kym nodded. She glanced at Tomark's sweat-covered face; he nodded too. Kym let go of him and pointed her hands at the Conduit. She imagined her energy floating from her fingers, surrounding the massive stone like it was water. The Conduit's energy—a violent, primal storm—pushed against hers. As subtly as she could, Kym pushed back. The power inside the Conduit shuddered, and Kym's heart thudded in her chest as her muscles seized. Kym gritted her teeth. This needed to work.

"On the count of three," Damon said, standing between Ashlyn and Tomark.

"Focus," Ashlyn said. "Nothing matters besides hitting him."

Kym took a deep breath and closed her eyes. She felt the Conduit's primal energy, but there was something more there. She felt her friends—their pain, their anger, their determination. Kym opened her eyes and stared over the Conduit at Thed. Ashlyn was right. Nothing else mattered.

"One…two…three!"

Kym pushed her hands forward like she was trying to shove Thed off a cliff. Her muscles tensed as she channeled her energy into the Conduit, lights popping in her eyes. A massive blast, neither fire nor smoke, burst from the crystal. It streaked through the air, filling Kym's eyes with brilliant, lilac light. Her arms shook, and the edges of her vison blurred as the force of the blast pushed her back several yards. She twisted her feet, trying to find some purchase on the ground. She couldn't stop now.

The blast collided with Thed in a brilliant lilac explosion. Shockwaves rippled through the air, and Kym flew back, unable to stop herself. She smashed into the ground, and her blood felt like acid burning through her veins as her muscles screamed in agony. Around her, she heard the others groan weakly.

Kym pushed herself up, the world spinning around her. Across the field, it looked like a bomb had gone off. Tree trunks and boulders littered the ground while a massive black scorch mark sat in the middle of a smoking crater. Tiny black filaments drifted through the air like weird, twisted snow. Kym squinted at them, trying to bring them into focus as her legs trembled. Had they done it?

The black filaments fused together, consolidating into one inky mass. Kym's heart fell as legs and arms sprouted from the black ooze. They hadn't beaten Thed. He was much smaller now—maybe ten feet tall—but now he was no longer featureless. He had a worn face and thin, shoulder-length hair—but there was no mistaking the glittering blue of his eyes and his inky skin.

"You are fools," Thed said, his voice reaching Kym like a whisper on the wind. *"Did you think you could destroy me? I am death. And death is eternal."*

Kym sank to her knees beside the spinning Conduit. Why did she think she could destroy death? Thed was right; death was inevitable. Kym stared at the glittering stone floating beside her. Why hadn't its power been enough to blast Thed back to Nothingness? She'd used the gods' magic, just like Reta told her to. It should've worked.

Kym touched the smooth surface of the crystal. Energy, more

energy than Kym had ever felt, surged through her. It burned through her veins, jolting life into Kym's sore limbs. Kym shook uncontrollably as the energy ravaged her mind, her heart, her soul.

She jerked her hand back, staring at her fingers. She'd felt like she had enough energy to blast a hole through the black mountain. With all that power at her command, Kym could do anything. Amber had been wrong. The Conduit wasn't the weapon. It was merely a vessel.

Kym took a deep breath, trying to calm her shaking nerves. Then, she placed her hand back on the Conduit. Energy surged through her once again, but this time, Kym swallowed her fear and didn't pull away. Glittering blue mist emerged from the depths of the crystal as Kym's insides burned with power, winding around her shaking arm.

"Kym, what are you doing?" Tomark asked, reaching up to grab her, but she shook her head. She couldn't stop.

Her feet left solid ground as more energy flowed into her. Her fingers lifted from the Conduit's crystal surface, but Kym knew it didn't matter as a warm sense of calm washed over her. Even though she wasn't touching the vessel for the gods' magic, blue mist continued to flow to her hands. She'd connected with the gods' magic. She didn't need to touch it anymore.

Off in the distance, Thed raised his skeletal hands. Jet-black flames shot from his fingers toward Kym, who heard the others cry out below her. They wanted her to move, but she didn't bother. She didn't need to.

Kym raised her hands, and a massive, glowing blue wave crested in front of her. The black flames exploded against it, but unlike Kym's previous defenses, it remained. Kym flicked her wrist, and the wave fell, crashing to the ground and surging toward Thed. It knocked him back, carrying him away on a tide of glittering blue water.

Kym drifted forward, the blue mist from the Conduit swirling around her. Somewhere, either inside of her or all around her, she felt her friends place their hands on the Conduit. She felt their friendship, their trust, and their love as green, purple, and yellow light filled the air. Kat, Ashlyn, and Xander joined Kym, their bodies surrounded in green, yellow, and purple mist.

"Surround him," Kym said, her voice oddly calm.

The others nodded, drifting forward to take their places around Thed, who was struggling back to his feet. Thed pointed his hands at Kym, and his black flames filled the air again. A tornado of shimmering silver air appeared in front of Kym, throwing Thed's fire away from her. Kym turned and saw Tomark floating beside her. Kym smiled as Amber, Jazin, and Damon joined her, Kat, Tomark, Ashlyn, and Xander, streams of multicolored mist connecting them to the Conduit. With her friends by her side, no feat was too large.

"*You cannot defeat me,*" Thed said, his deep voice trembling with anger. "*My gift is inevitable. You cannot destroy death.*"

Kym smiled. Thed was right, of course. Kym couldn't destroy death, and Kym didn't want to anymore. She closed her eyes and heard the happy voices of those who'd found their peace in Nothingness. She didn't want to take that from anyone. Death was necessary to nature and balance, but it had no place among the living.

Kym raised her hands, and energy from the Conduit surged through her. She focused her mind, letting everything else fade away until only a single thought remained. She let that thought fill her being, infusing every drop of the gods' magic burning through her.

"You don't belong here."

Bright blue energy shot from Kym's fingertips. It enveloped Thed, surrounding him in a cloud of blue mist. Green and silver energy surged forward on either side of Kym, as did red, black, yellow, purple, and white energy. Kym felt her friends' power mingle with her own, becoming indistinguishable from hers. Kym felt Thed's death within the cloud of energy, but it was no match for Kym and her friends. Was it the magic of the gods that was so strong, or something more?

Kym focused, letting her desire to send Thed back to Nothingness fill her whole being. The multicolored cloud spun around Thed like a tornado, lifting him into the air. She felt like a million bands were snapping against her soul as the cloud swirled faster, consolidating around Thed. She wondered what was happening, and the answer bloomed in some distant part of her mind. Thed's anchors to Princirum were finally breaking.

Kym shoved her arms forward, pushing harder than she ever had in her life, focusing even harder on her intent. The swirling cloud around Thed grew smaller as the snapping subsided. Kym felt the others' intent grow stronger and knew it was time. The multicolored cloud stopped swirling, now the size of a marble. Kym cried out, pushing with all her strength, and her energy descended on Thed.

The multicolored sphere exploded as a deep, low scream filled Kym's soul. She threw up her hands, and a shimmering blue sphere appeared around her. The energy collided with Kym's shield, forcing her back. However, the shield didn't crack as enormous trees were ripped up by the roots and a column of smoke rose in the air.

Silence pressed on Kym's ears as the dust settled around her. Kym closed her eyes, and the searing energy burning her veins felt oddly distant. The aches and pains of battle returned as the calming clarity eased from Kym's mind. She landed on the blackened, cracked earth, sinking gently to her knees. Kym gasped as the last traces of power trickled from her, digging her hands into the black sand, sweat dripping down her face.

Kym didn't look up for a long time. She continued to stare at the dead earth in front of her, waiting for something to happen. Tiny, bright green blades of grass pushed their way through the sand, which slowly shifted from black to brown. Kym's breath caught in her throat. Had they done it?

Finally, Kym made herself look up. All around her, new life continued to bloom from the places touched by death. Her eyes drifted to the side, and she saw Tomark. He was kneeling on the ground, tears streaming down his face as he slowly ran his hands through the newly brown earth.

Kym crawled over to him and wrapped her arms around

Tomark's neck. Warmth filled her as the built up tension inside her faded. White-hot tears fell from her eyes, stinging her skin. Other hands found their way onto Kym's body. They wrapped around her, their sobs mingling with Tomark's. No one spoke. They didn't need to. In that moment, Kym didn't care that she'd been a pawn in the gods' plan. The nightmare was finally over. Thed was gone. They'd won.

CHAPTER THIRTY-FOUR

THE WEIGHT OF
JUSTICE

"YOU NEED TO GET READY, MY DEAR."

"Just a minute!"

"The others aren't going to wait forever."

Kym sighed and sank under the sweet, rose-scented water, her irritation bubbling beneath her skin. She knew Veronica and Isabel meant well; they were the only reason she'd made it anywhere on time for weeks. But this wasn't an ordinary day, and Kym knew her maids had something special in mind. After all, it was the final day of the Rulers' trial.

Kym reluctantly climbed out of the enormous tub and wrapped herself with a towel. She considered telling Veronica she was done, but she needn't bother. Kym was barely dry when the bathroom door burst open. Veronica and Isabel hurried in, their arms full of so many fabrics, shoes, and hair ornaments it made Kym flinch. Did they mean for her to wear all of it? Kym prayed they didn't.

"Kym, why'd you take so long?" Isabel asked. She grabbed Kym's wrist and held her fingers close to her eyes. "You've gone all pruny."

"And your hair's in a state," Veronica said, running Kym's long blond hair through her fingers. "I asked you to take care of it last night."

"Sorry," Kym shrugged, failing to conceal her smile.

Her maids had been on edge since Kym moved back to Wadita. Returning hadn't been her idea, but she did see the benefits. If it had been up to Kym, she'd have returned to her home, the City of Contellus, or gone back to the Disciples to stay with her mother while she recovered. She got updates from Nurse Byrd and Dr. Gwin twice a day, but it wasn't the same as seeing her.

Kym closed her eyes, breathing through her nose as her maids set to work. She only needed to last a few more days, then her current state of madness would end. But if her maids kept upping their standards, Kym wasn't sure she'd be able to make it.

"Ryland stopped by earlier," Veronica said, running a comb through Kym's hair.

"Really?" Kym asked, her heart sinking. "What did he want?"

"To go see Aidan at Crystal Palace before the sentencing," Isabel said, her usual light, singsong voice somber. "And he's not the only one."

Kym bit her lip. She hated that Ryland thought he needed to ask her permission. And on top of that, Aidan was still recovering at Crystal Palace. He'd joined the Disciples when he'd been freed from the Unity but got attacked by a death demon before the battle was over. Kym had spoken with Damon the previous day, and he said Aidan needed at least another week to recover. And Aidan wasn't the only one. Nearly half the Favored who'd participated in the battle were still recovering.

"Of course, he can go," Kym said. "He knows Damon's door is always open to those wishing to visit the injured. And I told him he didn't need to keep asking permission."

"We know, my dear," Veronica said, and there was a little too much understanding in her voice. "But you know they have to ask, even if you don't want them to. We told him he had your blessing."

A shiver ran down Kym's spine that had nothing to do with her damp skin. Veronica was right, of course. No matter how many times Kym asked, Ryland and the other Water Favored sought her approval or permission for everything. She'd wanted to tell them to leave her alone, but she knew it wouldn't do any good.

"Anything else?" Kym asked, eager to change the subject as she rose from her chair.

"Actually, your agenda is pretty straightforward," Isabel said, following Kym into her bedchamber. "After the sentencing, you're visiting the Cities of Silvaura and Termubra to assess their rebuilding efforts. Then, of course, you have the final meetings with the families of the fallen."

"How many are there?" Kym asked, her heart falling. "I can push the city visits if I need to."

"That won't be necessary," Veronica said, emerging from Kym's closet with a lot of blue fabric in her arms. "There's only one left. Kenna's mother and brother will be here this afternoon."

Kym nodded, her face falling. After Kenna survived protecting Crystal Palace, she joined the fight on the side of the Disciples. Apparently, she killed five death demons before one finally got her. That death demon was the reason Aidan was still recovering at Crystal Palace. She gave her life so Aidan could live.

The family meetings were Tomark's idea since so many Favored had been separated from their loved ones for so long. Tomark had wanted to do something for them. Kym, Kat, Amber, Tomark, Ashlyn, Xander, Jazin, and Damon honored all of those who'd died in the battle as heroes, the way they had for Short. But the palace visits were more painful than the embarkments. Kym thought showing the families around their children's homes after not seeing each other for years was excruciating. But Kym knew Tomark was right. The families needed closure. She was grateful she'd gotten that with her father.

"Okay," Kym said, taking a few breaths to steady herself. "Anything else?"

"That's it," Isabel said, helping Veronica slip Kym's dress over her head.

Kym stared at herself in the mirror and still couldn't believe the person staring back at her was herself. The spiral scars on her arms had faded and were only a few shades off from her fair skin. Her blond hair hung in ringlets down her back, while glittering blue makeup covered the dark circles under her eyes. Even though it had only been two years since she'd first stepped foot in her bedchamber, Kym looked like she'd lived through a lifetime of pain. There was a glint missing from her eyes, and Kym wondered if she'd ever get it back.

"Finishing touches," Isabel said.

She picked up the water charm from its place on the jewelry table and draped it around Kym's neck. Kym's insides surged with energy as the crystal thread touched her skin, but she barely noticed anymore. Veronica appeared behind Kym, and Kym bent her knees, lowering herself as Veronica placed the massive, eight-pointed blue crown on Kym's head. Kym shivered as she looked in the mirror, and the Ruler of Water stared back at her.

"You look wonderful, My Lady," Isabel said, bending down to fuss with the hem of Kym's flowing blue dress.

The sound of Isabel properly addressing Kym made her want to run and hide. Of all the things that happened in the aftermath of the battle, this had been the most surprising. Kym and the others returned to Crystal Palace with the unconscious Rulers, who they'd magically bound. The fighting stopped, and all of the remaining fighters, both Favored and Disciples, knelt to Kym and the others. Less than an hour later, the Council voted to instate Kym and her friends as the New Rulers of Princirum. Kym wanted to refuse, but the excited cheers of the crowd overrode her rejections.

"You really should wear this more, My Lady," Veronica said.

Kym actually laughed. If her maids had their way, Kym wouldn't leave her bedchamber without her crown. But Kym had to draw a line somewhere. She only wore the crown for important occasions. Plus, Veronica and Isabel only called Kym 'My Lady' when she wore the crown, which made Kym want to wear it even less.

"Maybe," Kym shrugged and looked to the large clock on the wall. It was nearly ten. "I'm late."

"We know," Isabel said, her irritation breaking through her kind exterior as Kym hurried toward the door. "We've been telling you that for an hour."

Kym smiled as she hurried through the deserted halls and stairwells. It was strange how easily Kym adjusted to being back at

Wadita. She'd thought she'd never return, but the moment she arrived as the new Ruler of Water, she felt like she'd never left. But if Kym were honest with herself, it wasn't too surprising. She may have hated the Palace of Water, but it was the place where she found her purpose—it was her home.

A few Disciples, Protectorate, and servants were running around the entrance hall when Kym arrived. They stopped when they saw her, dropped to their knees, and placed their heads on the ground. Kym tried to ignore the lurch in her stomach as she hurried past them, but it was hard. Like the Water Favored, everyone started treating Kym like Nila when she became a Ruler, and she hated it.

Kym stepped onto the sweeping palace steps, the bright summer sun warming her face. She invoked her Marks and turned on the spot, water swirling around her. She focused on her destination and hurtled through space, exploding into a million tiny pieces as the rush of waves filled her ears. Her feet hit solid ground, and Kym blinked several times to clear her whirring vision.

"It's about time," an irritated voice said, making Kym smile. "It's already started."

Kym sighed as the rustling of leaves filled her ears. Kat glared at Kym, leaning against the trunk of a massive tree. Kym shook her head, unable to stop herself from laughing. She thought Kat looked absolutely ridiculous in her Ruler outfit, topped with a shimmering green crown that barely reached Kym's forehead.

"I'm here, aren't I?" Kym asked.

"Whatever," Kat smiled, punching Kym lightly on the arm. "C'mon, the others are already inside."

"They're not standing right in the middle of everything?" Kym asked, following Kat up Alfonburg's sweeping silver steps.

"If Amber had it her way, we'd be conducting the trial ourselves," Kat snorted. "But no. Jazin talked the Fire Princess out of that craziness, and Tomark's got us covered. He said no one will see us."

Kym smiled. She'd had a feeling Tomark would do something like this. He was just as uncomfortable with being the new Ruler of

Air as Kym was. She was happy they'd overrode Amber's idea to run the trial themselves. Kym couldn't handle all of those people staring at her, not to mention the pressure of deciding the fate of the people who murdered her.

Alfonburg's entrance hall was packed. Favored, Servitude, priest, Protectorate, Disciples, and people from the cities stood shoulder to shoulder, all looking toward the other side of the room. A raised platform sat against the curved wall, where five people looked over the crowd. Kym thought Anderson, Hale, Perla, and Mrs. Mizel looked perfectly at home sitting on the platform. Kym and the others hadn't wanted to preside over the Rulers' trial, so the Council was the next obvious choice. Kym felt a pang in her stomach as she looked to the seat that had been her father's. Nurse Byrd looked a little out of place, but Kym was happy she chose her to fill her father's seat.

Kym followed Kat around the edge of the hall and through the first door, and a very bizarre sight met her eyes. Amber, Jazin, Ashlyn, Tomark, Xander, and Damon were all inside, dressed in their new Ruler attire while they stared at a holoprojection floating above the table. It showed the Council's raised platform, as well as the open circle in front of it Kym hadn't seen. Pros and soldiers lined the perimeter while the Rulers sat in chairs in the circle's center. Kym thought they all looked strange, dressed in simple clothes without their crowns. Large metal cuffs sat on their wrists, and Kym saw the orange energy glowing from the intricate designs on them.

Kym didn't see the purpose of the storm restraints. The Rulers hadn't used their magic since Thed's defeat. Kym had a feeling the gods may have had something to do with that. With balance restored, the Rulers' magic should be as strong as ever. But Kym knew how unhappy Reta and the other gods were with their children. So actually, their lack of magic made perfect sense.

"She's here," Kat said, elbowing her way to the edge of the table. "Have they started?"

"Almost," Tomark said as Anderson stood up in the projection.

Kym stepped beside Tomark, who squeezed Kym's shoulders as she took off her crown.

Kym heard the crowd cheer through the holoprojector speakers as Anderson raised his hands, calling for silence. She couldn't help but smile at the look of pride shining on Anderson's round face. She may not like him, but he'd kept the last pocket of life going while all other resistances fell. Kym knew he deserved this moment. This was what he'd been working toward for so long.

"Quiet. Please, my friends," Anderson's worn voice rang out from the holoprojector as clearly as if he was standing in front of Kym. "Today, this Council will pass judgment on the children of the gods. This right was gifted to us by the Ruler of Life, Lord Damon Oren, and the Ruler of Death, Lord Jazin Ekert. We thank Lord Tomark Baskin, the Ruler of Air, for offering his palace to hold the trial. We've heard testimony from multiple sources, detailing the accuseds' abuse of power and their desire to plunge Princirum into chaos as they waged war on the gods."

The hairs on the back of Kym's neck stood on end as Anderson settled back in his seat. Two seats down, Perla stood, and Kym saw a determination in her face that Kym hadn't seen before. But while people cheered when Anderson stood, the crowd was silent as Perla looked down on them.

"For their crimes of treason and attempted deicide, it would be customary for the children of the gods to be sentenced to death. However, this is impossible, as the gods imbued them with eternal life and longevity. They cannot die. Therefore, the children of the gods will receive another fate."

Hale stood as Perla took her seat, and Kym couldn't ignore the crowd's disappointed murmur. Personally, Kym didn't want the Rulers killed. She'd experienced too much death in her life to wish for more. Besides, Nila and the others killed Kym, Tomark, Kat, and Ashlyn when they tried to leave. Kym knew they needed to be better. But clearly, the people of Princirum thought the Rulers deserved it.

"Given the special circumstances," Hale said, her clipped voice cracking like a whip, "we've come to an agreement we feel fits the crimes. As punishment for their crimes against Princirum and the gods, the children of the gods will be locked in the very prison they built to house their enemies.

"The Ruler of Darkness, Lord Xander Gatlin, has permitted us to use Tenbatter to house the children of the gods. The Ruler of Earth, Lady Katarein Prathor, has installed a new Warden—the Earth Master Lennax. The Rulers also pardoned all former inmates for their supposed crimes against the children of the gods.

"The children of the gods will remain in Tenbatter for the rest of time," Hale continued as the crowd clapped and cheered. "Unlike the treatment received by those imprisoned in Tenbatter during their reign, the children of the gods will be treated with dignity. The Ruler of Light, Lady Ashlyn Vale, and the Ruler of Fire, Lady Amber Mizel, will oversee the children of the gods' transport to Tenbatter with Commander Parker at sundown."

The crowd cheered even louder as Hale sat down. Kym smiled, resting her head on Tomark's shoulder. She'd known the Council's decision, since they'd requested Kym and the other Rulers' approval the previous day. But knowing it and seeing it in action were two different things. She was happy the Rulers were getting locked away, but a small part of Kym wanted there to be more of a punishment. They had made her life miserable, killed her and her friends, and nearly destroyed her home. But Kym knew this was the right thing, in the end.

Kym watched Parker and her soldiers lead the former Rulers from the entrance hall. The camera followed them out of the hall, and Kym caught a glimpse of Zara's face and saw the anger in her eyes. The sight made Kym's insides boil like lava. What did Zara expect would happen? She and the other Rulers almost plunged Princirum into chaos with their actions. Did she think they'd go back to being the Rulers after everything they'd done?

Kym watched the crowd thin in the holoprojector as the Council descended the stage. She sighed, the long list of things she needed to do running through her mind. She'd wanted to spend some time at Alfonburg with the others, but from the sound of it, they all had their plates full as well.

"We'd better go," Ashlyn said, picking up her yellow crown and placing it on her red hair. "We need to talk to Parker before we transport the Rulers."

"*We* are the Rulers," Amber said pointedly, her nose held slightly in the air. "But you're right. We should go."

"Amber, do us all a favor and shut up," Kat said, rubbing her eyes with the heel of her palm.

Kym, Jazin, and Ashlyn laughed as Amber's eyes narrowed. Kym couldn't help it. The fact that they were the Rulers while Zara and the others weren't was still hard to wrap her head around. Ashlyn, Kat, and Xander followed Amber out of the room, promising to see each other that night at Terradon.

"We should go too," Damon said, looking to Jazin. He smiled at Kym, and she knew exactly where they were going. "I'll send Veronica and Isabel an update on your mom."

"Thank you," Kym smiled.

She gave Damon and Jazin a quick hug before they rushed off, leaving Kym and Tomark alone. Kym sighed and pressed her forehead into Tomark's chest. So much had happened since they'd become Rulers that they hardly got any time alone. Yet another reason why Kym didn't enjoy being a Ruler.

"I wish we could visit the cities together," Tomark said, resting his chin on the top of Kym's head.

"Me too," Kym sighed. "But Kenna's family's coming to Wadita. I need to be there."

"I know," Tomark said. "Be sure to tell them about all the good times you had. She was your friend after all."

Kym nodded. She'd been thinking about it for days and knew what she was going to tell them. She'd show them Kenna's bedchamber and the training rooms. She'd tell them about the first time they met, and when Kenna trained Kym, as well as the times they'd spent together when Kym first arrived at Wadita. She'd tell them how Kenna gave her life protecting her best friend at Crystal

Palace, which was something Kym would never forget. She'd leave out their falling out when Kenna spied on Kym for Nila. Her family didn't need to know about that—Kenna had regretted those choices after all.

Kym placed her crown back on her head before exiting the room. The entrance hall was nearly deserted, with only the stragglers heading toward the door. Kym walked behind Tomark and tried to smile as people bowed to her.

"Lady Collins."

Kym jumped slightly at the sound of her official title. Parker was hurrying toward her, her eyebrows very close together. Kym shook her head. If she didn't know any better, she'd have thought Parker was nervous. But why? She was supposed to be getting ready to go to Tenbatter with Amber and Ashlyn. Kym stifled a groan. What had Amber done this time?

"What's up?" Kym asked.

"My Lady, the daughter of Reta has asked to speak with you," Parker said.

Kym's mouth fell open. Why would Nila want to talk to her? Kym hadn't had a proper conversation with Nila, free of Thed's influence, since before the Calling. What could Nila possibly have to say to her?

"What?" Tomark asked, clearly as stunned as Kym.

"I know," Parker said, shaking her head. "I don't understand either. But she's refusing to cooperate until she speaks with Lady Collins."

Kym glanced at Tomark. Her first instinct was to have him come with her. She didn't want to face Nila alone. But she knew she couldn't. Tomark needed to check on the rebuilding in the Cities of Contellus and Luxmont. He also had his own fallen Favored to deal with. She couldn't ask him to stay.

"I'll stay if you want," Tomark said.

"It's okay," Kym said. "Go do your job, Lord Baskin. I'll see you tonight."

"Don't worry," Parker added, her voice a little softer than before. "I'll look after her."

Tomark nodded and hugged Kym before walking out the front doors. Kym watched him leave, and part of her wanted to call him back. But he was gone, and Kym was alone with Parker. Kym nodded, and Parker took Kym to the door she'd taken Nila and the others after their sentencing.

The room was small. It may have been a storage room during Stailin's rein, but now, it looked more like a waiting room. Several small chairs sat around a table in the center of the room. There were no windows, but several torches sat in brackets on the swirly walls. The warm firelight reflected off the silver walls, making Kym feel like she was inside a cloud.

Nila sat in one of the chairs, her back straight and her face impassive. Kym walked past Parker, closing the space between her and Nila in a few strides. Nila's eyes narrowed as Kym approached, and she saw her nostrils flare. A shudder ran down Kym's spine, and she fought to keep her discomfort from her face. The sooner this was over, the better.

"Hello, Kymbralyn," Nila said slowly, emphasizing each syllable.

"This is Lady Collins," Parker snapped, stepping up beside Kym. "You will show the Ruler of Water the respect she deserves."

"My apologies," Nila said, venom dripping from her silky voice.

Kym wanted to slap Nila, but stopped herself. She didn't care that Nila didn't use Kym's proper title. Even here, with her hands bound in storm shackles and on her way to a life in prison, Nila still acted like she was better than Kym. Didn't Nila understand that her time was up? She was just trying to get under Kym's skin, and it was working.

"Give us a minute," Kym said, turning to look at Parker. Parker backed out of the room without hesitation.

"Well," Nila said the second the door closed behind Parker. "I see you got what you always wanted."

"I never wanted this," Kym said, shaking her head. "You know that."

"Are you certain?" Nila asked slowly. "Because from where I sit, this is the only outcome your disloyalty could have brought."

Kym bit her tongue, fighting to keep her fury in check. Arguing with Nila was pointless. She was trying to get a rise out of Kym because she'd lost all her power—the one thing Kym knew she truly cherished. But Kym wasn't sure how much of this she could take.

"Regardless of your intentions, Princirum is yours now," Nila continued, her eyes narrowing as she stared at Kym. "Her fate rests in your hands. May you do well guiding the Great Mother's creation into the future."

"We will," Kym said slowly. What was Nila getting at? Why was she congratulating Kym?

"Speaking of, I have a lot of work to do," Kym said, turning to leave the room. "So if you don't—"

"Before we part, I have something you may wish to hear," Nila said, her voice just as calm and silky as always. "As a former Ruler, to the new."

Even though she wanted to ignore Nila's words, something gnawed inside Kym. She turned to Nila and was surprised to see her standing. Kym hadn't heard her get up. Even without her crown and dressed in simple clothes, she towered over Kym and made her feel incredibly small.

"The children of the gods led Princirum for millennia," Nila said, taking a step closer to Kym. "And we did everything in our power to keep the gods' creation safe and secure."

"You did what you needed to do to keep your power," Kym said, also taking a step toward Nila. "Like always."

"Perhaps," Nila said. "Regardless of our motives, we kept Princirum safe from the outside world since the gods created us. Now, that task falls to you."

Kym shook her head. She must have misheard Nila. There was no outside world. Everyone knew that once you went far enough, you'd fall off the edge of the sea and into the void. Princirum was all there was.

"What are you talking about?" Kym asked slowly. "There is no outside world. The gods created Princirum, and that's all there is."

"Kymbralyn," Nila laughed, her lips splitting into a grotesque smile. "You really do not believe that, do you?"

"I...I do," Kym stammered, but the sight of Nila's smile made her resolve crack. "I know the stories. The gods created—"

"I thought you were smarter than that, Kymbralyn," Nila said, shaking her head. "You met my mother, after all. You know the gods are not exactly what the stories say."

Kym couldn't think. This was too much. Why should she believe Nila, the woman who'd made Kym's life miserable for years? Kym narrowed her eyes. Was it possible that Nila was lying? Kym knew better. Nila was many things, but a liar wasn't one of them. But Kym didn't understand why Nila was telling her this.

"Within our first century, the gods instructed us to conceal and isolate Princirum from the outside world, which was on the brink of war," Nila said, sounding almost bored. "We were meant to remove this protection when the world evolved past its barbaric ways, but we ignored the gods' instructions. And we were right.

"The outside world is primitive—they abandoned their gods, are disloyal to their governments, and their societal development is centuries behind our own. I believe they even tell primitive tales about us—stories of an advanced civilization swallowed by an angry sea. It is childish, isn't it? By isolating Princirum, we ensured her protection while Princirum thrived."

Kym's brain felt like Nila had shoved it through a meat grinder. Why was Nila telling her this? It made no sense. She could have kept this to herself, and Kym and the others never would've known the outside world existed. But now, the world as Kym knew it was forever changed. The world wasn't what she knew at all.

"Why are you telling me this?" Kym asked, her voice no more than a whisper.

"To warn you," Nila said, stepping so close to Kym there was barely an inch between them. "The world beyond the protective dome we created around Princirum is once again on the verge of collapse. They would not understand the utopia we built. It is now your job to maintain this paradise. If you do not, you will destroy all we worked to protect for millennia."

Kym didn't want to listen to Nila anymore. She needed to think and process what Nila said without her breathing down her throat. But no matter how much she wanted to deny it, Kym knew Nila was telling the truth, and the truth was too big for Kym to ignore. There was a world outside of Princirum, but what did that mean? She needed to find the others and tell them. This wasn't something she could decide on her own.

Kym turned her back on Nila's disturbing smile. She knocked on the door, and it opened at once. Kym stepped into the hall, fighting to keep her face calm as the world she'd known all of her life imploded around her. She nodded to Parker, who reached out to close the door.

"Best of luck to you and the new Rulers," Nila's silky voice reached Kym's ears as the door closed, making her skin crawl.

CHAPTER THIRTY-FIVE

RIGHTING THE WRONGS

KYM STARED OUT THE CARRIAGE WINDOW, THE VAST BLACK mountain looming ever larger. She squinted in the bright morning light, trying to find the spot where she and the others fought Thed. She saw it a little ways away, but could only tell because of a few key details—uprooted trees, a dip in the smooth ground, and a field of what looked like newly planted wildflowers. To the untrained eye, this field looked like any other. In a few years, no one would be able to tell the difference. But Kym knew better.

Kym settled back in her seat as the carriage wound up the mountain path. She rubbed her neck, trying to alleviate some of her tension. She didn't understand why she needed to arrive by carriage when she could've warped there in seconds. But everyone—Amber, Kat, Xander, Veronica, Isabel, Parker, Ryland, Aidan, and even her mother—shot down that idea. They said Kym shouldn't mess with tradition. So, Kym had to get up before sunrise to ride in a carriage all day from Wadita to Crystal Palace.

The carriage stopped, and Kym closed her eyes as her heart thudded in her chest. Why was she so nervous? It wasn't like she hadn't done stuff like this before. Maybe it was the excited hum of the crowd she could already hear outside the carriage. The door opened, and bright light and cheers of delight assaulted her. She took a deep breath and tried to contort her face into what she hoped was a happy expression. Kym stepped outside, her arm raised in greeting to the gathered crowd.

"Gods bless you, Lady Collins!"

"You saved us all!"

"May you rule for eternity!"

Kym's insides squirmed as she tried to force a happy expression onto her face. She, Tomark, Jazin, and Ashlyn had wanted to keep this day a secret, but the others voted against it. After all, this was a big day for Princirum, and Kym knew the people would be excited. This was a day for hope. Kym only hoped she didn't let all of these people down.

"Make way for the Ruler of Water!"

Veronica and Isabel appeared on either side of Kym, now wearing form-fitting Protectorate robes. They had their spears out, but the spear tips were retracted. They held them in front of Kym, carving a path through the cheering crowd to Crystal Palace's front steps.

Kym smiled as she stepped down from the carriage. Parker had suggested she have Pros with her—given the excitement around the day—but Kym still wasn't comfortable having Pros around her. Isabel and Veronica offered instantly to take up the spear for her again. She was happy they did. With them there, Kym didn't feel completely alone.

Kym walked forward as people reached out from the crowd, wanting to touch some part of the girl who'd saved them from death. Things hadn't changed since Kym returned from the fight with Thed. And even though it went against every impulse Kym had, she didn't pull away as their fingers brushed against her arms or touched her glittering blue dress. They deserved this just as much as she did.

Kym was grateful when she reached the top of the front steps. Two of Parker's Disciple soldiers stood on either side of the massive front doors, which Damon had restored after the battle. They wore multicolored sashes over their storm mesh uniforms, while multiple batons and spears hung from their belts. They opened the doors as Kym approached, and she gratefully hurried inside.

"That sucked," Kym sighed as the doors closed behind her, muffling the sound of the crowd.

"You did well," Veronica said, collapsing her spear and stowing it in her robes.

"Very well," Isabel smiled.

Kym nodded and walked to the curved staircases that led to the second floor. As she climbed, she saw someone waiting for her on the landing. Parker looked just like the Disciples at the front door, although the spear and batons on her belt were gold and her sash was slightly bigger. Kym smiled. When the Council asked Kym and the others to appoint a head of their security, Kym knew Parker was the right person.

"Good. You're here," she said curtly.

"I'm not late," Kym said defensively, although she couldn't help but smile.

"You're not," Parker nodded, shaking her head as she turned down the hallway. "You're the fifth to arrive. I imagine some of your fellow Rulers may want to make an…"

"Entrance?" Kym asked, raising an eyebrow.

"You said it, not me." The corners of Parker's mouth twitched, and Kym saw her eyes twinkle a little.

Kym followed Parker through the familiar halls, not really paying attention to where they were going. She didn't need to. She'd walked this path countless times. Even if it had been over a year since she'd been here, Kym's feet knew the way.

Her heart raced as she reached the end of the hall. It was a large, round space with pillars supporting the domed ceiling. Two large, wooden doors stood at the other end of the hall. The last time Kym saw those doors was when she'd been murdered. But that wasn't what made Kym's heart stop.

Nurse Byrd stood beside the wooden doors, another woman at her side. She was frail, and her skin looked like she hadn't seen the sun for years. Her long hair, which was the same blond color as Kym's, was thin and wispy and sat in a loose bun on the top of her head.

"Mom."

Kym broke into a run, not caring that she was the Ruler of

Water. She closed the distance between them and flung her arms around Elena's neck, burying her face into her mother's shoulder. Kym's insides melted as she felt the warmth radiating from her mother. Kym had feared she'd never feel her mother's warmth again.

"My girl," Elena said, stroking Kym's hair.

"How are you here?" Kym asked, her eyes burning with tears. She looked at Byrd, who was smiling weakly. "You said she wouldn't be out of bed for another week."

"I wasn't going to miss this," Elena said, wiping Kym's tears away with trembling fingers.

"She wouldn't listen to me, My Lady," Byrd smiled. "Seems to be a family trait."

Kym couldn't stop herself from laughing. Byrd was right, after all. Elena was a fighter, just like Kym. Kym had visited Elena several times at the Disciple's tower, where she was still recovering. Most days, she'd been asleep when Kym arrived, and Kym didn't have the heart to wake her. She'd always have to leave sooner than she wanted, given all the responsibilities she now had as the Ruler of Water.

Kym was happy to see Elena, but her presence only emphasized who wasn't there. The smile fell from Kym's face, and she rested her chin on her mother's thin shoulder. She couldn't look at her, not after everything that happened.

"I know," Elena said, her voice shaking. "I miss him too. But Kym, he'd be so proud of you today. I know it."

"Would he?" Kym asked, pulling away from her mother. Even though she'd been well for weeks, Kym hadn't had the heart to tell her everything that happened between Marek and her. "A lot happened when you were…sick."

"I know," Elena said, and there was a little too much under-standing in her voice. "But in the end, you did the right thing. So did your father. Marek chose to come here because he believed in you. And so do I."

Kym nodded, fighting to hold back her tears. It wasn't like she hadn't heard this before. Tomark had told it to her countless times over the past weeks, but hearing her mom say it was different. In the end, her father accepted who Kym had become, and that was all that mattered.

"I'll see you after?" Kym asked, looking around her mom to the vast wooden doors behind her.

"Of course," Elena smiled.

Kym walked past Elena and squeezed Byrd's hand, who smiled weakly. Kym was more indebted to Byrd than she could ever repay. She'd cared for Kym and her friends, comforted her dad on his deathbed, and now was nursing Elena back to health. No matter how hard Kym tried, she'd never be able to repay that debt.

The wooden doors opened as Kym approached. Kym walked inside while Veronica, Isabel, and Parker stayed outside with Byrd and Elena. Kym stepped into the next room, hastily wiping her face as she took several deep breaths. The throne room was round, with six thrones situated like the points of a hexagon around the edge. Two more thrones sat in the middle of the room on a raised platform, illuminated by a ray of light from the skylight above. The glittering white floor between the outer and inner thrones was several inches lower than that nearest the walls. Silks that matched each Rulers' element sat decoratively over each throne.

"Welcome," Damon said, standing on the sunken portion of the floor with Ashlyn, Tomark, and Xander. He was dressed in a glittering white vest and pants, his dark hair slicked back.

"How's the crowd?" Ashlyn asked. "It was crazy when I got here."

"Still nuts," Kym said, moving to stand beside Tomark. She grabbed his hand, wanting something to hold on to.

"I saw your mom," Tomark whispered so only Kym could hear. "She got here a few minutes before me. She seems good."

"She is," Kym said, her eyes growing hot once again. "I'm gonna see her after."

"Good," Tomark smiled, squeezing Kym's fingers.

It took a while for the others to arrive. Kat and Jazin got there a few minutes after each other. They waited with Kym and the others in the middle of the throne room as the minutes ticked by. Kym's impatience multiplied. What was taking Amber so long? Finally, Amber glided into the throne room, looking more like a Ruler than the rest of them combined. Kym fought the urge to smack her on the back of the head.

"Took you long enough, Fire Princess," Kat snapped, voicing what they all were thinking.

"The crowd was massive," Amber said calmly. "It took me time to get through."

"I'm sure it did," Xander snorted.

Kym's anger simmered beneath her skin. Amber knew how important this day was. There was so much they needed to do, and she decided to take her time to wave to the crowd. Kym took a breath, trying to calm her nerves. The last thing she wanted was to lose her cool.

"Should we begin?" Jazin asked pointedly, and Kym was happy to see Amber's face soften a little.

They all nodded. Kym turned and walked to the throne draped in blue silk nearest the doors. She sat, and a shiver ran down her spine. Sitting on Nila's throne felt very wrong. Kat took the throne to her left, while Xander took the one on her right. Damon and Jazin stepped onto the raised platform, taking the thrones draped in white and black. Tomark sat on the throne beside Xander, while Ashlyn sat on the one by Kat. Kym couldn't see Amber, who sat across from her behind Damon and Jazin.

"I call this Rulers' Summit to order," Damon said, his voice shaking slightly as his and Jazin's platform turned slowly on the spot. "We…um…have a lot to talk about."

Kym laughed, as did the others. Damon was right. They did have a lot to talk about, and Kym had no idea where they should start. Zara always told the Rulers what they were discussing at the Summits Kym attended. But they'd decided to do things differently. And after her conversation with Nila, Kym had plenty of things she wanted to discuss.

"I'll start," Kat shrugged, turning sideways in her throne so her feet dangled off the armrest. "This whole thing—it's gotta go."

"Could you be a little more specific," Amber drawled behind Damon and Jazin's thrones, which turned to face Kat.

"This," Kat said pointedly, waving her arms around the throne room. "The Rulers, the realms, the cities—it's all designed to fail. I know it. We all know it. We've been Rulers for a month, and the idiots outside are already worshiping us like we're the gods."

"And that's bad?" Kym asked, trying to keep a straight face. She couldn't and burst out laughing.

"See," Kat said, smiling at Kym from her throne. "This way of leading doesn't work. The Rulers proved it. We should do what the Disciples did."

"How's five people leading different from us?" Ashlyn asked. "The Council had their own issues."

"Then we make it better," Tomark said. "Let the people pick their leaders and set limits on it. No more of the same people ruling Princirum for millennia."

"No matter what we do, the people will still look to us for leadership," Amber said. "They've clearly chosen us to lead, so why would we deny what they've already chosen?"

"Because, Amber, having a crown and living in a palace isn't everything," Xander said. "The Rulers' love of their power is what plunged Princirum into chaos. I don't want that to happen to us."

Kym's heart swelled at Xander's words. She knew giving up power was a hard thing for him to do. The whole reason he was loyal to Melana for so long was to not lose the power and prestige being one of her three Pupils granted him. And the last thing she wanted was to be a Ruler for the rest of her life. The only reason she and the others were there was because it was the only form of government Princirum knew. But what Tomark and Xander suggested was better. Princirum needed to lead itself.

"We should also remove the walls surrounding the cities," Ashlyn said, and Damon and Jazin's thrones turned to face her. "They're only walled to keep them separate from the Rulers' realms. But with no more Rulers, the cities won't need to be walled anymore."

"That will help with the overcrowding," Xander nodded. "And will show we're serious about not being Rulers anymore. You can't really be a Ruler with no land to rule over."

Kym laughed, as did Kat and Jazin. Xander and Ashlyn were right. Kym knew the cities needed to expand. She'd spent too much of her childhood cleaning trash out of the river because people had nowhere else to put it. For so long, she'd dreamed of seeing the world outside the city walls. And now, that dream would be real for everyone.

"But what about the palaces?" Damon asked. "We can't just get rid of them."

Kym bit her lip. Getting rid of the city walls was one thing, but the palaces were a whole other problem. She wasn't even sure if they could get rid of them. When she first arrived at Wadita, Nila told Kym Reta made the Palace of Water herself. Kym doubted they'd be able to do anything to the palaces.

"That can be decided another time," Jazin said. "I think for now, we say the leaders of Princirum will no longer live at the Palaces."

"Let's vote," Damon said. "So, we're abolishing the Ruler-led government, letting the people elect their own representatives, and removing the walls around the cities. All in favor?"

Kym raised her hand without hesitation. This was by far one of the simplest choices she needed to make. After this Summit, she wouldn't be a Ruler anymore, and Kym couldn't wait for that massive weight to vanish from her shoulders. For the first time since Reta gave her magic, Kym's life would be hers again.

"The vote passes seven to one," Jazin said, and Kym couldn't help but smile.

"Who's next?" Kat asked.

"I'll go," Tomark said. "So, we all know the truth now. The gods aren't what we were taught when we were young. They're not perfect. They lied to us and manipulated us into doing their dirty work. They gave Kym, Kat and me magic and bet Princirum's future on the off chance we'd make the right choices at the right times. The people of Princirum deserve to know the truth about their gods."

Kym nodded. She'd talked with Tomark about this the previous night. Even though it would be hard for them to hear, she wanted to tell the people the truth. Sure, there'd be those who didn't like it, but Kym thought it was better if the people knew the truth about the beings they worshipped. The gods made Kym, Kat, and Tomark Favored so they could do their dirty work, but never actually cared about them. Kym thought the people deserved to know the truth about the gods.

"Sorry, Tomark," Kat said. "I'm all for telling people the truth, but you're talking about fundamentally changing what the people believe. Sure, the gods screwed with us, but we don't have the right to take people's faith from them."

Kym stared at Kat. Out of everyone, she'd thought Kat would agree with her and Tomark's desire to tell the people the truth. Kat was always the one pushing Kym to find answers and to make up her own mind about things, no matter the consequences. Why was she so worried about the consequences of telling the people the truth now?

"How can you say that?" Tomark demanded. "After everything they've done, we should—"

"Tomark," Ashlyn said, her bright voice gentle, "I know you're upset. The gods showed their true colors when they spoke to you, Kat, and Kym during the battle. But you can't use their manipulation of you as a reason to justify destroying Princirum's faith."

"I agree," Xander said. "It doesn't matter what they believe. They believe we are the Rulers because we brought peace back to Princirum, and that's not true. I say we let them believe what they want if it gives them hope."

"And," Amber added, "what of those whose faith is more… devout? If we tell them the truth, what would happen when some believe us and some don't?"

"But at least they'd know the truth," Kym said. She thought

more of them would be on her and Tomark's side. They'd complained about the gods for as long as she had known them.

"We just got out of a war, Kym," Jazin said. "I'm not keen to start another if we can avoid it."

"Let's vote," Damon said. "All in favor of telling the people the truth about the gods?"

Kym raised her hand; so did Tomark. She glanced at Kat and saw both of her hands clasped in her lap. Kym wasn't surprised. In Kat's mind, she was protecting the people's faith by not telling them the truth. And even if Kym didn't agree with her, she respected her choice. In her own way, Kat was trying to protect the people of Princirum.

"The vote fails three to five," Jazin said.

Kym closed her eyes. She'd really wanted to tell the people the truth. She hated the idea of keeping that information from them. But they'd all agreed to respect the choices they made during the Summit. So, even though she didn't want to, she'd keep this information to herself.

"So...um," Damon said, his and Jazin's thrones turning slowly on the spot. "Do we let magic continue to exist?"

Kym stared at Damon. What did he mean by 'letting magic exist'? During the days leading up to this Summit, Kym and the others had briefly spoken about what they wanted to discuss. Kym couldn't remember any of them mentioning this. And she would've, given how crazy it sounded.

"What are you talking about?" Xander asked.

"Why would we get rid of magic?" Amber asked.

"C'mon," Damon said, looking around like he was shocked by their responses. "Magic is the reason this mess happened in the first place. Without it, the Rulers wouldn't have been in power for so long, and we wouldn't have been at war. I thought magic was this great thing, but it's caused so much destruction."

"Damon," Tomark said, his voice gentle, "it's done some good too. You do good with it every day"

Kym shook her head. For as long as she could remember, she'd wanted nothing to do with magic. Then when she got it, she found it had a purpose. Even when she'd lost her magic, she'd fought to get it back—a decision that still shocked her sometimes. Kym knew there was more good she could do with magic if she used it the right way.

"Damon, I hated magic when I was little," Kym said. "It destroyed my family and took me from my parents. You're right; magic has done terrible things. But we saved Princirum with magic. The Favored can use magic the right way. We just have to give them the chance to."

"But who's gonna give them that chance?" Xander asked. "With the Rulers locked up, there's no one to teach the Favored how to use magic the right way."

"What are you talking about?" Amber drawled, and Kym could almost hear her rolling her eyes. "We'll teach the Favored, Xan."

"Seriously? Why us?"

"Because, my most powerful Lord Muscle Man, the almighty gods who are perfect and nice and don't lie chose us," Kat said in a very good impression of Zara.

Kym laughed, as did the others. She knew Kat was joking, but the sad thing was, she knew that's what Princirum was thinking. How could they teach the Favored to use magic for the right reasons? Kym knew her magical knowledge wasn't as vast as Amber's, or Lance's, or Lucia's. Why would anyone want to learn from her? What had she done to earn that right? All she'd done was not die fighting a god.

"But in all seriousness," Kat said, sounding uncharacteristically serious, "how are we gonna teach them?"

"For starters, I think we shouldn't just teach them to fight," Tomark said, and Kym couldn't help but smile. She knew how much Tomark hated only using his magic to fight. "While we fought death, we had to get creative with magic. We learned that magic's sole use isn't fighting. We need to teach that to the rest of the Favored."

"Some of them won't like that," Jazin said. "Especially the

Masters. Fighting is all they know."

"It'll take time," Kym nodded. "And we should make it their choice."

"What?" Damon asked. "You want to give them a choice?"

"I do," Kym said. "We didn't have a choice to learn magic. But since we're changing it, we need to give the Favored the opportunity to choose. Of course we'll teach the new Favored this new way of using magic if they want to be Favored. But if the Masters don't want to change their ways, they don't have to."

Kym sighed. In a perfect world, she'd like to teach all of the Favored and Masters the new things she and the others learned. But she knew Xander had a point. Kym couldn't imagine teaching Lance that there was more to magic than fighting.

"And we're not the Rulers," Ashlyn said softly. "The Favored aren't some strange extension of our power. They're people, and we'll treat them that way. No more pitting the Favored against each other."

"Or keeping us separated," Jazin nodded. "The Rulers kept the elements apart to maintain their control over us. We're proof that the elements can coexist. We need to show the Favored and Masters that this is the way now. Since we rose to power, we opened the palaces to all Favored, but they've retained the elemental divisions. We need to make a solid effort to show them the mistrust between the elements doesn't need to exist."

Kym nodded. She'd been trying to get the Water Favored to stay at whatever palace they wanted for weeks. While Aidan was recovering at Crystal Palace after the battle, Kym told Ryland to stay there so he could be with him. But Ryland insisted on returning to Wadita every night, saying that was where Water Favored belonged.

"And while we're discussing magic," Xander said, a cool note in his voice. "We need to do something about the Cladium."

"What about it?" Ashlyn asked.

"Thanks to the Unity, all Favored know how to use them," Jazin said. "They're no longer a vile secret known only by a few Masters."

"I used them," Amber said, and Kym heard the pain in her voice. "and I was wrong to. We need to make the Cladium illegal."

"And what would the punishment be?" Tomark asked, and Kym heard the judgment in his voice. Kym knew he wanted to outlaw the Cladium as much as she did, but she knew Tomark's heart was too kind to punish those who used it. Luckily, they had Kat.

"We have Tenbatter," Kat said. "And it's better than when we were in there. Lennax will treat the inmates fairly."

"Twenty years?" Jazin asked.

"That's a long time," Kym said. She'd only been in Tenbatter for a little over a year, but it had felt like an eternity.

"It's the Cladium," Amber said, peering around Jazin and Damon's throne to glare at Kym. "The punishment needs to be severe enough to prevent people from using it."

Kym opened her mouth to argue but stopped herself. If she wanted to stop people from using the Cladium, there needed to be a punishment for using them. As much as she didn't like it, it was better than letting people use the Cladium freely. Amber was right.

"Okay," Jazin said, "So we're voting on magic. All in favor of changing the way we teach it, and making the Cladium illegal?"

Kym raised her hand. She knew this would be hard for the Favored and Masters to wrap their heads around. They'd grown so used to the way things were under the Rulers. They were changing the way the Favored saw themselves. They weren't divine warriors who needed to serve their Rulers without question. From now on, the Favored could be whatever they wanted to be.

"The vote is unanimous," Jazin said.

"Okay," Damon said, his and Jazin's thrones turning to face Kym. "I think that just leaves one item left. Kym?"

Kym took a deep breath and stood. She stepped onto the sunken portion of the floor, her hands shaking slightly at her sides. She closed her hands, trying to make them stop. Why was she so nervous?

"Okay," Kym began, her voice cracking slightly. "So, as you know, Nila told me there's a world outside of Princirum. Three days ago, I went with Parker to the edge of the world. It looks just like the stories say—water falling off into the abyss. But when we activated a storm generator, that changed. We saw the ocean beyond the void. Nila was telling the truth. Princirum isn't all there is in the world."

Silence followed Kym's words while the others gawked at her. She hadn't told any of them what she'd found with Parker, not even Tomark or Kat. She even swore Parker to secrecy, fearing what people would do if the information got out before the Summit. If the people found out about the outside world before Kym and the others made a decision about it, it could cause a panic.

"What are you proposing?" Amber asked, her voice full of concern.

"We should take the dome down," Kym said plainly. "There's a whole world out there, but the Rulers made it so they think we don't exist. It's time they knew about us."

"Didn't Nila say the outside world was very underdeveloped?" Xander asked.

"Yes…" Kym said slowly. "But we could handle—"

"Kym, what do you think is going to happen when Princirum just appears?" Amber asked. "We're not a small island. They're going to notice when a massive landmass that they thought was a myth appears in their ocean. Nila told you the outside world spent the majority of its history fighting. What do you think they'll do when an advanced society, both technologically and magically, just appears out of the blue?"

"We'll figure it out," Tomark said. "Kym's right. It's time Princirum returned to the world."

"Nila said the gods told the Rulers to take the dome down centuries ago," Ashlyn said. "They didn't listen. Isn't that why we're here? To fix their mistakes?"

"How?" Kat asked. "We're not children of the gods, remember? We may be Rulers, but we don't have magic like they did."

"We'll need to use the Conduit again," Damon said. "It's still full of the Rulers' magic. It'll be enough to take down the dome."

"It won't be if we keep using it," Jazin said. "Shouldn't we save it in case Thed, or one of the other gods, decide to attack?"

Kym shook her head. She knew this would be a hard sell. They were trying to keep Princirum safe, but they were also hiding. They wanted to save the Conduit for a fight that may never come. There was a whole world suffering outside of Princirum, and Kym knew she could help if they could just get outside. But she needed all of her friends to make it happen.

"I think we should vote," Jazin said, and Kym returned to her throne. "All in favor of destroying the protective dome around Princirum?"

Kym closed her eyes as she raised her hand. The moment stretched on for an eternity. She didn't want to see how the others voted. If it failed, she didn't want to hold it against them. She just hoped enough of them were on her side.

"The vote passes five to three," Damon said.

Kym opened her eyes, excitement coursing through her like electricity. She couldn't believe it. Her vote passed. Kym breathed freely for the first time since Nila told her about the dome. Kym and her friends weren't going to make the same mistakes Nila and the others had.

"This concludes the final Rulers' Summit...ever," Jazin said quietly.

"I guess," Damon said, standing up, "there's only one thing left to do."

Kym stood with the others, and lifted the large, eight-pointed crown from her head. She set it on her throne, and her heart felt a million pounds lighter. Her time as a Ruler was over. If everything went according to plan, she wouldn't set foot in the throne room ever again. And Kym wanted nothing more.

"Alright," Damon said, stepping down from his throne, Jazin right behind him. "I guess we better go inform the masses."

Kym nodded. She walked to the massive throne room doors, which opened as she approached. Every step she took felt like she was leaving a dream. The others followed her into the hall, which was now deserted. Kym glanced over her shoulder as the doors closed silently on the throne room. It was oddly dark, with light no longer shining down from the skylight.

The others rushed past Kym, shouting hurried good-byes to each other. They were going to meet at their secret clearing once they'd seen the multitude of people needed to get things going. Kym couldn't wait. It was going to be just like old times.

"Are you ready?" Tomark asked, appearing beside Kym as they reached the balcony overlooking the entrance hall. Outside, Kym heard the crowd cheering their names

"For what?" Kym asked. She grabbed Tomark's hand, and his fingers intertwined with hers.

"To face this new world we created?" Tomark said, smiling down at Kym. "Everything's gonna change when we walk out those doors."

Kym leaned against Tomark and heard his heart thundering against his chest. He was right; everything was going to change, and it was all because of choices Kym and the others made. But for the first time in a long time, that didn't bother her. She looked into Tomark's dark green eyes, his long, wavy hair brushing his shoulders. It was odd, but as she stood on the verge of stepping into a new world full of unknown wonders, she felt perfectly calm.

"Whatever happens," Kym said as the cheers of the crowd grew louder, "we'll face it together."

"Are you sure?"

Kym stood on her tiptoes and pressed her lips to Tomark's. Warmth spread through her as the hairs on the back of her neck stood on end. Tomark caressed her face, and it took a long time before they finally pulled apart. Kym looked into his eyes, his tears glistening in the light streaming in from the many windows. Kym wasn't sure what this new world would look like, but she did know one thing—with Tomark and her friends at her side, there was nothing she couldn't face.

"Always."

THE END

AIDAN (AY-dihn) – Water Favored

ALFONBURG (AAL-fon-berg) – the Palace of Air, home to Lord Stailin and the Air Favored

AMBER – Fire Favored

PROFESSOR ANDERSON (Ahn-dehr-suhn) – leader of the True Disciples; head of the Disciple Council

ASHLYN (AASH-lihn) – Light Favored

BRONIX (BRAH-nics) – Tenbatter Pro

BYRD (BIHRD) – True Disiple; nurse; first name Jamie (JAYM-ee)

THE CALLING- a magical contest among the Favored; used to determine the will of the gods

CHARMS- one for each of the physical elements; lets wielder use their magic at its peak

THE CITY OF CONTELLUS – one of Princirum's four cities, located at the border of Contellus

THE CITY OF LUXMONT – one of Princirum's four cities, located at the border of Luxmont

THE CITY OF SILVAURA – one of Princirum's four cities, located at the border of Silvaura

THE CITY OF TERMUBRA – one of Princirum's four cities, located at the border of Termubra

CLADIUM (CLAAD-ee-um)- magic used to control an aspect of human existence; used by planal and physical elements

THE CONDUIT – Princirum's source of magic

CONTELLUS (Con-TEHL-uhs) – the realm of earth

CRYSTAL PALACE – the Palace of Life, home to Lady Zara

DAMON (DAY-muhn) – Life Favored; former Servitude at
Crystal Palace

DEATH DEMON – a creature infused with and radiating death

ELENA COLLINS (EH-layn-uh) – Kym's mother

EMBARKMENT (EHM-bahrk-mehnt) – religious service
where newly deceased receive the gods' last rites

EZARK (Eh-ZAHRK) – True Disciple soldier

FAVORED – those in Princirum who can magically control
one of the elements

FESTIVAL OF CREATION – Princirum's eight day religious
festival; celebrates the gods' creation of the known world

THE GREAT FORTRESS – the Palace of Darkness, home to
Lady Melana and the Darkness Pupils

DR. GWIN (GWIHN) – head doctor for the True Disciples

COMMANDER HALE (HAYL) – former commander of the
City Patrol; True Disciple; member of the Disciple
Council

HEIRRAPH (AIR-aaf) – god of fire and love

HIGH PRIEST- highest rank of the priesthood

HIGH PRO- highest rank of Protectorate in a city

IGMONTIS (Ihg-MOHNT-ihs) – the realm of fire

INALI (IHN-ahl-ee) – Tenbatter Pro

INFERON (Ihn-FAIR-on) – the Palace of Fire, home to Lord
James and the Fire Favored

ISABEL (IHS-uh-behl) – Kym's lady's maid

JAZIN (JAY-zihn)- Death Favored

JEAN (Jeen) – Water Favored

KATAREIN (KAAT-uh-rain) – Earth Favored, goes by Kat

KENNA (KEHNN-uh) – Water Favored

KENSRAD (KEHNS-raad) – goddess of darkness and bravery

KENSRIX (KEhns-rics)- Fire Favored

KYMBRALYN (KIHM-brah-lihn) – Water Favored, goes
by Kym

LADY EVANNA (EE-vaan-uh) – Ruler of Light and daughter of Thilg

LADY MELANA (Meh-LAHN-uh) – Ruler of Darkness and daughter of Kensrad

LADY NILA (NEYE-lah) – Ruler of Water and daughter of Reta

LADY ZARA (ZAR-ah) – Ruler of Life and daughter of Pheil

LANCE (Laans)- Water Master; Nila's most trusted master

LENNAX (LEHNN-aax)- Earth Master

LORD JAMES – Ruler of Fire and son of Heirraph

LORD KAI (KEYE)– Ruler of Earth and son of Thray

LORD PHILLIP- Ruler of Death; chosen by Thed as his Ruler

LORD STAILIN (STAY-lihn) – Ruler of Air and son of Rai

LUCIA (Loo-SEE-uh) – Fire Master; Lord James's most trusted Master

LUXMONT (LUHX-mont) – the realm of light

MAREK COLLINS (MAIR-ehk) – Kym's father; True Disciple; member of the Disciple Council

MASTER- title given to a Favored when they have completed their training

MRS. MIZEL (MEYE-zehl) –Amber's mother; True Disciple; member of the Disciple Council; Kat's former teacher

NOTHINGNESS – the realm of the dead

PARKER (PAHRK-her) – True Disciples Lieutenant

PERLA (PEHR-lah) – High Priest of the True Disciples; member of the Disciple Council; former Protectorate

PHEIL (FEEL) – goddess of life and family, the Great Mother, Queen of the gods

PHYSICAL ELEMENT- fire, water, air, and earth

PLANAL ELEMENT- light and darkness

PRIESTHOOD- a branch of the Princirum faith; sworn to guide the people through the gods' plan

PRINCIRUM (PRIHNC-ee-ruhm) – a land of magic created by the gods

PRIZED- title give to Favored competing in the Calling

PROTECTORATE- a branch of the Princirum faith; sworn to protect the temples and those loyal to the gods; given the title 'Pro'

PUPIL – name taken by all Darkness Favored

PURE ELEMENT- life and death; the original elements

RAI (RAY) – god of air and judgement

RETA (REHT-ah) – goddess of water and purification

ROETTA (ROH-ehtt-uh)- Water Master

RULER – title given to the children of the gods

RYLAND (REYE-lihnd) –Water Favored

SERVITUDE- a branch of the Princirum faith; sworn to serve those blessed by the gods

SHORT (SHOHRT) – True Disciples officer; first name Jeren (JEHR-ehn)

SILVAURA (SIHLV-ohr-uh) – the realm of air

SOLARIS (Sohl-ARE-ihs) – the Palace of Light, home to Lady Evanna and the Light Favored

THE STORM – an artificial energy that negates magic

SYRETA (SIH-rehtah) – Protectorate

TENBATTER (TEHN-baat-ter)- the Rulers' prison

TERADON (TEHR-ah-don) – the Palace of Earth, home to Lord Kai and the Earth Favored

TERMUBRA (TEHR-muh-bruh) – the realm of darkness

THED (THEHD) – god of death, King of Nothingness

THILG (THIHLG) – goddess of light and wisdom

THILG INSTITUTE OF HIGHER LEARNING – Princirum's university

THRAY (THRAY) – god of earth and the harvest

TOMARK (TAH-mark) – Air Favored

TRUE DISCIPLES – those who refuse to accept the Rulers as the new gods

UNDARUNCI (Uhn-duh-RUN-see) – the realm of water

THE UNITY – a singular, artificial consciousness connected to and controlling the Favored

VANQUISHER – Favored charged with destroying death
    demons; one for each element
VERONICA (Ver-ohn-ih-cuh) – Kym's lady's maid
VERRAPH (VEHR-ahf) – Protectorate
WADITA (Wah-DEE-tah) – the Palace of Water, home to
    Lady Nila and the Water Favored
THE WARDEN- Earth Favored; in charge of Tenbatter
XANDER (ZAAN-der)- Darkess Favored
ZAYVEN (ZAY-vehn) – Protectorate

A C K N O W L E D G M E N T S

WELL, THIS IS A SENTENCE I NEVER THOUGHT I'D WRITE—I'VE finished my first book series! For a long time, I never thought I'd reach this moment. I had the idea for this series in December of 2011 (and yes, I do know the day and time and what I was doing LOL). More than ten years have passed since that night, and for a while, I never thought I'd reach this third and final book. So many things had to happen to reach this point. I needed to write the first one, and then the second. This third and final book in Kym's journey has always been the light at the end of the tunnel. If I could just write the first two, then I'd get to do the third. But now that I'm here, I have to say it's very bitter sweet. Saying goodbye to something that been a part of my life for over a decade is harder than I thought it would be. But, telling Kym's story in the way I always intend to makes the parting a little easier to swallow (but only a little).

Over the past decade, there are so many people who have had to put up with me while I write, and rewrite, and complain, and disappear to write this series and this final installment.

To My Friends, thank you for putting up with my very strange behavior, like taking whole printed manuscripts on vacations (which I did a lot), and listening when I had a sudden idea.

I'd like to thank *My Family* for never letting me give up, even when they had no idea how to process or understand what I was doing. Thank you for getting me through all of the rejections (of which there were many) and for celebrating the random accomplishments of writing (like actually making deadlines, which was a struggle with this final book).

Dani—you are the best critique partner I could ever ask for. You pick every little thing apart, and tell me when things need a second look. But you also tell me what I need to hear, and not what I want you to say. This time around, that meant telling me the book was OK, and not a dumpster fire (which was what I called this book every time I thought of it).

KAYLA—your insights were as wonderful as ever. I love how much you cared for the smallest moments in this story. Your comments and questions made this story better in every way.

ALEX—you were new to my writing process, and were by far the most excitable BETA reader I've ever had! Your enthusiasm reinvigorated my passion for the story I've been telling for over a decade (especially when I wanted to throw my laptop against a wall).

SUZANNE—you are the best editor a writer could wish for! If it wasn't for you editing the first book almost three years ago, I wouldn't be here on the third one! Thank you for everything you've done for me and my books!

WESLEY—what can I say? Your artistic talent really knows no bounds! You brought the cover of this book to life in extraordinary detail, which was not easy given how detailed it turned out. Thank you for bringing my books to life.

And finally, these books wouldn't be here without you—*MY READERS.* I want to thank each and every one of you who have stuck with Kym through thick and thin. You are the best readers an author could as for, and you are the reason I want to keep telling stories. And just know, that even though Kym's story has come to an end, Princirum will always be there whenever you want to escape to a world with a little magic.

ABOUT THE AUTHOR

LOGAN YOUNG IS A COLORADO-BASED YOUNG ADULT AUTHOR. AS A child, his overactive mind never shut off, filling his head with new stories and worlds to explore. It didn't take long before those stories found their way onto paper. Deciding to pursue writing as more than a side passion, he attended the University of Colorado, Boulder and graduated in 2017 with a Bachelor of Arts in English, Creative Writing. When not writing, Logan enjoys an active lifestyle, but is always looking for his next idea.

Hear about LOGAN YOUNG's new releases, cover reveals, publishing news, and much more before anyone else!

WWW.IMLOGANYOUNG.COM

instagram.com/imloganyoung

amazon.com/author/imloganyoung

goodreads.com/imloganyoung

bookbub.com/authors/logan-young

facebook.com/imloganyoung

twitter.com/imloganyoung